The *Year's Best*
Fantasy and
Horror

The Year's Best Fantasy and Horror

FOURTH ANNUAL COLLECTION

Edited by Ellen Datlow
and Terri Windling

ST. MARTIN'S PRESS   NEW YORK

ISBN 0-312-06005-x (hbk)
ISBN 0-312-06007-6 (pbk)

First Edition: July 1991

10 9 8 7 6 5 4 3 2 1

A Bluejay Books Production

CONTENTS

Acknowledgments   xi
INTRODUCTION
    Summation: *1990: Fantasy* by Terri Windling   xii
    Summation: *1990: Horror* by Ellen Datlow   xxiii
    Horror and Fantasy in the Media by Edward Bryant   xlv
    Obituaries   lii
Charles de Lint FREEWHEELING   1
Nina Kiriki Hoffman COMING HOME   16
George Szanto THE SWEEPER   24
Joyce Carol Oates LADIES AND GENTLEMEN   38
Nancy A. Collins FREAKTENT   45
John Crowley MISSOLONGHI 1824   55
Thomas Ligotti THE LAST FEAST OF HARLEQUIN   64
David Memmott SOUNDING THE PRAISES OF SHADOW TO THE
    MERCHANTS OF LIGHT (poem)   92
Kristine Kathryn Rusch HARVEST   95
Susan Cooper FANTASY IN THE REAL WORLD (essay)   105
Dyan Sheldon THE DREAM   116
John Brunner MOTHS   123
Susan Prospere FROZEN CHARLOTTES (poem)   136
Rachel Simon LITTLE NIGHTMARES, LITTLE DREAMS   139
John Morressy TIMEKEEPER   148
Ellen Kushner SONATA: FOR TWO FRIENDS IN DIFFERENT TIMES
    OF THE SAME TROUBLE (poem)   165
Stuart Dybek DEATH OF A RIGHT FIELDER   168
David J. Schow NOT FROM AROUND HERE   172
Karen Joy Fowler LIESERL   198
Sharon M. Hall THE LAST GAME   205
Susan Palwick OFFERINGS   220
Vern Rutsala THE MUSES OF ROOMS (poem)   233
Nina Kiriki Hoffman A TOUCH OF THE OLD LILITH   236
David B. Silva THE CALLING   250
Haruki Murakami TV PEOPLE (translated from the Japanese
    by Alfred Birnbaum)   261
Steve Rasnic Tem IN THE TREES   276
Garry Kilworth TRUMAN CAPOTE'S TRILBY: THE FACTS   282
Ian R. MacLeod GREEN   290
Garry Kilworth DARK HILLS, HOLLOW CLOCKS   310
Jonathan Carroll THE PANIC HAND   318
Michael Blumlein BESTSELLER   326
Delia Sherman NANNY PETERS AND THE FEATHERY BRIDE   351

Jack Womack OUT OF SIGHT, OUT OF MIND   357
Éilís Ní Dhuibhne MIDWIFE TO THE FAIRIES   368
Joe R. Lansdale THE PHONE WOMAN   376
T. E. D. Klein LADDER   387
Steven Millhauser ALICE, FALLING   397
Angela Carter ASHPUTTLE: or, THE MOTHER'S GHOST   409
Adrian Cole FACE TO FACE   416
Karel Čapek THE DOG'S TALE (translated from the Czechoslovakian
     by Dagmar Herrmann)   428
Elizabeth Massie STEPHEN   435
Peter Straub A SHORT GUIDE TO THE CITY   454
R. A. Lafferty THE STORY OF LITTLE BRIAR-ROSE,
     A SCHOLARLY STUDY   463
K. W. Jeter THE FIRST TIME   469
Ian Frazier COYOTE v. ACME   481
Richard Christian Matheson AROUSAL   486
Gwen Strauss THE WAITING WOLF (poem)   491
                    THE BEAST (poem)   494
Michael Bishop SNAPSHOTS FROM THE BUTTERFLY PLAGUE   496
Isabel Allende TWO WORDS (translated from the Spanish
     by Margaret Sayers Peden)   510
Lucius Shepard and Robert Frazier THE ALL-CONSUMING   517
Jonathan Carroll THE SADNESS OF DETAIL   536
Honorable Mentions   545

Acknowledgments

I would like to thank Robert Killheffer; Gordon Van Gelder; Merrilee Heifetz; all the publishers who provided material; and the contributors. A special thanks to Jim Frenkel for his nudging, his feedback and his legwork; to Tom Canty for his gorgeous bookcovers; and Terri Windling, my partner in crime, for being a good friend and co-editor.

I'd also like to acknowledge Charles N. Brown's *Locus* magazine (Locus Publications, P.O. Box 13305, Oakland, CA 94611; $48.00 for a one-year first-class subscription, (12 issues) $35.00 second class) as an invaluable reference source throughout the Summation; and Andrew Porter's *Science Fiction Chronicle* (*S.F. Chronicle*, P.O. Box 2730, Brooklyn, NY 11202-0056; $36.00 for a one-year first-class subscription, (12 issues) $30.00 bulk rate), also an invaluable reference source throughout.

—Ellen Datlow

Many thanks to all the publishers, writers, artists, booksellers, librarians and readers who sent me material, recommended favorite titles, and shared their thoughts on the year in fantasy publishing with me; and to *Locus*, *SF Chronicle*, *Library Journal*, *Horn Book* and *Folk Roots Music Magazine* which are helpful sources for seeking out fantasy material. (Anyone wishing to recommend fantasy stories, novels, music or art released in 1991 for next year's volume can do so c/o The Endicott Studio, 2790 North Wentworth Road, Tucson, AZ, 85749.)

Special thanks to Wendy Memmott of the Castignetti Artists Building who worked as the editorial assistant on the fantasy half of this volume; to Midori Snyder for pointing out the Ní Dhuibhne story; to Bruce Shapiro at Tufts University for pointing out Čapek's work; to Ellen Kushner (at WGBH Radio), Robert Gould, Charles de Lint and Mike Korolenko for music recommendations; to Jane Yolen for children's book recommendations; to Will Shetterly and Emma Bull at Steeldragon Press for comic book recommendations; and to Tappan King, Beth Meacham, Valerie Smith, Ellen Steiber, Sheila Williams at *IASFM*, Don Keller at William Morrow and Company, Rob Killheffer at *Omni*, and the patient staffs in the Boston and Tucson Public Library periodicals rooms. Finally, as always, my deepest thanks to Jim Frenkel, Ellen Datlow, Gordon Van Gelder and Thomas Canty for their work on this volume.

—Terri Windling

The editors and packager would like to thank Ellen Zins for her help in making this book possible.

Summation 1990: Fantasy

"Fantasy," for those new to the field, is a confusing term because the realms of fantasy are as vast and mutable as the realms of Faery in old folk tales. Fantasy is a broad range of classic and contemporary literature with magical, fabulous or surrealistic elements, from novels set in imaginary worlds with their roots in folktale and mythology to contemporary stories of Magic Realism where the fantasy elements are used as metaphoric devices to illuminate the world we know. You need not have ever read J.R.R. Tolkien's *The Hobbit* or its imitators to have read fantasy, for it is a field that includes literature as diverse as Yeats's fairy poems and Oscar Wilde's fairy stories, selected works by Shakespeare, by Blake, by Chesterton and Thurber and countless others. Fantasy and fairy tales comprise humanity's literary heritage, for they are integral to the concept of storytelling.

For the past two decades, publishers and booksellers have used the label "fantasy" (or "adult fantasy") as a convenient handle to file supposedly similar (and in fact wildly dissimilar) books in a common section of the bookstore; usually next to, or even mixed in with, science fiction novels. This has the marketing advantage of identifying books with magical elements for the reader, and the critical disadvantage of segregating these books from readers of mainstream and literary fiction. A reader new to the fantasy field should thus keep in mind that a fantasy label on the spine of a book (or dragons and swords on the cover) is merely a publisher's marketing tool, and not a designation of quality or content—for beneath the fantasy label you will find a bewildering variety of books from stylistically complex literary works to uninspired but entertaining fantasy adventures that one writer has aptly dubbed the genre of Bathtub Reading. You will also find fantasy fiction, without the genre label, in many other sections of the bookstore such as the Magic Realist fantasy of mainstream authors like Mark Helprin or Margaret Atwood or Gabriel García Márquez; the ageless fantasy published as children's fiction by writers like Ursula K. Le Guin, Lloyd Alexander and Diana Wynne Jones; and in fiction and poetry classics from Mallory's *Morte D'Arthur* to William Morris's *News From Nowhere*.

Because there is so much fantasy fiction published each year both within and outside of the "adult fantasy" genre, it is the purpose of this anthology to seek out stories and poems from many different sources—genre magazines and anthologies, literary journals, children's books, mainstream story collections, foreign works in translation—and bring the best together in one volume. I can't claim to have read every magical or surrealistic work presented by every publisher here and abroad. Nor can this introduction give you more than a brief overview of fantasy in the contemporary arts in the year 1990. But I hope that through my experiences working as an editor with fantasy writers and artists across this country and England I can lead you to some works you may have overlooked or some new authors whom you might enjoy.

The Nineties are already proving an interesting decade for lovers of fantastical fiction. The hard reality is that the publishing industry is facing difficult times, and this affects what you find offered to you on the bookstore racks. Tight competition for a shrinking amount of national rack space (as retailers choose to display more profitable items, like videos) leads to an impossibly short shelf life for books by all but the best known authors, with no time for "word of mouth" advertising to help sell the work of newer writers. Recent tax law changes have made warehousing backstock titles costly, leading to short print runs and short backlists. In a field that once thrived upon the steady sales of the backlist (with the assumption that when you find a writer you like you will go back and buy their previous work), genre publishers are now letting books go quickly out of print, depending upon the big initial sale guaranteed by a small pool of bestselling authors to make their money.

Against this bleak backdrop, fantasy is nonetheless a healthy literary form. Genre fantasy enjoys a sizable and loyal audience of readers, and its books occasionally find their way to the bestseller lists. Magic Realism is becoming an increasingly visible and critically acceptable form in literary fiction both in the English language and abroad, due largely to the influence of modern Latin American writers. After decades of being dismissed as childish, pop, escapist or simply unfashionable, fantasy is suddenly a strong theme in all the contemporary arts. Despite the troubled state of trade book publishing (that is, books from large corporate publishing houses—not the small presses, which are thriving), the Nineties are an exciting time to be a creative artist working with the tools of myth and folklore. It has been said that literature is our way of conversing with people long dead and people who have yet to be born. How much more so in the fantasy field, with its traditions that are as ancient as they are international.

It is not difficult to understand the taste for fantasy in a postmodern society. Our culture has undergone a pendulum swing from the extreme idealism of the Sixties/Seventies to the cool urban "Fuck It" attitude of the Eighties, expressed both in the angry nihilism of the punk aesthetic and the solipsism of yuppie professionalism. The popularity of fantasy's dark sister, horror fiction (and film), particularly among young readers, seems to me a reaction against Eighties banality—not simply an expression of rage or terror, but a desire that there still be mystery in our lives, something more to life than what we can see or manufacture or buy with a Visa card, even if the only magic in which one can believe is dark and violent, like the world around us.

As we come out of the Eighties, taking a hard look at the ravages of consumerism and the philosophical emptiness of a culture directed by advertising, we see a definite reexamination of basic life values like family, community, creativity, and a mature reassessment of a need for philosophical ideals that would have been dismissed as sentimental or unimportant five years ago. This is seen in the enormous popularity of Joseph Campbell's work on the function of mythology in contemporary life; in John Bradshaw's explorations of the family (which also draw on the metaphoric value of myth and fairy tale), alongside Alice Miller's healing work on the subject of childhood; and in the popularity of Robert Bly's recent poetry and search for a contemporary mythology for men in the Nineties.

Magic Realism in literary fiction; worldbeat music that mixes traditional folk themes with modern instrumentation; an increasing acceptance of works of an unsentimentalized modern Romanticism in both the fine and illustrative arts; and the number of talented and intelligent writers who have chosen to dedicate themselves to genre forms like fantasy, horror and science fiction are all creating the groundswell of a fascinating movement that makes arbitrary barriers between genres and art forms unimportant. As we begin the hard task of looking at our world (and our arts) and saying, "What next?", fantasy provides images in which we can see ourselves and our futures. For fantasy at its best is a mirror held up to the world we live in; its magic lands are the lands of the human soul.

With this diversity of the ways fantasy can be used in fiction kept in mind, the following is a list of notable fantasy works published in 1990. If you have time to read only a handful of them, here's a baker's dozen of the novels I'd recommend you not miss (in alphabetical order):

The King, Donald Barthelme (Harper & Row). An enchanting slim novel that sets the Arthurian legend in the early days of World War II, gorgeously illustrated by master bookmaker Barry Moser.

Ghostwood (Pulphouse) or *Drink Down the Moon* (Ace), Charles de Lint. Urban fantasy bringing magic and folklore to the streets of modern Canada by one of the pioneers of this brand of fiction. The first is a sequel to *Moonheart*, the second to *Jack the Giant-Killer* so I am cheating wildly by actually recommending four books in the place of one.

Redwall, Brian Jacques (Avon). I admit, it's about talking rodents—but this is not just a kiddie novel or *Watership Down* redux; and the mice and other creatures in this indescribable fantasy are not overly precious. Jacques creates a complex and detailed society within the walls of a medieval castle, and the book is a pure delight.

Thomas the Rhymer, Ellen Kushner (Wm. Morrow). If you've been burned by too many badly written imaginary-world fantasy novels, Kushner will restore your sense of wonder with this evocative and very sensuous retelling of the story of the musician who spends seven years in the land of Faery.

Tehanu: The Last Book of Earthsea, Ursula K. Le Guin (Atheneum). This, the fourth volume in Le Guin's now classic Earthsea series, is controversial—some readers loved it and others were vastly disappointed. It is well worth picking up and deciding for yourself.

Lens of the World, R.A. MacAvoy (Wm. Morrow). MacAvoy is one of the best of the writers to emerge in the fantasy genre in the 1980s, and this medieval coming-of-age story is an intelligently magical fantasy tale.

The General in His Labyrinth, Gabriel García Márquez (Knopf). South American author García Márquez has influenced writers not only in the fantasy field but across the globe with the superb Magic Realism of novels like *One Hundred Years of Solitude* and *The Autumn of the Patriarch*. His latest transmutes history into a magical narrative, following the "great liberator" Simón Bolívar on a seven-month journey down the Magdelena River in Bogotá.

Haroun and the Sea of Stories, Salman Rushdie (Viking). A charmingly funny and magical adventure, recounted by the storyteller the Shah of Blah, from the author of *The Satanic Verses*.

Borgel, Daniel Pinkwater (Macmillan). An old man appears at the Spellbound family's door to take young Marvin on a search through time and space for the Popsicle God. Typically Pinkwater hyperdrive wackiness from a writer who is not so much a children's book author as a genre unto himself.

The Child Garden, Geoff Ryman (St. Martin's Press). A gorgeously written fantasy novel set in a bizarre, semi-tropical London that is quite simply one of the best books I've ever read, in its first U.S. edition. Don't miss it.

Cambio Bay, Kate Wilhelm (St. Martin's Press). A haunting and subtle story by a master fantasist that makes deft use of Native American legendry.

Sexing the Cherry, Jeanette Winterson (Atlantic Monthly Press). This lively and engaging Magic Realist fantasy novel about a young woman coming of age in an alternate England received a lot of attention in the U.K. and is in its first U.S. edition.

Castleview, Gene Wolfe (Tor). As always, Wolfe is witty, erudite and wondrous with this fantasy set in the small midwestern town of Castleview (named for the floating castle that sometimes appears overhead) where magic and reality intersect.

There is one more novel I would have liked to include with the very best of the year except, alas, it's not really fantasy, even if the author does invent (*à la* Tim Powers) two imaginary Victorian poets and their supposed works. (By that reasoning any book with invented characters could classify as fantasy. . . .) Nonetheless, I strongly recommend seeking out A.S. Byatt's *Possession*, which recently won England's prestigious Booker Prize. It is the story of two scholars researching the letters and love affair between a lionized 19th century poet and a reclusive Christina Rossetti–type writer of fairy poems—and while it is highly enjoyable if you are not a literary scholar, for readers with any knowledge of Victorian literature and personalities, and of the modern academic lit. crit. scene, it is wickedly funny.

The "Best Peculiar Book of the Year Award" goes to Serbian poet Milorad Pavić's *Landscape Painted With Tea*, a fantasy of the Orient complete with reader participation, in a gorgeously produced edition from Knopf.

The best first novels of the year are *Through the Arc of the Rainbow Forest* by Karen tei Yamashita, a lovely Magic Realist fantasy from Coffee House Press; and *Max Lakeman and the Beautiful Stranger* by Jon Cohen, contemporary fantasy set in a small American town, from Warner. Other notable debuts are Peter Gadol's southwestern Spiritwalk *Coyote* (Crown), and Annette Curtis Klau's coming-of-age novel *The Silver Kiss* (Delacorte), complete with a leather-jacket-wearing teenage vampire.

Other recommended titles of 1990: From Ace Fantasy/The Berkley Publishing Group: *Phoenix*, Steven Brust (more than just series fiction, Brust's "Vlad" novels have grown and matured along with the considerable skills of the author); *Drink Down the Moon*, Charles de Lint (excellent urban fantasy issued along with the first paperback edition of its prequel, *Jack the Giant-Killer* [Fairy Tale Series #2]); *Festival Week*, edited by Will Shetterly and Emma Bull (the closing book in the "Liavek" series, nicely rounding out this shared-world anthology that showcased some of the best new talent in fantasy in the last decade); *Fortress of the Pearl*, Michael Moorcock (a new "Elric" series novel from a writer who, even when he is "slumming" with adventure fantasy, is still intelligent and stylish); *The Work of the Sun*, Teresa Edgerton (last book in a trilogy by a writer to watch); *The Stalking Horse*, Constance Ash (a political intrigue fantasy by a writer with a real talent for characterization); and *Spell Bound*, Ru Emerson (a retelling of the Cinderella fairy tale set in 17th century Germany). The Ace list is most successful with their light fantasy: for lovers of humorous fantasy, the best of these in 1990 were *Revenge of the Fluffy Bunnies* by Craig Shaw Gardner, *Hooray for Hellywood* by Esther Friesner, and *Kedrigern and the Charming Couple* by John Morressy.

From Atheneum: *A Romance of the Equator*, Brian Aldiss (first U.S. edition of this excellent fat story collection); *The Stories of Eva Luna*, Isabel Allende (collected stories by the Chilean author of *In the Spirit House*); and *The Dogs of Paradise*, Abel Possee (a mystical, magical historical extravaganza from this Argentine author which I listed last year but which is, in fact, a January '90 publication).

The Atlantic Monthly Press: *Whilom*, Robert Watson (an interesting if not entirely successful Shakespearean satirical fantasy) and the above-mentioned *Sexing the Cherry* by Jeanette Winterson.

Available Press/Ballantine: *Max and the Cats*, Moacyr Scliar (three fascinating Magic Realist stories from Brazil, translated from the Portuguese.)

Avon: The above-mentioned *Redwall* and its sequel *Mossflower*, Brian Jacques; *Fire on the Mountain*, Terry Bisson (this is science fiction from a writer who has heretofore published fantasy novels, but Bisson's excellent depiction of an alternate-history America will appeal to his fantasy readers as well); and a reissue of *Midnight's Children*, Salman Rushdie (which is at least as good as, if not better than, the more notorious *The Satanic Verses*).

From Baen/Sign of the Dragon: Baen bills itself as "fantasy with rivets" and specializes in science-fantasy adventure tales—with the occasional notable exception: in 1990 it was the first paperback edition of the splendid literary fantasy *The Coachman Rat* by David Henry Wilson (a dark retelling of Cinderella from the coachman's point of view). Humorous fantasy readers should note the publication of *The Undesired Princess and the Enchanted Bunny* by L. Sprague de Camp (one of the inventors of this brand of fiction) and David Drake.

From Bantam/Spectra and Doubleday/Foundation: *Walker of Worlds*, Tom De Haven (don't be put off by the generic fantasy look of the book; it's intelligently written and very highly recommended); *Eight Skilled Gentlemen*, Barry Hughart (an excellent third Chinese fantasy from this World Fantasy Award–winning writer); *Dead Man's Hand*, edited by George R.R. Martin (#VII in the "Wild Cards" series, an extremely well-crafted "shared world" anthology containing short fiction that straddles the line between science fiction and dark fantasy); *Points of Departure*, Pat Murphy (a short story collection that includes fantasy from this very talented West Coast author); the first U.S. edition of *A Child Across the Sky*, Jonathan Carroll (unusual dark fantasy; highly recommended); and *Mary Reilly*, Valerie Martin (a fascinating look at Stevenson's story of Jekyll and Hyde from the housemaid's point of view).

From Bloomsbury: *Squed*, Richard Miller (a strange literary fantasy novel).

From Century Legend: *The Blood of Roses*, Tanith Lee (dark, dark fantasy; gorgeous and chilling); *The Last Guardian*, David Gemmell (sequel to *Wolf in Shadow*).

From Citadel Press: *Walford's Oak*, Jill M. Phillips (a ghostly tale within a tale as purportedly told to Samuel Taylor Coleridge).

From Clarkson Potter: *Black Water 2*, Alberto Manguel (excellent fat collection of primarily reprint stories).

From Coffee House Press: *Verging on the Pertinent*, Carol Emshwiller (a story collection from one of the field's most adventurous stylists—actually published in 1989, but I missed it last year); and the above-mentioned *Through the Arc of the Rain Forest* by Karen tei Yamashita.

From Crown: the above-mentioned southwestern American fantasy, *Coyote* by Peter Gadol.

From Dark Harvest: *The Leiber Chronicles*, edited by Martin H. Greenberg (an important omnibus volume of 44 stories covering 34 years of writing by one of fantasy's Grand Masters).

From DAW: Notable titles of magical adventure fantasy: *Magic's Price*, Mercedes Lackey (ends the very popular "Last Herald Mage" series); *Stone of Farewell*, Tad Williams (sequel to *The Dragonbone Chair*); and *Shadow's Realm*, Mickey Zucker Reichert (4th book in the "Bifrost Guardians" series).

From Del Rey: *The Dark Hand of Magic*, Barbara Hambly (excellent imaginary world story); *Chernevog*, C.J. Cherryh (Russian fantasy, the sequel to *Rusalka*, also a cut above the rest); *Call of Madness*, Julie Dean Smith (a coming-of-age fantasy that marks an interesting debut; *The Dragon's Carbuncle*, Elizabeth R. Boyer (fantasy with a Scandinavian touch); and *Sorceress of Darshiva*, David Eddings (Book #4 in the "Mallorean" series). Also of note is *The Scions of Shannara* by bestselling author Terry Brooks (imaginary world fantasy, consciously Tolkien-esque).

From Dedalus: a new edition of *Fantasy Tales* by Goethe.

From the Euto Group: *After Magic*, Bruce Boston (an interestingly surrealistic novella, illustrated by Lari Davidson).

From Farrar, Straus & Giroux: *Christopher Unborn*, Carlos Fuentes (a literary fantasy set in the future of Mexico, narrated by an unborn child); and *Absence*, Peter Handke (a surrealistic tale translated from the German).

Gollancz: *Casablanca*, Michael Moorcock (a splendid collection of stories and nonfiction); and *Good Omens* by Terry Pratchett and Neil Gaiman (here's the point where I have to admit that "funny fantasy" spoofs are just not my preferred reading—but even I found this one pretty funny).

From Grove Weidenfeld: *The Last Word*, Christoph Ransmayr (a metaphysical thriller concerning Ovid's *Metamorphoses*, translated from the German).

From Harper & Row: *The Underside of Stones*, George Szanto (a story cycle set in a small Mexican village, highly recommended); and the above-mentioned *The King* by Donald Barthelme and Barry Moser.

From Harper Perennial Library: the first U.S. edition of *Mother London*, Michael Moorcock (an extraordinary and stylistically fascinating novel, with some fantasy elements, that explores the city of London from World War II to the present through the eyes of several characters).

From Alfred A. Knopf: *Ah, Sweet Mystery of Life*, Roald Dahl (a collection from this highly original writer); *The Princess and the Dragon*, Robert Pazzi (a story about the brother of the last Tsar of Russia that blends the factual with the miraculous, translated from the Italian); and the above-mentioned *Landscape Painted With Tea* by Milorad Pavić.

From Little, Brown: *The Pearl of the Soul of the World*, Meredith Ann Pierce (book #3 of the "Darkangel" trilogy); and a new edition of *Arthur Rex* by Thomas Berger.

From Macdonald: *Scholars and Soldiers*, Mary Gentle (a volume of stories by this talented writer).

From Macmillan: *Borgel*, Daniel Pinkwater (you have to read him to believe him).

From McPherson & Co.: *All the Errors*, Giorgio Manganelli (metaphysical stories translated from the Italian); *I Hear Voices* (first U.S. edition of this surrealistic fantasy first published thirty years ago in Paris by Olympia Press); and *Twelve Ravens*, Howard Rose (a strange midwestern gothic fantasy back in print after thirty years).

From Mercury House: *Carmen Dog*, Carol Emshwiller (first U.S. edition of this allegorical novel).

From William Morrow: the above-mentioned *Thomas the Rhymer* by Ellen Kushner and *Lens of the World* by R. A. MacAvoy; *No Return*, Alexander Kabakov (first U.S. edition of a dystopian novel that has been very popular in the USSR); and several excellent SF novels with fantastical elements that may appeal to fantasy readers: *Only Begotten Daughter* by James Morrow; *The Hemingway Hoax* by Joe Haldeman; and *Brain Rose* by Nancy Kress.

From NAL/Roc: *Rats & Gargoyles*, Mary Gentle (dark medieval fantasy with a hint of Mervyn Peake; highly recommended); *Tigana*, Guy Gavriel Kay (imaginary-world fantasy with the flavor of Renaissance Italy); *Tempter*, Nancy A. Collins (this is horror set in New Orleans, but its energy and quirky characterization will appeal to many fantasy readers as well); and, for humorous fantasy readers, *Wyrd Sister* by Terry Pratchett.

From North Point Press: *The Hour of Blue*, Robert Froese (interesting ecological fantasy).

From Oceanview Press: *Short Circuits*, Bruce Boston (poetry collection).

From Overlook Press: *The Corn King and the Spring Queen*, Naomi Mitchison (a reprint edition of this mystical historical set in 228 B.C.).

From Pantheon: *Skeleton-in-Waiting*, Peter Dickinson (a mystery novel set in an alternate

England, the sequel to *King and Joker*, by one of the most masterful writers in the English language).

From Penguin: *Sunburn Lake*, Tom De Haven (collection of short fiction); and a new edition of G.K. Chesterton's *The Man Who Was Thursday*.

From Poseidon Press: *The Barnum Museum*, Steven Millhauser (collection of short fiction); and *Queen of Stars* by Persia Wooley (recommended to me but not seen).

From G.P. Putnam's Sons: *Hocus, Pocus or What's the Hurry, Son*, the latest from Kurt Vonnegut.

From Pulphouse Publishing: *Ghostwood*, Charles de Lint (sequel to his urban fantasy novel *Moonheart*).

From St. Martin's Press: the above-mentioned *Cambio Bay* by Kate Wilhelm and *The Child Garden* by Geoff Ryman.

From Simon and Schuster/Fireside: *Three-fisted Tales of "Bob"*, edited by Reverend Ivan Stang (a recommended collection of stories by William S. Burroughs, Robert Anton Wilson, Lewis Shiner and others based on the Church of the Subgenius).

From Syracuse University Press: *At Midnight on the 31st of May*, Josephine Young Case (a long out of print 1938 story in poetry form about a town that is suddenly cut off from the rest of 20th century America, finding itself surrounded by primeval forest. Recommended.).

From Tor: the above-mentioned *Castleview*, Gene Wolfe; *Maps in a Mirror*, Orson Scott Card (a fat volume of the short fiction, including fantasy and fables, of this highly original writer); *Ill Met in Lankhmar*, Fritz Leiber and *The Fair in Emain Macha*, Charles de Lint (two fantasy novellas by an old master and a new); *The Enchantments of Flesh and Spirit*, Storm Constantine (interesting fantasy with punk elements, controversial—some love it, some hate it); *Moon Dance*, S.P. Somtow (a horror novel about werewolves in the 19th century American West that fantasy readers may enjoy as well—another 1989 book that somehow slipped past me last year); *Time and Chance*, Alan Brennert (Jack Finney–esque fantasy, recommended); *Tales of the Witch World 3*, edited by Andre Norton (original stories set in Norton's "Witch World" series, which has been popular with readers for a generation); and paperback editions of *Snow White and Rose Red* by Patricia C. Wrede (a charming Elizabethan retelling of the fairy tale), and *White Jenna*, Jane Yolen (a splendid, Nebula-award nominated novel by one of the field's masters).

From TSR: among the adventure and Fantasy Gaming–oriented books produced by this publisher, Mary Herbert's *Dark Horse* stands out as an interesting first novel; she adds some freshness to standard material.

From Unwin Hyman: a new edition of the fairy tale retelling *Swan's Wing* by Ursula Synge (recommended).

From Viking: *Falling Out of Time*, O.R. Melling (a literary fantasy published jointly in the U.S. and Canada); *Antique Dust*, Robert Westall (first U.S. edition of the first adult collection of stories from a superb British writer of dark fantasy for children; highly recommended); Salman Rushdie's *Haroun and the Sea of Stories*, mentioned above; and *Wondermonger*, Michael Rothchild (a collection of New England stories that border on the fantastic; "A Land Without Fossils" is particularly recommended).

From Vintage: reprints of *The Best of Roald Dahl* and *Tales of the Unexpected* by Roald Dahl; *The Cockroaches of Stay More*, Donald Harrington (recommended, bizarre as it sounds); *Sleeping in Flame*, Jonathan Carroll (first U.S. edition of this dark fantasy; highly recommended); and *The Colorist*, Susan Daitch (peculiar literary fantasy about a cartoonist and her superhero).

From Warner: the above-mentioned *Max Lakeman and the Beautiful Stranger* by Jon

Cohen; *Geek Love*, Katherine Dunn (first paperback edition of an excellent dark fantasy; recommended).

From W.H. Allen: *Extraordinary Tales*, edited by Jorge Luis Borges and Aldolfo Bioy Casares (a good collection of reprint stories, largely but not entirely South American).

From The Women's Press: *The Start of the End of it All and Other Stories*, Carol Emshwiller (more good fiction from Emshwiller).

From Mark V. Ziesing: *A Short, Sharp Shock*, Kim Stanley Robinson (wonderful surrealistic fantasy, nicely illustrated by Arnie Fenner).

Some of the works we think of as adult fantasy were originally published as children's fiction, so it is always worth looking at the children's shelves in the bookstore or library when looking for a good fantasy read. In 1990, two new fantasy lines debuted. Jane Yolen Books, an imprint of Harcourt Brace Jovanovich edited by master storyteller Jane Yolen, specializing in fantasy and science fiction for teenagers, was launched with two excellent novels: *Dealing With Dragons* by Patricia C. Wrede and *Wren to the Rescue* by Sherwood Smith. Dragonflight, a line packaged by Byron Preiss Visual Publications for Atheneum, launched with *Letters from Atlantis*, light fantasy entertainment from Robert Silverberg, and Charles de Lint's lovely *The Dreaming Place*. The publication of *Tehanu: The Last Book of Earthsea* by Ursula K. Le Guin (along with a fascinating essay from Le Guin, published by Pulphouse, discussing why she felt compelled to return to the world of Earthsea) was the other notable event in children's fantasy in 1990.

In addition to these books, I would also recommend taking a look at the following excellent children's fantasy titles: *The Dragon's Boy*, Jane Yolen (Harper & Row); *The Ogre Downstairs*, Diana Wynne Jones (Greenwillow), *Hidden Turnings*, edited by Diana Wynne Jones (Greenwillow, first U.S. edition); *Mattimeo*, Brian Jacques (sequel to *Redwall* and *Mossflower*, published by Philomel); *Red Wizard*, Nancy Springer (Atheneum); *The Shining Company*, Rosemary Sutcliff (FS&G): *The Palace of Kings* and *Shadowlight*, Mike Jefferies (Harper & Row); *Dark Hills, Hollow Clocks*, Garry Kilworth (story collection, Methuen); *A Well Timed Enchantment*, Vivian Vande Velde (Crown), *High Wizardry*, Diane Duane (Delacorte); *A Fit of Shivers*, Joan Aiken (story collection, Gollancz); and *The Silver Kiss*, Annette Curtis Klaus (Delacorte).

Children's picture books are a forum not only for lovely short fantasy tales but for some of the best magical art and illustration since the Golden Age of illustrators like Rackham, Nielsen and Dulac. If you are a lover of fantasy art, you must particularly take a look at Gennadij Spirin's exquisite paintings illustrating Gogol's tale *Sorotchintzey the Fair* (David R. Godine) which are as rich as medieval miniatures and do amazing things with the layout of the page.

Other favorites this year are *The Merry Pranks of Till Eulenspiegel* (translated by Anthea Bell) and *Aesop's Fables* (both published by Picture Book Studio), beautifully rendered by the peerless young Viennese painter Lizbeth Zwerger, who recently won the prestigious Hans Christian Andersen medal for Life Achievement. Barry Moser is another of our most skilled illustrators and he has done a beautiful job with Jane Yolen's Native American story *Sky Dogs* (HBJ). Newbery Award–winning author Virginia Hamilton has put out a collection of dark folk tales called *The Dark Way: Stories from the Spirit World*, nicely illustrated by Lambert Davis (HBJ). Leo and Diane Dillon have illustrated Katherine Patterson's Chinese story *The Tale of the Mandarin Ducks* (Henry Holt); and Michael Hague has illustrated the old William Allingham poem *The Fairies* (Henry Holt). *Crow and Weasel* is a wonderful Native American tale told by Barry Lopez and charmingly illustrated by Tom Pohrt (North Point Press). And Jane Yolen's gentle retelling of the Scottish ballad *Tam Lin* has been illustrated by Charles Mikolaycak (HBJ).

In adult fantasy illustration we see two distinct schools prevalent these days. One has its roots in American illustration, following in the tradition of great illustrators like N.C. Wyeth, Howard Pyle and Norman Rockwell. The other has its roots in British Romanticism, following in the tradition of turn-of-the-century painters like the Pre-Raphaelites, Whistler and Waterhouse in England, Mucha and Klimt on the continent.

While artists fulfilling commercial assignments for fantasy book covers are under more marketing direction and constraints than illustrators in other fields such as picture books or adult comics (the cover of a book being not so much an artistic representation of what is inside the book as a "billboard" advertising it), there has nonetheless been some commendable work done within these constraints in 1990; Brian Froud's extraordinary painting on *The Dreaming Place* as well as Robert Gould's design work for the volume (by Charles de Lint, Atheneum); Robert Gould's own work on *Letters from Atlantis* (by Robert Silverberg, Atheneum); Mel Odom's distinctive work on *Tigana* (by Guy Gavriel Kay, NAL) and *Max Lakeman and the Beautiful Stranger* (by Jon Cohen, Warner); Thomas Woodruff's rich and mystical painting for *The General in His Labyrinth* (by Gabriel García Márquez, (Knopf); Yvonne Gilbert's delicately evocative *The Moonbane Mage* (by Laurie J. Marks, DAW); Jody Lee's beautifully designed *Magic's Promise* (by Mercedes Lackey, DAW); Thomas Canty's "American Romantic" work on *Little, Big* (by John Crowley, Bantam) and his charming mice on *Redwall* and *Mossflower* (by Brian Jacques, Avon) as well as Troy Howell's version of those same mice on *Mattimeo* (by Brian Jacques, Philomel); Graham Rust's sumptuously elegant *Landscape Painted with Tea* (by Milorad Pavić, Knopf); Rowena Morrill's lovely painting for the U.K. edition of *Prentice Alvin* (by Orson Scott Card, Legend); David Bergin's enchanted wood on the U.K. edition of *Moonheart* (by Charles de Lint, Pan); Trina Schart Hyman's engaging work on *Dealing With Dragons* (Patricia C. Wrede, HBJ); Kyle Baker's striking comic art for *The Further Adventures of the Joker* (Bantam collection); Dean Morrissey's richly detailed and humorous work such as *Kedrigern and the Charming Couple* (by John Morressy, Ace); Michael Whelan's window into another world for *Stone of Farewell* (by Tad Williams, DAW)—and this is the tip of the iceberg of laudable works from artists in our field (with my apologies to those I haven't room to list). Bantam deserves a particular commendation for unusual and interesting covers in 1990—particularly in their reissue of the Ray Bradbury backlist in which each book showcased the work of a different artist in the field (Michael Whelan, Barclay Shaw, Don Maitz, J.K. Potter, Thomas Canty, Kevin E. Johnson, Jim Burns, and Leo and Diane Dillon).

"In Dreams Awake," a large exhibit of fantasy work by a number of the major fantasy and comics illustrators including Michael Kaluta, Charles Vess, Jeffrey Jones, Michael Whelan, David Cherry, Ron Walotsky, Dennis Nolan, Jody Lee, Thomas Kidd, Don Maitz and Janny Wurts, was held in New York in 1990.

In England, some of the artists from the Ruralist movement along with fine British fantasy artists—like painters Brian Froud and Thomas Woodruff and sculptor Wendy Froud—put together an excellent exhibition on the theme of Alice in Wonderland, which traveled around the country and ended in London. A television play loosely based on the Ruralists (a Pre-Raphaelite–influenced group of fine artists who first banded together in the Sixties) was broadcast in Britain in 1990. British watercolorist Alan Lee was commissioned to paint fifty new works for a special edition of *The Lord of the Rings* by J.R.R. Tolkien; by the end of the year he had completed the assignment with a studio full of extraordinary paintings influenced by the magical Devon countryside. The book will be published in 1991 by Unwin Hyman.

Art books of interest this year: Rizzoli issued a new book of paintings by Victorian

Romantic J.W. Waterhouse (with text and pictures that overlap their previous book on the painter); Abrams issued a gorgeous new book on turn-of-the-century illustrator Arthur Rackham and a collection of the works of American mystical painter Albert Pinkham Ryder. Macmillan has published a huge James A. McNeill Whistler retrospective, which is of note because of the influence Whistler's paintings have had on many fantasy and adult comics illustrators.

An English edition of *The Art Of Yoshitaka Amano Hiten*, one of Japan's leading illustrators, is available from Nippon/US editions. Paper Tiger has published *Last Ship Home*, a collection of paintings and posters by Rodney Mathews. Pomegranate Press has completely sold out of the hauntingly beautiful "Goddess" calendar of paintings by Southwestern artist Susan Seddon Boulet (not to be confused with her annual "Shaman" calendar) so if you find it somewhere, snap it up—it's stunning and you needn't be a crystal-carrying New Ager to enjoy it. Author Piers Anthony has self-published a Xanth calendar, commissioning works from some of the fantasy field's best illustrators. GW Books has published *Ratspoil* containing the work of John Blanche and Ian Miller; and Fantagraphics has published the first of four Diary Sketchbooks by the late comic artist Vaughan Bodē.

In the area of adult comics, *Sandman* written by Neil Gaiman (DC Comics) remains the most consistently high quality series; I particularly recommend the September '90 issue illustrated by Charles Vess to fantasy readers. Dan Sweetman has published some gorgeous and dark drawings in the *Beautiful Stories for Ugly Children* comics put out by Piranha Press (DC). And I most highly recommend *Big Numbers*, written by Alan Moore and illustrated by Bill Sienkiewicz (Mad Love Publishing); the two issues I've seen thus far are truly adult comics—complex, thoughtful works by two of the most talented men working today.

Traditional folk music is of special interest to many fantasy readers because the old ballads, particularly in the English, Irish and Scots folk traditions, are often based on the same folk and fairy tale roots as fantasy fiction. And the current generation of worldbeat musicians, like contemporary fantasy writers, are taking traditional music and adapting it to a modern age. New listeners might try *Flight of the Green Linnet: Celtic Music—the Next Generation* as an introduction to the music; it features several of the best new bands such as Capercaille and Silly Wizard. (If you prefer music with a rock or punk edge to it, then I'd suggest starting out with a band like Boiled in Lead, the Waterboys, or Blowzabella.)

The veteran English folk band Pentangle released a new studio album, blending folk, jazz and blues, titled *So Early in the Spring*—their first really satisfying release in the last few years. Blowzabella is one of the best of the worldbeat bands that mixes music and instrumentation from many cultures; they released a new album titled *Vanilla* in 1990. *Hard Cash* is a companion to a BBC television series on "exploitation in the workplace" which has an all-star lineup and all new material by June Tabor, Martin Carthy, The Watersons, Dave Mattocks, the legendary Richard Thompson, and many others. The Scots band Tannahill Weavers has released *Cullen Bay*, their strongest work yet; and the Irish band Altan has released *The Red Crow* with gorgeous vocals by Mairead Ni Mhaonaigh. Johnny Cunningham (of Silly Wizard) has produced *Orealis: Musique Celtique*, introducing a fine new Canadian band that mixes modern and traditional music—like a quieter version of Rare Air. Ireland's Patrick Street has released *Irish Times*, and the Irish folk-rock band The Waterboys have released the wonderful *Room to Roam* which includes a George MacDonald poem set to music and the best version of "Raggle-Taggle Gypsies" that I've yet heard; highly recommended. Minneapolis band Cats Laughing, which includes fantasists Emma Bull and Steven Brust among its members, has released *Another Way to*

Travel (only available by writing to Spin Art, Box 7253, Minneapolis, MN 55407); and that city's excellent worldbeat "rock and reel" band Boiled in Lead have produced their best album yet, titled *Orb*.

Also recommended: *Blues for Transylvania* by the Hungarian band Muzsikas; *Yasimika* by Jali Musa Jawara, haunting African music from Guinea; the punk-folk blend of *Accordions Go Crazy*; the indescribably beautiful *Mouth Music*; the subtly mystical songs by Ferron on her new album, *Ferron*; *Invisible Means* (R. Thompson, French, Frith, and Kaiser); *Savuka*, from the South African musicians who formerly made up the Zulu and Celtic–influenced band Juluka; *Carry the Gift*, contemporary Native American music from R. Carlos Nakai; and powerful British vocalist June Tabor's latest release, *Some Other Time*.

1990 produced several noteworthy editions for fairy tale and folk tale libraries, the best of these being Angela Carter's *Old Wives' Fairy Book* from Pantheon.

I also recommend taking a look at: *The Complete Fairy Tales of Oscar Wilde*, Jack Zipes, ed. (NAL); *The Fairy Tales of Frank Stockton* (NAL); *Fairy Tales of Ireland*, William Butler Yeats—a new edition illustrated by P.J. Lynch (Delacorte); *The Hard Facts of Grimm's Fairy Tales*, Maria Tartar (Pantheon); *The Mythology of Mexico and Central America*, Jon Bierhorst (Wm. Morrow); *The Wind Children and Other Tales* from Japan, Samira Kirollos (Andre Deutsch, U.K.); *Mimekor Yisrael: Selected Jewish Folktales*, Micha Joseph Bin Gorion (Indiana University Press); *The Oxford Book of Canadian Ghost Stories*, Alberto Manguel, ed.; and *Folklore of Canada*, Edith Fowke (McClelland & Stewart). P.L. Travers (author of *Mary Poppins*) published a collection of essays on myth and story in 1989, unseen until now; Travers' *What the Bee Knows* is available from The Aquarian Press and highly recommended.

There were also a number of works of nonfiction published in 1990 of interest to fantasy readers. Notable titles:

C.S. Lewis: A Biography, A.N. Wilson (Norton); *The Letters of J.R.R. Tolkien*, Humphrey Carpenter, ed. (Unwin); *William Morris: The Construction of a Male Self, 1856–1872*, Frederick Kirtchoff (Ohio University Press); *The Godwins and the Shelleys*, William St. Clair (W.W. Norton); *The Poetic Fantastic: Studies in an Evolving Genre*, Patrick D. Murphy and Vernon Hayes, eds. (Greenwood); *The Rushdie File*, Sara Maitland and Lisa Appignanesi, eds. (Syracuse University Press); *Feminist Alternatives: Irony and Fantasy in the Contemporary Novel by Women*, Nancy A. Walker (University of Mississippi); and *Fantasy Literature: A Reader's Guide*, Neil Barron, ed. (Garland Publishing).

The 11th Annual Conference on the Fantastic in the Arts was held in March in Ft. Lauderdale, Florida. The Guests of Honor were Hal Clement, Jane Yolen, Brian W. Aldiss, and Stephen R. Donaldson.

The 1990 Fourth Street Fantasy Convention was held in June in Minneapolis. The Guests of Honor were author Samuel R. Delany and artist Don Maitz.

The 1990 World Fantasy Convention was held in November in Chicago. The Guests of Honor were authors F. Paul Wilson and L. Sprague de Camp, artist David Mattingly, and Susan Allison of the Berkley Publishing Group. Winners of the World Fantasy Award (for work in 1989) were: Best Novel: *Lyonesse: Madouc*, Jack Vance; Best Novella: "Great Work of Time," John Crowley; Best Short Fiction: "The Illusionist," Steven Millhauser; Best Collection: *Richard Matheson: Collected Stories* (horror), Richard Matheson; Best Anthology: *The Year's Best Fantasy: Second Annual Collection*, Ellen Datlow & Terri Windling, eds.; Best Artist: Thomas Canty; Special Award/Professional: Mark V. Ziesing Publications; Special Award/Nonprofessional: *Grue* Magazine (horror), Peggy Nadramia; Life Achievement Award: R.A. Lafferty. Judges for the award were: Michael Dirda, Pat

LoBrutto, Beth Meacham, Peter Straub and Rodger Turner. Next year's World Fantasy Convention will be held in October in Tucson, Arizona.

The British Fantasy Awards were presented in Birmingham, U.K. in September. The August Derleth Award for Best Novel went to: *Carrion Comfort* (horror), by Dan Simmons; Best Short Fiction: "On the Far Side of the Cadillac Desert with Dead Folks" (horror), by Joe R. Lansdale; Best Artist: Dave Carson. Special Award: British Fantasy Society organizer Peter Coleborn.

As always, there was an abundance of good fantasy fiction both within and outside of the genre in 1990, making it hard to choose a limited number of stories to reprint. Each year my final list of selected stories is slightly longer than we have room to publish, even in a fat anthology like this one, and so I'd like to point out the following 1990 publications as among the very best of the year (I hope you will seek them out): "Bones" by Pat Murphy (*Isaac Asimov's*, May); "Bears Discover Fire" by Terry Bisson (*Isaac Asimov's*, August); "And the Angels Sing" by Kate Wilhelm (*Omni*, May); "The Man Who Ran With Deer," Thomas Fox Averill (*The Sonoran Review* #18) and "The Haunted Boardinghouse" by Gene Wolfe (*Walls of Fear*).

I regret that there is little "imaginary world" fantasy fiction in this volume; it was not in general a strong year for short fiction of that sort. (Although you can find some very good imaginary world stories indeed in the Shetterly & Bull anthology *Festival Week* from Ace, and in Andre Norton's *Witch World* anthology from Tor (most notably the Wrede, Randall and McKillip contributions)—though in both these cases these are stories that work best when read together as part of the whole volume, particularly for readers unfamiliar with the background "worlds" they are set in.) You will also find a marked trend toward stories dealing with family and childhood themes, a subject that seems to be close to the bone for many writers right now.

All in all, 1990 was an excellent year for fantasy short fiction. I hope that you'll agree, and that you will enjoy the magical tales that follow.

—Terri Windling

Summation 1990: Horror

Horror in 1990 was a mixed bag. There were some outstanding books published, and some superlative shorter work appeared as well, but overall, the field's economic health was placed in some doubt. In November, amid cries of corporate censorship, Simon & Schuster announced the cancellation of its soon-to-be-shipped hardcover of Bratpacker Bret Easton Ellis's third novel, *American Psycho*. The media flap focused on intimations that the book was withdrawn because of pressure brought by the chief executive of the conglomerate parent, Marvin Davis, chairman of Paramount Communications, although he and Richard Snyder, chairman of Simon & Schuster, both deny this.

The book is about a yuppie psycho who coolly goes about slicing and dicing (after torturing) various men, women, and children. Snyder claims that the nature of the book first reached his attention when he saw a piece in *Time*, and after reading the novel, he made his decision to withdraw it. The Author's Guild immediately protested on behalf of Ellis while Snyder claimed it wasn't a First Amendment issue. Ellis said there had been "rumblings" in the company when the manuscript was first submitted a year earlier but that Charles Hayward, president of the trade division, and Robert Asahina, Ellis's editor, believed in the book and calmed everyone down. Apparently, the sales and marketing people had strong reactions when the book was presented to them at the publishing meeting during the summer of 1990, and the general feeling in-house was that it would lose money. The initial print order was to be 20,000 to 40,000 copies. The reported advance of $350,000 was not returned and Sonny Mehta, president of Knopf and Vintage, snapped the novel up for the prestigious trade paperback imprint, Vintage Contemporaries.

Having read the edited Simon & Schuster manuscript, I don't believe the violence is any worse than that in the works of genre horror writers Richard Laymon and C. Dean Andersson or for that matter in those of the Marquis de Sade. And Ellis's book has a lot more humor. In fact, it's a blackly humorous look at yuppiedom. The self-absorbed protagonist tries confessing his deeds to his self-absorbed friends, who either completely ignore what he says or take it as an in-joke. *American Psycho* is a sleazier, less funny *Bonfire of the Vanities*—without the style of Wolfe and with far more self-indulgence. The book has a dated feel to it; the prime year for publication would have been 1987 or so, before the downfall of the Yuppie. Now it seems almost nostalgic. The book is much too long, with loads of boring details of the yuppie lifestyle. It gets so dull that this reader was longing for some violence to break up the monotony of the drab lives. There's no doubt that the violence is graphic and horrifying, but surprisingly, the book also has some eroticism. There are hints that at least some of the violence is fantasy, but to me it is all so matter-of-fact that it didn't really get to me the way some depictions of violence do.

Okay. So is it a good book? No. Will horror fans like it? Probably not. But its notoriety has virtually ensured that *American Psycho* will make the bestseller lists and that it will earn back its advances (both of them). And *that's* the only obscenity involved here. If I didn't know better I'd voice suspicions that there's a conspiracy between the two publishers in order to make a fortune from this book.

André Schiffrin, longtime managing director of Pantheon Books, resigned in late February of 1990 after twenty-eight years with the Random House imprint. He resigned in protest of plans to cut the Pantheon list by one half or more; most of the original Pantheon staff has since quit; a demonstration held March fifth in front of the Random House headquarters was attended by James A. Michener, Studs Terkel and Kurt Vonnegut, along with other writers, agents, and editors and others in the book world. Pantheon's financial status lay at the crux of the developments. Alberto Vitale, brought in from Bertelsmann to replace Robert Bernstein (a longtime Pantheon supporter) as chief executive of Random House, claimed that "Pantheon had been losing a lot of money over the last several years . . ." although a highly placed employee who worked with Bernstein denied this. Former Pantheon editors insisted that the issue was the loss of a "cultural treasure" (Pantheon has published Samuel Beckett, William S. Burroughs, Václav Havel, Harold Pinter, Jean-Paul Sartre, Tom Stoppard and Fay Weldon) and not the bottom line. By now, the whole furor has died down, and under the editorial direction of Fred Jordan it seems to be business as usual for Pantheon, although it will be a while before the book industry sees the change—if any—in the direction for the imprint.

Edward L. Ferman, editor of the respected digest-sized *The Magazine of Fantasy & Science Fiction* for twenty-five years, has given up his position as editor to become full-time publisher and art director of the magazine. Kristine Kathryn Rusch was named the new editor late in 1990. Rusch won the John W. Campbell Award for best new writer in the fantasy and science fiction field for 1989. She is also senior editor of Pulphouse Publishing and won (along with Dean Wesley Smith) a 1989 World Fantasy Award for her editing work at Pulphouse. She will continue to edit book projects for Pulphouse, as well as overseeing other editorial projects, but she will no longer be editing short fiction for *Pulphouse* magazine. Kristine Rusch is the sixth editor of *F & SF* in its forty-two-year history. The founding editors, in 1949, were Anthony Boucher and J. Francis McComas. They were followed by Robert P. Mills, Avram Davidson, and Ferman. The magazine will be edited from Eugene, Oregon; the changeover is effective as of March 1, 1991.

In other news of interest to the horror field, Tor Books stopped publishing their horror as a separate line in January. These books are now listed and published instead as general fiction. Five years ago, Tor was the first company to start a separate horror line, in order to add another "lead" title to their list. In the future, books by horror writers such as Ramsey Campbell and John Farris will be treated as regular fiction leads.

The Berkley Publishing Group's Charter imprint was renamed Diamond Books effective August 1990. The renamed line is publishing eight category titles a month (two horror). Berkley and Jove will continue to do the occasional horror title.

Despite dire predictions by editors and publishers that the interest in horror novels has peaked, Dell Books, under editor Jeanne Cavelos, prepared to launch a new monthly horror line called Abyss. The first book, Kathe Koja's *The Cipher* (originally called *The Funhole*) was published February 1991, with novels by Brian Hodge, Ron Dee, J.M. Dillard and Melanie Tem to follow.

Author Thomas F. Monteleone announced the formation of Borderlands Press, a new hardcover imprint. The press's books will be slipcased, with an emphasis on quality design and graphics. Working with Monteleone on the press are businessmen Henry G. Curtis and James C. Dobbs. The company's first release, announced for February 1991, was a signed limited edition of *The Magic Wagon* by Joe R. Lansdale. Other books in the works are *Borderlands II*, an original horror anthology edited by Monteleone, a series of works by Harlan Ellison (none of which has ever appeared in hardcover), and an edition of *Gauntlet*, the magazine devoted to questions of censorship, which will include a signed essay by Stephen King.

In Great Britain: Publisher W.H. Allen closed down at the end of the week of January 22nd. Staff was given a day's notice before being dismissed. W.H. Allen published, among others, Dean R. Koontz, Shaun Hutson and Richard Laymon. Headline reportedly took on the Star imprint backlist of Koontz and Laymon titles. Unwin Hyman, one of the U.K.'s last small independent publishers of sf and fantasy was absorbed by Rupert Murdoch's HarperCollins.

Random Century has begun a program of publishing science fiction and horror novellas under the Legend line. The first four novellas, by Greg Bear, Jonathan Carroll, Ramsey Campbell and Lucius Shepard, have been bought in the U.S. by St. Martin's Press. What's unusual about the program is that the authors have been paid as much as for full-length novels. The books are expensive but beautifully illustrated and jacketed hardcovers with art by such artists as Dave McKean, Fred Gambino, and Jamel Akib, who illustrated two of the books. It's an ambitious project.

Also, David Pringle, editor and publisher of *Interzone,* has launched a new magazine called *Million: The Magazine of Popular Fiction*. It is devoted to popular and genre fiction in all forms and its purpose is to "provide a forum for discussion of, and information about, popular fiction and its audiences and creators." There will be one or two short stories per issue. Most of the contents will consist of profiles/interviews, book reviews, film reviews, bibliographies, short filler articles, etc.

There was a bit of a to-do when a new British magazine that recently went from fanzine to semi-prozine—*Skeleton Crew:* Portraits of Horror, published by Argus Specialist Press —fired its first editor, David Hughes, for refusing to remove certain offensive words from a reprint of Stephen King's story "The Reploids" in the second issue of the magazine. All copies of the second issue were withdrawn from circulation pending removal of the offending material. Management claims Hughes agreed to certain guidelines when he took the job and blatantly ignored those guidelines. The new editor is Dave Reeder. I've only seen the December issue but it looks like it could be an interesting addition to the British horror scene. It seems to be mostly nonfiction, with interviews with Joe R. Lansdale and Stephen Gallagher and a fascinating pictorial by British fantasy photographer Simon Marsden. The book coverage was brief and superficial, but the magazine has potential.

What follows is a list of the novels I enjoyed this year. Most are psychological thriller/horror rather than supernatural. This is because I (and the general horror reader) am so burned out by the generic supernatural horror novels being churned out as original paperbacks that I can hardly bear to look at one unless it's recommended to me. I can read a first page and know how the book is going to end. I take it as a positive sign that the major paperback publishers have cut back their horror lists. Now if the other ones would just follow the lead . . . But for those critics who claim the horror novel is passé, this just isn't true. Good supernatural horror will continue to sell. Stephen King is still able to surprise and delight readers, and so are other talented horror novelists.

A real boom has occurred in the psycho-killer sub-genre and this is the kind of book I found most interesting to read in 1990. Thomas Harris singlehandedly created it with his novel *Red Dragon* in the early 1980s (Robert Bloch's *Psycho*, of course, came first, but it didn't generate a slew of other psycho-killer novels as did *Red Dragon*). *Red Dragon* and *The Silence of the Lambs* shook up the thriller/mystery/horror field, and the trend is just now reaching its peak. Some of my favorite novels of the year:

Mercy by David Lindsey (Doubleday) is the hottest psycho-killer novel since *The Silence of the Lambs*. When an hispanic policewoman and a male FBI specialist on profiling sexual killers hunt a serial killer in Houston, they come across a group of bisexual S&M enthusiasts among the elite women of the city. Sexy, thought-provoking in its contention about the biases of sex crime gender profiling, and well-researched. Excellent except for the unnecessarily negative epilogue. Highly recommended.

Nightlight by Michael Cadnum (St. Martin's) is a spooky first novel by an award-winning poet. It's suggestive rather than overt in its horror until the climax, which is both frightening and macabre. A young man is asked by his aunt to check up on her son, who has disappeared in the California wine country. The missing cousin specialized in night photography and is obsessed with graveyards and tombstones. Excellent supernatural and psychological horror. Lovely use of language. The poet in the author shows.

Rules of Prey by John Sandford (Berkley) is a serial killer/police procedural with a likable cop protagonist who is a specialist in this sort of crime. A page-turner throughout the first half. Every time you think you've got the book pegged, the author surprises and goes against expectation. Unfortunately, the killer, who at first seems interesting, loses his edge as the book progresses. He's just a nerd who can't get attention any other way. The trip is exciting although the destination's a disappointment.

The Night Man by K.W. Jeter (Onyx) is a brutal, gritty and grim novel about a neglected ten-year-old bullied by the town football team, and his dreams of revenge. Controlled and sharp. Jeter's horror fiction gets better and better.

Soul/Mate by Joyce Carol Oates writing as Rosamund Smith (Onyx) might be a little slow at the start for some horror readers but it's carefully crafted and grows on you. The psychopath is beautifully rendered, the protagonist a bit too genteel for her age and her time. She'd be more realistic is the book was set in the back in the 1950s, which kind of puts the whole story out of whack. Despite this, it's chilling.

Nemesis by Rosamund Smith (Dutton) is another mystery/thriller from the author of *Soul/Mate*, quite a marked improvement over the last one. A scandal brought on by the alleged rape of a male student shakes up a small academic community, particularly when the accused, a Pulitzer Prize–winning composer, is subsequently murdered. Not horror, but of interest to horror readers.

The Book of Evidence by John Banville (Scribner's) was short-listed for the prestigious Booker Prize in England and has been compared to Camus's *The Stranger* and Dostoevsky's *Crime and Punishment*. A first-person account of a seemingly average Briton's descent into criminality and murder, it's about the banality of evil, or maybe just the indifference of the main character to other people. Not big on action, but this human monster is certainly more believable than a character like Chaingang (Slob) Bunkowski. May be too literary for its own good but not bad. Quiet crime/horror.

Lie To Me by David Martin (Random House)—the first thirty pages of this psychological thriller by a previously mainstream author are absolutely riveting. There is a subtle monstrous image that sucks you in as soon as you realize what's going on. I was doubtful that the author would be able to follow through but he does. The story is told from the alternating viewpoints of the psychopath (a very believable one) and the burned-out detective, who can always tell if someone is lying. Carefully written, stylistically interesting, terrifying and kinky—one of the best horror novels (although no one will call it such) of the year. Highly recommended.

Billy by Whitley Strieber (Putnam) is a powerful piece of writing about the abduction of a child. The first third is almost too upsetting to read. The point of view shifts from child to parents to psychotic abductor. It's a very controlled piece of writing by the author of *The Hunger* and *The Wolfen*.

"The Langoliers," by Stephen King (from *Four Past Midnight*) (Viking) is novel-length for anyone but Stephen King. In this collection, it's considered a novella. A spooky story about the nature of time, it begins with an airplane flight from which most of the passengers disappear and feeds on our fear of flying.

"Secret Window, Secret Garden" uses material that already has been mined extensively by King in *The Shining*, *Misery*, and *The Dark Half*—the creative process, the unconscious as a fearful force once it gets out of control, etc.

"The Library Policeman" contains some very interesting characters and an interesting milieu—Alcoholics Anonymous and those who are drawn to the organization. It starts with a premise that I suspect many adults would relate to—that there actually is a "library policeman" who will come after you if you don't return your library books. Of course, in King country, the "policeman" becomes far more—a powerful symbol for unacknowledged traumas of childhood—good, scary novella.

Good Omens by Neil Gaiman and Terry Pratchett (Workman) is a very funny novel about the coming apocalypse with a cast of thousands, including the four horsemen and the anti-christ. A giggle for those interested in the light side of the end of the world.

Kalimantan by Lucius Shepard (Legend) is the first of four novellas published in this distinguished series—this one is long enough to be a novel. The jacket copy accurately describes the book as a combination of *Heart of Darkness* and *Altered States*. A search for truth, beauty and redemption in the mystical jungles of Bornea. Terrific stuff. Beautiful and effective art by Jamel Akib.

Spider by Patrick McGrath (Poseidon)—The author continues to grow in his control of his prose. He's quite the expert on madness. A man returns to London after twenty years in an asylum. By trying to re-create his horrendous past, he once again descends into madness. Disturbing and powerful.

Bad Desire by Gary Devon (Random House) is an unpleasant yet impressive novel about obsession. Mayor Henry Lee Slater will stop at nothing to possess teenager Sheila Bonner. A disturbing psychosexual page-turner.

Night Secrets by Thomas H. Cook (Putnam) is not horror but mystery/suspense, private investigator Frank Clemons's third adventure. He's an interesting protagonist who takes on day/night cases which eventually come together in a surprisingly satisfying way. In this case, secret gypsy rituals and troublesome pasts dovetail for an excellent read.

The Night Mayor by Kim Newman (Carroll & Graf)—The City is the creation and refuge of the night mayor, arch-criminal Truro Daine of the 21st century. Tom Tunney alias private eye Dick Quick is sent into this cyberspace creation to capture the bad guy. This is sf/cyber/techno/noir. A fascinating combo with an artificial intelligence that controls everything. It isn't completely successful but it's fun and boasts appearances by Humphrey Bogart, Sydney Greenstreet, Lauren Bacall, and Mary Astor, who roam through the perpetual rainy 2:30 A.M. scene.

Mary Reilly by Valerie Martin (Doubleday) is *Dr. Jekyll and Mr. Hyde* from the point of view of the maidservant (who keeps a diary—unusual in that she's literate). Wonderful historical details but not all that suspenseful and not really horror despite the subject matter. Still, it's very readable.

Winterlong by Elizabeth Hand (Bantam/Spectra) is justly marketed as science fiction and has an sf feel to it, but there's definitely horror in this extraordinary first novel. Hand has created a carefully crafted world set in a latter-day Washington, D.C. after the "war of roses" (chemical warfare or acid rain), in which twins, unknown to each other, spend most of the novel inadvertently seeking their other half. One is autistic but sort of normalized by a scientific experiment, the other is a seductive courtesan (male). Macabre and beautiful. This novel isn't for every horror fan, but should interest those who also read sf. Highly recommended.

A Reasonable Madness by Fran Dorf (Birchlane Press)—A beautiful mother of three walks into a police station to confess to a heinous murder that she could not have committed. She claims she can cause death by thinking or dreaming of being angry at someone. The police don't believe her and send her to a psychiatrist. Is she crazy? Precognitive? Can she indeed cause someone's death? It's an interesting first novel that puts carefully detailed research into the psychoanalytic process and parapsychology to good use. Just a bit too much coincidence powers the plot, though.

Dreamer by Peter James (St. Martin's) is another novel about precognition. In this one, 32-year-old Samantha Curtis starts having nightmares about death. And there is always a hooded man in these dreams. Upon waking, she finds her dreams coming true. She begins to think she may be causing events rather than predicting them. Although there are similarities to *A Reasonable Madness*, it reads quite differently. As the nightmares continue, her confusion and her terror escalate until she's unsure as to what is dream and what is reality. Good supernatural thriller, high on the tension.

Trade Secrets by Ray Garton (Mark V. Ziesing) is a fast-paced thriller about a man who becomes involved with a woman running from powerful citizens who want to silence her before she implicates them in a massive conspiracy. Brutal and sexy and a good read.

The Scarred Man by Keith Peterson (Doubleday) is an excellent psychological suspense novel with horrific over- and undertones. A rootless young journalist meets the daughter of his boss at a Christmas gathering in the country and it's love at first sight for both of them. That is, until he is called upon to tell a ghost story, which he does and scares the bejesus out of his new found love, who has dreamed of the same "scarred man" of his story. Taut, absorbing and complicated, it holds together nicely.

Flesh by Gus Weill (St. Martin's) is a bizarre little oddity about a very wealthy family with monstrous secrets. A young lyricist is invited to the family island by his classmate to collaborate on a musical. Despite the fact that there is no mystery to the family's odd predilection, the book is surprisingly suspenseful, well-written, clever and kinky. Not a bad combination for horror fans.

The Revelation by Bentley Little (St. Martin's) is a good first novel by someone who has been building a reputation with his short stories in the various small presses. A well written book about a prophesied conflict between good and evil that is to take place in the small town of Randall, Arizona. Good characterizations, except for the hellfire preacher who turns out to be quite other than what he appears to be.

Other horror or borderline horror novels published in 1990 include: *Looker* by Jorge Saralegui (Charter), *Fiends* by John Farris (Tor), *Blood Alone* by Elaine Bergstrom (Jove), *Reborn* by F. Paul Wilson (Dark Harvest/Jove), *Silent Moon* by William Relling, Jr. (Tor), *Children of the Knife* by Brad Strickland (Onyx), *Tempter* by Nancy A. Collins (Onyx), *Rune* by Christopher Fowler (Century-UK), *Savage Season* by Joe R. Lansdale (Bantam), *Red Spider White Web* by Misha (Morrigan), *Othersyde* by J. Michael Straczynski (Dutton), *Second Child* by John Saul (Bantam), *The Jekyll Legacy* by Robert Bloch and Andre Norton (Tor), *Out of the House of Life* by Chelsea Quinn Yarbro (Tor), *Psycho House* by Robert Bloch (Tor), *Ghost Dance* by Kathryn Ptacek (Tor), *Torments* by Lisa Cantrell (Tor), *A Matter of Taste* by Fred Saberhagen (Tor), *Reign* by Chet Williamson (Dark Harvest), *Dead Voices* by Rick Hautala (Warner), *Mine* by Robert R. McCammon (Pocket Books), *Stunts* by Charles L. Grant (Tor), *The Stand* by Stephen King (expanded) (Doubleday), *Four Past Midnight*, four novellas by Stephen King (Viking); *The Witching Hour* by Anne Rice (Knopf); and *The Shaft* by David J. Schow (Macdonald).

There was a lot of good short horror published in 1990, partly because the publication of anthologies and single-author collections held steady and partly because the small press magazines improved markedly. Also, some of the professional magazines seemed to be publishing more horror fiction. David Silva's *The Horror Show* published its last issue, with a moody cover by Harry O. Morris, excellent fiction by Nancy A. Collins, Brian Hodge, Graham Masterton, Darrell Schweitzer, Jason van Hollander and others, profiles on Anne Rice and Charles L. Grant and interviews with Dennis Etchison, and special effects veteran Peter Chesney. I'm sad to see it go.

Fear, edited by John Gilbert, has gone monthly. While it still concentrates on all aspects of the horror film, it also carries mini-profiles of sf/fantasy and horror writers and news of the field. The fiction remains inconsistent but there were good stories by Nicola Germain, Ian Harding, Colin Davis, Peter T. Garrett, David L. Duggins, Ian Hunter, Brian Cooper, and Elizabeth R. Caine.

Fantasy Tales, edited by Stephen Jones and David Sutton, brought out spring and fall issues in its new book format. The magazine boasted effectively disquieting covers by J.K. Potter, reviews and articles, and some good fiction by Stephen Gallagher, Charles L. Grant, Steve Rasnic Tem, Darrell Schweitzer, Elsa Beckett, Garry Kilworth, and Gary William Crawford, and a good poem by Jessica Amanda Salmonson.

Despite persistent rumors of its imminent demise, *Amazing Stories*, the oldest sf magazine, seems to have acquired a new lease on life. Patrick Lucien Price, editor for four years, will finish out the current volume in digest form through the March 1991 issue. As of this writing, the magazine, with Kim H. Mohan, former editor of TSR's *Dragon*, at the helm, will be transformed into a full-color 96-page monthly slick with six to ten pieces of fiction, each with a color illustration, short excerpts from upcoming novels, articles, essays, opinion pieces, book reviews and computer gaming. The new format started with the May 1991 issue. *Amazing* rarely publishes horror, but among the few stories it did publish in 1990, Robert Frazier's, Nina Kiriki Hoffman's, N. Lee Wood's, and Kathe Koja's stood out.

Interzone, the British magazine of sf and fantasy, went monthly with issue #35 dated May 1990. Also, its circulation has reportedly gone over the 10,000-copy mark. Although they don't acknowledge it, for the last couple of years *Interzone* has been running stories that occasionally inhabit that twilight area of techno-horror and dark fantasy. Some of the best in 1990 were by Richard Calder, Ian R. MacLeod, Simon D. Ings, Susan Beetlestone, Nicholas Royle, Lisa Tuttle, Sherry Coldsmith, Jonathan Carroll and Sharon M. Hall.

Weird Tales, edited by John Betancourt, George H. Scithers, and Darrell Schweitzer, is getting better and better. The covers are usually attractive and effective, the design is clean and easy to read. The fall issue had the best mix of fiction I've yet seen in the magazine with excellent stories by Patricia Anthony, Chet Williamson, Ian Watson, Ian R. MacLeod, Peg Kerr, Darrell Schweitzer, and Jason van Hollander and a Stephen King reprint—the surprisingly good first story for which he was every paid. Other issues had good stories by David J. Schow, Nancy Springer, Ardath Mayhar, Jonathan Carroll, William F. Nolan, and Robert Sampson. The magazine is finally beginning to live up to its promise.

Midnight Graffiti is still publishing intermittently—only one issue in 1990, a "psycho" theme issue. The fiction was disappointing considering the impressive lineup of writers but there were decent stories by Nancy A. Collins, Mick Garris, and K.W. Jeter.

Pulphouse: The Hardback Magazine, edited by Kristine Kathryn Rusch, has ceased publication as a hardcover quarterly with its twelfth issue and has gone to a weekly 40–48 page 8½ × 11 format. Each issue will contain fiction, including serialized novels, nonfiction articles, and columns. Editorial duties have been taken over by publisher Dean Wesley Smith, as a result of Rusch's move to *F & SF*. The 1990 issues of *Pulphouse* contained good horror fiction by William F. Wu, Russell Roberts, Joyce Thompson, Bradley Denton, Susan Palwick, Edward Bryant, A.R. Morlan, Yvonne Navarro, Midori Snyder, Adrian Nikolas Phoenix, Nancy Holder, D.W. Taylor, Lisa Tuttle, Melinda M. Snodgrass, Don H. DeBrandt, Jerry Oltion, Mary Rosenblum, Marina Fitch, and Kelley Eskridge.

Omni Magazine (of which I am fiction editor) published horror or borderline horror by Pat Cadigan, John Skipp and Craig Spector, Gahan Wilson, Michael Bishop, Jonathan Carroll, and Gardner R. Dozois.

Isaac Asimov's Science Fiction Magazine, edited by Gardner R. Dozois, published some interesting horror by Greg Egan, Lewis Shiner, Kim Stanley Robinson, Bradley Denton, Lucius Shepard, Charles Sheffield, Bruce Boston, Ian Watson, John Griesemer, and Kim Antieau.

Fantasy & Science Fiction, edited by Ed Ferman, has been publishing more horror over the last couple of years. The most impressive stories of 1990 were by Michael Blumlein, Ray Aldridge, Robert Reed, Thomas Ligotti, Esther Friesner, Karen Haber, Daryl Gregory, Michael Cassutt, Sheri S. Tepper, John Maddox Roberts, Stephen King, and S. Newman.

Grue, edited by Peggy Nadramia, has great covers by Harry O. Morris, and #11 has a terrific back illustration by Harry Fassl. There were good stories by Tom Elliott, C.S. Fuqua, David Starkey, Brad Cahoon, Nina Kiriki Hoffman, and Howard Seabrook. In general, this magazine looks good and reads well.

Cemetery Dance, edited by Richard T. Chizmar, went to full-color covers with its summer issue and contained the best fiction I've yet seen in it. The writing has been consistently professional this year even if not every story is successful. The most impressive fiction was by Barb Hendee, David L. Duggins, David B. Silva, Thomas F. Monteleone, Ed Gorman, Jack Pavey, Kim Antieau, Carol Cail, Richard Christian Matheson and

William Relling, Jr., Barry Hoffman, Stefan Jackson, and Gary A. Braunbeck. The interviews are interesting and informative. The only major problem is the poor reproduction of book jackets in the review section—you can't see the art or read the titles.

Iniquities took a bit longer than it was supposed to—the first issue was about six months late, the second hasn't yet appeared—but the wait's worth it. The magazine is good-looking, well-designed and has a nice mix of fiction by Roberta Lannes, Chet Williamson, Tim Sullivan and others.

Noctulpa, edited by George Hatch, has become an annual with a new anthology format. Issue #4 looks good with illustrations by John Borkowski and powerful fiction by Norman Partridge, Mark Rainey, and Chet Williamson.

Deathrealm, edited by Mark Rainey, always has interesting graphics. The artists I liked the best in 1990 were Harry Fassl, Robert Baldwin and Jeffrey Osier. And there was good fiction by Fred Chappell, David A. Sydney, Gary L. Phillips, and Nina Kiriki Hoffman.

2 A.M., a large format quarterly magazine, published by Gretta M. Anderson had interesting fiction by Dean Wesley Smith, Gary David Johnson, and Michael R. Collings.

Eldritch Tales, edited by Crispin Burnham, published three issues in 1990 (the winter '89–'90 issue didn't reach me until '90). Good fiction can be found there by Ken Wisman, Bentley Little, and Judith R. Behunin, and Jessica Amanda Salmonson has an excellent poem in the magazine. There is a story by A.R. Morlan serialized in three parts over the year (A big mistake with anything published less often than monthly).

Thin Ice, edited by Kathleen Jurgens, is a digest that despite the difficulty in readability, had worthwhile fiction by Sherrie Brown, Dale White, Albert J. Manachino, and Raymond Marshall.

After Hours, edited by William G. Raley is in 8½ × 11 format and published impressive fiction by Rick McMahan, Gregor Hartmann, Kiel Stuart, Jeffrey Thomas, Gary A. Braunbeck, and William C. Orem.

Alfred Hitchcock's Mystery Magazine ran more than its usual share of horror and some of it was quite good, including stories by Taylor McCafferty, J.A. Paul, Nina Kiriki Hoffman, L.A. Taylor, Robert Hood, Karen Parker, Elliott Capon, and Kim Antieau. The digest-sized magazine is edited by Cathleen Jordan.

Its sister publication, *Ellery Queen's Mystery Magazine*, also ran quite a lot of horrific fiction this year including stories by Robert Twohy, Keith Peterson (Andrew Klavan), Glyn Hardwicke, James Sallis, Robert Barnard, J.W. Whitehead, Ruth Rendell, Harlan Ellison, and Barbara Owens. Its editor is Eleanor Sullivan.

Other magazines in and out of the field which published some good horror stories or poems are *The New Yorker, Tikkun, Harper's, New Pathways, Fantasy Macabre, New Blood, Weirdbook, The Blood Review, Tales of the Unanticipated, Playboy, Esquire, The Quarterly, Wigwag, West/Word 1, Doppelganger, Unique, The Tome, The Sterling Web, Starshore, Back Brain Recluse, REM, Star*Line, Haunts*, and *Not One of Us* by, variously, Susan Prospere, Joyce Carol Oates, David Ira Cleary, Elizabeth Hillman, Dennis Post, James Kisner, Tom Elliott, Joseph Payne Brennan, Peter Tremayne, Brian Lumley, Michael R. Collings, Kristine Larson, Lucius Shepard, Rachel Ingalls, Melinda Davis, Gahan Wilson, Alex Quiroba, Jana Hakes, Rick Shelley, John Rosenman, Ann K. Schwader, Mark Rainey, Scott D. Yost, Mike O'Driscoll, Rick Cadger, Simon D. Ings, William Marconette, Jr., and Jack Pavey.

Many small presses come out irregularly and are available only through subscription. Here are addresses and prices for some of the best. Only U.S. subscription prices are listed. For overseas information, query the publication. I'm including publications unavailable on U.S. newsstands. *Fear*, c/o Barry Hatcher, British Magazine Distributors Ltd., 598 Durham Crescent, Woodstock, Ontario N4S 5X3 Canada, U.S. $65, Canada $75; *Skeleton*

Crew, Wise Owl Worldwide Publications, 4314 W. 238th St., Torrance, CA 90505, U.S. $54 a year; *Interzone*, 124 Osborne Road, Brighton BN1 6LU, UK, $42 (surface mail), $52 airmail; *Cemetery Dance*, P.O. Box 858, Edgewood, MD 21040, $15 one year (4 issues); *Midnight Graffiti*, 13101 Sudan Road, Poway, CA 92064, $24 one year (has been extremely irregular); *Eldritch Tales*, c/o Crispin Burnham, 1051 Wellington Rd., Lawrence, KS 66049, $24 four issues; *Haunts*, Nightshade Publications, P.O. Box 3342, Providence, RI 02906, $13 four issues; *Grue* Magazine, c/o Hell's Kitchen Productions, Inc., P.O. Box 370, Times Square Station, New York, NY 10108-0370, $13 three-issue subscription; *Noctulpa*, c/o George Hatch, P.O. Box 5175, Long Island City, NY 11105, $8.95 per issue (176 pp.); *Deathrealm*, 3223–F Regents Park Lane, Greensboro, NC 27405, $13 one year (four issues) payable to Mark Rainey; *Iniquities*, 167 N. Sierra Bonita Ave., Pasadena, CA 91106, $19.95 one year (announced as quarterly, but as of Dec. 1990 only one issue has come out); *Thin Ice*, 379 Lincoln Ave., Council Bluffs, IA 51503, $12.50 one year (three issues) payable to Kathleen Jurgens; *2 A.M.* Publications, P.O. Box 6754, Rockford, IL 61125-1754, $19 four issues; *After Hours*, 21541 Oakbrook, Mission Viejo, CA 92692-3044, $14 one-year subscription (quarterly); *Not One of Us*, 44 Shady Lane, Storrs, CT 06268, $10.50 payable to John Benson for a three-issue subscription; *The Grabinski Reader*, Teawood Publications, Box 2398, New York, NY 10009, $9 for a three-issue subscription.

For more information on small press magazines subscribe to *The Scavenger's Newsletter*, 519 Ellinwood, Osage City, KS 66523-1329, $12.50 for a first class one-year subscription (twelve issues) payable to Janet Fox. Other invaluable sources of information on the horror/ dark fantasy field are: *The Scream Factory*, 145 Tully Road, San Jose, CA 95111, $17 (four issues) payable to Joe Lopez; *New Pathways*, c/o MGA Services, P.O. Box 863994, Plano, TX 75086-3994, $25 one year (six issues) payable to MGA Services; *Locus Publications* and *Science Fiction Chronicle* (subscription information on both is in acknowledgments); *Science Fiction Eye* for a provocative critical magazine dealing with sf, fantasy and horror subjects. Published irregularly by Stephen Brown. P.O. Box 43244, Washington, DC 20010-9244, $10 for three issues (one year—has been running behind); *The New York Review of Science Fiction*, P.O. Box 78, Pleasantville, NY 10570, $32 payable to Dragon Press for a one-year first class subscription (12 issues), $24 second class subscription; *The Blood Review*, edited by Ruben Sosa Villegas is a good-looking well-produced news magazine for the horror field. The January 1990 issue covered a timely and important topic—Women in Horror—and did an excellent job. P.O. Box 4394, Denver, CO 80204-9998, $25 for a one-year subscription (quarterly); *Fangoria* and *Gorezone* are the grand-daddies of blood and guts horror publishing. I'm not sure why the publishers put out two magazines of essentially the same material. They mostly cover movies and special effects but (very) occasionally have some thoughtful criticism and book reviews. But it's pretty much gore, gore, gore, from the gross-out covers to the numerous flack pieces for the film companies with more explicit gore. Both are available in specialty stores and newsstands as well as by subscription; *Nova Express*, edited by Michael Sumbera contains reviews and articles on sf, fantasy and horror, and the odd piece of fiction (P.O. Box 27231, Austin, TX 78755-2231, $10 for a one-year subscription—quarterly); *Mystery Scene*, edited by Ed Gorman contains articles, columns, and reviews of sf, mystery and horror books. (3840 Clark Road, SE, Cedar Rapids, IA 52403, $37.50 for six issues). Also, the new newsletter put out by Kathryn Ptacek (author of various horror novels and editor of *Women of Darkness I* and *II*) called *The Gila Queen's Guide to Markets* provides valuable up-to-date information and news on publishing, including markets of all kinds (Kathryn Ptacek, 28 Linwood Avenue, Newton, NJ 07860, $20.00 for a one year (12 issue) subscription).

Anthology and single-author collections held steady, with about the same as published last year.

Houses Without Doors, by Peter Straub (Putnam) is a collection of mostly original pieces, including two excellent short stories and two very fine original novellas, the chilling "Mrs. God" in the Aickman tradition and "The Buffalo Hunter," about a man going mad. Also included here are the reprints "Blue Rose" and "The Juniper Tree." Highly recommended.

Lost Angels by David J. Schow (Onyx)—Five longer works by Schow, including the award-winning "Red Light," and the brilliant and eerie "Pamela's Get." Includes an excellent original mainstream story called "Monster Movies." Together with his other collection, *Seeing Red* (Tor), also published in 1990, Schow's versatility as a writer is showcased. At the same time these books demonstrate the meaninglessness of the term "splatterpunk" and even the damage Schow does his own reputation by embracing it to define himself as a writer.

The SeaHarp Hotel edited by Charles L. Grant (Tor) The third book of stories about the imaginary community of Greystone Bay. The best things in the anthology are those that have least to do with the setting and could take place anywhere. Inconsistencies are creeping in. In one story the hotel has a swimming pool. In two others it does not. In one story a character is a murderess, while in others she's bland and barely figures in the plots. And a character's former lover makes an anachronistic reappearance later in the book under a different last name.

Skin of the Soul: New Horror Stories by Women edited by Lisa Tuttle (The Women's Press/Pocket Books)—While I feel the anthology may be a little heavy on the side of the "intimate fear," as Clive Barker puts it in the cover blurb, it isn't at all bad. And while I may not agree with its goals, it certainly does fulfill them.

The idea of an all-women horror anthology developed from the (correct) perception that the horror field in general and anthologies in particular were dominated by male writers. Kathryn Ptacek's *Women of Darkness* (1988) was conceived to remedy this. Its publication in itself brought needed attention to the perceived "problem," and in that, the book was successful. It engendered much controversy over, and an increasing sensitivity to, the problem. *Skin of the Soul*, though intended to address the same issues, has not yet generated the same level of discussion and debate, perhaps because it was published by a feminist press rather than a trade horror line, or perhaps because after *Women of Darkness* the all-women anthology is not so surprising.

I object to the single-gender anthology as a remedy. If more women edit horror anthologies, more women might be included. Of course, quality should always come first. I personally prefer to blur lines of gender and genre rather than bringing more attention to them and labeling them. There is an excellent essay by Jeannette M. Hopper in *The Blood Review* on women writing about stereotypically women's subjects. The argument, with which I agree, is that if women want to be read by the other half of the population, they need to write male characters who aren't stereotypical and two-dimensional, and they need to appeal to concerns of both men and women. These same truths hold for men and women; I'm dead sick of stories about battered women and children, just as I'm sick of stories by men that brutalize women for the eroticism of it. So where are we now? Similar complaints were made about science fiction fifteen years ago. Since then, women have come, if not to dominate the sf field, certainly to achieve considerable representation in it, as proven by the number of women who are now nominated for and win the Nebula and Hugo awards. Horror is just a few years behind.

Walls of Fear edited by Kathryn Cramer (Wm. Morrow)—Good follow-up to the World

Fantasy Award–winning *The Architecture of Fear* with excellent stories by Jack Womack, Chet Williamson, Ian Watson, Garry Kilworth, Gwyneth Jones, M.J. Engh and Karl Edward Wagner. Some of the stories are more fantasy than horror (e.g., Susan Palwick's). The introduction, though, starts out interestingly enough with the editor talking about how the anthology came to be, but veers off into philosophical gibberish three pages in.

Borderlands edited by Thomas F. Monteleone (Avon)—A couple of dogs but some real winners and for the most part a very satisfying anthology. Among the best are those by Elizabeth Massie, Karl Edward Wagner, and T.E.D. Klein. A good Harlan Ellison story that's more fantasy than horror and an unpolished but powerful story by Lee Moler. The ambition of the editor was to push the envelope of horror. I'm not convinced many of the stories do that, but most of the stories are absorbing. It's the first of a projected series.

The Further Adventures of the Joker edited by Martin H. Greenberg (Bantam)—Surprisingly good (since the *Batman* anthology was so lackluster) original anthology. Perhaps the Joker is just a more interesting character because he's so evil. Some inconsistencies creep up between stories (Barb, the commissioner's daughter, is crippled in one story, then fine in a later one). Excellent work by Robert R. McCammon, Stuart M. Kaminsky, Garfield Reeves-Stevens, and good work by everyone else.

Lovecraft's Legacy edited by Martin H. Greenberg and Robert E. Weinberg (Tor)—A good original anthology. Most of the stories use Lovecraftian lore but not all do. A couple are completely indifferent to it, despite claims by the individual authors that they were influenced by Lovecraft (not necessarily a bad thing, but these stories do stick out). Excellent novella by F. Paul Wilson.

Dark Voices 2 (formerly the Pan Book of Horror series) edited by David Sutton and Stephen Jones (Pan)—A mixed bag from excellent stories by John Brunner, Adrian Cole, and Cherry Wilder to very good to a couple of abominable ones by newer writers. Includes reprints by Ramsey Campbell, William F. Nolan, and Brian Lumley.

Methods of Madness by Ray Garton (Dark Harvest)—Garton's writing is still pretty rough although he's got lots of energy and a fascinating obsession with the dark side of male/female relationships. Unfortunately, though, because of this obsessiveness, all the stories have a sameness about them with the notable exception of "Dr. Krusadian's Method." This novella, like "Punishments" from *Hot Blood*, seems more carefully crafted and better under the writer's control than most of his shorter work.

Mummy Stories edited by Martin H. Greenberg (Ballantine)—Mediocre originals (five) and classic reprints by Conan Doyle, E.F. Benson, Edgar Allan Poe, and Robert Bloch, among others. One good original by Sharyn McCrumb.

Women of Darkness II edited by Kathryn Ptacek (Tor)—Pretty undistinguished reprise of #1 with an excellent story by Nina Kiriki Hoffman and good stories by Kristl Volk Franklin, Tanith Lee, Lisa Swallow, and Lynn S. Hightower (see above comments about *Skin of the Soul*). Nina Kiriki Hoffman is the writer who has stood out most in the short fiction field this year. As you'll see from the recommended list, she is all over the place, producing consistently excellent supernatural and psychological horror stories.

When the Black Lotus Blooms edited by Elizabeth Saunders Gregg (Unnameable Press)—Interesting idea, mixing prose, poetry and illustrations. The design is excellent and so are the illustrations by Harry O. Morris and others, but aside from a few good originals and reprints by Charles L. Grant, Janet Fox, Michael Bishop, Brad Strickland and James Robert Smith, the fiction in this dark fantasy volume is disappointing.

The Brains of Rats by Michael Blumlein (Scream/Press)—A collection of provocative sf, fantasy and horror by an American writer whose first stories appeared in the British magazine *Interzone*. Some of these stories are original to this volume. A must read for those who want to see where fantastic fiction should be going. Highly recommended.

Alien Sex edited by Ellen Datlow (Dutton)—An anthology of sf and horror fiction which is comprised of half originals, half reprints with original horror stories by K.W. Jeter, Richard Christian Matheson, Lewis Shiner, and a poem by Michaela Roessner.

Best English Short Stories II edited by Giles Gordon and David Hughes (Norton) is a collection of ostensibly mainstream short stories culled from various British magazines during 1989. I've just received a copy. Included are stories with horrific elements by Cecil Bonstein, Janice Galloway, Robert Grossmith, Russell Hoban, and Janette Turner Hospital.

The Call and Other Stories by Robert Westall (Viking UK)—This writer is better known for his young adult ghost stories than for his adult fiction but last year's adult collection, *Antique Dust*, was quite impressive. This collection, too, is definitely worth reading. I assume it will eventually appear in the U.S.

Night Visions 8 (Dark Harvest) Original anthology series. All new material by John Farris, Stephen Gallagher and Joe R. Lansdale. A pretty good story by John Farris, author of such novels as *Harrison High*, *All Heads Turn When the Hunt Goes By* and *Son of the Endless Night*. Gallagher is a newer writer just starting to make a name for himself. In this batch I particularly liked Gallagher's "Dead Man's Handle" but was impressed by three of the four. Lansdale once again demonstrates that he can write the redneck monster story better than anyone else around but it's getting tired—he seems to be trying to outdo himself on the gross-out factor. I was far more impressed by "The Phone Woman," which I found more subtle and chilling than the other three included in the collection.

New Crimes: New American and British Crime Writing, edited by Maxim Jakubowski (Carroll & Graf)—While there's no outright horror here, there are a couple of good stories verging on the horrific. Generally, a good anthology of crime fiction.

Sisters in Crime 2, edited by Marilyn Wallace (Berkley)—Good anthology of crime fiction but no real horror. As the above, some excellent material that verges on the horrific.

Zenith 2, edited by David S. Garnett (Orbit)—Some excellent fiction in here but very little horrific. Eric Brown's story, however, while definitely sf, is quite chilling. Michael Moorcock's fantasy novella is absolutely brilliant (although not horror at all). Discontinued by Orbit, this series will be published by Grafton as *New Worlds* in 1991.

Other anthologies and collections with some good original horror fiction were: *Miracles in America* by Sheila Kohler (Knopf); *Semiotext(e) SF* (Semiotext(e) #14)—Michael Blumlein and T.L. Parkinson; *Universe I* (Doubleday)—Scott Baker; *The Women Who Walk Through Fire* (Crossing)—J.L. Comeau and Elaine Bergstrom; *Monochrome: The Readercon Anthology*—Gene Wolfe; *The Start of the End of It All* by Carol Emshwiller (The Women's ' Press); *Splatterpunks* (St. Martin's)—Philip Nutman; *The Sixth Day and Other Tales* by Primo Levi (Summit); *Women of the West* (Doubleday)—A. R. Morlan and Melanie Tem; *The Barnum Museum* by Steven Millhauser (Poseidon); *Sisters in Crime 3* (Berkley)— Marcia Biederman, Janet LaPierre, and Sarah Shankman.

The following reprint anthologies were published in 1990: *Intensive Scare*, edited by Karl Edward Wagner (DAW), *The Year's Best Horror Stories XVIII*, edited by Karl Edward Wagner (DAW), *Devil Worshippers*, edited by Martin H. Greenberg and Charles G. Waugh (DAW), *Dark Voices: The Best From the Pan Book of Horror Stories*, edited by Stephen Jones and Clarence Paget (Pan), *The Best Horror from Fantasy Tales*, edited by Stephen Jones and David Sutton (Carroll & Graf), *Under the Gun: Mystery Scene Presents the Best Suspense and Mystery*, edited by Edward Gorman and Robert J. Randisi (Plume), *The New Edgar Winners: The Mystery Writers of America*, edited by Martin H. Greenberg (Wynwood), *Western Ghosts*, *Ghosts of the Heartland*, *Eastern Ghosts* and *New England Ghosts* all edited by Frank D. McSherry, Charles G. Waugh, and Martin H. Greenberg (Rutledge Hill Press), *Dinosaurs!* edited by Jack Dann and Gardner R. Dozois (Ace), *The*

Mammoth Book of Ghost Stories, edited by Richard Dalby (Carroll & Graf), *Urban Fantasies*, edited by William F. Nolan and Martin H. Greenberg (Dark Harvest), *Weird Tales: A Selection in Facsimile, of the Best of the World's Most Famous Fantasy Magazine*, Selected and Introduced by Peter Haining (Carroll & Graf), *Cults of Horror*, edited by Martin H. Greenberg & Charles G. Waugh (DAW), *Best New Horror*, edited by Stephen Jones and Ramsey Campbell (Carroll & Graf), *Invasions*, edited by Isaac Asimov, Martin H. Greenberg & Charles G. Waugh (Roc), *Black Water 2: More Tales of the Fantastic*, edited by Alberto Manguel (Clarkson Potter), *Horrorstory* volume four, edited by Karl Edward Wagner (Underwood-Miller), *Christmas on Ganymede*, edited by Martin H. Greenberg (Avon); *The Oxford Book of Canadian Ghost Stories*, edited by Alberto Manguel (Oxford University Press); *Rivals of Weird Tales: Fantasy and Horror Stories from the Pulps*, edited by Robert Weinberg, Stefan R. Dziemianowicz & Martin H. Greenberg (Bonanza); *The Best Horror Stories*, edited anonymously, 31 vintage horror stories (Mallard Press); *Lilith's Cave: Jewish Folktales of the Supernatural*, selected and retold by Howard Schwartz (Oxford University Press); *Chillers for Christmas 27 Christmas Ghost and Horror Stories*, edited by Richard Dalby (Gallery Books—1st U.S.); *Fifty Years of the Best of Ellery Queen* edited by Eleanor Sullivan (Carroll & Graf); *The Leiber Chronicles: Fifty Years of Fritz Leiber*, edited by Martin H. Greenberg (Dark Harvest); *Songs of a Dead Dreamer* by Thomas Ligotti (Carroll & Graf); *Escapes* by Joy Williams (Atlantic Monthly); *Author's Choice Monthly: Nina Kiriki Hoffman* (one original), *F. Paul Wilson*, and *Michael Bishop* (Pulphouse); *Her Pilgrim Soul* by Alan Brennert (Tor—one original), *Maps in a Mirror: The Short Fiction of Orson Scott Card* (Tor—a few originals); *Prayers to Broken Stones* by Dan Simmons (Dark Harvest—one original), *Points of Departure* by Pat Murphy (Bantam Spectra); *Her Smoke Rose Up Forever* by James Tiptree, Jr. (Arkham House); *Can Such Things Be?: Tales of Horror and the Supernatural* by Ambrose Bierce (Carol Publishing); *Dream of the Wolf* by Scott Bradfield (Knopf); *The Time-Lapsed Man and Other Stories* by Eric Brown (Pan—UK); *Dark Hills, Hollow Clocks: Stories from the Otherworld* by Garry Kilworth (Methuen—UK); *Ah, Sweet Mystery of Life: Stories by Roald Dahl* (Knopf); *Short Sharp Shocks* edited by Julian Lloyd Webber (Weidenfeld & Nicolson—UK); and *The Ghost Now Standing On Platform One* edited by Richard Payton (Souvenir Press—UK).

As usual, the small specialty presses were active, and continuing to take more chances than trade publishers on collections and oddball projects. Many of these are unseen by me but sound interesting. A few were published late in 1989 and I didn't see or receive them in time for last year's volume: Dunscaith Publishers Ltd., of the UK, published *The Faceless Tarot* by Keith Seddon and Jocelyn Almond. It is a sword & sorcery novel based on genuine mythology, with a color dustwrapper by Albrecht Dürer; Jwindz Publishing brought out *Look Back on Laurel Hills*, poetry by Joseph Payne Brennan, *Under the Skin*, a limited edition portfolio of art by Rodger Gerberding for adults only, and *Between Heaven and Hell* by Robert Lowry, a collection of short stories; the New England SF Association produced *Sung in Blood*, an original novel by Glen Cook with a color dustjacket by David Cherry; Tabb House of the UK published *Kipling's Lost World*, an anthology of stories, poetry, letters and speeches touching on literature and the creative imagination, edited and with an introduction by Harry Ricketts; Graham Stone of Australia published *The Burlesque of Frankenstein* by George Isaacs. It's a mid-19th-century Australian play, a humorous version of Frankenstein in rhymed verse, with songs. Originally published in an 1865 collection, this is its first solo publication; Mark V. Ziesing published *Trade Secrets*, with a full color cover by Bob Eggleton, and illustrated endpapers and frontispiece by Arnie Fenner, and *A Short, Sharp Shock*, with full color dustjacket and interior artwork by Arnie Fenner; Catbird Press published *Toward the Radical Center: A Karel Čapek Reader*, edited by Peter Kussi. It's the first complete and correct American translation of the play *R.U.R.* and also includes the play "The Makropulus Secret"; Kenneth W. Faig, Jr. published *To Yith and Beyond* by Duane W. Rimel, which is reprinted stories with new poetry and other material and updated autobiographical information; Dark Harvest published *Shadowfires*, a novel (originally brought out under the "Leigh Nichols" pseudonym) by Dean R. Koontz with a full-color cover and B&W illustrations by Phil Parks, *Reborn* by F. Paul Wilson with illustrations by Stephen Gervais, *Fiends* by John Farris with illustrations by Phil Parks, *Methods of Madness*, by Ray Garton with cover and illustrations by Paul Sonju, and *Reign* by Chet Williamson, illustrated by John and Laura Lakey; Fedogan & Bremer published *Colossus: The Collected Science Fiction of Donald Wandrei* with a color dustjacket by Jon Arfstrom and interior artwork by Rodger Geberding. It contains twenty-one stories, an essay by Richard L. Tierney and bibliography; University of Nebraska Press brought out a new edition of *The Strange Case of Dr. Jekyll and Mr. Hyde* by Robert Louis Stevenson, gorgeously illustrated by Barry Moser; Syracuse University Press reissued *At Midnight on the 31st of March*, a prose poem by Josephine Young Case about a small town in upstate N.Y. which suddenly finds that the rest of the world has disappeared; August House brought out *Classic American Ghost Stories: 200 Years of Ghost Lore* edited by Deborah A. Downer; The Eotu Group published *After Magic*, original fiction by Bruce Boston illustrated by Lari Davidson; Morrigan Publications's *Red Spider White Web* was illustrated by Don Coyote with foreword by Brian W. Aldiss and postscript by James P. Blaylock; Deadline Publications put out *Quick Chills: The Year's Best Horror Stories From the Small Press*, Volume I edited by Peter Enfantino; Scarborough House published *Lust for Blood: The Consuming Story of Vampires* by Olga Gruhzit Hoyt; Starmont House produced *Dark Transformations: Deadly Visions of Change*, poetry and stories by Michael R. Collings and *Faces of the Beast*, poetry by Bruce Boston, illustrated by Allen Koszowski; Arkham House published *Tales of the Cthulhu Mythos* by H.P. Lovecraft and Divers Hands with cover and illustrations by J.K. Potter and *Her Smoke Rose Up Forever*, with cover by Gustav Klimt, interior illustrations by Andrew Smith and introduction by John Clute; W. Paul Ganley published *The Compleat Khash, Vol. 1: Never a Backward Glance* by Brian Lumley and *Slab's Tavern and Other Odd Places* by John Gregory Betancourt; Necronomicon Press published *The Hashish-Eater* by Clark Ashton Smith with illustrations by Robert H. Knox, *The Events at Poroth Farm* by T.E.D. Klein, a Lovecraftian short story on which *The Ceremonies* was based, *H.P. Lovecraft: The Fantastic Poetry*, edited by S.T. Joshi, *The Parents of H.P. Lovecraft* by Kenneth W. Faig, Jr., and *"Sunset Terrace Imagery in Lovecraft" and other Essays* by Peter Cannon; Space & Time published *The Gift*, a gay horror novel by Scott Edelman; Gryphon Publications put out "Sherlock Holmes in the Adventure of the Ancient Gods" by Ralph Vaughan. It's a short pastiche in which Holmes faces Cthulhoid horrors; Donald M. Grant offered *At the Mountains of Madness* by H.P. Lovecraft in a limited deluxe leatherbound edition, with 15 color panels by Fernando Duval, individually signed by the artist, *The Adventures of Lucius Leffing, Thirteen Stories of the Occult Detective* by Joseph Payne Brennan, nine of them originals and *Post Oaks and Sand Roughs*, a semi-autobiographical novel by Robert E. Howard with cover design by Phil Hale; Lord John Press offered "Entropy's Bed at Midnight," a mainstream short story by Dan Simmons; Mirage Press published *The Harlan Ellison Hornbook*, essays and articles by Harlan Ellison; Underwood-Miller published *Dark Dreamers: Conversations With the Masters of Horror* by Stanley Wiater (reprinted by Avon); and Axolotl Press brought out *Ghostwood*, a novel by Charles de Lint.

Chapbooks and other specialty items:
Roadkill Press has begun a monthly series of chapbooks, including original stories by Gary
Jonas and Steve Rasnic Tem, pieces by Dan Simmons from his new novel *Summer of
Night* and a reprint by Edward Bryant. They're limited editions signed by the authors;
Chris Drumm published Bruce Boston's *Hypertales & Metafictions*, a collection of previously published but revised work; BBR Books of the UK put out *Blood & Grit*, an original
collection of fiction by British writer Simon Clark, whose work has mostly appeared in the
small press; *Dark Transformations: Deadly Visions of Change* is a collection of stories and
poems by Michael R. Collings from Starmont House; "After Magic" is an original story
by Bruce Boston, published by The Eotu Group; *Faces of the Beast* is poetry by Bruce
Boston illustrated by Allen Koszowski from Starmont House; "Midnight Mass" is an original
novella by F. Paul Wilson published by Axolotl Press; "Pelts," an original novella by F.
Paul Wilson was published by Footsteps Press; Triskell Press of Canada put out Charles
de Lint's annual Christmas story, "Ghosts of Wind and Shadow"; and Cliff Burns published
his own collection of short stories *Sex & Other Acts of the Imagination*.

Graphic Novels:
The Wasteland by Dave Louapre & Dan Sweetman (Piranha Press) is a cartoon book of
grotesquery, sick nasty jokes and some really funny stuff. Highly recommended.
   HORROR: *The Illustrated Book of Fears #2* (Northstar) has a good rendition of David
J. Schow's "Blood Rape of the Lust Ghouls," Masterton's "Hurry Monster," W.C. Ras-
mussen's "Little Holes," and James Kisner's "The Litter." The reprint material is better
than the original. Nicely disgusting cover.
   Fly In My Eye edited by Steve Niles (Arcane) is an interesting mix. The best piece is
the chilling autobiography of Ramsey Campbell (taken from his introduction to *The Face
That Must Die*) with illustrations by Bill Wray. It's more terrifying than any fiction. Some
great art by Ellman Brown, Clive Barker, J.K. Potter and John Bolton and a good graphic
novel by Potter and Tim Caldwell. An excellent interview with Gahan Wilson. Some
mediocre material but on the whole very good. A *Fly Inside the Eye* insert contains some
more odds and ends.
   Daughters of Fly in My Eye edited by Steve Niles (Arcane) has excellent covers by Jon
Muth (front) and John Bolton (back). There's also a wonderful rendition of Edgar Allen
Poe's "The Raven" by Ferdinand H. Horvath, an artist I'm unfamiliar with, and an
interesting piece on how to make shrunken heads by Peter Hayes. Good interior art by
John Bolton and some sophomoric pieces that stand out quite negatively compared to the
really good stuff.
   The Drowned Girl by Jon Hammer (Piranha Press)—Private Eye Dick Shamus wanders
around NYC in a drug haze searching for a Nazi fifth column. Weird. The gritty side of
NY with a nasty humor.
   The Elvis Mandible by Douglas Michael (Piranha Press)—Pokes fun at the "Elvis is
everywhere" phenomenon. Michael plays with this obsession, positing that Elvis's mandible
is what made him great and is a mystical source of power. Fun.
   Big Black Kiss by Howard Chaykin (Vortex)—adults only—is a three-parter about vampirism, transsexuality, cults, corrupt, vicious cops and sex sex sex. Suspense/horror that
some will find offensive but it packs a wallop. As the introduction states, it "drop kicks us
straight to hell."
   Arkham Asylum written by Grant Morrison and illustrated by Dave McKean (Warner)
follows in the tradition of *The Dark Knight* and *The Killing Joke*—dark, grim, impres-

sionistic art and a Freudian-influenced text. Brilliant mature work that's beautiful and chilling although a bit heavy on the angst.

Ed, The Happy Clown by Chester Brown (Vortex) is pretttty weird. Perverse, grotesque, funny and as one blurber is quoted as saying, "hideous and brilliant." A compilation of the Canadian comic series Yummy Fur. Most definitely offensive.

M Book 1 by Fritz Lang with illustrations by Jon J. Muth (Arcane/Eclipse) is a retelling of the classic movie, Lang's first talkie, in lovely black and white with splashes of color. The film starred Peter Lorre as a pathetic child-killer. The package includes a record with the murderer's theme and some other music from the film.

Meltdown by Walter and Louise Simonson, Jon J. Muth and Kent Williams (Epic) is a compilation of books 1–4 in this series about two mutant American superheroes, Havoc and Wolverine, who are caught up in a plot by another mutant—Russian—to take over the world. Great art and good writing.

Plastic Forks by Ted McKeever (Epic) is about some mad scientists who experiment on themselves and each other with the pineal gland, creating monsters. Great stuff—adventure, scary, horrific, disgusting and moving. Nicely drawn. A five-book series. Want to know where the title comes from? Plastic forks are disposable, like the people in this series.

The Sandman: The Doll's House by Neil Gaiman, Mike Dringenberg and Malcolm Jones III (DC) is a compilation of books 8–16 in this series. Covers by Dave McKean. The standout for me is the issue on the serial killer convention. Funny parody of convention-going with panels and talks and fun for all.

Also: *Dr. Jekyll & Mr. Hyde* by Robert Louis Stevenson and Guido Crepax (Catalan—for adults only); the *Sandman* series (DC) written by Neil Gaiman with various artists; the *Tapping the Vein* series (Eclipse) written by Clive Barker with various artists; *Beautiful Stories for Ugly Children* (Piranha) by Dave Lapoutre and Dan Sweetman; the *Chaingang* series by Peter Gross, Mark Nelson and Mort Castle; (Northstar); *Monster Masterworks* by Stan Lee and Jack Kirby (Marvel), collecting for the first time the old comics, *Where Monsters Dwell, Where Creatures Roam*, and *Fear*; the *Swamp Thing* series created by Len Wein and Bernie Wrightson, written by Alan Moore with various artists (DC Comics); and *V for Vendetta* by Alan Moore and David Lloyd (DC Comics).

Some odds and ends I found interesting this year were:

Amok: Fourth Dispatch catalog of books, audio and video. A "guide to the steamy undergrowths of the well-manicured fiction garden and a thorough directory of the extremes of information in print." Includes forensic medical texts and CIA torture manuals (with illustrations), behavior control techniques, biographies of serial killers and porno queens, fire-and-brimstone fundamentalist fulminations, etc. etc. and . . . cyberpunk sf, hard-boiled pulp writers, blaxploitation novels, surrealists, new wave. You name it, they've got it. Great stuff. Invaluable for research. 351 pages. Visit their store in Los Angeles.

Gauntlet: Exploring the Limits of Free Expression, contains some thought-provoking essays, both originals and reprints including opposing views on the exposure of female bodies, both written by women. Also Ray Bradbury's essay reprinted from a 1979 edition of his novel *Fahrenheit 451*, George Carlin's famous "filthy word" bit, an article on the problems Steven Bissette had in publishing the second issue of *Taboo*, plus (yet again) the "censored" snippets of Ray Garton's *Crucifax Autumn*. An important magazine in intent, but there isn't enough thought or discussion given to the consequences of totally unfettered free expression. The publishers come across as apologists for blatant racism, sexism and violence when they say that Andy Rooney is "stepping on the toes of minorities who are today's darlings of yuppie liberals." This is an offensive comment seemingly in support of hate-mongering. And this is the big problem with the first issue of the magazine—the publishers fail to put their articles on censorship into any context. Bias crimes are up all over the country yet the articles supporting Rooney (and I assume Jimmy Breslin as well) completely ignore the fact that these men appear on nationwide television and are in the public eye, influencing thousands of readers and listeners. There's no discussion about the responsibilities of citizens of a free society. *Gauntlet* is just a beginning; how about a more thorough examination of the issues?

Journal Wired edited and published by Andy Watson and Mark V. Ziesing and designed by Arnie Fenner—a quarterly that put out three excellent issues of critical essays, rantings (by Lucius Shepard) and fiction. Unfortunately, the publishers found it economically unviable. It was by subscription only and covered not only the field of fantasic literature but a wide range of material.

Classics Illustrated (First Comics/Berkley) is an attempt at reviving the old comic series from years ago. Too many of the illustrations are unimaginative, having taken the text far too literally. Exceptions are Bill Sienkewicz's *Moby Dick*, Gahan Wilson's *The Raven and Other Poe Pieces*, P. Craig Russell & Jay Geldhof's *Fall of the House of Usher* and J.K. Potter's cover (interiors are by someone else) for *The Island of Dr. Moreau*.

The Waste Land by Martin Rowson (Perennial) is a very clever parody of T.S. Eliot and Raymond Chandler. Lots of visual jokes. Private eye Chris Marlowe searches for his partner's murderer, and, at the same time, for the holy grail. I think to fully appreciate this excellent material, it would help to read or reread Eliot's "The Waste Land."

Crocodile Attack by Hugh Edwards (Avon). With a sensationalistic cover of a big croc with wide toothy grin and blurbs like "gut-wrenching . . . dramatic . . . hair-raising," and a subtitle that proclaims "Shocking true stories about the terrible reptiles and their human prey"—one might be surprised to find inside the covers a plea of understanding for this much maligned remnant of the age of dinosaurs. Interwoven with hair-raising stories of people decapitated, chomped on, and mutilated by crocs (apparently alligators, mostly found in the American South, don't eat people—although they might attack them), are explanations of why the victims were in the wrong place at the wrong time and how people who live near crocs need to become aware of crocodilian habits and treat them with the respect they deserve and require. So, despite the exploitation package for all you horror ghouls out there, there's also serious information imparted in this book.

In the House of Secret Enemies by George C. Chesbro (Mysterious Press) is a collection of stories about Mongo the dwarf, a former circus acrobat now expert criminologist/private detective. Ranging from 1971 and most of the '70s to the most recent story, published in 1988 in an anthology I missed (I'd probably have taken the story for that year's volume of the year's best if I'd seen it). Chesbro explains in his thoughtful introduction how the character developed and took on a life of his own, becoming the hero of the very popular series of novels. A must for Mongo fans.

Coup D'Etat: The Assassination of John F. Kennedy trading cards by Paul Brancato and Bill Sienkiewicz (Eclipse) is an introduction to the twisted maze of conspiracy theory. The only thing certain is that there had to be more than one gunman and that the truth of what happened November 22, 1963 isn't yet known and may never be. Fascinating material with excellent illustrations by Sienkiewicz.

Silent Cities: The Evolution of the American Cemetery by Kenneth T. Jackson & Camilio José Vergara (Princeton Architectural Press) is a history of the American cemetery. More than 350 color photographs. In its examination of more than three hundred cemeteries, the book combines architectural, historical, and sociological research, recounting the words of contemporary cemetery officials, caretakers, and mourners. Not seen by editor but sounds interesting.

Phantoms of the Isles: Further Tales of the Haunted Realm by Simon Marsden (Webb & Bower—UK) while unseen by me, is mentioned in the British magazine *Skeleton Crew* and looks hauntingly lovely, judging from the black and white cover and photographs, reproduced in the magazine. He did the illustrations for *Visions of Poe*, recommended last year.

There was an Old Lady by Nick Bantock (Viking). I admit it, I'm a sucker for pop-up books. Give me one and I'll be happy for hours (Ok, minutes). She eats a fly, a spider, a bird, etc. It's cute, it's clever, it's silly.

13 Plays of Ghosts & The Supernatural selected by Marvin Kaye (GuildAmerica Books)—Included are European and American plays by William Butler Yeats, Isaac Bashevis Singer, Eugene Ionesco, Parke Godwin and James M. Barrie among others. With a delicious jacket by Edward Gorey.

Biomechanics by H. R. Giger (Morpheus International). First U.S. edition. Originally published in Germany in 1988. This oversized, sumptuous hardcover priced at $69.50 contains an introduction by Harlan Ellison, commentary by Viennese fantastic realist Ernst Fuchs, as well as the artist's own commentary. At the heart of the book are more than 300 pieces of art, including full-color reproductions of numerous projects and pieces, accompanied by black and white sketches, and extensive biographical notes on the artist's career. An expensive but worthwhile package, with gorgeous design and good production values.

Clive Barker Illustrator, text by Fred Burke (Arcane/Eclipse) is an excellent collection of art by the author of *Books of Blood* and *The Great and Secret Show* and director of *Hellraiser*. Barker has experimented with a wide range of artistic styles, and I think his most interesting work is in B&W. With just a few lines he can suggest full-fledged figures. Also included are the color illustrations from the British hardcover edition of *Books of Blood*. The text is perceptive and generously quotes from Barker on his own artwork. Highly recommended.

The Jeffrey Jones Fantasy Collection (Lenar Fine Arts) is four 8″ × 10″ full color prints of art which first appeared on the covers of books by Fritz Leiber and Robert E. Howard plus two *Fantastic* covers.

The Stephen Fabian Fantasy Collection (Lenar Fine Arts) is also four prints in color.

The Year in Fear 1991 Calendar (Tundra Publishing Ltd.) with a color cover and 12 unbound duotone illos by Stephen R. Bissette.

1991 The Year in Darkness Wall Calendar (Bucky Montgomery) featuring the horrific art of John Borkowski, Alfred Klosterman, Jim Garrison, Allen Koszowski, Bucky Montgomery and others and the dark fiction of Jeanette Hopper, Bentley Little, David B. Silva, J.N. Williamson and others.

Heavy Metal July 1990—I haven't kept on top of this illustrated fantasy magazine but a recent copy has a portfolio of wonderful horror material by H.R. Giger and some good strips with borderline horror material.

Until You Are Dead: The Book of Executions in America by Frederick Drimmer (Citadel) is a very readable history of the development of capital punishment in the U.S. The book begins with the case history of the first man to be executed in the electric chair (which Thomas Alva Edison developed) and continues with the evolution of the "chair," the changeover to gas and then lethal injection. The author, by personalizing the various cases, draws the reader in. There are many interesting tidbits including the facts that Vanzetti (of Sacco & Vanzetti—two Italian immigrants now thought to be innocent) was reprieved at the last minute but the telegram failed to reach the warden in time; Utah allowed beheading as one of its possible means of execution (although never used); and most prison wardens were against capital punishment (as, surprisingly, were some of the executioners). This and other fascinating material make me recommend this odd book. Highly recommended.

Still Unsolved: Great True Murder Cases, selected, with an Introduction, by Richard Glyn Jones (Lyle Stuart) is an interesting compilation of some famous unsolved murders written about by Ngaio Marsh, Erle Stanley Gardner, Nancy Mitford, Colin Wilson, and others. The only problem with a book of this type is that it's kind of frustrating—if only they'd include a "solved" murder, but the reader is left hanging. . . .

Re/Search Publications:
Some interesting new material by the people who brought us tattooed and pierced body parts last year in their book *Modern Primitives*. Most of their material is 8½" × 11" with attractive slick covers and good interior design. The gem is a large-format, illustrated edition of *The Atrocity Exhibition*, the classic book of short stories/compressed novels by J.G. Ballard. In it are the infamous "Why I Want to Fuck Ronald Reagan" and "The Assassination of John Fitzgerald Kennedy Considered as a Downhill Motor Race." With five additional fiction pieces, extensive annotations, disturbing photographs by Ana Barrado and anatomically explicit medical illustrations by Phoebe Gloeckner. For those of you unfamiliar with the original book (shredded by Nelson Doubleday when it was still in the warehouse and eventually picked up by Grove Press as *Love and Napalm: Export USA*), it is a classic of science fiction but should be of interest to horror fans as well. *The Confessions of Wanda Von Sacher-Masoch*—Available for the first time in English, this is by the wife of Leopold Von Sacher-Masoch, for whose sexual games the term "masochism" was coined. From the catalogue: "A compelling study of a woman's search for her own identity, strength and ultimately—complete independence—this is a true life adventure story. . . . Underneath its unforgettable poetic imagery and almost unbearable emotional cataclysms reigns a woman's consistent unblinking investigation of the limits of morality and the deepest meanings of love." Sounds good to me. *Freaks: We Who Are Not As Others* by Daniel P. Mannix is another out-of-print classic based on Mannix's personal acquaintance with various sideshow stars. Eighty-eight photographs and additional material from the author's personal collection.

The Philosophy of Horror: or Paradoxes of the Heart, by Noel Carroll (Routledge—UK) An academic treatise on what puts the "horror" in horror—films and books. If you've always wondered what academics think about the subject of horror, this might be your cup of tea. Parts are a bit dry and some will irritate the casual reader, particularly the need of the author to repeat ideas and phrases several times to get his point across. I personally feel the author makes at least two major mistakes—he narrows the definition too much and he uses films and books interchangeably for his examples.

Some non-fiction books of interest to the horror reader are:
The Monster with A Thousand Faces by Brian J. Frost. Non-fiction reference guide to various types of vampirism in literature (Bowling Green University, Popular Press); *Contemporary Science Fiction, Fantasy and Horror Poetry: A Resource Guide and Biographical Dictionary* by Scott E. Green (Greenwood); *Horror Literature: A Reader's Guide* edited by Neil Barron (Garland); *The Shape of the Fantastic: Selected Essays From the Seventh International Conference of the Fantastic in the Arts*, edited by Olena H. Saciuk and *Contours of the Fantastic: Selected Essays from the Eighth ICFA*, edited by Michele K. Langford (Greenwood), see above; *The Weird Tale* by S.T. Joshi. N-F reference. A study of the works of six masters of the classic weird tale. (University of Texas Press); *Lovecraft Studies 20*, ed. by S.T. Joshi and *Studies in Weird Fiction #6* ed. by Joshi and *H.P. Lovecraft Letters to Henry Kuttner* edited by David E. Schultz and S.T. Joshi (Necron-

omicon Press); *The Aesthetics of Junk Fiction* by Thomas J. Roberts. N-F reference (University of Georgia Press); *Angels: An Endangered Species* by Malcolm Godwin (Simon & Schuster); *Of Kinkajous, Capybaras, Horned Beetles, Seladangs and the Oddest and Most Wonderful Mammals, Insects, Birds, and Plants of Our World*, by Jeanne K. Hanson and Deane Morrison (HarperCollins); *How I Made A Hundred Movies in Hollywood and Never Lost a Dime* by Roger Corman with Jim Jerome (Random House); *Hollywood Gothic: The Tangled Web of Dracula From Novel to Stage to Screen* by David J. Skal (Norton); *Universal Horrors: The Studio's Classic Films 1931–1946*, by Michael Brunas, John Brunas, and Tom Weaver; *Karloff and Lugosi: The Story of a Haunting Collaboration, with a complete Filmography of their Films Together* by Gregory William Mank, and *Images of Fear: How Horror Stories Helped Shape Modern Culture* (McFarland); *The Dark Shadows Companion: 25th Anniversary Collector's Edition* edited by Kathryn Leigh Scott (Pomegranate Press); *The Look of Horror: Scary Moments From Scary Movies* by Jonathan Sternfield (Running Press/Courage); *The Cabinet of Dr. Caligari: Texts, Contexts, Histories* edited by Mike Budd (Rutgers University Press); *Escape from Banality: The Fantastic Art of Clive Barker* by Gary Hoppenstad, *H.P. Lovecraft: The Decline of the West* by S.T. Joshi, *The "Shining" Reader* ed. by Anthony Magistrale, *In the Darkest Night: The Student's Guide to Stephen King* by Tim Murphy. *Fear to the World: Eleven Voices in the Chorus of Horror* ed. by Kevin E. Proulx, *Discovering Classic Horror Fiction* by Darrell Schweitzer, *The Devil's Notebook* by Clark Ashton Smith, *The Stephen King Short Story Concordance* by Chris Thomsen, *H.P. Lovecraft and the Cthulhu Mythos* by Robert M. Price and *The Horror of It All: Encrusted Gems From the Crypt of Cthulhu* (Starmont); *The Living of Charlotte Perkins Gilman: An Autobiography* (University of Wisconsin Press); *Clive Barker's Nightbreed: The Making of the Film* (HarperCollins/Fontana); *The Modern Horror Film* by John McCarty (Carol); *More Annotated Alice* by Lewis Carroll, an omnibus of *Alice's Adventures in Wonderland* and *Through the Looking-Glass* with fully revised annotations by Martin Gardner, Peter Newell illustrations. Some new material (Random House); *The Work of Charles Beaumont* by William F. Nolan. 2nd edition expanded and revised from orig. 1986 pamphlet (Borgo Press); *Rod Serling: The Dreams and Nightmares of Life in the Twilight Zone* by Joel Engel and *The Ghostly Gazetteer: American's Most Fascinating Haunted Landmarks* by Arthur Myers (Contemporary); and *Science Fiction, Fantasy, & Horror: 1989* by Charles N. Brown and William G. Contento (Locus Press).

The third Horror Writers of America weekend was held June 22–24 in Providence, Rhode Island. The recipients of the Bram Stoker Awards for outstanding achievement in horror literature were Novel: *Carrion Comfort* by Dan Simmons (Dark Harvest/Warner); First Novel: *Sunglasses After Dark* by Nancy A. Collins (Onyx); Novella/Novelette: "On the Far Side of the Cadillac Desert With Dead Folks," by Joe R. Lansdale (*Book of the Dead*); Short Story: "Eat Me," by Robert R. McCammon (*Book of the Dead*); Collection: *Richard Matheson: Collected Stories* (Scream/Press); nonfiction (tie): *Harlan Ellison's Watching* by Harlan Ellison (Underwood-Miller) and *Horror: 100 Best Books* by Stephen Jones and Kim Newman (Carroll & Graf); Robert Bloch, who was guest speaker at the banquet, received the HWA's Lifetime Achievement Award. For information on the Horror Writers of America, contact HWA c/o Matthew J. Costello, 22 Piping Rock Drive, Ossining, NY 10562.

The 1990 Readercon small press awards were announced. Novel: no award, Short Work: *A Dozen Tough Jobs* by Howard Waldrop (Ziesing). Collection: *Richard Matheson: Collected Stories* (Scream/Press). Anthology: *What Did Miss Darrington See?: An Anthology of Feminist Supernatural Fiction*, Jessica Amanda Salmonson, editor (Feminist Press). Non-fiction: *The Dark-Haired Girl*, Philip K. Dick (Ziesing). Reference/bibliography: no award. Reprint: *The Anubis Gates* by Tim Powers (Ziesing). Jacket Illustration: *The Anubis*

Gates, J.K. Potter, illustrator. Interior Illustration: *S. Peterson's Field Guide to Creatures of the Dreamlands*, Mark Ferrari and Tom Sullivan, illustrators (Chaosium); Value in Bookcraft: *Richard Matheson: Collected Stories*, Richard Matheson (Scream/Press); Magazine—fiction: *Interzone*, David Pringle, ed.; Magazine—criticism: *Science Fiction Eye*, Stephen P. Brown and Daniel J. Steffan, editors. Magazine-design: *Science Fiction Eye*. The awards, given for work appearing in 1989, were chosen by a panel of judges: Thomas M. Disch, John Shirley, Kathryn Cramer, Paul Chadwick, Jerry Kaufman, Greg Ketter, and Evelyn Leeper.

The Lambda Literary Awards were presented in Las Vegas June 1, 1990. Lesbian SF/ fantasy: *What Did Miss Darrington See?* Jessica Amanda Salmonson, ed. (Feminist Press). Gay Men's SF/Fantasy: *Somewhere in the Night*, Jeffrey N. McMahan (Alyson).

A campaign by three Lovecraft fans to convince the city of Providence, Rhode Island, to erect a bronze centennial plaque to the memory of H.P. Lovecraft has succeeded. The plaque—which was dedicated August 20, the centenary of Lovecraft's birth, at the John Hay Library, which houses Lovecraft's papers—has a profile of the author plus a poem about Providence.

A *Clockwork Orange* by Anthony Burgess, staged by the Royal Shakespeare Company, received mostly negative reviews when it opened in London in February 1990. The *Sunday Telegraph* called it "a clockwork lemon." The movie, filmed in 1968, was withdrawn from British circulation by its director, Stanley Kubrick, in 1972 because he was receiving death threats. Burgess said he wrote the stage play to deter others from doing it and according to the *Evening Standard* was quoted as saying, "It's a terrible book in some ways. I'm not prepared to defend it."

Dr. Jekyll & Mr. Hyde was interpreted and performed by Charles Ludlam's The Ridiculous Theatrical Company in New York. A witty parody of the melodrama.

Horror and Fantasy in the Media: 1990
by Edward Bryant

In 1990, the top fifty or so genre films (sf, fantasy, and horror) pulled in about a billion and a half dollars at the door. The gross for all films released in America was a bit more than three times that figure. The $5.02 billion in gross receipts was the second-best total in history. Ticket sales decreased by more than a tenth; ticket prices increased and made up the slack. It's all Monopoly money, anyway. Compare the total to Matsushita's paying $6.5 billion for MCA, which includes Universal Pictures and Putnam/Ace/Berkley Books. The new Japanese owners earned $38 billion last year.

Whatever the exact figures, it's a hell of a lot of popcorn. And what did we all get in exchange?

Well, one way to answer that is to say that the best science fiction film I saw on the big screen last year was *Blade Runner*. And yes, I *know* the movie's nine years old. But like *Lawrence of Arabia* and couple of other aged blockbusters, Ridley Scott's liberal adaptation of Philip K. Dick's *Do Androids Dream of Electric Sheep?* had a limited re-release in 70-millimeter in selected art houses. I had to think hard about going to see it. I'd viewed at least two different versions back in 1982: the preliminary preview version, with a bit more violence and a little more character interaction; and the release print, with its tacked-on voice-over narration and cheery ending. I'd much preferred the former, but hadn't really been knocked out by either.

Then, in a year in which I'd seen *Total Recall* and *Darkman* and *Dick Tracy*, I returned to the topless towers of L.A. 2019 and streets crawling with rogue replicants. Holy nostalgic revisionism, Batman! *Blade Runner*'s suddenly become a fuggin' masterpiece.

In other words, 1990 didn't see much breaking of new ground. One had to scrounge pretty deep for signs of innovation, courage and askew sensibilities.

But you'd never know it from most of the top-grossers. *Total Recall* was neither director Paul Verhoeven nor star Arnold Schwarzenegger's finest moment. Not that it didn't have nice production values, good effects, and occasional cute lines. But it funneled down to a monumentally stupid climax on the planet Mars which could have been doctored very easily and effectively, but hey, the producers never asked me, so what's a Monday morning quarterback to say? The result was a $40 or $50 million B-movie.

Spend a lot less and you got *Tremors*, a genuinely *good* B-movie. Kevin Bacon and Fred Ward did wonderfully well at fending off a clutch of huge, carnivorous sandworms busily digging their way under the Nevada desert. Ron Underwood directed. Part of the picture's real charm was that it was a classic '50s style movie, but one in which none of the characters did anything truly stupid. They all acted as though they were actually sentient beings. That's refreshing. The film was sharp, funny, exciting and entertaining. I can't say that about too many movies in *any* year.

Another good B-movie, though on a less consistent scale, was the direct-to-video release, *Circuitry Man*. This was a genuine cyberpunk chase movie. Steve Lovy directed. At the beginning the film had a fine, imaginative, retro look, sort of like Walter Hill's *Streets of Fire* or Alan Rudolph's *Trouble in Mind*. The melodramatic plot is about professional bodyguard Dana Wheeler-Nicholson and android gigolo Jim Metzler, in a '64 Ford Galaxie convertible, trying to keep a packet of expensive microchips out of the hands of Vernon Wells, a droll, pragmatic villain with a lot of cranial implants, named Plughead. The writers sometimes strain for humor, but the film generally succeeds with moments of real wit and a constant state of not taking itself too seriously.

On the other hand . . . *Ghost* was unbearably romantic and unspeakably manipulative. Audiences ate it up with gravy ladles. *Dick Tracy* boosted both Warren Beatty's and Madonna's careers, and generated lots of entertainment rag headlines. As a comic book translation, it looked great except when the aware viewer considered how much the backgrounds (Chester Gould tended never to draw them in the strip) were inspired, er, well, *derived* without credit from Will Eisner cityscapes. *Arachnophobia* showed that director Frank Marshall can still handle a second unit very well. Speaking as an arachnophobe myself, I was a bit disappointed that little happened on-screen that impelled me to run screaming from the theater. Too bad. Maybe Hollywood Pictures should have gone the William Castle route, arranging to have billions of harmless live spiders dropped from the ceiling at just the right moments.

One of the year's big surprises was the success of *Teenage Mutant Ninja Turtles*. It made a *lot* of money, and did it by cleverly doing double duty as both a kids' and an adult movie. The four hardshell comic book heroes sliced pizza and performed their martial arts duties admirably, and much of the film was genuinely funny. The human love-interest couple were particularly offbeat in their attractiveness.

Sequels slogged along with only a few bright spots. They tended to opt for attempting the high points of their predecessors, but rarely achieving that and, worse, adding nothing new. *Robocop II* had Peter Weller, but that was about it. It was, alas, junk. When it comes to bad films, there are two varieties: those that amuse, and those that don't. Another that joined *Robocop II* in the latter category was *Gremlins II: the New Batch*. It didn't have the wit of *Gremlins*, and the original had precious little of that commodity in the first place. *Predator II* had a great cast (Danny Glover, Ruben Blades, Maria Conchita Alonso, etc.) and squandered them all on a foolish pyramid scheme: "Hey, if *one* invisible alien in the jungle is killing humans, how about we put a *bunch* of invisible aliens in L.A. and let them kill humans?" It just didn't work. After the cheap, visceral, boy-adolescent, adrenaline rush of the first cops-vs.-drug dealers scene abated, there was nothing else to match.

The first *Child's Play* was taut and edgy, with the spirit of Brad Dourif's mad killer possessing the body of a toy doll. The only scare *Child's Play 2* contributed to western civilization was the rubber sucker-appendaged Chuckie dolls sported on the insides of a few automobile windows. At least he was a change from Garfield. *Leatherface: Texas Chainsaw Massacre III* had neither the raw energy of the first installment, nor the manic appeal of Dennis Hopper's performance in the second. It had a good director (Jeff Burr) and a good writer (David J. Schow). But everything seemed to come a cropper. Too bad. The moments were good.

Back to the Future III was inoffensive and entertaining. The three episodes form a continuous, unified whole, which is to their credit, and do a good job of translating the concept of time travel paradox to a broad audience. Christopher Lloyd continued as a fine mad scientist, and Michael J. Fox did a good job trying to look as young as the teen hero he was playing.

The best sequel of the year in the realm of the fantastic was *The Exorcist III*. William Peter Blatty directed from his own novel, and very well. George C. Scott lent a fair amount of authority. The nicest thing about the film was its old-fashioned approach to horror. Most of the movie sat on a firm base of slowly escalating atmosphere and tension. It took a long time before the grue become graphic. It worked well. This was literate, beautifully crafted, Catholic horror. If you're an agnostic, it still works. Madelyn Murray O'Hare, were she still alive, would probably have a tough time.

Speaking of religious horror, Margaret Atwood's *The Handmaid's Tale* was directed by

Volker Schlondorff from a script by Harold Pinter, and with a stellar cast. In this dystopian vision (well, depending on your orientation . . .) fundamentalist Christianity takes over the U.S., a plague sterilizes most women, and the remainder are forced into becoming baby factories. The whole movie seemed a bit sterile, lacking the gut-punching energetic power the material demanded and deserved. If a film were to get the "good try" award, it would be this one.

Another movie with a deeply religious underpinning was Adrian Lyne's *Jacob's Ladder*. Bruce Joel Rubin's script had knocked around Hollywood for a decade or so, gathering much praise but no takers. Tim Robbins does a splendid job as a protagonist who discovers that his reality is quite literally falling apart. Things change. Perspective shifts. The result may be a religious parable, or an enormous borrowing from Ambrose Bierce's "An Occurrence at Owl Creek Bridge," or something much stranger. A legitimate ambiguity is set up so that the viewer is obliged to participate in the decision- and analysis-making process. *Ghost* fans may find the movie infuriating. The horror aspects are sparingly and extremely effectively employed.

Sam Raimi's *Darkman* was a major disappointment. The director had the opportunity to create a new mythic pulp-fiction hero and muffed it. While there's plenty of the patented Raimi nonstop action (especially a car-and-helicopter chase scene), the movie is undercut at every turn by a sloppy script. Once again, there's an object lesson: plot logic costs no more than plot idiocy. Much the same charge can be leveled at *Flatliners*, an initially intriguing melodrama of medical students obsessively screwing around with near-death experience. The cast's pretty good and Julia Roberts is nice to look at, but the refrain, "That doesn't make *sense*," keeps popping up.

Of course both the above look much more like *Blade Runner* when you stack them up against Bill Cosby in *Ghost Dad* and the animated *Jetsons: The Movie*. There are some things that are totally unfunny, not because of their intrinsic subject matter, but simply in their execution. Both *Ghost Dad* and *Jetsons: The Movie* should indeed have been executed.

On the other hand, *I Come In Peace* with Dolph Lundgren actually has its amusing moments. It's got the familiar elements of alien cop pursuing alien criminal here on Earth, and a four-way imbroglio with the L.A. cops, the aliens, and the various drug gangs. But it's also got Jessie Vint in a cameo, and such funny touches as a vicious crack gang comprised of yuppie white boys (they actually call themselves that) with impeccable grooming and snazzy cars. Another entertaining bad movie is *Graveyard Shift*. Ralph S. Singleton directed from John Esposito's script based on a Stephen King short story. The film has great Maine location filming and some nice rat-wrangling. It's got one priceless moment when the camera fades in on a hapless rat sailing along a small basement river on a piece of wooden shingle while a boombox plays "Surfin' Safari." This is another case of many good moments, but no good whole.

King fared better in Rob Reiner's classy adaptation of *Misery*. William Goldman wrote the script of the best-selling romance novelist trapped in a Colorado winter by his greatest fan. James Caan did well as the writer, and Kathy Bates convinced as the latest incarnation of Big Nurse. While not exactly *Stand By Me*, *Misery* was surprisingly restrained. Nevada stood in for Colorado and Richard Farnsworth had a good supporting role as a lawman. The suspense was solid.

King also contributed one of the episodes to the anthology entry, *Tales From the Darkside: The Movie*. The film entertained, but unevenly, and didn't exactly bolster any kind of trend toward a new wave in big-screen anthologies. *Darkside* was produced by the folks at Laurel Entertainment, a prime supplier of decent pop-horror, one of whose founders wrote a remake of a horror classic. George Romero reworked the materials from his own *Night of the Living Dead* and Tom Savini directed. I thought Romero did a fine job of recapturing the past and then elaborating it in new directions. The original grainy, black-and-white frantic edge is gone, sacrificed for slicker wide-screen color, but there are some new benefits. The female lead is very much a courageous woman of the '90s, ultimately resourceful. Romero not only adds a few surprises parlayed on the original, he also suggests much more of the world-view background of a zombifying landscape. Additionally he covers some of the simple plot flaws of the original: "Well, how come you can't just *outrun* those lumbering, clumsy monsters?" It's a clean, spare, well-lit job.

You can't quite say the same about *The First Power*, a supernatural thriller in which Lou Diamond Phillips just doesn't carry a whole lot of authority as a tough homicide cop. He's trying to protect Melanie's half-sister, Tracy Griffith, from a body-jumping dead Satanist dude. It's a weaker version of *Shocker*. Same disappointment goes for *The Guardian*, an adaptation of Dan Greenburg's novel, *The Nanny*. This was William Friedkin's return to directing horror. Unfortunately his vision of a contemporary tree-spirit's eating up yuppie babies neither thrilled, nor horrified.

Science fiction drones had their own problems with mediocrity. Patrick Read Johnson's *Spaced Invaders* showed moronic Martians invading Earth after confusing themselves with a broadcast of the radio "War of the Worlds." The humor was broad and spotty, somewhere between *Attack of the Killer Tomatoes* on the down side, *Strange Invaders* on the up. Stuart Gordon's *Robot Jox* was finally released regionally. This parable of humanity's settling international disputes by having huge, human-guided robot gladiators duking it out was filmed from a Joe Haldeman script. One hopes the script was cut by other hands, since the result was simplistic and preachy. The low-budget special effects were pretty good. And it was nice seeing Paul Koslo working again (as the Soviet bloc champ).

Hardware was a major disappointment. British rock video director Richard Stanley's cyberpunked-out, futuristic horror creation looked gorgeous. Unfortunately virtually every element was derived from some previous, more successful science fiction film. Great looks, not a brain in its head.

Then there was David Lynch. His *Wild at Heart* was manic, inventive, and intermittently powerful. But unlike *Blue Velvet*, it ultimately never seemed to be *about* anything. All effect, nothing happening under the glitzy surfaces. Too bad. It entertained, but didn't nourish.

Another tough call was Clive Barker's *Nightbreed*. It didn't have the powerfully kinky sexual tension of a *Hellraiser*, but it did ambitiously attempt a complex tale of evil humans vs. sympathetic monsters. The picture gets a lot of points for effort, but seemed ultimately doomed by its distributor's incredibly inept promotional campaign.

Edward Scissorhands also had its share of disappointment. Directed by Tim Burton, this seemed deliberately aimed at being another *Beauty and the Beast* or *Phantom of the Opera*, treating the monster as sympathetic protagonist. Johnny Depp did well as the title character, an artificially created boy, but unfinished with monstrous shears in place of hands. Brilliant invention alternated with utterly dumb miscalculation, so that, sadly, this will never become a modern classic.

On the animation front, the re-release of *Fantasia* blew everything else out of the water. The re-release of *Jungle Book* did well too. Of the original features, *Ducktales* was pretty good, *The Nutcracker Prince* wasn't. *Rescuers Down Under* was quite good, especially with George C. Scott giving voice to the villain. Appropriately, the villain, an Outback poacher, was drawn to look like Scott. This is a movie that works equally well for adult and juvenile audiences. On a more unilaterally adult level, such compilations as *The Third Animation Celebration* toured well. In the latter, high points were many, but Mike Wellins and Mark

Swain's "This Is Not Frank's Planet" especially amused. *The XXIInd International Tourneé of Animation* included 18 pieces, one of the most outstanding being Jan Kounen's "Gisele Kerozene," an incredibly frantic example of stop-action pixillation in which cyberpunk demons chase each other on jet-powered broomsticks through an urban nightmare.

The most impressive piece of theatrical animation last year was Katsuhiro Otomo's *Akira*. This feature-length adaptation of Otomo's graphic novel was expensively budgeted, and looked it. It's a punked-out epic of gangs, revolution, and government conspiracy, all set in the post-holocaust Tokyo of 2019. This is animation aimed at adults; and, in its own way, it displays a complexity and depth that shames a film such as *Total Recall*.

Enough grousing for a while. Let's look at some interesting and rewarding works. On the documentary side, *For All Mankind* copped an Oscar nomination for its portrait of the Apollo moon flights. It was enough to renew one's sense of wonder—and generate profound sadness at the foundering space program.

For my money, one of the finest fantasy films of the year was Akira Kurosawa's *Dreams*. The Japanese master filmmaker crafted a compilation of short films incorporating elements of the fantastic. Some of the episodes were brilliant; others were a bit preachy and self-indulgent, something like later Heinlein. But in every case, the vignettes were lushly gorgeous and evocative. The opening sections, in which a young boy disobeys his mother's orders and spies on the foxes' wedding procession, suggest subtly that *Dreams* can be interpreted as the story not only of Kurosawa's, but of *any* committed artist's giving up a conventional, comfortable life to become an outsider and a creator.

Another very personal vision by a talented director—and one less formal and much weirder—is Alejandro Jodorowsky's *Santa Sangre*. This is the first film in a decade from the maker of the legendary *El Topo*. Lots of bizarre imagery (the elephant's funeral comes to mind), kinky sex, and surreal violence here. A grotesque Mexican circus and psychic possession of a son by his religiously obsessed mother form the core of Jodorowsky's dreamy nightmare. It's like having Norman Bates for a tour guide in a demented Disneyland of the mind.

Also in the category of strange fantasy, *Jesus of Montreal* earned considerable credibility. It was a Canadian film that suggested the actor playing the lead in a contemporary Passion Play might actually be the Christ Himself. It's a speculation about religious faith that is never pushy. Another thought-provoking film was the expanded re-release of Andrei Tarkovsky's *Solaris*. The 1972 Soviet adaptation of Stanislaw Lem's novel was cut by 35 minutes for its initial American release. I saw that first version and was hard-put to stay awake through the remaining two hours and twelve minutes. The longer version works beautifully. The pacing becomes dreamy, hypnotic in its intensity. I was awake and fascinated every moment. For something a little more melodramatic and paranoid, I recommend *Incident at Raven's Gate*. This Australian film about alien first contact and government conspiracy possesses a high level of intelligence. My benchmark for that judgment is the fact that this movie believes in making plot points just once, not the two or three repetitions that so many commercial films employ. What results is tense, chilly, and even a bit wonder-inspiring. *The Reincarnation of Golden Lotus* was just your basic political fantasy, involving traditional Chinese myth, reincarnation, revenge, and feminism. You know; the usual. Actually this feature by debut director, Shanghai-born Clara Law, is a beautiful and provocative examination of romantic myth.

I saw two movies that fascinated many, but simultaneously repelled a significant number of viewers so that they walked out. Peter Greenaway's *The Cook, the Thief, His Wife & Her Lover* played both the art circuit and at suburban malls, and seemed to startle moviegoers everywhere. Grim, biting, occasionally shocking and always hilarious, this romance and revenge play as hybridized by Monty Python on strange drugs, dealt with the eternal verities of sex and food. Exquisitely designed and shot, *The Cook, etc.* was as beautiful a film as any in the year, save perhaps *Dreams*.

"Beautiful" is not an adjective many would use with John McNaughton's *Henry: Portrait of a Serial Killer*. Too bad, because the film possesses a terrible beauty. Shot quick and cheap in the nastier underbellies of Chicago, *Henry* finally made it into commercial release. Based loosely on the careers of serial killers Henry Lee Lucas and Ottis Toole, funded by the guys who paid for *Faces of Death*, there was no reason to suppose *Henry* would turn out to be anything but the basest exploitation flick. Wrong. In our contemporary culture, horror we got. This movie brings it to unignorable life. People walked out of both screenings I attended; not, I think, because it was any more graphic than slice-and-dice features (and it's not), but because of the intensity, the utter conviction of the production. Michael Rooker does well in the title role. At Hollywood parties, it's possible he only converses with Anthony Hopkins, Hannibal Lector of *The Silence of the Lambs*, because no one else will talk to him. At any rate, *Henry* definitely gets the nod as the best, most convincing horror film of the year.

Finally, a pair of good, out-and-out fantasies. *Grim Prairie Tales* was an odd and distinctive anthology feature written and directed by Wayne Coe. No budget here, but a solid, intriguing production and a great cast. Somewhere in the later decades of the 19th century, eastern dude Brad Dourif finds himself out in the boonies sharing a fire with loutish bounty hunter James Earl Jones. As the flames wane, they tell each other stories, and those episodes make up the body of the picture. But in this film, the framing device isn't just a pretext for some spiffy, free-standing episodes. The content, the meaning of the whole movie, reflects back and forth between the developing relationship of the two men, their personalities, and what's going on in the internal episodes. Neatly done.

The Witches had everything going for it: Nicholas Roeg as director, a script by Roald Dahl, and Anjelica Huston starring. And it worked. This is a fantasy about the British witches' conspiracy to turn all the kids in the modern kingdom into mice. Fortunately for the Worldwide Witches Anti-Defamation League, not quite *all* the witches are utterly malign. This is what you might call a mature fantasy for kids of all ages. Like a traditional fairy tale, it's by turns genuinely amusing and frightening. The production does not talk down to its younger watchers. This one really *could* become a classic.

In the world of the small screen, TV had its ups and downs. *Star Trek: The Next Generation* finally surpassed its parent series in terms of number of episodes produced. It continues to be extremely popular. Some of the success of its 1990 season can probably be laid at the door of former story editor Melinda Snodgress. While Fox knew a good thing when it renewed the animated series, *The Simpsons*, it wimped out by canceling Kenneth Johnson's increasingly ambitious, complex, and adroit sf dramatic series, *Alien Nation*. There was some talk of producing a few *Alien Nation* made-for-TV movies, but nothing's come to fruition. HBO's anthology series, *Tales From the Crypt*, continued to attract good directors and scarfed up 12 ACE nominations, the Oscar of the cable field.

On the major networks, *Quantum Leap* continued its inspirational, increasingly metaphysical course, and *The Flash* slowly went downhill after an expensive and well-produced pilot movie. Vincent fans were crushed when CBS canceled the staggering *Beauty and the Beast*. An orchestrated fan write-in effort changed no minds at the network.

Stephen King's *It* was produced as a four-hour miniseries. The first two hours were pretty good; the second two hours dragged. The ending did not inspire. In December, the Richard Matheson–scripted *The Dreamer of Oz* starred John Ritter as L. Frank Baum. Good job.

The most ambitious and the most interesting series around was David Lynch and Mark

Frost's *Twin Peaks*. In the space of a year, the series appeared, dazzled viewers, was thoroughgoing weirdness from start to finish, and then began to sink in the ratings and in public interest. The large cast, the bizarre production touches, and the completely surreal atmosphere (including some sf/fantasy touches) all went completely against network stereotype. The future of *Twin Peaks* is now indeterminate, but dim.

After a heavy year of promotion, the Sci Fi Channel is gearing up for its takeover of the cable world.

The significance of such as the Baum bio-pic, *The Simpsons*, and *Twin Peaks* is that the small tube is not *always* a vast wasteland. Keep hoping. Continue writing letters in support of that which you respect and enjoy.

I'm afraid my consumption of live theater declined—temporarily, I hope—during 1990. About the only play that came close to the stage of the fantastic was the two-man speculative history, *The Boys in Autumn*. Walter Koenig and Mark Lenard played Huck Finn and Tom Sawyer as aging adults meeting each other in the early 1920s. Alan Hunt's direction, from the script by Bernard Sabath, worked fine, and Koenig proved he could recover quickly when the sound-tech muffed his cue and a Model T the actor was cranking didn't start when it should have.

Those dynamic equations in which both prose writing and music reflect and interact continued to apply. Just as writers sometimes sing, hum, or tap their feet to the rhythm of the word processor, so composers and musicians seem frequently to read—and to pay attention.

Not too surprisingly, most of the sf-, fantasy-, or horror-related music is in the pop field. I discovered plenty of people eager to make suggestions. The Cramps appeared far more frequently than, say, composers on the order of Holst.

Here, in no particular arrangement, is a hypothetical CD compilation album that one could use as accompaniment for reading just about any fantasy, dark or light: *I Am Stretched Out on Your Grave* by Lloyd Cole, Sinéad O'Connor's *Tomorrow, Wendy, Witchcraft* by Wishcraft, *Broken Bones* by Jinx Jones, Emotional Fish's *Gray Matter*, Chris Ria's *Road to Hell*, *Encounter* by Michael Stearns, *Space Sick* and *Creature From the Black Leather Lagoon* from the Cramps, all sorts of stuff by the Alien Sex Fiends, and, of course, all Julee Cruise's soundtrack music from *Twin Peaks*. Many thanks to Don Riley, Gary Jonas, Frank Day, and many other valiant, toe-tapping, lyric-intrigued readers for their leads and suggestions.

In the tradition of Warren Zevon's *Transverse City* and *Full Moon Fever* by Tom Petty, I found the biggest and best concentration of fantasy-related music on Concrete Blonde's *Bloodletting*. If Nancy A. Collins' *Sunglasses After Dark* ever becomes a feature film, the soundtrack could do much, much worse than use the title song from *Bloodletting* as the main theme. The tune is a driving, eerie, doomed-romance ("Love is a vampire/Drunk on your blood" says a line from "The Beast," another song on the album) ballad about vampires, lovers, and New Orleans. The major strengths of Concrete Blonde are the edgy lyrics and the powerful, distinctive delivery of vocalist Johnette Napolitano. This is driving, literate rock that functions perfectly well as music on its own terms; *however*, it also works fine if you want some background accompaniment as you orally drain the carotid of your beloved.

Obituaries

As in any year, 1990 saw the thinning of the ranks of those whose efforts contribute to the creation of fantasy and horror. Last year marked the passing of two key figures in the field. DONALD A. WOLLHEIM, 76, had a major influence on the development of fantasy, science fiction, and horror as a written form, for five decades. JIM HENSON, 53, redefined film and television fantasy and horror with his innovative and energetic vision of what had previously been a far more limited and limiting field.

Wollheim was primarily a book editor, though he also edited anthologies and wrote science fiction. Coming into the field as a very young man in the late 1930s, he edited perhaps the first SF anthology, *The Pocket Book of Science Fiction*, for Pocket Books in 1943. At Avon Books in the 1940s he edited many sf and fantasy books, including those of the bestselling A. Merritt. But it was at Ace, from its start in the early 1950s, that he made the contributions that would mark him as perhaps the single most important book editor in the field over a period of two decades. The list of major authors he brought to print in paperback to a wide audience is long and illustrious, including Brian W. Aldiss, John Brunner, C.J. Cherryh, Philip K. Dick, Tanith Lee, Ursula K. Le Guin, Andre Norton, and Roger Zelazny. He was one of a very few editors in the field to publish works by authors who wrote in languages other than English.

As Editor-in-Chief of Ace he had a hand in many books of other sorts, but sf and fantasy were his first love. He was a creative marketer for his time, inventing the Ace Double to bring short novels into paperback that had previously been published only in the sf magazines. He fostered young editors as well as young writers, most notably Terry Carr, who with Wollheim's approval developed and edited the Ace SF Specials, a series of outstanding paperbacks that to this day comprises an impressive list of speculative works.

He left Ace in 1971 as the company, which had changed hands several years earlier, endured difficult times financially. The company he then founded, DAW Books, focused solely on sf and fantasy. Many skeptics predicted quick failure, but he confounded them all, and DAW is still quite viable, in the hands of his daughter, Betsy Wollheim, and a longtime associate, Sheila Gilbert. Wollheim was known for his stubbornness and his willingness to take an occasional risk, as when he reprinted at Ace the works of Edgar Rice Burroughs, despite the objections of the estate, though the copyright on the books had lapsed. He also published the first U.S. editions of Tolkien's *The Lord of the Rings*, under circumstances which created an opportunity that he couldn't resist. He wrote a number of sf novels as David Grinnell, and in the 1960s began to edit a series of Best of the Year anthologies for which he became quite famous.

Jim Henson is probably best known for creating memorable "muppet" (he coined the term to describe his unique puppets) characters such as Kermit the Frog, Miss Piggy, and for *Sesame Street*, Big Bird and friends. Even in his early days as a puppeteer, Henson's sophisticated, adult humor gave him increasingly frequent exposure on major television showcases such as *The Ed Sullivan Show*, *The Tonight Show*, and *Saturday Night Live*. After establishing a cast of characters who have been staples on *Sesame Street* since the long-running children's educational show's inception, he created *The Muppet Show*, a unique variety show that showcased his favorite characters along with guest-star live performers to whom he gave an opportunity to break out of their usual form and go a little wild. For several years he maintained the frenetic pace of a weekly prime-time series while developing other projects. When he finally stopped producing new episodes of the series, he turned to theatrical motion pictures and TV specials, including the successful film *The Muppet Movie* and a variety of TV productions that were either successful adaptations of fairytales or new material. All of his productions, including his later series for cable, *Fraggle Rock*, reflected his generous creativity, his wit, sensitivity to human and ecological issues, and his deeply rooted humanism.

In addition to his own productions, Henson used his experience to create a completely new generation of special effects for film and television. Working with his talented, creative group of muppeteers and staff, Henson made "critters" who could play parts in film and TV productions that used not animation but live action. Films like *The Dark Crystal* and *Teenage Mutant Ninja Turtles* would have had no protagonists without characters created by Henson's people.

Henson said he was inspired by puppeteer Bil Baird, but Henson's own innovations have already proven to be of vastly more consequence, inspiring not only a new technological revolution in myth-making, but also a generation of young artists and writers who in emulating his style and ideals bring to millions the power and benign influence of Henson's positive, humanistic vision.

Some major writers died in 1990, including such mature authors as ROALD DAHL, 74, the wickedly literate author of barbed fantasy for readers young and old. His best known work was *Charlie and the Chocolate Factory*, filmed as *Willie Wonka*, but his short fiction for adults, collected in such volumes as *Switch Bitch*, was widely acclaimed as well. Important magic realist authors MANUEL PUIG, 57, and MANUEL DE PEDROLO, 72, also died this year, as did WALKER PERCY, 73, the National Book Award winner for *The Movie-goer*, and LAWRENCE DURRELL, 78, author of the acclaimed *Alexandria Quartet*.

In the genre, JOSEPH PAYNE BRENNAN, 71, known for his horror fiction, and ROBERT ADAMS, 56, whose young, violent adventure fantasies brought him great popularity in the 1980s, left the scene, as did CARL SHERRELL, 60, a writer of intriguing and quirky fantasy who was also a graphic artist. The major loss to the ranks of visual artists after Henson was ED EMSHWILLER, 65, who was one of the two or three major artists of paperback SF and fantasy art in the 1950s and 1960s. Emsh, as he signed his cover work, turned to film and then video, at a time when visual experimentation was very new. He pioneered in these media and continued to produce major works until illness forced him to stop shortly before his death. More famous and infinitely more commercially successful was BERNARD KLIBAN, 55, who at one time was a household word because of his drawings of cats, which drawings were reproduced not only as cartoons, but also on greeting cards, as stuffed toys, coffee cups—he was, in the 1970s, a one-man industry.

Other popular icons died as well. Among the film community, we lost JOHN PAYNE, 77, who is best remembered for the film he produced and starred in, *Miracle on 34th Street*, one of the great classic Christmas films. Other actors of note were the sensuous AVA GARDNER, 67, who brought to life *One Touch of Venus*, and was one of the hottest stars of the fifties, EVE ARDEN, 83, who was a deft comedienne in numerous films and on television, HOWARD DUFF, 76, who had a long and varied career as a romantic lead on TV, and essayed a variety of roles in film. DAVID RAPPOPORT, 38, was on his way to making great strides as a fine actor who avoided the stereotyping that has dogged the careers of most dwarfs, when he took his own life. Other actors who died this year who had roles big or small in fantasy or horror included LEE VAN CLEEF, 64, SILVANA MANGANO, 59, GORDON JACKSON, 66, JOCK MAHONEY, 70, and IAN CHARLESON, 40.

Songwriter SAMMY FAIN, 87, in addition to writing many hits in a glittering career, wrote songs for Disney productions of *Peter Pan* and *Alice in Wonderland*. Screenwriter ROBERT PIROSH, 79, who won an Oscar for his screenplay for *Battleground*, wrote the script for *I Married A Witch*, among several film fantasies. Composer JEFF ALEXANDER, 79, wrote music for numerous fine productions, including *Kismet*. Special effects art lost two innovators, JEAN IMAGE, 78, and THEODORE J. LYDECKER, 81. Art director LYLE WHEELER, 84, created the look for some great visual spectacles, among them *Journey to the Center of the Earth*. MICHAEL POWELL, 84, a director and producer, was active in hundreds of productions, none more exciting than *The Thief of Bagdad*. SIR JAMES CARREROS, 81, was head of Hammer Studios, which produced many low-budget horror films. AUBREY WISBERG, 78, a writer and producer died, as did Effects man BUD THACKERY, 81, and comic stalwart TERRY-THOMAS, 78, and actor ARTHUR KENNEDY, 75.

Many others connected to the publishing process and the written word died this year, including NED L. PINES, 84, publisher of *Thrilling Wonder Stories* and other pulp magazines, and then Popular Library paperbacks. HARRY ALTSHULER, 77, was primarily a newspaperman, but he was also an agent to numerous writers in the 1950s, helping a number of young, talented authors to get their work published in books. DONALD HUTTER, 57, was a distinguished, savvy trade editor who published some very successful fantasy in the 1970s when he was an editor at Holt, Rinehart, and Winston. Hutter had a keen eye for talent, and published some young authors who made him look very good: Stephen R. Donaldson and James Morrow are among his finds. WENDAYNE ACKERMAN, 77, translated books from her native German for publication in the U.S. She was also an active fan, and was married to, divorced from, and lived with Forrest J Ackerman. HELEN HOKE, 86, was a writer, and an anthologist of stories of fantasy and supernatural for children. She headed children's book divisions for several major publishers.

Other fantasy authors who died this year included LEO GIROUX, 55, author of *The Rishi*, DOROTHY JAMES ROBERTS, 96, the author of historical novels based on myth, including *The Enchanted Cup* (based on Tristan and Isolde), and *Fire in the Ice*, based on Icelandic myth. STELLA GIBBONS, 87, was the author of *Cold Comfort Farm*; JOSÉ DURAND, 64, was the Peruvian-born magic realist author of the classic *Ocasa de Sirenes*, among other works. GEORGE SELDEN THOMPSON, 60, wrote the children's classic Newbery Award winner, *The Cricket In Times Square*. And ELIZABETH PEARSE, 61, died. Not an author, she gave much to the field, though, organizing art shows at major SF and Fantasy conventions, and encouraging many talented young artists. She herself was quite talented, but chose to help others instead of fully devoting herself to her own career. She and all the others leave empty places in our lives than cannot be filled.

CHARLES DE LINT
Freewheeling

Canadian author Charles de Lint is a versatile and original writer, and one of the primary creators of the modern "urban fantasy" novel, mixing contemporary and streetwise characters with traditional folklore motifs, using myth and dream as a way to explore the modern world. Work in this vein includes *Moonheart* and its sequel *Ghostwood*, *Mulengro*, *Yarrow*, *Greenmantle* and *Jack the Giant-Killer: The Jack of Kinrowan*. His most recent novels are *The Little Country* and *The Dreaming Place*. He is also the author of several traditional fantasy novels and stories, and publishes horror fiction under the name Samuel Key.

"Freewheeling" is typical of de Lint's work and one of the very best stories of this year. Set in the mythical Canadian city of Newford, it is part of the author's story cycle about the punks, runaways and street people of that city and the magic that lurks in the city shadows, a magic that can be both wondrous and dark and, in de Lint's hands, always the catalyst for transformation. It is reprinted from *Pulphouse #6*.

De Lint is also a musician, specializing in Celtic folk music. He and his wife are members of the band Jump at the Sun, and make their home in Ottawa, Ontario.

—T.W.

Freewheeling

CHARLES DE LINT

There is apparently nothing that cannot happen.
—attributed to Mark Twain

There are three kinds of people: those who make things happen, those
who watch things happen, and those who wonder, "What happened?"
—message found inside a Christmas cracker

— 1 —

He stood on the rain-slick street, a pale fire burning behind his eyes. Nerve ends
tingling, he watched them go—a slow parade of riderless bicycles.

Ten-speeds and mountain bikes. Domesticated, urban. So inbred that all they
were was spoked wheels and emaciated frames. Mere skeletons of what their genetic
ancestors had been. They had never known freedom, never known joy; only the
weight of serious riders in slick-leather-seated shorts, pedaling determinedly with
their cycling shoes strapped to the pedals, heads encased in crash helmets, fingerless
gloves on the hands gripping the handles tightly.

He smiled and watched them go. Down the wet street, wheels throwing up
arcs of fine spray, metal frames glistening in the streetlights, reflector lights winking
red.

The rain had plastered his hair slick against his head, his clothes were sodden,
but he paid no attention to personal discomfort. He thought instead of that fat-
wheeled aboriginal one-speed that led them now. The maverick who'd come from
who knows where to pilot his domesticated brothers and sisters away.

For a night's freedom. Perhaps for always.

The last of them were rounding the corner now. He lifted his right hand to
wave good-bye. His left hand hung down by his leg, still holding the heavy-duty
wire cutters by one handle, the black rubber grip making a ribbed pattern on the
palm of his hand. By fences and on porches, up and down the street, locks had
been cut, chains lay discarded, bicycles ran free.

He heard a siren approaching. Lifting his head, he licked the rain drops from
his lips. Water got in his eyes, gathering in their corners. He squinted, enamored
by the kaleidoscoping spray of lights this caused to appear behind his eyelids.
There were omens in lights he knew. And in the night sky, with its scattershot

sweep of stars. So many lights. . . . There were secrets waiting to unfold there, mysteries that required a voice to be freed.

Like the bicycles were freed by their maverick brother.

He could be that voice, if he only knew what to sing.

He was still watching the sky for signs when the police finally arrived.

"Let me go, boys, let me go . . ."

The Pogues album *If I Should Fall From Grace With God* was on the turntable. The title cut leaked from the sound system's speakers, one of which sat on a crate crowded with half-used paint tubes and tins of turpentine, the other perched on the windowsill, commanding a view of rainswept Yoors Street one floor below. The song was jauntier than one might expect from its subject matter while Shane MacGowan's voice was as rough as ever, chewing the words and spitting them out, rather than singing them.

It was an angry voice, Jilly decided as she hummed softly along with the chorus. Even when it sang a tender song. But what could you expect from a group that had originally named itself Pogue Mahone—Irish Gaelic for "Kiss my ass"?

Angry and brash and vulgar. The band was all of that. But they were honest, too—painfully so, at times—and that was what brought Jilly back to their music, time and again. Because sometimes things just had to be said.

"I don't get this stuff," Sue remarked.

She'd been frowning over the lyrics that were printed on the album's inner sleeve. Leaning her head against the patched backrest of one of Jilly's two old sofas, she set the sleeve aside.

"I mean, music's supposed to make you feel good, isn't it?" she went on.

Jilly shook her head. "It's supposed to make you feel *something*—happy, sad, angry, whatever—just so long as it doesn't leave you brain-dead the way most Top 40 does. For me, music needs meaning to be worth my time—preferably something more than 'I want your body, babe,' if you know what I mean."

"You're beginning to develop a snooty attitude, Jilly."

"*Me?* To laugh, dahling."

Susan Ashworth was Jilly's uptown friend. As a pair, the two women made a perfect study in contrasts.

Sue's blonde hair was straight, hanging to just below her shoulders, where Jilly's was a riot of brown curls, made manageable tonight only by a clip that drew it all up to the top of her head before letting it fall free in the shape of something that resembled nothing so much as a disenchanted Mohawk. They were both in their twenties, slender and blue-eyed—the latter expected in a blonde; the electric blue of Jilly's eyes gave her, with her darker skin, a look of continual startlement. Where Sue wore just the right amount of makeup, Jilly could usually be counted on having a smudge of charcoal somewhere on her face and dried oil paint under her nails.

Sue worked for the city as an architect; she lived uptown and her parents were from the Beaches where it seemed you needed a permit just to be out on the sidewalks after eight in the evening—or at least that was the impression that the police patrols left when they stopped strangers to check their ID. She always had that upscale look of one who was just about to step out to a restaurant for cocktails and dinner.

Jilly's first love was art of a freer style than designing municipal necessities, but she usually paid her rent by waitressing and other odd jobs. She tended to wear baggy clothes—like the over-sized white T-shirt and blue poplin lace-front pants she had on tonight—and always had a sketchbook close at hand.

Tonight it was on her lap as she sat propped up on her Murphy bed, toes in their ballet slippers tapping against one another in time to the music. The Pogues were playing an instrumental now—"Metropolis"—which sounded like a cross between a Celtic fiddle tune and the old *Dragnet* theme.

"They're really not for me," Sue went on. "I mean if the guy could sing, maybe, but—"

"It's the feeling that he puts into his voice that's important," Jilly said. "But this is an instrumental. He's not even—"

"Supposed to be singing. I know. Only—"

"If you'd just—"

The jangling of the phone sliced through their discussion. Because she was closer—and knew that Jilly would claim some old war wound or any excuse not to get up, now that she was lying down—Sue answered it. She listened for a long moment, an odd expression on her face, then slowly cradled the receiver.

"Wrong number?"

Sue shook her head. "No. It was someone named . . . uh, Zinc? He said that he's been captured by two Elvis Presleys disguised as police officers and would you please come and explain to them that he wasn't stealing bikes, he was just setting them free. Then he just hung up."

"Oh, shit!" Jilly stuffed her sketchbook into her shoulderbag and got up.

"This makes sense to you?"

"He's one of the street kids."

Sue rolled her eyes, but she got up as well. "Want me to bring my checkbook?"

"What for?"

"Bail. It's what you have to put up to spring somebody from jail. Don't you *ever* watch TV?"

Jilly shook her head. "What? And let the aliens monitor my brainwaves?"

"What scares me," Sue muttered as they left the loft and started down the stairs, "is that sometimes I don't think you're kidding."

"Maybe I'm not," Jilly said.

Sue shook her head. "I'm going to pretend I didn't hear that."

Jilly knew people from all over the city, in all walks of life. Socialites and bag ladies. Street kids and university profs. Nobody was too poor, or conversely, too rich for her to strike up a conversation with, no matter where they happened to meet, or under what circumstances. Detective Lou Fucceri, of the Crowsea Precinct's General Investigations squad, she met when he was still a patrolman, walking the Stanton Street Combat Zone beat. Jilly was there, taking reference photos for a painting she was planning. When she had asked Lou to pose for a couple of shots, he tried to run her in on a soliciting charge.

"Is it true?" Sue wanted to know as soon as the desk sergeant showed them into Lou's office. "The way you guys met?"

"You mean UFO-spotting in Butler U Park?" he replied.

Sue sighed. "I should've known. I must be the only person who's maintained her sanity after meeting Jilly."

She sat down on one of the two wooden chairs that faced Lou's desk in the small cubicle that passed for his office. There was room for a bookcase behind him, crowded with law books and file folders, and a brass coat rack from which hung a lightweight sports jacket. Lou sat at the desk, white shirt sleeves rolled halfway up to his elbows, top collar undone, black tie hanging loose.

His Italian heritage was very much present in the Mediterranean cast to his complexion, his dark brooding eyes and darker hair. As Jilly sat down in the chair Sue had left for her, he shook a cigarette free from a crumpled pack that he dug out from under the litter of files on his desk. He offered them around, tossing the pack back down on the desk and lighting his own when there were no takers.

Jilly pulled her chair closer to the desk. "What did he do, Lou? Sue took the call, but I don't know if she got the message right."

"I can *take* a message," Sue began, but Jilly waved a hand in her direction. She wasn't in the mood for banter just now.

Lou blew a stream of blue-gray smoke towards the ceiling. "We've been having a lot of trouble with a bicycle theft ring operating in the city," he said. "They've hit the Beaches, which was bad enough, though with all the Mercedes and BMWs out there, I doubt they're going to miss their bikes a lot. But rich people like to complain, and now the gang's moved its operations to Crowsea."

Jilly nodded. "Where for a lot of people, a bicycle's the only way they *can* get around."

"You got it."

"So what does that have to do with Zinc?"

"The patrol car that picked him up found him standing in the middle of the street with a pair of heavy-duty wire cutters in his hand. The street'd been cleaned right out, Jilly. There wasn't a bike left on the block—just the cut locks and chains left behind."

"So where are the bikes?"

Lou shrugged. "Who knows. Probably in a Foxville chopshop having their serial numbers changed. Jilly, you've got to get Zinc to tell us who he was working with. Christ, they took off, leaving him to hold the bag. He doesn't owe them a thing now."

Jilly shook her head slowly. "This doesn't make any sense. Zinc's not the criminal kind."

"I'll tell you what doesn't make any sense," Lou said. "The kid himself. He's heading straight for the loony bin with all his talk about Elvis clones and Venusian thought machines and feral-fuc—" He glanced at Sue and covered up the profanity with a cough. "Feral bicycles leading the domesticated ones away."

"He said that?"

Lou nodded. "That's why he was clipping the locks—to set the bikes free so that they could follow their, and I quote, 'spiritual leader, home to the place of mystery.' "

"That's a new one," Jilly said.

"You're having me on—right?" Lou said. "That's all you can say? It's a new one? The Elvis clones are old hat now? Christ on a comet. Would you give me a break? Just get the kid to roll over and I'll make sure things go easy for him."

"Christ on a comet?" Sue repeated softly.

"C'mon, Lou," Jilly said. "How can I make Zinc tell you something he doesn't know? Maybe he found those wire cutters on the street—just before the patrol car came. For all we know he could—"

"He *said* he cut the locks."

The air went out of Jilly. "Right," she said. She slouched in her chair. "I forgot you'd said that."

"Maybe the bikes really did just go off on their own," Sue said.

Lou gave her a weary look, but Jilly sat up straighter. "I wonder," she began.

"Oh, for God's sake," Sue said. "I was only joking."

"I know you were," Jilly said. "But I've seen enough odd things in this world that I won't say anything's impossible anymore."

"The police department doesn't see things quite the same way," Lou told Jilly. The dryness of his tone wasn't lost on her.

"I know."

"I want these bike thieves, Jilly."

"Are you arresting Zinc?"

Lou shook his head. "I've got nothing to hold him on except for circumstantial evidence."

"I thought you said he admitted to cutting the locks," Sue said.

Jilly shot her a quick fierce look that plainly said, Don't make waves when he's giving us what we came for.

Lou nodded. "Yeah. He admitted to that. He also admitted to knowing a hobo who was really a spy from Pluto. Asked why the patrolmen had traded in their white Vegas suits for uniforms and wanted to hear them sing 'Heartbreak Hotel.' For next of kin he put down Bigfoot."

"*Gigantopithecus blacki*," Jilly said.

Lou looked at her. "What?"

"Some guy at Washington State University's given Bigfoot a Latin name now. *Giganto*—"

Lou cut her off. "That's what I thought you said." He turned back to Sue. "So you see, his admitting to cutting the locks isn't really going to amount to much. Not when a lawyer with half a brain can get him off without even having to work up a sweat."

"Does that mean he's free to go then?" Jilly asked.

Lou nodded. "Yeah. He can go. But keep him out of trouble, Jilly. He's in here again, and I'm sending him straight to the Zeb for psychiatric testing. And try to convince him to come clean on this—okay? It's not just for me, it's for him too. We break this case and find out he's involved, nobody's going to go easy on him. We don't give out rainchecks."

"Not even for dinner?" Jilly asked brightly, happy now that she knew Zinc was getting out.

"What do you mean?"

Jilly grabbed a pencil and paper from his desk and scrawled "Jilly Coppercorn owes Hotshot Lou one dinner, restaurant of her choice," and passed it over to him.

"I think they call this a bribe," he said.

"I call it keeping in touch with your friends," Jilly replied and gave him a big grin.

Lou glanced at Sue and rolled his eyes.

"Don't look at me like that," she said. "I'm the sane one here."

"You wish," Jilly told her.

Lou heaved himself to his feet with exaggerated weariness. "C'mon, let's get your friend out of here before he decides to sue us because we don't have our coffee flown in from the Twilight Zone," he said as he led the way down to the holding cells.

Zinc had the look of a street kid about two days away from a good meal. His jeans, T-shirt, and cotton jacket were ragged, but clean; his hair had the look of a badly mown lawn, with tufts standing up here and there like exclamation points. The pupils of his dark brown eyes seemed too large for someone who never did drugs. He was seventeen, but acted half his age.

The only home he had was a squat in Upper Foxville that he shared with a couple of performance artists, so that was where Jilly and Sue took him in Sue's Mazda. The living space he shared with the artists was on the upper story of a deserted tenement where someone had put together a makeshift loft by the simple method of removing all the walls, leaving a large empty area cluttered only by support pillars and the squatters' belongings.

Lucia and Ursula were there when they arrived, practicing one of their pieces to the accompaniment of a ghetto blaster pumping out a mixture of electronic music and the sound of breaking glass at a barely audible volume. Lucia was wrapped in plastic and lying on the floor, her black hair spread out in an arc around her head. Every few moments one of her limbs would twitch, the plastic wrap stretching tight against her skin with the movement. Ursula crouched beside the blaster, chanting a poem that consisted only of the line, "There are no patterns." She'd shaved her head since the last time Jilly had seen her.

"What am I doing here?" Sue asked softly. She made no effort to keep the look of astonishment from her features.

"Seeing how the other half lives," Jilly said as she led the way across the loft to where Zinc's junkyard of belongings took up a good third of the available space.

"But just look at this stuff," Sue said. "And how did he get that in here?"

She pointed to a Volkswagen bug that was sitting up on blocks, missing only its wheels and front hood. Scattered all around it was a hodge-podge of metal scraps, old furniture, boxes filled with wiring and God only knew what.

"Piece by piece," Jilly told her.

"And then he assembled it here?"

Jilly nodded.

"Okay. I'll bite. Why?"

"Why don't you ask him?"

Jilly grinned as Sue quickly shook her head. The entire trip from the precinct station, Zinc had carefully explained his theory of the world to her, how the planet Earth was actually an asylum for insane aliens, and that was why nothing made sense.

Zinc followed the pair of them across the room, stopping only long enough to greet his squat-mates. "Hi, Luce. Hi, Urse."

Lucia never looked at him.

"There are no patterns," Ursula said.

Zinc nodded thoughtfully.

"Maybe there's a pattern in that," Sue offered.

"Don't start," Jilly said. She turned to Zinc. "Are you going to be all right?"

"You should've seen them go, Jill," Zinc said. "All shiny and quiet, just whizzing down the street, heading for the hills."

"I'm sure it was really something, but you've got to promise me to stay off the streets for awhile. Will you do that, Zinc? At least until they catch this gang of bike thieves?"

"But there weren't any thieves. It's like I told Elvis Two, they left on their own."

Sue gave him an odd look. "Elvis too?"

"Don't ask," Jilly said. She touched Zinc's arm. "Just stay in for awhile—okay? Let the bikes take off on their own."

"But I like to watch them go."

"Do it as a favor to me, would you?"

"I'll try."

Jilly gave him a quick smile. "Thanks. Is there anything you need? Do you need money for some food?"

Zinc shook his head. Jilly gave him a quick kiss on the cheek and tousled the exclamation point hair tufts sticking up from his head.

"I'll drop by to see you tomorrow, then—okay?" At his nod, Jilly started back across the room. "C'mon, Sue," she said when her companion paused beside the tape machine where Ursula was still chanting.

"So what about this stock market stuff?" she asked the poet.

"There are no patterns," Ursula said.

"That's what I thought," Sue said, but then Jilly was tugging her arm.

"Couldn't resist, could you?" Jilly said.

Sue just grinned.

"Why do you humor him?" Sue asked when she pulled up in front of Jilly's loft.

"What makes you think I am?"

"I'm being serious, Jilly."

"So am I. He believes in what he's talking about. That's good enough for me."

"But all this stuff he goes on about . . . Elvis clones and insane aliens—"

"Don't forget animated bicycles."

Sue gave Jilly a pained look. "I'm not. That's just what I mean—it's all so crazy."

"What if it's not?"

Sue shook her head. "I can't buy it."

"It's not hurting anybody." Jilly leaned over and gave Sue a quick kiss on the cheek. "Gotta run. Thanks for everything."

"Maybe it's hurting him," Sue said as Jilly opened the door to get out. "Maybe it's closing the door on any chance he has of living a normal life. You know—opportunity comes knocking, but there's nobody home? He's not just eccentric, Jilly. He's crazy."

Jilly sighed. "His mother was a hooker, Sue. The reason he's a little flaky is her pimp threw him down two flights of stairs when he was six years old—not because Zinc did anything, or because his mother didn't trick enough johns that night, but just because the creep felt like doing it. That's what normal was for Zinc. He's happy now—a lot happier than when Social Services tried to put him in a foster home where they only wanted him for the support check they got once a month for taking him in. And a lot happier than he'd be in the Zeb, all doped up or sitting around in a padded cell whenever he tried to tell people about the things he sees.

"He's got his own life now. It's not much—not by your standards, maybe not even by mine, but it's his and I don't want anybody to take it away from him."

"But—"

"I know you mean well," Jilly said, "but things don't always work out the way we'd like them to. Nobody's got time for a kid like Zinc in Social Services. There he's just a statistic that they shuffle around with all the rest of their files and red tape. Out here on the street, we've got a system that works. We take care of our own. It's that simple. Doesn't matter if it's the Cat Lady, sleeping in an alleyway with a half dozen mangy toms, or Rude Ruthie, haranguing the commuters on the subway, we take care of each other."

"Utopia," Sue said.

A corner of Jilly's mouth twitched with the shadow of a humorless smile. "Yeah. I know. We've got a high asshole quotient, but what can you do? You try to get by—that's all. You just try to get by."

"I wish I could understand it better," Sue said.

"Don't worry about it. You're good people, but this just isn't your world. You can visit, but you wouldn't want to live in it, Sue."

"I guess."

Jilly started to add something more, but then just smiled encouragingly and got out of the car.

"See you Friday?" she asked, leaning in the door.

Sue nodded.

Jilly stood on the pavement and watched the Mazda until it turned the corner and its rear lights were lost from view, then she went upstairs to her apartment. The big room seemed too quiet and she felt too wound up to sleep, so she put a cassette in the tape player—Lynn Harrell playing a Schumann concerto—and started to prepare a new canvas to work on in the morning when the light would be better.

— 2 —

It was raining again, a soft drizzle that put a glistening sheen on the streets and lampposts, on porch handrails and street signs. Zinc stood in the shadows that had gathered in the mouth of an alleyway, his new pair of wire cutters a comfortable weight in his hand. His eyes sparked with reflected lights. His hair was damp against his scalp. He licked his lips, tasting mountain heights and distant forests within the drizzle's slightly metallic tang.

Jilly knew a lot about things that were, he thought, and things that might be, and she always meant well, but there was one thing she just couldn't get right. You didn't make art by capturing an image on paper, or canvas, or in stone. You didn't make it by writing down stories and poems. Music and dance came closest to what real art was—but only so long as you didn't try to record or film it. Musical notation was only so much dead ink on paper. Choreography was planning, not art.

You could only make art by setting it free. Anything else was just a memory, no matter how you stored it. On film or paper, sculpted or recorded.

Everything that existed, existed in a captured state. Animate or inanimate, everything wanted to be free.

That's what the lights said; that was their secret. Wild lights in the night skies, and domesticated lights, right here on the street, they all told the same tale. It was so plain to see when you knew *how* to look. Didn't neon and streetlights yearn to be starlight?

To be free.

He bent down and picked up a stone, smiling at the satisfying crack it made when it broke the glass protection of the streetlight, his grin widening as the light inside flickered, then died.

It was part of the secret now, part of the voices that spoke in the night sky.

Free.

Still smiling, he set out across the street to where a bicycle was chained to the railing of a porch.

"Let me tell you about art," he said to it as he mounted the stairs.

Psycho Puppies were playing at the YoMan on Gracie Street near the corner of Landis Avenue that Friday night. They weren't anywhere near as punkish as their name implied. If they had been, Jilly would never have been able to get Sue out to see them.

"I don't care if they damage themselves," she'd told Jilly the one and only time she'd gone out to one of the punk clubs further west on Gracie, "but I refuse to pay good money just to have someone spit at me and do their best to rupture my eardrums."

The Puppies were positively tame compared to how that punk band had been. Their music was loud, but melodic, and while there was an undercurrent of social conscience to their lyrics, you could dance to them as well. Jilly couldn't help but smile to see Sue stepping it up to a chorus of, "You can take my job, but you can't take me, ain't nobody gonna steal my dignity."

The crowd was an even mix of slumming uptowners, Crowsea artistes and the neighborhood kids from surrounding Foxville. Jilly and Sue danced with each other, not from lack of offers, but because they didn't want to feel obligated to any guy that night. Too many men felt that one dance entitled them to ownership—for the night, at least, if not forever—and neither of them felt like going through the ritual repartee that the whole business required.

Sue was on the right side of a bad relationship at the moment, while Jilly was simply eschewing relationships on general principle these days. Relationships required changes, and she wasn't ready for changes in her life just now. And besides, all the men she'd ever cared for were already taken and she didn't think it likely that she'd run into her own particular Prince Charming in a Foxville night club.

"I like this band," Sue confided to her when they took a break to finish the beers they'd ordered at the beginning of the set.

Jilly nodded, but she didn't have anything to say. A glance across the room caught a glimpse of a head with hair enough like Zinc's badly mown lawn scalp to remind her that he hadn't been home when she'd dropped by his place on the way to the club tonight.

Don't be out setting bicycles free, Zinc, she thought.

"Hey, Tomás. Check this out."

There were two of them, one Anglo, one Hispanic, neither of them much more than a year or so older than Zinc. They both wore leather jackets and jeans, dark hair greased back in ducktails. The drizzle put a sheen on their jackets and hair. The Hispanic moved closer to see what his companion was pointing out.

Zinc had melted into the shadows at their approach. The streetlights that he had yet to free whispered *careful, careful*, as they wrapped him in darkness, their electric light illuminating the pair on the street.

"Well, shit," the Hispanic said. "Somebody's doing our work for us."

As he picked up the lock that Zinc had just snipped, the chain holding the bike to the railing fell to the pavement with a clatter. Both teenagers froze, one checking out one end of the street, his companion the other.

"Scool," the Anglo said. "Nobody here but you, me, and your cooties."

"Chew on a big one."

"I don't do myself, *puto*."

"That's 'cos it's too small to find."

The pair of them laughed—a quick nervous sound that belied their bravado —then the Anglo wheeled the bike away from the railing.

"Hey, Bobby-O," the Hispanic said. "Got another one over here."

"Well, what're you waiting for, man? Wheel her down to the van."

They were setting bicycles free, Zinc realized—just like he was. He'd gotten almost all the way down the block, painstakingly snipping the shackle of each lock, before the pair had arrived.

Careful, careful, the streetlights were still whispering, but Zinc was already moving out of the shadows.

"Hi, guys," he said.

The teenagers froze, then the Anglo's gaze took in the wire cutters in Zinc's hand.

"Well, well," he said. "What've we got here? What're you doing on the night side of the street, kid?"

Before Zinc could reply, the sound of a siren cut the air. A lone siren, approaching fast.

The Chinese waitress looked great in her leather miniskirt and fishnet stockings. She wore a blood-red camisole tucked into the waist of the skirt which made her pale skin seem ever paler. Her hair was the black of polished jet, pulled up in a loose bun that spilled stray strands across her neck and shoulders. Blue-black eye shadow made her dark eyes darker. Her lips were the same color red as her camisole.

"How come she looks so good," Sue wanted to know, "when I'd just look like a tart if I dressed like that?"

"She's inscrutable," Jilly replied. "You're just obvious."

"How sweet of you to point that out," Sue said with a grin. She stood up from their table. "C'mon. Let's dance."

Jilly shook her head. "You go ahead. I'll sit this one out."

"Uh-uh. I'm not going out there alone."

"There's LaDonna," Jilly said, pointing out a girl they both knew. "Dance with her."

"Are you feeling all right, Jilly?"

"I'm fine—just a little pooped. Give me a chance to catch my breath."

But she wasn't all right, she thought as Sue crossed over to where LaDonna da Costa and her brother Pipo were sitting. Not when she had Zinc to worry about. If he was out there, cutting off the locks of more bicycles. . . .

You're not his mother, she told herself. Except—

Out here in the streets we take care of our own.

That's what she'd told Sue. And maybe it wasn't true for a lot of people who hit the skids—the winos and the losers and the bag people who were just too screwed up to take care of themselves, little say look after anyone else—but it was true for her.

Someone like Zinc—he was an in betweener. Most days he could take care of himself just fine, but there was a fey streak in him so that sometimes he carried a touch of the magic that ran wild in the streets, the magic that was loose late at night when the straights were in bed and the city belonged to the night people. That magic took up lodgings in people like Zinc. For a week. A day. An hour. Didn't matter if it was real or not, if it couldn't be measured or catalogued, it was real to them. It existed all the same.

Did that make it true?

Jilly shook her head. It wasn't her kind of question and it didn't matter anyway. Real or not, it could still be driving Zinc into breaking corporeal laws—the kind that'd have Lou breathing down his neck, real fast. The kind that'd put him in jail with a whole different kind of loser.

The kid wouldn't last out a week inside.

Jilly got up from the table and headed across the dance floor to where Sue and LaDonna were jitterbugging to a tune that sounded as though Buddy Holly could have penned the melody, if not the words.

"Fuck this, man!" the Anglo said.

He threw down the bike and took off at a run, his companion right on his heels, scattering puddles with the impact of their boots. Zinc watched them go. There was a buzzing in the back of his head. The streetlights were telling him to run too, but he saw the bike lying there on the pavement like a wounded animal, one wheel spinning forlornly, and he couldn't just take off.

Bikes were like turtles. Turn 'em on their backs—or a bike on its side—and they couldn't get up on their own again.

He tossed down the wire cutters and ran to the bike. Just as he was leaning it up against the railing from which the Anglo had taken it, a police cruiser came around the corner, skidding on the wet pavement, cherry light gyrating—screaming *Run, run!* in its urgent high-pitched voice—headlights pinning Zinc where he stood.

Almost before the cruiser came to a halt, the passenger door popped open and a uniformed officer stepped out. He drew his gun. Using the cruiser as a shield, he aimed across its roof at where Zinc was standing.

"Hold it right there, kid!" he shouted. "Don't even blink."

Zinc was privy to secrets. He could hear voices in lights. He knew that there was more to be seen in the world if you watched it from the corner of your eye, than head on. It was a simple truth that every policeman he ever saw looked just like Elvis. But he hadn't survived all his years on the streets without protection. He had a lucky charm. A little tin monkey pendant that had originally lived in a box of Crackerjacks—back when Crackerjacks had real prizes in them. Lucia had given it to him. He'd forgotten to bring it out with him the other night when the Elvises had taken him in. But he wasn't stupid. He'd remembered it tonight.

He reached into his pocket to get it out and wake its magic.

"You're just being silly," Sue said as they collected their jackets from their chairs.

"So humor me," Jilly asked.

"I'm coming, aren't I?"

Jilly nodded. She could hear the voice of Zinc's roommate Ursula in the back of her head—

There are no patterns.

—but she could feel one right now, growing tight as a drawn bowstring, humming with its urgency to be loosed.

"C'mon," she said, almost running from the club.

* * *

Police officer Mario Hidalgo was still a rookie—tonight was only the beginning of his third month of active duty—and while he'd drawn his sidearm before, he had yet to fire it in the line of duty. He had the makings of a good cop. He was steady, he was conscientious. The street hadn't had a chance to harden him yet, though it had already thrown him more than a couple of serious uglies in his first eight weeks of active duty.

But steady though he'd proved himself to be so far, when he saw the kid reaching into the pocket of his baggy jacket, Hidalgo had a single moment of unreasoning panic.

The kid's got a gun, that panic told him. The kid's going for a weapon.

One moment was all it took.

His finger was already tightening on the trigger of his regulation .38 as the kid's hand came out of his pocket. Hidalgo wanted to stop the pressure he was putting on the gun's trigger, but it was like there was a broken circuit between his brain and his hand.

The gun went off with a deafening roar.

Got it, Zinc thought as his fingers closed on the little tin monkey charm. Got my luck.

He started to take it out of his pocket, but then something hit him straight in the chest. It lifted him off his feet and threw him against the wall behind him with enough force to knock all the wind out of his lungs. There was a raw pain firing every one of his nerve ends. His hands opened and closed spastically, the charm falling out of his grip to hit the ground moments before his body slid down the wall to join it on the wet pavement.

Good-bye, good-bye, sweet friend, the streetlights cried.

He could sense the spin of the stars as they wheeled high above the city streets, their voices joining the electric voices of the streetlights.

My turn to go free, he thought as a white tunnel opened in his mind. He could feel it draw him in, and then he was falling, falling, falling. . . .

"Good-bye . . ." he said, thought he said, but no words came forth from between his lips.

Just a trickle of blood that mingled with the rain that now began to fall in earnest, as though it too was saying its own farewell.

All Jilly had to see was the red spinning cherries of the police cruisers to know where the pattern she'd felt in the club was taking her. There were a lot of cars here—cruisers and unmarked vehicles, an ambulance—all on official business, their presence coinciding with her business. She didn't see Lou approach until he laid his hand on her shoulder.

"You don't want to see," he told her.

Jilly never even looked at him. One moment he was holding her shoulder, the next she'd shrugged herself free of his grip and just kept on walking.

"Is it . . . is it Zinc?" Sue asked the detective.

Jilly didn't have to ask. She knew. Without being told. Without having to see the body.

An officer stepped in front of her to stop her, but Lou waved him aside. In her peripheral vision she saw another officer sitting inside a cruiser, weeping, but it didn't really register.

"I thought he had a gun," the policeman was saying as she went by. "Oh, Jesus. I thought the kid was going for a gun. . . ."

And then she was standing over Zinc's body, looking down at his slender frame, limbs flung awkwardly like those of a rag doll that had been tossed into a corner and forgotten. She knelt down at Zinc's side. Something glinted on the wet pavement. A small tin monkey charm. She picked it up, closed it tightly in her fist.

"C'mon, Jilly," Lou said as he came up behind her. He helped her to her feet.

It didn't seem possible that anyone as vibrant—as *alive*—as Zinc had been could have any relation whatsoever with that empty shell of a body that lay there on the pavement.

As Lou led her away from the body, Jilly's tears finally came, welling up from her eyes to salt the rain on her cheek.

"He . . . he wasn't . . . stealing bikes, Lou. . . ." she said.

"It doesn't look good," Lou said.

Often when she'd been with Zinc, Jilly had had a sense of that magic that touched him. A feeling that even if she couldn't see the marvels he told her about, they still existed just beyond the reach of her sight.

That feeling should be gone now, she thought.

"He was just . . . setting them free," she said.

The magic should have died, when he died. But she felt, if she just looked hard enough, that she'd see him, riding a maverick bike at the head of a pack of riderless bicycles—metal frames glistening, reflector lights glinting red, wheels throwing up arcs of fine spray, as they went off down the wet street.

Around the corner and out of sight.

"Nice friends the kid had," a plainclothes detective who was standing near them said to the uniformed officer beside him. "Took off with just about every bike on the street and left him holding the bag."

Jilly didn't think so. Not this time.

This time they'd gone free.

NINA KIRIKI HOFFMAN
Coming Home

Nina Kiriki Hoffman lives in Eugene, Oregon. Her excellent stories have appeared all over the horror field in 1990. In addition to the two stories chosen for this anthology, four more made the recommended list. She's someone to keep an eye on.

This story, from *Author's Choice Monthly* Issue 14, is about ghosts. One could say it's the dark side of the hit movie *Home Alone*.

—E.D.

Coming Home

NINA KIRIKI HOFFMAN

I love this house. Except that one closet. I don't think I'll ever, ever leave this house, no matter what happens or who lives here, even though I don't like the closet and it's so close to my room I hate to leave my room because then I have to go past. it. I know what happened in that closet, but I don't think about it, or where my brother Matt is. He's been dead longer than I have. I'm still not sure if he's here in the house or not.

My room is the big room at the sunrise side of the upstairs. There's a great big picture window I can see the mountains from, and I love looking at them when the moon slips up behind them, because that's when I'm strongest, in the cool moonlight, not like the mornings when the sun flames across the sky. The sun makes me feel pale. I think that's funny because it used to turn me brown every summer.

This house is like a white wedding cake with a piece cut out in front. The upstairs is smaller and sits on top of the downstairs, and a giant came and cut a piece out of the middle of the downstairs. I think it might have been the piece with the biggest rose. The house is frosted white as a wedding, and upstairs, doors lead out onto the roof so I can pretend to be the bride on top of the cake. Mama called this house adobe. I think it's like living inside a cake with windows.

My best friend Robin, ten, a year older than me, used to live next door in the flat, ordinary house I can see from one of my windows. She liked to come visit, especially after I told her about the cake. She wanted to be a scientist. She said, "Livvie, if I had your brain, I'd put it in a glass bowl and ask it questions all the time."

She didn't say that after Matt was in the closet. Nobody said anything nice to me for a long time after that. We moved away and I never saw Robin again.

*　*　*

After twenty-five years, I was going back to the house I couldn't ever remember calling home, though I lived there with four brothers and my parents the first nine years I was alive. When my husband Scott turned the van onto the private lane that led to the house, I felt as though a lump of ice formed in my chest, as though I were all alone, even with Scott in the driver's seat beside me and the eight kids yelling all around us. Sarah was in my lap and she was as squirmy as a puppy. Dion kept tugging on my braid and saying, "Are we there yet, Mommy? Can I have my own room?" Sterling said he was the oldest and deserved a room of his own if anybody did. Carol said who said Sterling was the oldest? He didn't know his real birthday, did he? Maybe she was older. They had this argument every year when it got to close to June 20th, when we celebrated their birthdays together. The adoption agency had told us they had no birth certificate for Sterling.

Nick yelled for everybody to shut up. He had a deep little voice that reminded me of a frog's croak. He said this was a special moment and Maria wanted it to be nice so shut up. He always spoke up for Maria; she was our newest, only with us seven months, and still shy and quiet. Sometimes I wondered if she really said any of the things Nick credited her with, but it didn't matter; she clung to him and he cared for her, and that was enough. Later, when she settled in, I would ask her how she felt about things.

Prudence said, "Is this it, Mommy? Is this where you lived when you were little?"

I said, "It must be." I felt cold, even though sunlight splashed down on the lush greenery of gardens on both sides of the car. "It must be, but I don't really remember. Except—" I saw a patch of pampas grass in somebody's front yard, and a drive bordered with fuchsia bushes. I felt a shiver ripple up my back. None of this was new. Yet, when I reached for memories, I found only gray fog. My life began at my grandmother's house in San Francisco, almost ten years after I was born.

I thought that was what it was like for our kids. They had lives behind them, mostly in institutions, where they waited for someone to want them; then we adopted them, and their lives really started. I remembered the first time I handed Sterling, our first child, a rolling pin and invited him to flatten out some gingerbread dough so we could cut cookies. He was six, and very solemn. I didn't know how to talk to him; children seemed like another species to me, a fascinating species I wanted to study, but I didn't know how to approach them. When I handed Sterling the rolling pin, his eyes brightened. When I gave him the raisins for the gingerbread boys' eyes, I remembered my grandmother reaching out to drop precious raisins in my small hand—almost my first-ever memory.

That first contact with Sterling had warmed me, kindling my desire to learn about and love children the way Scott did. Scott spent a lot of his work time doing custody determinations; he was always concerned that the children he worked with stay with the best parent for them.

"What's that?" Artie asked, leaning forward to point past my shoulder, nearly hitting Sarah on the head as he did it.

"A stone pine tree," I said. And how did I know?

It was like a bonsai left by a giant, an enormous twisted tree, standing in the center of the driveway in an elevated circle of ground ringed by stones. There was the big turnaround in front of the houses at the end of the drive. I stared at the white one, a piece of the old Southwest transplanted to this Southern California town, blocky white adobe with vigas poking out here and there, its unlikeliest features its huge windows—in real adobe buildings, the windows were small, the thick walls conserving heat in the winter and cool in the summer. I had studied the Indian cultures of the Southwest in my anthropology courses. The vanished cultures interested me the most.

Scott pulled the van to a stop in front of the white adobe house. The lawn that separated it from the suburban house on the left looked weedy and overgrown. "Who wants to mow the lawn?" Scott asked in his best cheery voice.

"I do!" yelled Nick. Dion chimed in. Sterling laughed. He knows a trick when he hears one.

"Okay, Nick, you and Dion can help me, just as soon as the moving van gets here."

"Honey. Let's get the furniture set up first, okay?" I said. I had never suspected Scott had a passion for yard work. In the rambling house on the edge of town we'd been living in until this house came open, he left the yard to me, and concentrated on keeping the furniture in good repair and the plumbing healthy. I planted the tulip bulbs and coaxed Prudence and Carol into helping me weed. I had wanted to stay there, but Scott kept griping. "Via, you *own* that enormous house, for heaven's sake. How easy is it going to be to find renters? Why don't we just move in? We're one of the few families I know of who could actually use all that space."

I couldn't explain my reluctance. There was something about that house. . . . Ever since my father's will had been read three years earlier and he left the house to me, I had felt something in some tucked-away corner of my mind. After hearing the clause that left me title to the house, I had looked at my three brothers, strangers to me, angry strangers, who stared back.

Douglas, the oldest, had smiled a terrible smile at me.

Karl's eyes had gone wide. Then he turned his face away from me.

Mark said, "No. He can't mean that." He slumped down, a slender insubstantial thirty-year-old who had never grown up.

"I don't need it," I said. "I'll deed it over to you."

"No, Olivia," said Douglas. "That house belongs to you. Keep it."

Karl shook his head, but he didn't say anything.

Since the house came to me I had let Scott take care of all the maintenance and yard work. I let him deal with the renters. I didn't even want to see the house, and I couldn't tell him why. He accepted it, the same way he accepted my blank-slate childhood: with a kiss, and a "That's all right, Via. I don't have to understand."

"Come on, troops," Scott said now, hopping down out of the van and going around to sling open the sliding door.

"Mommy, I want out," said Sarah, reaching for the door handle. I let her out, then descended to the gravelly drive myself and stood staring at the blank white façade of the house. The children trooped up the brick walkway toward the front courtyard, a cobblestone patio between the wings of the lower story.

"Open it, open it," Carol cried, tugging at the front door.

Scott fished keys out of his pocket and opened the front door. The children pushed past him into the house. My throat closed. I felt dizzy. "Scott, don't let them out of your sight."

"What?" He glanced after them. They went whooping through the house, scattering. "Via. Calm down. I've been through this place with the termite people and there isn't an unsound board in the whole house. It's great."

"Scott," I said, and gripped his arm. "Scott."

He put his arm around me. "What is it, honey?"

"There's a—" I took two staggering steps and I was over the threshold and into the house, Scott supporting me. "Doesn't it smell bad in here?"

"Lysol, maybe. I had professional cleaners in. The last tenants left a mess, but they left a big cleaning deposit too."

"Not that," I said. I eased out of his embrace and strode down the front hallway, toward the western wing.

"The master bedroom's through here," Scott said, pointing down a little hall.

I turned away from him and mounted the stairs. "Nick!" I called. I heard his voice, arguing with Sterling's, above us. "Nick? Where's Artie?"

Carol came to the top of the stairs. "Mom! Guess what? There's a closet up here big enough to be a bedroom!"

I ran up the stairs. "Get out of there!"

I don't like that closet. It's the one place in the house I don't like. I haven't for a long time. Even before it turned into Matt's closet. Before Matt was in the closet, I was in the closet. He locked me in all the time. He was only one year older than me but he was lots bigger. When he was really feeling mean he'd hide the key so the others couldn't let me out, except Doug would hear me screaming in the closet and go get Mama and she had a key that worked too. She always said, "I must get Daddy to take the lock off that door!" but she never did.

I spent a lot of time in that closet. It had all kinds of great games and puzzles and things in it because it was the upstairs playroom closet, and crayons and poster paints and sketch pads. But Matt locked me in and left the light off—the light switch was outside—so I couldn't do anything about it. Once I found crayons and marked all over the walls in the dark because I was just so mad and nobody was home to let me out. Mama gave me Windex and a razor blade and some scrubbing things and made me clean everything off. I cut myself. There were some marks back behind the costumes for dress-up I never did get off, but she didn't look very close.

Matt and I were always fighting. He was mad because I got the big bedroom with its own bathroom. He said that wasn't fair, when he had to share a room with Doug, and Karl and Mark had to share a room too. Mama said it was because I was a girl. Matt said that wasn't fair either. Daddy said nobody ever promised anybody life would be fair.

After Matt was in the closet, nobody would talk to me. It took Daddy and

Mama a long time to find a new house. They tried to sell our house but no one would buy it. So we stayed here.

I *do* love this house.

One night I ran down the stairs past Matt's closet and went to Daddy's study. At dinners and at breakfasts everybody looked at me and looked away. Nobody talked. I took a sack lunch to school and ate outside because nobody there would talk to me either. I went to Daddy and said, "Tell me you love me, Daddy. Please please. Just tell me you love me. Just once."

And he cried, and he said, "Livvie, I know you can't understand this, baby. We're doing the best we can."

Scott held me and said, "What's wrong? What's wrong?"

I said, "Don't let the children go into that closet! Not until you take the door off, Scott. Promise me."

Sterling looked sideways at me. Maria came and hugged my waist. I picked her up and hugged her, burying my face in her clean black hair. "Oh, baby," I whispered, "I love you, I love you."

Scott said, "You kids, you heard your mother. Nobody goes in that closet, all right? I mean it, now."

"But Daddy," said Carol, "there's nothing in there. It's just empty. Except there's some marks on the wall."

I went to the threshold and stared in. Way on the back wall, some faint scribbles in purple crayon—a child's stick figure drawing of a person with a big frown on its face. And lower down, in green, three words: "help help help."

Somebody's been sleeping in my bed.

It's not really my bed. I mean, I can sit on my bed. Most of the time I just walk through all the furniture new people bring into the house, and I can walk through the new people, too. But now there are two girls sleeping in my room, on a bed that's in the same place my bed is. I can see and hear them better than I usually do.

And one of them is having a nightmare.

"Mommy!" "Mami!"

I heard two voices. Scott stirred in the bed beside me. "Go back to sleep," I murmured, "it's probably just first-night-in-a-new-place jitters."

He mumbled something about first-day jitters and how many jitters could the world possibly hold. I kissed him and got my robe and went upstairs.

Carol and Maria got the big room at the east end of the upstairs. The voices were theirs. I ran up the stairs, looked at the playroom closet—which Scott had nailed shut for me, after I checked it three times to be absolutely certain none of the children was inside—and went to the girls' room.

"Mommy, Maria's having a nightmare," Carol said, sitting up in her white nightgown. Maria had a grip on Carol's hand, and her eyes were wide and frightened. "She wouldn't let me go get you."

"Mami! A spirit, a spirit!"

"What? What is it, baby?" I sat on the bed beside her and hugged her.

"Is my sister," she whispered. "The little one, oh, pobrecito."

"Maria," I whispered. "You have a sister?"

"Nick said she had a little sister but she died," said Carol.

"The agency didn't tell us. Oh, baby. I'm so sorry." And I thought, no, I was wrong. Their lives don't start when they join our family. Scott talks to them about their pasts. Whenever something like that comes up I turn it over to Scott. He remembers being a child. He knows what it is like to have a past, and how to live with one. "Would you like some warm milk with honey in it?" I asked Maria.

"Mami!" she cried, and pointed past my shoulder.

I looked, and saw a little girl shimmering there, in front of the closet door. Cold terror touched my heart. I hugged Maria tightly, more for my comfort than hers. Carol climbed onto the bed behind me, putting her arms around my shoulders. "Daddy!" she screamed.

"Shh," I said, "shh." And then a song woke in me, a lullaby, not one of Grandma's, though. I sang.

> Evening's come, and day is done,
> Gone are sing and shout
> Time to rest in blanket nest
> And blow the candles out.
>
> Down the road to dreams you'll go
> There to stay and play
> Nothing here but sleeping self
> Come to the end of day.
>
> Know I love you when you go
> Wherever you may roam
> I'll be here to welcome you
> When you come back home.

I heard my voice, and thought it wasn't really my voice. It was my mother's voice. I couldn't even remember my mother speaking to me, let alone singing to me. The little shimmering girl crept closer to us. I felt Carol's fingers tighten like talons on my shoulders. "Mama," said the little girl. Her voice sounded like someone talking underwater.

Maria let out a wail and buried her face against my breast.

"Mama," said the little girl. She reached out and touched my face—

—The little girl vanished.

The three of us sat on the bed and wailed and wailed, clutching at each other. And I remembered. . . .

I colored in my coloring book so carefully, staying inside the lines. Matt took a black crayon and marked across my three favorite pictures. I wanted to put them on my bulletin board. But he wrecked them.

I locked him in the closet.

Matt was in sailing camp with Robin's brother Tommy and he didn't want to leave the neighborhood. He was supposed to stay with Robin and Tommy while the rest of us went to visit Gramma in San Francisco. She was sick. I locked Matt in the closet right before we left.

And I forgot.

Matt was supposed to feed our cats while we were gone, even my cat, Little Explorer. They were outside cats and when they didn't get fed they all ran away.

When we came back from two weeks at Gramma's there was a smell in the house.

Tommy's and Robin's mother saw our big station wagon pull in and she came running across the lawn. "Isn't Matt with you?" she said. "I tried to call you and ask but I couldn't remember your mother's name." And she looked in the car and Doug and Karl and Mark and I looked back. I thought maybe Matt ran away. He used to talk about running away. So did I. Sometimes at night we snuck out on the roof together and talked about running away. Matt wanted to go to Mexico. He wanted to find an iguana and tame it for a pet. For a minute I thought maybe Matt went to Mexico, but then I remembered . . .

Carol's face was hot and wet, pressed into the back of my neck. I could feel Maria's hot tears soaking through my robe and nightgown. I felt a chill in me that even the heat of tears could not banish, as the nine-year-old child inside me began to speak.

GEORGE SZANTO
The Sweeper

George Szanto has lived and worked in England, the U.S., France, Germany, Canada and Mexico. Presently he divides his time between Mexico and Montreal. His first novel, *Not Working*, was published to acclaim in Canada in 1983; since then he has written stories, novels, plays and criticism.

I hope that fantasy readers will seek out Szanto's most recent story cycle, *The Underside of Stones*. The connected stories in this cycle are set in a small town in the central highlands of Mexico. They are evocative works of Magic Realism exploring the collision between societies, between ancient and modern ways of life—and the power of Story to transform them both. "The Sweeper," reprinted from this collection, is quite possibly the best, and certainly my favorite, fantasy story of the year.

—T.W.

The Sweeper

GEORGE SZANTO

Dead. I knew he was dead, I'd helped put him in the ground. An honor for any gringo, my neighbor Pepe who runs the Telecable told me. Except I hadn't understood the dead man's son Tomás nearly well enough to grasp the nature of this honor.

Tomás was the eldest. "My father willed it."

You don't argue with the eldest son of a dead man, not after less than three months in a town and your sweeper dies and the responsible son says you are a pallbearer, his father willed it. Despite too much recent contact with death, you go.

The culture about me is so foreign I could be in Kabul or Papua. I'm trying to write a novel. But the dead man, my sweeper, often interrupts. "You would like a story? I have a few little stories, let me tell you a story or two." This he'd said while he was alive. After he was dead he told me, There are hundreds of stories going on under your nose (under your eggs, he said; that took me a few seconds to figure out). Tiny stories and volcano-size stories, he said. You gringos are blind.

He's much ruder dead than alive.

When I'd learned to argue with him dead I said I thought most people were blind. After a while he conceded yes, I was right, partly; except I from my culture was blind in a worse way.

He does have a lot of stories. Anecdotes, anyway; rambles. Mostly I only have to listen. A few he's dragged me into the middle of. Like this one, about the statue. He wouldn't leave me alone about it: That's a man inside there.

Come on, it's a statue. Look, I said, its feet are poured cement, reinforced, it's only steel bars that're inside there, all the way up to its outstretched hand. Look.

He laughed. All you gringos believe that. Why are you only a stupid gringo, you, a writer, a professor of criminología?

I am, as charged, a criminologist; I have a split teaching position, Boston and Montreal. I'm here for a year in Michoácuaro in the Sierra Madre Occidentale mountains of Michoacán, to withdraw. Michoácuaro is a hillside town of thirty thousand where the streets were paved just three years ago for the first time in its four-century history, where burros mingle with muffler-free trucks, where pigs are allowed by ordinance to meander through town only on the end of a piece of clothesline held by kids not less than eight years old. Far from office meetings, from my telephone answering service. From hospitals. Not far at all from television, but at least that I can keep out of the house. Time to escape from a life of slow death. Time to write a novel.

What kind of novel?

I tried to explain. It would be about victims. And why certain people become one kind of victim, and others become different kinds of victims. That was my specialty in criminology, I told him. Not guns or police. Victims.

People don't *become* victims, he said. So there can be no reasons.

Of course there can. I began listing a few reasons—

Slowly he shook his head, and again. Those aren't reasons. Some people *are* victims. Those are excuses.

I got more technical. Talked about different theories of victimization—

I don't understand. Why do you want to write about victims anyway? Write a story about me.

I said maybe I would, one day. When I'd finished my novel about people becoming victims.

It'll be a lie.

Like this he insinuated his way into my life from the start.

Then there was his death. Monday he was there, Tuesday he wasn't. I was informed. I made the proper noises, the brief visit to the family and so on. Then came the invitation to the funeral. Command performance it felt like, with my specific participation. Dealing with death—

I asked advice from the jefe de policía, Rubén Reyes Ponce; I was renting one of his houses. Having already accepted, of course. There'd been no room to refuse the son's polite restrained insistence during the ten minutes of his visit. The advice I got was, "Wear a dark suit. Give the family five thousand pesos for refrescos. Maybe you can use what you see." Cynical smile, broken bits of laughter. Michoácuarans have an off-center sense of humor.

I helped carry the coffin. Gilt gray, worth—not worth, actually, just costing —more than I might pay him in a year, even two, of sweeping. They opened the coffin. I touched his cheek like a hundred fifty others. Some kissed it. I wasn't up to that myself. It was a tough face, lined, a worker's face. Thin nose and lips, eyes closed now but in life dark brown, thin gray hair brushed flat and trimmed since his death, the lobe of his right ear cut off—a barroom fight when he'd worked the docks in Veracruz. He wore a light-green formal shirt. The rest of the body, rigid, stiff, was covered. They closed the coffin, we carried it to the hill and halfway up. The old man weighed mightily. As did the gilt box his family had gone into debt for.

"Death? Death?" He'd spat it at me once, a late afternoon as I was trying to get to the beer depósito quickly, back in time for sunset and a drink with friends down from Colorado for a few days. "Death belongs to the dead."

My problem was I'd tried to dismiss him in my dreadful Spanish by saying—wrong idiom—I was dying of thirst.

"Death, we felt it around us all the time when I was a stevedore. On the docks death was easy. Everyone died, sooner or later. They didn't know what dying was so they gave themselves up and they died. They lost. You cannot die of thirst. You can die of letting thirst take you over. If you refuse to lose to death you can't die."

I'm pretty sure that's what he said. More or less. My comprehension was still pretty bad and I was only three-quarters listening because my friends from Colorado were dying of thirst even if I wasn't allowed the privilege. They hadn't been due till the next day so there was no beer in the house. Now I didn't want their even metaphoric death-from-thirst on my hands. "Amigo, amigo, you will live forever, but I have to go buy beer. Walk with me." With him this was the only way of not standing around all afternoon, me listening and barely understanding.

His (alive) stories go on; not just the ones he told me, also some I've gotten in exchange from other people since his death.

I found out he was still around through the sweeping. Sweeping was the link between death and life.

I think he saw me, three minutes after I got to Michoácuaro, as a great possibility. For him I represented money; however slight my means this unpaid year, they were far greater than his own. Also perhaps there'd be advantages, later, for his sons.

The day after the earthquake he'd helped me move in. Unrequested. He appeared at the gate and started lending a hand. He participated in placing the couch; he knew I'd like it better away from the window, more looking out, more down here so the TV (I didn't have one? "Get a set, Jorge, help you learn Spanish") could sit with its back to the light, good for the eyes, help me see what's going on in the world.

My Spanish then, less than seventy-two hours after crossing out of Texas, was so awful, gestures and miming television-watching were the best I could deal with. I guess I didn't understand ninety percent of his actual words.

He suggested the movers, the other movers, the ones I'd actually hired, might like a beer. He knew where to get cold Superior. He gestured for me to come along. He stopped off at his son's place—Tomás, the eldest of eleven—to pick up half a dozen empties so I wouldn't have to pay the depósito. "Entiende depósito, Jorge?" I understood; he'd saved me twenty pesos times six.

We got back with the bottles. The movers had my stuff in, they drank the cold beer gratefully, unquestioningly. I had done what was right for a gringo to do—or for any person, I realized, after my sense of being a total outsider began to diminish. I paid the movers and tipped them a thousand pesos (road-back-money, English for a single word in Mexican Spanish); I'd been advised it was the appropriate amount.

He hung around. Suggestions for plants, ideas about where to place the lounging chairs in the courtyard for maximum sun—"Your face is pale, Jorge, you do not look well"—or maximum shade. He refused to leave. Finally I realized what had to be done—after three days in Mexico some sense of how to proceed does set in, especially once polite norteamericano patterns have failed so dreadfully. For Moisés de Jesús (I'd learned his name only after he'd repeated it four times; Moisés de Jesús Gutierrez Humberto), for him a gratuity was appropriate. I brought out my wallet. Mute, I handed him a thousand pesos. Folded in discrete quarters. He took it. I said, "Muchas gracias."

Well, he was either insulted (friendship is not to be paid for, and never never in this manner) or deeply appreciative and thankful (a thousand pesos could buy his family twenty kilos of tortillas). My negligible Spanish left me with nothing to say. His immediate emotion took him, too, momentarily out of the conversation.

But he pulled himself together and stepped close. Suddenly his face was six inches from mine. With a curious twist of his head he was looking directly into my right eye, and then as with a shrug his hands were holding my upper arms, squeezing gently. "We are amigos, are we not?"

His lunch had included raw onions. I grinned. Feebly, I suspect. "Yes. I think so."

His two eyes never left my right one. "It was me who swept your sidewalk for the week before you arrived. It was me who organized your house so it is right for you. I will keep your sidewalk clean for you forever. I will help you in many ways while you are on my street. I am your amigo. Does one pay an amigo a thousand pesos?"

This came through not in a single exchange but from a series of stumblings. On both our parts. "I—I don't know." I was feeling, curiously, afraid.

His grip tightened. "A thousand pesos. It is not much money."

That I understood. And with instant relief. I realized I'd been terrified we were about to be locked into some kind of blood brotherhood forever. But a larger tip I could handle. "Amigo, I am new in Mexico. I do not know the customs of your country. What is good money for your work?"

There was no change in his expression. I'd expected a gentle smile—yes, he had finally got through to the ignorant gringo—or an embarrassed glance at the world beyond my ear. He never took his eyes off mine. Then my arms were free as his hands rose to my head. He pressed, lightly, index, middle and ring fingers of each hand to my temples. "Between you and me, Jorge, there is good friendship. I do not know the answer to your question. Only the gods know. The gods will bring you their answer." He closed his eyes and remained motionless.

The gods didn't bring me a damn thing. Except a couple of moments to reflect on how easy life suddenly was: just give him another thousand.

Which I started to do. I reached for my wallet. My right shoulder ached mightily, I'd gone that stiff.

The difficulty with the great solution was this: after all my other tipping I had only a five-thousand-peso note left. But anything to be rid of him. "I hope this is good." His open eyes blinked several times.

Yes, his gods-of-wallet-fortuna were watching over him and he knew it. "If the gods say this, then it is good." No gracias now, no bowing or scraping. That would be inappropriate among equals. He stood back proud. "Hasta la vista, Don Jorge." He left. It seemed I had bought myself a title.

A title, and his recognition that I was his great good luck, his patsy.

During the next weeks he thought of a dozen services he could perform for me, from providing a tour of the countryside to doing my shopping. All of course with the appropriate compensation; the gods would no doubt inform me of the amount. I wanted only a bit of peace to write my book, so after a couple of weeks of saying no to everything else I acceded to the sweeping: all the sidewalk, and halfway across the road, by eight every morning, according to the town ordinance. He would charge me four thousand pesos a month.

I had asked advice from the jefe. Yes it is an ordinance. His price? Steep.

"Okay, you're hired. A thousand pesos a month."

"Oh no, three."

"The gods have told me: fifteen hundred."

"Surely they must have said two thousand."

"Perhaps. Two thousand."

"Don Jorge, as you know, I have been sweeping your sidewalk since you arrived—"

"But I did not ask you to—"

"Your sidewalk is clean every morning at eight, you will pay me now a thousand pesos for two weeks."

The battle was between resilient pride and beating an old man out of three dollars. If I were going to be in Michoácuaro for more than ten months—five years, say, or a lifetime—I would have refused and fought. I gave him a thousand pesos.

We had put him in the ground with all his medals. He'd been dead for eight days, buried for five. I asked, "Why didn't you keep them, a memory of your father?"

Tomás shook his head. "It was his will to be buried with them on his chest."

I concurred as to how you can't argue with a man's wishes once he's dead.

The medals were for pistol competition. Tomás told me that three years in a row, when his father was twenty-six, twenty-seven, twenty-eight, he'd been Michoacán Champion both for Air Pistol and Conventional Pistol and the middle year also for the Rapid-fire Pistol. Each year he had been in the running for Mexico's national team, but never had made it. Later, as a stevedore, he'd won half a dozen more ribbons and four little cups for his pistol expertise. All these trophies were buried with him.

It had been my habit since arriving in Michoácuaro to jog around the plaza ten to fifteen times every morning before the town began to stir—that is, at the least hint of light, enough so I didn't trip myself up—and I would see, three or four times a week before he died, Moisés de Jesús sweeping away or washing down the dust. We'd chat briefly and I'd head in to take a shower. For the last week naturally I hadn't seen my sweeper, but the sidewalk was continuously clean.

Probably one of the sons, I figured. An early morning, a Friday, I'd been up at four to make some notes and wasn't able to sleep after so I headed down to the plaza for my run.

A mistake. In front of the dark tostada stands my foot squished into the middle of a dropped soggy item, forgotten five or six hours ago, now found by me. My foot shot sideways and I landed flathanded and hip down. I swore, picked myself up, checked the damage—mostly a skinned palm, a hip that'd complain for a couple of days and an agony in the right shoulder from jerking my arm trying for impossible balance. The shoulder wanted streams of hot water and I wanted to forget being sensibly healthy. I walked slowly up the hill to the house. And there he was.

In the barest pre-light I assumed it was the son. I began, "Buenos días, o buenos noches—" when he turned, and it was old M. de J. himself.

Buenos días, Don Jorge. I am glad to see you. You owe me two thousand pesos. For the month.

Naturally I assumed I was dreaming. Which would've been fine because then I'd have been dreaming the pain in my shoulder too. I tried the usual check-out-if-you-are-asleep devices, speaking aloud: What're you doing here? and thrashing my arms, which hurt, and the cliché of pinching. But I was wide awake.

And he answered my question: Sweeping. You can see that. He spoke clearly, normally.

Look, this may sound foolish, but—well, aren't you dead?

You buried me. I was pleased you did. Tomás told me he did not think you would. He was wrong. As usual.

I suppose among my reactions there might have been fear. But no, none. I remember telling myself, you're talking to a ghost—ghosts being one of our normalizing categories for irrational phenomena. I touched him. No ectoplasm. Solid, like in life. I wondered if he'd fade with the coming light. The sky was barely dark gray.

I could make no intelligent sense of this. The worst, somehow (thinking back now, to have reached for instant better/worse gradations seems weird, but I suppose so does the rest of this on those scales of reason), was I'd always thought, according to our Judeo-Christian folklore, death was a release. Moisés de Jesús was dead. Yet he was getting up at this ungodly hour to sweep my sidewalk for two thousand pesos a month. I asked him if he minded.

No. If you are dead you don't sleep. So you don't have to get up.

In a perverse way that was a relief. Had he been around, well, ever since he died?

I can't remember much before yesterday. But since then, yes.

Always here? In town? I meant, I supposed, had he been to what gets called heaven or hell.

Of course I've been around here. I am from Michoácuaro, where else should I go?

Do you talk to many people? Like this?

I told you before I died. He looked angry now. Most people are blind. They are also deaf. They cannot hear me so I cannot talk to them. They are blind, so they do not know I am here.

Everybody?

Not everybody. Obviously not you, Don Jorge. Two or three others. Two friends, the ones that listened. Before. Also a woman. Sometimes she sees me, mostly not. Not my wife. I did not expect you would be able to.

I wasn't sure I wanted to be the exception. I wasn't sure I wanted that kind of honor. I was feeling the offer of blood brotherhood again and I didn't understand its implications. Or maybe it had already gone beyond the offer stage.

We continued to talk, the longest conversation of our acquaintance. The day got lighter. He didn't disappear. A couple of cars drove by, one backfiring like a burst of gunfire, neither paying any attention. I wondered what would happen if people walked past. The miracle, looking back, was more my ability to understand his Spanish and to make myself understood than the fact that this conversation was taking place at all. Did that mean it's easier to understand the dead than the living? Because they focus more? And what kind of metaphor was I letting myself in for here?

I don't remember how we stopped talking. Nothing like, Will I see you again? or, Have a good day, in any of their Spanish forms. Just the vaguest memory of opening the door and passing through the courtyard to turn on the water heater for the shower. No sense, either, of the fifteen minutes or so it takes for the water to get hot. The first clear subsequent image was me in the shower and the relief of a hot water spray massage on my shoulder.

We kept on meeting. There was usually no one else around. When I tried to get him to explain why he preferred seclusion he avoided the question. I suspect he was a bit afraid of being seen, and heard. It'd maybe disprove his absolute theories about people being blind and deaf. I asked him once, If gringos are so damn ignorant in the senses, how come I'm one of the few select? and if he wanted complete freedom for wandering around in the open, why didn't he go to the U.S. or Canada?

All he said was, Too cold.

Too cold for a dead man?

He looked at me as if I were stupid.

Often he appears, just like that, in my courtyard, the door locked, for a chat. Several times we've run into each other, if that's the right phrase, at the market. Shopping?

We all have to eat.

If it were only his one-liners I think I'd find him tiresome, whatever his state of existence. But, as I said, he has stories. I've spent months being his audience.

I wanted to know about being dead. Alaine, my wife of nineteen years, had spent the last four of them dying—being kept alive, dying with infinite slowness. Only a few weeks after the funeral I had left her there, up north, to come here. I had thought she was gone from me. Now—I pulled my courage together: Could you get any sense of her, being dead too?

Don't use me, Don Jorge.

Look, I'm sorry—

I can't see or hear other dead people. Anyway, not now. And if I could why should I tell you? If I wanted to be with dead people I wouldn't bother with you. Don't use me for a connection. You want to talk to me, go ahead.

Alaine's death, supposedly permanent. Then for a moment, the tiny hope. Now suddenly, a curious sorrow; new, yet less pain—

He was insistent too about the statue. I made him meet me there one morning while I was jogging so we could take a good look before people came into the square. It is a statue of Abelardo Carosuelto Núñez, an obscure lieutenant who served with Benito Juarez in the 1860's and later became part of his government. After Juarez's death Abelardo returned to Michoácuaro, his birthplace, married the heiress to a huge sugar cane plantation and died wealthy. To his honor, his unearned wealth one presumes, the statue is dedicated. It stands on a pedestal nearly two meters high. Lieutenant Abelardo is dressed in full uniform, his long coat coming down to his knees, Hessian boots rising to the hem of the coat. He is hatless, has flowing hair, a graceful mustache and a goatee. His left arm hangs at his side. His right is outstretched, rising above shoulder level. In this hand he holds a pistol. I am told it's an old Colt .45 but given my specialization I know even less about antique firearms than of contemporary ones. The pistol points across the breadth of the plaza. There, in the early morning moonlight, it glowed slightly.

Look, I said. Solid. Here. Feel it. I jumped up on the base of the pedestal. Touch the boots.

Boots are hard. Touch the coat.

I pulled myself up to the top of the pedestal. The statue is probably half again as tall as me. I held it around the waist. Solid poured cement, I said. It felt warm, as if it had soaked up the day's hot sun and was releasing it slowly. A kind of capacitor.

Maybe it feels solid to you. I know it is a man.

Amigo—

You can see me. Others cannot. Yet you refuse to believe it when I say that is a man.

Follow a path like this, you go crazy. In fact, some days I wasn't sure I wasn't there already. Talking with dead men is usually understood as some kind of aberrance of mind. When it isn't a religious act, anyway. None of which kept me from asking, Can you talk to him?

No.

Then how do you know?

I can see him.

Can he see you?

How should I know? Just because he's in a statue doesn't mean he isn't blind. Or deaf, for that matter.

Stone deaf! I laughed.

Moisés de Jesús didn't find that a bit funny. Alive he hadn't had much of a sense of humor either.

We weren't getting anywhere. I quickly found myself jogging again.

* * *

In early January a man was found dead on the plaza with a bullet in his skull. No one knew who did it. Someone claimed to have heard a shot, about three in the morning. But the sound could just as easily have been a car backfiring. Moisés de Jesús told me the statue shot the man.

Why?

Target practice.

Come on.

Sure. You get rusty, standing on that pedestal all day, not being allowed to move. Besides, they were both drunk.

A statue? Drunk? I laughed again, more uncomfortably.

Again irritation from him. You haven't learned anything at all, Don Jorge. Someday soon you won't be able to see me anymore.

And I knew I'd be sorry. It was becoming a strange kind of privilege. I've tried to explain to myself, dozens of times, how it could happen that I, a rational norteamericano, could have these conversations with Moisés de Jesús after he died. But there's no clarification that makes sense in our terms. When we talked it was as friends rather than acquaintances. Yet I would hardly have called Moisés de Jesús a friend, we'd barely known each other; still, now we talked. And it was with the openness of friendship, I mean; letting nothing stay hidden; nothing conscious, anyway. I mentioned Alaine now and then, when I couldn't stop myself. He wouldn't follow in this direction. Still, he'd got me over one hurdle: I was after all talking to him.

They'd found out in town that I am a criminologist. I'd given two talks, one to the Michoácuaro Lions Club and one to the Law Enforcement Association— I think that's the right term—of Michoacán; both with simultaneous translation, though by then I was getting so I understood some of the less complicated questions. My neighbor Pepe asked me if I would talk on television about the murder—the local news, put on by Telecable Michoácuaro.

I didn't much want to. You look like a fool when you can't really speak the language, and television exaggerates that. But Rubén, who as jefe of police had been very helpful in getting my tourist card renewed (knew a man who knew the man who with just a few thousand pesos—), Rubén urged me to; he hadn't found the killer and I sensed he was losing face. He didn't say so of course but he was asking me, a gringo, if I wouldn't mind mentioning something like how baffling this case was, and probably even with the most sophisticated methods of criminology it'd be very hard to find the killer, and so on. I agreed to the interview.

The case had become deeply disturbing to some of the citizens. It was all very well for campesinos to kill each other out in the cane bush, or for a couple of drunks to go at each other with knives or machetes in one of the cantinas. Somebody gets killed that way on an average of once a month. But when people start shooting each other in the town plaza? Across from the kids' library, and the cathedral half a block away? What was happening in town?

No one had been able to learn anything about the dead man either. The postmortem showed he'd been drunk when killed, as expected. Shot by a bullet from a nineteenth-century Colt .45.

Moisés de Jesús laughed darkly when I told him this. And did he become a victim?

What do you mean?

It doesn't matter. On the television, how will you explain it?

How did you hear?

Word gets around.

Among your dead friends?

What will you say?

I suddenly wanted out of the conversation. The truth.

How a statue shot him and made him a victim? Ha!

Go away, amigo.

In there, it is a man!

Should I say that?

Of course.

Who is he?

Moisés de Jesús suddenly looked grim, very uncomfortable, and stayed silent.

Well? You can't expect me to say there's a man in there unless you tell me who he is. That would be stupid.

It has been—different people.

I laughed. What people?

He glowered. Dead people.

Oh. Great. Dead people living inside a statue. Terrific.

Dead like me.

Look. First of all, there's nobody inside that statue. Secondly, if there were and it made any difference, they'd have to be alive for me to worry about it. Dead men in statues don't concern me, okay? If somebody in there were alive, well, we'd try to get them out, I said. I couldn't believe I was prattling this nonsense. It starts when you talk to dead people, I suppose. We'd pull the statue down, we'd shatter it so nobody, dead or alive, would—Which was when it hit me. You! You're afraid of being in there yourself!

Now he wouldn't meet my eye at all. He folded his arms and looked skyward.

Don't worry, amigo, because there's no one, *no one*, inside that statue. And you never will be.

When it is dark, come. I will show you. Suddenly he wasn't around.

It was all becoming, improbably, a story I might want to write one day. And who was the victim? I thought, Okay. I really will go down to the plaza, look at it again, fix it in my mind.

I got there about eleven. The tostada and carne asaka stands were closing up. People loitered in the lit center of the plaza around the fountain. There was no one by the statue.

Moisés de Jesús stepped out from behind it. I didn't think you would come. He was almost angry. Look. Look at it. Do you see the light from the inside? There he is.

I looked. True, the statue was caught in a curious light, especially at the folds of its coat. But that came from the moonlight. I said so.

Touch it. Climb up and feel it.

Look, I did that last time.

Do you want to remain stupid all your life?

It was as if his words scraped, I don't know why, a raw nerve. I sacrificed my dignity and climbed up. I touched Abelardo on the hips. He was indeed warm, certainly warmer than last time. But it was also six or seven hours earlier and the statue still retained a lot of the day's heat. I climbed down and explained that to M. de J.

You are lost, he said. And walked away.

I worked out what I would tell the interviewers. First I'd outline my procedure, then explain how usually some knowledge of the victim leads to an understanding of the purpose of the crime, which could result in finding the perpetrator. In this case, with nothing known of the victim, the police having done all they could in trying to identify—And so on.

About two in the morning on the day of the interview, I was awakened by, I figured, a truck backfiring. I guessed what M. de J. would say and couldn't get back to sleep. All the night-thoughts roared through my head: Alaine before the cancer struck, before the chemotherapy, before her hair—And the novel that was proceeding so slowly, and the interview itself, and Moisés de Jesús in his coffin. I got up, made myself a flour tortilla with melted cheese, wondered if my typewriter would wake anybody up at nearly 3:00 A.M. and heard the backfire again. Or—the statue shooting at someone else? I tried to read. No concentration. Maybe a little tequila? No, I wanted to be clear-headed for the damn interview. So I did the only thing a fool would do, I got dressed and walked—slowly, it was a cloudy night, dark—down to the plaza to check out the statue. Which wasn't there.

That's not exactly correct. The pedestal was there. On it, a kind of shape like Abelardo, except it was a glowing outline of the statue. I don't want to exaggerate this, it was hardly a fireball; much more a brighter version of what I had seen a few nights before. Except I couldn't explain it away by talking about reflected moonlight because the moon was behind thick clouds. I reached up. I was unable to stop myself, I put my hand into the glow. A sharp clip of fear hit me between the shoulder blades, passed through my gut and fled down my legs—fear of being burned, or just plain afraid, I don't know. I had the unexplainable sense of passing my hand through flesh that wasn't there—Then out the other side; and nothing.

No burn, no explanation. I dropped to the ground. What to do? Wait? I sat, focused on the glow. It changed very little. Or maybe not at all. I waited possibly half an hour. Then something, somebody, human in shape, wearing the same kind of glow, appeared at the far end of the plaza. He approached, fifty feet, thirty, twenty. He looked respectable enough in clothing, slacks, a shirt. Except for the glow it could have been any Michoácuaran. Except also, I noticed then, he carried a pistol. I couldn't swear it was a nineteenth-century Colt .45 but it looked a lot like the thing the statue always held. I couldn't help myself. I stepped out of the shadow. He saw me. And pointed the pistol.

Panic. I turned and ran. I heard a shot, no car backfire this time, but didn't feel anything. Except, now, pure fear. I kept running, reached the first cover, the tostada stands, dived around the nearest and bashed my head on a kind of sticking out counter. I remember thinking, if all I get is a bang on the skull I'll be lucky. I stared out at the pedestal. Carefully. There was the statue, standing on top, dull now in the dark light, pointing its pistol out across the plaza. Unless it shifted its traditional pose I was out of the line of fire.

I stayed beyond it, kept to the shadows for three blocks and got home. How to understand, by what process, the last hour? I half expected Moisés de Jesús there, grinning gleefully, bantering, See? See?

Then I was stuck: Forget all this for the interview and retain my credibility? Or tell Michoácuaro they had a ghost of a sniper in their statue?

Only one possibility, really. After explaining everything that was appropriate from my professional perspective, and it being line-for-line translated, I would tell the reporters and the TV audience, wryly, another explanation was also possible: The dead man had been shot by a statue.

In the studio everyone laughed. A little nervously, yes, but they must have needed to fill in more airtime because they followed my, so to speak, line of reasoning.

"Why would the statue do that?"

So I went on about the man in the statue. That since it had been put there, there were always men in the statue.

"Who kill?"

"Only sometimes. When they are seen."

"Why are they there in the first place?"

"I don't know."

"You've seen this man?"

"Well, I happened to be out on the plaza at three in the morning, and—" We went on for another ten minutes, me recounting the night's events in bravura style. The two reporters were delighted; usually their interviews proved a lot more, well, usual. I told them I'd had fun too, thank you.

The producer, Pepe, drew me aside. He wasn't sure my tactic had been wise, a long time since anybody took the ghost-of-Abelardo stories seriously, Michoácuaro was still in many ways fighting its way out of the Middle Ages, now my joke would revive all that superstition, and so on. But it was done. So he thanked me too.

I was fascinated. An ancient story. And old guess-who was waiting for me in the courtyard: I had almost lost hope, Don Jorge. But he said it with a grin and a shrug. There was something curious, different, about him. I realized what only after he'd left. The right earlobe, it was all there.

My friend the jefe laughed and slapped me on the back and told me I was terrific, best joke he'd heard in a long time. He thanked me too for the good word about the difficulties of the investigation. I couldn't help thinking I heard a nervous edge to the laughter.

People stopped me on the street for probably three weeks after. It was as if they knew me, I was a friend, talkable to. Two groups of people: I had a fantastic sense of humor, a humor fit for a Michoácuaran, how could a gringo have such a fine sense of humor? That was the larger group. The others would shake my hand and nod wisely, pull me aside and tell me I was a brave man, not often did one hear the truth on television, it was good to speak the truth even on television. These were mostly older people. I would thank them in return for their kindness, the appreciation. Terrific, that. I'd never been so popular before.

I still jog in the mornings. But only after first light. Moisés de Jesús comes by from time to time, and I meet him in accidental places. The sidewalk is always swept. With the inflation here he demanded, last week, three thousand a month. I've agreed to twenty-five hundred.

JOYCE CAROL OATES
Ladies and Gentlemen

Joyce Carol Oates was brought up in the countryside of New York State and currently lives in New Jersey. She is the author of numerous novels, short stories, poems, plays and essays and though she is published in the literary mainstream, her work often has overtones of dark fantasy or psychological horror. Her novel *Bellefleur* is particularly recommended to readers of fantasy. Oates won the National Book Award for her novel *Them* and she has twice been a recipient of the O. Henry Award for Continuing Achievement.

"Ladies and Gentlemen" is an acerbic piece of dark fantasy, commenting on the "yuppie" lifestyle of the 1980s with deadly black humor. It comes from the pages of *Harper's* magazine. I also recommend seeking out a second dark fantasy work by Oates published this year in *Tikkun* magazine (Vol. 5, No. 4): "Why Don't You Come Live With Me It's Time."

—T.W.

Ladies and
Gentlemen

JOYCE CAROL OATES

Ladies and gentlemen: a belated but heartfelt welcome aboard our cruise ship
S.S. *Ariel*; it's a true honor and a privilege for me, your captain, to greet you all
on this lovely sun-warmed January day—as balmy, isn't it, as any June morning
back north? I wish I could claim that we of the *Ariel* arranged personally for such
splendid weather, as compensation of sorts for the, shall we say, somewhat rocky
weather of the past several days, but, at any rate, it's a welcome omen indeed
and bodes well for the remainder of the cruise and for this morning's excursion,
ladies and gentlemen, to the island you see us rapidly approaching, a small but
remarkably beautiful island the natives of these waters call the "Island of
Tranquillity"—or, as some translators prefer, the "Island of Repose." For those
of you who've become virtual sailors with a keen eye for navigating, you'll want
to log our longitude at 155 degrees east and our latitude at 5 degrees north,
approximately 1,200 miles north and east of New Guinea. Yes, that's right! We've
come so far! And as this is a rather crucial morning, and your island adventure
an important event not only on this cruise but in your lives, ladies and gentlemen,
I hope you will quiet just a bit—just a bit!—and give me, your captain, your
fullest attention. Just for a few minutes—I promise! Then you will disembark.

As to the problems some of you have experienced: Let me take this opportunity,
as your captain, ladies and gentlemen, to apologize, or at least to explain. It's
true, for instance, that certain of your staterooms are not *precisely* as the advertising
brochures depicted them; the portholes are not quite so large, in some cases the
portholes are not in evidence. This is not the fault of any of the *Ariel* staff; indeed,
this has been a sore point with us for some years, a matter of misunderstandings
and embarrassments out of our control, yet I, as your captain, ladies and gentlemen, offer my apologies and my profoundest sympathies. Though I am a bit your
junior in age, I can well understand the special disappointment, the particular
hurt, outrage, and dismay that attend one's sense of having been cheated on what,

for some of you, probably, is perceived as being the last time you'll be taking so prolonged and exotic a trip. Thus, my profoundest sympathies! As to the toilets that have been reported as malfunctioning, or out of order entirely, and the loud throbbing or "tremors" of the engines that have been keeping some of you awake, and the negligent or even rude service, the over- or undercooked food, the high tariffs on mineral water, alcoholic beverages, and cigarettes, the reported sightings of rodents, cockroaches, and other vermin on board ship—perhaps I should explain, ladies and gentlemen, that this is the final voyage of the S.S. *Ariel*, and it was the owners' decision, and a justifiably pragmatic decision, to cut back on repairs, services, expenses, and the like. Ladies and gentlemen, I am sorry for your inconvenience, but the *Ariel* is an old ship, bound for dry dock in Manila and the fate of many a veteran seagoing vessel that has outlived her time. God bless her! We'll not see her likes again, ladies and gentlemen!

Ladies and gentlemen, may I have some quiet? *Please?* Just five minutes more, before the stewards help you prepare for your disembarkment? Thank you.

Yes, the *Ariel* is bound for Manila next. But have no fear: You won't be aboard.

Ladies and gentlemen, *please*. This murmuring and muttering begins to annoy.

(Yet, as your captain, I'd like to note that, amid the usual whiners and complainers and the just plain bad-tempered, it's gratifying to see a number of warm, friendly, *hopeful* faces; and to know that there are men and women determined to enjoy life, not quibble and harbor suspicions. Thank *you!*)

Now to our business at hand: Ladies and gentlemen, do you know what you have in common?

You can't guess?

You *can* guess?

No? Yes?

No?

Well—yes, sir, it's true that you are all aboard the S.S. *Ariel*; and yes, sir—excuse me, *ma'am*—it's certainly true that you are all of "retirement" age. (Though "retirement" has come to be a rather vague term in the past decade or so, hasn't it? For the youngest among you are in your late fifties—the result, I would guess, of especially generous early-retirement programs; and the eldest among you are in your mid-nineties. Quite a range of ages!)

Yes, it's true you are all Americans. You have expensive cameras, even, in some cases, video equipment for recording this South Seas adventure; you have all sorts of tropical-cruise paraphernalia, including some extremely attractive bleached-straw hats; some of you have quite a supply of sun-protective lotions; and most of you have a considerable quantity, and variety, of pharmacological supplies. And quite a store of paperbacks, magazines, cards, games, and crossword puzzles. Yet there is one primary thing you have in common, ladies and gentlemen, which has determined your presence here this morning, at longitude 155 degrees east and latitude 5 degrees north; your fate, as it were. Can't you guess?

Ladies and gentlemen: *your children.*

Yes, you have in common the fact that this cruise on the S.S. *Ariel* was originally your children's idea; and that they arranged for it, if you'll recall. (Though you have probably paid for your own passages, which weren't cheap.) Your children, who are "children" only technically, for of course they are fully grown, fully adult; a good number of them parents themselves (having made you proud grandparents—yes, haven't you been proud!); these sons and daughters, who, if I may speak frankly, are *very* tired of waiting for their inheritances.

Yes, and *very* impatient, some of them, *very* angry, waiting to come into control of what they believe is their due.

Ladies and gentlemen, please!—I'm asking for quiet, and I'm asking for respect. As captain of the *Ariel*, I am not accustomed to being interrupted.

I believe you did hear me correctly, sir. And you too, sir.

Yes, and you, ma'am. And *you*. (Most of you aren't nearly so deaf as you pretend!)

Let me speak candidly. While your children are in many or at least in some cases genuinely fond of you, they are simply impatient with the prospect of waiting for your "natural" deaths. Ten years, fifteen? Twenty? With today's medical technology, who knows, you might outlive *them*!

Of course it's a surprise to you, ladies and gentlemen. It's a *shock*. Thus you, sir, are shaking your head in disbelief, and you, sir, are muttering just a little too loudly, "Who does that fool think he is, making such bad jokes!" and you, ladies, are giggling like teenage girls, not knowing what to think. But remember: Your children have been living lives of their own, in a very difficult, very competitive corporate America; they are, on the face of it, "well-to-do," even affluent; yet they want, in some cases desperately need, *your* estates—not in a dozen years but *now*.

That is to say, as soon as your wills can be probated, following our "act of God" in these tropical seas.

For, however your sons and daughters appear in the eyes of their neighbors, friends, and business colleagues, even in the eyes of their own offspring, you can be sure that *they have not enough money*. You can be sure that they suffer keenly certain financial jealousies and yearnings. And who dares calibrate another's suffering? Who dares peer into another's heart? Without betraying anyone's confidence, I can say that there are several youngish men, beloved sons of couples in your midst, ladies and gentlemen, who are nearly bankrupt; men of integrity and "success" whose worlds are about to come tumbling about their heads— unless they get money, or find themselves in the position of being able to borrow money against their parents' estates, *fast*. Investment bankers, lawyers, a college professor or two—some of them already in debt. Thus, they decided to take severe measures.

Ladies and gentlemen, it's pointless to protest. As captain of the *Ariel*, I merely expedite orders.

And you must know that it's pointless to express disbelief or incredulity; to roll your eyes, as if *I* (of all people) were a bit cracked; to call out questions or demands; to shout, weep, sob, beg, rant and rave, and mutter, "If this is a joke it isn't a very funny joke!" "As if my son/daughter would ever do such a thing to me/ us!"—in short, it's pointless to express any and all of the reactions you're expressing and have been expressed by other ladies and gentlemen on past *Ariel* voyages to the South Seas.

* * *

Yes, it's the best thing, to cooperate. Yes, in an orderly fashion. It's wisest not to provoke the stewards (whose nerves are a bit ragged these days—the crew is only human, after all) into using force.

Ladies and gentlemen, these *are* lovely azure waters, exactly as the brochures promised! But shark-infested, so take care.

Ah yes, those dorsal fins slicing the waves, just beyond the surf—observe them closely.

No, we're leaving no picnic baskets with you today. Nor any bottles of mineral water, Perrier water, champagne.

For why delay what's inevitable? Why, cruelly, protract anguish?

Ladies and gentlemen, maybe it's a simple thing, maybe it's a self-evident thing, but consider: You are the kind of civilized men and women who brought babies into the world not by crude, primitive, anachronistic *chance* but by systematic *deliberation*. You planned your futures, you planned, as the expression goes, your parenthood. You are all of that American economic class called upper-middle; you are educated, you are cultured, you are stable; nearly without exception, you showered love upon your sons and daughters, who knew themselves, practically in the cradle, to be privileged. The very best, the most exclusive nursery schools—private schools—colleges, universities. Expensive toys and gifts of all kinds, closets of clothing, ski equipment, stereo equipment, racing bicycles, tennis lessons, riding lessons, snorkeling lessons, private tutoring, trips to the Caribbean, to Mexico, to Tangier, to Tokyo, to Switzerland, junior years abroad in Paris, in Rome, in London. Yes, and their teeth were perfect, or were made to be; yes, and they had cosmetic surgery if necessary or nearly necessary; yes, and you gladly paid for their abortions or their tuition for law school, medical school, business school; yes, and you paid for their weddings; yes, and you loaned them money "to get started," certainly you helped them with their mortgages, or their second cars, or their children's orthodontist bills. Nothing was too good or too expensive for them, for what, ladies and gentlemen, would it have been?

And, always, the more you gave your sons and daughters the more you seemed to be holding in reserve; the more generous you displayed yourself the more generous you were hinting you might be, in the future. But so far in the future —when your wills might be probated, after your deaths!

Ladies and gentlemen, you rarely stopped to consider your children as other than *your* children—as men and women growing into maturity, distinct from you. Rarely did you pause to see how patiently they were waiting to inherit their due—and then, by degrees, how impatiently. What anxieties besieged them, what nightmare speculations? For what if you squandered your money on medical bills? Nursing-home bills? The melancholic impedimenta of age in America? What if—worse yet!—addlebrained, suffering from Alzheimer's disease (about which they'd been reading suddenly, it seemed, everywhere), you turned against them? Disinherited them? Remarried someone younger, healthier, more cunning than they? Rewrote your wills, as elderly fools are always doing?

Ladies and gentlemen, your children declare that they want only *what's theirs*.

They say, laughingly, *they* aren't going to live forever.

(Well, yes: I'll confide in you, off-the-cuff, in several instances it was an *in-law* who looked into the possibility of a cruise on the S.S. *Ariel*; your own son or daughter merely cooperated, after the fact, as it were. Of course, that isn't the same thing!)

Ladies and gentlemen, as your captain, about to bid you farewell, let me say: I *am* sympathetic with your plight. Your stunned expressions, your staggering-swaying gait, your damp eyes, working mouths—"This is a bad joke!" "This is intolerable!" "This is a nightmare!" "No child of mine could be so cruel, inhuman, monstrous," etc.—all this is touching, wrenching to the heart, altogether *natural*. One might almost say *traditional*. Countless others, whose bones you may discover, should you have the energy and spirit to explore the "Island of Tranquillity" (or "Repose"), reacted in more or less the same way.

Thus, do not despair, ladies and gentlemen, for your emotions, however painful, are time-honored; but do not squander the few precious remaining hours of your life, for such emotions are futile.

Ladies and gentlemen: The "Island of Tranquillity" upon which you now stand shivering in the steamy morning heat is approximately six kilometers in circumference, ovoid in shape, with a curious archipelago of giant metamorphic rocks trailing off to the north, a pounding hallucinatory surf, and horizon, vague, dreamy, and distant, on all sides. Its soil is an admixture of volcanic ash, sand, rock, and peat; its jungle interior is pocked with treacherous bogs of quicksand.

It *is* a truly exotic island! But most of you will quickly become habituated to the ceaseless winds that ease across the island from several directions simultaneously, air as intimate and warmly stale as exhaled breaths, caressing, narcotic. You'll become habituated to the ubiquitous sand fleas, the glittering dragonflies with their eighteen-inch iridescent wings, the numerous species of snakes (the small quicksilver orange-speckled baja snake is the most venomous, you'll want to know); the red-beaked carnivorous macaw and its ear-piercing shriek; bullfrogs the size of North American jackrabbits; 200-pound tortoises with pouched, thoughtful eyes; spider monkeys as playful as children; tapir; tarantulas; most colorful of all, the comical cassowary birds with their bony heads, gaily hued wattles, stunted wings—these ungainly birds whom millions of years of evolution, on an island lacking mammal-predators, have rendered flightless.

And orchids: Some of you have already noticed the lovely, bountiful orchids growing everywhere, dozens of species, every imaginable color, some the size of grapes and others the size of a man's head, unfortunately inedible.

And the island's smells—are they fragrances or odors? Is it rampant fresh-budding life or jungle-rancid decay? Is there a difference?

By night (and the hardiest among you should survive numerous nights, if past history prevails) you'll contemplate the tropical moon, so different from our North American moon, hanging heavy and luminous in the sky like an overripe fruit; you'll be moved to smile at the sport of fiery-phosphorescent fish frolicking in the waves; you'll be lulled to sleep by the din of insects, the cries of nocturnal birds, your own prayers perhaps.

Some of you will cling together, like terrified herd animals; some of you will wander off alone, dazed, refusing to be touched, even comforted by a spouse of fifty years.

Ladies and gentlemen, I, your captain, speak for the crew of the S.S. *Ariel*, bidding you farewell.

Ladies and gentlemen, your children have asked me to assure you that they *do* love you—but circumstances have intervened.

Ladies and gentlemen, your children have asked me to recall to you those years when they were, in fact, *children*—wholly innocent as you imagined them, adoring you as gods.

Ladies and gentlemen, I now bid farewell to you as children do, waving good-bye not once but numerous times, solemn, reverential—good-bye, good-bye, good-bye.

NANCY A. COLLINS

Freaktent

Nancy A. Collins is a native of Arkansas and now lives in New Orleans. *Sunglasses After Dark* (Onyx) won the 1989 Bram Stoker Award for first novel and earned her a nomination for the John W. Campbell Award for Best New Writer. Her second novel, *Tempter*, was recently published by Onyx.

Her stories often reflect her southern upbringing. "Freaktent" certainly does. It appeared in the last issue of *The Horror Show* and is about a side of life most people rarely see or think about any more: carnival sideshows. Genetic engineering will soon be able to ensure that freaks will no longer be born. What happens then? For, as one character in this story notes, "There'll always be people who'll want to look."

I highly recommend another of Collins's stories published in 1990, "The Two-Headed Man," (*Pulphouse* Issue 9), mainstream, but written in the southern gothic tradition of Flannery O'Conner.

—E.D.

Freaktent

NANCY A. COLLINS

My hobby is sideshow freaks. Some call them "Special People." I used to call them that too, until the Seal-Boy (who was seventy at the time) laughed in my face.

It's taken fifteen years of hanging around mess tents and caravans of the few Podunk carnivals that still tour the rural areas to build enough trust amongst these people so they'd agree to sit for me. They guard their private lives, their *real*selves, jealously. In the carny, there's no such thing as a free peek. You see, I'm a photographer.

Two summers back I befriended Fallon, a human pincushion turned sideshow boss. Fallon's little family isn't much to write home about. There's the usual dwarf, fat lady, and pickled punk. Their big draw, however, is Rand Holstrum, The World's Ugliest Man.

Rand suffers from acromegaly. It is a disease that twists the bones and the flesh that covers them. It is a disease that makes monsters.

Rand Holstrum was born as normal as any child. He served in Korea and married his high school sweetheart. He fathered two beautiful, perfectly normal children. And then his head began to mutate.

The acromegaly infected the left side of his face, warping the facial bones like untreated pine boards. The flesh on that side of Rand's face resembles a water balloon filled to capacity. The upper forehead bulges like a baby emerging from its mother's cervix, its weight pressing against his bristling browridge. The puffy, bloated flesh of his cheek has long since swallowed the left eye, sealing it behind a wall of bone and meat. His nose was the size and shape of a man's doubled fist, rendering it useless for breathing. His lips are unnaturally thick and perpetually cracked. His lower jaw is seriously malformed and his teeth long since removed. Talking has become increasingly difficult for him. His hair was still dark, although the scalp's surface area had tripled, giving the impression of mange.

But these deformities alone did not make Rand Holstrum the successful freak that he is today. While the left half of his face is a hideously contorted mass of bone and gristle, like a papier-mâché mask made by a disturbed child, the other half is that of a handsome, intelligent man in his late fifties. *That* is what draws the fish. He is one of the most disturbing sights you could ever hope to see.

Had his disease been total, Rand Holstrum would have been just another sideshow performer. But due to the Janus-nature of his affliction, he's become one of the few remaining "celebrity" freaks in a day and age of jaded thrill seekers and Special People.

When I heard Fallon's carny had pulled into town I grabbed my camera and took the day off. The fairground was little more than a cow pasture dotted with aluminum outbuildings that served as exhibition halls. Everything smelled of fresh hay, stale straw, and manure. I was excited the moment I got out of my car.

The AirStream trailers that housed the carnies were located a few hundred feet beyond the faltering neon and grinding machinery of the midway. The rides were silent, their armature folded inward like giant metal birds with their heads tucked under their wings. I recognized Fallon's trailer by the faded Four Star Midways logo on its side.

As I stepped onto the cinderblock that served as the trailer's front stoop the door flew open, knocking me to the ground. An old man dressed in a polyester suit the color of cranberries flew from the interior of the trailer, landing a few feet from where I was sprawled.

"Gawddamn fuckin' *pre-vert*!" Anger and liquor slurred Fallon's voice. "I don't wanna see your face *again*, unnerstand? Go and peddle your monsters somewheres else!"

The old man picked himself up with overstated dignity, dusting his pants with liver-spotted hands. His chin quivered and his lips were compressed into a bloodless line. His dime-store salt-and-pepper toupee slid away from his forehead.

"You'll be sorry 'bout this, Fallon! How much longer you reckon Holstrum'll be around? Once your meal ticket's gone, you'll be coming 'round beggin' for ole Cabrini's help!"

"Not fuckin' likely! Now git 'fore I call the roustabouts!"

The old man looked mad enough to bite the head off a live chicken. He pretended to ignore me, walking in the opposite direction with a peculiar, storklike gait, his knobby hands fisted in his pockets.

"What the hell? . . ." I checked to make sure my light meter had survived the spill.

"Sorry 'bout all that, son. Didn't realize you was on the outside." Fallon stood over me, one scarred hand outstretched to help me up. He was still in his undershirt and baggy khakis, his usual off-hours uniform.

Fallon was in his late fifties but looked older. Thirty-five years in the carnival will do it to you. Especially the kind of work Fallon specialized in. For years he had been a pincushion; running skewers through his own flesh for the amusement of others. The marks of his trade could be glimpsed in the loose skin of his forearms, the flabby wattle of his neck, the webbing between thumb and forefinger, the underside of his tongue, and the cartilage of his ears. His face was long boned and heavily creased about the eyes and mouth, the cheeks marked by the hectic ivy blotches of broken blood vessels. As a younger man his hair had been the color of copper, but the years had leeched away its vitality, leaving it a pale orange. With his bulbous nose and knotty ridge of brow, Fallon would never be mistaken for handsome, but his was the kind of face the camera loves.

Fallon's mouth creases deepened. "Come on inside. I'll tell you all about it."

The interior of Fallon's trailer was a cramped jumble of old papers, dirty laundry, and rumpled bed linen. I sat down on the chair wedged beside the fold-down kitchen table while Fallon busied himself with finding two clean jelly glasses.

"I reckon you'd like to know what that hoo-ha was all about." He tried to sound nonchalant. If I hadn't known him better, I would have been taken in. "Seeing how's you got knocked ass over teakettle, can't says I blames you." He set a jelly glass in front of me and poured a liberal dose of whiskey. Even though it was well after three in the afternoon, it was breakfast time for Fallon. "What you just saw was none other than Harry Cabrini, one of th' sleaziest items found in the business, which is, believe me, sayin' something!" Fallon drained his glass with a sharp flex of the elbow.

"Who is this Cabrini? What does he do?"

Fallon hissed under his breath and poured another slug into his glass. "He sells freaks."

"Huh?" I put my whiskey down untouched. "What do you mean by 'sells'?"

"Exactly what I meant." Fallon was leaning against the kitchen counter, arms folded. He was almost hugging himself. "How d'ya think they find their way into th' business? They drive out on their own when they hear a circus is in town? Well, some do. But most freaks don't have much say 'bout where they end up. Most get sold by their folks. That's how Smidgen got into show biz. Hasn't seen his folks since Eisenhower was in office. Sometimes they get sold by the doctors that was lookin' after 'em. That's how Rand got into it. Before he was th' World's Ugliest Man, he was laid up in some gawdforsaken V.A. hospital. Then this intern heard about me lookin' for a good headliner and arranged it so's I could meet Rand. I paid him a good hunk'a change for the privilege. Haven't regretted it since. I'm sure he didn't think of it as 'selling.' More like being a talent scout, I reckon."

"And you've—bought—freaks?"

"Don't make it sound like slavery, boy! It's more like payin' a finder's fee. I give my folks decent wages and they're free to come an' go as they see fit! The slave days are long gone. But Cabrini . . . Cabrini is a whole other kettle of fish." Fallon looked as if he'd bitten into a lemon. "Cabrini ain't no agent. He's a slaver . . . at least, that's *my* opinion. Maybe I'm wrong. But the freaks Cabrini comes up with . . . there's something *wrong* about 'em. Most of 'em are feebleminded. Or worse. I made the mistake of buyin' a pickled punk offa him a few years back, and he's been hounding me ever since. Wants me to buy one'a his live 'uns! Buyin trouble is more like it! Here, look and see for yourself if I ain't right." Fallon leaned over and plucked a color Polaroid snapshot out of the tangle of dirty clothes and contracts. "He left one of his damn pictures behind." He handed it to me without looking at the photo.

I could understand why. In all the years I'd spent photographing flesh malformed by genetics and disease, nothing had prepared me for the wretched creature trapped inside the picture. The naked, fishbelly-white freak looked more like a skinned, mutant ape than anything born from the coupling of man and woman. Its hairless, undeveloped pudendum marked the unfinished thing as a child.

"Where'd he come up with a freak that young?" Fallon's whisper was tight and throaty. "Most of 'em that age, nowadays, are either in state homes or special schools. Where's its mama? And how come he's got more than one of 'em?"

I dropped in on Rand after leaving Fallon's trailer. I always visit Rand Holstrum when I have a chance. I never know when I might have another opportunity to photograph him. Rand isn't as young as he used to be, and his ailment is a temperamental one. He's been told he could die without any warning. Despite the doctors' prognosis, he remains as cheerful and life-affirming as ever.

I have dozens of photographs of Rand. They hold a weird fascination for me. By looking at them in sequence, I can trace the ravages of his disease. It is as if Rand is a living canvas, a quintessential work in progress.

Rand was in the freaktent, getting ready for that evening's show. He was still in his smoking jacket, a present from his daughter. His wife Sally was with him.

Rand extended a hand in greeting. It was a purely symbolic gesture. The acromegaly had spread there as well, twisting his knuckles until his hands were little more than flesh-and-blood catcher's mitts.

"You remember the wife, don't you?" he gasped.

Sally Holstrum was decent looking, as carny wives go. She nodded at me while she hammered up the chicken-wire screen that protected Rand from the crowd while he was on display. The fish get pretty rowdy at times, and a well-placed beer bottle could prove fatal to her husband.

Rand fished out his wallet, producing a couple of thumb-smudged prints for me to admire. Randy, the Holstrums' son, was dressed in a cap and gown, a diploma clutched in one hand. June, Rand's favorite, stood next to her husband, a toddler in her arms. "Randy's a dentist now . . . Got a practice in . . . Sheboygan . . . Little Dee-Dee can say . . . her ABCs . . ." Rand slurped.

"Time flies," I agreed. "Oh, I happened to run into some guy named Harry Cabrini today . . ."

Sally stopped what she was doing and turned to look at me. "Cabrini's here?"

"He *was* here. Fallon threw him out of his office. I don't know if he's still around or not . . ."

"He *better* not be!" she spat, wagging the claw hammer for emphasis. "If I find that slimeball skulkin' round this tent again, I'll show 'im where monkeys put bad nuts!"

"Now, Sally . . ."

"Don't you 'now Sally' me, Rand Holstrum! The trouble with you is that you're too damn nice! Even to people who don't deserve more'n what you'd give a dog on the street!"

Rand fell silent. He knew better than to argue with Sally.

"You know what I caught that crazy motherfucker doin'?" She resumed her hammering with vigor. "I came back from the Burger King and found that nutcase taking *measurements* of Rand's face!"

"It was . . . nothing . . . I've been measured before, Sal—"

"Yeah, by *doctors*. What business does some screwball like Harry Cabrini have doing shit like that?"

Rand shrugged and his good eye winked at me. Just then one of the roustabouts came into the tent with a take-out sack from one of the local burger joints. The grease from the fast food had already turned the paper bag translucent. "Got yer food, Mr. Holstrum." Rand paid off the roustabout while Sally got out the food processor.

"Go change your clothes, honey. You don't want to get that nice smoker June gave you dirty," Sally said as she dropped the cheeseburgers one by one into the hopper. Rand grunted in agreement and shuffled off to change.

The malformation of his jaw and the loss of his teeth has made chewing a thing of the past for Rand. Everything he eats has to be liquified.

"Uh, I'll see y'all later, Sal . . ."

"Sure, hon. Let me know if you see that Cabrini creep hangin' around."

"Sure thing."

I left just as the stainless steel rotary knives whirred to life, mulching the half-dozen cheeseburgers into a protein-rich soup.

I lied to Sally. I didn't mean to, but I ended up doing it anyway.

Twilight arrived at the carnival, and with it, life. The cheesy rides and midway attractions took on a magical aura once the sky darkened from cobalt to indigo and the neon was switched on. The rubes came to gawk and be parted from their hard-earned cash. The air was redolent of cotton candy, corndogs, snow cones, diesel fumes, and vomit. Taped music blared from World War II surplus public-address systems. The motors propelling the death-trap rides roared like captive animals and rattled their chains, yearning to break free.

The exhilarated shriek-laugh of the carnivalgoer echoed from every mouth. I began to feel the same excitement I'd known as a kid. The sights, sounds, and smells of the carnival sparked a surge of nostalgia for days that seemed simpler compared to the life I lived now.

I passed a gaggle of school kids gathered near the Topsy Turvy. They were searching the sawdust for loose change shaken from the pockets of the passengers, although they risked retribution at the hands of the roustabouts and being puked on by the riders. I smiled, remembering how I used to scuttle in the sawdust in search of nickels and dimes.

That's when I saw him.

He was weaving in and out of the crowd like a wading bird searching for minnows. His hands were jammed into his pockets. His toupee slid about on his head like a fried egg on a plate. His suit was a size too big for him, and all that kept him from losing his pants was a wide white patent leather belt. He had loafers to match.

I hesitated a moment, uncertain as to what I should do. He was headed for the parking lot. I wavered. The image of the twisted freak-child rose before my eyes and I followed him.

Cabrini got into a secondhand panel truck that had once belonged to a baked goods chain. The faded outline of a smiling, apple-cheeked little girl with blonde ringlets devouring a slab of white bread slathered in butter could still be glimpsed on the side of the van. It was easy enough to follow Cabrini from the fairground to a decrepit trailer park twenty miles away.

He lived in a fairly large mobile home set in a lot full of chickweed and rotting newspapers. Uncertain as to what I should do, I opted for the direct approach. I knocked on the trailer's door frame.

There was scurrying inside, then the sound of something being knocked over. "Who the fuck is it?"

"Mr. Cabrini? Mr. Harry Cabrini?"

"Yeah, I'm Cabrini—what's it t'ya?"

"Mr. Cabrini, my name is Kevin Malone. I was told by a Mr. Fallon that you had . . . something of interest to me." Silence. "Mr. Cabrini?"

The door opened the length of its safety chain. Cabrini's face, up close, was as storklike as his movements. His nose was a great stabbing beak overshadowing his thin-lipped mouth and flat cheekbones. The store-bought toupee was gone, revealing a smooth, liver-blotched scalp and a graying fringe ruff level with his ears. Cabrini stared at me, then at the camera slung around my neck. He grunted, more to himself than for my benefit, then shut the door. A moment later I heard him fumbling with the chain and the door jerked open. The toupee was back— still slightly askew—and Cabrini motioned me inside.

"C'mon, dammit. No point in lettin' every dam skeeter in the county in with you."

The interior of the trailer was hardly what I'd expected. The front section normally reserved for the living room and kitchen area had been stripped of all furnishings except for the refrigerator and stove. Gone was the built-in wet bar, pressboard room divider, imitation oak paneling, and wall-to-wall shag carpeting. In their place was a small formica table, a couple of Salvation Army–issue kitchen chairs, and one of the best-equipped workbenches I've ever seen. The rest was a labyrinth of lumber, varying from new two-by-fours to piles of sawdust. I noticed a spartan army cot in the corner next to a mound of polyester clothes.

"Yer that fella what takes pictures of freaks," he said flatly. "Flippo the Seal-Boy tol' me 'bout you."

"And Fallon told me about you."

Cabrini's spine stiffened. "Yeah? Well, what d'ya want? I ain't got all night . . ."

I reached into my jacket and withdrew the Polaroid he'd left at Fallon's trailer. "A picture. Just one. I'll pay you." It made me sick to speak to him, but I found myself saying the words nonetheless. I knew from the moment I saw its picture that I had to add it to my collection.

He looked into my eyes and it was like being sized up by a snake. He smiled then, and it was all I could do to keep from smashing his stork face into pulp.

"Okay. Hunnert bucks. Otherwise you walk."

My bank balance reeled at the blow, but I fished two fifties out of my wallet. Cabrini palmed them with the ease of a conjurer and motioned for me to follow him down the narrow hallway that led to the back of the trailer.

There were two bedrooms and a bathroom connected by the corridor. I glanced into what would have been the master bedroom and saw four or five small crates stacked in the darkness. Cabrini quickly closed the door, indicating that the second, smaller bedroom was what I wanted.

The room stank of human waste and rotten food. I fought to keep from gagging on the stench. Cabrini shrugged. "What can I do? They're morons. Jest like animals. Don't clean up after themselves. Don't talk. Shit whenever and wherever th' mood strikes 'em."

There were three of them. Two girls and a boy. They sat huddled together on a stained bare mattress on the filthy floor. Their deformities were strikingly similar: humped backs, twisted arms, bowed legs, warped rib cages resting atop their pelvises. Their fingers curled in on themselves, like those of an ape. They were pallid, with eyes so far recessed into their orbits as to resemble blind, cave-dwelling creatures. Their features were those of a wax doll held too close to an open flame. Their hair was filthy and matted with their own waste.

The odd thing was that their limbs, albeit contorted into unnatural angles, were of normal proportions. The stunted children looked like natives of some bizarre heavy-gravity planet, their torsos compressed into half the space necessary for normal growth.

But what truly shocked me was the look of animal fear on their ruined faces. I remember Slotzi the Pinhead; despite her severe imbecility, she enjoyed singing and dancing and was affectionate and curious in a disarmingly childlike way. She was locked into an eternal childhood, her mental development arrested somewhere between three and five years of age. Compared to Cabrini's trio of freak-babies, Slotzi was Nobel prize material. One thing was certain; these monstrously distorted children had never laughed, nor had they known any joy or love in their brief lives. Without really thinking of what I was doing, I adjusted the focus and checked the light. And then I had my picture.

Cabrini closed the door, propelling me back into the hall. I stared at him, trying to make sense of what I had seen.

"Those children . . . are they related?"

Cabrini shook his head, nearly sending his toupee into his face. "Drugs."

"Drugs?"

Cabrini's voice took on the singsong of a barker reciting his spiel. "LSD. Speed. Heroin. Crack. Who knows? Maybe an experimental drug like that thalidomide back in the sixties. They were all born within the same year. Ended up in a home. Until I found them."

We were back in the front room, amongst the lumber and sawdust. Cabrini was looking at me, an unpleasant smile twisting his lips. Averting my eyes, I found myself staring at a pile of papers scattered across the workbench. Amongst them were several detailed sketches of Rand Holstrum's face.

Cabrini brought out a plastic milk jug full of homemade popskull and placed a pair of Dixie cups on the workbench.

"Don't get too many visitors out this way. Reckon you deserve a free drink for yer hunnert bucks." White lightning sloshed into the cups and onto the bench. I half-expected it to eat into the wood, hissing like acid.

As much as I loathed Cabrini and all he represented, I found him perversely intriguing. For fifteen years I'd actively pursued knowledge concerning the secret lives of freaks. I'd listened to stories told by men with too many limbs, women with beards, and creatures that walked the blurred borders of gender. I'd talked shop with people who make their living displaying their difference to the curious for a dollar a head. I was aware that by the end of the century their way of life would be extinct and no one would know their story. Harry Cabrini—seller of freak-babies—comprised an important, if unsavory, portion of that history.

"Y'know, I've run across quite a few of yer kind in this business. Fellers who take pictures."

"Izzat so?" I sipped at the deceptively clear fluid in the paper cup. It scalded my throat on the way down.

"Yeah. Some were doctors or newspaper men. Others were arteests." He smirked. "They was like you. Thought I was dirt, but still paid me for the honor of lookin' at my babies! Y'all treat me like I ain't no more than some kinda brothelkeeper. But what does that make *you*, Mr. Arteest?" He tossed back his head to laugh, nearly dislodging his toupee.

"Where did you find those children?"

He stopped laughing, his eyes sharp and dangerous. "None of yer fuckin' business. All you wants is pictures of freaks. Why you wanna know where they come from? They come from normal, God-fearin' folk. Like they all do. Just like you 'n me." He poured himself a second shot of squeeze. I wondered what Cabrini's guts must look like. "The freak business is dyin' out, y'know. Been dyin' since the war." Cabrini's voice became nostalgic. "People learned more 'bout what makes freaks for real. Used t'think they was th' sins of the parents made flesh. That they didn't have no souls cause of it. That they weren't like real people. Hell, now that there March of Dimes has got rid of most that what used to reel th' fish in. Don't get me wrong. There'll always be people who's willin' to look. I think it makes 'em feel good. No matter how fuckin' awful things might be, at least you can walk down th' street without makin' people sick, right? But who wants to pay an' see dwarfs? Midgets? Fat ladies? Pinheads? Sure they're gross, but you can see 'em for free at th' Wal-Mart any ol' day of the week! No, you gotta have something that really *scares* 'em! Shocks 'em! Repulses 'em! Something that makes 'em forget they're lookin' at another human! Tall order, ain't it?"

"Uh, yeah."

"I got to readin' one time about these here guys back in Europe. During what they called the Dark Ages. These guys was called Freak Masters. Nice ring to it, huh? Anyways, these Freak Masters, when times were tough an' there weren't no good freaks around, they'd kidnap babies . . ."

Something inside me went cold. Cabrini was standing right next to me, but I felt as if I were light-years away.

" . . . and they'd put 'em in these here special cages, so that they'd grow up all twisted like. And they'd make 'em wear these special masks so their faces would grow a certain way, what with baby meat being so soft, y'know . . ."

Images of children twisted into tortured, abstract forms like human bonsai trees swam before my eyes. I recognized the expanding bubble in my rib cage as fear. Adrenaline surged through me, its primal message telling me to get the fuck *outta* there. My gaze flickered across the jumble on the workbench. Foul as he was, Cabrini was a genius when it came to working with his hands. I saw the partially completed leather mask nestled amidst the sketches and diagrams; it was a near-exact duplicate of Rand Holstrum's face. Only it was so small. Far too small for an adult to wear . . .

" . . . they fed 'em gruel and never talked to 'em, so they came out kinda brain-damaged, those that di'nt die. But the kings an' popes an' shit back then di'nt care. They bought freaks by the truckloads! Pet monsters!" Cabrini laughed again. He was drinking straight from the jug now. "They didn't have freaktents back then. But it don't matter. There's always been freaktents. We carry 'em with us wherever we go." He tapped his temple with one unsteady finger. The toupee fell off and landed on the floor; it lay amidst the sawdust and scraps of leather like a dead tarantula.

That's when he lunged, scything the air with one of the leather-cutting tools he'd snatched from the workbench. There was something feral in his eyes and the show of yellowed teeth. The stork had become a wild dog. I staggered backward, barking my shins on a pile of two-by-fours. I'd just missed having the hooked blade sink into my chest.

Cursing incoherently, Cabrini followed me. The knife sliced within millimeters of my nose. I heard the muffled, anguished cries of the idiot children coming from the other room as I threw the contents of my cup into Cabrini's face. He screamed and let go of his knife, clawing at his eyes. Cabrini reeled backward, knocking over the kitchen table in his blind flailing. I headed for the door, not daring to look back.

I could still hear Cabrini screaming long after I'd made my escape. "Damn you! Goddamn you, you fuckin' lousy *freak!*"

JOHN CROWLEY
Missolonghi 1824

I can make no bones about the fact that John Crowley is a writer who simply takes my breath away with his use of language, and with a clarity of vision akin to that of a fine painter. I believe him to be one of the important writers of our time. He is the author of *The Deep; Beasts; Engine Summer; Little, Big; Aegypt;* and a recent collection of short fiction, *Novelty*. Crowley and his wife and children live in the Berkshire Mountains of western Massachusetts.

"Missolonghi 1824" is an evocative 19th century fantasy set in Missolonghi, Greece. It comes from the March issue of *Isaac Asimov's*.

—T.W.

Missolonghi 1824

JOHN CROWLEY

The English milord took his hands from the boy's shoulders, discomfited but unembarrassed. "No?" he said. "No. Very well, I see, I see; you must forgive me then . . ."

The boy, desperate not to have offended the Englishman, clutched at the milord's tartan cloak and spoke in a rush of Romaic, shaking his head and near tears.

"No, no, my dear," the milord said. "It's not at all your fault; you have swept me into an impropriety. I misunderstood your kindness, that is all, and it is you who must forgive me."

He went, with his odd off-kilter and halting walk, to his couch, and reclined there. The boy stood erect in the middle of the room, and (switching to Italian) began a long speech about his deep love and respect for the noble lord, who was as dear as life itself to him. The noble lord watched him in wonder, smiling. Then he held out a hand to him: "Oh, no more, no more. You see it is just such sentiments as those that misled me. Really, I swear to you, I misunderstood and it shan't happen again. Only you mustn't stand there preaching at me, don't; come sit by me at least. Come."

The boy, knowing that a dignified coldness was often the safest demeanor to adopt when offers like the milord's were made to him, came and stood beside his employer, hands behind his back.

"Well," the milord said, himself adopting a more serious mien, "I'll tell you what. If you will not stand there like a stick, if you will put back on your usual face—sit, won't you?—then . . . then what shall I do? I shall tell you a story."

Immediately the boy melted. He sat, or squatted, near his master—not on the couch, but on a rag of carpet on the floor near it. "A story," he said. "A story of what, of what?"

"Of what, of what," said the Englishman. He felt the familiar night pains beginning within, everywhere and nowhere. "If you will just trim the lamp," he said, "and open a jar of that Hollands gin there, and pour me a cup with some *limonata*, and then put a stick on the fire—then we will have 'of what, of what.' "

The small compound was dark now, though not quiet; in the courtyard could still be heard the snort and stamp of horses arriving, the talk of his Suliote soldiers and the petitioners and hangers-on around the cookfires there, talk that could turn to insults, quarrels, riot, or dissolve in laughter. Insofar as he could, the noble foreign lord on whom all of them depended had banished them from this room: here, he had his couch, and the table where he wrote—masses of correspondence, on gold-edged crested paper to impress, or on plain paper to explain (endless the explanations, the cajolings, the reconcilings these Greeks demanded of him); and another pile of papers, messy large sheets much marked over, stanzas of a poem it had lately been hard for him to remember he was writing. Also on the table amid the papers, not so incongruous as they would once have struck him, were a gilt dress-sword, a fantastical crested helmet in the Grecian style, and a Manton's pistol.

He sipped the gin the boy had brought him, and said: "Very well. A story." The boy knelt again on his carpet, dark eyes turned up, eager as a hound: and the poet saw in his face that hunger for tales (what boy his age in England would show it, what public-school boy or even carter's or ploughman's lad would show it?), the same eagerness that must have been in the faces gathered around the fire by which Homer spoke. He felt almost abashed by the boy's open face: he could tell him anything, and he believed.

"Now this would have happened," he said, "I should think, in the year of your birth, or very near; and it happened not a great distance from this place, down in the Morea, in a district that was once called, by your own ancestors a long time ago, Arcadia."

"Arcadia," the boy said in Romaic.

"Yes. You've been there?"

He shook his head.

"Wild and strange it was to me then. I was very young, not so many years older than you are now, hard as it may be for you to imagine I was ever so. I was traveling, traveling because—well, I knew not why; for the sake of traveling, really, though that was hard to explain to the Turks, who do not travel for pleasure, you know, only for gain. I did discover why I traveled, though: that's part of this story. And a part of the story of how I come to be here in this wretched marsh, with you, telling you of it.

"You see, in England, where the people are chiefly hypocrites, and thus easily scandalized, the offer that I just foolishly made to you, my dear, should it have become public knowledge, would have got both us, but chiefly me, in a deal of very hot water. When I was young there was a fellow hanged for doing such things, or rather for being caught at it. Our vices are whoring and drink, you see; other vices are sternly punished.

"And yet it was not that which drove me abroad; nor was it the ladies either —that would come later. No—I think it was the weather, above all." He tugged the tartan more closely around him. "Now, this winter damp; this rain today, every day this week; these fogs. Imagine if they never stopped: summer and winter, the same, except that in winter it is . . . well, how am I to explain an English winter to you? I shall not try.

"As soon as I set foot on these shores, I knew I had come home. I was no citizen of England gone abroad. No: this was my land, my clime, my air. I went upon Hymettus and heard the bees. I climbed to the Acropolis (which Lord Elgin was just conspiring to despoil; he wanted to bring the statues to England, to teach the English sculpture—the English being as capable of sculpture as you, my dear, are of skating). I stood within the grove sacred to Apollo at Claros: except there is no grove there now, it is nothing but dust. You, Loukas, and your fathers have cut down all the trees, and burned them, out of spite or for firewood I know not. I stood in the blowing dust and sun, and I thought: *I am come two thousand years too late.*

"That was the sadness that haunted my happiness, you see. I did not despise the living Greeks, as so many of my countrymen did, and think them degenerate, and deserving their Turkish masters. No, I rejoiced in them, girls and boys, Albanians and Suliotes and Athenians. I loved Athens and the narrow squalid streets and the markets. I took exception to nothing. And yet . . . I wanted so much not to have *missed* it, and was so aware that I had. Homer's Greece; Pindar's; Sappho's. Yes, my young friend: you know soldiers and thieves with those names; I speak of others.

"I wintered in Athens. When summer came, I mounted an expedition into the Morea. I had with me my valet Fletcher, whom you know—still with me here; and my two Albanian servants, very fierce and greedy and loyal, drinking skinfuls of Zean wine at eight paras the oke every day. And there was my new Greek friend Nikos, who is your predecessor, Loukas, your *type* I might say, the original of all of you that I have loved: only the difference was, he loved me too.

"You know you can see the mountains into which we went from these windows, yes, on a clear cloudless day such as we have not seen now these many weeks; those mountains to the south across the bay, that look so bare and severe. The tops of them *are* bare, most of them; but down in the vales there are still bits of the ancient forests, and in the chasms where the underground rivers pour out. There are woods and pasture: yes, sheep and shepherds too in Arcady.

"That is Pan's country, you know—or perhaps you don't; sometimes I credit you Greeks with a knowledge that ought to have come down with your blood, but has not. Pan's country: where he was born, where he still lives. The old poets spoke of his hour as noon, when he sleeps upon the hills; when even if you did not see the god face to face—woe to you if you did—you could hear his voice, or the sound of his pipes: a sorrowful music, for he is a sad god at heart, and mourns for his lost love Echo."

The poet ceased to speak for a long moment. He remembered that music, heard in the blaze of the Arcadian sun, music not different from the hot nameless drone of noontide itself, compounded of insects, exhalation of the trees, the heated blood rushing in his head. Yet it was a song too, potent and vivifying—and sad, infinitely sad: that even a god could mistake the reflection of his own voice for love's.

There were other gods in those mountains besides great Pan, or had been once; the little party of travelers would pass through groves or near pools, where little stelae had been set up in another age, canted over now and pitted and mossy, or broken and worn away, but whose figures could sometimes still be read: crude nymphs, half-figures of squat horned bearded men with great phalluses, broken or whole. The Orthodox in their party crossed themselves passing these, the Mussulmen looked away or pointed and laughed.

"The little gods of woodland places," the poet said. "The gods of hunters and fishermen. It reminded me of my own home country of Scotland, and how the men and women still believe in pixies and kelpies, and leave food for them, or signs to placate them. It was very like that.

"And I doubt not those old Scotsmen have their reasons for acting as they do, as good reasons as the Greeks had. And have still—whereby hangs this tale."

He drank again (more than this cupful would be needed to get him through the night) and laid a careful hand on Loukas's dark curls. "It was in such a glen that one night we made our camp. So long did the Albanians dance and sing around the fire—'When we were thieves at Targa,' and I'm sure they were—and so sympathetic did I find the spot, that by noon next day we were still at ease there.

"Noon. Pan's song. But we became aware of other sounds as well, human sounds, a horn blown, thrashings and crashings in the glen beyond our camp. Then figures: villagers, armed with rakes and staves and one old man with a fowling-piece.

"A hunt of some sort was up, though what game could have been in these mountains large enough to attract such a crowd I could not imagine; it was hard to believe that many boar or deer could get a living here, and there was uproar enough among these villagers that they might have been after a tiger.

"We joined the chase for a time, trying to see what was afoot. A cry arose down where the forest was thickest, and for an instant I did see some beast ahead of the pack, crashing in the undergrowth, and heard an animal's cry—then no more. Nikos had no taste for pursuit in the heat of the day, and the hunt straggled on out of our ken.

"Toward evening we reached the village itself, over a mountain and a pass: a cluster of houses, a monastery on the scarp above where monks starved themselves, a *taberna* and a church. There was much excitement; men strutted with their weapons in the street. Apparently their hunt had been successful, but it was not easy to determine what they had caught. I spoke but little Romaic then; the Albanians knew none. Nikos, who could speak Italian and some English, held these mountain people in contempt, and soon grew bored with the work of translating. But gradually I conceived the idea that what they had hunted through the groves and glens was not an animal at all but a man—some poor madman, apparently, some wild man of the woods hunted down for sport. He was being kept caged outside the town, it seemed, awaiting the judgment of some village headman.

"I was well aware of the bigotries of people such as these villagers were; of Greeks in general, and of their Turkish masters too if it come to that. Whoever started their fear or incurred their displeasure, it would go hard with them. That winter in Athens I had interceded for a woman condemned to death by the Turkish authorities, she having been caught in illicit love. Not with me: with me she was not caught. Nonetheless I took it upon myself to rescue her, which with much bluster and a certain quantity of silver I accomplished. I thought perhaps I could help the poor wretch these people had taken. I cannot bear to see even a wild beast in a cage.

"No one welcomed my intervention. The village headman did not want to see me. The villagers fled from my Albanians, the loudest strutters fleeing first. When at last I found a priest I could get some sense from, he told me I was much mistaken and should not interfere. He was tremendously excited, and spoke of rape, not one but many, or the possibility of them anyway, now thank Christ avoided. But I could not credit what he seemed to say: that the captive was not a madman at all but a man of the woods, one who had never lived among men. Nikos translated what the priest said: 'He speaks, but no one understands him.'

"Now I was even more fascinated. I thought perhaps this might be one of the Wild Boys one hears of now and then, abandoned to die and raised by wolves; not a thing one normally credits, and yet . . . There was something in the air of the village, the wild distraction of the priest—compounded of fear and triumph —that kept me from inquiring further. I would bide my time.

"As darkness came on the people of the village seemed to be readying themselves for some further brutishness. Pine torches had been lit, leading the way to the dell where the captive was being held. It seemed possible that they planned to burn the fellow alive: any such idea as that of course I must prevent, and quickly.

"Like Machiavel, I chose a combination of force and suasion as best suited to accomplishing my purpose. I stood the men of the village to a quantity of drink at the *taberna*, and I posted my armed Albanians on the path out to the little dell where the captive was. Then I went in peace to see for myself.

"In the flare of the torches I could see the cage, green poles lashed together. I crept slowly to it, not wanting whoever was within to raise an alarm. I felt my heart beat fast, without knowing why it should. As I came close, a dark hand was put out, and took hold of a bar. Something in this hand's action—I cannot say what—was not the action of a man's hand, but of a beast's; what beast, though?

"What reached me next was the smell, a nose-filling rankness that I have never smelled again but would know in a moment. There was something of hurt and fear in it, the smell of an animal that has been wounded and soiled itself; but there was a life history in it too, a ferocious filthiness, something untrammeled and uncaring—well, it's quite impossible, the language has too few words for smells, potent though they be. Now I knew that what was in the cage was not a man; only a furbearer could retain so much odor. And yet: *He speaks*, the priest had said, *and no one understands him.*

"I looked within the cage. I could see nothing at first, though I could hear a labored breath, and felt a poised stillness, the tension of a creature waiting for attack. Then he blinked, and I saw his eyes turned on me.

"You know the eyes of your ancestors, Loukas, the eyes pictured on vases and on the ancientest of statues: those enormous almond-shaped eyes, outlined in black, black-pupiled too, and staring, overflowing with some life other than this world's. Those were his eyes, Greek eyes that no Greek ever had; white at the long corners, with great onyx centers.

"He blinked again, and moved within his cage—his captors had made it too small to stand in, and he must have suffered dreadfully in it—and drew up his legs. He struggled to get some ease, and one foot slid out between the bars below, and nearly touched my knee where I knelt in the dust. And I knew then why it was that he spoke but was not understood."

At first he had thought there must be more than one animal confined in the little cage, his mind unwilling to add together the reaching, twitching foot with its lean shin extended between the bars and the great-eyed hard-breathing personage inside. Cloven: that foot the Christians took from Pan and Pan's sons to give to their Devil. The poet had always taken his own clubbed foot as a sort of sign of his kinship with that race—which, however, along with the rest of modern mankind, he had still supposed to be merely fancies. They were not: not this one, stinking, breathing, waiting for words.

"Now I knew why my heart beat hard. I thought it astonishing but very likely that I alone, of all these Greeks about me here, I alone perhaps of all the mortals in Arcadia that night, knew the language this creature might know: for I had been made to study it, you see, forced with blows and implorings and bribes to learn it through many long years at Harrow. Was that fate? Had our father-god brought me here this night to do this child of his some good?

"I put my face close to the bars of the cage. I was afraid for a moment that all those thousands of lines learned by heart had fled from me. The only one I could think of was not so very appropriate. *Sing, Muse*, I said, *that man of many resources, who traveled far and wide . . .* and his eyes shone. I was right: he spoke the Greek of Homer, and not of these men of the iron age.

"Now what was I to say? He still lay quiet within the cage, but for the one hand gripping the bars, waiting for more. I realized he must be wounded—it seemed obvious that unless he were wounded he could not have been taken. I knew but one thing: I would not willingly be parted from him. I could have remained in his presence nightlong, forever. I sought his white almond eyes in the darkness and I thought: *I have not missed it after all: it awaited me here to find.*

"I would not have all night, though. My Albanians now discharged their weapons—the warning we'd agreed on—and I heard shouts; the men of the village, now suitably inflamed, were headed for this place. I took from my pocket a penknife—all I had—and set to work on the tough hemp of the cage's ropes.

"*Atrema*, I said, *atrema, atrema*—which I remembered was 'quietly, quietly.' He made no sound or movement as I cut, but when I took hold of a bar with my left hand to steady myself, he put out his long black-nailed hand and grasped my wrist. Not in anger, but not tenderly; strongly, purposefully. The hair rose on my neck. He did not release me until the ropes were cut and I tugged apart the bars.

"The moon had risen, and he came forth into its light. He was no taller than a boy of eight, and yet how he drew the night to him, as though it were a thing with a piece missing until he stepped out into it, and now was whole. I could see that indeed he had been hurt: stripes of blood ran round his bare chest where he had fallen or rolled down a steep declivity. I could see the ridged recurving horns that rose from the matted hair of his head; I could see his sex, big, held up against his belly by a fold of fur, like a dog's or a goat's. Alert, still breathing hard (his breast fluttering, as though the heart within him were huge) he glanced about himself, assessing which way were best to run.

"*Now go*, I said to him. *Live. Take care they do not come near you again. Hide from them when you must; despoil them when you can. Seize on their wives and daughters, piss in their vegetable gardens, tear down their fences, drive mad their sheep and goats. Teach them fear. Never never let them take you again.*

"I say I said this to him, but I confess I could not think of half the words; my Greek had fled me. No matter: he turned his great hot eyes on me as though he understood. What he said back to me I cannot tell you, though he spoke, and smiled; he spoke in a warm winey voice, but a few words, round and sweet. That was a surprise. Perhaps it was from Pan he had his music. I can tell you I have tried to bring those words up often from where I know they are lodged, in my heart of hearts; I think that it is really what I am about when I try to write poems. And now and again—yes, not often, but sometimes—I hear them again.

"He dropped to his hands, then, somewhat as an ape does; he turned and fled, and the tuft of his tail flashed once, like a hare's. At the end of the glen he turned—I could just see him at the edge of the trees—and looked at me. And that was all.

"I sat in the dust there, sweating in the night air. I remember thinking the striking thing about it was how *unpoetical* it had been. It was like no story about a meeting between a man and a god—or a godlet—that I had ever heard. No gift was given me, no promise made me. It was like freeing an otter from a fish trap. And that, most strangely, was what gave me joy in it. The difference, child, between the true gods and the imaginary ones is this: that the true gods are not less real than yourself."

It was deep midnight now in the villa; the tide was out, and rain had begun again to fall, spattering on the roof tiles, hissing in the fire.

It wasn't true, what he had told the boy: that he had been given no gift, made no promise. For it was only after Greece that he came to possess the quality for which, besides his knack for verse, he was chiefly famous: his gift (not always an easy one to live with) for attracting love from many different kinds and conditions of people. He had accepted the love that he attracted, and sought more, and had that too. *Satyr* he had been called, often enough. He thought, when he gave it any thought, that it had come to him through the grip of the horned one: a part of that being's own power of unrefusable ravishment.

Well, if that were so, then he had the gift no more: had used it up, spent it, worn it out. He was thirty-six, and looked and felt far older: sick and lame, his puffy features grey and haggard, his moustache white—foolish to think he could have been the object of Loukas's affection.

But without love, without its wild possibility, he could no longer defend himself against the void: against his black certainty that life mattered not a whit, was a brief compendium of folly and suffering, not worth the stakes. He would not take life on those terms; no, he would trade it for something more valuable . . . for Greece. Freedom. He would like to have given his life heroically, but even the ignoble death he seemed likely now to suffer here, in this mephitic swamp, even that was worth something: was owed, anyway, to the clime that made him a poet: to the blessing he had had.

"I have heard of no reports of such a creature in those mountains since that time," he said. "You know, I think the little gods are the oldest gods, older than the Olympians, older far than Jehovah. Pan forbid he should be dead, if he be the last of his kind . . ."

The firing of Suliote guns outside the villa woke him. He lifted his head painfully from the sweat-damp pillow. He put out his hand and thought for a moment his Newfoundland dog Lion lay at his feet. It was the boy Loukas: asleep.

He raised himself to his elbows. What had he dreamed? What story had he told?

NOTE: *Lord Byron died at Missolonghi, in Greece, April 19, 1824. He was thirty-six years old.*

THOMAS LIGOTTI
The Last Feast of Harlequin

Ligotti's short fiction has been appearing in various small press horror magazines for several years. Most of those stories have been collected in *Songs of a Dead Dreamer*, first published by Silver Scarab Press in a limited edition in 1985 and recently released by Carroll & Graf. A new collection, *Grimscribe*, is forthcoming.

"The Last Feast of Harlequin" was the very first story Ligotti wrote that he actually kept. He also tells us that he worked on it for twelve years before he felt it was finished. Like so much of his fiction, this novelette, taken from *Fantasy & Science Fiction*, is complicated in structure, baroque in style.

—E.D.

The Last Feast of Harlequin

THOMAS LIGOTTI

I

My interest in the town of Mirocaw was first aroused when I heard that an annual festival was held there which promised to include, to some extent, the participation of clowns among its other elements of pageantry. A former colleague of mine, who is now attached to the anthropology department of a distant university, had read one of my recent articles ("The Clown Figure in American Media," *Journal of Popular Culture*), and wrote to me that he vaguely remembered reading or being told of a town somewhere in the state that held a kind of "Fool's Feast" every year, thinking that this might be pertinent to my peculiar line of study. It was, of course, more pertinent than he had reason to think, both to my academic aims in this area and to my personal pursuits.

Aside from my teaching, I had for some years been engaged in various anthropological projects with the primary ambition of articulating the significance of the clown figure in diverse cultural contexts. Every year for the past twenty years I have attended the pre-Lenten festivals that are held in various places throughout the southern United States. Every year I learned something more concerning the esoterics of celebration. In these studies I was an eager participant—along with playing my part as an anthropologist, I also took a place behind the clownish mask myself. And I cherished this role as I did nothing else in my life. To me the title of Clown has always carried connotations of a noble sort. I was an adroit jester, strangely enough, and had always taken pride in the skills I worked so diligently to develop.

I wrote to the State Department of Recreation, indicating what information I desired and exposing an enthusiastic urgency which came naturally to me on this topic. Many weeks later I received a tan envelope imprinted with a government logo. Inside was a pamphlet that catalogued all of the various seasonal festivities of which the state was officially aware, and I noted in passing that there were as many in late autumn and winter as in the warmer seasons. A letter inserted within the pamphlet explained to me that, according to their voluminous records, no festivals held in the town of Mirocaw had been officially registered. Their files, nonetheless, could be placed at my disposal if I should wish to research this or similar matters in connection with some definite project. At the time this offer was made I was already laboring under so many professional and personal burdens that, with a weary hand, I simply deposited the envelope and its contents in a drawer, never to be consulted again.

Some months later, however, I made an impulsive digression from my responsibilities and, rather haphazardly, took up the Mirocaw project. This happened as I was driving north one afternoon in late summer with the intention of examining some journals in the holdings of a library at another university. Once out of the city limits the scenery changed to sunny fields and farms, diverting my thoughts from the signs that I passed along the highway. Nevertheless, the subconscious scholar in me must have been regarding these with studious care. The name of a town loomed into my vision. Instantly the scholar retrieved certain records from some deep mental drawer, and I was faced with making a few hasty calculations as to whether there was enough time and motivation for an investigative side trip. But the exit sign was even hastier in making its appearance, and I soon found myself leaving the highway, recalling the roadsign's promise that the town was no more than seven miles east.

These seven miles included several confusing turns, the forced taking of a temporarily alternate route, and a destination not even visible until a steep rise had been fully ascended. On the descent another helpful sign informed me that I was within the city limits of Mirocaw. Some scattered houses on the outskirts of the town were the first structures I encountered. Beyond them the numerical highway became Townshend Street, the main avenue of Mirocaw.

The town impressed me as being much larger once I was within its limits than it had appeared from the prominence just outside. I saw that the general hilliness of the surrounding countryside was also an internal feature of Mirocaw. Here, though, the effect was different. The parts of the town did not look as if they adhered very well to one another. This condition might be blamed on the irregular topography of the town. Behind some of the old stores in the business district, steeply roofed houses had been erected on a sudden incline, their peaks appearing at an extraordinary elevation above the lower buildings. And because the foundations of these houses could not be glimpsed, they conveyed the illusion of being either precariously suspended in air, threatening to topple down, or else constructed with an unnatural loftiness in relation to their width and mass. This situation also created a weird distortion of perspective. The two levels of structures overlapped each other without giving a sense of depth, so that the houses, because of their higher elevation and nearness to the foreground buildings, did not appear diminished in size as background objects should. Consequently, a look of flatness, as in a photograph, predominated in this area. Indeed, Mirocaw could be compared to an album of old snapshots, particularly ones in which the camera had been upset in the process of photography, causing the pictures to develop on an angle: a cone-roofed turret, like a pointed hat jauntily askew, peeked over the houses on a neighboring street; a billboard displaying a group of grinning vegetables tipped its contents slightly westward; cars parked along steep curbs seemed to be flying skyward in the glare-distorted windows of a five-and-ten; people leaned lethargically as they trod up and down sidewalks; and on that sunny day the clock tower, which at first I mistook for a church steeple, cast a long shadow that seemed to extend an impossible distance and wander into unlikely places in its progress across the town. I should say that perhaps the disharmonies of Mirocaw are more acutely affecting my imagination in retrospect than they were on that first day, when I was primarily concerned with locating the city hall or some other center of information.

I pulled around a corner and parked. Sliding over to the other side of the seat, I rolled down the window and called to a passerby: "Excuse me, sir," I said. The man, who was shabbily dressed and very old, paused for a moment without approaching the car. Though he had apparently responded to my call, his vacant expression did not betray the least awareness of my presence, and for a moment I thought it just a coincidence that he halted on the sidewalk at the same time I addressed him. His eyes were focused somewhere beyond me with a weary and imbecilic gaze. After a few moments he continued on his way and I said nothing to call him back, even though at the last second his face began to appear dimly familiar. Someone else finally came along who was able to direct me to the Mirocaw City Hall and Community Center.

The city hall turned out to be the building with the clock tower. Inside I stood at a counter behind which some people were working at desks and walking up and down a back hallway. On one wall was a poster for the state lottery: a jack-in-the-box with both hands grasping green bills. After a few moments, a tall, middle-aged woman came over to the counter.

"Can I help you?" she asked in a neutral, bureaucratic voice.

I explained that I had heard about the festival—saying nothing about being a nosy academic—and asked if she could provide me with further information or direct me to someone who could.

"Do you mean the one held in the winter?" she asked.

"How many of them are there?"

"Just that one."

"I suppose, then, that that's the one I mean." I smiled as if sharing a joke with her.

Without another word, she walked off into the back hallway. While she was absent I exchanged glances with several of the people behind the counter who periodically looked up from their work.

"There you are," she said when she returned, handing me a piece of paper that looked like the product of a cheap copy machine. *Please Come to the Fun*, it said in large letters. *Parades*, it went on, *Street Masquerade, Bands, The Winter Raffle*, and *The Coronation of the Winter Queen*. The page continued with the mention of a number of miscellaneous festivities. I read the words again. There was something about that imploring little "please" at the top of the announcement that made the whole affair seem like a charity function.

"When is it held? It doesn't say when the festival takes place."

"Most people already know that." She abruptly snatched the page from my hands and wrote something at the bottom. When she gave it back to me, I saw "Dec. 19–21" written in blue-green ink. I was immediately struck by an odd sense of scheduling on the part of the festival committee. There was, of course, solid anthropological and historical precedent for holding festivities around the winter solstice, but the timing of this particular event did not seem entirely practical.

"If you don't mind my asking, don't these days somewhat conflict with the regular holiday season? I mean, most people have enough going on at that time."

"It's just tradition," she said, as if invoking some venerable ancestry behind her words.

"That's very interesting," I said as much to myself as to her.

"Is there anything else?" she asked.

"Yes. Could you tell me if this festival has anything to do with clowns? I see there's something about a masquerade."

"Yes, of course there are some people in . . . costumes. I've never been in that position myself . . . that is, yes, there are clowns of a sort."

At that point my interest was definitely aroused, but I was not sure how much further I wanted to pursue it. I thanked the woman for her help and asked the best way to get back to the highway, not anxious to retrace the labyrinthine route by which I had entered the town. I walked back to my car with a whole flurry of half-formed questions, and as many vague and conflicting answers, cluttering my mind.

The directions the woman gave me necessitated passing through the south end of Mirocaw. There were not many people moving about in this section of town. Those that I did see, shuffling lethargically down a block of battered storefronts, exhibited the same sort of forlorn expression and manner as the old man from whom I had asked directions earlier. I must have been passing through a central artery of this area, for on either side stretched street after street of poorly tended yards and houses bowed with age and indifference. When I came to a stop at a street corner, one of the citizens of this slum passed in front of my car. This lean, morose, and epicene person turned my way and sneered outrageously with a taut little mouth, yet seemed to be looking at no one in particular. After progressing a few streets farther, I came to a road that led back to the highway. I felt detectably more comfortable as soon as I found myself traveling once again through the expanses of sun-drenched farmlands.

I reached the library with more than enough time for my research, and so I decided to make a scholarly detour to see what material I could find that might illuminate the winter festival held in Mirocaw. The library, one of the oldest in the state, included in its holdings the entire run of the Mirocaw *Courier*. I thought this would be an excellent place to start. I soon found, however, that there was no handy way to research information from this newspaper, and I did not want to engage in a blind search for articles concerning a specific subject.

I next turned to the more organized resources of the newspapers for the larger cities located in the same county, which incidentally shares its name with Mirocaw. I uncovered very little about the town, and almost nothing concerning its festival, except in one general article on annual events in the area that erroneously attributed to Mirocaw a "large Middle-Eastern community" which every spring hosted a kind of ethnic jamboree. From what I had already observed, and from what I subsequently learned, the citizens of Mirocaw were solidly midwestern-American, the probable descendants in a direct line from some enterprising pack of New Englanders of the last century. There was one brief item devoted to a Mirocavian event, but this merely turned out to be an obituary notice for an old woman who had quietly taken her life around Christmas time. Thus, I returned home that day all but empty-handed on the subject of Mirocaw.

However, it was not long afterward that I received another letter from the former colleague of mine who had first led me to seek out Mirocaw and its festival. As it happened, he rediscovered the article that caused him to stir my interest in a local "Fool's Feast." This article had its sole appearance in an obscure festschrift of anthropology studies published in Amsterdam twenty years ago. Most of these papers were in Dutch, a few in German, and only one was in English: "The Last Feast of Harlequin: Preliminary Notes on a Local Festival." It was exciting, of course, finally to be able to read this study, but even more exciting was the name of its author: Dr. Raymond Thoss.

II

Before proceeding any further, I should mention something about Thoss, and inevitably about myself. Over two decades ago, at my alma mater in Cambridge, Mass., Thoss was a professor of mine. Long before playing a role in the events I am about to describe, he was already one of the most important figures in my life. A striking personality, he inevitably influenced everyone who came in contact with him. I remember his lectures on social anthropology, how he turned that dim room into a brilliant and profound circus of learning. He moved in an uncannily brisk manner. When he swept his arm around to indicate some common term on the blackboard behind him, one felt he was presenting nothing less than an item of fantastic qualities and secret value. When he replaced his hand in the pocket of his old jacket this fleeting magic was once again stored away in its well-worn pouch, to be retrieved at the sorcerer's discretion. We sensed he was teaching us more than we could possibly learn, and that he himself was in possession of greater and deeper knowledge than he could possibly impart. On one occasion I summoned up the audacity to offer an interpretation—which was somewhat opposed to his own—regarding the tribal clowns of the Hopi Indians. I implied that personal experience as an amateur clown and special devotion to this study provided me with an insight possibly more valuable than his own. It was then he disclosed, casually and very obiter dicta, that he had actually acted in the role of one of these masked tribal fools and had celebrated with them the dance of the *kachinas*. In revealing these facts, however, he somehow managed not to add to the humiliation I had already inflicted upon myself. And for this I was grateful to him.

Thoss's activities were such that he sometimes became the object of gossip or romanticized speculation. He was a fieldworker par excellence, and his ability to insinuate himself into exotic cultures and situations, thereby gaining insights where other anthropologists merely collected data, was renowned. At various times in his career there had been rumors of his having "gone native" à la the Frank Hamilton Cushing legend. There were hints, which were not always irresponsible or cheaply glamorized, that he was involved in projects of a freakish sort, many of which focused on New England. It is a fact that he spent six months posing as a mental patient at an institution in western Massachusetts, gathering information on the "culture" of the psychically disturbed. When his book *Winter Solstice: The Longest Night of a Society* was published, the general opinion was that it was disappointingly subjective and impressionistic, and that, aside from a few moving but "poetically obscure" observations, there was nothing at all to give it value. Those who defended Thoss claimed he was a kind of super-anthropologist, while much of his work emphasized his own mind and feelings, his experience had in fact penetrated to a rich core of hard data which he had yet to disclose in objective discourse. As a student of Thoss, I tended to support this latter estimation of him. For a variety of tenable and untenable reasons, I believed Thoss capable of unearthing hitherto inaccessible strata of human existence. So it was gratifying at first that this article entitled "The Last Feast of Harlequin" seemed to uphold the Thoss mystique, and in an area I personally found captivating.

Much of the content of the article I did not immediately comprehend, given its author's characteristic and often strategic obscurities. On first reading, the most interesting aspect of this brief study—the "notes" encompassed only twenty pages—was the general mood of the piece. Thoss's eccentricities were definitely present in these pages, but only as a struggling inner force which was definitely contained—incarcerated, I might say—by the somber rhythmic movements of his prose and by some gloomy references he occasionally called upon. Two references in particular shared a common theme. One was a quotation from Poe's "The Conqueror Worm," which Thoss employed as a rather sensational epigraph. The point of the epigraph, however, was nowhere echoed in the text of the article save in another passing reference. Thoss brought up the well-known genesis of the modern Christmas celebration, which of course descends from the Roman Saturnalia. Then, making it clear he had not yet observed the Mirocaw festival and had only gathered its nature from various informants, he established that it too contained many, even more overt, elements of the Saturnalia. Next he made what seemed to me a trivial and purely linguistic observation, one that had less to do with his main course of argument than it did with the equally peripheral Poe epigraph. He briefly mentioned that an early sect of the Syrian Gnostics called themselves "Saturnians" and believed, among other religious heresies, that mankind was created by angels who were in turn created by the Supreme Unknown. The angels, however, did not possess the power to make their creation an erect being and for a time he crawled upon the earth like a worm. Later, the Creator remedied this grotesque state of affairs. At the time I supposed that the symbolic correspondences of mankind's origins and ultimate condition being associated with worms, combined with a year-end festival recognizing the winter death of the earth, was the gist of this Thossian "insight," a poetic but scientifically valueless observation.

Other observations he made on the Mirocaw festival were also strictly etic; in other words, they were based on secondhand sources, hearsay testimony. Even at that juncture, however, I felt Thoss knew more than he disclosed; and, as I later discovered, he had indeed included information on certain aspects of Mirocaw which suggested he was already in possession of several keys which for the moment he was keeping securely in his own pocket. By then I myself possessed a most revealing morsel of knowledge. A note to the "Harlequin" article apprised the reader that the piece was only a fragment in rude form of a more wide-ranging work in preparation. This work was never seen by the world. My former professor had not published anything since his withdrawal from academic circulation some twenty years ago. Now I suspected where he had gone.

For the man I had asked for directions on the streets of Mirocaw, the man with the disconcertingly lethargic gaze, had very much resembled a superannuated version of Dr. Raymond Thoss.

III

And now I have a confession to make. Despite my reasons for being enthusiastic about Mirocaw and its mysteries, especially its relationship to both Thoss and my own deepest concerns as a scholar—I contemplated the days ahead of me with no more than a feeling of frigid numbness and often with a sense of profound depression. Yet I had no reason to be surprised at this emotional state, which had little relevance to the outward events in my life but was determined by inward conditions that worked according to their own, quite enigmatic, seasons and cycles. For many years, at least since my university days, I have suffered from this dark malady, this recurrent despondency in which I would become buried when it came time for the earth to grow cold and bare and the skies heavy with shadows. Nevertheless, I pursued my plans, though somewhat mechanically, to visit Mirocaw during its festival days, for I superstitiously hoped that this activity might diminish the weight of my seasonal despair. In Mirocaw would be parades and parties and the opportunity to play the clown once again.

For weeks in advance I practiced my art, even perfecting a new feat of juggling magic, which was my special forte in foolery. I had my costumes cleaned, purchased fresh makeup, and was ready. I received permission from the university to cancel some of my classes prior to the holiday, explaining the nature of my project and the necessity of arriving in the town a few days before the festival began, in order to do some preliminary research, establish informants, and so on. Actually, my plan was to postpone any formal inquiry until after the festival and to involve myself beforehand as much as possible in its activities. I would, of course, keep a journal during this time.

There was one resource I did want to consult, however. Specifically, I returned to that outstate library to examine those issues of the Mirocaw *Courier* dating from December two decades ago. One story in particular confirmed a point Thoss made in the "Harlequin" article, though the event it chronicled must have taken place after Thoss had written his study.

The *Courier* story appeared two weeks after the festival had ended for that year and was concerned with the disappearance of a woman named Elizabeth Beadle, the wife of Samuel Beadle, a hotel owner in Mirocaw. The county authorities speculated that this was another instance of the "holiday suicides" which seemed to occur with inordinate seasonal regularity in the Mirocaw region. Thoss documented this situation in his "Harlequin" article, though I suspected that today these deaths would be neatly categorized under the heading "seasonal affective disorder." In any case, the authorities searched a half-frozen lake near the outskirts of Mirocaw where they had found many successful suicides in years past. This year, however, no body was discovered. Alongside the article was a picture of Elizabeth Beadle. Even in the grainy microfilm reproduction one could detect a certain vibrancy and vitality in Mrs. Beadle's face. That an hypothesis of "holiday suicide" should be so readily posited to explain her disappearance seemed strange and in some way unjust.

Thoss, in his brief article, wrote that every year there occurred changes of a moral or spiritual cast which seemed to affect Mirocaw along with the usual winter metamorphosis. He was not precise about its origin or nature but stated, in typically mystifying fashion, that the effect of this "subseason" on the town was conspicuously negative. In addition to the number of suicides actually accomplished during this time, there was also a rise in treatment of "hypochondriacal" conditions, which was how the medical men of twenty years past characterized these cases in discussions with Thoss. This state of affairs would gradually worsen and finally reach a climax during the days scheduled for the Mirocaw festival. Thoss speculated that given the secretive nature of small towns, the situation was probably even more intensely pronounced than casual investigation could reveal.

The connection between the festival and this insidious subseasonal climate in Mirocaw was a point on which Thoss did not come to any rigid conclusions. He did write, nevertheless, that these two "climatic aspects" had had a parallel existence in the town's history as far back as available records could document. A late nineteenth-century history of Mirocaw County speaks of the town by its original name of New Colstead, and castigates the townspeople for holding a "ribald and soulless feast" to the exclusion of normal Christmas observances. (Thoss comments that the historian had mistakenly fused two distinct aspects of the season, their actual relationship being essentially antagonistic.) The "Harlequin" article did not trace the festival to its earliest appearance (this may not have been possible), though Thoss emphasized the New England origins of Mirocaw's founders. The festival, therefore, was one imported from this region and could reasonably be extended at least a century; that is, if it had not been brought over from the Old World, in which case its roots would become indefinite until further research could be done. Surely Thoss's allusion to the Syrian Gnostics suggested the latter possibility could not entirely be ruled out.

But it seemed to be the festival's source in New England that nourished Thoss's speculations. He wrote of this patch of geography as if it were an acceptable place to end the search. For him, the very words "New England" seemed to be stripped of all traditional connotations and had come to imply nothing less than a gateway to all lands, both known and suspected, and even to ages beyond the civilized history of the region. Having been educated partly in New England, I could somewhat understand this sentimental exaggeration, for indeed there are places that seem archaic beyond chronological measure, appearing to transcend relative standards of time and achieving a kind of absolute antiquity which cannot be logically fathomed. But how this vague suggestion related to a small town in the Midwest I could not imagine. Thoss himself observed that the residents of Mirocaw did not betray any mysteriously primitive consciousness. On the contrary, they appeared superficially unaware of the genesis of their winter merrymaking. That such a tradition had endured through the years, however, even eclipsing the conventional Christmas holiday, revealed a profound awareness of the festival's meaning and function.

I cannot deny that what I had learned about the Mirocaw festival did inspire a trite sense of fate, especially given the involvement of such an important figure from my past as Thoss. It was the first time in my academic career that I knew myself to be better suited than anyone else to discern the true meaning of scattered data, even if I could only attribute this special authority to chance circumstances.

Nevertheless, as I sat in that library on a morning in mid-December I doubted for a moment the wisdom of setting out for Mirocaw rather than returning home, where the more familiar *rite de passage* of winter depression awaited me. My original scheme was to avoid the cyclical blues the season held for me, but it seemed this was also a part of the history of Mirocaw, only on a much larger scale. My emotional instability, however, was exactly what qualified me most for the particular fieldwork ahead, though I did not take pride or consolation in the fact. And to retreat would have been to deny myself an opportunity that might never offer itself again. In retrospect, there seems to have been no fortuitous resolution to the decision I had to make. As it happened, I went ahead to the town.

IV

Just past noon, on December 18, I started driving toward Mirocaw. A blur of dull, earthen-colored scenery extended in every direction. The snowfalls of late autumn had been sparse, and only a few white patches appeared in the harvested fields along the highway. The clouds were gray and abundant. Passing by a stretch of forest, I noticed the black, ragged clumps of abandoned nests clinging to the twisted mesh of bare branches. I thought I saw black birds skittering over the road ahead, but they were only dead leaves and they flew into the air as I drove by.

I approached Mirocaw from the south, entering the town from the direction I had left it on my visit the previous summer. This took me once again through that part of town which seemed to exist on the wrong side of some great invisible wall dividing the desirable sections of Mirocaw from the undesirable. As lurid as this district had appeared to me under the summer sun, in the thin light of that winter afternoon it degenerated into a pale phantom of itself. The frail stores and starved-looking houses suggested a borderline region between the material and nonmaterial worlds, with one sardonically wearing the mask of the other. I saw a few gaunt pedestrians who turned as I passed by, though seemingly not *because* I passed by, making my way up to the main street of Mirocaw.

Driving up the steep rise of Townshend Street, I found the sights there comparatively welcoming. The rolling avenues of the town were in readiness for the festival. Streetlights had their poles raveled with evergreen, the fresh boughs proudly conspicuous in a barren season. On the doors of many of the businesses on Townshend were holly wreaths, equally green but observably plastic. However, although there was nothing unusual in this traditional greenery of the season, it soon became apparent to me that Mirocaw had quite abandoned itself to this particular symbol of Yuletide. It was garishly in evidence everywhere. The windows of stores and houses were framed in green lights, green streamers hung down from storefront awnings, and the beacons of the Red Rooster Bar were peacock green floodlights. I supposed the residents of Mirocaw desired these decorations, but the effect was one of excess. An eerie emerald haze permeated the town, and faces looked slightly reptilian.

At the time I assumed that the prodigious evergreen, holly wreaths, and colored lights (if only of a single color) demonstrated an emphasis on the vegetable symbols of the Nordic Yuletide, which would inevitably be muddled into the winter festival of any northern country just as they had been adopted for the Christmas season. In his "Harlequin" article Thoss wrote of the pagan aspect of Mirocaw's festival, likening it to the ritual of a fertility cult, with probable connections to chthonic divinities at some time in the past. But Thoss had mistaken, as I had, what was only part of the festival's significance for the whole.

The hotel at which I had made reservations was located on Townshend. It was an old building of brown brick, with an arched doorway and a pathetic coping intended to convey an impression of neoclassicism. I found a parking space in front and left my suitcases in the car.

When I first entered the hotel lobby it was empty. I thought perhaps the Mirocaw festival would have attracted enough visitors to at least bolster the business of its only hotel, but it seemed I was mistaken. Tapping a little bell, I leaned on the desk and turned to look at a small, traditionally decorated Christmas tree on a table near the entranceway. It was complete with shiny, egg-fragile bulbs; miniature candy canes; flat, laughing Santas with arms wide; a star on top nodding awkwardly against the delicate shoulder of an upper branch; and colored lights that bloomed out of flower-shaped sockets. For some reason this seemed to me a sorry little piece.

"May I help you?" said a young woman arriving from a room adjacent to the lobby.

I must have been staring rather intently at her, for she looked away and seemed quite uneasy. I could hardly imagine what to say to her or how to explain what I was thinking. In person she immediately radiated a chilling brilliance of manner and expression. But if this woman had not committed suicide twenty years before, as the newspaper article had suggested, neither had she aged in that time.

"Sarah," called a masculine voice from the invisible heights of a stairway. A tall, middle-aged man came down the steps. "I thought you were in your room," said the man, whom I took to be Samuel Beadle. Sarah, not Elizabeth, Beadle glanced sideways in my direction to indicate to her father that she was conducting the business of the hotel. Beadle apologized to me, and then excused the two of them for a moment while they went off to one side to continue their exchange.

I smiled and pretended everything was normal, while trying to remain within earshot of their conversation. They spoke in tones that suggested their conflict was a familiar one: Beadle's overprotective concern with his daughter's whereabouts and Sarah's frustrated understanding of certain restrictions placed upon her. The conversation ended, and Sarah ascended the stairs, turning for a moment to give me a facial pantomime of apology for the unprofessional scene that had just taken place.

"Now, sir, what can I do for you?" Beadle asked, almost demanded.

"Yes, I have a reservation. Actually, I'm a day early, if that doesn't present a problem." I gave the hotel the benefit of the doubt that its business might have been secretly flourishing.

"No problem at all, sir," he said, presenting me with the registration form, and then a brass-colored key dangling from a black plastic disc bearing the number 44.

"Luggage?"

"Yes, it's in my car."

"I'll give you a hand with that."

While Beadle was settling me in my fourth-floor room it seemed an opportune moment to broach the subject of the festival, the holiday suicides, and perhaps, depending upon his reaction, the fate of his wife. I needed a respondent who had lived in the town for a good many years and who could enlighten me about the attitude of Mirocavians toward their season of sea green lights.

"This is just fine," I said about the clean but somber room. "Nice view. I can see the bright green lights of Mirocaw just fine from up here. Is the town usually all decked out like this? For the festival, I mean."

"Yes, sir, for the festival," he replied mechanically.

"I imagine you'll probably be getting quite a few of us out-of-towners in the next couple days."

"Could be. Is there anything else?"

"Yes, there is. I wonder if you could tell me something about the festivities."

"Such as . . ."

"Well, you know, the clowns and so forth."

"Only clowns here are the ones that're . . . well, picked out, I suppose you would say."

"I don't understand."

"Excuse me, sir. I'm very busy right now. Is there anything else?"

I could think of nothing at the moment to perpetuate our conversation. Beadle wished me a good stay and left.

I unpacked my suitcases. In addition to regular clothing I had also brought along some of the items from my clown's wardrobe. Beadle's comment that clowns were "picked out" here left me wondering exactly what purpose these street masqueraders served in the festival. The clown figure has had so many meanings in different times and cultures. The jolly, well-loved joker familiar to most people is actually but one aspect of this protean creature. Madmen, hunchbacks, amputees, and other abnormals were once considered natural clowns; they were elected to fulfil a comic role which could allow others to see them as ludicrous rather than as terrible reminders of the forces of disorder in the world. But sometimes a cheerless jester was required to draw attention to this same disorder, as in the case of King Lear's morbid and honest fool, who of course was eventually hanged, and so much for his clownish wisdom. Clowns have often had ambiguous and sometimes contradictory roles to play. Thus, I knew enough not to brashly jump into costume and cry out, "Here I am again!"

That first day in Mirocaw I did not stray far from the hotel. I read and rested for a few hours and then ate at a nearby diner. Through the window beside my table I watched the winter night turn the soft green glow of the town into a harsh and almost totally new color as it contrasted with the darkness. The streets of Mirocaw seemed to me unusually busy for a small town at evening. Yet it was not the kind of activity one normally sees before an approaching Christmas holiday. This was not a crowd of bustling shoppers loaded with bright bags of presents. Their arms were empty, their hands shoved deep in their pockets against the cold, which nevertheless had not driven them to the solitude of their presumably warm houses. I watched them enter and exit store after store without buying; many merchants remained open late, and even the places that were closed had left their neons illuminated. The faces that passed the window of the diner were possibly just stiffened by the cold, I thought; frozen into deep frowns and nothing else. In the window I also saw the reflection of my own face. It was not the face of an adept clown; it was slack and flabby and at that moment seemed the face of someone less than alive. Outside was the town of Mirocaw, its streets dipping and rising with a lunatic severity, its citizens packing the sidewalks, its heart bathed in green: as promising a field of professional and personal challenge as I had ever encountered—and I was bored to the point of dread. I hurried back to my hotel room.

"Mirocaw has another coldness within its cold," I wrote in my journal that night. "Another set of buildings and streets that exists behind the visible town's facade like a world of disgraceful back alleys." I went on like this for about a page, across which I finally engraved a big "X." Then I went to bed.

In the morning I left my car at the hotel and walked toward the main business district a few blocks away. Mingling with the good people of Mirocaw seemed like the proper thing to do at that point in my scientific sojourn. But as I began laboriously walking up Townshend (the sidewalks were cramped with wandering pedestrians), a glimpse of someone suddenly replaced my haphazard plan with a more specific and immediate one. Through the crowd and about fifteen paces ahead was my goal.

"Dr. Thoss," I called.

His head almost seemed to turn and look back in response to my shout, but I could not be certain. I pushed past several warmly wrapped bodies and green-scarved necks, only to find that the object of my pursuit appeared to be maintaining the same distance from me, though I did not know if this was being done deliberately or not. At the next corner, the dark-coated Thoss abruptly turned right onto a steep street which led downward directly toward the dilapidated south end of Mirocaw. When I reached the corner I looked down the sidewalk and could see him very clearly from above. I also saw how he managed to stay so far ahead of me in a mob that had impeded my own progress. For some reason the people on the sidewalk made room so that he could move past them easily, without the usual jostling of bodies. It was not a dramatic physical avoidance, though it seemed nonetheless intentional. Fighting the tight fabric of the throng, I continued to follow Thoss, losing and regaining sight of him.

By the time I reached the bottom of the sloping street the crowd had thinned out considerably, and after walking a block or so farther I found myself practically a lone pedestrian pacing behind a distant figure that I hoped was still Thoss. He was now walking quite swiftly and in a way that seemed to acknowledge my pursuit of him, though really it felt as if he were leading me as much as I was chasing him. I called his name a few more times at a volume he could not have failed to hear, assuming that deafness was not one of the changes to have come over him; he was, after all, not a young man, nor even a middle-aged one any longer.

Thoss suddenly crossed in the middle of the street. He walked a few more steps and entered a signless brick building between a liquor store and a repair shop of some kind. In the "Harlequin" article Thoss had mentioned that the people living in this section of Mirocaw maintained their own businesses, and that these were patronized almost exclusively by residents of the area. I could well believe this statement when I looked at these little sheds of commerce, for they had the same badly weathered appearance as their clientele. The formidable shoddiness of these buildings notwithstanding, I followed Thoss into the plain brick shell of what had been, or possibly still was, a diner.

Inside it was unusually dark. Even before my eyes made the adjustment I sensed that this was not a thriving restaurant cozily cluttered with chairs and tables—as was the establishment where I had eaten the night before—but a place with only a few disarranged furnishings, and very cold. It seemed colder, in fact, than the winter streets outside.

"Dr. Thoss?" I called toward a lone table near the center of the long room. Perhaps four or five were sitting around the table, with some others blending into the dimness behind them. Scattered across the top of the table were some books and loose papers. Seated there was an old man indicating something in the pages before him, but it was not Thoss. Beside him were two youths whose wholesome features distinguished them from the grim weariness of the others. I approached the table and they all looked up at me. None of them showed a glimmer of emotion except the two boys, who exchanged worried and guilt-ridden glances with each other, as if they had just been discovered in some shameful act. They both suddenly burst from the table and ran into the dark background, where a light appeared briefly as they exited by a back door.

"I'm sorry," I said diffidently. "I thought I saw someone I knew come in here."

They said nothing. Out of a back room others began to emerge, no doubt interested in the source of the commotion. In a few moments the room was crowded with these tramplike figures, all of them gazing emptily in the dimness. I was not at this point frightened of them; at least I was not afraid they would do me any physical harm. Actually, I felt as if it was quite within my power to pummel them easily into submission, their mousy faces almost inviting a succession of firm blows. But there were so many of them.

They slid slowly toward me in a wormlike mass. Their eyes seemed empty and unfocused, and I wondered a moment if they were even aware of my presence. Nevertheless, I was the center upon which their lethargic shuffling converged, their shoes scuffing softly along the bare floor. I began to deliver a number of hasty inanities as they continued to press toward me, their weak and unexpectedly odorless bodies nudging against mine. (I understood now why the people along the sidewalks seemed to instinctively avoid Thoss.) Unseen legs seemed to become entangled with my own; I staggered and then regained my balance. This sudden movement aroused me from a kind of mesmeric daze which I must have fallen into without being aware of it. I had intended to leave that dreary place long before events had reached such a juncture, but for some reason I could not focus my intentions strongly enough to cause myself to act. My mind had been drifting farther away as these slavish things approached. In a sudden surge of panic I pushed through their soft ranks and was outside.

The open air revived me to my former alertness, and I immediately started pacing swiftly up the hill. I was no longer sure that I had not simply imagined what had seemed, and at the same time did not seem, like a perilous moment. Had their movements been directed toward a harmful assault, or were they trying merely to intimidate me? As I reached the green-glazed main street of Mirocaw I really could not be sure what had just happened.

The sidewalks were still jammed with a multitude of pedestrians, but now they seemed to be moving and chattering in a more lively way. There was a kind of vitality that could only be attributed to the imminent festivities. A group of young men had begun celebrating prematurely and strode noisily across the street at midpoint, obviously intoxicated. From the laughter and joking among the still sober citizens I gathered that, mardi-gras style, public drunkenness was within the traditions of this winter festival. I looked for anything to indicate the beginnings of the Street Masquerade, but saw nothing: no brightly garbed harlequins or snow white pierrots. Were the ceremonies even now in preparation for the coronation of the Winter Queen? "The Winter Queen," I wrote in my journal. "Figure of fertility invested with symbolic powers of revival and prosperity. Elected in the manner of a high school prom queen. Check for possible consort figure in the form of a representative from the underworld."

In the pre-darkness hours of December 19 I sat in my hotel room and wrote and thought and organized. I did not feel too badly, all things considered. The holiday excitement which was steadily rising in the streets below my window was definitely infecting me. I forced myself to take a short nap in anticipation of a long night. When I awoke, Mirocaw's annual feast had begun.

V

Shouting, commotion, carousing. Sleepily I went to the window and looked out over the town. It seemed all the lights of Mirocaw were shining, save in that section down the hill which became part of the black void of winter. And now the town's greenish tinge was even more pronounced, spreading everywhere like a great green rainbow that had melted from the sky and endured, phosphorescent, into the night. In the streets was the brightness of an artificial spring. The byways of Mirocaw vibrated with activity: on a nearby corner a brass band blared; marauding cars blew their horns and were sometimes mounted by laughing pedestrians; a man emerged from the Red Rooster Bar, threw up his arms, and crowed. I looked closely at the individual celebrants, searching for the vestments of clowns. Soon, delightedly, I saw them. The costume was red and white, with matching cap, and the face painted a noble alabaster. It almost seemed to be a clownish incarnation of that white-bearded and black-booted Christmas fool.

This particular fool, however, was not receiving the affection and respect usually accorded to a Santa Claus. My poor fellow-clown was in the middle of a circle of revelers who were pushing him back and forth from one to the other. The object of this abuse seemed to accept it somewhat willingly, but this little game nevertheless appeared to have humiliation as its purpose. "Only clowns here are the one's that're picked out," echoed Beadle's voice in my memory. "Picked *on*" seemed closer to the truth.

Packing myself in some heavy clothes, I went out into the green gleaming streets. Not far from the hotel I was stumbled into by a character with a wide blue-and-red grin and bright baggy clothes. Actually he had been shoved into me by some youths outside a drugstore.

"See the freak," said an obese and drunken fellow. "See the freak fall."

My first response was anger, and then fear as I saw two others flanking the fat drunk. They walked toward me and I tensed myself for a confrontation.

"This is a disgrace," one said, the neck of a wine bottle held loosely in his left hand.

But it was not to me they were speaking; it was to the clown, who had been pushed to the sidewalk. His three persecutors helped him up with a sudden jerk and then splashed wine in his face. They ignored me altogether.

"Let him loose," the fat one said. "Crawl away, freak. Oh, he flies!"

The clown trotted off, becoming lost in the throng.

"Wait a minute," I said to the rowdy trio, who had started lumbering away. I quickly decided that it would probably be futile to ask them to explain what I had just witnessed, especially amid the noise and confusion of the festivities. In my best jovial fashion I proposed we all go someplace where I could buy them each a drink. They had no objection and in a short while we were all squeezed around a table in the Red Rooster.

Over several drinks I explained to them that I was from out of town, which pleased them no end for some reason. I told them there were some things I did not understand about their festival.

"I don't think there's anything *to* understand," the fat one said. "It's just what you see."

I asked him about the people dressed as clowns.

"Them? They're the freaks. It's their turn this year. Everyone takes their turn. Next year it might be mine. Or *yours*," he said, pointing at one of his friends across the table. "And when we find out which one you are—"

"You're not smart enough," said the defiant potential freak.

This was an important point: the fact that individuals who play the clowns remain, or at least attempted to remain, anonymous. This arrangement would help remove inhibitions a resident of Mirocaw might have about abusing his own neighbor or even a family relation. From what I later observed, the extent of this abuse did not go beyond a kind of playful roughhousing. And even so, it was only the occasional group of rowdies who actually took advantage of this aspect of the festival, the majority of the citizens very much content to stay on the sidelines.

As far as being able to illuminate the meaning of this custom, my three young friends were quite useless. To them it was just amusement, as I imagine it was to the majority of Mirocavians. This was understandable. I suppose the average person would not be able to explain exactly how the profoundly familiar Christmas holiday came to be celebrated in its present form.

I left the bar alone and not unaffected by the drinks I had consumed there. Outside, the general merrymaking continued. Loud music emanated from several quarters. Mirocaw had fully transformed itself from a sedate small town to an enclave of Saturnalia within the dark immensity of a winter night. But Saturn is also the planetary symbol of melancholy and sterility, a clash of opposites contained within that single word. And as I wandered half-drunkenly down the street, I discovered that there was a conflict within the winter festival itself. This discovery indeed appeared to be that secret key which Thoss withheld in his study of the town. Oddly enough, it was through my unfamiliarity with the outward nature of the festival that I came to know its true nature.

I was mingling with the crowd on the street, warmly enjoying the confusion around me, when I saw a strangely designed creature lingering on the corner up ahead. It was one of the Mirocaw clowns. Its clothes were shabby and nondescript, almost in the style of a tramp-type clown, but not humorously exaggerated enough. The face, though, made up for the lackluster costume. I had never seen such a strange conception for a clown's countenance. The figure stood beneath a dim streetlight, and when it turned its head my way I realized why it seemed familiar. The thin, smooth, and pale head; the wide eyes; the oval-shaped features resembling nothing so much as the skull-faced, screaming creature in that famous painting (memory fails me). This clownish imitation rivalled the original in suggesting stricken realms of abject horror and despair: an inhuman likeness more proper to something under the earth than upon it.

From the first moment I saw this creature, I thought of those inhabitants of the ghetto down the hill. There was the same nauseating passivity and languor in its bearing. Perhaps if I had not been drinking earlier I would not have been bold enough to take the action I did. I decided to join in one of the upstanding traditions of the winter festival, for it annoyed me to see this morbid impostor of a clown standing up. When I reached the corner I laughingly pushed myself into the creature—"Whoops!"—who stumbled backward and ended up on the side-walk. I laughed again and looked around for approval from the festivalers in the vicinity. No one, however, seemed to appreciate or even acknowledge what I had done. They did not laugh with me or point with amusement, but only passed by, perhaps walking a little faster until they were some distance from this street corner incident. I realized instantly I had violated some tacit rule of behavior, though I had thought my action well within the common practice. The thought occurred to me that I might even be apprehended and prosecuted for what in any other circumstances was certainly a criminal act. I turned around to help the clown back to his feet, hoping to somehow redeem my offense, but the creature was gone. Solemnly I walked away from the scene of my inadvertent crime and sought other streets away from its witnesses.

Along the various back avenues of Mirocaw I wandered, pausing exhaustedly at one point to sit at the counter of a small sandwich shop that was packed with customers. I ordered a cup of coffee to revive my overly alcoholed system. Warm-ing my hands around the cup and sipping slowly from it, I watched the people outside as they passed the front window. It was well after midnight but the thick flow of passersby gave no indication that anyone was going home early. A carnival of profiles filed past the window and I was content simply to sit back and observe, until finally one of these faces made me start. It was that frightful little clown I had roughed up earlier. But although its face was familiar in its ghastly aspect, there was something different about it. And I wondered that there should be two such hideous freaks.

Quickly paying the man at the counter, I dashed out to get a second glimpse of the clown, who was now nowhere in sight. The dense crowd kept me from pursuing this figure with any speed, and I wondered how the clown could have made its way so easily ahead of me. Unless the crowd had instinctively allowed this creature to pass unhindered through its massive ranks, as it did for Thoss. In the process of searching for this particular freak, I discovered that interspersed among the celebrating populous of Mirocaw, which included the sanctioned festival clowns, there was not one or two, but a considerable number of these pale, wraith-like creatures. And they all drifted along the streets unmolested by even the rowdiest of revelers. I now understood one of the taboos of the festival. These other clowns were not to be disturbed and should even be avoided, much as were the residents of the slum at the edge of town. Nevertheless, I felt instinc-tively that the two groups of clowns were somehow identified with each other, even if the ghetto clowns were not welcome at Mirocaw's winter festival. Indeed, they were not simply part of the community and celebrating the season in their own way. To all appearances, this group of melancholy mummers constituted nothing less than an entirely independent festival—a festival within a festival.

Returning to my room, I entered my suppositions into the journal I was keeping for this venture. The following are excerpts:

> There is a superstitiousness displayed by the residents of Mirocaw with regard to these people from the slum section, particularly as they lately appear in those dreadful faces signifying their own festival. What is the relationship between these simultaneous celebrations? Did one precede the other? If so, which? My opinion at this point—and I claim no conclusiveness for it—is that Mirocaw's winter festival is the later manifestation, that it appeared after the festival of those depressingly pallid clowns, in order to cover it up or mitigate its effect. The holiday suicides come to mind, and the subclimate Thoss wrote about, the disappearance of Elizabeth Beadle twenty years ago, and my own experience with this pariah clan existing outside yet within the community. Of my own experience with this emotionally deleterious subseason I would rather not speak at this time. Still not able to say whether or not my usual winter melancholy is the cause. On the general subject of mental health, I must consider Thoss's book about his stay in a psychiatric hospital (in western Mass., almost sure of that. Check on this book & Mirocaw's New England roots). The winter solstice is tomorrow, albeit sometime past midnight (how blurry these days and nights are becoming!). It is, of course, the day of the year in which night hours surpass daylight hours by the greatest margin. Note what this has to do with the suicides and a rise in psychic disorder. Recalling Thoss's list of documented suicides in his article, there seemed to be a recurrence of specific family names, as there very likely might be for any kind of data collected in a small town. Among these names was a Beadle or two. Perhaps, then, there is a geneological basis for the suicides which has nothing to do with Thoss's mystical subclimate, which is a colorful idea to be sure and one that seems fitting for this town of various outward and inward aspects, but is not a conception that can be substantiated.

> One thing that seems certain, however, is the division of Mirocaw into two very distinct types of citizenry, resulting in two festivals and the appearance of similar clowns—a term now used in an extremely loose sense. But there is a connection, and I believe I have some idea of what it is. I said before that the normal residents of the town regard those from the ghetto, and especially their clown figures, with superstition. Yet it's more than that: there is fear, perhaps a kind of hatred—the particular kind of hatred resulting from some powerful and irrational memory. What threatens Mirocaw I think I can very well understand. I recall the incident earlier today in that vacant diner. "Vacant" is the appropriate word here, despite its contradiction of fact. The congregation of that half-lit room formed less a presence than an absence, even considering the oppressive number of them. Those eyes that did not or could not focus on anything, the pining lassitude of their faces, the lazy march of their feet. I was

spiritually drained when I ran out of there. I then understood why these people and their activities are avoided.

I cannot question the wisdom of those ancestral Mirocavians who began the tradition of the winter festival and gave the town a pretext for cele-bration and social intercourse at a time when the consequences of brood-ing isolation are most severe, those longest and darkest days of the solstice. A mood of Christmas joviality obviously would not be sufficient to counter the menace of this season. But even so, there are still the suicides of individuals who are somehow cut off, I imagine, from the vitalizing activities of the festival.

It is the nature of this insidious subseason that seems to determine the outward forms of Mirocaw's winter festival: the optimistic greenery in a period of gray dormancy; the fertile promise of the Winter Queen; and, most interesting to my mind, the clowns. The bright clowns of Mirocaw who are treated so badly; they appear to serve as substitute figures for those dark-eyed mummers of the slums. Since the latter are feared for some power or influence they possess, they may still be symbolically confronted and conquered through their counterparts, who are elected for precisely this function. If I am right about this, I wonder to what extent there is a conscious awareness among the town's populace of this indirect show of aggression. Those three young men I spoke with tonight did not seem to possess much insight beyond seeing that there was a certain amount of robust fun in the festival's tradition. For that matter, how much awareness is there on the *other side* of these two antagonistic festivals? Too horrible to think of such a thing, but I must wonder if, for all their apparent aimlessness, those inhabitants of the ghetto are not the only ones who know what they are about. No denying that behind those inhumanly limp expressions there seems to lie a kind of obnoxious intelligence.

Now I realize the confusion of my present state, but as I wobbled from street to street tonight, watching those oval-mouthed clowns, I could not help feeling that all the merrymaking in Mirocaw was somehow allowed only by their sufferance. This I hope is no more than a fanciful Thossian intuition, the sort of idea that is curious and thought-provoking without ever seeming to gain the benefit of proof. I know my mind is not entirely lucid, but I feel that it may be possible to penetrate Mirocaw's many complexities and illuminate the hidden side of the festival season. In particular I must look for the significance of the other festival. Is it also some kind of fertility celebration? From what I have seen, the tenor of this "celebrating" sub-group is one of *anti*-fertility, if anything. How have they managed to keep from dying out completely over the years? How do they maintain their numbers?

But I was too tired to formulate any more of my sodden speculations. Falling onto my bed, I soon became lost in dreams of streets and faces.

VI

I was, of course, slightly hung over when I woke up late the next morning. The festival was still going strong, and loud blaring music outside roused me from a nightmare. It was a parade. A number of floats proceeded down Townshend, a familiar color predominating. There were theme floats of pilgrims and Indians, cowboys and Indians, and clowns of an orthodox type. In the middle of it all was the Winter Queen herself, freezing atop an icy throne. She waved in all directions. I even imagined she waved up at my dark window.

In the first few groggy moments of wakefulness I had no sympathy with my excitation of the previous night. But I discovered that my former enthusiasm had merely lain dormant, and soon returned with an even greater intensity. Never before had my mind and senses been so active during this usually inert time of year. At home I would have been playing lugubrious old records and looking out the window quite a bit. I was terribly grateful in a completely abstract way for my commitment to a meaningful mania. And I was eager to get to work after I had had some breakfast at the coffee shop.

When I got back to my room I discovered the door was unlocked. And there was something written on the dresser mirror. The writing was red and greasy, as if done with a clown's make-up pencil—my own, I realized. I read the legend, or rather I should say *riddle*, several times: "What buries itself before it is dead?" I looked at it for quite a while, very shaken at how vulnerable my holiday forti- fications were. Was this supposed to be a warning of some kind? A threat to the effect that if I persisted in a certain course I would end up prematurely interred? I would have to be careful, I told myself. My resolution was to let nothing deter me from the inspired strategy I had conceived for myself. I wiped the mirror clean, for it was now needed for other purposes.

I spent the rest of the day devising a very special costume and the appropriate face to go with it. I easily shabbied up my overcoat with a torn pocket or two and a complete set of stains. Combined with blue jeans and a pair of rather scuffed- up shoes, I had a passable costume for a derelict. The face, however, was more difficult, for I had to experiment from memory. Remembering the screaming pierrot in that painting (*The Scream*, I now recall) helped me quite a bit. At nightfall I exited the hotel by the back stairway.

It was strange to walk down the crowded street in this gruesome disguise. Though I thought I would feel conspicuous, the actual experience was very close, I imag- ined, to one of complete invisibility. No one looked at me as I strolled by, or as they strolled by, or as we strolled by each other. I was a phantom—perhaps the ghost of festivals past, or those yet to come.

I had no clear idea where my disguise would take me that night, only vague expectations of gaining the confidence of my fellow specters and possibly in some way coming to know their secrets. For a while I would simply wander around in that lackadaisical manner I had learned from them, following their lead in any way they might indicate. And for the most part, this meant doing almost nothing and doing it silently. If I passed one of my kind on the sidewalk there was no speaking, no exchange of knowing looks, no recognition at all that I was aware of. We were there on the streets of Mirocaw to create a presence and nothing more. At least, this is how I came to feel about it. As I drifted along with my bodiless invisibility, I felt myself more and more becoming an empty, floating shape, seeing without being seen and walking without the interference of those grosser creatures who shared my world. It was not an experience completely without interest or even pleasure. The clown's shibboleth of "here we are again" took on a new meaning for me as I felt myself a novitiate of a more rarified order of harlequinry. And very soon the opportunity to make further progress along this path presented itself.

On the other side of the street, going the opposite direction, a pickup truck slowly passed, gently parting a sea of zigging and zagging celebrants. The cargo in the back of this truck was curious, for it was made up entirely of my fellow sectarians. Farther down the street the truck stopped and another of them boarded it over the back gate. One block down I saw still another get on. Two blocks down, the truck made a U-turn at an intersection and headed in my direction.

I stood at the curb as I had seen the others do. I was not sure the truck would pick me up, thinking that somehow they knew I was an imposter. The truck did, however, slow down, almost coming to a stop when it reached me. The others were crowded on the floor of the truck bed. Most of them were just staring into nothingness with the usual indifference I had come to expect from their kind. But a few actually glanced at me with some anticipation. For a second I hesitated, not sure I wanted to pursue this ruse any further. At the last moment, some impulse sent me climbing up the back of the truck and squeezing myself in among the others.

There were only a few more to pick up before the truck headed for the outskirts of Mirocaw and beyond. At first I tried to maintain a clear orientation with respect to the town. But as we took turn after turn through the darkness of narrow country roads, I found myself unable to preserve any sense of direction. The majority of the others in the back of the truck exhibited no apparent awareness of their fellow passengers. Guardedly, I looked from face to ghostly face. A few of them spoke in short whispered phrases to others close by. I could not make out what they were saying but the tone of their voices was one of innocent normalcy, as if they were not of the hardened slum-herd of Mirocaw. Perhaps, I thought, these were thrill seekers who had disguised themselves as I had done, or, more likely, initiates of some kind. Possibly they had received prior instructions at such meetings as I had stumbled onto the day before. It was also likely that among this crew were those very boys I had frightened into a precipitate exit from that old diner.

The truck was now speeding along a fairly open stretch of country, heading toward those higher hills that surrounded the now distant town of Mirocaw. The icy wind whipped around us, and I could not keep myself from trembling with cold. This definitely betrayed me as one of the newcomers among the group, for the two bodies that pressed against mine were rigidly still and even seemed to be radiating a frigidity of their own. I glanced ahead at the darkness into which we were rapidly progressing.

We had left all open country behind us now, and the road was enclosed by thick woods. The mass of bodies in the truck leaned into each other as we began traveling up a steep incline. Above us, at the top of the hill, were lights shining somewhere within the woods. When the road levelled off the truck made an abrupt turn, steering into what I thought was the roadside blackness or a great ditch. There was an unpaved path, however, upon which the truck proceeded toward the glowing in the near distance.

This glowing became brighter and sharper as we approached, flickering upon the trees and revealing stark detail where there had formerly been only smooth darkness. As the truck pulled into a clearing and came to a stop, I saw a loose assembly of figures, many of which held lanterns that beamed with a dazzling and frosty light. I stood up in the back of the truck to unboard as the others were doing. Glancing around from that height I saw approximately thirty more of those cadaverous clowns milling about. One of my fellow passengers spied me lingering in the truck and in a strangely high-pitched whisper told me to hurry, explaining something about the "apex of darkness." I thought again about this solstice night; it was technically the longest period of darkness of the year, even if not by a very significant margin from many other winter nights. Its true significance, though, was related to considerations having little to do with either statistics or the calendar.

I went over to the place where the others were forming into a tighter crowd, and in which there was a sense of expectancy in the subtle gestures and expressions of its individual members. Glances were now exchanged, the hand of one lightly touched the shoulder of another, and a pair of circled eyes gazed over to where two figures were setting their lanterns on the ground about six feet apart. The illumination of these lanterns revealed an opening in the earth. Eventually the awareness of everyone was focused on this roundish pit, and as if by prearranged signal we all began huddling around it. The only sounds were those of the wind and our own movements as we crushed frozen leaves and sticks underfoot.

Finally, when we had all surrounded this gaping hole, the first one jumped in, leaving our sight for a moment but then reappearing to take hold of a lantern which another one handed him from above. The miniature abyss filled with light, and I could see it was no more than six feet deep. Near the base of its inner wall the mouth of a tunnel was carved out. The figure holding the lantern stooped a little and disappeared into the passage.

One by one, then, the members of the crowd leaped into the darkness of this pit, and every fifth one took a lantern. I kept to the back of the group, for whatever subterranean activities were going to take place, I was sure I wanted to be on their periphery. When only about ten of us remained on the ground above, I maneuvered to let four of them precede me so that as the fifth I might receive a lantern. This was exactly how it worked out, for after I had leaped to the bottom of the hole a light was ritually handed down to me. Turning about face, I quickly entered the passageway. At that point I shook so with cold that I was neither curious nor afraid, but only grateful for the shelter.

I entered a long, gently sloping tunnel, just high enough for me to stand upright. It was considerably warmer down there than outside in the cold darkness of the woods. After a few moments I had sufficiently thawed out so that my concerns shifted from those of physical comfort to a sudden and justified preoccupation with my survival. As I walked I held my lantern close to the sides of the tunnel.

They were relatively smooth and even, as if the passage had not been made by manual digging but had been burrowed by something which left behind a clue to its dimensions in the tunnel's size and shape. This delirious idea came to me when I recalled the message that had been left on my bedroom mirror: "What buries itself before it is dead?"

I had to hurry along to keep up with those uncanny spelunkers who preceded me. The lanterns ahead bobbed with every step of their bearers, the lumbering procession seeming less and less real the farther we marched into that snug little tunnel. At some point I noticed the line ahead of me growing shorter. The processioners were emptying out into a cavernous chamber where I, too, soon arrived. This area was about thirty feet in height, its other dimensions approximating those of a large ballroom. Gazing into the distance above made me uncomfortably aware of how far we had descended into the earth. Unlike the smooth sides of the tunnel, the walls of this cavern looked jagged and irregular, as though they had been gnawed at. The earth had been removed, I assumed, either through the tunnel from which we had emerged, or else by way of one of the many other black openings that I saw around the edges of the chamber, for possibly they too led back to the surface.

But the structure of this chamber occupied my mind a great deal less than did its occupants. There to meet us on the floor of the great cavern was what must have been the entire slum population of Mirocaw, and more, all with the same eerily wide-eyed and oval-mouthed faces. They formed a circle around an altar-like object which had some kind of dark, leathery covering draped over it. Upon the altar, another covering of the same material concealed a lumpy form beneath.

And behind this form, looking down upon the altar, was the only figure whose face was not greased with makeup.

He wore a long snowy robe that was the same color as the wispy hair berimming his head. His arms were calmly at his sides. He made no movement. The man I once believed would penetrate great secrets stood before us with the same professorial bearing that had impressed me so many years ago, yet now I felt nothing but dread at the thought of what revelations lay pocketed within the abysmal folds of his magisterial attire. Had I really come here to challenge such a formidable figure? The name by which I knew him seemed itself insufficient to designate one of his stature. Rather I should name him by his other incarnations: god of all wisdom, scribe of all sacred books, father of all magicians, thrice great and more—rather I should call him *Thoth*.

He raised his cupped hands to his congregation and the ceremony was underway.

It was all very simple. The entire assembly, which had remained speechless until this moment, broke out in the most horrendous high-pitched singing that can be imagined. It was a choir of sorrow, of shrieking delirium, and of shame. The cavern rang shrilly with the dissonant, whining chorus. My voice, too, was added to the congregation's, trying to blend with their maimed music. But my singing could not imitate theirs, having a huskiness unlike their cacaphonous keening wail. To keep from exposing myself as an intruder I continued to mouth their words without sound. These words were a revelation of the moody malignancy which until then I had no more than sensed whenever in the presence of these figures. They were singing to the "unborn in paradise," to the "pure unlived lives." They sang a dirge for existence, for all its vital forms and seasons. Their ideals were those of darkness, chaos, and a melancholy half-existence consecrated to all the many shapes of death. A sea of thin, bloodless faces trembled and screamed with perverted hopes. And the robed, guiding figure at the heart of all this—elevated over the course of twenty years to the status of high priest—was the man from whom I had taken so many of my own life's principles. It would be useless to describe what I felt at that moment and a waste of the time I need to describe the events which followed.

The singing abruptly stopped and the towering white-haired figure began to speak. He was welcoming those of the new generation—twenty winters had passed since the "Pure Ones" had expanded their ranks. The word "pure" in this setting was a violence to what sense and composure I still retained, for nothing could have been more foul than what was to come. Thoss—and I employ this defunct identity only as a convenience—closed his sermon and moved back toward the dark-skinned altar. There, with all the flourish of his former life, he drew back the topmost covering. Beneath it was a limp-limbed effigy, a collapsed puppet sprawled upon the slab. I was standing toward the rear of the congregation and attempted to keep as close to the exit passage as I could. Thus, I did not see everything as clearly as I might have.

Thoss looked down over the crooked, doll-like form and then out at the gathering. I even imagined that he made knowing eye-contact with myself. He spread his arms and a stream of continuous and unintelligible words flowed from his moaning mouth. The congregation began to stir, not greatly but perceptibly. Until that moment there was a limit to what I believed was the evil of these people. They were, after all, only that. They were merely morbid, self-tortured souls with strange beliefs. If there was anything I had learned in all my years as an anthropologist it was that the world is infinitely rich in strange ideas, even to the point where the concept of strangeness itself had little meaning for me. But with the scene I then witnessed, my conscience bounded into a realm from which it will never return.

For now was the transformation scene, the culmination of every harlequinade.

It began slowly. There was increasing movement among those on the far side of the chamber from where I stood. Someone had fallen to the floor and the others in the area backed away. The voice at the altar continued its chanting. I tried to gain a better view but there were too many of them around me. Through the mass of obstructing bodies I caught only glimpses of what was taking place.

The one who had swooned to the floor of the chamber seemed to be losing all former shape and proportion. I thought it was a clown's trick. They were clowns, were they not? I myself could make four white balls transform into four black balls as I juggled them. And this was not my most astonishing feat of clownish magic. And is there not always a sleight-of-hand inherent in all ceremonies, often dependent on the transported delusions of the celebrants? This was a good show, I thought, and giggled to myself. The transformation scene of Harlequin throwing off his fool's facade. O God, Harlequin, do not move like that! Harlequin, where are your arms? And your legs have melted together and have begun squirming upon the floor. What horrible, mouthing umbilicus is that where your face should be? *What is it that buries itself before it is dead?* The almighty serpent of wisdom—the Conqueror Worm.

It now started happening all around the chamber. Individual members of the congregation would gaze emptily—caught for a moment in a frozen trance—and then collapse to the floor to begin the sickening metamorphosis. This happened with ever-increasing frequency the louder and more frantic Thoss chanted his insane prayer or curse. Then there began a writhing movement toward the altar, and Thoss welcomed the things as they curled their way to the altar-top. I knew now what lax figure lay upon it.

This was Kora and Persephone, the daughter of Ceres and the Winter Queen: the child abducted into the underworld of death. Except this child had no supernatural mother to save her, no living mother at all. For the sacrifice I witnessed was an echo of one that had occurred twenty years before, the carnival feast of the preceding generation—*O carne vale!* Now both mother and daughter had become victims of this subterranean sabbath. I finally realized this truth when the figure stirred upon the altar, lifted its head of icy beauty, and screamed at the sight of mute mouths closing around her.

I ran from the chamber into the tunnel. (There was nothing else that could be done, I have obsessively told myself.) Some of the others who had not yet changed began to pursue me. They would have caught up to me, I have no doubt, for I fell only a few yards into the passage. And for a moment I imagined that I too was about to undergo a transformation, but I had not been prepared as the others had been. When I heard the approaching footsteps of my pursuers I was sure there was an even worse fate facing me upon the altar. But the footsteps ceased and retreated. They had received an order in the voice of their high priest. I too heard the order, though I wish I had not, for until then I had imagined that Thoss did not remember who I was. It was that voice which taught me otherwise.

For the moment I was free to leave. I struggled to my feet and, having broken my lantern in the fall, retraced my way back through cloacal blackness.

Everything seemed to happen very quickly once I emerged from the tunnel and climbed up from the pit. I wiped the reeking greasepaint from my face as I ran through the woods and back to the road. A passing car stopped, though I gave it no other choice except to run me down.

"Thank you for stopping."

"What the hell are you doing out here?" the driver asked.

I caught my breath. "It was a joke. The festival. Friends thought it would be funny. . . . Please drive on."

My ride let me off about a mile out of town, and from there I could find my way. It was the same way I had come into Mirocaw on my first visit the summer before. I stood for a while at the summit of that high hill just outside the city limits, looking down upon the busy little hamlet. The intensity of the festival had not abated, and would not until morning. I walked down toward the welcoming glow of green, slipped through the festivities unnoticed, and returned to the hotel.

No one saw me go up to my room. Indeed, there was an atmosphere of absence and abandonment through that building, and the desk in the lobby was unattended.

I locked the door to my room and collapsed upon the bed.

VII

When I awoke the next morning I saw from my window that the town and surrounding countryside had been visited during the night by a snowstorm, one which was entirely unpredicted. The snow was still falling and blowing and gathering on the now deserted streets of Mirocaw. The festival was over. Everyone had gone home.

And this was exactly my own intention. Any action on my part concerning what I had seen the night before would have to wait until I was away from the town. I am still not sure it will do the slightest good to speak up like this. Any accusations I could make against the slum populous of Mirocaw would be resisted, as well they should be, as unbelievable. Perhaps in a very short while none of this will be my concern.

With packed suitcases in both hands I walked up to the front desk to check out. The man behind the desk was not Beadle and he had to fumble around to find my bill.

"Here we are. Everything all right?"

"Fine," I answered. "Is Mr. Beadle around?"

"No, I'm afraid he's not back yet. Been out all night looking for his daughter. She's a very popular girl, being the Winter Queen and all that nonsense. Probably find she was at a party somewhere."

A little noise came out of my throat.

I threw my suitcases in the backseat of my car and got behind the wheel. On that morning nothing I could recall seemed real to me. The snow was falling and I watched it through my windshield, slow and silent and entrancing. I started up my car, routinely glancing in my rearview mirror. What I saw there is now vividly framed in my mind, as it was framed in the back window of my car when I turned to verify its reality.

In the middle of the street behind me, standing ankle-deep in snow, was Thoss and another figure. When I looked closely at the other I recognized him as one of the boys whom I surprised in that diner. But he had now taken on a corrupt and listless resemblance to his new family. Both he and Thoss stared at me, making no attempt to forestall my departure. Thoss knew that this was unnecessary.

I had to carry the image of those two dark figures in my mind as I drove back home. But only now has the full weight of my experience descended upon me. So far I have claimed illness in order to avoid my teaching schedule. To face the normal flow of life as I had formerly known it would be impossible. I am now very much under the influence of a season and a climate far colder and more barren than all the winters in human memory. And mentally retracing past events does not seem to have helped; I can feel myself sinking deeper into a velvety white abyss.

At certain times I could almost dissolve entirely into this inner realm of awful purity and emptiness. I remember those invisible moments when in disguise I drifted through the streets of Mirocaw, untouched by the drunken, noisy forms around me: untouchable. But instantly I recoil at this grotesque nostalgia, for I realize what is happening and what I do not want to be true, though Thoss proclaimed it was. I recall his command to those others as I lay helplessly prone in the tunnel. They could have apprehended me, but Thoss, my old master, called them back. His voice echoed throughout that cavern, and it now reverberates within my own psychic chambers of memory.

"He is one of us," it said. "He has *always* been one of us."

It is this voice which now fills my dreams and my days and my long winter nights. I have seen you, Dr. Thoss, through the snow outside my window. Soon I will celebrate, alone, that last feast which will kill your words, only to prove how well I have learned their truth.

To the memory of H. P. Lovecraft

DAVID MEMMOTT

Sounding the Praises of Shadow to the Merchants of Light

The following poem addresses the trend that became prevalent during the Victorian era and continues today of extracting the dark elements from the fairy and folk tales we give our children, sanitizing them to the point where they lose their metaphoric power and consequently leave children with lasting impressions of Might-Equals-Right heroes and catatonically passive heroines.

David Memmott is part of a lively small press scene of writers and graphic artists in the Pacific Northwest; his poetry, drawings, and reviews have appeared in various small press venues. Memmott's new collection *House on Fire* contains, besides this poem a range of work from dark fantasy to surrealism. It is published by Alan Newcomer's Hypatia Press in Eugene, Oregon and is illustrated by Joey Shea.

—T.W.

Sounding the Praises of Shadow to the Merchants of Light

DAVID MEMMOTT

It takes a darker dark to realize a brighter bright.
You serve us the sun but not the space around it.
You intrude on reality by offering only your reality,
feeding us light until we flare and burn out
like used up stars collapsing into black holes.
We prefer the twilight glimmer of ogre breath,
the howl of bigbadwolves in the too near distance
and the ominous spectre of the giant's castle
spearing the clouds with its hermetic spires.
Our world consists of fables relived
with storybook princes and Brothers Grimm
leaping full-grown from a quiet mind,
Sherlock Holmes resurrected in a mild-mannered boy
who sniffs out Moriarty in a magical maze,
the slow Tarzan who swings through internal jungles
calling all animals to rescue a dizzy Jane
who wanders the halls looking for a perfect date.
We occupy a place you only dream about
but dare not discover in the light of day.

I hope to someday be a self-sufficient,
harmless and eccentric old fool
who dares to dress up in costumes
and hang around the school.
Though you would have me locked up,
I will be Robin Hood
stealing back the sacred fire

kept barely alive in a small chest
and loose it in the night
to skulk through the tangled tinder of sleep
and I will blow and blow
until your children dream dreams.

KRISTINE KATHRYN RUSCH

Harvest

Kristine Kathryn Rusch is a young Northwestern writer who has recently won the Campbell, an award for new talent in the science fiction and fantasy fields. She was the editor of *Pulphouse* magazine published out of Eugene, Oregon and has recently become the new editor of *The Magazine of Fantasy & Science Fiction* published out of Connecticut.

Rusch has been outspoken in her *Pulphouse* editorials on the subject of dysfunctional families and family issues. The following story first published in *Amazing*, explores this theme. It is a beautiful example of the way fantasy can be used as metaphor to portray characters and situations that are very, very real.

—T.W.

Harvest

KRISTINE KATHRYN RUSCH

—with thanks to poet Elizabeth Bishop

1

Time to plant tears, said the almanac, and so Kerry took the bucket she had carefully stored away at the back of the cupboard and went into the darkened bedroom. She took out each tear—perfectly formed, perfectly remembered, perfectly stored—cupped her hand around it so that the light from the hallway wouldn't catch the drop, and gently, ever so gently, tucked each tear in the fertile heart of the sleeping child.

2

Steam beaded the wallpaper. Amanda shut off the burner and moved the whistling teakettle. The morning was cold and gray. She felt chilled even though it was the beginning of summer. She set a tea bag in the mug Daniel had given her for her thirtieth birthday, and poured the water. Steam rose, fogging her glasses. She took them off, leaving the world a blur of greens and grays, grabbed a towel, and wiped the lenses. When she put her glasses back on, she saw that the tea bag had already stained the liquid brown.

She picked up the mug, happy for its warmth against her cold hands. Then she leaned against the refrigerator and sighed. She hated mornings like this. A stack of orders waited for her in her workroom, and she barely had enough energy to make a cup of tea. Part of the problem was the grayness. It oppressed her, brought out buried aches and pains. How could she sew when her hands were tight with cold, when the artificial light clashed with the darkness of a cloudy morning, making her stitches nearly impossible to see?

She made herself cross the living room into the workroom. Half-finished clothes lined the walls. The dress for Missy Anderson's wedding, still lacking a hem; the shirt for Carleton Meyer with the intricate hand-stitching undone; the pile of fabric that should already have been skirts for the high school's swing choir—all faced her like an accusation. The problem was the quilt that lay half-finished on the cluttered deacon's bench, the quilt that Amanda wanted to give Grandmother Kerry on her birthday only a week away.

Quilts were Amanda's specialty, but no one wanted quilts anymore. It was easier and cheaper to buy mass-produced things at the department stores down at the mall. Custom-made quilts were a luxury, like custom-made clothes, but for some reason people were willing to spend the money on a dress that they would use once rather than a quilt that would cover their bed for the next fifty years.

Amanda looked at the projects hanging on the wall, and then at the others stacked in her workbasket. She set her teacup down on the end table covered with pins and patterns, then grabbed the stack of swing choir skirts. They would take her half a day if she set her mind to the work.

She moved her worktable over, picked up the bolt of fabric, and laid it on the floor. The dark green velvet seemed ostentatious for a high-school group, but they had chosen it. She smoothed out the first segment, measured to see if she had the correct amount, and cut off the end of the fabric. Then she grabbed the pattern and pulled the tightly wrapped tissue pieces out of their paper folder.

Carefully, Amanda smoothed the tissue over the material. The thin paper crinkled as she worked. She checked knaps and widths, making sure that everything lined up properly, so that the skirt would be as beautiful as possible. Then she pinned the tissue to the velvet, shoving the slender silver pins in with a force unnecessary to her task. She pinched the fabric tightly, and shoved. The third pin went straight through both layers of velvet, shot across the tissue, and dug deep into the index finger of her left hand.

Amanda stared at the pin jutting out of her finger. Then the pain announced itself in a hard, burning jab. She pulled her finger away, squeezed the injured area, and watched the blood well into a tiny, tear-shaped drop. She put the fingertip in her mouth. It tasted of salt and iron.

A small smear of blood stained the green velvet. Tears rose in her eyes. She couldn't do anything right. She knew that she had to move quickly to make sure that the bloodstain wouldn't be permanent, but she remained still, sitting like a child, one finger in her mouth, and knees tucked under her body until her tears slowly slid back into the tear ducts where they belonged.

3

The clock in the dining room chimed midnight as Daniel unlocked the door and stepped in. The house felt heavy and oppressive in the dark. He flicked on the switch, and the soft lights scattered across the room, leaving corners filled with shadows. Amanda's tea mug sat on the floor beside the couch. A book, face down, leaned against the mug. A pillow, still bearing Amanda's headprint, had been crushed into the corner of the couch, and on the other end, a quilt had been thrown messily back.

He felt a twinge of guilt. Amanda had waited up for him and then, when she could wait no longer, had stumbled off to bed. He knew how he would find her, curled up like a child, fist against her face, hair sprawled against the pillow. He sighed. He lost track of time so easily, forgetting that she was here, waiting for him. And he found things that made it easy to forget. He hadn't needed that drink after work with Rich. Or to meet Margot for dinner. They could have discussed the Johnson account at the office, with a desk between them, instead of sitting hip to hip in Harper's while soft jazz echoed in the background.

Daniel left Amanda's mess—he had long ago stopped picking up after her—and went into the kitchen. She had left the light above the stove on for him, like she always did.

On the wall beside the teakettle, water beaded the wall. As he watched, one droplet slowly ran down and fell onto the oven's smooth metal surface. She had to stop facing that kettle toward the wall. The steam would ruin the wallpaper. He grabbed a paper towel and wiped the water away. Then he shut off the stove light and headed to bed.

The bedroom was dim, but not completely dark. Amanda had left the bathroom light on as well, and it fell softly across the bed, illuminating her slender form. She was curled up on her right side, one hand stretched across his pillow. The quilt had fallen off her shoulder, revealing soft skin and one well-formed breast.

He grabbed the knot of his tie, slipped it down, and slid the tie from his neck. Then he took off his clothes and carefully folded them, setting them on the rocking chair beneath the shaded windows. As he crawled into bed, he picked up her hand and ran it down his body, setting it on his groin so that as she awakened she could feel his arousal.

"Amanda," he said softly.

She stirred. He caressed her, touched every part of her, and then slipped inside of her. She didn't wake up until her first orgasm and then she cried, "Daniel!" as if he had surprised her. He buried his face in her shoulder, smelling the musky scent of her, as he came. He grabbed her waist, rolled over onto his side, holding them together so that they faced each other and let sleep drift through his body. The bathroom light shone in his eyes, but he didn't care. Amanda stirred, awake now, and he thought he felt a shudder run through her, like a sob. But when he reached up to touch her cheek, the skin was smooth, soft, and dry.

4

Amanda set the tea tray down on the coffee table. She picked up the porcelain teapot and poured. The thin liquid filled the fragile cup. Carefully, she handed the cup to her grandmother, then poured another cup. Kerry seemed frail and tired that morning, but as strong as ever. She wore a dainty summer dress of pale pink and kept her lacy off-white shawl about her shoulders.

Amanda sighed and settled back into the armchair. The rain pattered outside, dousing everything in grayness. Kerry reached over and wiped a bead of water from the teapot. Since she had arrived, she had wiped water off the wall in the kitchen, the bathroom, even the foyer where the swing choir skirts hung, waiting for the director to pick them up.

"I don't know what it is, Grandma," Amanda said. "I think it's the rain causing the dampness in the house."

Kerry shook her head. "The house is well-sealed," she said. "It's time you had children, Amanda."

Amanda looked up sharply. The non sequitur surprised her. Kerry had never said a word about children before. "I don't have time for children."

"You need them." Kerry set down her teacup. She squirmed uncomfortably, wiped another water bead off the wall, and frowned. "I can't sit here any longer. I have to go home, Amanda."

Amanda set her own teacup down, feeling a sense of panic build in the pit of her stomach. Her grandmother was in her eighties. Perhaps something had happened to her to make her so vague, something Amanda hadn't known about. "You all right, Grandma?"

Kerry leaned heavily on her cane as she got to her feet. "I'll be fine once I get home. You just remember what I said."

Amanda grabbed a sweater, wrapped it around her shoulders, and walked her grandmother to the door. Though it had stopped raining, Amanda asked, "You going to be okay walking home, Grandma?"

Kerry nodded. "It is only a block, Amanda. I haven't fallen apart yet."

Amanda smiled. Her grandmother was feisty even when she was vague. Amanda went out onto the porch and watched as Kerry made her way down the sidewalk. Two houses down, she stopped, turned, and looked at Amanda. "You'll have my birthday?"

"I won't miss it," Amanda said. Her grandmother kept walking, slowly, toward her own home. Amanda frowned. The discussion had bothered her. For the first time, her grandmother had seemed unfocused, slightly out of touch. But she was getting older. And in some ways, loss was inevitable. Or at least, that was what Daniel would say.

Daniel. Amanda grabbed the porch door and let herself back inside. He had left before she was up that morning. She rarely saw him anymore. Supposedly they spent weekends together, but he usually went off to play golf with clients or back to the office to work. He was a workaholic, a man who barely had time enough for his own wife. And her grandmother wanted Amanda to have children with him. Children were a partnership, a joint gift that a couple gave each other. If she had children now, she would merely be taking, for herself.

5

Kerry closed the door. Her house smelled like flowers and lemon furniture polish, not damp like Amanda's had. All the water on the walls, threatening to break through, and Amanda living there, working there, every day. Kerry made her way to the book on the shelf beside the stove. She picked it up, rubbing her hands across its worn leather cover before thumbing past the ripped and stained pages to the last page with writing on it, the page that had been blank the day before. She knew what she would find.

Time to plant tears, the almanac said.

Kerry closed the almanac and set it back on the shelf. Then she stared at the cupboard where her bucket was hidden, had been hidden for thirty years since Amanda's mother had used it months before her death. The bucket was dry and empty. Poor Amanda, Kerry thought as a wave of guilt twisted through her stomach. In some ways it was already too late. Amanda didn't want children, that was clear, and if she didn't have any, the water would burst through the walls and engulf her. Amanda would drown beneath the weight of her family's accumulated sorrows.

Kerry remembered her own grandmother explaining the process. *Children are stronger. They can carry the pain with ease—and pass it on when the pain grows too much for them.*

It sounded so simple, except when someone wanted to take the pain back. Kerry was old. She could die and take all those hurts with her. But she knew that she could never reclaim her gift of tears; her grandmother had told her that it was impossible.

So she would take the only other solution, the only other way she could help her beloved Amanda, even though it would cost them some of their family heritage. Kerry opened the almanac to the first page and ran down the list of names until she found Steiger's. Steiger would hold the water at bay until Amanda decided to have children. He had done it before.

6

Amanda was finishing the hand-stitching on Carleton Meyer's shirt while the radio blared a talk show. The topic, apparently planned weeks in advance, was how to keep cool in the summer heat. Callers reminded the poor host that the only heat they had felt so far had been from furnaces running to protect them from the chill outdoor damp.

The shirt was lovely. The stitching gave it an elegant, western look that would accent Carleton's appearance rather than detract from it. Three new projects sat on her worktable, waiting for her to start them. And the quilt pieces still lay on the deacon's bench, silently reproaching her. Her grandmother's birthday was only two days away. Amanda had nothing else to give her.

A firm rap on the front door brought her attention away from the shirt. A woman's voice echoed from the radio, suggesting dry ice in the bathtub as the best cure for the summer doldrums. Amanda gripped the ribbed dial and turned off the radio as she walked to the entrance.

The man standing on her porch was not a client. She could tell that immediately. He wore sturdy Levis and a workshirt under his rain gear. Water dripped from the brim of his hat onto the dry concrete under the overhang. She pulled open the door and adopted her best anti-salesman pose.

"Name's Steiger, ma'am." He handed her his business card. "I do house care. Been going door to door in this wet weather, asking folks if they're having troubles with mildew and damp."

Amanda frowned. She saw his truck parked near the curb. It was large and white, with STEIGER'S painted in blue along the cab. Underneath was a phone number and a slogan: SPECIALIZING IN LOST DREAMS AND MEMORIES. She glanced down at the card. The same phrase ran along the bottom. She pointed to it.

"What's that mean?"

Steiger grinned. He had a solid face, rather ordinary. She thought that if she had to describe it to Daniel, she would say Steiger had no distinguishing features. "Lost dreams and memories," he repeated and then shrugged. "Just personal fancy, ma'am. I like to think houses are part of their people. When they first buy the place, it's a dream come true. Then it becomes a headache filled with memories. Me, I try to turn it back into a dream again."

The idea pleased her. She felt a slight release as she stepped away from the door. "I have water dripping down my walls, Mr. Steiger. What would you charge to fix that?"

"Depends on the problem, ma'am." He shook the water out of his coat, removed his hat, and walked in. Then he hung everything on the coat-tree near the door, careful to move the tree so that the rainwater dripped onto the tile entry instead of the carpet. "Let's take a look."

She led him into the kitchen where water still beaded near the stove. She had turned the teapot that morning so that the steam exploded against empty air, but the beading remained. He examined the water as closely as a jeweler examined a diamond. Then he let out air gently. "You need my services, ma'am."

"What will you do?"

"First, I'll clean up the water. Then I'll see what I can do to dam it up."

"How much will it cost?" Amanda clutched her hands tightly together. She felt tense.

He continued to stare at the water. "Seventy-five dollars."

"Per hour?"

He shook his head. "Just seventy-five dollars."

No wonder he was going door to door; he couldn't make any money at the prices he charged. "I'll pay you by the hour," Amanda said.

He looked at her. His eyes were dry and inwardly focused, like the eyes of a person who had been reading for hours. "You're very kind, ma'am. But all I charge is seventy-five dollars. Feels like I'm cheating you at that rate."

Amanda wasn't going to argue with him. She ran a hand through her hair. "Will it take you long?"

"A few hours, at most. You have this anywhere else?"

"In the bathroom." A memory touched her mind, a small one, of waking up alone. "And I think some are starting on the ceiling in the bedroom."

He nodded, as if he had expected her to say that. "Don't worry, ma'am. I'll take care of it for you. You just go back to whatever it was you were doing, and leave the rest to me."

Amanda returned to her office as he ran to his truck. Carleton's shirt lay crumpled where she left it, needle still piercing the fabric. She started to flick on the radio, but stopped. Her hand went to the quilt, and this time, she didn't stop.

7

Daniel couldn't explain why he was driving home in the middle of the day, but when he arrived and saw the unusual truck parked outside, he knew that his sixth sense had been working overtime. Amanda had gotten in trouble. He could feel it.

He opened the door and stepped into the house. It was quiet. The damp smell he had been noticing over the past month was barely there. A raincoat and hat he didn't recognize hung on the coat-tree by the door. A light trailed down the hallway from the sewing room. The bedroom was dark, but he heard rustlings coming from it and suddenly felt ill.

He had been neglecting Amanda this past year, and she had not complained. He had never thought that she would see someone else, that slowly she was replacing him as the center of her life. His breathing became shallow as he walked. He rounded the corner into the bedroom door, expecting to find Amanda as only he had seen her, cheeks flushed with passion, eyes bright, hair flowing across her well-formed, naked body. Instead, he found a man he had never seen before scraping the ceiling.

"What the hell are you doing?" Daniel demanded.

The man stopped working. He took the little vial he had been holding in his hand and shoved it in his pocket. "I'm done," he said as he stepped off the stool he had been standing on.

"Let me see what you have there," Daniel said. He knew that the man had taken something valuable, could feel it in his bones.

"Sorry," the man said. "I contracted this work with your wife."

Daniel turned. "Amanda!"

She came out of the sewing room into the hall. Her expression was sleep-blurry, and her hair was mussed. In her right hand, she clutched an oval-shaped quilt piece. "I didn't know you were home," she said.

"Damn right. What is this man doing here?"

Amanda smiled. "He's cleaning out the water."

"He's been stealing from us." Daniel could feel it as firmly as he had felt the impulse to come home. The man had been stealing. Valuable things. Family heirlooms. Things passed from generation to generation.

Amanda shook her head. "Don't be silly, Daniel. There's nothing to steal."

"I want him out of here," Daniel said. "Now."

The man opened his hands, bowed slightly at Daniel, but spoke to Amanda. "I'm sorry," he said. "It's nearly finished."

"Let me walk you to the door." Amanda walked beside the man. Daniel followed, feeling angry, betrayed, as if she had dismissed him and sided with the thief. She picked up her purse from the bench near the door and handed the man some money.

"Amanda!" Daniel cried. "The man has been stealing."

"Thank you," she said without a glance at Daniel.

The man took the money, stuffed it in his shirt pocket, then put on his rain gear. "You are too kind for this," he said. "I wish you the best, Amanda."

He walked out into the rain. Daniel leaned out the door and memorized the license off the truck. Then he went to the phone.

"What are you doing?" Amanda asked.

"Calling the cops." Daniel pushed the buttons, dialing as fast as he could. "He was robbing from us. And you paid him."

Amanda reached over, took the receiver from his hand, and hung it up. "It was my money. And he wasn't stealing. He was cleaning. Tell me what he took."

Family heirlooms. Treasures passed from generation to generation. "I don't know," Daniel said slowly. "But I could feel something—"

"You don't feel," Amanda snapped. She walked down the hall to the sewing room and closed the door. Daniel stood in the darkened hallway. She had rebuked him, turning his words to another meaning. For the first time with Amanda, he felt unsure of himself and a little frightened.

8

Amanda sat on the deacon's bench. While Steiger had been there, she had nearly finished the quilt. She wished he had stayed, had been able to finish the job. Somehow, now, she felt that the burden was on her. Her eyes were tired and her back ached. She hadn't meant to snap at Daniel, but he was so self-important. He had offended her and, she realized, it had not been the first time. He always assumed she would be there, but he treated her as if she were replaceable, as if she didn't matter. A tear formed in her eye and rolled down her cheek. She shivered as the warm drop traced her jawbone and settled on her chin. It had been a long time since she cried. She couldn't remember the last time.

Carleton's shirt still lay crumpled on the floor. An accusation. Shirts made money. Quilts did not. She picked up the shirt and stroked its fine handwork. Only an hour's work left on that versus an evening with the quilt. She sighed, thinking that if she still had energy when she finished the shirt, she would work on the quilt.

She could hear Daniel slamming about in the kitchen, trying to call attention to himself with the noise he was making. This time she would not go and try to calm him. This time she would take care of herself.

The shirt felt heavy in her hands. Carleton could wait an extra day for the shirt. She wanted to work on the quilt. No project had ever absorbed her like that one. She took the thick material and ran it across her lap. The tear dripped from her chin into the fabric. A round moisture stain appeared for a moment, and then faded. Amanda squeezed the material. It felt thicker where the tear had landed, but not wet. She nodded, feeling her eyes overflow. Slowly, she stitched and ignored the tears as they fell.

9

The presents sat at Kerry's feet like obedient schoolchildren. Conversation hummed around her. Aunts, cousins, second cousins, friends all filled Amanda's living room. But Kerry didn't watch them. She watched Amanda flow through the crowd with a grace the girl had never had before. Amanda poured herself a glass of punch, then came and sat beside Kerry.

"You're not socializing," Amanda said.

"I've been watching you." Kerry took her granddaughter's dry hand into her own. "You're not pregnant, are you? You have that glow."

Amanda shook her head and lowered her gaze, but not before Kerry saw what was in it. No children. Not then. Not ever—at least, with Daniel. "I want to talk to you, Grandma, but not today."

Kerry nodded. She didn't want to hear it today. At least Steiger had helped, a little.

Amanda reached down and grabbed the largest box. It was wrapped in silver paper and tied with a large red bow. "It's from me, Grandma. Open it."

Kerry took the package and set it on her lap. It felt heavy and oppressive. Her hands shook as she reached for the red bow. Slowly she untied it, then slipped her fingers through the cool paper. As she pulled off the lid her heart thudded against her chest.

"It's a quilt, Grandma," Amanda said. "I made it for you."

But Kerry didn't have to hear the words. She knew that the quilt was hers. She recognized the tears woven into every stitch. She touched the first and saw the day her father died, that stark, cold gray day when her father's face had matched the sky. And the next tear—the day Thomas first hit her. Married only a month and already he had drawn blood. And older tears, memories that weren't hers, but that she had carried for years until she had harvested them along with her own crop and planted the seeds with the next generation. She had thought of taking them, but she had never realized that a child could give them back.

The gift had been given, the seeds planted. But there would never be another harvest.

"Is it okay, Grandma?" Amanda sounded worried. "I thought you would like it."

Kerry looked up and saw that her granddaughter was happy for the first time. "I love you, child," Kerry said, hugging the quilt tightly to her chest.

SUSAN COOPER

Fantasy in the Real World

Susan Cooper was born in the U.K., read English at Oxford, and now resides in the U.S. near Boston. A journalist and writer of screenplays, she has also published a number of children's books including a sequence of splendid fantasy novels that have become classics of our field: *Over Sea, Under Stone; The Dark is Rising* (a Newbery Honor Book); *Greenwitch; The Grey King* (winner of the Newbery Award); and the final book in the sequence, *Silver on the Tree.* Cooper set these books in her native Buckinghamshire, reworking Celtic myth and legend with a deft touch and strength of narrative that one reviewer called "as rich and eloquent as a Beethoven symphony." They are highly recommended even to those readers tired of Celtic "high" fantasy. These are not imitations; these are the real thing.

Though fantasy has been a staple of children's literature (and, indeed, of adult literature) since literature began, there are still those (reviewers, educators and librarians among them) who turn up their noses at it, or go further to assert that it is actively bad for children. In the pages of *Horn Book,* a journal about children's literature published out of Boston, Cooper eloquently addressed this issue, shedding light on the value of fantasy fiction for adults in the process. This essay was previously a speech made by Ms. Cooper at the New York Public Library. I am very pleased to be able to include this essay *about* fantasy with the year's best fantasy stories. I also recommend Emma Bull's moving essay "Why I Write Fantasy" published in the Winter 1990 issue of *Pulphouse* magazine.

—T.W.

Fantasy in the Real World

SUSAN COOPER

Once upon a time, when I was writing a sequence of books called *The Dark Is Rising*, I began having a recurrent dream. It was a fragment of dream, really: a set of images, short on narrative. In the dream I found myself in a library, a big wood-paneled room full of book-crammed shelves and heavy wooden tables and chairs, all set on an odd mixture of levels. As I walked through this library, I saw people reading, sitting at the tables, but although I spoke to one or two of them, they paid me no attention; it was as if I wasn't really there. As indeed I wasn't, of course.

I noticed that one long wall of the room was completely lined with bookshelves, but that the opposite wall had none. And then suddenly, as I looked, that bookless wall vanished away, leaving only blank space, and I was looking down over the edge of the floor into the dark, shadowy auditorium of a vast theater. The library and I were high above its stage, facing row upon row of empty seats stretching back into the darkness.

Then by another of those flicker-changes of dream I was down in the theater, out in the auditorium, looking back up at the library. There it hung, suspended, as if it were a long gallery above the stage. The theater was dark; only that hovering room and its books were brightly lit, and the readers, absorbed, sat unheeding at their tables and read on.

And at that point, always, I woke up.

I dreamed this dream three or four times in a period of, I suppose, three or four years. Eventually, when I was writing the last book in my sequence, *Silver on the Tree*, I came to a point in my story where two boys walked through a door. I left them there, walking through, at the end of one writing day. I didn't know what they would find on the other side. The next day, when I began to write about what they saw, I found myself describing the strange library-theater of my dream—and I've never dreamed about it since. Perhaps it wanted a life of its own, a chance to get into other imaginations than mine, and was now content that it had been set free. For this of course is what happens to any character or place or image that a writer puts into a story: born in one imagination, he, she, or it is then born again, over and over, in the separate imaginations of every reader of that story, until the last copy of the book falls apart or the last reader forgets. No wonder Tolkien called storytelling "subcreation."

My dream itself had the usual echoes in it of the past, present, and future of the dreamer. All my life I had been rooted in libraries, both as a reader of other people's books and writer of my own. All my life I had been stage-struck, haunted by the theater. Within a year of finishing *Silver on the Tree*, and my sequence of novels, I was writing scenes for John Langstaff's *Christmas Revels* at Sanders Theatre in Cambridge and beginning to collaborate with the actor Hume Cronyn on a play called *Foxfire*, which eventually made its way to Broadway. The wall of the library had melted away, and I was down in the theater which had been waiting beyond. I've been moving between the two ever since.

But if we detach that little dream from personal experience, it can be a useful metaphor of another kind. Take a man or woman at an early age, in the condition which is known as childhood, and put him or her into a library. Give the child a book to read. (I am using my library to stand for any nook or cranny in which a child may read, from the bedroom to the subway, from the breakfast table to —well, the library.) Once the child's imagination is caught up in that book, particularly if it deals with experiences beyond his own world, beyond reality— then boundaries vanish, walls disappear, and he finds himself facing a wonderful space in which anything can happen. He's transported into my dream theater.

The theater. Consider the image. A magical place, quiet and dark most of the time—sometimes for months on end, if its owner is unlucky—but a place which once in a while is brilliant with light and life and excitement. It lies there sleeping, closed up, its doors all locked—until suddenly one day the doors are open and you can go in, and find wonder and delight. That isn't a bad image of the unconscious mind.

Fantasy, our subject and my preoccupation, comes from and appeals to the unconscious. It draws all its images from that dark wonderland, through the mysterious catalyst of the creative imagination. Nobody has ever described the process better than that great librarian, Lillian H. Smith, in her book *The Un-reluctant Years*. "Creative imagination," she said, "is more than mere invention. It is that power which creates, out of abstractions, life. It goes to the heart of the unseen, and puts that which is so mysteriously hidden from ordinary mortals into the clear light of their understanding, or at least of their partial understanding. It is more true, perhaps, of writers of fantasy than of any other writers except poets that they struggle with the inexpressible. According to their varying capacities, they are able to evoke ideas and clothe them in symbols, allegory, and dream."

Symbols, allegory, and dream. Like ritual and myth, those other mighty ances-tors of fantasy, they have in recent years been much more widely discussed than is usual in this country, thanks to the television journalist Bill Moyers. First, public television gave us "Moyers: Joseph Campbell and the Power of Myth," Moyers's six one-hour interviews with the mythologist Joseph Campbell, and then

Doubleday published what I suppose should be called the book of the series, *The Power of Myth*. The interviews were watched by two-and-a-half million people, and the book was on the *New York Times* best-seller list for six months. Between them they made Campbell's ideas far more accessible than his own books had done over the last forty years; he was a good writer but a better teacher, and *The Power of Myth*, both on film and on the page, is captivating.

When Joseph Campbell talks about myth, he is talking about the tree of which fantasy is a branch—or more accurately, a whole cluster of branches. And his great complaint is that we live today in a demythologized world: a society without the guidelines of ritual, a society which lacks the unconscious awareness of long-established patterns of civilized behavior, and falls into destructive violence as a result. The United States, says Campbell, has no ethos. "Ethos" had me reaching for my dictionary, because to me it meant character, and you could hardly accuse the United States of having no character. In the *Oxford English Dictionary* I found a more specific meaning, deriving from Aristotle on Rhetoric: "The characteristic spirit, prevalent tone of sentiment, of people or community; the 'genius' of an institution or system." So, back to Campbell. The United States, he says, has no ethos: as a vast jumble of people from different nationalities and traditions, it lacks the web of assumptions about social behavior that you find in a deep-rooted homogeneous culture—"an unstated mythology, you might say." Instead it is held together by law. Our children in America share with all mankind a deep and ancient hunger for myth, but there are no myths for them to inherit—so some of them make up their own. "This is why we have graffiti all over the city," says Campbell. "These kids have their own . . . morality, and they're doing the best they can. But they're dangerous, because their own laws are not those of the city."

He is talking only about a particular stratum of urban youth, but there is no question that we live in the most violent society in the so-called civilized world. One statistic will do. In one year—1983—the number of people killed with guns in Japan was thirty-five; in Switzerland, twenty-seven; in Australia, ten; in Canada, six. In Great Britain, eight people were shot. The population of the United States is four times as large as that of Great Britain. Multiply the British figure by four and you get thirty-two. But the number of people killed with guns in the United States that year wasn't thirty-two; it was 9,014.

For Joseph Campbell, this is the violence of a cultural chaos: a civilization without mythological foundation. Myths are "stories about the wisdom of life," he says. "What we're learning in our schools is not the wisdom of life. We're learning technologies, we're getting information." Whenever he lectured, he says, he found a real hunger in his students, because "mythology has a great deal to do with the stages of life, the initiation ceremonies as you move from childhood to adult responsibilities . . . the process of throwing off the old [role] and coming out in the new."

He says: "[Myths] are the world's dreams. They are archetypal dreams, and deal with great human problems. I know when I come to one of these thresholds now. The myth tells me about it, how to respond to certain crises of disappointment or delight or failure or success. The myths tell me where I am."

The myths tell me where I am. Fantasy tells me where I am.

Perhaps I shouldn't use these two words interchangeably, in this context, without justifying what I am doing. Joseph Campbell, as you might expect, is eloquent in defining myth. "A dream is a personal experience of that deep, dark ground that is the support of our conscious lives, and a myth is the society's dream. The myth is the public dream and the dream is the private myth. . . . Myth must be kept alive. The people who can keep it alive are artists of one kind or another. The function of the artist is the mythologization of the environment and the world."

He's saying that artists have inherited the mythmaking function of the shaman and the seer, and of course he's right. Where the art of writing is concerned, his point applies most of all to the poets and to the writers of fantasy. Both deal with images, and with their links to and within the unconscious mind. And the fantasist—not one of my favorite words—deals with the substance of myth: the deep archetypal patterns of emotion and behavior which haunt us all whether we know it or not.

All of us who write fantasy are creating, in one way or another, variations on a single theme: we have a hero—or heroine—who has to cross the threshold from his familiar world into the unknown. In search of some person or thing or ideal, he has a series of adventures, undergoes trials, survives dangers and disasters, until he achieves his goal, his quest. And having achieved it, he comes home again a wiser person, better prepared for the longer journey which is now ahead of him, the adventure of living his life.

This is not a blueprint which every writer deliberately follows: God forbid. Indeed many try assiduously to keep away from it. But when you look back over a book of genuine fantasy, you can always see the pattern lurking inside it, in however shadowy a form. The echo of myth runs through fairy tales and folk tales from every culture, every tradition; in our own literature it runs through *Pilgrim's Progress* to *Gulliver's Travels*, *Alice in Wonderland* to *The Wizard of Oz*; from Macdonald to Tolkien, from Lewis to Le Guin. When I look at my own books, I see a continual reiteration of the quest theme; not only in the *Dark Is Rising* books and my other fantasy novels, *Seaward* and *Mandrake*, but even in the nonfiction. I wrote a book called *Behind the Golden Curtain* which was, now I come to think about it, my personal quest in search of the nature of America; I wrote a biography of the English author J. B. Priestly which spent much of its time portraying him as a man in search of his own lost youth. And as I reflect on the book I'm writing now, I can see it is already taking on the pattern of a leaving and a search, to be followed no doubt (though I haven't the least intention of this at the moment) by a return. I am clearly stuck: so deeply imbued with the archetypes of fantasy and myth that I can't write about anything else. Well, I'm in some good company.

It is quite possible that I *need* these archetypes, not just as an artist, but personally. After all, writers are at the mercy not only of the quality of imagination they inherit, but the quality of character that came along with it. What is certainly true is that certain *readers* seem to need that archetypal pattern.

The children who write to authors of fantasy novels fumble to explain why they like such books, and come up with sentences like these from my own mail. From a thirteen-year-old in Texas: "Your books are my escape from the world I live in. I often wish I were one of the Old Ones, fighting the Dark and protecting Mankind from harm." A thirteen-year-old in Britain: "When I open your books I feel myself slipping out of this world and into another. I am one of those people who long for Adventure, and reading your books is the closest I have ever come to being in one." From a twenty-year-old in Illinois: "You give all of us the chance to leave the mundane struggles we face and enter a slightly grander struggle for a while." A sixteen-year-old in Sweden: "I get such a feeling when I read your books. It's like I want to climb up to the pages and walk straight into it and help Will and his friends." And from a twelve-year-old in Britain, the simplest and perhaps the most accurate: "Your books seem to fit me just right."

All of us need adventure, though of course it's easier to handle vicariously, through the pages of a book, than when it actually arrives. The celebrated cathartic effect, that mixture of pity and fear which is supposed to refresh the soul, is better acquired by watching *King Lear*, or reading about him, than by actually being King Lear. Just consider being King Lear. You have two psychotic daughters who murder each other, your best friend has his eyes torn out, and you go raving mad on a stormy heath, and end up dying of a broken heart with your third daughter's body in your arms. A memorable life, but not an enjoyable one. Fantasy, unlike real life, offers amazing adventures with no price tag; all you have to do is open a book. And afterwards, if one of its adventures does ever happen to overtake you, somewhere in your unconscious mind you will be equipped to endure or enjoy it.

We all need heroes, too, and not only when we're children. In story, in myth, the hero may die, but he must be replaced. The king is dead; long live the king! Among the few societies which still keep this pattern alive, Great Britain is a fortunate country; there is a great deal to be said for constitutional monarchy. The actual governing is all done by a democratically elected Parliament; the monarch has no power at all, but leads a benevolent and very public life as a figurehead, a focus for ritual and emotion—a hero. Popularity is less important for a British prime minister than for an American president, since in Britain the public can focus all its adoration, all its hero-worship, upon the Queen—not to mention Prince Charles, Princess Di, and the rest. The allure of royalty even spreads beyond national boundaries, to wistful millions in kingless, queenless countries: when Charles and Diana were married in 1981 it was estimated that the wedding was watched on television by an eighth of the population of the globe. And if Prince Charles ever manages to succeed to the throne, he will instantly acquire new stature throughout the world; through the ritual of the coronation, the magic of monarchy, he will become a new worldwide hero.

We are short of such figures in the United States. (I take the liberty of saying "we" even though I'm not an American, because I have after all lived here for twenty-five years.) We have rich and powerful men and women; we have people of great talent or intelligence or beauty, or all three—but where are the figures to attract that deep, worshipful fervor drawn out by the mystique of the ritual hero? Who are *our* heroes? Ronald Reagan? Donald Trump?

There have been figures with the stature of heroes: John Fitzgerald Kennedy, Martin Luther King, Jr. But they're dead, assassinated, and their stature has been vastly increased by the fact that they did die, as if they were powerful images of ritual sacrifice. They died, but they weren't replaced. Today, in general, we don't have heroes; we have celebrities—people well known not for their gigantic accomplishments but simply for being well known. Joseph Campbell was appalled by the results of a questionnaire which was sent round a high school in Brooklyn, asking the students, "What would you like to be?" Two-thirds of them ticked off the answer: "A celebrity." They didn't aspire to achievement, Campbell unhappily noted; they wanted simply to be known, to have name and fame. It's small wonder, with this scale of values in place, that we have such depressing presidential elections, with the candidates judged less by their ability or potential or beliefs than by their charisma, their image—or lack of it.

This is a very, very young country. Yes, we need outlets for the longing for mythic adventure, and we need mythic heroes. But you can't expect development that in other lands took three thousand years to be accomplished here in less than three hundred. The history of England, for instance, is a long layering of different traditions, as one culture after another came invading the island and taking control from the one which had invaded last time. There were lots of invaders, and each *one* of them lasted at least three hundred years. The English have ended up as an extraordinary interbred mix of Pict, Celt, Angle, Saxon, Jute, Dane, Roman, Norman—but time has merged all those different elements into a kind of rich compost, out of which an unmistakably English character and way of life slowly grew. America, now—America is an extraordinary mix of English, Italian, Irish, German, Scandinavian, African, Polish, Japanese, Chinese, Spanish, Russian, West Indian—you name it. But they haven't blended; they haven't had enough centuries; and the first invaders (who came from England) didn't even *try* to blend with the culture that was here before them—instead they did their level best to destroy it. The myths and imagery of the native American could have become as potent a basis for this country's cultural development as the classical and Celtic myths were for Western Europe—but that didn't happen, and now it can never happen. The nation had to grow too fast; there wasn't time—and there certainly isn't time now. Almost every one of the older nations of the world has a slow-grown mythological foundation: what Campbell called its own ethos. The United States, instead, has a gap.

I think perhaps that the task of fantasy, in our contemporary world, is to help fill that gap.

Our society itself tries to fill the gap, without knowing it, but it does so from the wrong end; it tries to put in a foundation by stuffing things into the attic. Let me digress, in order to explain.

When I first came to this country in 1962, as a wide-eyed young newspaper reporter, I was hit very hard by two overwhelming impressions. The first was wonderful; it was the sense of opportunity, "anybody can do anything"—the sense of freedom that always enraptures visitors from England's comparatively rigid structure of tradition and behavior.

The second impression was less wonderful, but fascinating: a more gradual realization that this freedom-loving society was gripped by a longing for rituali-zation. It began from the moment I stepped off the airplane in Washington; the first thing I saw, after the startling glimpse of policemen wearing real guns, was a line of about twenty-five teenage girls all dressed as Little Bopeep, marching through the airport, chanting. I said to my American escort, *"What's that?"* He looked slightly embarrassed and he said, "Oh, they're from a sorority. That's something they have to do, to join it. A kind of initiation rite."

I'd never heard of Joseph Campbell then.

Fraternities and sororities, the Elks and the Kiwanis and the Sons of Italy, the golf clubs and the country clubs—they all thrive on rituals of membership. Then there's American football, an amazing ritualization of the relatively simple game of rugby. The players no longer wear simple shorts and shirts; they are all decked about with special helmets and padding, as ceremonially armored as medieval knights approaching a joust. They huddle together to murmur ritual numbers to one another; they launch into a sequence of ritual movements—and then someone waves a flag or blows a whistle, and they all stop, in order that the ground may be ritually measured and the ceremony start all over again. During any pause, groups of nubile young women leap in unison beside their team, and chant ritual chants to the God Ra (as in Rah! Rah! Rah!). At a central break in the ceremony, another group of acolytes moves in stylized patterns over the sacred ground, playing musical instruments, while a priest figure makes ritual motions with a sacred stick. On particularly sacred dates all this may be watched by as many as one hundred million people on small ritual boxes containing a glass screen.

Other kinds of ritualization are more insidious, based on the second of the two founding principles of the United States: freedom, and the right to make a profit. There are no longer any sacred festivals in the American calendar, religious or otherwise; there are only celebrations of commerce, filling the stores with Christ-mas goods in October and turning Thanksgiving into the year's biggest buying weekend. Eighty-five per cent of the load carried by the average American mailman consists of ritual pieces of paper exhorting folk to spend money. Alternatively, they ask them to give money away. Charities have adopted the complex and manipulative ceremonies of advertising—and so have senators, who reach their positions of power not simply by free election but by raising an average of three million dollars for their election campaign—ten thousand dollars for every week of a six-year term. The only known exception has been Senator William Proxmire of Wisconsin, who claimed to have spent on his last election campaign in 1982 a total of $145.10, all out of his own pocket. And he won.

The newest and fastest growing ritual imposed on modern life is that of the computer, whose complex ceremonial amounts to a new secret language and way of thinking. *The Power of Myth* rehearses the story of President Eisenhower, confronted with the first major computer complex and told that he can ask it any question he pleases. The president eyes the machine and asks, "Is there a God?" And the lights flash, and the wheels turn, and after a while a voice says, *"Now there is."*

The computer is an Old Testament God, says Joseph Campbell, with a lot of rules and no mercy. I think of that every time I try to communicate with my

Macintosh, and it shows me a small frowning face or says, like the Mad Hatter, "No Room!"

The kinds of ritualization I've been contemplating here are those which a society unconsciously imposes on itself out of a deep, unwitting sense of need. But they can't satisfy the need. Instead they produce phenomena like those high-school children whose dream was not heroism, not achievement, but celebrity. Underneath, there is still the gap—down there in civilization's basement, in the collective unconscious. If fantasy is the only thing with a chance of filling the empty basement of what Campbell calls "our demythologized world," what are its chances of success?

It would be nice to be able to say: let's make all the children in the country read more, and let's introduce more of them to fantasy. Make sure curricula and reading lists are full of the myths of the founding civilizations—Greek, Roman, Norse, Celtic, native American, and so on. Make sure too that children have the chance to read new fantasy, in which—let us hope—patterns for the future emerge from the mythic echoes of the past. Yes, we must do these things. But a great proportion of our children will never voluntarily open a book outside the doors of school, mostly because their parents don't. They may never even be able properly to read, but become part of the mind-boggling percentage of functional illiterates which our educational system lets slip through the cracks. You can be pretty sure that when these children were between the ages of two and eleven, they were at the very high end of the scale which in a recent report produced an *average* figure, for children in that age group, of twenty-eight hours of television watched every week. Twenty-eight hours a week! Four hours a day, including schooldays! That's my idea of hell, not pleasure—proof, if it were needed, that television is a drug.

The screen, small or large, is not intrinsically a bad thing. Like most other drugs, it can serve wonderful ends. The pressure of commerce keeps its standards low, but individuals of talent and determination can use the screen to re-create a mythological pattern as powerful as any story written down, or told aloud. And if one of them does it well, the results can be astounding. *Star Wars* and *E.T.* are both variants of the fantasy hero pattern that I was describing earlier; Luke Skywalker's quest runs through a "galaxy far, far away," and the little Extra-Terrestrial comes from his world to ours and back again. More people have seen those two films, throughout the world, than have seen any other film ever made; not because they are the best films ever made, but because they managed, for a couple of hours, to satisfy the longings of the collective unconscious. "Mum!" said my children, as we left the cinema after seeing *Star Wars* twelve years ago, "it's all about your books!" They sounded indignant, as if they felt George Lucas had been cribbing from *The Dark Is Rising*, but of course he hadn't; their indignation only served to point up the fact that where the archetypes of myth are concerned, there is no such thing as a new story. There is only, as Professor Tolkien observed, the cauldron of story, which is available to all of us through the unconscious, and from which we all draw. Nearly every fantasy author I've ever met has had the experience of having a glorious new idea for a story, only to find that some bard or minstrel had the same idea eight hundred years ago.

Television does not produce fantasy of the quality of *Star Wars*. Nor very often does the cinema, for good and simple reasons. A few years ago I had an idea for what I thought was a fantasy novel, but when I began to work on it I found it wanted to be a film. *The Cloud People*, it was called. So I wrote it as a film treatment. It went to a number of producers from Steven Spielberg on down, and it came back again, and although there's now an Englishman who has hopes for it, I very much doubt whether it will ever get made, even assuming it's good of its kind. The trouble with my small story is that to become a film it would require a budget of at least thirty million dollars, and at the requisite ration of two-and-a-half to one, it would have to earn at least seventy-five million before it could even break even, let alone make a profit. That's a large risk for a producer to take. I really wish *The Cloud People* had wanted to be a book.

So fantasy and its archetypal patterns are not going to reach a mass audience very often today. Even amongst that limited part of the population which reads books—books, not newspapers or magazines or escapist thrillers or romances—even amongst them, it isn't going to reach everyone. Every teacher or librarian knows the sturdy child who is a dogged realist and thinks fantasy is for the birds. There are more children like that than there are fantasy readers, and from a practical point of view that's probably just as well. Back in the mists of time, as everyone sat around the campfire listening to the shaman telling the sacred stories, there was always the realist in the group. "I don't want to listen to those boring old myths," he said, and he went off on his own and invented the wheel.

"Your books seem to fit me just right," said the little girl. *Those* are the children we have to reach: to drop into the shadowy pool of their unconscious minds a few images that—perhaps, with luck—will echo through their lives and help them understand and even improve their world, our world. If America doesn't have what Aristotle and Mr. Campbell call an ethos, if instead there is a gap, we need to make sure that our children are given an early awareness of the timeless, placeless archetypes of myth. And since we have no one single myth, that has to mean all the different—and yet similar—mythic patterns we inherit, collectively, in this country from our very diverse beginnings. I am speaking not only of ancient myth but of the modern fantasy which is its descendant, its inheritor. Like poetry, these are the books which speak most directly to the imagination. As Ursula Le Guin once wrote, "It is by such statements as 'Once upon a time there was a dragon,' or 'In a hole in the ground there lived a hobbit'—it is by such beautiful non-facts that we fantastic human beings may arrive, in our peculiar fashion, at the truth."

Parents, teachers, librarians, authors, publishers; we are the people with the responsibility for putting together the right child and the right book. Any child and any book will do, but it helps if they match. The biggest truism of our professional lives is that hugely important fact too many civilians still forget: *every child should be encouraged to read books, words on a page, for his or her own pleasure, in his own time, dreaming his own—and the author's—dream.* When December comes, I shall be found whispering to people I know (and wanting to shout to a great many I don't): "For every toy you buy a child this Christmas, add to the package a paperback book." In a demythologized world, where the sunlight of the imagination has to filter past the great looming skyscrapers of the computer and television set, books need all the help they can get.

Down I went, in my dream, into the mysterious theater of the unconscious, where all manner of fantastical scenes could be played out—and will be played out, as long as one human mind can respond to another. But high above me, brightly lit, was the place where it all began, full of people lost in their imaginations, reading books. I dreamed about a library, once upon a time.

DYAN SHELDON
The Dream

Dyan Sheldon is the author of the novels *Victim of Love* and *Dreams of an Average Man*. Her short stories have been included in various British anthologies. She lived in London for many years, and recently moved back to her native New York.

This story holds a special terror for the reader. Nothing violent happens, nothing bad. It's just life. Right.

—E.D.

From the mutable border between reality and dream (as well as the border between fantasy and horror) comes some of the most powerful of fantasy stories. Sheldon's tale, both lovely and disquieting, walks in the shadows along that border.

—T.W.

The Dream

DYAN SHELDON

This is the dream. She wakes up screaming. The covers are twisted around her legs, holding her like hands. The room is lightless. There is no sound. The clock isn't ticking. Her brothers aren't whispering or snoring across the hallway. Her mother isn't hurrying up the stairs. There is only her screaming. She screams and screams. Screams and screams. But the door doesn't open. The door doesn't open, letting in the rest of the house: the lamp with the pink shade on the small table outside her room, the narrow green rug, the flowered wallpaper, the painting of a woman walking by a lake, and, downstairs, the carpet from Persia, the polished tables, the maroon sofa, the ottoman she sits on when her mother reads to her, the figurines on the mantel—the sweet-faced ballerina whose left foot is chipped and the smiling young man—her father reading in his armchair, her grandmother by the fire, talking to the shadows, the old black dog curled up at her feet. There are no sounds. No movements. Her mother doesn't come. She screams and screams.

This dream is nothing like the other bad dreams Megan sometimes has—the nightmares. Nightmares about monsters hiding under her bed, or about being stolen by gypsies or witches, or about being carried up into the sky in the claws of a gigantic vulture. Nothing like the spider dream or the tiger dream or the dream where she is lost and can't find her way back home. When she has those dreams she really does wake up screaming, shaking and crying, holding on to the quilt. When she wakes up from those dreams she can still see the bright red eyes of the monster or the tiger's sharp smile, feel the heat, the touch of a long rough tongue. But even though her eyes are shut and she is crying and calling out, even though, she always knows that her mother is running up the stairs, always knows that in a few seconds the door will open and the light will rush in from the hallway, and her mother will be sitting on the bed with her, taking her in her arms, saying, "There, there, darling, it's all right, it's all right, it was only a bad dream."

After she's calmed down, her mother always makes her a cup of tea and stays with her until she falls back to sleep. Sometimes—after the spider dream and after the dream about getting lost—Megan's mother takes her into her bed, where even the sheets smell like her and it is possible, if Megan barely breathes, to hear her mother's heart beat.

"It was because we saw that poster about the circus," her mother will say the next morning as she's fixing the breakfast, talking over her shoulder as she works at the stove. "It was because you ate that piece of cake before bedtime, Megan," her mother will say, wiping her hands on her apron, setting Megan's bowl in front of her with a solid thump. "It was too heavy for so late." "It's the boys always teasing you, Meg. They think they're funny, your brothers. You just pay them no attention." After one of those nightmares, her mother will let her have toast and hot milk with sugar as a special treat. "It's those stories your father's always telling you," her mother will say. "It's because the milkman's horse frightened you." "It's the full moon."

"All the girls in our family have bad dreams," says her grandmother, breaking her toast into her tea because of her teeth, because she doesn't have any teeth— no teeth, no meat on her bones, thin white hair. "Did I ever tell you how I used to scream the house down? Screamed it down. And my sister, Ellie, Ellie had the second sight." Megan's grandmother is a tiny doll of a woman always dressed in black or navy blue, all wrinkles and veins, her ankles swollen, her fingers misshapen. There is always something trickling (food or spittle, a milky line of tea) from the corner of her mouth. Megan has to smile when her grandmother talks about being a girl, as if she ever was, but her mother just says, "Oh, for heaven's sake, Ma, don't start scaring the child more."

She is in a room. She is in a room and she is all alone. So alone that she can hear the tap dripping in the kitchen, low voices next door, someone laughing outside. She is in the front room, but it isn't the front room, not really. If she didn't know it was the front room she would think it was some other room, in a place she's never been. Most of the furniture is gone—her father's chair, the large china lamp and the brass one with the satin shade that her mother sits under when she knits, the pie-top tables and the writing desk—and instead of the rug from Persia there is a faded grey carpet on the floor; instead of the lace curtains, yellowing net. The room smells of cats. In places, the dingy paper peels from the walls. The room is dark, or perhaps not dark really, not so dark that she can't see—she can see the floor, the windows, the walls, the bed in the corner where the bookshelves should be—but everything is dim, drained of color, faded as an old photograph. She is standing at the window, looking out at the street. And the street, too, is different. No, not just because the dairy across the road now has tables of vegetables outside, or because the elm tree is gone from in front of the house, but because it seems so far away. There are the houses and the shops, people walking by—jostling schoolchildren, swaggering young men, giggling girls, busy adults with places to go and things to do—hurrying, pushing their babies or looking at their watches or carrying their groceries, stopping to talk to one another, smiling and laughing, nodding heads, shaking hands, embracing in the moment of good-bye. But she can't hear them, somehow, can't touch them, watches them as though they're in a film, up there on the screen in another world, unaware that she is standing at the window, so close her breath mists the surface. It's a dream, she tells herself in the dream. That's the way of dreams—everything the same but different, everything familiar but changed. In dreams you see people you know and they don't recognize you, you recognize people you know but they don't look the same. In dreams you are always by yourself. She stands at the window, unsure of the season or the time of day, looking at the flat sky for signs of rain. Trapped behind the glass like a ghost trapped by time.

Her brothers like to scare her. Boys will be boys, her mother always says. Her brothers think it's funny, the way she always falls for their tricks, the way she starts and drops the cup she was carrying, plops on the floor with her doll tight in her arms and tears down her cheeks.

"Ooooooh, Megan Coleman," a wobbly, screechy voice will call from underneath the stairs. "Ooooooh, I'm going to get you, Megan, I'm going to get you, get you . . ." jumping out with a scream.

"Watch out, Megan," one of them will say to her over supper, the others grinning at each other, passing secret looks, "I saw a monster in the garden last night, and he was looking for you. He was staring up at the windows, looking for your room," and then they laugh, choking on their food, until her father says in his quiet voice, "That's enough of that now."

They leave things in her bed—dead spiders and clumps of horsehair, wet socks. They blindfold her and hide. But it's only a game. "It's only a game, Megan," they laugh, hugging her, picking her up in their strong, sure arms. "We're only teasing you, you know."

And then one of them will give her a sweet, or take her to the park, or fix a broken toy, or play with her for hours while the afternoon turns dark outside and the smells of supper being cooked begin to fill the house. And they watch out for her. They won't let anyone else scare her. When she walks down the street with her brothers she never feels frightened of dogs, or traffic, or the rough boys who stand together in little clumps, watching everybody who passes, liquor on their breath and nothing in their eyes. When she is with her brothers she doesn't get confused, never worries about getting lost or being knocked over, about people yelling at her: "What are you doing?" "Get out of the way!" "What did you want?" "Why are you here?" "Can't you remember what you want?" Not like when she's on her own.

She doesn't want to go out. She knows that she has to go out—there is something she needs out there, something for which she must walk down the nine steps of the front stoop and out on the pavement, something for which she must cross at the corner. She lets the curtain fall back in place. Maybe it isn't that she has to go out to get something but simply that she has to get out. Get out of this room. She looks over her shoulder. The walls are moving in. She sees them move. She's sure she sees them move. An inch at a time. A half an inch. Not every minute —but every few minutes. She turns away, turns back quickly. Minute after minute, hour after hour, an inch or a half an inch, maybe even less. That's why I have to get out, she tells herself, the room is shrinking, the walls are closing in. She looks around for the door, but the door isn't there. Where the door should be is only wall. There is no way out to the hall with the frosted entrance door and the mirror and the hat-stand and the bannister so polished that it shines. Where is the door? She can't leave the room. Who could have moved the door? "I'll wake up soon," she says out loud, "I'll wake up soon." She looks over her shoulder. The walls move in.

Her mother says she thinks the problem is that Megan spends too much time in the house.

"The boys are so much older," her mother tells her grandmother, "she's always on her own, amusing herself. I'm sure it's made her imagination over-active."

Megan's grandmother takes a bit of the pastry Megan's mother is rolling and pops it in her mouth. Megan's grandmother used to make the best apple pie in the world, but now her hands hurt too much to roll the crust or peel the fruit, so she sits at the table, saying things like, "I never liked it too thin," "You need a bit of lemon and a little more cinnamon, Eleanore," "I always brushed the top with cream." "All the girls in my family had a good imagination," says Megan's grandmother. "She gets it from me."

Megan and her mother go out together. If they are going to the shops, Megan's mother wears her blue coat with the silver butterfly pin and a blue hat with a single feather, and over her arm she carries the basket. If they are going visiting, Megan wears one of her best dresses and a ribbon in her hair. They walk quickly, briskly, her mother calls it, her mother's footsteps sounding like someone counting, one two one two one two, Megan giving a little skip every few steps just to keep up, down to the end and cross at the corner, look where you're going, don't dally, don't run ahead, don't drag your feet, don't step on a crack. Her mother walks with her back straight and her head up, chatting as they go along, "Did you see that puppy?" "What's that in the window?" "What sort of tree is that?" "Maybe we'll have ginger cake for tea." Her mother knows everyone. The men touch their hats, the women nod. "Good morning, Mrs. Coleman." "Good afternoon, Mrs. Coleman." "Nice day." "Fine weather." "How's the family then?" "I'm going your way, let me help you with your things." And "Megan," they say, "how you're growing," "how pretty you look," "I think I've got something in my pocket for you."

She is standing at the end of a long long street. It must be their street. It must be their street, because here she stands, outside the house, holding on to the iron railing and staring at the number on the transom. It is her house but the door has been painted red and the glass etched with flowers has been replaced with plain. There is something wrong with the road itself as well. Something she can't quite put her finger on, and some of the houses that line it have changed color or shape, seem smaller somehow, and one or two have disappeared, the Begleys'

and the Littlejohns', but there is their house, still with the knocker Uncle John
brought back from Italy. She wants to go back inside. There are dogs on the street,
large dogs, running free, large young men behind them, dangling chains. Go
back inside, she says to herself, go back inside. Her heart is pounding. That's all
she can hear—not the traffic, or the passersby, or the birds in the trees—just the
pounding of her own heart. But she has to get down to the end, to the end of
the street. There is some reason why it is very important that she reaches the end,
gets down to the corner, but she doesn't know now what it is. Can't remember.
She knew it before, though; she's sure of that, she knew it before. She tries to
concentrate. She says to herself, think, think, why did you come outside? She
looks around. It is a cold day, bright and sunny, and the street is crowded. But
there is no one she recognizes. Face after face. No one she knows. A color of
eye, a wave of hair, a shape of nose, a walk, a smile that makes her catch her
breath, makes her look again. Isn't that . . . ? Could it be . . . ? Surely that's
. . . But then the person turns or comes closer—and it's always someone else,
always someone she doesn't know. The street is full of people, but when she raises
her hand no one sees her. When she calls out, "Excuse me, excuse me," no one
hears her. No one stops to tell her why she has to get to the end of the road. A
voice in her head screams, "Why do I have to get to the end of the road? Just
tell me that, why do I have to get to the end of the road?" Her heart pounds.
There must be a hundred people on the street—two hundred eyes, not one smile.
And she. They know, they must know—she knows they know—but they won't
look at her, they won't tell her. No one will help her. She starts to walk. One
step and then another step, one step and then another step, one step and then
one step more. But when she finally stops, breathless, she is no closer to the end,
it is still in the distance, so far she can't see it. One step and then another step,
one step and then another, willing her feet to walk, her body to move. But when
she looks up again she is still near the house. Like walking in treacle. Walking
in a dream. Left foot, she thinks, right foot, left foot, right foot, everyone else
hurrying by, running, shoving her out of the way, bikes flying past, just keep
going, she tells herself, just keep going, one step and then another step, one step
and then another step. Slow motion dream. She must step from the curb. Into
traffic. Cars speeding, horns shouting, brakes sharp and shrill. She stands there.
The road is feet beneath her. Miles. She is balanced on the edge of a cliff and
the ground is miles away. She stands there. Forward? Backward? Left? Right?
Voices are screaming at her. Move. Move. Move. People push past her. Move.
Move. Get out of the way. And she stands there. Trembling. Stands there.
Shaking. Stands there, and stands there, and stands . . .

She wakes up in her bed. Sunlight bursts through the window, making the coverlet
look as white as the summer clouds that drift by outside, making the tiny pink
roses on the wallpaper as bright as the roses in the garden. She is warm in the
sunlight, safe in her bed, her head against the pillow-case her grandmother embroidered for her with her stiff old hands, violets and honeysuckle, her name in
blue thread, her arm around her worn stuffed bear. She can hear the boys laughing
across the hallway.

"Last one up's a lazybones," they shout through her door. "Hurry up! Hurry up! It's the picnic today." She can hear her mother in the kitchen, smell apple pie. The milkman whistles as he walks up the path, and her mother calls up the stairs, "Megan, Megan, you're not going to stay in bed all day, are you? You're not going to stay in bed all day?" And she thinks about the picnic, about the boat ride on the river, about running through the field with her brothers, the sky so blue and the trees so green and she behind the others, "Wait for me, wait for me," but laughing, breathless and laughing, her mother standing up with a hand to shield her eyes, watching that they don't go too far, "You watch out for your sister, you hear me?" A child again, her brothers still alive, still children, her mother still living, still young, and she, with the sunlight on her and the day just waiting to befriend her, to surprise her and wrap her in wonders, she so happy with life, so far from death.

And that is the dream.

JOHN BRUNNER
Moths

John Brunner has won the British Fantasy Award and the Hugo Award, among others. He is best known for his science fiction novels *Stand on Zanzibar*, *The Sheep Look Up*, *The Shockwave Rider* and his fantasy story cycle *The Compleat Traveller in Black*. He doesn't often write horror, so I was especially surprised and pleased to read "Moths" in *Dark Voices 2*, the newly refurbished *Pan Book of Horror*. There are other stories in the anthology that I highly recommend, particularly Adrian Cole's terrifying sf/horror story "Face to Face" and Michael Marshall Smith's "The Man Who Drew Cats."

"Moths" has the feeling and sense of poetic justice of a fairy tale and it's one of the few historicals I've chosen for this volume. Along with conveying a sense of growing unease, "Moths" provides a fascinating portrait of rural France in the late eighteenth or early nineteenth century.

—E.D.

Although ultimately a horror story, "Moths" is also a splendidly written fantasy tale, albeit a dark one, reminiscent of the French folk tale tradition of the wicked eldest sister and abused youngest who sits by the hearth and spins. . . .

—T.W.

Moths

JOHN BRUNNER

The rooms at the back of the house had no windows, so Mathilde was accustomed to being told to bring and hold a lamp for her half-sister Chantal when she needed something from one of them during the day.

What she was not prepared for . . .

The shop that provided the Arrieux sisters with their meager living was temporarily empty. Occupying the entire ground floor, it had been a stable; before that, when this was the only house on the north side of what was now called *la Grande Place*, the main square of Pilières, it had served as a feed-store and before that again, a pigsty. Now its walls were lined with crude shelves bearing stocks of the necessities the local people could not provide themselves: salt, nails, bolts of cloth, buttons, knives, cooking-pots, and a barrel of the mouth-wrenching factory-made acid that the older villagers insisted on for their salads, claiming ordinary vinegar lacked taste.

Gathering her skirt above her knees, since there were no men present, Chantal practically scuttled up the ladder giving access to the upper floors. She had on new stockings of bright blue. For a moment Mathilde wondered dully where she had got them. Then the answer became obvious. Her *fiancé* must have given them to her.

Sometimes Mathilde suspected that Chantal was glad her mother was dead. Not her own mother: Wilhelmine, who was Mathilde's. She had been their father's second wife. Because she spoke in a strange accent and had different habits people accused her of being a witch, and there had been a time, when she was a little girl, when Mathilde had wept because she feared it might be true. But the *pasteur* had been kind—the old one who had retired last year, not the new gruff one who had taken his place—and explained that she spoke strangely because she came from a foreign country called Belgium, and had been brought up to a different version of the faith, called Catholic.

That had upset Mathilde even more, good Protestant as she was, but, tolerant, the *pasteur* had assured her that God was merciful toward those born into a situation that they couldn't help. Besides, her mother had converted on marrying, so it made no difference where she hailed from.

More slowly, Mathilde negotiated the ladder, and not just because she had the lamp to cope with. Compared to Chantal she was heavy and clumsy, despite being the younger by four years. As for her looks . . .

She reached the top of the ladder and held up the lamp. She saw by the yellowish gleam it cast across the floor of creaking planks that Chantal was raising the lid of the huge oak chest in which Wilhelmine's *trousseau* had been brought from her faraway home on carts with creaking wheels and filthy-tempered drivers. Mathilde hadn't seen that, of course, but she had often been told about it.

Scarcely daring to believe her eyes, she clambered up the last of the ladder's rungs and advanced across the room.

First Chantal removed a layer of tissue-paper; then a folded table-cloth with a lace fringe. A musty smell grew oppressive in the air, the stale reek of what had been sweet herbs, lavender and pennyroyal. Then more, and more, until the stack beside the chest grew higher than it was.

A sick suspicion gathered in Mathilde's mind.

And finally, with a cry of triumph, Chantal found what she was looking for, right at the bottom of the chest. She snatched it up hastily, heedlessly tearing the tissue it was interlayered with, and spun round, holding it against her shoulders: lace, beautiful lace, a whole gown made of it, and a bridal veil.

"It'll fit me as though it had been made for me!" she declared.

Very slowly Mathilde set the lamp on a nearby shelf. She said after a long pause, "That's *my* mother's wedding-dress. Not *your* mother's. Put it back."

"Oh, don't be silly!" The gown swirling before her, Chantal danced towards the light. "Can you imagine me in *my* mother's wedding-dress? She was dumpy! She must have weighed ten kilos more than I do. Whereas this is just my size, isn't it?"

She was lovely. Even Mathilde had to admit that. She was slim, dark-haired, with brilliant dark eyes and a red, red mouth. If only she hadn't also been selfish, demanding, lazy . . . !

What did her fool of a *fiancé* see in her? Or she in him, come to that? What had possessed her to accept a *huissier*, a bailiff, hated by half the people of Pilières because they or their relatives had suffered at the hands of the lawyer whose agent he was, and feared by the other half because the way things were going they too might one day receive a call from him, saying their farms and even houses were forfeit by due process of law?

It could only be her good looks that had ensnared him, and his expected wealth that had captivated her.

She was about to say again, "Put it back!" But suddenly Chantal exclaimed, holding the gown up before the lamp.

"The moths have been at it!"

Mathilde blinked and leaned to look. It was true. The delicate lace was holed, here, here, there again, in dozens of different places. Straightening with a sense of relief, she said, "Well, in that case you won't want to borrow it after all."

She stressed the "borrow" meaningfully.

"May the devil take me if I don't!" Chantal blurted. And, before Mathilde could bridle at the shocking phrase she must have picked up from her *fiancé*, she had changed her mood again, mercurially, and was drawing closer with a beseeching look and a wheedling tone of voice.

"Mathilde *chérie*, you can mend it. You're the only person in Pilières who knows how."

And that, in fact, was so. As a girl Wilhelmine had made lace for a living like the rest of her family; her bridal gown and veil, along with all the other marvellous articles that had accompanied her in the oaken chest, had been made by her, her mother, and two of her aunts. Seemingly they had been impressed by the fact of her marrying a foreigner, albeit a Protestant, for they had outdone themselves with the fineness and intricacy of her *trousseau*. And, although from the hard work demanded of her by her French husband her hands had rapidly grown coarse and clumsy, eventually stiff with rheumatism, she had been at pains (how apt the term was, to one who had watched her struggle to locate pins in the pillow on her knee and braid the thread between them!) to instruct her daughter.

Who dutifully tried to learn, and did to some extent, but had thick un-deft fingers, and had never attempted—though the family had pressured her—to produce anything for sale, contenting herself with undertaking occasional repairs that at least helped to supplement their income.

"Here!" Chantal whispered, proffering the veil. "See where the threads are broken by the moths? You can mend those at least, can't you?"

Mathilde hesitated, passing the veil from hand to hand. In addition to the stale odor of long-decayed herbs, she could now detect another smell. On the spiderweb-fragile fabric she felt a dusty trace, perhaps from scales shed by the guilty moths. She knew them all too well. Everyone did who had stored smart and precious garments and neglected to bring them out and air them every spring. Now and then one saw the greyish-yellow moths themselves, but it wasn't they who did the actual damage. No, it was their larvae, hatched from eggs laid especially along the seams of clothing put away unwashed. But how could one wash thick velvet, heavy plush, elaborate brocade, and not lose their brilliance to soap and water?

Of such domestic questions was her life compounded, and would doubtless be forever. Chantal was beautiful and going to be rich. She herself was heavy-set and plain, despite the mass of bright blond hair that once—just once!—she had been complimented on. Also, some said because she was over-fond of sweets, her teeth were going bad.

"Let me see the dress," she said at last, knowing she was going to give in.

Chantal passed it to her, and she held it up before the lamp. Dim though it was, the light sufficed to show that the damage was even more severe than she'd imagined.

"Oh, come on!" Chantal urged. "When word gets around that I'm going to wear this—and I'll make sure it does!—people who were going to send apologies will decide to turn up for the wedding after all!"

Mathilde bit back harsh words to the effect that it was indecent to get married before the time of mourning ran out for their mother . . . Yes, she had been Chantal's mother too, for most of her life. At any rate it had been she who kept the family together when their father Pierre fell ill; it had been she who suggested turning the ground floor into a shop and somehow raised the money to stock it; it had been she who argued stoutly with the lawyers after Pierre's death and found a loophole in the contract of tenure that enabled them to hang on to the house . . . In a sense, Mathilde reflected, it had been she who brought Chantal and her *huissier* together, for had Wilhelmine not been so obstinate his master would never have dispatched his best agent Jacques Lefèbre to Pilières, and he would never have been smitten by those black eyes and ruby lips . . .

A shout came from below. Someone had entered the shop, demanding service.

"Say you will!" Chantal pleaded. "Say you'll mend it!"

Mathilde was on the verge of yielding. Suddenly she felt an access of stubbornness, due perhaps to her still-smouldering annoyance that Chantal should plan to go ahead with the wedding when Wilhelmine was scarcely cold in her grave. Folding the gown and veil together on her left arm, she said, "What are you and—and Jacques going to do about this house?"

She hadn't dared ask for precise assurances before.

Chantal blinked. "Why, sell it, of course! Jacques has a bigger one, with land!"

Gratingly: "So what's to become of me?"

"Oh, Mathilde! So that's what's been making you so grumpy recently! I didn't think I'd have to spell it out! We've always been so much a part of one another's lives!"

"That's not an answer," muttered Mathilde.

"You come and live with us, of course, what else? We've talked it over—" *not with me*, glossed Mathilde "—and you will have a room much nicer than you do here!"

And I'll be expected to fetch and carry, wash and cook—won't I? Mathilde added silently. Yet, the gown and veil weighing curiously heavy on her arm, all she did was shrug and start to turn away.

There was another shout from below. This time it included a name. Chantal clenched her fists.

"It's Monsieur Pasquelier! I've got to see him about slaughtering the pigs we're roasting at the wedding feast!"

And at the top of her voice, "*Attendez encore un moment, je vous en prie! J'arrive!*"

Then hastily, cajolingly, "Mathilde, you will mend the lace, won't you?"

Mathilde's brain was not among the fastest-working of all humanity, but during the past few minutes it had dawned on her that if she consented she would have an ideal excuse to avoid the other duties Chantal would otherwise foist on her. The prospect of having to take care of every single detail involved in organizing food and wine and tables and knives and forks and glasses and everything right down to the borrowing of salt-cellars and making a list of whose house they came from—that daunted her.

This was her way of escape. At least for a little while.

She forced a smile. "Yes, of course I will. Because you want it so much, don't you?"

Chantal flung her arms around her half-sister and gave her a smacking kiss before rushing towards the ladder, once again kilting up her skirts. Apparently she didn't mind if M. Pasquelier saw her legs.

Maybe it was because she was so proud of her bright new stockings.

But, just as her head was about to vanish below the floor, she checked and called out: "Mathilde!"

"Yes?"

"I don't know why you aren't looking forward to my wedding. Everybody else is! You should be too! Lots and lots of people are going to turn up—maybe one of the men will propose to you! Then you can have a wedding of your own!"

And she vanished, laughing.

If she hadn't laughed . . .

But she did. It was in that moment that Mathilde realized how much she hated her half-sister.

The hatred seethed during the next two weeks. Knowing it was sinful, she nonetheless made no attempt to conquer it. Never in her life had she felt such strong emotion. In some strange way it lent her a sense of power. Daily, she sat out before the house—the tumbledown house for which, perhaps, a purchaser would be found even more miserable and desperate than the sisters Arrieux had been, to take on the boring hopeless task of wringing a livelihood from the shop—and to the surprise and occasional admiration of the local children demonstrated that when she put her mind to it she could imitate, even match, the techniques that Wilhelmine whom they'd mocked as a witch had brought from Belgium. Her hands moved slower than her mother's, but they were no less sure.

The veil would be comparatively easy to deal with, so she was—of malice aforethought—leaving it to last. But she had had to unstitch the worst-affected portions of the gown, then wash the lot and hang it out to dry before attempting repairs. The intricacy of her work attracted much attention; more than once old biddies who had previously made a public show of despising this child of a second marriage (hereabouts the strict believers felt remarrying insulted God) halted, and stared, and said at last, "I wish I'd had a skill like yours when I was young."

For the first time Mathilde was able to believe that, had things turned out differently, she might have found a place in the community instead of being shunned and isolated because her mother was a foreigner. She even began to imagine that Chantal could have been right when she joked about someone proposing to her at the wedding—

No. Stop. Were she, for the sake of argument, to find a prospective husband, it would necessarily be someone who couldn't pick on anybody better: a young man with a harelip or a game leg, a widower who'd worn his first wife out with childbirth—in or near Pilières there were a score of those, including Jacques's father—or some other sort of left-over.

Besides, if the said hypothetical person did indeed propose to her at Chantal's wedding, for which barrels of wine were already being delivered by the drayload, he would more than likely be drunk out of his mind.

Wouldn't he?

Resigned to her inevitable fate, wishing she didn't hate her half-sister so fiercely, wishing now and then that she shared her mother's version of Christianity that permitted confession (but the new *pasteur*, to whom she had mentioned the practice, had condemned it as a loathsome heresy), Mathilde worked over the seemingly endless mass of lace that flowed across her lap.

And now and then found, close beneath the tight-sewn seams she had to unpick and would have to restitch, small grey ovoids: stuck to the fabric, seeming somehow to have survived her careful washing.

Had it really been so careful?

The first time she found a batch of them, her reaction had been to scrape them clear and throw them away. Even as she poised her broadest needle, though, she felt her hand checked as though by a power greater than herself.

Pausing and drawing breath, she recognized it.

Her all-consuming hate.

Under the dusty-leaved trees that grew before the door of her home, whose roots would eventually tilt the front wall so far off the vertical it must collapse, Mathilde pretended she was only mending lace. She let no one's attention fall on the bowl at her side where she kept spare lace-makers' pins and basting-pins against the final re-assembly of the bridal gown . . . and the tiny grey eggs that had escaped her careful laundering.

Had it really been so careful?

Day after day Chantal descended from the carriage drawn by a clatter-hoofed horse that took her to and brought her back from *rendez-vous* with Jacques her *fiancé*. Day after day she shouted to Mathilde that such-and-such now must be done, and Mathilde reveled in the freedom she herself had generated.

For she could always say, "If you want to wear this gown I have to fix the damage that the moths have done!"

Whereat, sullen-faced, Chantal would go indoors. But Mathilde would work outside until the light was spent, then gather up the pieces—who would have imagined that one dress could incorporate so many?—and take them up the ladder to her lamp-lit bedroom.

There she would sit on her hard uncomfortable bed and set the tiny ovoids she'd retrieved back among the seams whence she'd removed them, not piercing them or stitching them, just placing them. The work strained her eyes, but she felt she had to do it.

Somehow, it seemed to her, the moths had acted in her interest. Had they been allowed to complete their work of destruction, the dress and veil would have escaped the clutches of pretty, greedy Chantal. And since her own dreams were never likely to become reality . . .

All this was vague. Had someone questioned her—the *pasteur*, for example, who called once or twice to discuss details of the wedding ceremony—Mathilde might have found words to express her feelings with. But since he had been so scathing of the religion Wilhelmine had been brought up to, she was disinclined to talk to him again.

Constantly, however, she found herself thinking, "They called her a witch, didn't they? Chantal takes after her mother—temperamentally, that is, not physically. I've seen pictures, never understood why *papa* who must have liked plump cuddly women chose Wilhelmine, as slim as Chantal who's going to look fantastic when she dons my mother's dress—the witch's dress . . ."

And, eventually, inevitably: "If Chantal takes after her mother, I guess I must take after mine."

Whereupon, uttering words beneath her breath that were not quite a prayer, she would insert yet another of the indestructible grey ovoids in the seams of the dress she was painstakingly reconstructing from its twenty-three individual segments.

As passersby came up to her and for the first time made polite conversation, she began to realize a second truth: how much she hated the people she'd grown up among.

But there was never any doubt about how much she hated Chantal. It endured irrespective of the fury with which her half-sister, as the wedding-day drew closer, shouted at her to do this, do that, find chairs, find cups, find extra tables . . . only to be met with the bland counter: "Do you or do you not want to wear this dress? Let me get on!"

And, shutting out Chantal's complaints and curses, she bent again to her needlework. Now she dared to sew the moths' eggs into place out here, outdoors, for no one knew what fate she was hatching for Chantal, no one would dream of it. And when eventually it struck—as she was sure it would—she in her turn would certainly be doomed. If the people of Pilières had called Wilhelmine a witch because of her strange accent and her Catholic upbringing, what would they call her, this fat clumsy Mathilde whom no man save a desperate one would look at twice, when she proved she could, she really could . . . ?

But—could she?

"That's fine work!"

A shrill voice was uttering a compliment. By now she had heard enough not to care any more. Automatically she glanced up, forced a smile, recognizing one of the black-clad old women she dismissed as "biddies," and carried on.

This passerby, though, was not to be so easily dismissed. Hunchbacked with age, her black dress—possibly her only garment—dragging on the ground and turning yellow with dust around the hem, she tapped forward on the hedge-cut stick she needed for support.

"Interesting design you've added!" she croaked.

What design? All I'm doing is repair the lace!

A bony finger reached out while Mathilde was still lost in confusion, and pointed to a newly, neatly mended section of the gown.

"A butterfly, is it?" the ancient voice suggested.

Mathilde stared. So far as she was aware, she'd merely been drawing together the surviving threads and filling in the gaps; more than that, for Chantal's marriage, she was not prepared to do. Yet, now it was pointed out to her, she could see what the old woman meant. That last hole she had filled in had taken on the rough shape of an insect . . .

"No!" she exclaimed.

Offended, the old woman reared back, clutching her stick as though fearing an attack.

"I only meant to compliment you!" she said haughtily, and made to turn away.

Mathilde caught her sleeve. "I'm sorry! I only wanted to say, it's not a butterfly! At any rate, it isn't meant to be."

Suspicious, but relaxing, the old woman said, "Now I look again—these old eyes aren't so clear, you know, not nowadays—I see what you mean. So what is it?"

A sense of total certainty overtook Mathilde.

"A moth."

Why?

The old woman said something, and she responded, and in a moment the tapping of her stick resumed as she made her way down the irregular flagstones that long ago, when the village belonged to a rich landowner, had been laid in front of the houses so that their occupants might walk dryshod in all but the wettest weather.

Mathilde was left wondering about two things.

How could anybody mistake a moth for a butterfly, when even children were taught that the latter rested with wings upraised together and the former with wings parallel or overlapping?

And how was it that—now she looked, she saw—without her noticing, whenever she had to draw the broken threads of the lace together, she had formed them into a pattern much like the resting posture of the very moths that had caused the damage in the first place?

The question was too deep. In any case, she was interrupted in her musing. Yet again Chantal trundled up in her husband-to-be's carriage. And she shouted:

"Mathilde, for heaven's sake! You aren't still at it? You can't be! The wedding is *tomorrow!*"

The words lifted a burden from Mathilde's mind. She folded the piece she was working on and began to gather up the others.

"You'll have it to put on before you go to church. That is, provided you leave me alone until I'm finished."

"But you've been at it for ages!"—panting and glaring. "Are you trying to make sure of spoiling things on the most important day of my life?"

Yes.

The word leapt to the tip of Mathilde's tongue, but she bit it back. It would be stupid to let Chantal know how much she was detested before the time was ripe.

After all, it had been Chantal who nearly persuaded her half-sister that the rumors about Wilhelmine being a witch must hold at least a grain of truth.

Until this moment, Mathilde had forgotten that. The old *pasteur*, the one who had retired, must have encouraged her to dismiss it from her mind, and she had dutifully obeyed. Now he was gone, and the new one was going to celebrate Chantal's marriage to her horrible *huissier*—tomorrow.

So that's why I hate her so much. It wasn't just her joke about someone proposing to me. It goes back.

It goes back a very long way.

Perfectly calm, Mathilde rose and made to head indoors.

"Just you leave me alone and I promise you can wear it in the morning."

And along with it all the misery my mother—not yours, not though she brought you up, but the mother who bore me in her body—suffered because of you. All the taunts, the cruelty, the persecution that turned her lovely hands to thick and clumsy grippers, knob-knuckled, useless for lace-making, the trade I wasn't good enough to follow.

Yet somehow I've found out a way to do what she could not. And I'm not going to tell you what it is.

That, you have to find out.

Chantal was stamping her foot, shouting about all the things that must be done before the morning—precisely what Mathilde had foreseen. But, advancing up the slope of the *Grande Place* like a sluggish flood, here came women to assist, to light fires, gut pigs, make sausages, bake bread, peel vegetables, boil soup . . .

"I'll need our best lamp," said Mathilde composedly. "The dress is ready, so I only need to patch the veil. I promise you, I'll finish it if I have to sit up all night. But I shall need proper light."

"Then take it and be damned to you!" shrieked Chantal.

The dress and veil were ready, and she hadn't even had to sit up very late. She helped Chantal to put the dress on over a new cream satin slip, and when the bride looked at herself in the mirror she seemed tempted for a moment to say something kind.

Indeed, she started to. She said, "Hmm! I don't think anyone could guess where the holes were, could they?"

Mathilde smiled, where her reflection could not be seen.

"You didn't get it very white, though, did you?" Chantal went on, her normal peevish tone returning.

Aloud, Mathilde excused herself. "It is old, you know, and even stored in the chest it was bound to fade a bit. But it tones very well with the cream."

In the privacy of her head, however, very different words were running through her mind.

It's exactly the shade of a clothes-moth's wing.

Hooves rattled outside, and wheels ground as a carriage was backed and turned.

"Don't tell me they're here already!" Chantal cried.

Running to the window, Mathilde looked out. "Yes!" she reported. "It's for us!"

"You aren't even dressed yet! If you make me late—!"

"I only have to take off this dress and put my best one on," Mathilde countered, suiting action to word.

"You haven't finished my hair!"

"It'll only take a second . . ." Wriggling, for her "best dress" was two years old and she had put on weight since it was new. "That's it! Now pass me the brush and comb."

Three quick flicks, and the job was done. Ceremoniously she lifted the veil from where it rested on a nearby table and placed it over her half-sister's head, securing it with a jewelled pin—yet another gift from Jacques.

"There! You'll cause a sensation, you really will! Now don't forget your bouquet! And don't for goodness' sake snag the dress as you go down the ladder!"

With extreme care, she didn't. And, followed by oohs and aahs from a crowd of children, paraded solemnly to the waiting carriage on the arm of a distant cousin of their father's, recruited to give her away.

He was polite enough to help Mathilde into the carriage also, and seat her opposite his elderly wife, but it was Chantal that he couldn't tear his eyes away from.

Naturally.

By the ancient clock on the church tower they arrived ten minutes late, but it was probably wrong anyway. Wheezy music was being not so much conjured forth as dug up from the organ, which was as old and poorly-maintained as the clock. Pilières had fallen on hard times. Perhaps one might charitably ascribe the *pasteur*'s gruffness to his being assigned this parish; it was not a place one would opt for given a free choice.

As they entered the west door, Mathilde holding up Chantal's train, to find the congregation, the bridegroom and the minister awaiting them, Mathilde was chiefly conscious of a pungent smell, not the customary one of hot and seldom washed bodies. More clothes than the wedding-dress had obviously been brought out of store today. Moving slowly up the aisle, she glanced covertly from side to side, seeking the signs of hasty repair that would commemorate the depredations of the clothes-moth.

But the church's windows were small, and its interior was very dark compared with the bright day outside.

The music stopped; the service got under way, the *pasteur* rattling through it as though eager to have it over and done with. Standing directly behind Chantal, ready to take her bouquet when she needed her hand free to accept the ring, Mathilde was gratified to notice her fidgeting occasionally. At first it was a mere shift of posture which might have been due to sore feet—her shoes, after all, being brand new, were doubtless stiff and tight—but little by little it grew more marked, as though she were beginning to itch and fighting the impulse to scratch. That of course would never have done when all eyes were on her. Most undignified!

Once or twice she adjusted her veil, especially where it brushed her neck. It seemed to go on moving for some while after she let her hand fall again.

Mathilde's tension was growing by the moment. She was so rapt, she almost failed to react when called on to take the bouquet, but she covered her hesitation well. Stepping back to her former position, she endured, in a frenzy of impatience, the delivery of the ring. Then, in his usual glum tone, the *pasteur* instructed the bride to raise her veil and let the bridegroom kiss her.

Sickly, Mathilde let the hand that held the bouquet fall to her side, and lowered her eyes. Nothing was going to happen after all. She must have been off her head these last two weeks, truly insane. The rest of her life was fixed: she would live with Jacques and Chantal, in the "much nicer room," and be treated like an unpaid servant—

"What's wrong?" demanded someone loudly. "He hasn't kissed her!"

Mathilde started and looked again. Indeed he hadn't. Hands poised to grasp her shoulders and draw her toward him, he stood rigid, petrified, eyes wide and mouth ajar. The *pasteur* had half-turned away; now, realizing something was amiss, he glanced around. Instantly his face became a mask of dismay.

Her attitude eloquent of puzzlement, after another moment Chantal moved slightly forward, as though concluding that Jacques expected her, not him, to close the gap between them.

He yelled!

Spun on his heel!

Ran full tilt back down the aisle and out the door, which had been left open since the day was warm.

So astonished were the congregation that they all followed him with their eyes. It wasn't until they turned back that they saw what Mathilde had seen already, what had caused bright and hellish joy to warm her icy heart.

From under the lifted veil, among her hair, on her forehead and her cheeks and temples, over her shoulders where they showed pink beneath the open lace: *moths.*

Hundreds of them. Thousands of them. Starting now to spill to the floor, greyish-whitish-yellowish, the very colour of the faded dress.

What dress?

It was falling apart, no more than a tangle of threads, and along with it the bodice of the satin underslip, gnawed into holes, into scraps, into fragments. Too weak to stay in place against the weight of its own skirt, the garment dropped away, startling a cloud of moths to flight.

A child screamed. The *pasteur* called futilely for calm, but he looked as though he wanted to be sick. A man began praying aloud and others swiftly joined in:

"But deliver us from evil!" When they reached that line it was almost a shout, and most had covered their eyes.

Not Mathilde.

Grasping the bouquet in both hands now, she watched with absolute attention, not wanting to miss a second of her triumph. Now her clothes were gone, Chantal stood stunned and naked—bar her stockings, preyed on by a few remaining moths—on the cold flags of the church's pavement, and one could see the holes.

In the youthful skin she'd been so proud of, that her husband would no doubt have so enjoyed: holes.

There was no blood. Just raw red flesh, uncountable patches of it ranging from pinprick size to that of a five-franc piece, showing where the skin had been devoured.

Also her hair was falling out.

I hope you're satisfied. Mathilde spoke wordlessly to those around her. *You said my mother was a witch, and mocked and threatened her. It was a lie. But thanks to what you did to her you've driven me to be a real one.*

Suddenly, without a sound, Chantal collapsed. People from the front pews rushed to help her, swatting aside the moths with cries and curses.

Mathilde waited no longer. Tossing the bouquet to the ground, she turned and walked slowly down the aisle, wondering amid a cloud of dusty wings what else she might have time to accomplish with her new-found power before they heard about what she'd said to that old biddy with the hedge-cut stick and came with clubs and scythes to claim her life.

SUSAN PROSPERE

Frozen Charlottes

Susan Prospere was born in Oak Ridge, Tennessee. She has a law degree from Tulane University in New Orleans and a Master's Degree in Creative Writing from the University of Houston. She has had poetry published in *The New Yorker, Antaeus, Poetry, Field*, and *The Nation*. She won *The Nation*/Discovery Award and the PEN Southwest Houston Discovery Award. She has received an Ingram Merrill grant. A forthcoming collection of her poems, to be published by W.W. Norton & Company, will be titled *Sub Rosa*.

"Frozen Charlottes" appeared in *The New Yorker*. It's about an innocent hobby, doll collecting, that Prospere deftly imbues with an undercurrent of menace.

—E.D.

Frozen Charlottes

SUSAN PROSPERE

Far down into the dark reaches
               of human waste
                        and sorrow,
          you go in search of Frozen Charlottes—
                    porcelain dolls tossed into privies
                         under the tupelos
                    by children bored
with the way they lay so still.
          And now, whiter than snow,
                    they're lined in rows
inside your glass cabinet—moonglow, glacial,
          gardenias floating all day
                              on silver racks
          in the icebox. Sometimes they are whole,
and sometimes they're broken,
                    though not, I'd say, in spirit,
          so stoic they look, so
                    disdainfully composed. I'd like
          to know the secret
                    of these fallen women,
          that I, too, could lie peacefully
                    beside your Flow Blue china,
          having come at last
                    beyond defilement into lustre.

Because you're my brother, I do not ask you
          how you woo them, though I know

> of men who find women
>   flagrante delicto
>   and lift them out of the mire
> long enough to love them,
>   or to love themselves
>   for their own goodness. To the one
> who loves, it hardly matters. Do
> they love you back or, having been exposed,
>   do they turn
>   into themselves, pearling
> forever in bewildering beauty? When
>   you walk along the creek meanders,
>   where the deer blow warning
>   in the understory,
>   do you wish sometimes for me
>   someone would hold me?

Smoking grapevine, you go
                 down the loess roads, far
     into the canebrake, past the lady's slippers,
                 and the nodding lady's tresses,
                                  to dig into the midden
                 with your pick and shovel,
                 lowering your bucket
                         on a rope into the hole
                 to draw up trap-door
     spiders, half dimes, minié balls, and Light
                 Dragoon buttons, and you bring
                                  these female dolls
                 into the open, turning them
                         in your hands over
                                  and over—brushing
                 the earth from their shining
                         buttocks, an arm outstretched
                 with hand extended, their legs
     pressed together so tightly
                         they are one limb
                 that cannot be parted.

RACHEL SIMON

Little Nightmares, Little Dreams

Rachel Simon is a young writer whose stories have begun appearing in literary magazines since she won the Writers at Work fiction competition in 1988. She has also won the Philadelphia Phiction Award and had her work adapted for the stage. She currently lives wherever she can "find a quiet room and a hospitable library."

"Little Nightmares, Little Dreams" comes from Simon's first collection of stories. Also titled *Little Nightmares, Little Dreams*, published by Houghton Mifflin/Seymour Lawrence, the collection is a striking debut containing sixteen stories that range from the stark realism of contemporary urban street life to ribald humor to phantasmagorical tales like the one that follows of an elderly couple's haunting love.

—T.W.

Little Nightmares, Little Dreams

RACHEL SIMON

And now, he wants us to share our dreams. Not just talk about them in the morning over coffee, like we usually do. He means we should dream them together, at the same time. Try doing it this very afternoon.

I say to him, "Fabian, isn't it enough we've been married fifty-three years, that we've known no one in a biblical way but each other, and we've always made a point of having a real conversation every night in bed? That sounds about as close as any two people can get. This doctor you've been seeing—did he put something funny into one of those pills?"

"No," Fabian says, and he lowers his teacup to the saucer. He's used saucers since the day we were married. I like how he respects the furniture, even now that he's retired, sitting around eating cream cheese sandwiches and listening to talk shows on the radio. He never leaves a ring on the wood. Not even after he's bought a can of soda on the way back from the doctor, and when he makes it up the front steps all he can do is fall into the nearest chair. Even then, he remembers to use a coaster.

He says, "Elsie, maybe there are ways to get even closer. Wouldn't that be something—dreaming together?"

"Yeah, it'd be something."

"And I think I know how we can manage it. I've been doing some reading. Seems like it might just be a matter of physical position and will." I look at him, smile, and shake my head. "Come on, Elsie. It'll be easy. It'll be worth it."

This is what he said about all his get-closer ideas, and he's been pushing them since the night he carried me over the threshold. First it was doing the marital act with the lights on. This was not too hard for me, as I was young and curious about the curves and angles of the human body which I'd never been privileged to see before. Then, it was using the commode with the door open. I resisted this till I started shuffling diapers like stacks of soiled playing cards. After that, who can be modest? It's no longer a secret what happens at the far end of our intestines. And, of course, those talks at night. His idea. And a good one too, I came to see. Those talks kept us linked all through the problems of loud music and sibling wars and dreary wedding ceremonies and two-home grandchildren.

I used to wonder why it mattered so much to him to be close. This was not what people I knew expected out of marriage. He couldn't have gotten the idea from the relatives who raised him. They were private people. They were good people—if a few too many in number. Once we took a vacation and drove by all his old homes; our route looked like we'd dropped a handful of lentils on the map of the United States, and they'd scattered to every corner.

His only buddies—besides me, that is—have been my girlfriends' husbands. Married couples would come to our house and split apart the moment they stepped inside, the wives drawing me away to the kitchen so we could talk about our marriages and children, the husbands urging Fabian to come out front and see the new car, or play a few rounds of gin rummy. Now, the few friends who visit come alone; they've all become widows. Fabian, for the last few years, took classes at the community center downtown. Legends of Imaginary Animals, Extraterrestrial Influence in Human History. I'd ask him, "Did you meet anyone?" He'd shrug, "Yes, but they're too busy. Everyone's too busy." Recently he stopped going, saying the doctor visits take enough out of him as it is. Now all he does is sit in the house or backyard, reading and listening to the radio. With such a life, I'd be lonely. But he says he doesn't need anyone except me.

The closeness Fabian and I have had, it's satisfied us both. Till the last few months, that is. Suddenly, get-close ideas are all he thinks about. Why, just a few weeks ago he set up two checkerboards, one in my sewing room upstairs, the other in his toolshed out back. My set had the red pieces, his the black. He said, "You move one man every other night, I go on the nights in between." "How will I know where your men are?" I asked. "Marriage ESP," he said.

Now, sitting beside me in the kitchen, he says, "So I found this dream book at that flea market where I got those embroidered handkerchiefs you like so much. And this book, it says there are ways to dream together."

"You know, you've also read books that said the sun was going to blink off at six A.M. Christmas Day three years ago. And then there was that whole Inca power series you thought was so good."

"I know, I know. But those books, they didn't give me any ideas on how we can make our lives better. They were just interesting to think about."

"They were." This I had to admit.

Fabian says, "Let me show you the book. Then you can decide." He gets up and shuffles across the linoleum to the living room. The sun's coming through the window, lighting up his hair like a crown.

Fabian's still the most handsome man I've ever seen. Though to be truthful, since I got to be able to tell time by the different ways my limbs creak during the day, I have been noticing younger men. There's one that lives across the street, divorced, women in and out of there every few days like he keeps trying them on but can't find the one that suits him. He's good-looking, this man; I almost want to put on rouge when I take out the garbage.

Still, other men, though I think about them, they're nothing to me. It's been so long since Fabian and I walked up the aisle. Then and now, we keep each other from falling. That's what those talks before bed are about. Holding out our arms as we stumble through life together, working each other loose if one of us gets stuck in some bad situation.

He comes back into the kitchen, lays the book on the table. It's dusty, smells like a basement, has mold crawling across the cover. *The Greatest Intimacy*. I have to put on my glasses; the words are hard to read, all squiggly like dripping batter. Like those posters Peggy used to pin to her wall back when she kept skipping school and staying in her room all day, smoking what kids did then, we later found out.

"Looks like one of those Leary treatises," I say.

"Don't knock it, Elsie," he says. "Not everyone back then was a—what did James used to call them?"

"Airhead."

"Yeah. Give it a chance, don't fight this like you did some of my other ideas."

The book crackles as I open it. Fabian lowers himself slowly into the chair. "I picked this up because of that talk we had a few nights ago, remember? That talk where you said—how'd you put it?—that we could lay the maze of our minds on top of each other and they'd lock together just about perfectly."

He was right, I'd said that. Me and my mouth. I say things that sound grand, and I don't mean them fully. See, he'd been talking about entering us in this Couple of the Year contest the local park's planning to hold in a few weeks. Couples will sit under a tent and get asked questions to see how well they know each other. Like some game on TV, I'm told, though we don't watch TV. Anyway, I said then that we were a shoo-in if we entered. Being married so long, we don't even need to talk, when it comes to things like what's for dinner and what our bodies are feeling and what mood we're in. The kinds of questions I expect they'd ask in that contest. Skin questions, as Peggy called them when she was on her anti-superficiality kick. Nothing that shows you really *know* someone, know the parts of him he can't put into words himself. Maybe even know something before he does.

Truth is, though I admire Fabian's get-close ideas, I'm of the opinion—and I do tell him this from time to time, but he likes to forget—that you have to have some private place inside you. Not for secrets, necessarily, though that's nice too. But for a feeling of yourself and what it means to be alone, on two legs instead of four. Because I'm no fool, I know it's all good now, but the time will come when one of us will be gone. Then where will the survivor be, if our I's have always been we's? I'll tell you, this is my little nightmare.

But I said what I said, and in marriage the words you speak to your mate are never forgotten. "So you really want to do this. But I still don't even know if we're playing the same game of checkers."

"We'll look at each other's boards tomorrow, OK? And as for this dreaming stuff—it'll be fun. At the very least, we'll have a nice afternoon together in bed. And it's been a while since we've taken naps together, hasn't it?"

I think for a second. "Only about forty-five years."

"So we're long overdue."

"Well, what makes it happen? Some weird contraption? Hypnosis?"

"Says here"—and he flips through the book—"that all you have to do is lie on your backs with the arms that meet in the middle hooked together and the arms on the sides propped up on pillows. Says doing it in daylight is good too, because the sleep levels don't drop as low, so it's more likely you can dream."

"Sounds a little too easy."

"Humor me."

"First, tell me this: Do you make up a dream together? Or does one of you start and then the other joins in?"

"It didn't go into that," he says, pushing his bifocals up on his nose and turning to the dog-eared pages. Then he looks at me. "Does it matter?"

Well, actually it might. For the past few weeks, Fabian's felt tired all day long. He keeps calling the doctor, who tells him to come by for more tests. They've tried five different kinds of medicine so far. I offer to go with him, but he's got too much pride to let me come along, and I don't push the issue. So, when he leaves, I lie on the beach chair on the front porch and wait for him to return. And this is why dreaming together might matter: once, while I was on that chair, I took a little nap, and dreamt about the man across the street. I'm almost embarrassed to admit it—in the dream the man took me into his house and, well, I actually felt a little guilty when I woke up. But now, sitting here across the table from Fabian, thinking about that dream, I realize: once the clothes came off, I was no longer with the man across the street; I was with my husband. "No, it doesn't matter," I say.

I peer at him, with his white hair and white eyebrows, his brown eyes the color of coffee. Except for this dream with the man across the street, I don't do anything without Fabian at my side in my dreams. He's like the smell of my own body, the way my hair feels on my neck—something I don't think about, he's so much a part of me. And it's nice, because when my dreams fade into waking, he's next to me still.

Sometimes I forget what Fabian looks like. I forget I'm there too; I can just feel us together. This is the opposite of how it was when we first met, my eyes following his lips as he spoke to me, following the skimming of his fingers over my porch railing as we stood in the brisk winter chill. I watched him so closely, I swear I could see his cells reproduce. When I turned away, it was only because my parents were calling me inside.

In marriage, for years, this was how it went too. With each other but separate. Especially in our bed: very *me* and *he*. Air all around us, between us. Two bodies touching self-consciously, even when in rhythm hearing our own inner beat.

Then—when did it happen? And how? The difference between me and Fabian just seemed to disappear. This even when we had to lock the door to keep the kids out, or when Barbara ran away to Montana and we were so worried. This even through my fifties, when my hormones surfed out of me on waves of sweat, and I dried up inside my private parts. And I can remember when our last grandchild was born. We got off the phone and stretched out on the sofa. Even there, we fell into step, didn't hear anything but our own breathing, mixing with the sighing of the furnace. And this is how it is now, even when all we do is lie back and hold each other.

"Come on," he says, rising to his feet and tugging on the sleeve of my housedress.

"You wanted to try marijuana too, after we read about it in *Life* magazine," I tell him. "Look where we'd be now if we'd done that."

He shrugs. "As bad off as Louise, but as good as Peggy. Who can say what will happen?" He lowers his head and coughs. "Please. Do this for me."

I tell him, "All right. OK. I'll try it this once."

We go upstairs. I have to walk beside him on the steps so I can hold his elbow for support. I move slowly because lately he's had to.

In our bedroom he lowers the shade. The afternoon sun lights it up from behind, and the shadows of branches and leaves lie across it like lace.

I stand by the bed. He comes toward me. I raise my arms, and he works my dress over my hips, belly, breasts, head. Then he peels off my underthings. I am doing this to him too, unbuttoning, unbelting.

We lie down. There is no blanket, just sheets, and we do not get under them. We breathe, the window shade taps against the sill. What does my body look like? My friends complain about theirs, about how fat or thin or weak they are, about how their imperfect bodies made them avoid intimacy when their husbands were alive. Me, somehow I always forget to notice my body when I'm with Fabian. And he's with me all the time; I am never naked alone.

Always we roll to face each other. But this time we don't. Instead we each take one of the extra pillows at the top of the bed and fit it beneath our outside elbows.

"And now what do we do?" I ask.

"We lock arms," he says.

He lifts his left arm and hooks it into my right.

"What do you want to dream about?" I ask him.

"I don't know. I just want to see what happens."

We lie there, looking at the ceiling. A few cars buzz by outside. A little girl down the street calls for her friend.

Then I start giggling, and in a moment Fabian joins in. There we are in bed, in this crazy position, laughing. "I feel too silly to do this," I say.

"So do I," he says. "Wouldn't you just die if the kids could see us?"

This makes me laugh more. I go on like this for a while, the laughter rolling out of me, the bed trembling. I go on until I realize Fabian is no longer laughing with me, and then it occurs to me that I feel more nervous than silly. I am panting as I laugh, the way a child does when he's lying.

I close my eyes. Fabian is breathing deeply already. He twitches, that teetering-on-the-edge-of-sleep twitch. I follow his breath like it is a broom sweeping my path clear. Time passes, I think I will never get there, I jolt awake, I sink back down.

And then finally I fall asleep.

*   *   *

The dream opens to me slowly. We are sitting on the sofa in our living room. At first this dream feels no different from any other; how can I tell if Fabian is having it too? "Are you with me?" I ask him. "I think so," he says, but a look flashes across his face and then he adds, "Where are we?" "We're at home," I say, "See? There's the lamp Louise made in school and the family photograph we got for our fortieth anniversary and that fern you bought last week." "Yes," he says, "I see."

Someone knocks on the front door. Fabian rises to answer and, since our arms are locked together, even in this dream, I must rise with him. Side by side we make our way across the room.

When we open the door, the porch is empty. But then Fabian says, "Is that a man or a woman?" as he peers into the darkness.

I am not sure if I should tell him I don't see anyone. I can feel him getting scared. "What are you doing, just standing there?" he asks the invisible—to me —stranger. "What do you want from me?"

I turn to Fabian. His eyes are wide, and he is sweating. "Is this your dream?" I ask him. "Or is it mine?"

"It's not my dream," he says, still staring ahead. "It's my nightmare."

My back tingles and I look away from him, down at my legs. They're thick and netted with varicose veins. My eyes sweep up my body and I see myself now, as if I'm naked for the first time in my life. The dimples on my stomach, the wrinkles that fan down my breasts, my navel gaping like an open mouth. So this is how I look.

I want to tell him this, and I raise my head to speak directly to him. But it is in that moment that I wake up.

He is still beside me, breathing deeply. I look at his profile. I know every pore on that face.

Lying there, watching him, this is what I feel: his nightmare was telling me something. Though maybe it was *my* nightmare, and all it was doing was making clear a fact I've suspected for the past few weeks but haven't wanted to face. And maybe I haven't faced it because he hasn't yet, either.

I unlock my arm from his and sit up. I could wake him to ask what he dreamt, see if it overlapped in any way with what I dreamt. I want to; but I can't bring myself to do that. Not right now.

I roll off the bed and throw on my dress. In the dying sunlight I see his body, white and covered with hair, his love handles and the smiles under his knees. I leave the bedroom and close the door.

Light no longer shines into the hallway, so it must be near dusk. I walk downstairs. I'm not sure why I don't go to my sewing room, where his shirts sit in my basket, waiting for buttons. I have let them pile up for months; now I wonder if I can finish them in time.

I go through the living room and the kitchen, out the back door. The sky is deep blue, receding into black at the tree line. I pad across the grass, noticing his sandals, a book he was reading, a glass half empty. When I reach the toolshed, I hear crickets, rising around me like hymns.

It is dark inside the shed. I have to wave my arms in the air as I creep forward until one hand brushes against the hanging light bulb. I click it on.

Everything—floor, tools, worktable—is covered with sawdust, as it was the last time I was in here. When was that? At least a few years. But there is regular dust now too, thick on everything, even the air. Well, almost everything. Not the checkerboard.

I walk over and look down. A few of his checkers sit along the side of the table. I guess he thought I jumped them. I close my eyes and try to envision my whole board. That man here, that one there, those three kings. . . . And when the picture is sharp, I open my eyes and lay it on top of the board in front of me. He was right, we can play the same game without even looking. We do have marriage ESP.

On the chair in front of the board is one of his shirts, a red flannel shirt that he wore all last winter. It has no dust on it. I pick it up and hold it to my face. It smells like a shirt; no, like *his* shirt. He does have a smell, I just never notice it; I forget and think it is me.

I lift my dress up over my head and drop it on the chair. Then I fit myself into his shirt. It is large. I don't button it; I wrap it around me, like his arms.

It is dark when I make my way across the yard, back into the house, and upstairs. I feel my way along the wall. The house is so quiet when I think of him gone.

In our room I raise the shade, and moonlight beams in. He looks like he's covered with snow. As I sit on the bed, he groans and turns his head toward me.

"You're up?" he says.

"Not for long," I say. "What did you dream?"

"Oh," he says, rubbing his eyes, rolling over to face the ceiling. "I couldn't figure out where I was." He pauses for a moment. "You were with me. I asked you where we were, and you said we were at home. But it didn't look like home to me. It looked like a combination of the houses I grew up in. Familiar and strange at the same time.

"And then there was a knock on the door. I had to tug on your hand to get you up to answer it. I opened the door, and there was—someone or something. Not really a person. I asked who it was, and it wouldn't answer, it just stood there, staring. I wanted to lock it out, but when I turned to ask you to help me close the door, you were looking down, away from me. That thing—I was looking at it again—wanted me to step onto the porch. I didn't want to, but I couldn't walk away. All I could do was stand there like I was frozen. And then I realized that you weren't holding my hand anymore; you were gone. It was just me and it. And we stared at each other so long . . ."

My skin grows cold beneath his shirt; I grab it tighter around me. "Fabian," I say, "that was the same dream I had."

"I knew we could do it," he says, but he doesn't sound happy. He takes hold of my hand. "It scared me, Elsie. It made me feel like something terrible's going to happen. Did you feel that? Did you feel that in your dream?"

I want to reply that it won't be terrible, but I know it will. And I cannot be dishonest; after all, we have marriage ESP. I lie down on the bed and stroke his chest. His hair tickles my palm. I have not been aware of this, of him and me, for so long now. "Fabian," I whisper, telling myself to remember how his hair feels beneath my hand, how his body feels next to mine, "I'm sure we'll be all right."

JOHN MORRESSY
Timekeeper

John Morressy lives in New Hampshire, and teaches at a small New England college. In the fantasy field, he is best known as the author of the humorous "Kedrigern" series of stories that have appeared in *The Magazine of Fantasy & Science Fiction*, and in novels from Ace Books including *Kedrigern and the Charming Couple* published in 1990.

The following story is, in tone, a departure from the author's tongue-in-cheek "Kedrigern" spoofs. "Timekeeper" is a beautifully written work of dark fantasy set in a small New England town, reminiscent of Oscar Wilde's fairy tales, or James Thurber's as seen through a dark glass. It is reprinted from *The Magazine of Fantasy & Science Fiction*.

—T.W.

"Timekeeper" was first read by me as a submission to *Omni*. Even though it wasn't appropriate for the magazine, I was very impressed and asked John to keep me apprised as to its publication so Terri and I could consider it for our *Year's Best*. A beautiful fairy tale, it contains that touch of darkness all fairy tales possess.

—E.D.

Timekeeper

JOHN MORRESSY

A single lantern was the only source of light in the shop. Two men stood in the center of the room, spilling out broadening shadows across the floor and against the counter and the empty walls.

The shorter and heavier of the men, the bearer of the lantern, moved. Shadows swooped, and the floor creaked under his weight. He pushed a box into place, stepped on it, and reached up to hang the lantern from a hook depending from the ceiling. This done, he took a few steps to the counter. He blew a swirl of dust from the glass top and rubbed the surface clear with his handkerchief.

"It's only dust, Mr. Bell," he said. "If you decide to take this place, we'll have it spotless before you move in."

The taller man said nothing. With the light behind and above him, only a slight distance over his head, his face was obscured, and his expression could not be seen. The other man continued.

"You won't find a better location in this town, Mr. Bell. You have two nice rooms upstairs for your living quarters, and a large room in back for storage or a workshop. And there's the big display window on the street," he said earnestly.

"I'll take it, Mr. Lockyer," the tall man said.

"A wise decision, Mr. Bell. There's no property in this town more suitable for a jeweler's shop."

"I'm not a jeweler, Mr. Lockyer," Bell corrected him.

Lockyer shook his head vigorously and waved his hand as if to brush away his error. "No, of course not. You're a clockmaster. You mentioned that. Sorry, Mr. Bell."

"I make and repair timepieces. I do not deal in trinkets."

"You're certainly needed here, Mr. Bell. Do you know, if anyone wants a clock or a watch repaired, he has to take it all the way down to Boston? That's a long trip, and, more often than not, it's a waste of time."

"I never waste time, Mr. Lockyer."

"People are going to be mighty glad you came here. And you will be, too. You'll do well here, Mr. Bell," the smaller man said. He paused, smiling at the dark outline of the other, then he went on. "As a matter of fact, I have a watch you might look at when you're all set up. It was my grandfather's originally. Kept perfect time for nearly a century, that watch did, but last year I dropped it on the stone floor down at the railroad station, and that was the end of it. I took it to the best jeweler in Boston, and those people held on to it for nearly six months, and then told me they couldn't do a thing; it was beyond repair."

"Bring it to me."

"Do you think you might be able to replace the works?"

"I'll repair it, Mr. Lockyer," Bell said. "Take it to your office tomorrow."

"I will, Mr. Bell. I'll have the lease all ready for your signature. My men will get to work here first thing tomorrow morning. You'll be able to move in by the end of the week."

"I'll do my own cleaning and move in tomorrow. Just give me the keys."

Lockyer looked uncomfortable. "Well now, it's always been our policy not to turn a place over to a tenant until it's spotless," he said, looking around at the dusty surfaces and cobwebbed corners. "I appreciate your hurry, but I just wouldn't feel right giving you a place in this condition. It needs a good cleaning."

"I always do my own cleaning. Let me have the keys, and I'll be open for business tomorrow afternoon," the tall man said.

"You'll never manage that, Mr. Bell," said the other. "There's too much to be done."

"I know how to make the best use of time, Mr. Lockyer. Come by at six tomorrow, and your watch will be ready."

Lockyer entered the shop a few minutes before six the following evening. He was astonished at the changes that had been wrought in a single day. The windows, the glass countertop, and the display case were all spotless. The floors and wood-work gleamed freshly polished. The shelves were filled with an assortment of clocks. Some were quite ordinary; others were like none that Lockyer had ever seen before.

Bell was not in the shop. Lockyer went to the display case and stooped for a closer look at the clocks behind the glass front. The hour struck, and he was immersed in a medley of sound. Tiny chimes tinkled like tapped crystal; deep-tolling bells and reverberant mellow gongs vied with chirps and whistles and birdsong in a brief fantasia. Scores of tiny figures came forth to mark the hour each in its own way.

Lockyer found himself drawn to the capering figures of a Harlequin turning handsprings, one for each of the six peals of the little silver bell at the very top of the clock. The figure was smaller than his thumb, yet it moved with supple smoothness, free of the awkward lurching of the clock figures he had seen so many times before. At the sixth stroke the Harlequin turned its final handspring, bowed, and retreated inside a pair of gaily painted doors that shut firmly behind it. Lockyer leaned close, stooping, his hands on his knees, fascinated by the tiny figure's grace. He started at the sound of the clockmaker's voice and straightened quickly to find Bell standing behind the display case.

"I'm sorry if I startled you," the tall man said.

"I was watching. . . . I was fascinated by this," said Lockyer, his eyes returning to the clock now placidly ticking its way to another hour and another performance. "I've never seen a clock like this . . . like any of these."

"You must come again when the hour is striking, and see the others. Some are quite unusual."

"They must be very expensive."

"Some are priceless. Others are less expensive than you might think."

Lockyer leaned down to look more closely at the Harlequin clock. He touched his pudgy fingers to the glass of the case in a childlike gesture, and drew them back quickly in embarrassment. Looking at Bell, he said, "How much is that one?"

"That one is not for sale, Mr. Lockyer. I've been offered a great deal of money for it, but I'm not prepared to let my little Harlequin go."

"It's a marvelous piece of work. Everything is the shop is marvelous . . . and you've set it all up so quickly!" Lockyer said with a frank, ingenuous smile. "It's incredible that you accomplished so much in less than a day."

"Would you like your watch, Mr. Lockyer?"

"Oh, surely you haven't had enough time. . . ." Lockyer broke off his protest as Bell drew out his grandfather's watch, bright and new-looking, and held it up for Lockyer to hear. The watch was ticking very softly. Lockyer took it, looked at it in amazement, and held it to his ear again.

"It will keep time for your grandchildren, Mr. Lockyer. And for their grand-children, too."

Lockyer's expression grew somber, but only for an instant. He asked, "How did you do it? The watchmaker in Boston told me it was ruined. He said no one could fix it."

"There are very few things that can't be fixed. Perhaps I've had more experience than others."

Looking from the watch to Bell in silent wonder, Lockyer said after a time, "It looks brand-new. I must admit, I didn't think you could fix it."

"It was a pleasure, Mr. Lockyer."

The smaller man looked at his watch again, held it to his ear, and shook his head bemusedly. He tucked the watch into his vest pocket and reached for his wallet. "How much will it be?"

Bell raised his hand in an arresting gesture. "There is no charge."

"But you must have put a lot of time and work into this."

"I never charge my first customer."

"You're very generous." Lockyer looked at the shelves behind the display case. "Perhaps . . . you mentioned that some of your clocks are not too expensive, and perhaps . . . I'm sure my wife would be pleased with a nice clock for the mantel."

"Then we shall find one to her liking," Bell said. He walked slowly down the length of shelves, paused, retraced his steps, and at last stopped to take down a clock mounted atop a silver cylinder embellished with enameled swans on a woodland lake. He placed it on the countertop. The clock was silent; its hands were fixed at a minute before twelve.

"It's waiting for its proper owner," he explained.

He touched something at the back, and the clock began to tick. When the hands met at twelve, the cylinder opened, and, to the accompaniment of a sweet melody, a little dark-haired ballerina stepped forth, bowed, and began to dance. Lockyer stared at the figure in astonishment and murmured the single word "Antoinette."

At the last stroke, the tiny dancer withdrew, and the cylinder closed around her. Lockyer continued to stare for a moment, then he rubbed his eyes and looked up at Bell.

"It's uncanny," he said, his voice hushed and slightly hoarse. "We had a daughter. She loved to dance. We hoped that she'd be a ballerina, but it wasn't to be. She died of pneumonia two years ago."

"I'm very sorry, Mr. Lockyer. I hope I've not caused you pain."

"No! Oh no, Mr. Bell. That little dancer is the image of Antoinette as she was when we lost her."

"Then you have your daughter back. Every time the hour strikes, she will dance as she once did."

"My wife would be so happy," said Lockyer, his eyes fixed on the clock. He spoke like a man voicing his private thoughts. "She's never gotten over it, really. She seldom leaves the house anymore. But that clock. . . . I know it must be very expensive, but I'll manage to pay for it somehow."

Bell stated the price. Lockyer gaped at him, and at last cried, "But that's ridiculous! You could sell this clock for a hundred times that much!"

"I choose to sell it to you for exactly that price, no more and no less. Will you have it?"

"I will!"

"Then it is yours," the clockmaster said. He made a quick adjustment at the back, turning the hands to the proper time, and then he took up the clock and handed it back to Lockyer. "It's properly set now. It will require no further adjustment. I hope it brings pleasure to you and your wife."

"It's certain to do that. Thank you, Mr. Bell," Lockyer said as he backed from the counter, the clock cradled in his arms.

The clockmaker's shop soon became a point of interest in the town. Schoolchildren and idlers clustered outside the window to observe the hourly spectacle. Customers came in increasing numbers, some to bring a watch or clock for repair or adjustment, and some to buy one of the timepieces that Bell sold at such modest prices. All who entered the shop stayed long, entranced by the marvels of workmanship that filled the display case and lined the shelves.

Lockyer was a regular visitor. At least once each week, usually more than that, he showed up at Bell's shop to report on the remarkable accuracy of his watch, to thank Bell for the ballerina clock, and then to examine the latest product of Bell's workshop. He was awed by the speed with which the clockmaker could create his marvelous mechanisms. Every week brought something new.

Late in the year, when Lockyer stopped in the shop on a rainy afternoon, Bell was placing a new clock in the display case. At the sight of Lockyer, the clockmaker smiled and set the clock on the glass top, extending his hand in welcome.

"Would you care to see it work?" he asked.

"Yes, Mr. Bell," said Lockyer eagerly. He put his umbrella in the stand by the door and came to the display case.

He saw a dark sphere, about the size of a cannonball. It appeared to be of crystal, so deep blue that it was almost black. Atop the opaque crystal was a small white-and-gold clock no bigger than a child's fist. The hands of the clock stood at one minute to twelve.

Lockyer studied the crystal, and could distinguish nothing within but darkness. The clock was exquisite, the crystal flawless, but this seemed a disappointingly simple timepiece to come from one who was capable of the intricate and subtle mechanisms that filled the shop.

As if he had read Lockyer's thoughts, Bell said, "It is not quite so simple as it appears." Lockyer glanced sharply up in embarrassment. Bell smiled and set the clockwork going.

It appeared to Lockyer that by the time the hands had met, the darkness in the crystal had softened somewhat. At the first stroke of twelve, a light appeared at the center. With each successive stroke, a new light glowed somewhere in the crystal, and all grew steadily brighter. The outer lights moved about the central one, brightest of them all, and smaller lights, hardly more than pinpoints against the rich blue that now suffused the sphere, circled some of the outer lights. Silent and serene, they moved in stately procession around the bright center. At the ninth revolution, the lights began to fade and the darkness deepen. When the twelfth revolution was completed, only the faint glow at the center of the crystal remained, and then suddenly it was gone, and all within was darkness once again.

"That's marvelous! It's . . . it's the universe!" Lockyer blurted.

"Only a representation of one small part," said Bell, lifting the sphere and placing it in the case.

"It's incredible, Mr. Bell. Incredible. Those lights . . . and the way they move . . . how did you do it?"

"I have my secrets. I thought you'd enjoy seeing this one, Mr. Lockyer. It will not be here after today."

"Are you actually selling that? Who could afford such a—" Lockyer silenced himself abruptly, more embarrassed than before. Bell's dealings were no one's business but his own; if he undervalued his own work, the fact did not seem to trouble him, or to do him any harm.

"I charged a fair price. And the woman who ordered this very special clock for her husband can well afford it."

"Sutterland. It can only be Elizabeth Sutterland." Bell nodded, but said nothing, and Lockyer went on, "Well, maybe I shouldn't say this, but it hurts me, Mr. Bell, it really hurts me, to think of a beautiful piece of workmanship like this clock being in the hands of a man like Paul Sutterland. He doesn't deserve it."

"Mrs. Sutterland seems to think he does."

"Elizabeth has forgiven him a hundred times, taken him back when he's done things. . . ." Lockyer stopped himself. He gestured angrily, and stood with reddened face, glaring at the dark sphere.

"Perhaps she loves him, Mr. Lockyer."

"If she does, she's a fool. I'm not a prying man, but I can't help hearing things, and if only a fraction of the things I hear about Paul Sutterland and that crowd of his friends are true, Elizabeth should have left him long ago."

"Things may improve, Mr. Lockyer. People do change."

Bitterly, Lockyer said, "Some people do. I know Sutterland, and I know that he'll never change, not if he lives to be a hundred."

"We must hope."

Lockyer nodded impatiently and went to the door. He took his umbrella, put his hand on the doorknob, and then turned to Bell. "Look, Mr. Bell, I'm sorry. I had no right to say the things I said. I got angry for a moment. Elizabeth is an old friend. A lot of people in this town respect her."

"It's perfectly all right, Mr. Lockyer."

"It isn't all right. That's what troubles me. Sutterland is cruel to his wife and children. He treats his servants brutally. And to think of her giving him something so exquisite. . . ." He gestured helplessly.

"As I said, we must hope. Perhaps this anniversary present will mark a turning point for the Sutterlands."

Mrs. Sutterland arrived late that afternoon. She was a beautiful woman, her fine features almost untouched by time, her thick hair a glowing auburn; but years of unhappiness had left their mark in other ways. Her manner was cool and formal, and there was a tautness in her voice that served as a barrier to all but essential conversation.

The sight of the clock changed her. She folded back her veil and looked with unfeigned delight at the motion of the tiny worlds within the sphere. When the last light faded, she turned eagerly to the clockmaker, her eyes aglow, her expression animated.

"Mr. Bell, this is a wonder! I've never seen anything to rival it. My husband will be overwhelmed!" she said exuberantly.

"I'm happy to see you so pleased, Mrs. Sutterland."

"I'm delighted. It's quite beyond anything I expected, Mr. Bell." She placed her gloved hands on the crystal and looked into its dark depths, and as she looked, her expression hardened and weariness seemed to enfold her like a shadow. When she addressed him again, the barrier was in place. "If by any chance the clock should be damaged, Mr. Bell—we will, of course, take the greatest care of such a delicate mechanism, but children and servants can be clumsy—if some mischance should occur—"

"I will repair it," said Bell.

This town, like all towns, had its share of idlers and wastrels. Some of them were frequent observers of the noontime display in Bell's shop window, but, being the sort of men to whom punctuality was not so much a virtue as an imposition, they did not become patrons. Nearly a full year passed from his arrival before one of them visited the shop, and he came only to amuse himself at the clockmaker's expense.

His name was Monson, and he was given to this kind of amusement. He was a portly, florid-faced man with handsome features and a confident manner, well-dressed and well-spoken. He belonged to a prominent and prosperous family, though he himself showed no signs of industry or concern for good repute. He came to the shop one morning, spent a quarter hour examining the clocks on display, and then introduced himself to Bell. "People say you repair damaged clocks and watches," he went on.

"I do," said Bell.

"I've heard that you can repair any watch, no matter how badly it's been damaged."

"People have been satisfied by my work. Perhaps they exaggerate."

"Well, if you're as good as they say, I have a little job for you. It should be no trouble at all for a man of your abilities." Monson drew a dirty rolled-up handkerchief from his pocket, laid it on the countertop, and unfolded it to reveal a jumble of wheels, springs, and tiny bits of metal; a cracked dial; and a bent and battered watchcase. All were encrusted with dried mud, and the case was scored and scratched. When Bell remained silent, Monson said, "Too much for you?", and favored him with a bland smile.

"Perhaps not, Mr. Monson," said Bell.

Monson's smile wavered in the face of this calm response, but he quickly recovered. "It slipped from my fingers and rolled into the roadway. A horse trod it into the dirt, and the wagon wheels rolled right over it. I thought it was beyond fixing, but this watch has sentimental value to me, and so I kept the pieces. Then, when I heard everyone in town singing your praises, I told them I'd bring the watch to you and let you show how good you really are." His smile was a mocking challenge.

"Come back tomorrow at four," Bell said, taking up the handkerchief full of fragments.

"So soon, Mr. Bell? You work fast."

"I do not waste time, Mr. Monson, neither mine nor other people's," Bell replied.

Monson left, and when he joined the friends who had waited for him outside, their laughter could be heard inside the shop. The next day all three came at the appointed hour. Three other men, all well-dressed and in very high spirits, were also present, having entered only a few minutes earlier. They joined the others around Monson when he greeted the clockmaker, placed his palms on the top of the display case, and said boldly, "My watch, if you please, Mr. Bell."

"Your watch, Mr. Monson," said the clockmaker. He placed a small box on the glass and opened it. Inside was a spotless white handkerchief—Monson's own, as the monogram attested—which he unfolded to reveal a watch in excellent condition. The hands were at two minutes past four.

"No, no, Mr. Bell. You must have misunderstood me. I want my own watch, not a replacement," said Monson, shaking his head.

"This is your watch."

Monson took up the watch and inspected it front and back. After a time he said, "It may be my watchcase . . . either the original or a damned clever imitation . . . but even if it is my own, the rest of it. . . ." He put the watch down and shook his head emphatically. "I didn't authorize you to replace the works, I told you to repair them, and you said you would."

"I replaced only those parts that were missing," Bell said. "I repaired your watch. Mr. Monson."

"Nobody could have repaired that watch," said Monson flatly. "I handed you a lot of junk."

"You did indeed. Nevertheless, I repaired the watch. Do you want it, Mr. Monson?"

"Of course I do. It's my watch, isn't it? You said so yourself. But if you think you're going to charge me some outrageous price, you'd better think again. I'm on to that trick."

Bell quoted the price of his repairs. The men with Monson grinned at one another. One of them laughed. Whether Monson, or Bell, or the situation in which they found themselves, was the source of their amusement was not clear; but Monson did not appear to share their feelings. He took the coins from his pocket and dropped them with a clatter on the glass top. He took up the watch, turned, and stalked from the shop without another word.

Later that week, two of the men who had been with Monson came to Bell's shop. They looked over the clocks on display carefully and critically, and finally informed Bell that they intended to buy a clock for their clubroom at the hotel. Nothing on the shelves or in the display case was precisely what they had in mind, one of them explained further, but there were three that might be acceptable, provided the price was low enough. They pointed out the three, and when Bell told them the prices, they gaped at him in astonishment.

"What do you mean, asking prices like those?" one demanded. "There's nobody in this town can pay that kind of money for a clock!"

"I hear that if you like people, you sell them a clock for practically nothing. What's wrong with us that you ask so much? Do we look like fools?" said the other angrily.

"My prices vary," said Bell. "You saw how little I asked from your friend."

"Well then, treat us the same way, if you don't want trouble," said the second man.

Bell did not reply at once. Then, as if he had not heard the threat, or had chosen to ignore it, he said, "You gentlemen have chosen three of the most expensive clocks in my shop. I have others that cost much less."

"If we wanted a cheap clock, we'd go to the general store. We're willing to pay good money for good workmanship, but we won't be gouged."

"Perhaps I can show you something else. The clocks you selected are very delicate. I may have others more suitable for a gentlemen's clubroom," Bell said.

They blustered a bit, but were mollified by what they took as his apology. He went to his storeroom and brought out several sturdy clocks set in brass and polished mahogany, with deep-resounding bells to mark the hour. The price of these clocks was absurdly low. The men examined them and selected one; but even as Bell was packing it carefully in a box for them, one of the men looked longingly at the first clock they had chosen.

"That clock with the little acrobat is still my favorite. Will you reconsider the price?" he asked.

"I set my prices very carefully, gentlemen. It is impossible for me to bargain."

"How does that acrobat work?" asked the other. "That's what fascinates me. I didn't see any wires."

"I didn't see wires on any of them. Be damned if I can figure out how those little people operate. What's your secret, Bell?"

Bell smiled, but said nothing.

"Probably just as well for us to get a good, sturdy clock and not one of those others. They're interesting, but they wouldn't last long once things got boisterous down at the club," said one of the men. The other laughed, and said, "Even a good, solid clock like this one may not last long, What do you say, Bell—if someone bounces this off a wall, will it keep on telling proper time?"

"If anything happens to this clock, come to me," Bell said.

Elizabeth Sutterland revisited the clockmaker's shop in the spring. Bell was at the door, awaiting her arrival, and she waved to him as her carriage pulled up. She entered the shop with the light step of a girl. Folding back her veil, she looked around the shelves and turned to Bell, beaming.

"Mr. Bell, I came at a perfect time—you have a score of new creations on your shelves!" she exclaimed.

"I trust the clock you purchased last year is performing satisfactorily?"

"It hasn't lost a second. And it's such a pleasure to watch. It seems to be just a bit different every time it strikes. The children love it, and Mr. Sutterland is absolutely fascinated by it. He keeps saying that he intends to come here himself and tell you how much pleasure he's gotten from it."

"I look forward to his visit, Mrs. Sutterland."

"Well, I hope he gets to it soon. He seems so very tired lately."

"These are busy times," said Bell, ushering Mrs. Sutterland to the counter and seating her.

"Oh, it isn't overwork. He just seems weary. It's almost as if he's gotten much older in the last few months," she said, looking up at the shelves.

Bell did not reply. He followed her gaze, and then reached up to take the clock that had attracted her eye. He set it on top of the counter. She leaned closer, examined it, then looked at him and smiled expectantly. "It's a lovely scene, Mr. Bell. So peaceful. I can't imagine what I'll see when it strikes."

The hands stood at two minutes to three. The clock face was set in a gold dome that canopied a woodland scene; a still pond surrounded by willows. A rowboat about the size of a child's little finger floated near the center of the pond. In it was a figure in a straw hat, dangling a fishing pole in the water. All was serene. When the first chime struck, the fisherman pulled up a tiny fish, unhooked it, and cast his line again, to land a fish at each stroke. The three fish flopped and thrashed in the bottom of the boat. The fisherman took them up and dropped them back into the water. As the ripples spread and faded, he settled in his seat, tilted his hat against the declining sun, lowered his line, and returned to his fishing.

Mrs. Sutterland clapped her hands together in an innocent gesture of sheer delight. "That's wonderful, Mr. Bell!" she exclaimed.

"Thank you, Mrs. Sutterland," he said, taking up the clock to replace it on the shelf. "Is there any other you'd like to see?"

"I love them all, Mr. Bell, but I'm really here to look for something suitable for my mother's birthday."

"Have you a special clock in mind?"

"I was hoping you might have another clock like the one I bought for my husband."

"Alas, no. Each clock is unique," said Bell. "But let me think. I may have something more suitable." He swept the shelves with a slow, searching gaze, then studied the contents of the display case. He stood for a time, frowning, a finger pressed to his lips; then, excusing himself, he withdrew to his workroom. Some minutes later he emerged bearing a delicate white vase that contained twelve red rosebuds.

"A clock, Mr. Bell?" she asked.

He nodded, pointing to a small dial near the base, its hands at one minute to twelve. He set the clock going and placed it before Mrs. Sutterland. As the clock struck, a rosebud opened at each stroke, and a growing fragrance filled the air. She exclaimed softly in wonder and delight.

"Oh, Mr. Bell, it's absolutely perfect!" she said when the last rose was full-blown. "My mother adores roses. I couldn't give her a nicer present."

"I completed this clock only yesterday, Mrs. Sutterland."

"Just in time for Mother's birthday!"

"Exactly on time, it appears," Bell said.

Late in the summer, Paul Sutterland died quietly at his home. He was in his early forties, and showed no evidence of disease; but in his last days, he was a shrunken white-haired man, drained and feeble in body and mind. His widow mourned him sincerely, but there were many in town who counted her fortunate to be free of him.

In the fall, on a dark, rainy day of empty streets, Monson and two of his friends brought their damaged clock to Bell's shop. Monson stood it on top of the display case and stepped back, laughing. The others joined in as Monson pointed to the shattered face.

"One of the lads fancies himself a marksman, Bell. How long will it take you to fix this one?" he asked.

Bell took up the clock and examined it, turning it in his hands. His expression was grave.

"Well, how long? We want it tomorrow. You're a fast worker, aren't you?" said one of the men, glancing at his companions and laughing.

"Too much for you, Bell?" asked Monson. "If you can't fix it, we'll take another one to replace it. A fancy one, one of your special models this time," he added, gesturing toward the shelves.

"Those clocks are not for sale," Bell said.

"You're a hell of a businessman, Bell. You don't want to sell your best goods, and what you do decide to sell, you sell at crazy prices."

"He makes enough on the ones he sells to rich women. Is that it, Bell?" one of Monson's companions asked.

"Yes, what are you up to with Liz Sutterland?" Monson asked. "She spends a good bit of time here, some people say. Don't get any ideas about her, Bell, do you hear me?"

"Leave my shop," said Bell.

"Leave? We're customers, Bell. You're a shopkeeper, and you'll treat us with respect. We want to look over these precious clocks of yours, all these not-for-sale treasures you're hoarding, and you'll show us what we tell you to show us."

"Leave my shop," Bell said once again, his voice level and unchanged. He put down the ruined clock and took a step toward them.

"How about this one?" said Monson, moving swiftly to the shelves and picking up a creation of gold and porcelain and brightly enameled metal on which a single uniformed guardsman stood smartly at attention. "Don't do anything to upset me, now, Bell. I might drop it."

Bell's voice was calm and icy cold. "Put down the clock and leave my shop."

Monson looked at his two friends and grinned. He cried sharply, "Oops! Careful, now!", and feigned dropping the clock, laughing loudly. At his motion the figure was jarred and fell to the floor. Monson quickly replaced the clock on the shelf. "I didn't mean to do that. You should have just kept quiet, Bell. We didn't intend any harm."

"Of course you intended harm. And you've accomplished it."

The atmosphere in the shop had changed in an instant. Bell seemed to loom over the three men; and they, though all of them were more powerfully built than he, and some years younger, now shrank from him. He bent, very gently took up the fallen figure, and raised it close to his eyes.

"You can fix it, Bell," one of the men said.

"Yes, you can fix things like that easily," said the other. "It's not as if we hurt anyone."

"Don't bother about the clock we brought in. It was a joke. Just a joke," said the first.

Monson stepped forward and thrust out his jaw defiantly. His voice was forced and unnaturally loud. "Just a minute. Bell can fix that clock of ours, and there's no reason why he shouldn't. If I did any damage—any real damage—I'm willing to pay for it, as long as it's a fair price. We have nothing to apologize for. We'll pay, and that's the end of it."

Bell raised his eyes from the broken figure in his hand. "I will calculate the proper payment," he said.

The disappearance of Austin Monson and two of his cronies was a matter of general discussion and much speculation around town in the following months.

Explanations of all sorts, from the ridiculous to the lurid, circulated for a day or two, then gave way to newer. But as time passed, interest waned, and soon the three vanished men were spoken of only by their friends.

In the year that followed this cause célèbre, Bell's clientele grew to include nearly everyone in town. Even the poorest family, it seemed, could afford to own a clock from his shop. And all his clocks, whatever the price, however simple or elaborate, kept perfect time. No customer was ever dissatisfied.

Bell was always available to a customer or a casual visitor, always willing to demonstrate some ingenious new timepiece. By this time, Lockyer and his wife had become regular weekly visitors; and every week, Bell had a new clock to display, ever more ingenious, sometimes close to magical. When the hour struck, one might see birds take wing or porpoises leap from a miniature sea or bats fly from a ruined belfry; woodsmen felled trees, skaters swooped and spun and cut intricate figures, a trainer put tiny lions and tigers through their paces, jugglers tossed Indian clubs smaller than a grain of rice, archers sent their all but invisible arrows into targets smaller than a fingernail; a sailor danced a hornpipe, a dervish twirled in ecstasy, a stately couple waltzed serenely while a quintet of periwigged musicians played. And never were the movements of these little figures awkward or mechanical, but always smooth and natural; no wires or levers or tracks could be seen, only graceful and disciplined motion, time after time.

Bell seemed to sell his clocks as quickly as he could make them. Even those that were not for sale left the shop, to be replaced on the shelves by new ones. Only a few were permanent. The little Harlequin whose acrobatics had captivated Lockyer on his first visit to the shop was still in place. The fire-breathing dragon on his hoard of gold and precious gems and skeletons in armor was still in a corner of the window, slouching forth every hour to the terror and delight of all the children. And a trim little pavilion of gold and porcelain and bright stripes of red and blue enameled metal, before which a single uniformed guardsman marched and countermarched every hour while a piper and a drummer marked the beat, stood where it had been for as long as Lockyer could recall; a year, at the very least.

During the holiday season, Bell's shop was a crowded, busy place, cheerful and lively. Those few townspeople who did not yet own one of his clocks were finally about to make a purchase, and others wished to buy one as a special gift for a relative or a friend. How he managed to do it no one knew, but Bell met the increased demand and even produced a magnificent new clock, a lighted cathedral with carolers before its steps and a choir of angels hovering over its spires. He placed it in the window three days before Christmas, and every passerby stopped to marvel.

In the cold, dark days of the new year, the mood of the town changed. No one criticized Bell or his work, or complained of his prices, but now the shop was often empty, no customers visiting for two or three days running. The Lockyers still came regularly, sometimes bringing their infant daughter. They noticed no change in Bell's manner and heard no word of complaint from him, but they sensed a difference that they could not explain to one another.

New rumors had begun in the clubroom where Monson's friends still gathered. Here they drank, and brooded, and their idle minds dwelt on the still-unexplained disappearance of their old companions. As rumors do, their stories fed on themselves, and interwove one with another, corroborating exaggeration with misstatement and validating both with falsehood. In time they became firmly convinced of their own imaginings.

Bell was the culprit, said the rumormongers. Why? Envy, of course. That was plain to anyone who knew the facts. Monson had shown him up, made him look foolish. The ridiculous clockmaker had thought himself a rival for the widow's affections—fancy a woman like her wedded to a shopkeeper!—and when he learned of her preference for Monson, jealousy added to envy had pushed him to desperation. Monson had put him in his place, and he had sought revenge. It was obvious. Just what he had done to his rival, and how, and why he had included others in his deed, was not clear—Bell was too crafty to leave evidence that would give him away; no one questioned his shrewdness—but he was the guilty party, that was plain to any reasonable person, and he must be brought to justice.

At first the townspeople laughed at these wild tales, considering their source and their probable motive. But they heard them again and again, and in time a tiny seed of something—not quite doubt, but perhaps a vague and reluctant uncertainty—took root in their minds. What was said so often, so earnestly, could not be completely without foundation, they told themselves. Not that they believed a word of it—but Bell was a mysterious man; no one would deny that. Where had he come from, and why had he come to this town? How could a man price his wares so erratically and stay in business, even prosper? Who bought those expensive clocks, and what became of the ones that were not for sale but nevertheless vanished from the shelves? How could anyone produce mechanisms of such delicacy and precision so quickly and yet so perfectly, and still turn out sturdy, serviceable clocks at bargain prices? And if it was indeed true that Monson and his friends had been talking about visiting Bell on the very day of their disappearance, then the clockmaker owed the town an explanation. No amount of good workmanship, not even genius, exempted a man from the common judgment, said the good citizens. The rumors grew more insistent, the issue more troublesome, the questions more pointed, as spring drew near.

One evening, when the shop was closed and the streets empty, Lockyer tapped at the clockmaker's back door. Bell was in his workroom, as he usually was in the evening hours, and he opened the door after a short delay.

"Mr. Bell, you must seek protection," Lockyer said without preamble when the door opened.

"I need no protection," Bell replied.

"You do," Lockyer insisted. "You must know the stories that are going around town."

"I have heard foolish rumors," Bell conceded.

"You and I know that they're foolish, but others in town are beginning to believe them. There's talk of coming to your shop and demanding an account of Monson's disappearance."

Bell's voice was unperturbed. "My shop will be open at the usual hour. I have always been willing to answer reasonable questions. Will you come in, Mr. Lockyer?"

"No, no, I can't," said Lockyer, drawing back. "But you must do something to protect yourself. Monson's friends are behind this, and they want to hurt you. They may break in on you in the night."

"Will the townspeople permit this?"

Lockyer hesitated, then lamely replied, "No one wants anything to happen to you. But Monson's friends have everyone confused. They have a lot of influence in this town; some of them do, anyway. And the people have heard so many stories that they don't know what to believe. They're confused."

"So I must fear the actions of a lawless mob."

"I'm afraid that's the case. You must protect yourself."

"I will, Mr. Lockyer," said Bell. Without another word, he closed the door. Lockyer heard the bolt slide into place.

They came to the shop later that night, eleven men strong. Others waited outside, at front and back. Several had been customers at one time or another, and some had come on occasion to observe the clocks as they struck the hour, or watched the display in the window. Three who had been present when Bell had presented Monson with his repaired watch were the leaders. The others did not speak.

"We're here to find out what you did to our friends, Bell. We're not leaving until we're satisfied," said one, planting himself in front of the clockmaker.

"Why do you blame me?" Bell asked, looking calmly down on him.

"They said they were coming here. We all heard them say that. And then we never saw them again. You're the one behind their disappearance, all right."

"Just admit it, Bell. We can make you tell us everything, if you force us to," one of the others said. He raised a walking stick and tapped it on the glass top of the display case.

"We can smash this place to bits, and you with it," said the first. "Now, tell us what you did to our friends."

Bell looked down at him, then at the man with the walking stick, then at such others as met his glance. He raised his hand and pointed to the door. "It is best that you leave my shop," he said.

"Best for you, that's certain. But we're not leaving," said the first man, and several of the others, under the challenge of his ferocious gaze, murmured their agreement.

"Don't try to bluff us, Bell. You've bluffed this whole town for too long. Answer our questions, or it's going to get mighty unpleasant," said the second. He brought his stick down sharply. The glass cracked.

Then, suddenly, at exactly nine minutes past the hour of one, all the clocks in the shop began to strike in unison. Deep gongs and crystalline chimes, resonant bells and the sound of tiny drums and trumpets, music and birdsong and a din of indistinguishable pealings and tollings and clangings, all blended to engulf the intruders in a wave of sound; and on and on they struck, twelve times and twelve more and twelve times twelve more, rapidly at first, and then steadily diminishing in volume and rapidity, fading as if they were receding at a steady rate, becoming ever fainter until they could be heard no more.

The men stood benumbed by the assault of sound. They felt no pain and sensed no restraint by external force. Not one of them carried any trace of physical harm as a result of that night. Their breath came freely; they could move their eyes and hear every sound. But their bodies were held, as if the air had grown viscid and glutinous, clinging to them, dragging at them like thick mud or heavy snow, but a thousand times more inhibitive than mud or snow because, invisible and insensible as it was, it clung not only to their feet and legs, but to their hands, arms, heads, and bodies. They felt as if time itself had crawled almost to a halt, congealing and trapping them within it like insects in amber.

Those who spoke of that night—and few of them ever did so, and those few reluctantly, after long silence, and still fearful of ridicule—agreed on several points. Bell, they all said, was untouched by the phenomenon. He removed the clocks from the shelves and the window and the display case, one by one, carefully and lovingly, and took them into his workroom. This process took some time, several hours at least, but none of the men felt the pain or cramping that such a long period of enforced immobility, or near immobility, would be certain to cause. Bell worked methodically, ignoring the intruders, his attention confined to his clocks.

On these facts all agreed, but each had his own particular memory of that night. According to one man, the shop grew steadily darker; another said that the light remained constant, but Bell himself moved ever more swiftly, until at last he moved too fast for the eye to follow, and vanished from sight; a third man claimed that Bell grew more insubstantial and wraithlike with each timepiece he removed, and at last simply faded into nothingness. One man recalled a sight of a fly that passed before his face so slowly that he could count the beats of its wings. The fly progressed no more than a foot; and yet the man swore that its passage consumed three hours, at the very least. One of his companions spoke of the disturbing sight of ash fallen from the cigar in the hand of a man standing near him: it fell to the ground so slowly that in all the time he stood confined, no less than four hours by his calculation, it had not reached the floor. Two other men mentioned their awareness of each tick of a clock, separated by an agonizing interval. One claimed a full hour's space, while the other spoke only of "a horrible long wait" between one tick and the next.

Whatever happened on that night, however it happened, when the men could move—and their immobility ended in an instant, without warning—Bell and all the clocks were gone.

Five men fled the shop in terror the instant they had command of their legs. Those who remained did so more from fear of showing fear than from courage, or even anger. They looked to one another uncertainly, awaiting direction, and finally someone said, "We have to go after him."

The workroom was dark and empty. They drew the bolt on the back door, and one shouted to the others waiting outside, "Did you see him?"

A man carrying a pick handle emerged from the shadows. "Didn't see nobody. Nobody's come out that door."

"Are you sure?"

"Of course we're sure, damn it!" called an unseen voice near at hand. "What happened? Bell get away from you?"

They did not reply. They returned to the shop, and noticed something that had escaped them in the first shock of freedom. The shop was thick in dust, and cobwebs hung from the ceiling and rounded the upper corners of the shelves. The air was stale, like that of a room long sealed. As they looked around them, the clock in the town hall struck the quarter hour. One man looked at his watch and announced in a hushed voice, "One-fifteen."

No one ever learned what became of the clockmaker. No clocks like his were ever seen again by any of the townspeople, even those who traveled widely and took an interest in such things. Those that he sold have been passed on through three or four or even five generations. They keep perfect time, and have never required repair.

ELLEN KUSHNER

Sonata: For Two Friends in Different Times of the Same Trouble

Ellen Kushner is the author of two highly acclaimed novels, *Swordspoint* and *Thomas the Rhymer*, and four adventure books for children; and editor of the fantasy anthology *Basilisk*. She has published short fiction and poetry in *Elsewhere I & II*, *Heroic Visions*, *Whispers*, the *Borderland* urban fantasy series, and *F & SF*. She is also host (and script writer) for the Nakamichi International Music Series of classical music concerts broadcast nationally on NPR and APR, as well as host of a weekly worldbeat music show on WGBH in Boston and a liaison for European radio. Kushner lives in Somerville, Massachusetts.

The following poem deftly incorporates the Cinderella fairy tale as the author addresses the subject of painful endings of romantic relationships. It comes from the Readercon anthology *Monochrome*, published by Broken Mirrors Press.

—T.W.

Sonata:
For Two Friends
In Different
Times
Of the Same
Trouble

ELLEN KUSHNER

Yes, it will have been worth it after all.
If Cinderella had stayed at the ball
She'd be the heroine of quite another tale.
The twelfth chime would have struck, and all turned pale
To see their proud prince dancing with a slut.
Let's face it: Nobody knows what
Precisely would have happened next.
Allow me the pomposity of guess:
The delicate pretender had her chance—
Lucky at all to have gotten to the dance.
(And disobeying orders, while a shame,
Is sometimes the best way to break the game.)
So think of her, if not nude, in a dress
Of rotten rags. It would have hurt her less,
Maybe, because it was not new
For her to be the lowest thing on view—
But for her to see herself despised,
Reborn as garbage in the prince's eyes
That lately loved—made harder by his caring—
Hurt like low death, hurt almost past all bearing.

She bore it though. I know she did not run.
She was both brave and forthright. And she won
No lasting peace. No comfort there at all,
Only another chance at some grim ball
Or other, more demands on her life;

Lucky to live as mistress, never wife;
Lucky to be in any tale at all
As it continued. She lived through the ball.

Perrault doesn't sing this one, nor does Grimm:
An odiously modern, graceless hymn
To heartbreak and to heroines who fall
And fall hard. (Baby, when you're at the ball,
You're lucky to get asked to dance at all.)
Their tales ended in marriage. Pace to
Hymen, Juno, and all that holy crew.
There's nothing wrong with union as end,
Either real or artistic. And to mend
Breaches is noble, in a quiet way.
But think of Endings.

Ignore what I say
If that's what's best. Why do my friends'
Hurts hurt so much harder? All the ends
I can come up with are not half so good
As one good folk-tale ending as it should.

The times are hard. The way is long. The tale
Is being told. Go on, spin out, regale
The graceless fairies with a tale that's new—
You'll be the heroine of that one, too.

STUART DYBEK
Death of a Right Fielder

Stuart Dybek grew up in Chicago and now lives with his wife and children in Kalamazoo, Michigan. He teaches at Case Western University. Dybek's stories and poetry have appeared in *The Atlantic Monthly*, *The New Yorker*, *The Iowa Review*, *Antaeus*, *Ploughshares*, and the O. Henry prize story collections. He is the author of *Childhood and Other Neighborhoods* and the recent *The Coast of Chicago*, as well as the poetry collection *Brass Knuckles*.

"Death of a Right Fielder" is a quietly eerie piece that plays with a purely American mythology: the game of baseball. Dybek's brief excursion into the realm of Magic Realism appeared in *Harper's* magazine.

—T.W.

Death of a Right Fielder

STUART DYBEK

After too many balls went out and never came back, we went out to check. It was a long walk—he always played deep. Finally we saw him; from a distance he resembled the towel we sometimes threw down for second base.

It was hard to tell how long he'd been lying there, sprawled on his face. Had he been playing infield, his presence, or lack of it, would of course have been noticed immediately. The infield demands communication—the constant, re-assuring chatter of team play. But he was remote, clearly an outfielder. The infield is for wisecrackers, pepper pots, gum-poppers; the outfield is for loners, onlookers, brooders who would rather study clover and swat gnats than holler. People could pretty much be divided between infielders and outfielders. Not that one always has a choice. He didn't necessarily choose right field so much as accept it.

There were several theories as to what killed him. From the start, the most popular was that he'd been shot. Perhaps from a passing car, possibly by that gang calling themselves the Jokers, who played sixteen-inch softball in the center of the housing project on the concrete diamond with painted bases, or by the Latin Lords, who didn't play sports, period. Or maybe some pervert with a telescopic sight, shooting from a bedroom window, or a mad sniper from a water tower, or a terrorist with a silencer from the expressway overpass, or maybe it was an accident, a stray slug from a robbery, or shoot-out, or assassination attempt miles away.

No matter who pulled the trigger, it seemed more plausible to ascribe his death to a bullet than to natural causes like, say, a heart attack. Young deaths are never natural; they're all violent. Not that kids don't die of heart attacks. But he never seemed the type. Sure, he was quiet, but not the quiet of someone always listening for the heart murmur his parents repeatedly warned him about since he was old enough to play. Nor could it have been leukemia. He wasn't a talented enough athlete to die of that. He'd have been playing center, not right, if leukemia was going to get him.

The shooting theory was better, even though there wasn't a mark on him. Couldn't it have been, as some argued, a high-powered bullet traveling with such velocity that its hole fused behind it? Still, not everyone was satisfied. Other theories were formulated, rumors became legends over the years: He'd had an allergic reaction to a bee sting; been struck by a single bolt of lightning from a freak, instantaneous electrical storm; ingested too strong a dose of insecticide from the grass blades he chewed on; sonic waves, radiation, pollution, etc. And a few of us like to think it was simply that, chasing a sinking liner, diving to make a shoestring catch, he broke his neck.

There *was* a ball in the webbing of his mitt when we turned him over. His mitt had been pinned under his body and was coated with an almost luminescent gray film. The same gray was on his black high-top gym shoes, as if he'd been running through lime, and it was on the bill of his baseball cap—the blue felt one with the red C that he always denied stood for the Chicago Cubs. He may have been a loner, but he didn't want to be identified with a loser. He lacked the sense of humor for that, lacked the perverse pride that sticking with a loser season after season breeds, and the love. He was just an ordinary guy, .250 at the plate, and we stood above him not knowing what to do next. By then the guys from the other outfield positions had trotted over. Someone, the shortstop probably, suggested team prayer. But no one could think of a team prayer. So we all just stood there, silently bowing our heads, pretending to pray while the shadows moved darkly across the outfield grass. After a while the entire diamond was swallowed and the field lights came on.

In the bluish squint of those lights, he didn't look like someone we'd once known—nothing looked quite right—and we hurriedly scratched a shallow grave, covered him over, and stamped it down as much as possible so that the next right fielder, whoever he'd be, wouldn't trip. It could be just such a seemingly trivial stumble that would ruin a great career before it had begun, or hamper it years later the way Mantle's was hampered by bum knees. One can never be sure the kid beside you isn't another Roberto Clemente; and who can ever know how many potential Great Ones have gone down in the obscurity of their neighborhoods? And so, in the catcher's phrase, we "buried the grave" rather than contribute to any further tragedy. In all likelihood, the next right fielder, whoever he'd be, would be clumsy too, and if there was a mound to trip over he'd find it and break *his* neck, and soon right field would get the reputation as haunted, a kind of sandlot Bermuda Triangle, inhabited by phantoms calling for ghostly fly balls, where no one but the most desperate outcasts, already on the verge of suicide, would be willing to play.

Still, despite our efforts, we couldn't totally disguise it. A fresh grave is stubborn. Its outline remained visible—a scuffed bald spot that might have been mistaken for an aberrant pitcher's mound except for the bat jammed in the earth with the mitt and blue cap hooked over the handle. Perhaps we didn't want to make it disappear completely—a part of us was resting there. Perhaps we wanted the new right fielder, whoever he'd be, to notice and wonder about who played there before him, realizing he was not the only link between past and future that mattered.

As for us, we walked back, but by then it was too late—getting on to supper, getting on to the end of summer vacation, time for other things, college, careers, settling down and raising a family. Past thirty-five the talk starts about being over the hill, about a graying Phil Niekro in his forties still fanning them with the knuckler as if it's some kind of miracle, beating the odds. And maybe the talk is right. One remembers Willie Mays, forty-two years old and a Met, dropping that can-of-corn fly in the '73 Series, all that grace stripped away and with it the conviction, leaving a man confused and apologetic about the boy in him. It's sad to admit it ends so soon, but everyone knows those are the lucky ones. Most guys are washed up by seventeen.

DAVID J. SCHOW
Not From Around Here

Elsewhere in this book, I take great pains to point out that most of Schow's fiction is not in the splatterpunk mode, and that by describing himself as a major practitioner, he does a great disservice to his skill as a writer. As examples, I like to point out the subtle chiller, "Pamela's Get," which appeared in the first volume of this anthology and the gentle mainstream story "Monster Movies," published in 1990.

On the other hand, "Not From Around Here" is bright and vicious and nasty and graphic and has monsters in it. I love it. It was originally published in his short story collection *Seeing Red*.

—E.D.

Not From Around Here

DAVID J. SCHOW

This morning I saw an alley cat busily disemboweling a rail lizard. I watched much longer than I had to in order to get the point.

Townies call little hamlets like Point Pitt "bedroom communities." Look west from San Francisco, and you'll see the Pacific Ocean. Twenty minutes by car to any other compass point will bring you to the population-signless borders of a bedroom community. El Granada. Dos Piedras. Half Moon Bay. Summit. Pumpkin Valley (no kidding).

Point Pitt rated a dot on the roadmaps only because of a NASA tracking dish, fenced off on a stone jetty, anchored rock-solid against gales, its microwave ear turned toward the universe. Gatewood was four and three-quarter miles to the north. To drive from Point Pitt to Gatewood you passed a sprawling, loamy-smelling acreage of flat fields and greenhouses, where itinerant Mexicans picked mushrooms for about a buck an hour. I saw them working every morning. They were visible through my right passenger window as I took the coast road up to San Francisco, and to my left every evening when I drove home. On the opposite side of the road, the ocean marked time. The pickers never gazed out toward the sea; they lacked the leisure. My first week of commuting eroded my notice of them. The panorama of incoming surf proved more useful for drive-time meditation. I no longer lacked the leisure.

You had to lean out a bit, but you could also see the Pacific from the balcony rail of our new upstairs bedroom, framed between two gargantuan California pines at least eighty years old. Suzanne fell for the house as soon as we toured it under the wing of the realtor. Our three-year-old, Jilly, squealed "Cave!" and jumped up and down in place, in hyperactive circles of little kid astonishment. Hard to believe, that this cavernous place was ours, that we weren't visiting a higher social class and would soon have to go home. This *was* home, and we were in love . . . goofy as that may sound.

I did not fall in love with the idea that all the decent movies, restaurants, and other urban diversions were still up in San Francisco. Gatewood boasted a single grease-griddle coffee shop that opened two hours before my morning alarm razzed and went dark promptly at five—up here, dinner was obviously a meal eaten at home, with family. Nearby was a mom-and-pop grocery that locked up at 9:00 P.M. Several miles away, in Dos Piedras, was an all-nighter where you could get chips and beer and bread and milk.

It sure wasn't the city. As a town, it wasn't vast enough to merit a stoplight. Point Pitt was no more than a rustic clot of well-built older homes tucked into a mountainside, with an ocean view. Voilà—bedroom community. Any encapsulation made it sound like a travel-folder wet dream, or an ideal environment in which to raise a child. I suspect my shrink knew this. He fomented this conspiracy, with my doctor, to get me away from my beloved city for the sake of my not-so-beloved ulcers.

I became a commuter. The drive was usually soothing, contemplative. I calmed my gut by chugging a lot of milk from the all-night market. We popped for cable TV—sixty channels. We adjusted fast.

It was required that I buy a barn-shaped rural mailbox. Suzanne jazzed it up with our name in stick-on weatherproof lettering: TASKE. The first Sunday after we moved in, I bolted it to the gang post by the feeder road, next to the boxes of our nearest neighbors. The hillside lots were widely separated by distance and altitude, fences and weald. There was much privacy to be had here. The good life, I guessed.

When a long shadow fell across the gang post from behind, I looked up at Creighton Dunwoody for the first time. His box read MR & MRS. C. DUNWOODY. He had the sun behind him; I was on my knees, wrestling with a screwdriver. It just wouldn't have played for me to say, *You have me at a disadvantage, sir,* so I gave him something else sparkling, like, "Uh . . . hello?"

He squinted at my shiny white mailbox, next to his rusty steel one. It had a large, ancient dent in the top. "You're Taske?" He pronounced it like *passkey*; it was a mistake I'd endured since the first grade.

I gently corrected him. "Carl Taske, right." I stood and shifted, foot-to-foot, the essence of nervous schmuckdom, and finally stuck out my hand. Carl Taske, alien being, here.

I almost thought he was going to ignore it when he leaned forward and clasped it emotionlessly. "Dunwoody. You're in Meyer Olson's old house. Good house." He was taller than me, a gaunt farmer type. His skin was stretched over his bones in that brownly weathered way that makes thirty look like fifty, and fifty like a hundred and ten. Like a good neighbor coasting through meaningless chat, I was about to inquire as to the fate of Meyer Olson when Dunwoody cut in, point-blank. "You got any kids?"

"My daughter Jill's the only one so far." And Jilly had been well-planned. I couldn't help thinking of farm families with fourteen kids, like litters.

He chewed on that a bit. His attention seemed to stray. This was country speed, not city rush, but I felt like jumping in and filling the dead space. It wouldn't do to appear pushy. I might have to do this a lot with the hayseed set from now on.

"Any pets?" he said.

"Not today." A partial lie. Suzanne had found an orphaned Alsatian at the animal shelter and was making the drive to collect it the next day.

"Any guns in your house?"

"Don't believe in guns." I shook my head and kept my eyes on his. The languid, directional focus of his questions made my guard pop up automatically. This was starting to sound like more than the standard greenhorn feel-up.

"That's good. That you don't." We traded idiotic, uncomfortable smiles.

In my new master bedroom there were his and hers closets. A zippered case in the back of mine held a twelve-gauge Remington pumpgun loaded with five three-inch Nitro Mag shells. My father had taught me that this was the only way to avoid killing yourself accidentally with an "unloaded" gun, and Suzanne was giving me hell about it now that Jilly was walking around by herself. It was none of Dunwoody's business, anyway.

"How old's your girl?"

"Three, this past May."

"She's not a baby anymore, then."

"Well, technically, no." I smiled again and it hurt my face. The sun was waning and the sky had gone mauve. Everything seemed to glow in the brief starkness of twilight gray.

Dunwoody nodded as though I'd given the correct answers on a geography test. "That's good. That you have your little girl." He was about to add something else when his gaze tilted past my shoulder.

I turned around and saw nothing. Then I caught a wink of reflected gold light. Looking more intently, I could see what looked to be a pretty large cat, cradled in the crotch of a towering eucalyptus tree uphill in the distance. Its eyes tossed back the sunset as it watched us.

Dunwoody was off, walking quickly up the slope without further comment. Maybe he had to feed the cat. "I guess I'll see . . . you later," I said to his back. I doubt if he heard me. His house stood in shadow off a sharp switchback in the road. A wandering, deeply-etched dirt path wound up to the front porch.

Not exactly rudeness. Not the city brand, at least.

The moon emerged to hang full and orange on the horizon, like an ebbing sun. High in its arc it shrank to a hard silver coin, its white brilliance filtering down through the treetops and shimmering on the sea-ripple. Suzanne hopped from bed and strode naked to the balcony, moving out through the French doors. Moonbeams made foliage patterns on her skin; the cool nighttime breeze buffeted her hair, in a gentle contest.

Her thin summer nightgown was tangled up in my feet, beneath the sheets. We'd dispensed with it about midnight. The one advantage to becoming a home-owner I'd never anticipated was the nude perfection of Suzanne on the balcony. She was a blue silhouette, weight on one foot and shoulders tilted in an unconsciously classical pose. After bearing Jilly and dropping the surplus weight of pregnancy, her ass and pelvis had resolved into a lascivious fullness that I could not keep my hands away from for long.

We fancied ourselves progressive parents, and Jilly had been installed in our living room from the first. We kept our single bedroom to ourselves. On hair triggers for the vaguest noise of infant distress, Mommy and Daddy were then besieged with the usual wee-hour fire drills and some spectacular demonstrations of eliminatory functions. Marital spats over the baby came and went like paper cuts; that was normal, too. Pain that might spoil a whole day, but was not permanent. Jilly's crib was swapped for a loveseat that opened into a single bed. And now she did not require constant surveillance, and was happily ensconced in her first private, real-life room.

Recently, Suzanne had shed all self-consciousness about sex, becoming adventurous again. There was no birth control to fret over. That was a hitch we still didn't discuss too often, because of the quiet pain involved—the permanent kind.

"Carl, come here and look." She spoke in a rapid hush, having spied something odd. "Hurry up!"

I padded out to embrace her from behind, nuzzling into the bouquet of her hair, then looking past her shoulder.

A big man was meandering slowly up the road. The nearest streetlamp was more than a block away, and we saw him as he passed through its pool of light, down by the junction with the coast highway. He was large and fleshy and fat and as naked as we were.

I pulled Suzanne back two paces, into the darkness of the bedroom. The balcony was amply private. Neither of us wanted to be caught peeking.

He seemed to grow as he got closer, until he was enormous. He was bald, with sloping mountain shoulders and vast pizza-dough pilings of flesh pulled into pendant bags by gravity. His knotted boxer's brow hid his eyes in shadow, as his pale belly hung to obscure his sex, except for a faint smudge of pubic hair. The load had bowed his knees inward, and his *lumpen* thighs jiggled as he ponderously hauled up one leg to drop in front of the other. We heard his bare feet slapping the pavement. His tits swam to and fro.

"There's something wrong with him," I whispered. Before Suzanne could give me a shot in the ribs for being a smartass, I added, "No—something else. *Look* at him. Closely."

We hurried across to the bedroom's south window so we could follow his progress past the mailboxes in front of the house. He was staring up into the sky as he walked, and his chin was wet. He was drooling. His arms hung dead dumb at his sides as he gazed upward, turning his head slowly one way, then another, as though trying to record distant stars through faulty receiving equipment.

"He's like a great big *baby*." Suzanne was aghast.

"That's what I was thinking." I recalled Jilly, when she was only a month out of the womb. The slack, stunned expression of the man below reminded me of the way a baby stares at a crib trinket—one that glitters, or revolves, or otherwise captures the eye of a being who is seeing this world for the first time.

"Maybe he's retarded."

A shudder wormed its way up my backbone but I successfully hid it. "Maybe he's a local boy they let run loose at night, y'know, like putting out the cat."

"Yeeugh, don't say that." She backed against me and my hands enfolded her, crossing to cup her breasts. Her body was alive with goosebumps; her nipples condensed to solid little nubs. She relaxed her head into the hollow of my shoulder and locked her arms behind me. Thus entangled, we watched the naked pilgrim drift up the street and beyond the light. My hands did their bit and she purred, closing her eyes. Her gorgeous rump settled in. "Hm. I seem to be riding the rail again," she said, and chuckled.

She loved having her breasts kneaded, and we didn't lapse into the dialogue I'd expected. The one about how her bosom *could* be a *little bit* larger, didn't I think so? (What I thought was that every woman I'd ever known had memorized this routine, like a mantra. Suzanne played it back every six weeks or so.) Nor did she lapse into the post-sex melancholy she sometimes suffered when she thought of the other thing, the painful one.

Eighteen months after Jilly was born, Suzanne's doctor discovered ovarian cysts. Three, medium-sized, successfully removed. The consensus was that Jilly would be our only child, and Suzanne believed only children were maladjusted. While there was regret that our power of choice had been excised, Suzanne still held out hope for a happy accident someday. I was more pragmatic, or maybe more selfish. I wasn't sure I wanted more than one child, and in a sense this metabolic happenstance had neatly relieved me of the responsibility of the vasectomy I'd been contemplating. I was hung up on getting my virility surgically removed in an operation that was, to me, a one-way gamble with no guarantees. Frightening. I prefer guarantees—hard-line, black-and-white, duly notarized. A hot tip from a realtor on a sheer steal of a house had more to do with reality than the caprices of a body that turns traitor and hampers your emotional life.

And when Suzanne's tumors were a bad memory, a plague of superstitions followed. For several months she was convinced that I considered her leprous, sexually unclean. From her late mother she had assimilated the irrational fear that says once doctors slice into your body with a scalpel, it's only a matter of borrowed time before the Big *D* comes pounding at the drawbridge.

The whole topic was a tightly twined nest of vipers neither of us care to trespass upon anymore. God, how she could bounce back.

Passion cranked up its heat, and she shimmied around so we were face-to-face. The way we fit together in embrace was comfortingly safe. Her hand filled and fondled, and I got a loving squeeze below. "This gets enough of a workout," she slyly opined. Then she patted my waistline. "But we need to exert this. When we get the dog, you can go out running with it, like me."

It was depressingly true. Bucking a desk chair had caused a thickening I did not appreciate. "Too much competition," I muttered. I was afraid to challenge the ulcerations eating my stomach wall too soon. She was in much better physical shape than me. Those excuses served, for now. Her legs were short, well-proportioned, and athletic. Her calves were solid and sleek. Another turn-on.

"Mmm." Her hands slid up, around, and all over. "In that case, come back to bed. I've got a new taste sensation I know you're just dying to try."

The following morning, I met the huge bald man.

He was wearing a circus-tent-sized denim coverall, gum-soled work boots, and an old cotton shirt, blazing white and yellowed at the armpits. He was busily rummaging in Dunwoody's mailbox.

I played it straight, clearing my throat too loudly and standing by.

He started, looking up and yanking his hand out of the box. His head narrowed at the hat-brim line and bulged up and out in the back, as though his skull had been bound in infancy, ritually deformed. His tiny black eyes settled on me and a wide grin split his face. Too wide.

"G'morn," he said with a voice like a foghorn. My skin contracted. I got the feeling he was sniffing me from afar. His lips continued meaningless movements while he stared.

"Ormly!"

Creighton Dunwoody was hustling down the path from his house. The hillside was steep enough to put his cellar floor above the level of our roof. He wore an undershirt and had a towel draped around his neck; he had obviously interrupted his morning shave to come out and yell. Drooping suspenders danced around his legs as he mountaineered down the path.

Ormly cringed at the sound of his name, but did not move. Birds twittered away the morning, and he grinned hugely at their music.

For one frozen moment we faced off, a triangle with Ormly at the mailboxes. I thought of the three-way showdown at the climax of *The Good, the Bad and the Ugly*.

Dunwoody stopped to scope us out, made his decision with a grunt, and resumed his brisk oldster's stride toward me. He realized the burden of explanation was his, and he motioned me to approach the mailboxes. His mouth was a tight moue of anger or embarrassment. Maybe disgust. But he bulled it through.

"Mister Taske. This here's Ormly. My boy." He nodded from him to me and back again. "Ormly. Mister Taske is from the city. You should shake his hand."

Dunwoody's presence did not make it any easier to move into Ormly's range. Without the work boots he would still be a foot taller than I was. I watched as his brain obediently motivated his hand toward me. It was like burying my own hand in a catcher's mitt. He was still grinning.

The social amenities executed, Dunwoody said, "You get on back up the house now. Mail ain't till later."

Ormly minded. I've seen more raw intelligence in the eyes of goldfish. As he clumped home, I saw a puckered fist of scar tissue nested behind his left ear. It was a baseball-sized hemisphere, deeply fissured and bone white. A big bite of brains was missing there. Maybe his pituitary gland had been damaged as part of the deal.

Dunwoody batted shut the lid to his mailbox; it made a hollow *chunk* sound. "S'okay," he said. "Ormly's not right in the head."

I was suddenly embarrassed for the older man.

"Sometimes he gets out. He's peaceful, though. He has peace. Ain't nothing to be afraid of."

I took a chance and mentioned what I'd seen last night. His eyes darted up to lock onto mine for the first time.

"And what were *you* doin' up that time of night anyhow, Mister Taske?" That almost colonial mistrust of newcomers was back.

"I woke up. Thought I heard something crashing around in the woods." The lie slipped smoothly out. So far, I'd aimed more lies at Dunwoody than truth. It was stupid for me to stand there in my C&R three-piece, calfhide attaché case in hand, judging his standards of honesty.

"This ain't the city. Animals come down from the hills to forage. Make sure your garbage-can lids are locked down or you'll have a mess to clean up."

I caught a comic picture of opening the kitchen door late at night and saying howdy-do to a grizzly bear. Not funny. Nearly forty yards up the hill, I watched Ormly duck the front door lintel and vanish inside. Dunwoody's house cried out for new paint. It was as decrepit as his mailbox.

Dunwoody marked my expression. "Ormly's all I got left. My little girl, Sarah, died a long time ago. The crib death. Primmy—that's my wife; her name was Primrose—is dead, too. She just didn't take to these parts. . . ." His voice trailed off.

I felt like the shallow, yuppie city slicker I was. I wanted to say something healing, something that would diminish the gap between me and this old rustic. He was tough as a scrub bristle. His T-shirt was frayed but clean. There was shaving lather drying on his face, and he had lost a wife, a daughter, and from what I'd seen, ninety percent of a son. I *wanted* to say something. But then I saw his bare arms, and the blood drained from my face in a flood.

He didn't notice, or didn't care.

I checked my watch, in an artificial, diversionary move Dunwoody saw right through. It was a Cartier tank watch. I felt myself sinking deeper.

"Mind if I ask you a question?"

"Uh—no." I shot my cuff to hide the watch, which had turned ostentatious and loud.

"Why do you folks want to live here?" There it was: bald hostility, countrified, but still as potent as snake venom. I tried to puzzle out some politic response to this when he continued. "I mean, why live here when it makes you so late for everything?" His eyes went to my shirtsleeve, which concealed my overpriced watch.

He shrugged and turned toward his house with no leave-takings, as before. All I could register in my brain were his arms. From the wrists to where they met his undershirt, Dunwoody's arms were seeded with more tiny puncture marks than you would have found on two hundred junkies up in the Mission district. Thousands and thousands of scarred holes.

My trusty BMW waited, a sanctuary until the scent of leather upholstery brought on new heartstabs of class guilt. It was simple to insulate oneself with the trappings of upward mobility, with *things*. My grand exit was marred by sloppy shifting. The closer I drew to the city the better I felt, and my deathgrip on the wheel's racing sleeve gradually relaxed.

Maybe our other neighbors would make themselves apparent in time. Oh bliss oh joy.

* * *

Brix became the dog's name by consensus. I stayed as far away from that decision as politely possible. Dad the diplomat.

Jilly had thrilled to its reddish-brown coat, which put her in mind of "bricks," you see. Suzanne went at tedious length about how Alsatians reacted best to monosyllabic names containing a lot of hard consonants. In a word, that was Brix—and he was already huge enough for Jilly to ride bareback. He could gallop rings around Suzanne while she jogged. He never got winded or tired. He looked great next the fireplace. A Christmas card snapshot of our idyllic family unit would have made you barf from the cuteness: shapely, amber-haired Mom; angelic blond Jillian Heather; Brix the Faithful Canine . . . and sourpuss Dad with his corporate razor cut and incipient ulcers. We were totally nuclear.

I didn't bother with Dunwoody or Ormly again until the night Brix got killed.

It was predestined that the dog's sleeping mat would go at the foot of Jilly's hide-a-bed. While Suzanne and I struggled patiently to indoctrinate the animal to his new name and surroundings, he'd snap to and seek Jilly the instant she called him. They were inseparable, and that was fine. The dog got a piece of Jilly's life; Suzanne and I were fair-traded a small chunk of the personal time we'd sacrificed in order to be called Mommy and Daddy. This payoff would accrue interest, year by year, until the day our daughter walked out the door to play grown-up for the rest of her life. It was a bittersweet revelation: starting right now, more and more of her would be lost to us. On the other hand, the way she flung her arms around Brix's ruff and hugged him tight made me want to cry, too.

Since we'd assumed residence in Point Pitt, our lives really *had* begun to arrange more agreeably. Our city tensions bled off. We were settling, healing. Sometimes I must be forced to drink the water I lead myself to.

Brix quickly cultivated one peculiar regimen. At Jilly's bedtime he'd plunk his muzzle down on the mat and play prone sentry until her breathing became deep and metered. Then he'd lope quietly out to hang with the other humans. When our lights went down, he'd pull an about-face and trot back to his post in Jilly's room. Once or twice I heard him pacing out the size of the house in the middle of the night, and when the forest made its grizzly-bear commotions, Brix would return one or two barks of warning. He never did this while in Jilly's room, which was considerate of him. Barks sufficed. In his canine way, he kept back the dangers of the night.

So when he went thundering down the stairs barking loudly enough to buzz the woodwork, I woke up knowing something was not normal. Suzanne moaned and rolled over, sinking her face into the pillows. I extricated myself from the sleepy grasp of her free arm in order to punch in as Daddy the night watchman. The digital clock merrily announced 3:44 A.M. And counting.

Point Pitt was not a place where residents bolted their doors at night, although that was one habit I was in no danger of losing, ever. Because the worst of summer still lingered, we had taken to leaving a few windows open. It wasn't completely foolish to assume some thief might be cruising for a likely smash-and-grab spot. By the time the sheriffs (the district's only real law enforcement) could be summoned, even an inept burglar would have ample time to rip off all the goodies in the house and come back for seconds. While this sort of social shortcoming was traditionally reserved for the big bad city, there was no telling who might start a trend, or when.

Besides, if there were no bad guys, I might be treated to the surreal sight of a live bear consuming my rubbish.

Downstairs a window noisily ceased existence. Breaking glass is one of the ugliest sounds there is. I picked up speed highballing down the stairs.

I thought of the claw hammer Suzanne had been using while hanging plants in her little conservatory and hung the corner wildly, skidding to a stop and embedding a flat wedge of glass into the ball of my right foot. I howled, keeled over, and obliterated a dieffenbachia mounted in a wire tripod. The entire middle section of leaded-glass panes was blown out into the night. Pots swung crookedly in their macramé slings where Brix had leapt through.

Somewhere in the backyard he was having it rabidly out with the interloper, scrabbling and snapping.

Grimacing, I stumped into the kitchen and hit the backyard light switches. Nothing. The floodlamps were still lined up on the counter in their store cartons, with a Post-it note stuck to the center one, reminding me of another undone chore. Outside the fight churned and boiled and I couldn't see a damned thing.

My next thought was of the shotgun. I limped back to the stairs, leaving single footprints in blood on the hardwood floor. Brix had stopped barking.

"Carl?"

"I'm okay," I called toward the landing. To my left was the shattered conservatory window, and the toothless black gullet of the night beyond it. "*Brix!* Hey, Brix! C'mon, guy! Party's over!"

Only one sound came in response. To this day I can't describe it accurately. It was like the peal of tearing cellophane, amplified a thousand times, or the grating rasp a glass cutter makes. It made my teeth twinge and brought every follicle on my body to full alert.

"Carl!" Suzanne was robed and halfway down the stairs.

"Get me a bandage and some peroxide, would you? I've hacked my goddamn foot wide open. Don't go outside. Get my tennis shoes."

I sat down on the second stair with a thump. When Suzanne extracted the trapezoidal chunk of glass, I nearly puked. There was a gash two inches wide, leaking blood and throbbing with each slam of my heartbeat. I thought I could feel cold air seeking tiny, exposed bones down there.

"Jesus, Carl." She made a face, as though I'd done this just to stir up a boring night. "Brixy whiffs a bobcat, or some fucking dog game, and you have to ruin our new floor by bleeding all over it. . . ."

"Something turned him on enough to take out the conservatory window. Jesus Christ in a Handi-Van. Ouch! Even if it *is* a bobcat, those things are too bad to mess with."

She swept her hair back, leaving a smear of blood on her forehead. She handed over the peroxide and left my foot half taped. "You finish. Let me deal with Jilly before she freaks out."

"Mommy?" Jilly's voice was tiny and sleep-clogged. She'd missed the circus.

I sure hadn't heard her roll out of the sack, but Suzanne apparently had. Mommy vibes, she'd tell me later.

After gingerly pulling on my shoes, I stumped to the kitchen door and disordered some drawers looking for a flashlight. Upstairs, Suzanne was murmuring a soothing story about how Daddy had himself an accident and fell on his ass.

I didn't have to look far to find Brix. He was gutted and strewn all over the backyard. The first part I found was his left rear leg, lying in the dirt like a gruesome drumstick with a blood-slicked jag of bone jutting from it. My damaged foot stubbed it; pain shot up my ass and blasted through the top of my head. His carcass was folded backward over the east fence, belly torn lengthwise, organs ripped out. The dripping cavern in the top of his head showed me where his brain had been until ten minutes ago.

The metallic, shrieking noise sailed down from the hills.

And the lights were on up at Dunwoody's place.

When the sheriffs told me Brix's evisceration was nothing abnormal, I almost lost it and started punching. Calling the cops had been automatic city behavior; a conditioned reaction that no longer had any real purpose. Atavistic. There hadn't been enough of Brix left to fill a Hefty bag. What wasn't in the bag was missing, presumed eaten. Predators, they shrugged.

In one way I was thankful we'd only had the dog a few days. Jilly was still too young to be really stunned by the loss of him, though she spent the day retreated into that horrible quiet that seizes children on the level of pure instinct. I immediately promised her another pet. Maybe that was impulsive and wrong, but I wasn't tracking on all channels myself. It did light her face briefly up.

I felt worse for Suzanne. She had been spared most of the visceral evidence of the slaughter, but those morsels she could not avoid seeing had hollowed her eyes and slackened her jaw. She had taken to Brix immediately, and had always militated against anything that caused pain to animals. There was no way to bleach out the solid and sickeningly large bloodstain on the fence, and I finally kicked out the offending planks. Looking at the hole was just as depressing.

The sheriffs were cloyed, too fat and secure in their jobs. All I had done was bring myself to their attention, which is one place no sane person wants to be. Annoyed at my cowardly waste of their time, they marked up my floor with their boots and felt up my wife with their eyes.

Things were done differently here. That was what impelled me to Dunwoody's place, at a brisk limp.

I had not expected Ormly to answer the door; I couldn't fathom what tasks were outside his capabilities and simply assumed he was too stupid to wipe his own ass. He filled up the doorway, immense and ugly, his face blank as a pine plank (with a knot on the flip side, I knew). He was dressed exactly as before. Perhaps he had not changed. It took a couple of long beats, but he did recognize me.

"Fur paw," he said.

The back of my neck bristled. When Ormly's brain changed stations, he haunted the forest, starkers, in the dead of night; what other pastimes might his damaged imagination offer him? When he spoke, I half expected him to produce one of

Brix's unaccounted-for shanks from his back pocket and gnaw on it. Then I realized what he had said: *For pa*.

"Yeah." I tried to clear the idiocy out of my throat. "Is he home."

"Home. Yuh." He lurched dutifully out of the foyer, Frankenstein's Monster in search of a battery charge.

I waited on the stoop, thinking it unwise to go where I wasn't specifically beckoned or invited. Another urban prejudice. Wait for the protocol, go through the official motions. Put it through channels. That routine was what had won me the white-lipped holes blooming in my stomach.

Dunwoody weaved out of the stale-smelling dimness holding half a glass of peppermint schnapps. He was wearing a long-sleeved workshirt with the cuffs buttoned.

"I'm sorry to bother you, Mr. Dunwoody, but my dog was killed last night." No reaction. He showed the same disinterest the cops had, and that brought my simmering anger a notch closer to boiling. "More to the point, he was pelted and hung on my back fence with his head scooped out and his guts spread all over the yard. The fence bordering *your* property, Mr. Dunwoody."

"I heard him barking." He looked down and away. "Saw you kick the slats out." His words billowed toward me in minty clouds; he was tying on a nice, out-of-focus afternoon drunk. "You said you didn't have no pets."

It was an accusation: *If you hadn't lied, this would not have happened.*

I felt obligated to be pissed off, but my soul wasn't really in it. My need to know was stronger. "Sorry—but look, you mentioned wildcats coming out of the hills. Or bears. Maybe I'm no authority on wildlife feeding habits, but what happened was . . ." I flashed on Brix's corpse again and my voice hitched. "That was far beyond killing for food."

"I didn't see it." His voice wasn't a full slur. Not yet, but soon. "Woke me up. But I didn't see it. I'm glad I didn't. That part I don't fancy, sir." He scratched an eyebrow. "I think y'all should leave. Go."

"You mean leave Point Pitt?"

"Move somewhere else. Don't live here." He took a long drag on his glass and grimaced, as though choking down cough medicine. "See what happens? This ain't for boys like you, with your fag hairdo's and your little Japanese cars and your satellite TV . . . aahhh, Christ . . ."

Ormly loomed behind him, recording all the pain with oddly sad eyes, so much like a dog himself.

A cloudy tear slipped down Dunwoody's face, but his own eyes were clear and decisive as they looked from me to the north. "Go home," he said. "Just go home, please." Then he shut the door in my face.

Dinner was flavorless, by rote. Suzanne had tried to nap and only gotten haggard. Jilly told me she missed Brix.

After bestowing my customary bedtime smackeroo, Jilly asked again about getting another pet *right now*. Her mom had run the same idea past me downstairs. Between them I'd finally be goaded into some reparation.

Suzanne reached for me as soon as I hit my side of the bed. She had already divested herself of clothing, and her movements were brazen and urgent. She wanted to outrun the last twenty-four hours in a steambath of good therapeutic fucking. Her nerves were rawed, and close to the surface; she climaxed with very little effort and kept me inside her for a long, comforting while. Then she kissed me very tenderly, ate two sleeping pills, and chased oblivion in another direction.

My foot felt as if I had stomped on a sharpened pencil. I hobbled to the bathroom, pretending I was Chester in *Gunsmoke*. The dressing was yellowed from drainage and shadowed with dry brown blood. It gave off a carrion odor. I took my time washing and swabbing and winding on new gauze. I was still pleasantly numb everywhere else.

There was a low thrumming, like that of a large truck idling on the street outside. I felt it before I actually heard it. I checked the window across from the bathroom door, but there was nothing, not even Ormly making his uniformless predawn rounds. With my Bay City paranoid's devotion to ritual, I hobbled downstairs and jiggled all the locked doors. The boarded-up plant nook was secure. I sneaked a couple of slugs of milk straight from the carton. Ulcer maintenance.

Jilly's room was on the far side of the bathroom. When I peeked stealthily in, the vibrational noise got noticeably louder.

Triplechecking everything constantly was as much a habit of new parenthood as security insecurity. Jilly was wound up in her Sesame Street sheets. I decided to shut the window, which was curtained but half-open.

The sheet-shape was grotesque enough to suggest that Jilly's entire platoon of stuffed animals was bunking with her tonight. I'd tucked in Wile E. Coyote myself. No more Brix. My throat started to close up with self-pity. I crept closer to plant a sleeptime kiss on Jilly's temple—another parental privilege, so Suzanne told me. Jilly's hair was just beginning to shade closer to the coloring of my own.

The low, fluttering noise was coming from beneath her sheets. And something smelled bad in the room. Perhaps she had soiled herself in sleep.

Hunched into Jilly's back was a mass of oily black fur as big as she was. At first my brain rang with a replay of Brix's horrifying inside-out death. The thing spooning with my daughter had one fat paw draped over her sleeping shoulder, and was alive. And purring.

I had the sheet peeled halfway down to reveal more of it when it twisted around and bit me on the wrist.

I took one panicked backward step, jerking away. Jilly's plush brontosaurus was feet-up on the floor; I stumbled over it, savaging my injured foot and crashing, sprawl-assed, down on Brix's rug, which smelled doggish and was dusted with his red hair. I had to get up, fast, tear the thing from her back, get the shotgun, to—

I tried to chock my good leg under me and could not. Both had gone thick and unresponsively numb. Then, shockingly, warmth spread at my crotch as my belly was seized by a sudden and powerful orgasm. My arms became as stupid as my legs. Then even my neck muscles lost it, and my forehead thunked into Brix's rug. And I came again.

And again.

Within seconds it was like receiving a thorough professional battering. I was having one orgasm for every three beats of my heart. My useless legs twitched.

Saliva ran from the corner of my mouth to pool in my ear; even my vocal cords were iced into nonfunction. And while I lay curled up on the floor, coming and shuddering and coming, the creature that had been in bed with my daughter climbed down to watch.

Its eyes were bronze coins, reflecting candlefire. I thought of the thing I had seen monitoring me from the tree on my first day as a Point Pitt resident.

It was bigger than a bobcat, stockier, low-slung. The fur or hair was backswept, spiky-stiff and glistening, as though heavily lubricated. Thick legs sprouted out from the body rather than down, making its carriage ground-gripping and reptilian. I heard hard leather pads scuff the floor as it neared, saw hooked claws, hooded in pink ligatures, close in on my face.

It was still purring. The head was a cat's, all golden eyes and pointed felt ears, but the snout was elongated into a canine coffin shape. The chatoyant pupils were X-shaped, deep-glowing crosscuts in the iris of each eye, and they widened like opening wounds to drink me in. It yawned. Less than a foot from my face I saw two bent needle fangs, backed by triangular, sharkish teeth in double rows. Its breath was worse than the stink of the congealed bandage I had stripped from my foot.

One galvanic sexual climax after another wrenched my insides apart. I was dry-coming; about to ejaculate blood. The creature dipped its head to lick some spittle from my cheek. Its tongue was sandpapery.

I had to kill it, bludgeon its monster skull to mush, blast it again and again until its carcass could hold no more shot. I orgasmed again. I could barely breathe.

It ceased tasting me and the hideous eyes sparked alive, hot yellow now. It padded back to the bed and leaped silently up. Jilly remained limp. I didn't even know if she was already dead or not.

It looked, to make sure I could see. Then it settled in, gripping Jilly's shoulders from above with its claws and licking her hair. It opened its mouth. Cartilage cracked softly as its jawbones separated, and the elastic black lips stretched taut to engulf the top of her head.

It sensed how much I hated it. Hate glittered back at me from those molten gash-eyes—my own hate, absorbed, made primal and total, and sent back to me.

Of hate, it knew.

My traitorous body continued its knifing spasms, and tears of pain blurred the view that I was incapable of commanding my eyelids to block out. The lips wormed forward, side-to-side, the slanted teeth seating, then pulling backward. The mouth elongated to full bore and the eyes fixed in a forward stare, glazed as though intoxicated by this meal.

With a mindless alien malice, it looked like it was smiling.

Blackness sucked me down before I could hear the abrasive, porcelain sound of those teeth grinding together, meeting at last through the pale flesh of my little girl's throat.

Moonlight delineated the window in blue-white.

I tried to sit up and rub my face. I was sweat-soaked, and lacquered in scales of dry semen. My balls were crushed grapes. Half my mind tried to wheedle me back into unconsciousness, begging to flee from what it had recorded. The less craven half had kicked me until I awoke, feeling like a frayed net loaded with broken bones, unable to stand or walk. I crawled on my belly to Jilly's bed. Lowering groans slipped from my throat.

I've seen snakes eat their prey. I didn't have to see what was left in Jilly's bed to know what had happened. But to get my legs back, and finish the work begun this night, I forced myself to look.

I took it all in without even a gasp. Only the drapes whispered furtively together, unable to remain still or quiet.

So much blood, blackening the Sesame Street sheets. Her tiny outthrust hand was speckled with it, and cold to the touch. Her pillow was a saturated dark sponge.

I slumped and vomited into my own lap. Nothing much came up as my guts were rent, the sore muscles pulling themselves to tatters. My hand went out and skidded into something like warm gelatin next to the bedpost.

It was the skin of our visitor, piled there like an enormous scalp, greasy black spines rooted in an opaque membrane. It reminded me of Brix's empty pelt. Here was the broad, flat sheath of the back; here, the sleeve of each leg. The reversed tissue was coated with a kind of thick, veined afterbirth that smelled like shit and rotten hamburger. My stomach clenched at the hot stink, and the pain almost put me under again. I swallowed a surge of bile and held.

It was slippery, as heavy as a waterlogged throw rug when I dragged it out of the room.

I knew there was a handful of speed and painkillers waiting for me in the bathroom. I filled the basin from the cold tap and immersed my head. I stared into the clean white gorge of the toilet and decided not to heave.

Suzanne was still safe in the depths of drugged sleep, where there are no true nightmares. On wobbly wino's feet I locked the balcony doors. The bedroom door had a two-way skeleton-key lock that could be engaged from the outside.

My Levi's jacket and shoes were downstairs on the sofa. And the shotgun was where it had been patiently waiting since the day we moved in.

Dunwoody's house was just up the hill.

My shoulder stung as the Remington's recoil pad kicked it, and the works on Dunwoody's back door, mostly shit, blew away to floating wood chaff and fused shrapnel. The door skewed open on its upper hinge, and the inside knob rebounded from the kitchen wall with a clacking cueball noise. It spun madly in place until its energy was used up. The echo of the blast returned softly from the hills.

Two rooms down a narrow hallway, Dunwoody sat watching a black-and-white television that displayed only test-pattern bars. The screen bounced rectangles of light off his wire-rim glasses and made his old-fashioned undershirt glow blue in the darkness. He turned to look at the intruder stepping through the hanging wreckage of his back door, his gaze settling with resigned indifference on the twelve-gauge in my hand. He sighed.

My right wrist was throbbing as though fractured; mean red coronas of inflammation had blossomed around the twin punctures there, and I didn't know how many more shots it could stand before breaking. The smell of dry puke swam richly through my head, chased by the fetor of my prize. My eyes were pinpricks; the black capsules were doing their dirty work in the solvents of my stomach. It was the dope as much as the backwash of nausea that made me giddy—dark, toxic waves slopping up on a polluted beach, then receding.

Stiff-legged, lead-footed, I moved into the house. I knew where I was going and what to do when I arrived. My life had a purpose.

I jacked back the slide to reload, retrieved the reeking mess of shed skin with my free hand, and clumped forward. I was going to nestle the barrel right on the bridge of Dunwoody's thin hickory nose. He just sat there, watching my approach. There were no hidey-holes, and Ormly was probably out cruising at this time of night.

"You look foolish with that pumpgun, city boy."

"Foolish enough to spread your reedy old ass all over the wallpaper." My voice was dry and coarse, a rusted thing.

"You want all kind of answers." He spoke like the keeper of knowledge and wisdom, shifting in his easy chair with a snort of contempt. "Big-city know-it-all finds out he *don't* know it all. Don't know shit." He gulped schnapps from a fingerprinty glass.

I couldn't buy his casual disdain for the gun. Perhaps he thought I wouldn't use it. To dash that little misconception from his mind, I stepped into the room and brought the shotgun to bear.

It tore violently out of my grasp like a runaway rocket, skinning my index finger on the trigger guard. Momentum yanked me the rest of the way into the room, and I got my crippled foot down to keep from falling. It wasn't worth it.

Ormly had been stationed in ambush behind the doorway and had acted with a speed startling for his bulk and presumed intellect. He stood there with the shotgun locked in his bulldozer grip, upside down, while Dunwoody watched drops of blood from my hand speckle the floor like small change.

"Get Mister Taske a cloth for his hand, Ormly." Each order was slow, metered, portioned out at rural speed. "Take care of his pumpgun; I'm sure he paid a lot of money for it. And bring me my bottle. You might as well have a seat, Mister Taske. And we'll talk."

The tar-colored pelt had slithered from my grasp and piled up in an oily heap on the floor. It slid around itself, never settling, as if it refused to give up the life it once contained. Dunwoody looked at it.

"It's stronger now, quicker. At its best, since it dropped a hide. Don't gawp at me like I'm nuts. You saw it the first day you was here, and you didn't pay it no mind."

"I thought it was . . . some kind of cat," I stammered lamely. "Mountain lion, or . . ."

"Yeah, well, you know so goddamn much about mountain cats, now don't you?" he said with derision. "You said you didn't have no pets, no guns. See what happens? It ain't no cat."

Jesus. Anybody with two dendrites of intelligence could see that it *weren't no cat*. Arguing that now would only keep the old man off the track. I decided to shut up, and he seemed satisfied that I was going to let him talk without any know-it-all city-boy interruptions. Ormly lumbered back with the schnapps, which Dunwoody offered to me perfunctorily. *Let's retch!* my stomach announced, and I waved the bottle away.

Ormly backed into his corner like the world's largest Saint Bernard sentry, keeping his eyes on me.

"Ormly was whip-smart," Dunwoody began. "He was my Primmy's favorite. Then she had Sarah. Little Sarah. You'da seen that baby girl, Mister Taske, she woulda busted your heart left and right, she was so perfect. Like your little girl."

"Jilly's dead." It was shockingly easy to say it so soon. "It—that thing, it—"

"I know. And I know you think me and Ormly is up to something, squirreled away up here, that we're somehow responsible. We ain't. I'd never hurt a little girl, and Ormly's never harmed no person nor animal. It's just . . . there's a certain order of things, here."

I had begun watching the ugly shed skin, still yielding, relaxing. It might reinflate and attack.

"Primmy and I kept a henhouse. We loved fryers and fresh eggs. One day I went out and all our chickens had been killed." The drama replayed behind his eyes. "You know how chickens run around after you cut off their heads, too dumb to know they're dead? Christ almighty. Twenty chickens, and half of them still strutting around when I got there. Without heads. It came down that night to eat the heads. And left the chickens. We'd been living in Point Pitt about two months."

My brain dipped sickeningly toward blackout. It was an almost pleasing sensation. Ebb tide of the mind; time to go to sleep. I sat down hard in the chair next to Dunwoody's and swallowed some schnapps without even tasting it.

"I had two hounds, Homer and Jethro, and an old Savage and Fox double-barrel, not as fancy as that pumpgun you got, but mean enough to stop a runaway truck dead. I laid up in the chicken coop the next night. 'Long about two in the morning, it stuck its head in and I let it have both barrels in the face. It was as close as you are to me. It yowled and ran off into the woods, and I set Homer and Jethro on it. Next morning, I found them. That thing took two loads of double-ought buckshot in the face and still gutted both my dogs. Ormly loved them old mutts."

I remembered the sound it made, the ground-glass screech. I didn't have to ask whether Dunwoody's dogs had been found with their heads intact.

Dunwoody cleared his throat phlegmatically and hefted himself out of the chair, to pry open a stuck bureau drawer behind the TV set. "Next night, it came back again. Walked into my home bold as you please and took my baby Sarah. It was slow getting out the window. Sluggish, with its belly full. I shot it again like a fool. Didn't do no good. Let me show you something."

He handed across a brown-edged, fuzzy piece of sketchbook paper. "Careful with it. It's real old."

It was a pencil rendering of the Dunwoody house, done in a stark and very sophisticated woodcut style. The trim and moldings stood out in relief. The building was done in calm earth tones, complimented by trees in full bloom. The forest shaded up the hillside in diminishing perspective. The strokes and

chiaroscuro were assured. The drawing deserved a good matte and frame. I tilted
it toward the light of the television and made out a faded signature in the lower
right, done with a modest but not egocentric flourish.

O. Dunwoody.

He handed me a photograph, also slightly foxed, in black-and-white with waffled
snapshot borders. A furry diagonal crease bisected a robustly pregnant woman
packed into a paisley maternity dress. She had the bun hairdo and slight bulb
nose that had always evoked the 1940s for me—World War II wives, the Andrews
Sisters, all of that. Hugging her ferociously was a slim, dark-haired boy of nine
or so, smiling wide and unselfconsciously. He had his father's eyes, and they
blazed with what Dunwoody would call the smarts.

I tried to equate the boy in the photo with Ormly's overgrown, cartoonish body,
or to the imbecilic expression on his face as he stood placidly in his corner. No
match.

"Night after it took baby Sarah, it came back. We were laying to bushwhack
it outside. It flanked us. Ormly came in for a drink of water, and there it was,
all black and bristly and eating away on his mamma. He couldn't do nothing but
stand there and scream; all the starch had run right out of him. He looked kinda
like you do right now. I ran back in. That was the first time it bit me."

I extended my wrist for him to see, and his eyes lowered with guilt.

"Then you know that part already," he said.

Ormly stood parked like a wax dummy while his father went to him and looked
over the wasteland of his son, hoping perhaps to read a glimmer of the past in
the dull eyes. There was no light there, only the reflected snow of the TV set,
now tuned to nothingness.

"Ormly was crazy with fear and wanted to run. He loved his mamma and his
little sister and the dogs, but he knew the sense in running. I was full up with
ideas of what a man should do. A man didn't go beggin' to the police. The police
don't understand nothing; they don't care and don't want to. A man should settle with his own grief, I thought, and Ormly wanted to be a man, so he hung
with me."

Brave kid, I thought. *Braver than me.*

"Ormly came up with the idea of setting it on fire. He'd seen some monster
movie where'd they'd doused the monster with kerosene and touched it off with
a flare gun. We set up for it, we knew it was coming back, because it knew we
didn't like it and would try to kill it. It *knew* how we felt. We were the ones that
had intruded on its territory, and when you do that, you either make peace or
you make a stand. Or you run. And that's what we shoulda done, because we
were prideful and we didn't know what we were up against. We shoulda run like
hell."

Dunwoody was stoking his own coals now, like a stump revival preacher getting
ready to rip Satan a new asshole.

"Sure enough, the son of a bitch came down after us that night. You couldn't
have convinced me there was another human soul in Point Pitt. All the houses
were dark. They all *knew*, that is, everyone but me. When I spotted it crossing
the backyard, in the moonlight, it was different than before. It'd dropped its hide,

just like a bullsnake." He indicated the rancid leftover on the floor with a weak wave of his hand, not wanting to see it.

He did not look at Ormly, either, even as he spoke of him.

"The boy was perfect, by god. He stepped out from his hiding place, exposed himself to danger just so he could dump his pail of gasoline right smack into that thing's open mouth. I set my propane torch to it and it tagged me on the back of the hand—just a scratch, no venom. Or maybe the gas all over my hand neutralized it. We watched it shag ass into the hills, shrieking and dropping embers, setting little fires in the bushes as it ran. We hooted and jumped and clapped each other on the back like we were big heroes or something, and the next morning we tried to find it. All we turned up was a shed skin, like that one. And when the sun went down again, it came back. For Ormly. I swear to you, Mister Taske, it knew who had thought of burning it. But it didn't kill Ormly." The memory shined in Dunwoody's welling eyes. He had witnessed what had happened. "Didn't kill him. It took a big, red mouthful out of the back of his head, and . . . and . . ."

He extended his scarred arms toward me, Christ-like, seeking some absolution I could not give. Bite marks peppered them everywhere, holes scabbing atop older holes.

"You get so you can't go without," he said dully. "You won't want to. You'll see."

I was aware of speaking in an almost sub-aural whisper. "Why didn't you leave?"

He shook his head sadly, ignoring me. "One day it just showed up. That's all anybody knows. Whether it came down out of the hills or crawled out of the ocean don't really matter. What matters is it came here and decided to stay. Maybe somebody fed it."

The speed maxed out in my bloodstream, hitting its spike point. The murky room resolved to sharp-edged clarity around me in a single headlong second. I'd broken through, and rage sprang me from my chair, to brace Dunwoody so he could no longer retreat into obfuscations or babble.

"Why the hell didn't you leave?" I screamed in his face.

He flinched, then considered his ruined arms again, and avoided the easy answer. "We don't like the city."

I remembered Suzanne, browsing the house. All her remarks about getting back to nature, slowing down, escaping the killer smog, hightailing it from the city as though it was some monster that had corrupted us internally and conspired to consume us. The big, bad neon nightmare. What penetrated now was the truth—that the state of nature is the last thing any thinking being would want. The true state of nature is not romantic. It is savage, primal, unforgivingly hostile. Mercy is a quality of civilization. Out here, stuck halfway between the wilds and the cities, a man had to settle his own grief. And if he could not . . .

My father, the guy who'd taught me to keep all guns loaded, had another adage I'd never had to take seriously yet: *If you can't kill it with a gun, son—run.*

"You've squared off with it," Dunwoody said. "That choice was yours. Believe me when I say it knows you don't like it." The provincial superiority was seeping back into his tone. "Have you figured it out yet, or has all that toe-food crap turned your brain to marl?"

Near the nub of his right elbow, the old man had sustained a fresh bite. It was all I could see. The thing had bitten Dunwoody recently—and Dunwoody had let it.

He sighed at my thickness. "It's coming back. Might even come back tonight. You're new here, after all."

I bolted then, with a strangled little cry. It was a high sound, childish, womanish. A coward's bleat, I thought.

Ormly had left my shotgun on the kitchen table, and I snatched it up as I ran, hurdling the demolished door, heedless of the stabbing pains in my hand, or the blood I could feel welling from the ruptured wound on my foot. My shoe had turned crimson. I ran so fast I did not see Dunwoody nodding to himself, like a man who has made the desired impression, and I missed his final words to his huge, dull-witted son.

"Ormly, you go on with Mister Taske, now. You know what you have to do."

Three feet more.

Three feet more, and the world would be set right. Three feet more to reach the hole in the fence, where Brix had died. Then came three more feet to reach the back door, to the stairs, to our bedroom. Three seconds more and I could shake Suzanne awake, pack her into the BMW, and bust posted limits red-lining it out of this nightmare. If the city wanted us back, no problem. We could scoot by on our plastic for months. My life was not a spaghetti western; I did not bash through my degree and get ulcers so I could do symbol-laden combat with monsters.

And Jilly . . .

The south window had been shoved neatly up. The drapes fluttered and there was no hint of broken glass, of the horrorshow trespass my brain had pictured for me. The creature was snuggled between Suzanne's legs on the bed. Eating. It looked very different without its skin.

Thick braids of exposed sinew coiled up each of its legs, filament cable that bunched and flexed. The knobs of its spine were strapped down by double wrapping of inflated, powerful muscle tissue as smoothly grooved and perfect as plastic. It no longer required an envelope of skin. An absurd little triangular flap covered its anus like a pointed tail.

Suzanne's eyes were slitted, locked. She was beyond feeling what was being done to her. Another orgasm hissed past her teeth, gutturally. Nothing more.

The skeleton key dropped from my trembling fingers and bounced on the hardwood floor. The thing on the bed had cranked its blood-slathered muzzle around to dismiss me. I was no big deal.

With a sidelong yank of its head, it worried loose some morsel anchored by stubborn tendons to the chest cavity. It was about halfway to its favorite part. The scraps it had sampled and discarded littered the bed wetly. If it had chanced across any tumors during its methodical progress toward the brain, I was sure it had crunched them up like popcorn. Piggishly, it lapped and slurped.

Suzanne looked at me as she came again, convulsing as much as her sundered body would let her. A thin stringer of frothy lung blood leapt onto her chest.

I kept my eyes in contact with hers as I snapped the trigger of the Remington, thinking how much I loved her.

The Nitro Mag load tore our bed to smithereens. Suzanne's dead arm jerked up, flopped back. Bloodstained goosedown took to the air, drifting. I worked the slide one-handed and fired again. The French doors disintegrated. Rickrack jumped from the bedstands to shatter on the floor.

The creature eased out its caked snout and saw what had just befallen that part of the feast it had been saving for last. Its impossibly wide, hinged maw dropped open to screech at me, as though I owed it something and had reneged. I shot it in the face, as Dunwoody had done years ago. It snapped at the incoming shot like a bloodhound at gnats, then obstinately sank its nose back into its grisly dinner.

Suzanne was no longer on the bed. The corpse was not identifiable as anything but dead, butchered meat.

I slammed the bedroom door hard; don't ask why. There was an instant when I might have jammed the barrel between my teeth and swallowed that last shot myself. Instead, a pungent odor hauled me, staggering, to the stair landing.

Downstairs, the floor was wet and sloppy, glistening. Ormly waited for me, a ten-gallon jerry can of gasoline in each massive hand, smiling.

The buffeting heat was so intense that we had to back across the street to avoid getting our eyebrows flash-fried.

I watched the south window of our bedroom grow dreamy behind a sheet of orange flame. There was absolutely no exterior access. The thing had crawled up the front of the house like a fly, and clinging, had opened the window with one paw.

Neither of us saw it jump out, trailing sparks. The expression on Ormly's face frightened me. It was the closest thing to a glimmer of abstract thought I'd yet seen mar his slablike, mannequin countenance. He stared, unblinking, into the skyrocketing licks of fire.

"Hotter," he said. "Stronger. Better this time."

By dawn we were down to smoldering debris. I did not want to scrutinize the wreckage too closely, for fear of recognizing blackened bones.

Ormly stood in the backyard, his face dead with a kind of infinite sadness. I followed his gaze to the ground, and saw a deeply-dug, charred clawprint. The foot that had embossed itself there had been so hot that the grass had been cooked into an unmistakable pattern.

Ormly's mitt-sized hands pushed me toward my BMW, parked past the mailboxes. When I dug in my heels, he plucked me up and carried me. It was too easy to know why.

When night fell, the ground-glass shriek would waft down from the forest, and Point Pitt's new god would return.

Back in the arms of the city, I waited around for fate to come crashing down on my head with charges of murder and arson. Civilized accusations. No one came knocking.

Like I said earlier, this morning I sat and watched a cat disembowel a rail lizard. I watched much longer than I had to in order to get to the point. Then my eyelids pushed down to allow swatches of stop-and-go sleep.

The nightmares of my past replaced those of the here and now.

A week after I'd turned thirteen, the school sadist at my junior high decreed that the day had come to pound every last speck of shit out of my rasty white body. Ross Delaney was the eldest son of a local garbageman—to be fair, he took a lot of socially maladjusting crap just for that. He was coasting through his third encore performance at the seventh-grade level. A seventh-grader who had a down mustache, drove his own jalopy to school, smoked, and hung out with peers destined for big things: aggravated assault, rape, grand theft auto . . .

Ross had made me loan him a pen once in study hall and he'd dismantled it after scrawling on the back of my shirt and laughing like I was the world's biggest a-hole. My buddy Blake and I had discovered a bunch of disposable hypodermic needles while scrounging for intriguing goodies in the trash dumpster of a health clinic, reasoning that it was against some law for them to throw out anything really *dangerous*, right? Those hypos made primo mini-squirt guns, and that's all Blake and I thought of using them for. They were tech, they were cool. They were enormously appealing to Ross, who threatened to put out my eye with a Lucky if I didn't give him one. Right before lunch, Ross was scooped up by Mr. Shanks, *El Principal* of the humorless specs and full-length gray plastic raincoat. Needles in school were serious business, and I soon found myself being paged for an interview. I denied everything. Ross' eyes, yellow-brown, settled on me like a pronouncement of execution by hanging.

He laid for me in the parking lot. There was no way around him. He loomed above me. I wanted to say something pacifying, babble that might exonerate us both as rebels cornered by an unfair system. Ross' brain lacked the logic links such a ploy needed to work. Trying to appease him had always been a pussy's game with an automatic loser. Guess who.

The next thing I knew, I was catching Ross' hand with my face.

My neckbones popped as my head snapped around, and my hand made the mistake of contracting into a fist. My left eye filled up with knuckles and stopped seeing. He snagged a handful of my hair and used his knee to loosen all the molars on the side of my head nearest the pavement. I bit tarmac and tasted blood. I curled up. He started kicking me with his Mexican pimp boots, shouting incoherently, his face totally glazed.

My deck was discarded, so I called for my mom. I honestly thought it was my moment to die, and so reverted to instant babyhood, bawling and dribbling and yowling for my mother. Ross' cohorts ate it up. What a queer, what a pussy, he wants he momma. Ross kicked again and I felt a lung try to jump out my throat. He yelled for me to shut up. Something cracked sharply inside me.

Then something *burst* inside me.

It wasn't my liver exploding. It was something slag-hot, bursting brightly outward, filling me, popping on full bore like sprinkler systems during a fire, or an airbag in a car crash. The only sensation I can compare it to is the time my cardiologist broke an ampule of amyl nitrate under my nose, to test my pump. Only my internal ampule was full of something more like PCP. I was flooded to the brim—WHAM! My fingertips tingled. Both hands locked into fists. I scared the crap out of myself; I think I yelped. Instead of stopping the tip of Ross' next incoming bonebreaker, I rolled out, stood up, and faced him.

Then I kicked the shit out of him, impossibly enough.

Hesitation scampered behind his eyes when he saw me get up. But there was no mystery in it for him. The medulla section of his primate mind saw an opportunity to stomp some serious ass and would not be denied. If I could stand, the massacre would just be more interesting. Ross roared and came in like a freight train. His fist was black and sooty and callused.

I snatched that meteor out of the air and diverted his momentum, planting my elbow in his mouth, then whip-cracking him into a one-eighty snap that left his gonads open to my foot. They decompressed with a squish and he hit the pavement on hands and knees . . . and then *I* was kicking *him*, blood flushing my face. Every bullshit, picayune adolescent injustice ever suffered now rushed home, and I went at Ross like a berserk wolverine spiked on crank. Ribs staved inward. Snot and blood lathered his chin.

And I felt *good*.

Mr. Shanks, the principal, yanked me off of Ross Delaney, school tyrant. He was too horrified by the damage he saw to wonder how I'd done it. I got my fine white ass suspended.

That school had been my introduction to life in the city. Since then, the city had treated me right. My apartment never got robbed; my car never got boosted. Degree. Master's. Wife. Promotion. Child. Success. Suzanne and Jilly had been excited by our move to Point Pitt; I had been the reluctant one.

Now my city had repudiated me. I'd come crawling back after giving it the finger, and the only thing it would show me was an ugly orange tabby tearing the intestines out of a lizard that wasn't dead all the way yet.

In its reptile eyes, the suffering as it was eaten.

I wanted to file a complaint. To protest that none of this was my fault. I didn't want to leave; they made me do it. That would be like trying to make nice to Ross Delaney. Too late for that.

I had spent the night in a parking lot and there was dry snot on my face, from crying. Returning to the city had not erased Suzanne or Jilly or poor old goddamn Brix. So much for the snapshot.

The BMW's motor caught on the third try. I noticed blood staining the walnut of the gearshift as I backed out of the alleyway.

I wanted my mommy. But she wasn't around this time, either. Not here.

The blackened garbage dump that, yesterday, had been my new home had cooled. If anyone had come out to investigate, they were gone now. Birds twittered in the forest, above all this folly.

Dunwoody finally spotted me and came out; I have to credit him for having that much iron left. He motioned me into his squalid little home and we sat drinking until the sun went down. I watched Ormly shamble about. Such a waste, there.

The shrieking I expected began to peal down from the woods after dusk. My hands quivered on the arms of Dunwoody's dusty easy chair. They had not stopped shaking since last night.

"You forgot your pumpgun," said Dunwoody. "Had Ormly fetch it. Only two loads innit though." He drained his schnapps glass and burped, half-in, half-out, a state he clearly wanted to maintain.

The clear liquor trickled into me like kerosene. I thought of it as fuel. I noticed the barrels of the shotgun were warm; that seemed odd, somehow.

Clutching the Remington, I left limping, favoring my gashed foot. Breathing was a chore. My eyes pulsed in time to the pounding of my metabolism as I picked my way to the center of my burned-out grave of a home. One end of the barbequed sofa jutted from the debris like the stern of a sinking ship. Here was the banister—fissured, carbonized, its stored heat energy bled free. Over here, smashed shards of terra cotta from Suzanne's conservatory. Skeletal junk, all exuding the reek of an overflowing ashtray. Soft clouds of soot puffed up with each step I took.

On the border of the feeder road, the streetlamp sputtered blue, then white, throwing tombstone shadows down from the row of mailboxes. The residents of Point Pitt had drawn their curtains. The houses on the hillside were dark against whatever might come in the night. Not secure. Just lacking light and any form of human sympathy.

Dunwoody was the exception. I saw his drawn face appear in a crack of drape, then zip away, then return. I'd lost my Cartier watch, so I used Dunwoody's periodic surveillance to mark time. I couldn't recall losing the watch, not that it mattered. Night vapors tingled the hair on my arms. My last bath had been yesterday afternoon, eons ago, and by now I was as aromatic as stale beef bouillon.

"Come on, come *on!*" I lashed out at a fire-ravaged plank and it crumbled into brittle charcoal cinders. My voice echoed back from the treeline twice.

Lava-colored eyes emerged to assess me from behind the still-standing brick chimney. Chatoyant pupils tossed back the street light in dual crosscut shapes.

A conventional defensive move would draw it out, confident of its own invincibility. I chambered a round as loudly as I could. "This is for you! Come on— it's what you want, right?"

Motion, hesitant, like Ross Delaney, unsure. There was a smear of bright bronze as the eyes darted to a new vantage.

"Come on, bag of shit!" Fuck reaction time. The gun went boom and a mean bite leapt out of the chimney. Pointed chunks of brick flew into the creature's face. It did not blink. The Remington's report settled debris all around.

I dropped the gun into the ashes.

Its outer tissue was pinkish, as though battened with blood from an earlier feed. The alien eyes blazed. When it saw me lose the shotgun, it decided, and in three huge bounds the distance between us was reduced to nothing. I saw it in midair, rippling, its thorny claws extruded from their cowls and coming for my face.

I braced myself, the memory of grabbing Ross Delaney's deadly fist still hot. I spoke softly to the woods, to the forest in the distance, to the sea behind me.

"Help me. Mother."

It smashed me down like a truck pasting an old lady in a crosswalk. The opaque talons sank to their moorings in my shoulder. I grabbed, to keep the jaws from my throat, and its fangs pierced the palm of my hand, one-two.

"*Mother! Help me!*"

I got my other hand up and seized its snout, which was feverishly hot. Stale blood-breath misted into my eyes and the black lips yawned wide for me. Those lips had caressed my daughter's face as they engulfed her. They had made an intimate, ghastly smorgasbord of Suzanne.

I clenched my fist. It tried to jerk its paw back to slash me into confetti, but the claws were trapped in my muscle tissue and would not slide free. The X-shaped eyes dimmed in surprise. It backpedaled, preparing to dig in with its hind legs and free my intestines.

I sat up with its movement, taking a firmer grip and twisting until its lower jaw came away in my hand. Think of halving a head of lettuce; that was the sound it made. Think of pulling a drumstick from a whole tom turkey. It jammed, then wrenched loose, dripping, trailing ruptured tatters of sinew.

It shrieked. Without a mouth, in pain.

Purple blood, thick and gelid, spurted into my face. Under the vapor lamp it looked like chocolate syrup; it stank of vomit or hydrochloric acid. The eyes went from golden to dead ochre, the color of dry leaves.

"You're done here," I rasped in its face. Still holding the snout, I punched my fist down the ruined wet maw of glottus. My fingers locked around something slick and throbbing and I tore it out. The body on top of me shuddered hideously and lost tension. The legs scrabbled, then went slack, pitching more feebly.

I stared fixedly into the eyes as their incandescence waned.

The residents of Point Pitt had come out at last, to watch. My new neighbors. They dotted the street, milling uncertainly, none daring closer than the mailboxes. They watched as their old god screeched and died. As with department-store mannequins, it had been so simple for them to be led, to be arranged.

What difference? That was ended now.

When I extracted the claws from my shoulder, my own blood jetted briefly out. I was still that human. Eyes cold, the limp and stinking carcass slid as I rose. Another shedding. A steel rail of an erection was trying to fight its way out of my pants.

They all stood, nothing more declarative. Silently they waited. The last to arrive were Dunwoody and Ormly, coming down the trail from their home. No one else moved to attack, or assist, or anything. It was not their place to.

Thank you . . .

Reflexively, the dead claws had folded in upon themselves. When I picked up the corpse, it crackled, still seeming to weigh too much for its mass. I remembered the awful sound its discarded skin had made. Purple goo dripped from the jawless mouth. The flat paws dangled harmlessly as I lifted the fatal wound to my lips and drank in long, soul-kiss draughts, quaffing with a passion almost primitive in its purity.

Thank you. Mother.

My communion raced through me to work its changes. My arm ceased bleeding and clotted up. I stopped shaking at last; all of me at once. My vision began to blur. Soon I would be able to see things imperceptible to normal, circular pupils.

I motioned to Ormly and he dutifully clumped forward. He had to be the first one. There was plenty for everybody, but Ormly had to be first.

Things evolve. Always have. Even in the country, things change when it's time. There was growth potential here.

Dunwoody nodded his old man's brand of approval. If I needed any indication that I was going to be benevolent, that was it.

KAREN JOY FOWLER

Lieserl

Karen Joy Fowler studied at Berkeley and the University of California at Davis, receiving an M.A. in North Asian Studies. She is the author of *Artificial Things*, a powerful debut collection of short fiction that is highly recommended. "Lieserl" was originally published in the author's second collection, a volume that is Issue #6 in the *Author's Choice Monthly* series from Pulphouse in Eugene, Oregon.

Fowler begins the story with a real life event drawm from the recently published letters from Albert Einstein as a young man to the woman he later married. In these letters, Fowler writes, the birth of his daughter was an occasion for joy; yet after this letter she is never mentioned again, not in his autobiography, subsequent letters, nor the numerous biographies of his life. Fowler takes this mystery into a flight of speculative fantasy that explores the complex realities of human nature.

—T.W.

Lieserl

KAREN JOY FOWLER

Einstein received the first letter in the afternoon post. It had traveled in bags and boxes all the way from Hungary, sailing finally through the brass slit in Einstein's door. *Dear Albert*, it said. *Little Lieserl is here. Mileva says to tell you that your new daughter has tiny fingers and a head as bald as an egg. Mileva says to say that she loves you and will write you herself when she feels better.* The signature was Mileva's father's. The letter was sent at the end of January, but arrived at the beginning of February, so even if everything in it was true when written, it was entirely possible that none of it was true now. Einstein read the letter several times. He was frightened. Why could Mileva not write him herself? The birth must have been a very difficult one. Was the baby really as bald as all that? He wished for a picture. What kind of little eyes did she have? Did she look like Mileva? Mileva had an aura of thick, dark hair. Einstein was living in Bern, Switzerland, and Mileva had returned to her parents' home in Titel, Hungary, for the birth. Mileva was hurt because Einstein sent her to Hungary alone, although she had not said so. The year was 1902. Einstein was twenty-two years old. None of this is as simple as it sounds, but one must start somewhere even though such placement inevitably entails the telling of a lie.

Outside Einstein's window, large star-shaped flakes of snow swirled silently in the air like the pretend snow in a glass globe. The sky darkened into evening as Einstein sat on his bed with his papers. The globe had been shaken and Einstein was the still, ceramic figure at its swirling heart, the painted Father Christmas. Lieserl. How I love her already, Einstein thought, dangerously. Before I even know her, how I love her.

The second letter arrived the next morning. *Liebes Schatzerl*, Mileva wrote. *Your daughter is so beautiful. But the world does not suit her at all. With such fury she cries! Papa is coming soon, I tell her. Papa will change everything for you, everything you don't like, the whole world if this is what you want. Papa loves Lieserl. I am very tired still. You must hurry to us. Lieserl's hair has come in dark and I think she is getting a tooth.* Einstein stared at the letter.

A friend of Einstein's will tell Einstein one day that he, himself, would never have the courage to marry a woman who was not absolutely sound. He will say this soon after meeting Mileva. Mileva walked with a limp although it is unlikely that a limp is all this friend meant. Einstein will respond that Mileva had a lovely voice.

Einstein had not married Mileva yet when he received this letter, although he wanted to very badly. She was his Liebes Dockerl, his little doll. He had not found a way to support her. He had just run an advertisement offering his services as a tutor. He wrote Mileva back. *Now you can make observations,* he said. *I would like once to produce a Lieserl myself, it must be so interesting. She certainly can cry already, but to laugh she'll learn later. Therein lies a profound truth.* On the bottom of the letter he sketched his tiny room in Bern. It resembled the drawings he will do later to accompany his Gedanken, or thought experiments, how he would visualize physics in various situations. In this sketch, he labeled the features of his room with letters. Big B for the bed. Little b for a picture. He was trying to figure a way to fit Mileva and Lieserl into his room. He was inviting Mileva to help.

In June he will get a job with the Swiss Civil Service. A year after Lieserl's birth, the following January, he will marry Mileva. Years later when friends ask him why he married her, his answer will vary. Duty, he will say sometimes. Sometimes he will say that he has never been able to remember why.

A third letter arrived the next day. *Mein liebes, boses Schatzerl!* it said. *Lieserl misses her Papa. She is so clever, Albert. You will never believe it. Today she pulled a book from the shelf. She opened it, sucking hard on her fingers. Can Lieserl read? I asked her, joking. But she pointed to the letter E, making such a sweet, sticky fingerprint beside it on the page. E, she said. You will be so proud of her. Already she runs and laughs. I had not realized how quickly they grow up. When are you coming to us? Mileva.*

His room was too small. The dust collected over his books and danced in the light with Brownian-like movements. Einstein went out for a walk. The sun shone, both from above him and also as reflected off the new snowbanks in blinding white sheets. Icicles shrank visibly at the roots until they cracked, falling from the eaves like knives into the soft snow beneath them. *Mileva is a book, like you,* his mother had told him. *What you need is a housekeeper. What you need is a wife.*

Einstein met Mileva in Zurich at the Swiss Federal Polytechnical School. Entrance to the school required the passage of a stiff examination. Einstein himself failed the General Knowledge section on his first try. *She will ruin your life,* Einstein's mother said. *No decent family will have her. Don't sleep with her. If she gets a child, you'll be in a pretty mess.* It is not clear what Einstein's mother's objection to Mileva was. She was unhappy that Mileva had scholastic ambitions and then more unhappy when Mileva failed her examinations twice and could not get her diploma.

Five days passed before Einstein heard from Mileva again. *Mein liebstes Schatzerl. If she has not climbed onto the kitchen table, then she is sliding down the banisters,* Mileva complained. *I must watch her every minute. I have tried to take her picture for you as you asked, but she will never hold still long enough. Until you come to her, you must be content with my descriptions. Her hair is dark and thick and curly. She has the eyes of a doe. Already she has outgrown all the clothes I had for her and is in proper dresses with aprons. Papa, papa, papa, she says. It is her favorite word. Yes, I tell her. Papa is coming. I teach her to throw kisses. I teach her to clap her hands. Papa is coming, she says, kissing and clapping. Papa loves his Lieserl.*

Einstein loved his Lieserl whom he had not met. He loved Mileva. He loved science. He loved music. He solved scientific puzzles while playing the violin. He thought of Lieserl while solving scientific puzzles. Love is faith. Science is faith. Einstein could see that his faith was being tested. Science feels like art, Einstein will say later, but it is not. Art involves inspiration and experience, but experience is a hindrance to the scientist. He has only a few years in which to invent, with his innocence, a whole new world that he must live in for the rest of his life. Einstein would not always be such a young man. Einstein did not have all the time in the world.

Einstein waited for the next letter in the tiny cell of his room. The letters were making him unhappy. He did not want to receive another so he would not leave, even for an instant, and risk delaying it. He had not responded to Mileva's last letters. He did not know how. He made himself a cup of tea and stirred it, noticing that the tea leaves gathered in the center of the cup bottom, but not about the circumference. He reached for a fresh piece of paper and filled it with drawings of rivers, not the rivers of a landscape, but the narrow, twisting rivers of a map.

The letter came only a few hours later in the afternoon post, sliding like a tongue through the slit in the door. Einstein caught it as it fell. *Was treibst Du Schatzerl?* it began. *Your little Lieserl has been asked to a party and looks like a princess tonight. Her dress is long and white like a bride's. I have made her hair curl by wrapping it over my fingers. She wears a violet sash and violet ribbons. She is dancing with my father in the hallway, her feet on my father's feet, her head only slightly higher than his waist. They are waltzing. All the boys will want to dance with you, my father said to her, but she frowned. I am not interested in boys, she answered. Nowhere is there a boy I could love like I love my papa.*

In 1899 Einstein began writing to Mileva about the electrodynamics of moving bodies, which became the title of his 1905 paper on relativity. In 1902 Einstein loved Mileva, but in 1916 in a letter to his friend Besso, Einstein will write that he would have become mentally and physically exhausted if he had not been able to keep his wife at a distance, out of sight and out of hearing. You cannot know, he will tell his friends, the tricks a woman such as my wife will play.

Mileva, trained as a physicist herself, though without a diploma, will complain that she never understood the special theory of relativity. She will blame Einstein who, she will say, has never taken the time to explain it properly to her.

Einstein wrote a question along the twisting line of one river. Where are you? He chose another river for a second question. How are you moving? He extended the end of the second river around many curves until it finally merged with the first.

Liebes Schatzerl! the next letter said. It came four posts later. *She is a lovely young lady. If you could only see her, your breath would catch in your throat. Hair like silk. Eyes like stars. She sends her love. Tell my darling Papa, she says, that I will always be his little Lieserl, always running out into the snowy garden, caped in red, to draw angels. Suddenly I am frightened for her, Albert. She is as fragile as a snowflake. Have I kept her too sheltered? What does she know of men? If only you had been here to advise me.* Even after its long journey, the letter smelled of roses.

Two friends came for dinner that night to Einstein's little apartment. One was a philosophy student named Solovine. One was a mathematician named Habicht. The three together called themselves the Olympia Academy, making fun of the serious bent of their minds.

Einstein made a simple dinner of fried fish and bought wine. They sat about the table, drinking and picking the last pieces of fish out with their fingers until nothing remained on their plates but the spines with the smaller bones attached like the naked branches of winter trees. The friends argued loudly about music. Solovine's favorite composer was Beethoven, whose music, Einstein suddenly began to shout, was emotionally over-charged, especially in C minor. Einstein's favorite composer was Mozart. Beethoven created his beautiful music, but Mozart discovered it, Einstein said. Beethoven wrote the music of the human heart, but Mozart transcribed the music of God. There is a perfection in the humanless world which will draw Einstein all his life. It is an irony that his greatest achievement will be to add the relativity of men to the objective Newtonian science of angels.

He did not tell his friends about his daughter. The wind outside was a choir without a voice. All his life, Einstein will say later, all his life, he tried to free himself from the chains of the *merely personal*. Einstein rarely spoke of his personal life. Such absolute silence suggests that he escaped from it easily or, alternatively, that its hold was so powerful he was afraid to ever say it aloud. One or both or neither of these things must be true.

Let us talk about the merely personal. The information received through the five senses is appallingly approximate. Take sight, the sense on which humans depend most. Man sees only a few of all the colors in the world. It is as if a curtain has been drawn over a large window, but not drawn so that it fully meets in the middle. The small gap at the center represents the visual abilities of man.

A cat hears sounds that men must only imagine. It has an upper range of 100,000 cycles per second as opposed to the 35,000 to 45,000 a dog can hear or the 20,000 which marks the upper range for men. A cat can distinguish between two sounds made only 18 inches apart when the cat, itself, is at a distance of 60 feet.

Some insects can identify members of their own species by smell at distances nearing a mile.

A blindfolded man holding his nose cannot distinguish the taste of an apple from an onion.

Of course, man fumbles about the world, perceiving nothing, understanding nothing. In a whole universe, man has been shut into one small room. Of course, Einstein could not begin to know what was happening to his daughter or to Mileva, deprived even of these blundering senses. The postman was careless with Mileva's next letter. He failed to push it properly through the door slit so that it fell back into the snow where it lay all night and was ice the next morning. Einstein picked the envelope up on his front step. It was so cold it burnt his fingers. He breathed on it until he could open it.

Another quiet evening with your Lieserl. We read until late and then sat together, talking. She asked me many questions tonight about you, hoping, I think, to hear something, anything I had not yet told her. But she settled, sweetly, for the old stories all over again. She got out the little drawing you sent her just after her birth; have I told you how she treasures it? When she was a child she used to point to it. Papa sits here, she would say, pointing. Papa sleeps here. I wished that I could gather her into my lap again. It would have been so silly, Albert. You must picture her with her legs longer than mine and new gray in the black of her hair. Was I silly to want it, Schatzerl? Shouldn't someone have warned me that I wouldn't be able to hold her forever?

Einstein set the letter back down into the snow. He had not yet found it. He had never had such a beautiful daughter. Perhaps he had not even met Mileva yet, Mileva whom he still loved, but who was not sound and who liked to play tricks.

Perhaps, he thought, he will find the letter in the spring when the snow melts. If the ink has not run, if he can still read it, then he will decide what to do. Then he will have to decide. It began to snow again. Einstein went back into his room for his umbrella. The snow covered the letter. He could not even see the letter under the snow when he stepped over it on his way to the bakery. He did not want to go home where no letter was hidden by the door. He was twenty-two years old and he stood outside the bakery, eating his bread, reading a book in the tiny world he had made under his umbrella in the snow.

Several years later, after Einstein has married Mileva and neither ever, ever mentions Lieserl, after they have had two sons, a colleague will describe a visit to Einstein's apartment. The door will be open so that the newly washed floor can dry. Mileva will be hanging dripping laundry in the hall. Einstein will rock a baby's bassinet with one hand and hold a book open with the other. The stove will smoke. How does he bear it? the colleague will ask in a letter which still survives, a letter anyone can read. That genius. How can he bear it?

The answer is that he could not. He will try for many years and then Einstein will leave Mileva and his sons, sending back to them the money he wins along with the Nobel Prize. When the afternoon post came, the postman had found the letter again and included it with the new mail. So there were two letters, only one had been already opened.

Einstein put the new letter aside. He put it under his papers. He hid it in his bookcase. He retrieved it and opened it clumsily because his hands were shaking. He had known this letter was coming, known it perhaps with Lieserl's first tooth, certainly with her first dance. It was exactly what he had expected, worse than he could have imagined. *She is as bald as ice and as mad as a goddess, my Albert*, Mileva wrote. *But she is still my Liebes Dockerl, my little doll. She clings to me, crying if I must leave her for a minute. Mama, Mama! Such madness in her eyes and her mouth. She is toothless and soils herself. She is my baby. And yours, Schatzerl. Nowhere is there a boy I could love like my Papa, she says, lisping again just the way she did when she was little. She has left a message for you. It is a message from the dead. You will get what you really want, Papa, she said. I have gone to get it for you. Remember that it comes from me. She was weeping and biting her nails until they bled. Her eyes were white with madness. She said something else. The brighter the light, the more shadows, my papa, she said. My darling Papa. My poor Papa. You will see.*

The room was too small. Einstein went outside where his breath came in a cloud from his mouth, tangible, as if he were breathing on glass. He imagined writing on the surface of a mirror, drawing one of his Gedanken with his finger into his own breath. He imagined a valentine. Lieserl, he wrote across it. He loved Lieserl. He cut the word in half, down the *s* with the stroke of his nail. The two halves of the heart opened and closed, beating against each other, faster and faster, like wings, until they split apart and vanished from his mind.

SHARON M. HALL
The Last Game

Sharon M. Hall was born in 1958 and lives with her husband and children in Notting-hamshire, U.K. "The Last Game" is a disturbing and beautifully rendered tale of dark fantasy that appeared in the British magazine *Interzone*.

The author works with the symbols of fairy tales, using these symbols as potent metaphors to tell the story of a young girl whose innocence is lost—or stolen from her. Like the best of the old fairy tales, before the Victorians and Disney pulled their sharp teeth, Hall's story ventures deep into the human psyche, a journey that is both wondrous and frightening.

—T.W.

The Last Game

SHARON M. HALL

At the end of time there is a wall, and beyond the wall there is a garden. It is a quiet garden, old and rambling and friendly, and of proportions such that a child, playing in the stream that passes through it, or running down its long slope of lawn, would find in it a world.

The garden is entered, if enter it you may, via a door in what we might call the north-eastern corner, where the dense undergrowth of forest east meets with the rough stone of the wall. From here the lawn slopes downward to the stream, beyond which there is an orchard and a vegetable patch, a glasshouse and— concealed beneath the overhanging branches of a weeping willow tree—a dark shed.

To the west, where the lawn rises steeply to meet the wall, a castellated playhouse has been built into the bank. Its stone walls enclose two rooms, one upper, one lower, and one half room, in which there is a basin and a hole. Narrow corridors, secret passageways and steep, twisted stairways connect the rooms, interspersed, en route, with small, dark, hidey holes. Hidey holes of proportions such that a child could sit in them in comfort and imagine herself safe. Outside there is a turret, topped by a flagless flagpole, and a balcony, which forms the roof of the lower room.

In front of the castle a bed of creepers—purple-blue lobelia and soft grey lambs-ears—moves slowly back and forth across the lawn, and on the plateau beside the castle there is a maze of walking hedges. The child of the garden is not afraid of the hedges, but she does not often venture into the maze. Its tall green passageways hold no enticement for her, and she has no desire to reach the wooden beams and rough-roped nets which form the sculptured playground at its centre.

From the plateau, and more especially from the turret of the castle, it is possible to see the whole of the garden: from the forest which borders it to the west, to the forest which borders it to the east, and from the forest south, to the wall. Viewed thus the garden appears to be small, contained, not at all the wild free place that a child, whilst climbing trees in its orchard, or dangling daringly from the small wooden bridge which spans the stream, might think that it is.

The child of the garden, Amaranthe, is seven years old. She is a wiry child, slender yet agile, with strong brown hands, scratched knees, and a quick, shy smile. Her hair is black: dusty black, like a cat's, and her eyes are the color of stepping stones. She has been seven years old for as long as she can remember.

The child is not alone in the garden. A pair of blackbirds, Titua and Alvin, are nesting in the conifer hedge that shields the orchard, and rabbits live along the edge of the forest. One of them in particular, a soft white baby called Brere, is Amaranthe's friend. Fish swim in the stream, tiny darting silver-backs, and beneath the bridge a frog prince sings to his love. Amaranthe knows all the occupants of the garden, but none better than the phinx who sleeps in the castle, and the peacock who lives on the lawn. The peacock is her lover, sometimes. Other times he is her brother, or her father, or her familiar. A king, a prince, a magician, a fool.

Today, since Amaranthe is an Asian princess, he is her lover, changed by magic into the form of a bird by her wicked . . . Amaranthe hesitates, she had been about to think Uncle.

"Father," she says, loudly, so that the whole garden might hear. "My lover, Prince Tamil, has been changed into the form of a bird by my wicked father. Oh, what shall I do?"

Titua and Alvin, who are patrolling the lawn, pause. Titua peers at Amaranthe, then at Tamil. Then noticing that Alvin has spotted a worm, she hops toward him, dipping her head, begging.

Amaranthe rises majestically, turns toward the castle and walks sadly away. She is naked. When she returns, some moments later, she is struggling with a strip of blue-gold silk. She winds it somewhat haphazardly around her waist, then throws the loose end over her shoulder. Her shoulders straighten, she tips her nose into the air.

"I shall visit the wild ones beyond the river," she says. "They will know what to do."

She rushes toward Tamil, hugs him to her, then turning, runs toward the stream.

A day has passed. By the stream she stops to rest. She removes the silk and bathes for a while, lying with her head between the stepping stones, enjoying the cold gush of the water as it tumbles over her shoulders. Then, with her hair still dripping wet, and leaving the silk, forgotten, at the other side of the stream, she curls up and sleeps. While she sleeps she listens to the stream, to the chitter-chatter of Titua and Alvin, and the summery buzz of insects. The frog prince croaks, and a playful breeze whispers through the forest. Perhaps this is why she does not hear the door open. Or perhaps it is simply that the door is smooth and silent in its opening. Or perhaps it is because the opener wishes it this way. But whatever the reason, Amaranthe remains unaware of her visitor, until, having slept enough, she opens her eyes.

A boy is sitting on the other side of the stream, legs crossed, watching her. He is tall and slender; his limbs are golden, his hair is fair. It gleams in the sunlight, highlighting the lines of his shins and forearms, and forming a halo above his prettily pious face. He looks to be twelve years old, or thereabouts, and as usual he is wearing only a shirt. Sleeveless, knee-length. It rests across his thighs, revealing, rather than concealing, the podgy pink penis between his legs. This is the first thing that Amaranthe sees, and quickly she averts her eyes, looking, startled, into his face.

He smiles. "Hello, sleepy-head."

Amaranthe makes no reply. She rolls quickly up onto her knees and, sitting on her heels, places her hands in her lap. She glances at the silk, lying sodden on the other side of the stream. Tamil, tail splayed, struts across the lawn; the creepers creep; Titua and Alvin fly overhead, squabbling.

"No, hello?" her visitor asks. "Not even a smile? Cat got your tongue?"

Amaranthe shakes her head.

"Well, then."

"Hello, Uncle."

"David. I've told you, call me David. Uncle sounds so old." He laughs. "You don't think I'm old, do you?"

Amaranthe shrugs uncertainly. Old is something of which she has little knowledge. Old is . . . a gnarled tree; or a smooth stone. In stories it is wily, or wise, or foolish. Or else it is something, Amaranthe frowns, *past*. Something that goes away and never comes back . . . and her uncle always comes back.

"No, I don't think you are old," she says.

Her uncle smiles, pleased. "Good." He stretches out his legs, dips his toes into the stream. "Go and dress."

Amaranthe stands and wades quickly through the stream, her shins cutting bluntly through the knee-deep water. Droplets splash onto the pure white of her uncle's shirt, but he says nothing. The lawn is firm beneath her running feet, the soil cool and damp beneath the warm, dry grass. Tamil calls to her, but she does not answer. She slows only when she reaches the safety of the castle.

In the lower room, a crystal window overlooks the garden. Carved with petals it fractures the outer colours, tumbling them, at the least movement, like shards in a kaleidoscope. Beneath the window there is a table. A low table, as dark as the shed on the other side of the stream. There are cushions around it—large and small, patterned and plain—and in its center there is a rose. Part way between bud and bloom, the rose rests in a stem vase just a little too large. Amaranthe has placed it there, sometime, and has not yet had the whim to remove it. She does not stop to do so now, but moves, with hurried steps, toward a curtain-covered passageway.

In the upper room there is a hand-shaped mattress. It is soft and warm, and at night it embraces her, rocking her to sleep. A cover lies crumpled within its palm, a cover iridescent with greens and blues and bronze-lidded eyes. Curled within the cover there is a small cat-like form. Its skin is grey, furless, but there are a few wispy hairs on the tips of its ears and whiskers on its nose. This is Amaranthe's companion. The phinx, Ankh Tut.

He looks up as Amaranthe enters, fixing her with a piercing blue gaze, and feeling the touch of his question. Amaranthe shakes her head. She has no time to talk. If she isn't quick, her uncle will come looking for her.

She moves across to the dressing box and, kneeling, begins to search through it. Scraps of material fly over her shoulder, capes and feathers and beads. Furs and leathers; slinkies and enhancers; tiger jaws and hair puffs. At the bottom of the box, beneath a shape-shift, she finds what she is looking for, and stands, pulling it over her head. Tut yawns disapprovingly and settles back to sleep.

Outside, Amaranthe's uncle is waiting for her. He looks at her ribbonless hair, at her naked feet, and frowns. Amaranthe shuffles nervously and smoothes her hand over the dress. It is a party dress, peach satin, trimmed with white bows and a lace collar. The stiff petticoats itch against her thighs. Her uncle holds up his hand, circles a finger in the air, and Amaranthe turns, showing off the hastily fastened bow at the rear.

"Really, Amaranthe," he says, and steps forward. His hands slide down her back, then tug roughly at the sash. He fastens it tightly, neatly, then turns her to face him. "My dear, you are the most unseemly child," he says. He leans forward to kiss her, but Amaranthe turns away, and his lips merely brush her cheek. He frowns. "First no hello, and now no kiss. You are cold Amaranthe. I don't know why I bother with you."

Amaranthe says nothing, she merely looks at him with her stepping-stone eyes until he looks away.

"You can't even dress yourself properly," he continues and, kneeling, reaches beneath the satin and tugs at the petticoats. His knuckles brush against her legs. Amaranthe does not move. She stands as still as a statue. As still as stone. He is right, she thinks: I am cold.

"That's better." He smoothes down the satin, and his hands are brown and strong, like her own, but larger. "Now, a present."

"I don't want anything."

"Ungrateful too, aren't you?"

"I have everything I need."

"Silly, presents are things you don't need. Like . . . close your eyes and hold out your hands. I'll show you."

Amaranthe hesitates, thinking to protest again, but then, seeing the furrow of impatience forming above her uncle's eyes, she quickly closes her own and holds out her hands. They are dirty, but her uncle seems not to notice this. Something tickles her palm. Swallowing, she opens her eyes. There is a feather in her hands. It shimmers in the sun, glistening with greens and blues and a single, bronze-lidded "eye."

"From Tamil!" She gasps. "How could you? How dare you? I—I—" She starts to run, her feet pounding on the grass. "Tamil! Where are you? Tamil!"

"He flew off into the forest. He'll be back tomorrow, as good as new."

"The forest? No . . . he couldn't."

"The orchard then. Do you want to go and look for him? Shall I help you?"

Amaranthe shakes her head, then nods. She wipes a hand across her cheek and finds to her dismay that she is crying.

"I didn't know it would upset you," her uncle says, appearing beside her. "I thought you would like it. You could wear it . . ." He shrugs. "There's no harm done."

"You hurt him."

"He hurt me, too. Look . . ." Her uncle pushes his arm in front of her and Amaranthe notices, for the first time, the bright red scratches that run from wrist to elbow. "Tried to peck it off," he says, and smiles.

Amaranthe returns the smile and for a moment, just for a moment, something glistens in her stepping-stone eyes, like sun on water.

"So, what do you want to do?" her uncle asks. "Play hide and seek? Go fruit picking? Mage the stones?"

"We could pick strawberries," Amaranthe says.

Her uncle nods. Between them, filling the air like a swarm of butterflies, are the words she does not say . . . for tea. Strawberries for tea.

They turn, together, not touching, and walk toward the bridge.

"You're supposed to be picking them, not eating them," Amaranthe says.

"I know." Her uncle grins across at her from his position in the middle of the strawberry patch. His white shirt is dirty and crumpled and stained with red, like his fingers. There are a few strawberries in his lap, but far more in his belly. "I just can't resist," he says. "Weak willed, I am." He pops another strawberry ceremoniously into his mouth, and smiles.

Amaranthe shakes her head, but he looks so happy that she smiles too.

"Most unseemly," she says.

"*Most* unseemly," he agrees; and they smile again.

The strawberries occupy her uncle's hands and mouth, and their sweetness has infected his eyes. He looks at her softly, and the blue of his eyes is the blue of the sky, wide and warm and undemanding. She is as dirty and crumpled as he, but he makes no move to rectify the matter, and does not comment when, kneeling on the dress and reaching too far, there is an ominous sound of tearing. Once, Amaranthe remembers, when playing hide and seek, she had hidden too well— in the compost heap—and afterwards he had insisted on washing her himself, pushing her again and again under the cold rushing water of the stream. And once, when she had torn the dress whilst climbing a tree, he had ripped it from her, blindfolded her, and made her walk along the southern wild edge, among the nettles and thistles and briars, so that she might know what it felt like to be torn. But now he smiles. So Amaranthe smiles too.

A butterfly passes between them, fluttering from plant to plant on route to the cabbages. Her uncle catches it, holds it trapped within his strong brown hand, then releases it with a smile. He picks another strawberry, places it solemnly between his teeth and bites it in two. One half he rests upon his tongue, opening his mouth to show it to her, the other he places on his palm, proffering it with a flourish. Amaranthe accepts it and puts it carefully with the others in her satin lap.

"No, no—eat," he says, curling the words around the strawberry on his tongue.

Amaranthe hesitates—then, picking up the half, places it quickly in her mouth. For some reason her uncle finds this amusing. He throws back his head, laughing, showing his own empty throat. His teeth are startling white against the redness of his throat and tongue and lips. "I love it, I love it, I love it . . ." He throws himself backwards and rolls among the tender plants.

"You're crushing them!"

Her uncle stops and stares up at her. "What do you care?" he says, "they'll be back, tomorrow . . . and tomorrow and tomorrow . . . you will always have strawberries."

"I know, but . . . all the same," Amaranthe hesitates. This is not the first time he has made such a comment, and she has heard, before, the same resentful tone in his voice. Uncertainly, she asks: "Don't you have strawberries in your garden?"

"No." Her uncle smiles, but his lips are twisted and ugly. "I don't have strawberries in my garden." And like his smile the words are twisted, their meaning sullied.

Amaranthe swallows, knowing that she has irritated him, and that now the happy time is over. "I'm sorry," she says.

"Me, too." Her uncle sits up and, turning, looks down at the crushed plants. He examines them slowly, in silence, the fingers of one hand patiently parting the leaves, probing, exploring. Amaranthe shivers.

"You don't remember the beginning, do you?" he asks abruptly.

Amaranthe starts. "The beginning?"

"Your first day in the garden," he says angrily. "Or the time before—your parents, for instance, do you remember your parents?"

"I dream about them sometimes . . ."

"Dreams aren't memories. Memories are real; dreams aren't. Do you remember me, when I'm not here?"

"Sometimes."

Her uncle nods, then sighs. "I wonder how long we've been here. Really; how long."

"Always," Amaranthe says.

"No! We were somewhere else, once. But something happened, something bad. Our parents sent us here. To wait."

Amaranthe frowns. "To wait?"

"To be safe."

"Then why didn't they come too?"

Her uncle shrugs. "They couldn't. They were too old, I think. Too polluted . . . too busy. It wouldn't have worked." He sighs again, then falls silent.

Amaranthe tries to imagine what somewhere else might look like, but she does not ask, and after a while her uncle says quietly, as if to himself: "I shouldn't be here." And then, standing, "Time for tea."

*   *   *

In the lower room of the castle, on the dark table, there are two dishes of cream. Amaranthe sits, legs crossed, hulling the strawberries before dropping them, with a satisfying plop, into the bowls. Spilt cream mingles with the hulls on the table. Her uncle sits opposite her, watching her. His legs are stretched beneath the table, his toes touch her knees. In front of him there is a pile of rose petals. The stem vase lies broken beneath the crystal window. Tomorrow, Amaranthe's uncle says, it will be whole.

Amaranthe, unable to bear the tense silence, the waiting, asks quietly: "What is your garden like?"

"My garden," her uncle says, accenting the word so that Amaranthe will know that it is not the correct word, but that nevertheless it amuses him to use it, "my *garden* is a box. There are things in the box, things such as you cannot remember, or imagine. There is a chair that walks, a friend that talks—nonsense, mostly— and a . . ." He frowns, searching for words that she will understand, "a dream-maker. A magic hat. There are mountains and seas in that hat. Alien worlds, creatures, history . . . all kinds of things."

"Is your friend pretty?" Amaranthe asks. "Like Tamil."

Her uncle sighs. "Pretty, yes. Like Tamil, no. Like the window perhaps. Or rather, like the colors shining through the window. Untouchable." As he says this, his toe presses into her knee. Amaranthe adds the last strawberry to the dishes of cream and pushes one towards him. They eat in silence.

When they have finished her uncle says: "I want to show you something. Come here."

Amaranthe does not move, and frowning he says again: "Come here. I won't hurt you. I only want to show you something." He smiles a false smile.

Amaranthe stands and moves around the table.

Her uncle pulls up his shirt. "Look," he says. "Here, look: hairs."

Amaranthe looks. Above the podgy-pink penis there are a few wispy hairs, like those on Ankh Tut's ears.

"And my voice," her uncle continues, "sometimes it changes. I try to speak and it comes out all wrong, like a growl . . ."

Amaranthe looks from the hairs to his eyes. "You're different," she says. And in her eyes and voice wonder mingles with fear.

Her uncle nods. "I'm getting old." He smiles and, because he expects it, Amaranthe smiles too.

"No," she says. "You cannot."

Her uncle shrugs, and reaching towards her, catches her wrist in his hand. "I have to go soon," he says. "Shall we play the last game?"

Amaranthe hesitates. Her stomach contracts, she feels sick, trapped, like the butterfly. Caught in his strong brown hand. Once, she remembers, she refused him. She will not do so again.

"I don't feel well," she says.

Her uncle's face looks concerned, but his eyes glow with pleasure. "Too many strawberries, I expect," he says, "but I'd better take a look at you all the same. Get onto the table."

Amaranthe steps onto the table and lies down. She looks at the ceiling, at the colors cast by the crystal window. She tries to think of Tamil, of the sky, but her uncle's hands fill her mind. She bites her lip.

"Where does it hurt?" her uncle asks.

"There," Amaranthe says.

It is enough. Her uncle kneels beside the table and gently lifts her dress.

"I'm leaving now."

Amaranthe nods. She is standing beside the table. A trickle of blood runs down her leg.

"You'll be all right in the morning," her uncle says. "Good as new."

Amaranthe nods. Her eyes are like stepping stones, flat and grey. Her uncle stops at the door, and turns.

"I love you," he says.

Time passes. It is, to Amaranthe, a pattern of dreams and games, of dark and light, of sleeping and eating. She does not bother to count the days, they are not a progression. Nothing changes. Every morning when she wakes she throws aside the peacock cover and examines herself. But no hairs appear, and when she speaks, calling Ankh Tut to her side, her voice does not growl, but remains strong and true. Ankh Tut, who watches this morning ritual from the comfort of the dressing box, leaps onto the mattress and begins to wash his face. Look behind you, he says. Perhaps you've grown a tail.

Amaranthe is sitting in the stream, beneath the shelter of the willow, when she hears someone call her name. She lifts her hand, allowing the tiny silver-back caught within the corral of her fingers to return to its shoal, and listens. There is only one person it can be, the door will admit no-one else, and yet . . . the voice calls again, impatiently, and peeping between the branches of the willow Amaranthe sees her uncle striding across the lawn toward the bridge. Once on the bridge he hesitates, listening, then calls again. He is wearing a shirt, white, sleeveless. The sun shines in his hair, forming a dazzling halo that reaches down to his shoulders. The shirt seems small.

After a moment he leaves the bridge and follows the path to the orchard. Amaranthe hears his footsteps, a flurry of protest from Titua and Alvin, the crunching sound of teeth biting into an apple. He does not call her again. He moves across to the vegetable patch. Amaranthe can see him, through the leaves of the willow and the clear panes of the glasshouse. She is standing now, silent, her toes buried in silt. Water drips silently down her legs. Her uncle strides from row to row, holding onto his shirt with one hand, picking and pulling and storing with the other. The hairs are still there, beneath the bulge of the shirt. They seem thicker.

When the shirt will hold no more he returns to the stream, strides across the stepping stones, and drops his load onto the grass. He glances upstream, toward the willow, then pulls off his shirt and places it beside the collection of vegetables and fruit. The clean fruit he places directly onto the shirt. Others, root vegetables and the like, he washes in the stream. The clumps of soil separate, drifting with the current, toward Amaranthe. Finally he washes his hands and sits up.

"I'm having a picnic," he says, looking again at the willow. "Won't you join me?" He selects a carrot and begins to eat.

Slowly Amaranthe steps out from her hiding place and walks upstream. She watches him carefully, and notices that the hairs have spread to his chest and face. They are soft and pale, like downy breast feathers, but they are there. Her uncle returns her gaze, his eyes as bright and piercing as a kingfisher's.

"Still the same, I see," he says. "Like an apple?"

Amaranthe nods and he tosses one towards her. She catches it, but does not eat.

"We're celebrating," her uncle says. "I've come to stay."

"No . . ." She says the word softly. Whispers it, like the breeze. And then she screams: "no!"

She turns, runs, hears him splash after her. Her chest aches with fear, her heart pounds with anger, the path is hard beneath her feet. But still he is quicker. He catches her beside the blackcurrants and spins her to the ground. She struggles, squirming in the dirt, but he is stronger. His hands hold her wrists, he sits astride her. Within the bushes Ankh Tut moves like a pale shadow, belly to the ground, muscles gathering to leap.

"No," Amaranthe says.

"I have to." Her uncle leans his face close to hers. "Amaranthe—I have to. Something has gone wrong . . . chair limps and my friend, my friend has gone."

"Gone?"

"Faded, ceased, is not there!" Her uncle sits up, releasing her arms.

Ankh Tut lies in the dust, watching.

"What goes, comes back," Amaranthe says.

Her uncle shakes his head. "I kicked the chair," he says. "It didn't come when I called, so I kicked it, and now it limps."

"It will be all right tomorrow."

"No. There have been tomorrows. It still limps."

Amaranthe says nothing. She lies still, looking at the sky, and eventually her uncle moves, releasing her. He sits beside her, knees drawn up to his chest, staring at nothing.

After a while Amaranthe says: "You have hairs on top of your lip."

Her uncle sighs. "I know."

There is a pause. Titua and Alvin swoop past and dive into the conifers. The trees tremble with movement, then still. Ankh Tut lifts his head and, pretending indifference, slips away.

Amaranthe watches him go. She knows the exact position of the nest. She knows that there are three eggs inside, pale blue with soft brown freckles. She knows that inside each egg there is a tiny creature that will never be born; and she knows that Ankh Tut will never catch Titua or Alvin—but that he likes to try. She turns to her uncle. "What is wrong?" she asks.

"I don't know."

Amaranthe stands and looks down at her uncle, noticing the way his spine presses against the skin of his back, the way his shoulder-blades form budding wings, the way his golden hair spills over his shoulders. "The garden might not like it if you stay," she says.

He sighs. "I know."

The pattern changes. Amaranthe's uncle occupies much of the garden, sitting morosely on the lawn, or tending the vegetable patch, or standing, legs apart, hands on hips, on top of the turret. Amaranthe plays, but quietly now, secretly, confining herself to the hidey holes within the castle or the far edges of the garden. Tamil sulks in the orchard. Ankh Tut walks like a shadow at Amaranthe's feet.

At night, while Amaranthe lies secure in the hand of her mattress, and her uncle sleeps wrapped in the peacock cover on the floor beside her, the dark shed murmurs to itself. It is a soft sound, smooth and soothing, like a cat's purring. Or a child's snoring. It is the sort of sound that a pebble might make as it skims across the surface of a stream—if the stream was a stream of time, and the pebble a refractor. It is a sound which seeps into the garden, becoming, in places, an angry sound, like the irritating buzz of an insect.

Beneath the willow, the air seems to vibrate. The shadows deepen. Upstream, the frog prince calls out to his love. And in the lower room of the castle, the table hums.

The dark shed is many things: refractor, restorer, repertory, and in part it is a part of Amaranthe. The part that heals . . . the part that dreams.

Amaranthe dreams of her uncle leaving. But he has nowhere to go.

In the vegetable patch a small white rabbit is gnawing on a discarded carrot. Amaranthe stands behind the glasshouse, watching her uncle through gaps in the vines within. Her uncle, stick in hand, is creeping toward the rabbit.

Ankh Tut presses himself against Amaranthe's leg. His back is arched, a low hiss escapes his curled lips. Now? No, wait.

Closer, closer . . . her uncle raises the stick slightly. Abruptly Amaranthe darts from the shelter of the glasshouse and runs, screaming, toward the rabbit. Her uncle shouts; Ankh Tut dives between them growling. As Amaranthe reaches Brere her uncle brings the stick down across her back. She cries out, but the pain does not stop her sweeping the startled rabbit into her arms. She heads back toward the glasshouse, then runs on, to the dark shed. There, between its wall and a thornless bramble, she releases Brere. The rabbit hesitates, then disappears into the undergrowth as her uncle, detained briefly by Ankh Tut, catches up with her. He grabs hold of her arm, twisting her to face him, and Amaranthe, expecting anger and abuse, is chilled by the calm coldness of his eyes. "You will pay for that," he says.

He drags her, terrified but as yet unprotesting, through the stream and across the lawn, up the long shallow steps—where she begins to struggle—and finally, into the maze. He strides quickly between the hedgerows, and Amaranthe, guessing his intentions, finds her voice.

"Please, Uncle, Brere is my friend . . . I've always fed him and I forgot . . ."

Her uncle stops, shakes his head. "You must not forget. The garden is no longer yours, but ours. You must remember that Amaranthe."

"I will—I will remember. I won't do it again."

"I know."

"Then you won't punish me?"

"I must."

"No . . . not—" Amaranthe hesitates. "Wouldn't you rather play the game instead?"

Her uncle lets out an exclamation and all but throws her from him. Amaranthe stumbles, falls. She allows herself a moment to recover from the pain, then parting her legs slightly, she licks her lips. Her eyes are large, pleading, and her uncle hesitates, reaches down . . . and hits her. Amaranthe scrambles away, ducking beneath the hedge, pressing herself against its feet. But her uncle's hands find her.

"Bitch," he says. "Hussy!" And then he is on top of her, invading her, while his hands bind her wrists and his teeth grate against her lips, silencing her screams.

And somewhere within the tearing pain Amaranthe realizes that this time the game has changed. That this time the invasion is for real.

Amaranthe lies in the stream, her head resting on a stepping stone, her eyes half-closed. Black hair fans around her shoulders. Her feet move in desultory circles within the cool, numbing water. She has known pain before, but never upon waking. Her skin has been torn, but never scarred. She lifts her arm from the water and inspects her wrist. It is red, marked with the pattern of rope.

There are marks on the sides of the bridge upstream, too, where her uncle has scratched his name—David—so that she might remember it. And in the orchard pale tears shine against the bark of an apple tree. Nothing is as it should be.

Her uncle emerges from the castle, looks quickly around the garden, and seeing her lying in the stream trots down the slope of lawn. He sits on the grass beside her, dangles his feet into the water.

Behind him, on the flagpole above the castellated playhouse, a tattered white shirt blows in the breeze.

"I'm sorry," he says. "Yesterday, I lost my temper. I acted harshly. It won't happen again."

Amaranthe says nothing. She has moved her arms beneath her, concealing her wrists.

He smiles. "That looks like fun . . . may I?" He slides into the water beside her, not waiting for an answer. Amaranthe edges away from him and he grabs her arm, pulling her back. "Let's be friends," he says. "Please Amaranthe. Forgive me."

Amaranthe swallows. There are tears at the back of her eyes. Dry stinging tears. Her uncle finds her hand and brings it towards his lips. Stops. She feels a wet finger trace the pattern of the rope, and then, so softly that she barely hears, he says: "No. And your back?"

When Amaranthe does not move he touches her shoulder and turns her gently onto her side. He stares at her for a moment, then releases her.

"You must sleep on the table tonight," he says. "I'll stay away, far away. I'll sleep in the orchard. The table will help you . . . it's . . . like a hand, see? An amplifier. You'll be all right."

Amaranthe looks doubtful, but her uncle smiles.

"Trust me," he says. "I love you."

Night, and a starless twilight engulfs the garden. Amaranthe lies on top of the dark table with Ankh Tut wrapped in her arms. The table vibrates, deep in its heart, like a cat purring. Ankh Tut lifts his head; listening. Amaranthe dreams.

Her uncle lies in the furthermost corner of the garden, where forest west meets forest south. He wears a strip of silk, tied around his loins, and has about him a peacock cover and a fur stole. Beneath his head there is a cushion. He wakes occasionally, disturbed by the sounds of the forest and the purring of the ground.

Twice during the night a short but heavy rain falls.

When dawn breaks he rises and makes his way quickly to the castle. Amaranthe wakes as he enters, and together they examine her wrists. The marks have much improved, faded now to a soft pink blur. Likewise, the bruises and cuts that cover her back have almost healed.

"I told you," her uncle says.

Amaranthe nods, but she does not smile.

"Breakfast then," her uncle says. "Put something on."

Amaranthe hurries upstairs and searches the dressing box for something that will please him. She returns with a torn strip of peach satin which she wraps around her waist.

After breakfast they play games: "hide and seek," "queen of the stones" and "roll the hill." Amaranthe's uncle is jolly, tender, appeasing.

At midday he declares that he will eat only fish, and that caught by his own hand. His antics, in trying to catch one of the wily silver-backs, amuses Amaranthe. At length she smiles.

"Am I forgiven then?" her uncle chances to ask.

Amaranthe touches her wrists. "Ask the garden," she says.

Her uncle smiles and, standing, calls loudly: "Am I forgiven?"

The garden does not answer, but a short while later he succeeds in catching one of the tiny fish.

"It will need a dressing," Amaranthe says. "Wait."

She rises quickly, crosses the stream, and begins picking her way through the vegetable patch. The plants are dreary. Some have yellow leaves and patches of brown. The lettuce is limp, the carrots are soft, and the fruits are covered by a fluffy grey mould. Amaranthe thinks of the table but, afraid of her uncle's rancour, picks what there is. Titua and Alvin swoop past, calling loudly, and disappear into the wild patch. Ankh Tut, ears twitching, drops to his belly and follows them, only to return, moments later, full of excitement. Haughty blue eyes stare up at Amaranthe, Tut turns his head, like an arrow, toward the wild patch. Come, come see.

Amaranthe frowns. "What?"

Come see . . .

Tut sets off, and Amaranthe, fearing that he has finally caught one of the birds, chases after him. He leads her past the greying blackberries and faded redcurrants to a bush on the edge of the forest. Surrounded by the soft pink flowers of rosebay and tangled with bindweed, the bush stands aloof, vibrant with berries: yellow, black and red, shiny and fresh. See?

Amaranthe smiles and curls her finger under Tut's chin, rubbing gently. I see. The berries are strange to her, but she fears nothing from the garden and picks one. They have a sharp taste, strange, but pleasant. Happily she adds them to her load and quickly returns to her uncle.

He is crouching beside the bridge, staring beneath it. He has a large stone in his hand. As Amaranthe approaches he motions her to be quiet, then abruptly hurls the stone. There is a sharp sound, stone on stone, and with a yelp of victory he scurries beneath the bridge. Amaranthe waits, coldly afraid. As he emerges she lets out a scream, and dropping her load, runs, sobbing, toward the castle. Her uncle, the frog prince dangling from his hand, calls after her in vain.

Later, tears subsided, she hears him calling her again. She does not answer at first, but waits, and when he calls again she hears, clearly, the tones of pain in his voice. She moves to the door, and peering out sees her uncle lying on the lawn. His knees are pulled up tight to his chest whilst his arms, uncertain, cling first to his chest and then fly out, beating against the grass.

"Amaran—" This time his voice breaks off, subsiding to a groan, and Amaranthe runs towards him.

"What is it?" she asks. "What can I do?"

"I don't know." He groans again and sweat breaks out on his forehead.

Amaranthe crouches beside him. She touches a hand, uncertainly, to his head and he grips it in his own, squeezing it as the pain squeezes him.

"Make it stop," he gasps. "I'll go away, but please, make it stop."

He releases her suddenly; and not knowing what she does, or why, Amaranthe runs across the grass, across the stream, to the dark shed. She bangs her fist against its smooth black sides, crying, pleading, demanding. The dark shed does nothing. If there is an inside, it is unseen. It has neither door nor windows.

After a while, her hands aching, Amaranthe stops. She rests a moment, leaning against the shed with her eyes closed, then slowly, afraid of her failure, she returns to the stream. Unthinking, she dips her hands into the coolness of the water, and then, more certainly, she removes the satin from her waist, and wetting it, returns to her uncle.

While she has been away, he has been sick. Vibrant yellow bile lies upon the grass and in his hair. Threads, like spider webs, lead from his mouth. Her uncle grabs at the satin and wipes his face.

"Thank you," he says.

Amaranthe says nothing. She sits beside him and waits. When he asks she holds his hand. Twice she returns to the stream and wets the satin.

Later, he says: "I love you."

And later still: "I never meant to hurt you."

Night settles over the garden, and seeing that her uncle is sleeping, Amaranthe returns to the castle.

In the morning her first thought is for her uncle. She runs from the castle, takes a few steps across the grass, and stops. In the place where her uncle lay there is only the bed of creepers. Amaranthe calls, searches; then, remembering her uncle's promise, returns to the castle to breakfast alone.

That night a storm rips the tattered white shirt from the flagpole and tosses it into the forest. The marks on the bridge begin to fade, and in the orchard, the pale tears of the apple tree are smothered by bark.

The creepers no longer creep, and the frog prince does not sing beneath the bridge, but otherwise everything in the garden is as always. Except that the child of the garden no longer walks across the lawn, or plays in the stream, but sits in the turret of the castle, waiting. And sometimes, when it is cold, she wears a peach satin dress which seems a little too small.

SUSAN PALWICK
Offerings

Susan Palwick is a graduate of Princeton University's Creative Writing Program and the Clarion West Writers' Workshop; she is currently pursuing a doctorate in comparative literature at Yale. Her science fiction, fantasy and horror stories have appeared in *Isaac Asimov's*, *Amazing* and *Pulphouse* magazines, and her poem "The Neighbor's Wife" won the Rhysling Award. Her first novel will soon be published by Tor Books.

While not wanting to "typecast" this versatile author, some of her best work to date (including her forthcoming novel) has focused on the subject of childhood and its dangers, looking back from an unflinching adult perspective. "Offerings" is an excellent story in this vein, bringing folk-tale motifs into a contemporary suburban setting. "Offerings" is reprinted from *Pulphouse* magazine.

—T.W.

Offerings

SUSAN PALWICK

"The little people feed on anything that's evil," Matthew's mother told him when he was very young. "They're like the spiders in the garden, Matthew, which look ugly but are really good, because they eat the bugs which kill the flowers."

Matthew didn't like spiders, and he didn't like Mother's description of the little people, who smelled like old leaves and had small teeth as sharp as razors. "They really aren't that different from Nutmeg," Mother always said, but she made Matthew bathe the dog once a week and screamed whenever she found another dead squirrel in the kitchen, so he guessed that she wasn't as fond of smells and teeth as she claimed. Nutmeg redeemed herself by fetching sticks and sleeping in a warm heap at the foot of Matthew's bed every night, but he knew from his mother's stories that the little people were neither playful nor comforting.

"They saved your grandfather's life," she told Matthew. She'd tell him the story when he was helping her bake cookies in the kitchen, or when she was knitting sweaters for him to wear to school, or on wet days when he couldn't play outside. "It was when I was a little girl. He used to drink all the time and he'd turned bad, oh so bad, Matthew. He was running around with other women, and one night my mother tried to kick him out and he broke all her best dishes, the set from England that was decorated with real gold leaf—just took them down off the shelves and started smashing them on the floor. She tried to stop him and he hit her, and then he tried to hit me too but she got between us. She was a big woman. So she hit *him* and he fell and knocked his head against the table— maybe he passed out then, I don't know, but anyhow she dragged him outside and left him there and locked the door. It was raining. I made her go back out and turn him on his side instead of on his back, so he wouldn't drown from the water running in his nose . . . oh, I was scared. I thought he was going to die, and Mother kept saying, 'Your real daddy died a long time ago; your real daddy was loving and faithful and didn't break things. The whiskey killed him, Miriam. Don't cry for that mean drunk out there.'

"But I did anyway. I went to bed and cried myself to sleep, and in the middle of the night I woke up because he'd started screaming, out there in the rain. He kept screaming, 'Go away, go away! Stop hurting me!' I ran into my mother's room and got under the covers with her, and she said, 'Don't be scared. Nobody's hurting him but his own demons,' and finally we heard him say, 'All right, all right, I'll stop, I promise,' and then he stopped screaming. Mother got up and let him back in—oh, he was scared, white as a sheet and shaking like a leaf. He told us how the little people had come up to him in the dark and bitten him, bitten him all over with their sharp little teeth. There were too many of them to count, he said; they gnawed at his fingers and toes and nibbled on his legs and chewed on his nose, and they drank his blood the way he drank whiskey. He knew he was going to die and he promised that if they didn't kill him he'd stop drinking and fooling around and hitting us—and the minute he said that all the wounds healed up like they'd never been there at all, and all the little people went away, because he wasn't evil anymore. And he kept that promise, too: he never touched a drop after that, and he got a good job and bought my mother new dishes and never looked at anybody else. He was a wonderful man after that, loving and faithful just like my mother had said, and whenever anybody asked him what had made him change he said, 'It was the little people. I thought they were going to kill me, but they really saved my life.' "

Matthew was fascinated by the story; Matthew's father hated it. "It's crazy nonsense, Miriam! Matthew, your grandfather was having DTs and seeing things, that's all. That's why the bite marks healed up like they'd never been there: they hadn't! You've never seen one of these critters, have you?"

"Have you ever seen a germ?" his mother countered. "No, of course not. But they still make you sick, just like the little people made my father well."

Germs smelled like Listerine and the little people smelled like dead leaves. These invisibilities were every bit as real to Matthew as Mother herself, who smelled like warm cookies, or Miss Summersong at school, who smelled like lavender and gave him special books to read, or Daddy, who smelled like gin.

As Matthew grew taller Nutmeg became progressively better at killing squirrels, and the books Miss Summersong gave Matthew became more difficult. Daddy smelled like gin more and more often, and Mother like cookies less and less. They fought in the evenings when Matthew was supposed to be sleeping, as he lay in bed with Nutmeg curled heavily on his feet, chasing squirrels in her sleep; to escape the words Mother and Daddy hurled at each other Matthew thought about Miss Summersong's books, some of which were about magical kingdoms and some of which were about science.

Matthew believed as completely in both as he still did in the little people. He knew from the rustlings and scamperings he heard at night that they lived in the woods just beyond the house; sometimes, during a lull in his parents' fighting, he heard soft chewing noises outside and imagined the little people feasting on evil, but he could no longer tell if they were a protection or a threat.

"Squirrels," Daddy said once when Matthew described the noises, but it couldn't be squirrels. Nutmeg, who could hear a squirrel from three miles away through a thunderstorm, always slept soundly through these disturbances.

"You see?" Mother said. "Nutmeg isn't scared of them and neither should you be, Matthew. Your father, on the other hand—"

"Raccoons," Daddy said, refilling his orange juice glass with gin. "Muskrats. Maybe a bunch of bunny rabbits are having an orgy and the dog isn't interested because their tails aren't long enough, okay? Jesus, Miriam! You'll have the kid believing in flying saucers if you keep this up."

"You're disgusting," she said. "Eat some breakfast like a decent—"

"I'm not decent and I don't want breakfast; I want a drink."

"I hope they come and nibble you bare as a corncob and take all your bottles—"

"And do what? Pour them down the sink the way you do? Hey, Matt, the little critters actually live in the plumbing, didja know that? Your mother's been treating them to a party every night, or else she likes 'em a lot less than she says she does and she's trying to drown them. But it doesn't matter. There's enough for all of us. Here, kid—try some."

Matthew's mother started screaming at Daddy then, but Daddy only laughed. "I'd better go wait for the bus," Matthew said, ignoring the proffered glass and giving his last piece of bacon to Nutmeg. His stomach ached, as it always did at breakfast. He knew he'd feel better as soon as he got on the school bus.

One morning when Matthew was ten the bus didn't come. There had been a heavy snowstorm the night before, and when Matthew had been waiting in front of the house for an hour, Mother came to fetch him back inside.

"The bus isn't coming, Matthew; they just said so on the radio. The roads are too bad. There won't be any school today."

Matthew followed her into the house along the narrow path he'd shoveled for himself earlier that morning. Daddy sat in the kitchen, his hands clenched around a mug which held nothing but coffee. Mother must have emptied his bottles the night before, although Matthew wasn't sure when she'd had time. The fighting from his parents' bedroom had gone on until dawn, long past Matthew's ability to block it out by thinking about schoolwork. He hadn't even been able to hear the little people over the din.

"Look what you're doing to Matthew," Mother had yelled, and Daddy had answered just as loudly, "Matthew's fine, nothing's wrong with him, what's Matthew got to do with it anyway?"

"I want to go to school," Matthew told them, his stomach clenching. He didn't want to have anything to do with it. He wanted to be with Miss Summersong with her silver braided hair, Miss Summersong who had been giving him books since he was five, who could make him forget about the drinking and the fighting and living in the woods so far from everyone else. "Why can't I go to school?"

"Because of the roads," Mother said.

Daddy let go of the coffee mug and pressed his hands flat on the table to keep them from shaking. It didn't work. "Matthew, if you really want to go I'll drive you. Get in the truck."

"No! You're in no shape to drive, or the truck to be driven, or the roads to be driven on. The school's probably closed, anyway. Matthew, take your coat off."

Daddy clenched his hands into fists and jammed them into his pockets. "The radio said it was open. You heard it, Miriam."

"Well, I'm sure Miss Summersong won't be there."

"Miss Summersong's always there," Matthew told her.

"Matthew, he doesn't really want to take you to school! He's just looking for an excuse to go to town and buy more liquor. Don't you understand?"

He understood, but he didn't care. His father would go to town anyway, and if anything was moving toward the schoolhouse Matthew wanted to be in it. The truck was aged and rusting, the roads nearly impassible; Daddy cursed and clutched the steering wheel while Matthew prayed and clutched his books. He prayed to Miss Summersong and to the little people, both of whom were much closer than God.

His prayer to Miss Summersong was simple: please be there. He asked more complex things of the little people, things he knew they probably couldn't grant, things he didn't know if they'd be able to understand because he wasn't sure he understood them himself. Please don't say I'm evil, he prayed, please don't call me evil for wanting to go to school and giving Daddy an excuse to go to town, please stay outside the house, please leave me alone and leave Mother and Daddy alone too, don't eat us, I don't want to be eaten and I don't want them to be eaten because then where would I live? I'll give you anything you want, but leave the three of us alone.

He prayed all the way to school, but he didn't know if his supplications were appeasing the little people or only catching their attention. As Matthew walked into the schoolroom that morning it seemed as if the little people must be very close and very hungry, and not even the sight of Miss Summersong waiting for him, smiling because he was the only one of her fifteen students who'd managed the trip through the snow, could make him feel less afraid.

"I won't give you regular work today, Matthew, because the other children aren't here. We'll just do special things." So they talked about the books she'd given him, about the Arabian Nights and Oz and the biology book which had pictures of a man's body stripped of its skin, of its muscles, finally even of its organs, so that just the bones were left; they talked about rocks and stars and animals, but through all of it Matthew kept thinking about Daddy driving in the snowstorm and the little people in the woods. Finally Miss Summersong said, "Matthew, what's the matter? You seem unhappy today."

"Nothing's the matter," Matthew told her. It was too complicated, and if he told her what had happened she might be angry at him for coming to school at all. He wondered if she could tell he was lying.

But she only sighed and said, "I have something to show you—I'd meant to save it until the others were here too, but I think maybe today would be a good day for it. Wait here."

She went to the closet at the back of the room and came back with a microscope. Matthew had only seen microscopes in books, being used in clean, orderly rooms by people who wore white coats and wise expressions. Microscopes were as foreign and incomprehensible as banks and satellites, and it had never occurred to Matthew that he might one day be allowed to handle such a thing.

The slides Miss Summersong showed him, of bits of flowers and seeds like battleships under the lens and tiny insects' eyes grown into faceted jewels, managed to make him forget about the snow and his parents for a little while. He looked at a speck of dust and saw a mountain; he examined a downy feather and saw filaments as rough and gigantic as a monster's tentacles. But as he was putting away the most beautiful slide, a fragment of butterfly wing as intricate as some distant city, it slipped from his hand the same way the road had slid under the wheels of the truck, and shattered to shards on the schoolroom floor.

Matthew cried out and bent to retrieve the pieces, but they were too small; even had he been able to gather them all up again he never would have been able to reassemble them. "I'm sorry, Miss Summersong, I'm so sorry, I didn't mean to do it, really I didn't—"

She frowned at him and said, "Of course you didn't, Matthew. It's all right. We'll clean it up."

He watched her sweep up the bits of glass with a broom and dustpan and pour them into the trashcan, and he knew he never should have been allowed to touch the microscope at all. She was still frowning and the windows rattled as if someone were trying to get in, and for a moment Matthew heard the soft, wet noises of the little people licking their lips. "I'll do extra homework if you want me to, Miss Summersong. I'll pay for it—"

"It was an accident, Matthew. You don't have to do anything." Her frown deepened, and Matthew stared at the floor, wondering if she'd stop giving him books, now that she knew he couldn't be trusted with anything. But she only said, very gently, "Matthew, look at me. Do you like yourself?"

He stared at her, bewildered. He could easily have answered questions about fractions or muscles or flying carpets, but this one defeated him. Miss Summersong watched him steadily, as if he were a slide under the microscope. He didn't know what she wanted him to say. If it hadn't been for the storm and the little people in the woods, he'd have turned and run outside.

His father's horn honked from the road, and for once Matthew welcomed the sound. "I have to go now, Miss Summersong."

"Saved," she said, and Matthew wondered why she sounded sad. "Well, Matthew, I guess I'll see you tomorrow."

"Are you going to give me any homework?"

She looked thoughtful for a moment. "Yes—yes, I am. Tomorrow morning I want you to tell me three things you like about yourself."

He blinked at her, feeling lost. "That's my homework? No reading?"

"No reading. Reading's gotten too easy for you. My job's to challenge you, Matthew." She smiled then, but she didn't look happy.

The trip home was worse than the trip to school had been. The minute Matthew got into the truck he knew that Daddy hadn't gone home at all, but instead had spent the entire day in town drinking gin. The inside of the car reeked of it; a half empty bottle sloshed on the dashboard, and a full case slid in the back of the truck. "Stocked up," said his father, remarkably coherent. "Got lots this time. She'll never find it all. Did you have a good time at school?"

"I broke a butterfly slide," Matthew said.

"Yeah? So? Have some gin, kid. You'll feel better."

"No. I don't want to." That was the money for groceries, he thought. For milk and bacon and dog food. They won't do anything but fight once we get home, and there won't be anything to eat for dinner, and Mother will blame it all on me because I wanted to go to school.

His mother met them at the door, crying as he had known she would be. "Matthew—Matthew, sweetheart, come inside—"

"What about me, Miriam? Do I get to come inside too?"

"Do whatever you want," she said, tugging Matthew into the house, and he knew that something was very wrong. Something terrible must have happened, for her not to start screaming because Daddy was drunk.

"Matthew," she said, "sweetheart, I'm afraid—"

"Where's Nutmeg?" The dog always threw herself on Matthew the minute he got home. The house felt empty, and too quiet. "What happened to Nutmeg?"

"I—" His mother twisted her hands and turned away from him. "She—this afternoon she started barking the way she does when there's a squirrel, you know. I didn't want to let her out because of the snow but she kept barking and scratching at the door, so finally I did and off she runs into the woods and—"

"Oh Christ," Daddy said. "Is that all? The dog isn't back yet and it's a national calamity? What's for dinner?"

"Leftovers. You spent the grocery money on liquor; do you think I don't know you by now? Matthew, I went out and called her and I even looked for her in the woods, but she didn't come back—"

"It was the little people," Matthew said, remembering his prayer on the way to school. I'll give you anything you want, but leave the three of us alone. "The little people took her." Three, he'd prayed, three and not four: he should have said four. How could he have forgotten about Nutmeg? And now she was gone, vanished into the snow, made into a meal for horrible creatures with teeth sharper than hers.

"Nobody took her," Daddy said. "She ran off after a squirrel, that's all. She'll be back. Everybody calm down."

Matthew shook his head. "If she's not back by now she's not coming. She never stays out so long. She's dead. They ate her—"

"Matthew, it was a squirrel! A squirrel, all right? You heard what your mother said, how she was barking and all. Aren't you the one who says she doesn't bark at these pixies? She ran outside after something real, and she'll come back when she's caught it. Let's eat dinner!"

"I can't eat," Matthew said. "I feel sick."

His mother knelt beside him and felt his forehead. "Matthew, why would the little people—"

"There aren't any little people! Miriam, can't you see what these stories have—"

"Shut up! Matthew, why would they take Nutmeg?"

Because he had promised her to them without knowing it; but if he told Mother that he'd have to tell her about his prayer, how terrified he was that everyone in the house would be eaten for being evil, how he lay awake at night listening to the fighting. Even if he'd been able to tell his mother that he thought she was evil, he'd have been too ashamed to admit that he'd forgotten Nutmeg in his prayers.

So he lied. "She—she pooped in my bed the other night and I cleaned it up but maybe the little people took her because she was bad—"

"No," his mother said gently. "Matthew, she's a good dog. Having an accident doesn't make you evil, and the little people only eat evil things, harmful things. That's why your grandfather was such a good man after—"

"Miriam, cut it out! Stop feeding him this garbage and feed me some supper."

"No! Why should I? You should have bought food and you didn't. You bought liquor instead—fine, so make that your dinner! I don't care anymore! They should come for you, the little ones should—oh, you'd make a lovely meal for them!"

Matthew clutched at her hand. She was undoing his prayer of safekeeping, inviting the little people into the house to feed on Daddy, and if that happened Nutmeg would have died for nothing. Daddy hated them so much he wouldn't believe in them even if he saw them. He'd think he was just imagining things even when they were devouring him, and he'd die too. "Mother, stop it! Don't say that. The little people will hear you—"

"Matthew," Daddy said, very quiet now, "there's no one to hear her. The little people don't exist; that's just a scare story . . . let's fix those leftovers, eh? Nutmeg's playing in the snow. She'll be back soon."

But he was wrong. As anxiously as Matthew waited through the evening, Nutmeg didn't come back. The little people came instead, to claim the meal Mother had promised them.

Matthew awoke to find his room perfectly illuminated with moonlight reflected from the snow outside. "It's sunlight, Matthew," Miss Summersong had said that day, "all light is sunlight, moonlight too, which stops somewhere else on its way from the sun before it reaches us" but whatever heat this light had taken from the sun had been lost long ago. The room was icy in a draft from the hall, and the blankets on Matthew's bed did nothing to warm him without the familiar weight on his feet. He got up, shivering, to close whatever window had been left open.

Halfway down the hall to his parents' room he began to smell a stench of rotting leaves and dead things far too vile to belong to Nutmeg. The bedroom door was open, and Matthew saw the little people climbing in through the open window which was causing the draft.

They crept in one by one, as silent as cats, to gather around the bed where Matthew's parents slept, oblivious, his father unconscious from gin and his mother from despair. They looked incredibly old, those little ones, standing no higher than Matthew's knee and dressed in tattered clothing woven from moss and twigs and bits of shredded fabric they must have found in the woods. Their faces were as wrinkled as raisins around gleaming eyes and teeth which shone like needles in the moonlight. And they were thin: skeleton-gaunt, bones like twigs poking through their decaying garments. For all the times Matthew had heard them feasting, they looked as if they'd starved for centuries.

Nearly gagging from the smell, Matthew crouched in the hallway just outside the door. He was too afraid of drawing attention to himself to call out, "He's not evil, not always, some things about him are good!" How could he explain to the little people how parts of his father could be loving and other parts so horrible, when he couldn't understand it himself?

They kept climbing in the window; it looked as if there were hundreds of them now, swarming around the bed, clambering onto each other's shoulders. Matthew imagined them taking Daddy apart like the man in the biology book, stripping away first the skin and then the muscles and organs, until they found the part of him that was evil. Maybe they only wanted his liver; Miss Summersong said that the liver took poisons out of the blood, and the doctor said that Daddy's liver was swollen. Matthew remembered, too, a fairy tale about a witch who stole people's livers to make magic with. But even if the little people only took Daddy's liver, he'd still be dead. Could Matthew somehow convince them to take something which could grow back—a strand of hair, a fingernail, a cell?

And then he remembered the biology book again, which told him that he'd grown from two cells, one from each of his parents, and he knew those cells must have been bad ones. Daddy was evil for drinking and Mother was evil for summoning the little people, but Matthew had helped his father get out of the house to buy liquor, and he'd called the little people before Mother had. He'd prayed that they wouldn't think he was evil, but even the prayer had only proven how bad he was, because he'd forgotten to include Nutmeg. The little people didn't want Daddy at all: Matthew was the one they'd come for.

He turned to run, knowing he was not only wicked but a coward, and the little people saw him at last and scampered to surround him before he could move. They began making a low, horrible sound, a cross between a chuckle and an idling motor, as their eyes and teeth caught glints of moonlight. The smell was unbearable. As they crowded closer Matthew tried frantically to think of some charm or spell, some magic which would drive them away, but all he could remember was his homework assignment.

"Tell me three things you like about yourself," Miss Summersong had said. Three was a number which could make powerful magic, according to any story Matthew had ever read; perhaps Miss Summersong, who knew everything else, had known that the little people would come, and had given him that odd riddle as a weapon against them.

"I like myself because Miss Summersong thinks I'm smart," Matthew whispered as the little people pressed against him. Their eyes brightened, and the chuckling grew louder.

"I like myself because I took good care of Nutmeg and didn't mean to hurt her," Matthew said desperately, shrinking away from them and thinking as hard as he could of the smell of lavender. Accidents weren't evil, Mother had said, and he'd left Nutmeg out of his prayer by accident. He'd been thinking too hard about his parents, but that couldn't be evil, could it? Could trying to protect people be evil?

One more and he might be safe, if the magic worked, if it were strong enough—what, what? He squeezed his eyes shut, trembling, certain he'd feel those teeth tearing into his flesh at any moment, and cried, "I like myself because I love Mother and Daddy!"

There was a gust of wind and stabbing cold. When he opened his eyes the little people were gone, having taken their stench and their uncanny laughter with them. In the pool of moonlight which bathed his parents' bed Mother muttered something in a dream, and Daddy began snoring very softly.

It was years before he understood what had happened. Nothing changed after that night. His father kept drinking and his mother kept nagging; the fights were as loud as ever, and Miss Summersong's books even more alluring. Nutmeg never came back, and Matthew never saw the little people again. In time, he came to believe that their visit had been nothing but a nightmare inspired by his mother's vivid, gruesome stories.

He moved away to go to college, and never moved back. He studied biology and chemistry and chose a career in research, becoming one of the wise, solitary men in white coats he had admired so as a child. He traveled to many cities and never ceased finding them beautiful and comforting; wilderness unnerved him, although he could not have said why. Nor could he have explained fully why he neither prayed nor drank, why he handled lab equipment with a care considered extraordinary even by his colleagues, why he married a woman whom he had first noticed because she smelled like lavender.

He was successful in his work and happy in his marriage. He and Molly bought a spacious house in a suburb luxurious with lawns and swimming pools, and had a daughter who grew livelier and more inquisitive with each passing year. He gave Katie the books he had loved as a child, but he wasn't displeased when she spent more time ice-skating and playing softball than doing homework. Her ability to make friends awed him. Because his daughter's childhood was happier than his own, he believed himself safe.

When Katie was sixteen she began coming home from parties later than she should have, her eyes glassy and her breath smelling of beer. Molly talked to her, gently; Matthew tried to be gentle, and failed. When Katie's grades slipped he screamed at her, and saw her withdrawing from him. When she began stealing small amounts of money he retaliated by searching her room; preoccupied with his daughter, he became careless at work. He dropped a culture dish on the lab floor one day, and couldn't understand why it took him an hour to stop shaking.

One Saturday afternoon in May when Katie had stormed out of the house, hurling curses over her shoulder, Matthew went on another search and destroy mission. He found two cans of beer stashed inside Katie's winter boots and carried them, as if they were live grenades, to the kitchen sink. His stomach clenched at the noise the liquid made running into the drain.

"No," he heard behind him, and turned to find Molly standing in the kitchen doorway. "Matthew, that won't work. She's just out buying more; you know she is. Or getting someone to buy it for her." She took a few steps closer and put a hand on his arm. "Matthew—you're doing what your mother did. You know it didn't do any good. Don't you remember?"

He pulled away from her; he didn't want to remember. For a brief, bitter moment he regretted having ever described his parents to his wife. When he spoke, his own voice sounded foreign to him. "What should I do, then?"

"Talk to me," Molly said, and he noticed for the first time how dark the circles had grown under her eyes. "You never talk anymore. Here: come here. Sit down."

She led him to the kitchen table as if he were blind. "You're scared," she said. "I'm scared. Your father died from drinking and now Katie's doing it and you can't save her any more than you could save him, and it isn't fair. But destroying yourself won't change anything. I love you as much as I love her, Matthew, and I don't know which of you is harder to live with anymore. Do you understand?"

"Don't lecture me," he said, and it was that stranger with the hoarse voice talking again, not himself at all. "I don't know what we did wrong, but I'm not going to stand by and watch her—"

"For God's sake, Matthew! We're better parents than most, and of course you're standing by and watching her. That's all you've been doing for months. Watching and yelling."

"Now you're blaming me," he said.

"No, I'm not! You're blaming yourself. You think she inherited the tendency from you and that means you have to do something about it. Well, you can't do a damn thing. Nothing you've tried has worked."

Matthew rubbed a hand over his eyes. His palms smelled of beer, and suddenly he felt ill. All those years of work, of study, of success; the beautiful home in the beautiful place, the family vacations, the piano lessons. Molly was right: he'd done everything he could think of to protect Katie, and it hadn't worked. It hadn't been good enough. He'd failed.

A breeze smelling of warm, wet earth blew in through the kitchen window, and he thought he heard a throaty chuckling noise outside. Silly, he told himself. There are no forests for miles, and it was just a dream. But suddenly his tongue tasted of garbage and rotting leaves, and he was cold despite the warmth of the day.

"Matt?" Molly said. "What's wrong?"

He couldn't look at her. He stared at his fingers, remembering the sharp pieces of butterfly slide on the schoolroom floor, the gleam of moonlight on pointed teeth. Could trying to protect people be evil? If he'd let the little people feast on his father, that winter night, would Katie have been safe?

"Matthew, your hands are shaking. What is it?"

He swallowed. "Did I ever tell you about that nightmare I had when I was a kid?" He knew he hadn't; he'd never told anyone. Why should he? He'd outgrown his mother's superstitions. It had only been a dream.

"No," Molly said. "Tell me now."

So he did, trying to laugh as he told her about his mother's stories, about Miss Summersong and Nutmeg and the freezing midwinter night when the little people had come to claim the evil in the house. "It was just a dream," he said when he was finished; and then, smelling her perfume across the table, "I think I fell in love with you because you reminded me of Miss Summersong."

"Thank you," she said gravely, and smiled. "I fell in love with you because you were the first man I'd ever met who admired bacteria and remembered the titles of all the Narnia books. Matthew, what if the little people were real?"

"If they were, it didn't do any good." The taste of garbage was gone; all he could smell now was honeysuckle. He got up and went to the window. The front yard stretched smooth and vibrant and empty to the road; a red sportscar sped by, too fast, filled with shouting teenagers. Katie, Matthew thought, his fear returning. "I drove them away with Miss Summersong's charm. I didn't let them have anything evil because I was afraid they'd hurt us. I was afraid my father wouldn't believe in them even when he saw them there, and that they'd kill him."

"I think you're wrong," she said. "I think they went away because you fed them."

"Then why didn't anything change? Why didn't the evil stop?"

"Because it wasn't evil at all, but illness and ignorance. Because the only evil you can give away is your own. Look—your grandfather gave up the behavior that was hurting him and his family, right? Well, maybe what you fed the little people that night was your *belief* that you were evil. Maybe that's what was hurting you most. Does that make sense?"

"No," he said, and heard chuckling again. He gripped the windowsill and peered outside, into the beginnings of dusk. No one was there. Go away, he thought. Go away and leave me alone. "If I gave it to them, why do I still have it?"

"Because it grew back," Molly said softly. "Like a fingernail, or a strand of hair." She came up behind him and held him for a long time, her arms around his waist and her face pressed against his shoulder. He allowed himself to be enveloped by the familiar smell of lavender, and finally he turned and kissed her.

"There's a meeting at the high school in half an hour," she said into the hollow of his breastbone. "For parents who are scared about drugs." She laughed, sounding embarrassed, and Matthew realized how hard she was working to keep her voice steady. "You know—what to look for, where to get help, that kind of thing. Do you want to come with me?"

"No," he said. He couldn't face it in public, not yet. "Come back and tell me about it."

"All right." She pulled away from him and gathered up her purse and keys. "Try not to yell at Katie if she comes home."

He nodded numbly and went back to stand, unseeing, at the kitchen window. He wondered if he could still remember the titles of all the Narnia chronicles, and found that he could. I like myself because I like good books, he thought. I like myself because I'm a good scientist. I like myself because I've been as good a parent as I knew how to be, even if it wasn't enough, even if I made too many mistakes.

It occurred to him that maybe he had loved Katie too much, been too proud of her, jinxed her somehow. "Take whatever bad stuff you want," he said aloud, speaking quietly because he felt foolish. He wondered if the neighbors could hear him through the open window. "Take away as much garbage as you can carry, but leave me what I love. Give me back what I love and I'll never ask you for anything again."

All he could smell was honeysuckle. And what good would it do, even if they were real? What could they return to him? His parents were dead, and at last he realized, aching, that Molly was right: Katie belonged only to herself. She'd have to make her own offerings.

He was very tired. He closed his eyes, leaning against the windowsill, and breathed in the smell of flowers. A dog barked in the distance, and when Matthew opened his eyes again he saw Nutmeg, as spry as she'd been on the day she vanished, trotting across the tranquil twilit lawn with a squirrel in her mouth.

VERN RUTSALA

The Muses of Rooms

Vern Rutsala is the author of seven books of poetry, including *Ruined Cities* from Carnegie-Mellon. He teaches at Lewis and Clark College in Portland, Oregon.

"The Muses of Rooms" comes from the January '90 issue of *Poetry* magazine, published in Chicago. Like the best Magical Realist fiction, it can be read and enjoyed both as fantasy and as metaphor.

—T.W.

The Muses of Rooms

VERN RUTSALA

Some of your rooms have more than
one—take the kitchen
where the dishwasher goes through
her obsessive Lady Macbeth routine—
washing, rinsing, washing—
in her own kind of meter.
And that lover of paradox, the refrigerator
keeps your food cold with heat
and gives birth to ice cubes
neat as haiku and epigrams.
They're all stealthy and silent,
calling no attention to themselves
like the one in the dining room
who spends all her time embroidering
the slow legends of tarnish
in a kind of half sleep.
And there's that closet reserved
for the muse of self-pity
and the dumbwaiter frozen between floors—
your muse of writer's block.
You find the most honest ones
in the attic—they look like faded snapshots
and clothes gone out of style,
flapper muses, bohemian muses
all black leotards and guitars
endlessly playing with the exhausted toys
of childhood—broken dolls and bicycles

that lost their way for good.
Dusty alexandrines and rhyme royal
gather here with ottava rima
and shopworn rondeaux.
The house keeps them all going—
old native meter breathing
with the furnace, sprung rhythm
creaking in the floorboards.
They hover, generously sharing space
with their cousins—lares and penates.
They go on doing their odd jobs,
that muse with bedroom eyes keeping
you asleep by pretending to be a pillow
while the others whistle odd tunes up the chimney
swirling out into the pocked darkness,
tunes you almost remember before they die.

NINA KIRIKI HOFFMAN

A Touch of the Old Lilith

In "A Touch of the Old Lilith," first published in *Women of Darkness II*, a young woman denies, then tries to come to terms with her heritage. Completely different in tone from Nina Hoffman's other story in this collection, "Coming Home," this effective story shows her versatility.

—E.D.

A Touch of the Old Lilith

NINA KIRIKI HOFFMAN

Grandma said there was a touch of the old Lilith in all the Meander women, and she flexed her finger, beckoning, to prove it, saying that under the right circumstances the bones of one's finger became the spine of a snake. "Lilith was the first tempter, who took men one step away from God. She offered them the poison of death. Lilith was a Meander, and you's a Meander woman, little Clea. Don't you forget it."

I didn't understand the connection between Lilith and snakes until later, but I didn't forget anything Grandma told me the summer I turned eleven.

That summer comes back to me whenever I smell aromatic pipe tobacco or violet water. Grandma and I spent a lot of time on the porch together in the evenings while waiting for the air to cool enough for us to sleep. She patted violet water on her throat when the sun beat down, saying violets only grew in shadows, so the scent was cool. She smoked fragrant tobacco in a lady's pipe and blew the smoke at me, saying it would help keep off the mosquitos. She sat in the ladderback rocker like a little old toad, her short white hair boiling around her head, her gray eyes bright as thick summer stars. Her fingersnaps particularly pleased me; my mother had slammed all her fingers in a door before I was born, and her knuckles were scarred, their movements restricted.

Grandma was full of strange tales. Two of them in particular she told me over and over—the touch of Old Lilith one, with no explanations, and the bogey one—and I was a long time getting to sleep each night because of them that summer. She came to live with us just after her house burned down and Grandpa died. Daddy griped about that. Mom was the youngest of seven kids. "She has so many children she doesn't know what to do—why pick on us?" said Daddy. But our house had a guest room, so Grandma came to us first.

I asked Grandma about the fire. She said the police asked questions about why she wasn't home at two in the morning—when a neighbor first smelled smoke and saw flames, but too late to save Grandpa. Grandma was out picking flowers. "Phases of the moon," she said, waving a copy of the *Farmer's Almanac* at the police. She had carried it with her the night of the fire. "Got to harvest in the dark of the moon. Poor old Harvey—if only he didn't have that 'rithmatic in his bones—couldn't take the dew chill, otherwise he might have been out with me and alive today."

The last time I saw Grandpa Harvey had been the family Christmas party when I was still ten. His eyes had white shields over them and he couldn't see, and his hands shook. Grandma whispered to me that the shields saved him from seeing all the wickedness in the world; they were called cataracts, which meant waterfalls which meant cleansing and tears. I never understood that either. Mom said Grandpa had been blind since before she was born.

Investigation proved it to have been an electrical fire, bad wiring in the kitchen walls, nobody's fault. Everybody said I was too young to go to a funeral, so they left me with Lizzy Burns next door when they went off to bury Grandpa. When they got back, Mom's eyes were swollen and the tip of her nose was red, but Grandma looked just as chipper as ever.

That night, when I couldn't sleep, I snuck outside and crept around the side of the house until I was just under Mom's and Daddy's bedroom window. I had had the sense all summer that everybody was protecting me from things without telling me what I was supposed to be afraid of, and I hated not knowing, so I was always seeking out information any way I could. Somehow when I turned eleven in the spring, I figured out the whole world was in cahoots to keep everything quiet, but it was time for me to know. Wasn't I almost a teenager? When I was ten everybody still thought I was a baby, but it was time for that to change now, whether the grown-ups thought so or not.

Mom and Daddy were talking in the dark. "Poor old Pa," said Mom. "Never hurt a soul."

"Probably a merciful release," said Dad. "I would have done anything to get away from your mother. Maybe even set the fire myself. I might do it yet."

Mom said it was lucky the evidence was so clear, otherwise Grandma made a great suspect, her not shedding a tear over Grandpa or grieving over the loss of the house.

Daddy said, "Will you cry when I'm gone?"

"Peter, you know I will," said Mom, her voice tender.

"Oh, so you're planning to outlive me, are you?"

When I was younger I wished Daddy had a sense of humor like Mom's, but he never did. If he had said that with a smile in his voice, it would have been all right. But he hadn't.

I leaned my chin on my knees and waited for Mom's reply. Around me her carefully tended rose bushes whispered to each other, the flowers spilling a heavy rich scent on the night air. The dark, moist earth chilled me through my thin cotton nightgown and the soles of my feet. After a moment, Mom's voice came again, drifting out the open window of their bedroom.

"We Meander women are long-lived," said Mom in her slow, flat, Scriptures-reading voice.

"You Meander women," Daddy said, his voice sneering. "You sound like your mother. Why do you call yourself Meander? Your maiden name was Stone."

He was off, telling her again how stupid she was.

And when he had finished, run out of voice, she murmured, "Hush." I heard the sheets rustle, and the slide of flesh on flesh, like the sound a snake's belly makes as it crawls across tiles.

I resolved for the fifty-sixth time never, ever, to get married. I wished I hadn't lain awake thinking about the long-fingered bogey that hid under girls' beds and reached up to inject them with zombie juice the instant their breathing slowed in sleep. "When you wake up the next morning, you feel dead," Grandma said. "The bogey whispers the orders for the day and you follow them. You never make another move unless he tells you to. Nobody else notices anything wrong with you, and you can't tell nobody about it." Then she laughed. "I once knew a girl who was bogey-bit and nobody found out till sixteen years later. Nothing to do but kill her, poor thing. They just get too used to being zombies; real life ain't natural to 'em anymore, even if you *could* clean the juice out of their blood. It builds up in the brain."

Between Grandma's stories and Mom's and Dad's fights that summer, I didn't sleep much at all. I was even relieved when I started seventh grade in the fall, though I was at a new school with a lot of older kids at it, when I had gotten used to being in the most senior class. Grandma moved out the week before school started. I thought Daddy must have had something to do with that; he had been nagging Mom about Grandma since the fire. I learned later that Mom wanted Grandma gone just as much as Daddy did. Grandma went to live with my Uncle Kyle, a bachelor who managed an apartment complex—he fixed up a basement for her, and Daddy said that was only appropriate.

With hard work and a lot of reading, I managed to close up my memories over all Grandma's stories, but they still lay under the floor of my mind, like seeds buried deep and forgotten but full of growth potential, with the right sort of care.

When Daddy died two years later, and Grandma came to the funeral, I looked at her in her black clothes and little slivers of summer memory struggled free. She kissed my cheek, and her violet scent brought my eleventh summer back in a rush.

That night as I lay in bed, I bit the heels of my hands, trying to cry for my father. True to her word, my mother had cried for him, but I had not been able to; the funeral seemed to be happening on television, with me a distant watcher. So after I crawled in between the cold sheets and turned out the light, I concentrated on the times Daddy took me to the park down the street and taught me how to catch tadpoles with a pet store fishnet. I remembered him buying me a baseball glove when I was twelve, and playing catch in the yard with me. That eased my mind somewhat; nobody at school played with me much, so it was nice to have someone to come home to—when Daddy was in the mood.

Consciously I reached for what had been my favorite memory of Daddy: when I was nine, he came into the room where I was sitting on the floor, watching some show on television. I couldn't remember the show, I just remembered him sitting on the couch behind me, stroking my hair gently. I leaned against his knee and closed my eyes, feeling his hand on my head, a safe caress. I loved him completely in that moment, but it never happened again.

Though I had cherished these memories of him even while he was alive, they refused to stay with me that night. Instead I relived Grandma's summer at our house, her snapping her index finger at me like a striking snake, her old voice murmuring to me like the buzz of a summer fly on a winter window, the words slipping into my mind before I could shut them out. That night I dreamed, not of my father, but of the bogey under the bed, and I woke with a scream in my throat, lodged there like a bone.

A year later, my mother remarried. His name was Patrick, and he was large and loud and friendly, completely different from my small dark father. Grandma came to the wedding. She wore the same clothes she had worn to my father's funeral, and she shook her head no through the whole ceremony. "Eh, Mother, I saw you objecting," Patrick said at the reception after kissing Grandma's cheek.

"I'm an old woman, boy," she said—or I thought she said; she might have said "bogey." "Old women get shaky."

I didn't understand why Danny invited me to the senior prom. Nobody had asked me out on a date during my entire high school career, and I was satisfied with that; whenever anyone came near, I felt somewhere within me the lidless, ever-open eyes of snakes looking out at them, waiting to strike. I let those snakes look out through my eyes, and people always backed away.

I thought Danny must have been dared to do it, but facts were hard to come by later, when he was gone. I only know that when he took my hand and led me out on the floor for the first slow dance, I was more terrified than I ever had been before. His arms around me, his hands at the back of my waist, where I couldn't see them. My own hands out of sight behind his neck, where my fingers might have been flexing any moment, without my volition. I felt intensely aware of everything, the fragile orchid touching my wrist, the heat of Danny through his suit, his hands like solid sunlight warming my back, his smell, a mixture of aftershave and an oily human scent I had never been so close to before. The music we walked on, as though it were a staircase. Fear was so strong in me I felt as if the ground had vanished. My hands shook like Grandpa Harvey's had. I felt sweat trickle down my spine.

They said later it was heart attack. His family had a history. But never so young before.

There was a year between high school and college when I ran away. I chased forgetting. When I found it, I came home again.

Being the first one to arrive Monday mornings, I got to wheel the cart away from the library drop chute and check in all the returned books. As I pulled due-date cards out of the pockets and replaced them with check-out cards, I noticed a name: Jeffry Chase. He had checked out a whole stack of books on photography.

I remembered I had encountered a stack like this the week before, books on darkroom techniques, with his name on the check-out cards. This week, I found big picture books about the work of Diane Arbus, Eugene Atget, Richard Avedon, Edmund Weston. I paused, opened the books one at a time, looked at an image in each. Here was a man, wife and large-headed baby, all so much closer to the camera than they would be to a person in the normal course of conversation that their imperfections seemed glaring. Here was a street in Paris at the turn of the century, the road surfaced with wet paving stones, the buildings faced with wrinkled and torn posters and, in the misty distance, a bare-branched tree; here, an ultra-slender woman from the sixties with black kohl heavy around her eyes, her hair cut in a pageboy, her clothes short and stark; here, a bell pepper, photographed in black and white, its smooth curves sensuous and startling.

I closed the books slowly and put them on the filing cart, wondering about Jeffry. I tried to picture him in my mind, though I hadn't checked out any of these books for him. Was he a little old man, taking up a new hobby? Trying to connect with a past he remembered but could not picture clearly? Was he a teenager doing a project for high school? Maybe he had been given a list of books to check out. Maybe he was in college, like I was, doing a photographic internship like my library one.

My supervisor Jenna came in then and got mad at me for forgetting to start the coffee and for sitting over books with my eyes unfocused when there was work to be done.

But later, when a young man came to the desk, his hair curly black and his eyes the color of amethysts, I suspected him of being Jeffry; of course, he also had a stack of large photo books. I thought if I looked as gorgeous as he did, I would probably be interested in photography, too, wanting to preserve my own image in as many ways as possible, and studying which images had survived from the past.

I was the only one at the desk when he came and put down his books and a red backpack. Jenna had taken first lunch, leaving me in charge. I knew that, and still, when he smiled at me, I looked behind me to see if there was someone else who deserved that smile. I went over to the stack of due-date cards and offered him a timid smile in response.

"Hello," he said as I opened his books and took cards out of them. "I'm Jeff Chase, and I've been waiting three weeks for this moment."

"Pardon me?"

"Watching you work, hoping the moment would come when I could speak with you."

I touched my necklace, an amber pendant Grandma had sent me for my sixteenth birthday. I felt an urge to look behind me again, certain this fairy-tale prince must be talking to someone else.

"Why?" I said, and would have stepped on my own foot if I had been someone else watching me, to stop me from being so gauche.

"You have a certain beauty—not just in the common run, you know. I was hoping I could talk with you—ask you—I know this must sound like a line—if I could take pictures of you. I'm trying to put together a portfolio."

"Pictures? Of me?" My tone was full of doubt.

He gave me that smile again, his eyes catching light. "So many people say they'll break my camera. It amazes me! Look." He opened the outer pocket on his backpack and took out a snapshot. I looked at a face leaning on a hand, a spill of chestnut hair framing the features. Her pale eyes dreamed, and a smile touched one edge of her wide mouth. She had dark curved brows.

I got an eerie feeling from the picture, the sensation that it was a fossil found locked in a rock, and I wondered why it struck that chord. I turned the picture sideways. No clues.

Suddenly I realized I was looking at myself, a me I never saw in the mirror, where I always focused first on my blemishes, and second on getting the eyeliner on straight. I stared up at the man.

"I took that with my little Pentax three weeks ago. Would you model for me? I can't pay much, but I'll give you proof sheets. Maybe a few prints of the better shots."

I swallowed my first no, and thought a minute. He must have been nuts. Why would anyone look twice at me, especially a man like this? But this picture, maybe there was a me I didn't know how to look for. If we could keep the camera between us, we should be safe. It might be fun. I might see someone I wouldn't recognize who was also a part of me.

"Saturday?" I said.

He had some clothes he gave me to wear, a black dress with gold embroidery, a little large on me, and a black velvet cloche hat. He had asked me to bring black tights if I had them, and black high heels. I found some tights in a suitcase in the closet, among clothes I had been thinking about getting rid of but couldn't bear giving away. I brought the tights and my church shoes.

We talked about makeup; I never met a man who knew anything about makeup before. He had some rice powder he said Geisha girls used to pale their complexions. I sat in a chair with a towel over the black and gold dress and closed my eyes as he brushed the powder across my face, another strange caress, light as the touch of a butterfly's wing on my cheek. With expert hands he outlined my eyes in black, touched pale pink on my lips.

He handed me a mirror and again I saw someone I didn't know. My sense of myself as fossil returned, ancient and somehow horrible. My eyes looked clear and bottomless, my mouth silent, my expression remote. I could not smile at myself. In some buried corner of my mind, my grandmother's index finger snapped.

Jeffry took me to the graveyard.

He positioned me between the marble pillars of a Greek-style mausoleum. "The contrast between cold stone and warm flesh," he said, smiling at me. I looked at my pale hand against the white marble and thought he was right: my hand looked translucent, but it had its own beauty against the solid rock, a misty, living reality.

As Jeffry told me to turn and lean, to look toward the sky and think of flying, to glance at the ground and think of autumn, I felt disturbed on some other level. What were we really doing here, with me dressed as a corpse in mourning and posing with lambs and little angels on the graves of long-dead children? I leaned my cheek on a lichen-laced rough-hewn stone, smelling centuries locked in rock, and the acid tang of molding oak leaves. I listened to Jeffry's camera click. If he really wanted to contrast life with death, I should have been wearing red, or green. I felt I had wandered into someone else's dream.

The day was overcast. "Pearl light," Jeffry called it. "A diffuse, indirect light that softens edges." The grass and earth stayed wet with yesterday's rain; I shivered, remembering Grandpa Harvey, burned to death because he couldn't take the dew chill. Jeffry asked me to kneel on a grave beside a tombstone that bore a photographic tile depicting a little dead girl. Her face beamed above the date of her death, fifty years earlier. I touched the tile, wondering about parents marooning their child's image in this death camp. My memory jogged. I wondered if this child had died of bogey-bite.

"Can you get her expression on your face?" Jeffry asked.

"No," I said, standing up. "No."

He studied me for a minute, then nodded. "Let's go get some coffee. I bet you're cold."

In the coffeeshop I went to the women's room and splashed water on my face, hoping I could wash away the stranger Jeffry had photographed. I scrubbed my face with the gritty, pink institutional-scented soap. Then I looked at myself in the mirror. The warm water and the soap brought the blood back to my cheeks, and my lips looked dark pink again, but my eyes still frightened me. The day before, I had believed them blue, but this day they looked steel gray. I stared at myself but felt as if someone else were studying me.

When I got back to the table, Jeffry looked at me. "Coffee's not enough," he said. "Can I take you out to dinner tonight?"

The chill began to seep out of me. "All right," I said. "But this time I get to choose my own clothes."

He brought some black-and-white prints with him when he came to pick me up that night. I glanced at them, then put them back inside the envelope, not wanting to think about them. I left them on the table by my front door, and we went out to a place with a wine list, and napkins on top of two layers of tablecloths. Jeffry watched me during the meal. He liked how I looked, in my jewel-red dress, my hair in a chignon. I could sense his intense appreciation. It felt wonderful. It scared me.

I clung tight to my hard-earned forgetting.

We went to his apartment after supper. When he touched me, it was with reverence, and even in the heat that followed, I had the sense that he worshiped me.

I went home for Thanksgiving. I wanted Jeffry to come, but his mother wanted him at her house, and it was too soon, he said, to tell his mother about us. "I've never missed a Thanksgiving with Mother," he said. "I don't want her getting suspicious."

Grandma was at Mom's when I got there. "Hello, little Clea," she said to me as she always did, though I was taller than she. She looked exactly the same age as she had when I was eleven, and this time she was wearing colors—a purple and magenta dress, and a straw hat with a large droopy brim and sprays of fake cherries on it.

Patrick greeted me with a big kiss on the cheek and took the pumpkin pie I had bought at Safeway the day before. His bright hair had started to gray, and he was thickening through the middle. He vanished with the pie toward the kitchen. I smelled the rich holiday smell of turkey baking, and wondered why I didn't feel cheerful.

After grace, Patrick carved the turkey and Mom served, silent. I ate a lot of everything, following some instinct I didn't understand—I ate until I felt sick, without really tasting the food. No one talked during the meal, but afterward, when Patrick went in to watch football, Grandma and Mom and I cleared and started cleaning up. I took Jeff's pictures out of my satchel and showed them to Mom and Grandma. "My boyfriend took these," I said. He had tacked prints of me up all over his apartment, so I was getting used to them. "I wanted to bring him, but he couldn't make it."

They were both rock silent as they looked at the black-and-white photographs of my cool perfection among the tombstones. Mom's eyes seemed to grow shallow. Grandma said, "Oh, child. Oh, child." She reached out and took Mom's hand in hers, stroking the scarred knuckles. A tear spilled down her cheek. "I tried to give you everything, little Clea, but I couldn't. So the killing starts."

"What killing, Grandma?" I felt disturbed, as if I knew what she was talking about but didn't want to admit it. An image of Danny's face surfaced in my mind. I drowned it again, a reflex. Grandma had never known about Danny's death.

"Killing you into something other than what you are," she said. "Why can't people leave people alone?"

"Oh, Ma, you know we're put on this earth to be something to somebody," said my mother, pulling her hand away from Grandma and shoving both hands into her apron pockets.

"Don't you do what your Mama done, Clea," Grandma said. "Don't you help him kill you."

"What do you mean?" I asked. My face felt hot now, both with the meal and the tension. I felt sick.

"I'm going for a nap now," said Grandma. She blinked three times and walked out of the kitchen.

"Mom—"

"She's an evil woman," said my mother.

"What?" I asked. I had never heard my mother speak with more conviction.

"She filled my head with tales when I was little. She told us stories every night. Sometimes she told us Bible stories, but she talked as if the people were all relatives. She told you stories that summer, didn't she?"

I remembered. "Yes," I said, feeling again the overpowering dread that kept me lying sleepless in my bed night after night.

"That's why I begged Kyle to take her away. I didn't want her filling you up with all those evil thoughts. I didn't want you to do what I did, and what Jan and Suzle did in their own ways."

I hadn't heard Aunt Suzle's name since I was thirteen. I was looking at a picture book of Mom's family, laughing because my aunt and my mother and my four uncles looked so strange as children. There was another girl in many of the pictures. "That's your Aunt Suzle," Mom had said. "She's dead."

Mom stared at the floor. "Ma told us—oh, Clea, you're too young to hear this. I don't want you to be scared the way I was."

I looked at the pictures spread out on the kitchen table. In one of them, I stared straight into the camera. Behind me, a stone angel prayed with lowered lids. "Mom, if you don't tell me, I'll make up things worse than any reality," I said.

"I don't know if you could," she said. She stood still a moment, staring through the kitchen table. She sighed. "She told us we were powerful women and if we ever married we'd kill our husbands on our wedding nights. She said we had snakes inside us—in our fingers. And she told all the boys to go out and find wives. Then she laughed. We always knew she was scared of the boys, anyway, once they got taller than her. It was like telling them to go find someone to kill them. She said Lilith was Adam's first wife, but Adam didn't like Lilith because she wanted to be on top. Ma said God was a bully, and Lilith was the only one with integrity. Adam wanted women to serve him, but Lilith walked upright— till he rejected her, then she came back as a snake. She brought death to everyone. And there's a touch of the old Lilith in all Meander women." Her voice came out higher, like a little girl repeating a catechism. Then she began to laugh. "It's so stupid," she gasped, and laughed and laughed. "Hearing it out loud. It's so stupid, Clea!"

I got her a glass of water. She sat on a kitchen chair and laughed her throat raw. After gulping water, she calmed down again. "It was stupid, but it hurt us, because we were children and didn't know any better. Suzle fell in love with a boy when she was sixteen. She was so afraid she'd hurt him, and she loved him so much, she killed herself." Mom stared up at me, her eyes wide, her pupils large and dark. "I found her," she said. "She was lying in the bathtub and she had these wounds on her wrists. She didn't bleed to death, Clea. She poisoned herself. The wounds looked like snakebites."

I sat down, too, feeling sick. "What did Aunt Jan do?"

"Jan became a ballerina. She starves herself, and stays away from men. Her life for art. I wish you'd known her when she was younger, Clea. She was such a funny girl, a little bit plump, but with a wicked tongue and a wild eye. Then when she got to be fifteen or so, she went through this phase where she had a crush on movie stars. She was crazy about James Dean and Steve McQueen. She plastered her walls with pictures out of movie magazines. But she'd been dancing since she was six. One day I came home and all the pictures had come down, the walls were white in her room, and she didn't eat anything anymore except a couple lettuce leaves and a few spoonfuls of cottage cheese. She's saving mankind by staying away from them."

I remembered the one Christmas my Aunt Jan came out. She was pale and thin, with circles under her eyes, and she couldn't seem to look at me without wincing. "You had a girl," I heard her say to Mom. "It just goes on and on."

"What did you do, Mom?" I asked.

"Oh, I was practical! When I fell in love with Peter, I thought through all Mom's stories and figured out that the only real harm I could do him was with my fingers. I used to play piano, you know." She took her hands out of her apron pockets and stared at them. "Snakes' heads. If I could just rid myself of the snakes' heads. I propped open the coal cellar door with a stick, then put my hands on the doorsill and knocked the stick away. I broke all my fingers. How I screamed! It hurt for months, but I smiled through it all. Peter married me while my hands were still in bandages. No wedding ring." She smiled down at her crippled hands, her face softened with memories.

After a long moment, she glanced at me. "We're only human, after all, Clea. Ma fed us a pack of lies. I wanted to save you from that, and I did the best I could. I'm so glad you've found a boyfriend."

"But Mom—" I looked down at the pictures. Had Jeff photographed some real piece of me I didn't want to believe in? Who was this haunted woman? I picked up a picture of me next to a small pale angel, my pale eyes looking at her, my hand raised to her. My fingers looked curved in a gradual arc that defied human bones.

"Oh, come on. Do you think models in magazines are anything like their pictures? Your boy seems to have a weird sense of beauty, but you aren't what he makes you look like," she said. She gathered all the pictures together, the top one face down so none of them were visible, and put them in my satchel. "Now, come on. We have dishes to do and food to put away. Do you want some turkey to take home?"

Jeffry came to my apartment when we both got back from our Thanksgiving vacations.

Grandma had taken me shopping Friday morning, braving the sale crowds at the Plaza. I found myself a little afraid of her, and I wasn't pleased with her gift to me—a silver apple on a chain. But she insisted. "Don't take away an old woman's happiness," she said, tugging on my hair to get me to bend over far enough so she could fasten the pendant around my neck. "I had seven children, and you're the only granddaughter I got, little Clea. Leave me do things for you."

"Am I the last Meander woman?" I asked her.

"No, no," she said. We stood still in the center of the mall corridor between stores, and chattering people streamed past us on both sides, but I could hear her clearly. "There's no end to Meander women. Maybe every woman is a Meander woman."

We got home around noon, and I had a last family lunch with Mom and Patrick and Grandma. Then I drove the two-and-a-half hours back to my apartment. I remembered applying to colleges all over the state, but when I got accepted at the university and decided it was my college of choice, Mom seconded me. "Close enough to visit, but not close enough for me to look over your shoulder all the time," she had said.

I sat in my yard sale armchair, all the lights in the apartment off, my overnight bag on the living room floor in front of me, as daylight faded beyond the gauze curtains. I held my hand closed around the silver apple. It warmed to my flesh.

Presently I heard Jeffry's key in the lock. I wanted to jump up and turn on some lights, maybe put water on for coffee, but I waited. "Clea? You back yet?" he asked, flicking on the entry light. He carried red roses in rustling cellophane; beads of water shone on his hair. I realized I had been hearing the quiet dance of rain on shingles for some time.

"Yes," I said.

"Why so dark? Are you okay? Did something happen at your mother's?"

"I'm just tired."

He turned on the living room lights and came to me, setting the roses in my lap. Stepping back, he looked at me, and I considered my appearance: my chestnut hair spilling over the wide lapels of my long gray coat; my face, undoubtedly pale; the spray of roses as dark as fall apples, with its accompanying haze of white babies' breath and dark green fern, splashing across my lap; and black tights and black Chinese shoes, under a forest-green velvet dress. If he had brought one of his cameras, Jeffry would be focusing now, trying to decide whether to use a flash, and what to bounce it off.

He smiled at me. "Shall I put water on for coffee?"

"Please."

He walked toward the kitchenette, glancing back at me twice. His smile was almost smug. I felt a flick of anger, like a little bruise inside. Did he think because he liked the way I looked that he had created me?

Hadn't he? Didn't we choose this steel gray coat—"the color of your eyes"— together? Hadn't he bought me this green velvet dress at a second-hand shop, and didn't I drag these tights out of an old suitcase because he asked me to?

I lifted the roses, crackling in their cellophane shroud, and sniffed them, but they proved scentless. As I touched the lip-soft petals, I remembered my childhood resolve never to marry.

"Don't you want to put those in water?" Jeffry asked, coming back and sitting on the couch across from me.

I went to the kitchen and retrieved my yard sale vase, a strange twist of blue-and-clear glass as long as my forearm. As I ran water into it I glanced back at Jeffry. "Thank you for the flowers," I said. I turned off the water, unwrapped the roses, and inserted them into the vase.

"They reminded me of you. I was glad to have something nice to think about, after that turkey dinner with my mother."

Holding his roses, I stood and studied him. His gaze seemed fixed on the ceiling. "Rough?" I asked.

"It's the same every year," he said, and pressed his face into his hands. After a moment, he ran his hands through his hair, startling raindrops loose, then stared at his wet hands as if they were bloodstained. "She's done so much for me," he told his hands. "I know she loves me. I don't understand why I feel terrible after I see her. She raised me all by herself, you know, and she paid my way through college, and she loves my photography; she supports my choices. I hate her knowing what I do. I don't want her to like it, because then it isn't mine. I don't want her ever to find out about you. Oh, Clea, I know how that sounds, but I just feel—she would steal you from me, too."

"Hush," I said. I set the vase on the counter behind me and walked to him. He stood up. I buried my face in his shoulder, hugging him. He smelled of wet wool, and male animal, and clean wet human hair, but other odors were trapped in his shirt—cigarette smoke and violet water; instantly Grandma was somewhere in the room with us.

He must have felt my arms tighten. "What?" he whispered.

Paralyzed, I tried to sense my fingers on his back. Were they curved, or straight? If I looked in the mirror, would that fossil self show in my face, full of ancient purpose that had nothing to do with me? I wished all the lights were off. Perhaps then my identity would rest totally in my thoughts.

Jeffry knew me as image, though.

I let go of him, putting my hands behind my back. "Let's go to bed." He would take off the shirt and drape it over a chair, leaving his mother and my grandmother out of it. I could lose all these thoughts and live just under the surface of my skin, and we would climb the mountain together—

"You look so strange tonight," he said, and then the teakettle went off. He went into the kitchenette. "Still want coffee?"

"No—unless you do—"

He took the kettle off the heat and came back out to me. We turned off the living room light and retreated to my bedroom together.

I lay awake listening to his deep, even breathing, staring at a narrow slice of streetlight on the ceiling. Leaf shadows danced across the light, responding to a silent wind. I was blinking, ready to fall asleep, when I saw my own hands rise in the air. Silhouetted against the dim light, I saw my index fingers lash out, fluid movement that looked humanly impossible. I couldn't feel my hands at all; they seemed to belong to someone else.

In that state between dream and waking, I had no feelings about what I witnessed, except a sleepy wonder. Jeffry murmured in his sleep, and my hands, of their own volition, reached toward him.

Waking washed over me like a bucketful of cold water; I was across the room in an instant, the wood floor cold against my bare feet, goosebumps rising along my arms and hackles on the back of my neck.

I went into the bathroom and pulled the chain to turn on the light.

In the blind time before my eyes adjusted, I felt utterly silly and young. I knew I had imagined everything, and it was all Grandma's fault. I closed the toilet lid, put a towel on top, and sat down, studying my hands. They looked very pink and human in the bare-bulb light, and beautiful: I had always loved my slender-fingered hands. It was just a dream; if I had been alone in the house, I would have turned on the radio, gotten out a book, and closeted the fears again, drifting into a quieter sleep.

Like I had been doing so often lately.

I flexed my forefingers. They formed three sides of a bent rectangle. I sighed, and felt tension easing out of my shoulders.

My right forefinger whipped out as though it were as spineless as rope. It struck the side of the sink, leaving a drop of clear, glistening liquid on the white porcelain.

The breath coming from my throat had an edge of voice to it, the shadow of sobs. I thought of Aunt Suzle, entombing herself in bathroom white, mastering her forefingers enough to make them strike her own wrists—was it involuntary, or could one control it? I thought of Grandpa Harvey, whose eyes had been milky and whose mind wandered. Would a touch of venom only half kill? I thought of Grandma whipping her fingers at my four uncles, scaring them all into bachelorhood.

I thought of Jeffry, lying defenseless in my bed. If I went to the living room and finished out the night on the couch, he would surely wonder when he woke alone. And I would not tell him about my strange heritage, though I thought he must know, somehow, considering the contexts he chose to picture me in.

I thought about my favorite bread knife, with its serrated edge. If I just decapitated my fingers—cut off the first knuckle—would that suffice?

I felt cold and sad. I rooted an old cosmetics case out from under the sink, and found two Ace bandages inside, from sprained ankles in my past. I wound the bandages around my fingers, mummywrapping them, leaving only the thumbs free, until I felt constricted and mittened and safe. Then I crept into bed, keeping my back to Jeffry and curling my wrapped hands against my stomach.

"You're cold," he whispered, and he hugged me. His warmth felt comforting. I closed my eyes, and began to drift off to sleep.

Just as the world behind my eyelids began to gyrate in slow, hypnotic loops, I felt the tiny cold prick of a needle. Before my mind stilled, I remembered my grandmother's other favorite story from my eleventh summer.

We moved to New York two years later, the gallery demands for Jeff's work were so great. New York has graveyards dating back centuries.

Jeff's most famous picture of me depicts me as Ophelia, floating with eyes closed in shallow water, my hair rayed out about my head, and flowers huddled in the folds of my pale gauze gown. Only I know that within the long slender hands folded on my chest I hold my grandmother's apple.

DAVID B. SILVA
The Calling

Until a couple of years ago, David B. Silva—although his fiction has been appearing in various magazines and anthologies—was primarily known for his editorship of *The Horror Show*. The prestigious magazine's last issue came out this past spring, giving Silva more time to write.

As in Dyan Sheldon's "The Dream," the true horror of this story comes from an inexorable physical process, rather than the supernatural, although there may be an element of the supernatural in "The Calling." It appeared in the anthology *Borderlands*.

—E.D.

The Calling

DAVID B. SILVA

It never stops.

The whistle.

The sound is hollow, rising from a cork ball enclosed by red plastic. His mother no longer has the strength to blow hard—the cancer has made certain of that—so the sound comes out as a soft song, like the chirring of a cricket somewhere off in another part of the house, just barely audible. But there. Always unmistakably there.

Blair buries his head beneath his pillow. He feels like a little boy again, trying to close out the world because he just isn't ready to face up to what is out there. Not yet. Maybe never, he thinks. How do you ever face up to something like cancer? It never lets you catch up.

It's nearly three o'clock in the morning now.

And just across the hall . . .

Even with his eyes closed, he has a perfect picture of his mother's room: the lamp on her nightstand casting a sickly gray shadow over her bed, the blankets gathered at her feet. Behind her, leaning against the wall, an old ironing board serves as a makeshift stand for the IV the nurse was never able to get into his mother's veins. And the television is on. And the bars on the side of the bed are up to prevent her from falling out. In his mind, Blair sees it all. Much too clearly.

He wraps himself tighter in the pillow.

The sound from the television is turned down, but he still thinks he can hear a scene from *Starsky and Hutch* squealing from somewhere across the hallway.

Then the whistle.

A thousand times he has heard it calling him . . . at all hours of the night . . . when she is thirsty . . . when she needs to go to the bathroom . . . when she needs to be moved to a new position . . . when she is in pain. A thousand times. He hears the whistle, the soft whirring call, coming at him from everywhere now.

It is the sound of squealing tires from the street outside his bedroom window. It is the high-pitched hum of the dishwasher, of the television set, of the refrigerator when it kicks on at midnight.

Everywhere.

He has grown to hate it.

And he has grown to hate himself for hating it.

An ugly thought comes to mind: *why . . . doesn't she succumb? Why hasn't she died by now?* It's not the first time he's faced himself with this question, but lately it seems to come up more and more often in his mind. Cancer is not an easy thing to watch. It takes a person piece by piece . . . .

"My feet are numb."

"Numb?"

"Like walking on sandpaper."

"From the chemo?"

"I don't know."

"Maybe . . ." Blair said naively, "maybe your feet will feel better after the chemo's over." He had honestly believed that it would turn out that way. When the chemo stopped, then so would her nausea and her fatigue and her loss of hair. And the worst of the side effects *had* stopped, for a while. But the numbness in her feet . . . that part had stayed on, an ugly scar left over from a body pumped full of dreadful things with dreadful names like doxorubicin and dacarbazine and vinblastine. Chemicals you couldn't even pronounce. It wasn't long before she began to miss a step here and there, and soon she was having to guide herself down the hallway with one hand pressed against the wall.

"Sometimes I can't even feel them," she once told him, a pained expression etched into the lines of her face.

She knows, Blair had thought at the time. *She knows she's never going to dance again. The one thing she loves most in the world, and it's over for her.*

The heater kicks on.

There's a vent under the bed where he's trying to sleep. It makes a familiar, almost haunting sound, and for an instant, he can't be sure if he's hearing the soft, high-pitched hum of the whistle. He lifts his head, listens. There's a hush that reminds him of a hot summer night when it's too humid to sleep. But the house seems at peace, he decides.

She's sleeping, he tells himself in a whisper. *Finally sleeping.*

For too long, the endless nights have haunted him with her cancerous likeness. She is like a butterfly: so incredibly delicate. She's lying in bed, her eyes half closed, her mouth hung open. Five feet, seven inches tall and not quite ninety pounds. The covers are pulled back slightly, her nightgown is unbuttoned and the outline of her ribs resembles a relief map.

She's not the same person he used to call his mother.

It's been ages since he's seen that other person. Before the three surgeries. Before the chemotherapy. Before the radiation treatments. Before he finally locked up his house and moved down state to care for her . . .

*   *   *

She cried the first time she fell. It happened in her bedroom, early one morning while he was making breakfast. He heard a sharp cry, and when he found her, her legs were folded under like broken wings. She didn't have the strength to climb back to her feet. For a moment, her face was frozen behind a mask of complete surprise. Then suddenly she started crying.

"Are you hurt?"

She shook her head, burying her face in her hands.

"Here, let me help you up."

"No." She motioned him away.

He retreated a step, maybe two, staring down at her, studying her, *trying* to put himself in her position. It occurred to him that she wasn't upset because of the fall—that wasn't the reason for the tears—she was crying because suddenly she had realized the ride was coming to an end. The last curve of the roller coaster had been rounded and now it was winding down once and for all. No more corkscrews. No more quick drops. No more three-sixties. Just a slow, steady deacceleration until the ride came to a final standstill. Then it would be time to get off. The fall . . . marked the beginning of the end.

It had been a harsh realization for both of them.

He began walking with her after that, guiding her one step at a time from her bedroom to the kitchen, from the kitchen to the living room, from the living room to the bathroom. A week or two later, she was using a four-pronged cane. A week or two after that, she was using a wheelchair.

Everything ran together those few short weeks, a kaleidoscope of forfeitures, one after the other, all blended together until he could hardly recall a time when she had been healthy and whole. . . .

She's going to die.

Blair has known that for a long time now.

She's going to die, but . . .

but . . .

how long is it going to take?

It seems like forever.

A car passes by his bedroom window. It's been raining lightly and the slick whine of the tires reminds him of that other sound, the one he's come to hate so much. He hates it because there's nothing he can do now. There's no going back, no making things better. All he can do is watch . . . and wait . . . and try not to lose his sanity to the incessant call of the whistle.

He bought the whistle for her nearly two and a half weeks ago in the sporting goods section of the local Target store. A cheap thing, made of plastic and a small cork ball. She wears it around her neck, dangling from the end of a thin nylon cord. Once, when it became tangled in the pillowcase, she nearly choked on the cord. But he refuses to let her take it off. It's the only way he has of keeping in touch with her at night. Unless he doesn't sleep. But he's already feeling guilty about the morning he found her sleeping on the floor in the living room. . . .

*　*　*

When he went to bed—sometime around 1:30 or 2:00 in the morning—she'd been sleeping comfortably on the couch, and it seemed kinder not to disturb her. Seven hours later, after dragging himself out of the first sound night's sleep in weeks, he found her sitting on the floor.

"Jesus, Mom."

She was sitting in an awkward position, her legs folded sideways, one arm propped up on the edge of the couch, serving as a pillow. No blanket. Nothing on her feet to keep them from getting cold. And to think—she had spent the night like that.

He knelt next to her.

"Mom?"

Her eyes opened lazily. It wasn't terribly rational, but he held out a distant hope that she'd been able to sleep through most of the night. "I'm sorry," she said drowsily. "I couldn't get up . . . my legs wouldn't . . ."

"I shouldn't have left you out here all night." He managed to get her legs straightened out, to get her back on the couch, under a warm blanket, with a soft pillow behind her head.

That afternoon, he bought her the whistle.

"When you need me, use the whistle. You got that?"

She nodded.

"Night or day, it doesn't matter. If you need me for something, blow the whistle." He paused, hearing his own words echo through his mind, and a cold, shuddering realization swept over him. He didn't know when it had happened, but somewhere along the line they had swapped roles. He was the parent now, she the child.

"What if I can't?"

"Try it."

Like everything else, her lungs had slowly lost their strength over the past few months, but she was able to put enough air into the whistle to produce a short, high-pitched hum

"Great."

That was—what?—three weeks ago?

Blair sits up in bed. The streetlight outside his window is casting a murky blue-gray light through the bedroom curtains. The room is bathed in that light. It feels dark and strangely out of balance. He fluffs both pillows, stuffs them behind him, and leans back against the wall. Across the hall, the light flickers, and he knows the television is still on in his mother's room. It seems as if it's far away.

He shudders.

Let her sleep, he thinks. Let her sleep forever.

Sometimes the house feels like a prison. Just the two of them, caught in their life and death struggle. The ending already predetermined. It feels . . . not lonely, at least not in the traditional sense of the word . . . but . . . *isolated*. Outside these walls, there is nothing but endless black emptiness. But it's in here where life is coming to an end. Right here inside this house, inside these walls.

The television in her room flickers again.

Blair stares absently at the shifting patterns on the bedroom door across the hall. He used to watch that television set while she was in the bathroom. Sometimes as long as an hour, while she changed her colostomy bag . . .

"I'll never be close to a man again," she told him a few months after the doctors had surgically created the opening in the upper end of her sigmoid colon. The stoma was located on the lower left side of her abdomen. "How could anyone be attracted to me with this bag attached to my side? With the foul odor?"

"Someone will come along, and he'll love you for you. The bag won't matter."

A fleeting sigh of hope crossed her face, then she stared at him for a while, and that was that. She hadn't had enough of a chance to let it all out, so she kept it all in. The subject never came up again. And what she did on the other side of the bathroom door became something personal and private to her, something he half decided he didn't want to know about anyway.

If he had a choice.

"How're you doing in there?" he asked her late one night. He'd had to help her out of bed into the wheelchair, and out of the wheelchair onto the toilet. That was all the help she ever wanted. But she'd been in there, mysteriously quiet, for an unusually long time.

"Mom?"

"I'm okay," she whispered.

"Need any help?"

More quiet.

"Mom?"

"What?"

"Do you need any help?"

"I've lost the clip."

"The clip?"

"For the colostomy bag. It's not here."

"You want me to help you look for it?"

"No. See if you can find another one in one of the boxes in the closet."

"What does it look like?"

"It's . . . a little plastic . . . clip."

He found one, the last one, buried at the bottom of a box. It had the appearance of a bobby pin, a little longer, perhaps, and made of clear plastic instead of metal. "Found one."

"Oh, good."

He pulled the sliding pocket door open, more than was necessary if all he had intended to do was hand her the clip. The bathroom was smaller than he remembered it. There was a walker in front her, for balance if she ever had to stand up, and the toilet had metal supports on each side to help her get up and down. It seemed as if the entire room was filled with aids of one kind or another.

"Is this what you're looking for?"

She was hunched over, leaning heavily against one of the support bars, her nightgown pulled up around her waist. Her face was weighted down with a weariness he'd never seen before and for the first time he understood how taxing this daily—sometimes three or four times a day—process had become for her. When she looked up at him, she seemed confused and disoriented.

"Are you okay?"

"I can't find the clip." She showed him the colostomy pouch for the first time. He couldn't bring himself to see how it was attached to her. Partly because he didn't want to know, and partly because that would have been like checking out her scars after surgery. Some things are better left to the imagination. More important, there was a woman in front of him whose ribs were protruding from her chest, whose face was a taut mask stretched across her skull, whose fingers were frail sticklike extensions of her hands; and this woman, looking so much like a stranger, was his mother. God, this was the woman who had given him birth.

"I've got the clip right here."

"Oh." She tried a smile on him, then glanced down at the bag in her hands. The process was slow and deliberate, but after several attempts she was finally able to fold the bottom side of the bag over.

Blair slid the clip across it. "Like this?"

She nodded.

And he realized something that should have occurred to him long before this: it was getting to be too much for her. As simple as emptying the bag might be, it was too confusing for her to work through the procedure now.

"Okay, I think we've got it."

"Oh, good."

"Ready to get out of here?"

"I think so." She whispered the words, and before they were all out, she started to cry.

"Mom?"

She looked up, her eyes as big as he'd ever seen them.

God, I hate this, he thought, taking hold of her hand and feeling completely, despairingly helpless. I hate everything about this.

"I didn't hurt you, did I?"

Her crying seemed to grow louder for a moment.

"Mom?"

"I didn't want for you to have to do that."

Lovingly, he squeezed her hand. "I know."

"I'm sorry."

"There's nothing to be sorry about. It's not a big deal." He pulled a couple of squares of toilet paper off the roll and handed them to her. "Things are hard enough. Don't worry about the small stuff. Okay?"

By the time he got her back into bed again, she had stopped crying. But he'd never know if it was because of what he'd said, or if it was because she didn't want to upset him anymore. They were both bending over backwards trying not to upset each other. There was something crazy about that.

*   *   *

The whistle blows.

At least he thinks it's the whistle. Sometimes, it's so damn hard to tell. There's that part of him, that tired, defeated part of him, that doesn't want to hear it anyway. How long can this thing drag on? Outside, all of thirty or forty feet away, a man jogs by with his dog on the end of a leash. People who pass this house don't have the slightest inkling of what's going on behind these walls. A woman's dying in here. And dying right alongside her is her son.

He pulls the covers back, hangs his feet over the edge of the bed.

For several days, she hasn't been able to keep food down. That memory comes horribly clear to him now. . . .

"Feel better?"

She shook her head, her eyes closed, her body hunched forward over the bowl. Then suddenly another explosion of undigested soup burst from her mouth.

He held the stainless steel bowl closer; it felt warm in his hands. This had been going on for nearly three days now. It seemed like it might never stop. "You've got to take some Compazine, Mom."

"No."

"I can crush it for you and mix it with orange juice."

No response.

"Mom?"

No response.

"It'll go down easier that way."

"No."

"Christ, Mom, you've got to take something. You can't keep throwing up forever."

"The pills make me sick."

"Sicker than this?"

"They make me sick."

The whistle.

Blair slips a T-shirt over his head, pulls on a pair of Levi's. He tries to convince himself it'll stop. Maybe if he just leaves it alone, the sound will quietly drift into the background of the television set, and he'll be able to go back to sleep again. . . .

"It'll stop on its own," she tried to convince him.

"But if it doesn't, you'll dehydrate."

At last the vomiting appeared to have run its course. At least for the time being. She sat up a little straighter, taking in a deep breath. When she opened her eyes, they were faraway, devoid of that sparkle that used to be so prominent behind her smile.

"Please, just take one Compazine."

"No."

Her skin began to lose its elasticity a few days later. The nausea stopped on its own, just like she'd said it would. But now, the only liquid she was taking was in the form of crushed ice, and there was the very real fear that dehydration might eventually become too painful for her.

"We can try an IV," the visiting nurse told him. "It won't help her live longer, but it'll probably make her more comfortable."

"Her veins aren't in very good shape."

"I've done this before."

They had to lean the ironing board up against the wall behind the headboard of her bed, because they didn't have an IV stand. The nurse hung the solution bag from one of the legs, and it seemed to work well enough. Then she tried to find a vein in his mother's right arm. It wasn't as easy as she'd thought it would be.

After several new entries, he turned away.

His mother began to whimper.

"The needle keeps sliding off." The nurse switched to her left arm, still struggling to find a workable vein, still failing miserably.

"That's enough," he finally said. "Let's just forget it."

"Her veins are so—"

There was a tear running down the cheek of his mother, and her mouth was twisted into a grimace which seemed frozen on her face.

"I'm sorry, Mom. I didn't mean to hurt you."

She rolled over, away from him. . . .

He's standing at her bedroom door now, and she's in that same position: with her back turned toward him. He can see the black cord of the whistle tied around her neck, but the whistle is out of sight.

"Mom?"

The television flickers, drawing his attention. The scene is from *Starsky and Hutch*, shot inside a dingy, gray-black interrogation room. There's a young man sitting in an uncomfortable chair, Starsky standing over him, badgering him. It seems faraway and unimportant, and Blair's attention drifts easily back to his mother.

"You need anything?"

He moves around the foot of her bed, stops alongside her, the stainless steel bowl on the floor only a few inches away from his feet. "Mom?"

Her eyes are closed. She looks peaceful. Her nightgown is partially open in front. There's a thick tube running up the right side of her body and over her collarbone, running underneath the skin—like an artery—where the doctors had surgically implanted a shunt just a few short weeks earlier. Inside that tube, flowing out of her stomach, up her body, and back into her bloodstream, there's an endless current of cancerous fluid the tumor has been manufacturing for months.

In her left hand, wrapped around a long, thin finger, she's holding the nylon cord. He can almost hear the whistle's high-pitched hum calling to him from somewhere else. Sometimes it sounds as if it's singing his name—*Bl-air*—and he wonders if he'll ever be able to hear his name out loud again without being swept away by the strange concoction of resentment and helplessness that overwhelms him.

He touches her arm.

For a moment, everything is perfect: she's sleeping soundly, the house is quiet, the whistle stilled. Too good to be true.

"Mom?"

He places the palm of his hand over her chest, not believing what's going through his mind now. No intake of breath. No beat of heart. Instead, she feels cool to the touch, and . . . and absolutely . . . motionless.

"Jesus . . ."

"I don't want to talk to anyone."

"You sure?" he asked, holding his hand over the mouthpiece of the phone.

"They'll want to visit."

"Maybe not."

"I don't want anyone to see me like this."

It had happened so gradually: first the phone calls, then the visitors, finally the mail, and before he had realized what had happened, they had isolated themselves from the outside world. It was just the two of them, alone, inside the house, waiting for the cancer to run its course. . . .

One more time, he places the palm of his hand ever so lightly across her chest.

"Mom? Please, Mom."

The wall above her bed flickers with the light from the television set, reflecting dully off the underside of the ironing board. He glances up, staring at the IV tube still dangling from the leg of the board, remembering too clearly, too vividly how much pain she went through the night the nurse had struggled to find a good vein in her arms.

"I never should have let her do that to you."

It feels cold inside the house. The room seems darker, smaller, a lonelier place.

He stands next to the bed, careful not to disturb her, though somewhere in the back of his mind he's already aware that she's finally at peace now. She's lying near the edge, her legs bent at the knees, her arms bent at the elbows. She looks as if she's praying. For a moment longer, he stares, failing to remember a time when the flesh wasn't pulled taut like a death mask across her face. This is the way he'll always remember her. It's all he has left.

The television draws his attention again, and that tiny distraction is somehow enough to stir him. He turns toward the door, wanting to be out of the room, thinking it can't be over . . . he doesn't want it to be over . . . maybe if he comes back later . . .

Then he hears it again.

The whistle. A soft, echoing sound. Calling him.

Bl-air.

"Mom?"

He expects different when he turns back, but he finds her eyes still closed, her chest still motionless. The nylon cord hangs loosely around her neck, the whistle lost somewhere inside her cotton nightgown. He sits on the edge of the bed, studying her, suddenly feeling like a little boy. It's a lonely feeling.

Bl-air.

It sounds again.

The whistle.

With care, he unwraps her finger from around the black cord. Then he opens the front of her nightgown and follows the cord down . . . down *there* . . . down to where the whistle is softly blowing, to where the cancer has been growing. The incision from her last surgery is open, the tissue curled back, and inside the cavity—ash gray and darker, pulsing—the cancer is wrapped like a kiss around the mouthpiece of the whistle, exhaling a soft humming song—

Bl-air.

It never stops.

The cancer never stops.

HARUKI MURAKAMI
TV People

Haruki Murakami was born in Kobe, Japan in 1949. He studied Greek Drama and managed a jazz bar in Tokyo before turning to writing full time in 1981. He is the author of *A Wild Sheep Chase* (which won Japan's Noma Literary Award); *The Edge of the World and the Hardboiled Wonderland* (winner of the Tanizaki Prize); *Dance, Dance, Dance*; and *Norwegian Wood* (an international bestseller). He has also translated novels by F. Scott Fitzgerald, John Irving, Paul Theroux and Raymond Carver into Japanese. Murakami presently lives in Rome, Italy.

It is a great pleasure to be able to include Murakami's work in this volume with a surreal and off-beat tale translated from the Japanese by Alfred Birnbaum, reprinted from *The New Yorker*.

—T.W.

TV People

HARUKI MURAKAMI

It was Sunday evening when the TV PEOPLE showed up.

The season, spring. At least, I think it was spring. In any case, it wasn't particularly hot as seasons go, not particularly chilly.

To be honest, the season's not so important. What matters is that it's a Sunday evening.

I don't like Sunday evenings. Or, rather, I don't like everything that goes with them—that Sunday-evening state of affairs. Without fail, come Sunday evening my head starts to ache. In varying intensity each time. Maybe a third to a half of an inch into my temples, the soft flesh throbs—as if invisible threads lead out and someone far off is yanking at the other ends. Not that it hurts so much. It ought to hurt, but, strangely, it doesn't—it's like long needles probing anesthetized areas.

And I hear things. Not sounds, but thick slabs of silence being dragged through the dark. *KRZSHAAAL KKRZSHAAAAAL KKKKRMMMS*. Those are the initial indications. First, the aching. Then, a slight distortion of my vision. Tides of confusion wash through, premonitions tugging at memories, memories tugging at premonitions. A finely honed razor moon floats white in the sky, roots of doubt burrow into the earth. People walk extra loud down the hall just to get me. *KRRSPUMK DUWB KRRSPUMK DUWB KRRSPUMK DUWB*.

All the more reason for the TV PEOPLE to single out Sunday evening as the time to come around. Like melancholy moods, or the secretive, quiet fall of rain, they steal into the gloom of that appointed time.

Let me explain how the TV PEOPLE look.

The TV PEOPLE are slightly smaller than you or me. Not obviously smaller—*slightly* smaller. About, say, twenty or thirty per cent. Every part of their bodies

262

is uniformly smaller. So rather than "small" the more terminologically correct expression might be "reduced."

In fact, if you see TV PEOPLE somewhere, you might not notice at first that they're small. But even if you don't, they'll probably strike you as somehow strange. Unsettling, maybe. You're sure to think something's odd, and then you'll take another look. There's nothing unnatural about them at first glance, but that's what's so unnatural. Their smallness is completely different from that of children or dwarfs. When we see children, we *feel* they're small, but this sense of recognition comes mostly from the misproportioned awkwardness of their bodies. They are small, granted, but not uniformly so. The hands are small, but the head is big. Typically, that is. No, the smallness of TV PEOPLE is something else entirely. TV PEOPLE look as if they were reduced by photocopy, everything mechanically calibrated. Say their height has been reduced by a factor of 0.7, then their shoulder width is also in 0.7 reduction; ditto (0.7 reduction) for the feet, head, ears, and fingers. Like plastic models, only a little smaller than the real thing.

Or like perspective demos. Figures that look far away even close up. Something out of a trompe-l'oeil painting where the surface warps and buckles. An illusion where the hand fails to touch objects close by, yet brushes what is out of reach.

That's TV PEOPLE.

That's TV PEOPLE.

That's TV PEOPLE.

There were three of them altogether.

They don't knock or ring the doorbell. Don't say hello. They just sneak right in. I don't even hear a footstep. One opens the door, the other two carry in a TV. Not a very big TV. Your ordinary Sony color TV. The door was locked, I think, but I can't be certain. Maybe I forgot to lock it. It really wasn't foremost in my thoughts at the time, so who knows? Still, I think the door was locked.

When they come in, I'm lying on the sofa, gazing up at the ceiling. Nobody at home but me. That afternoon, the wife has gone out with the girls—some close friends from her high-school days—getting together to talk, then eating dinner out. "Can you grab your own supper?" the wife said before leaving. "There's vegetables in the fridge and all sorts of frozen foods. That much you can handle for yourself, can't you? And before the sun goes down, remember to take in the laundry, O.K.?"

"Sure thing," I said. Doesn't faze me a bit. Rice, right? Laundry, right? Nothing to it. Take care of it, simple as *SLUPPP KRRRTZ*!

"Did you say something, dear?" she asked.

"No, nothing," I said.

All afternoon I take it easy and loll around on the sofa. I have nothing better to do. I read a bit—that new novel by García Márquez—and listen to some music. I have myself a beer. Still, I'm unable to give my mind to any of this. I consider going back to bed, but I can't even pull myself together enough to do that. So I wind up lying on the sofa, staring at the ceiling.

The way my Sunday afternoons go, I end up doing a little bit of various things, none very well. It's a struggle to concentrate on any one thing. This particular day, everything seems to be going right. I think, Today I'll read this book, listen to these records, answer these letters. Today, for sure, I'll clean out my desk drawers, run errands, wash the car for once. But two o'clock rolls around, three o'clock rolls around, gradually dusk comes on, and all my plans are blown. I haven't done a thing; I've been lying around on the sofa the whole day, same as always. The clock ticks in my ears. *TRPP Q SCHAOUS TRPP Q SCHAOUS.* The sound erodes everything around me, little by little, like dripping rain. *TRPP Q SCHAOUS TRPP Q SCHAOUS.* Little by little, Sunday afternoon wears down, shrinking in scale. Just like the TV PEOPLE themselves.

The TV PEOPLE ignore me from the very outset. All three of them have this look that says the likes of me don't exist. They open the door and carry in their TV. The two put the set on the sideboard, the other one plugs it in. There's a mantel clock and a stack of magazines on the sideboard. The clock was a wedding gift, big and heavy—big and heavy as time itself—with a loud sound, too. *TRPP Q SCHAOUS TRPP Q SCHAOUS.* All through the house you can hear it. The TV PEOPLE move it off the sideboard, down onto the floor. The wife's going to raise hell, I think. She hates it when things get randomly shifted about. If everything isn't in its proper place, she gets really sore. What's worse, with the clock there on the floor, I'm bound to trip over it in the middle of the night. I'm forever getting up to go to the toilet at two in the morning, bleary-eyed, and stumbling over something.

Next, the TV PEOPLE move the magazines to the table. All of them women's magazines. (I hardly ever read magazines; I read books—personally, I wouldn't mind if every last magazine in the world went out of business.) *Elle* and *Marie Claire* and *Home Ideas*, magazines of that ilk. Neatly stacked on the sideboard. The wife doesn't like me touching her magazines—change the order of the stack, and I never hear the end of it—so I don't go near them. Never once flipped through them. But the TV PEOPLE couldn't care less: they move them right out of the way, they show no concern, they sweep the whole lot off the sideboard, they mix up the order. *Marie Claire* is on top of *Croissant*; *Home Ideas* is underneath *An-An.* Unforgivable. And worse, they're scattering the bookmarks onto the floor. They've lost her place, pages with important information. I have no idea what information or how important—might have been for work, might have been personal—but whatever, it was important to the wife, and she'll let me know about it. "What's the meaning of this? I go out for a nice time with friends, and when I come back the house is a shambles!" I can just hear it, line for line. Oh, great, I think, shaking my head.

Everything gets removed from the sideboard to make room for the television. The TV PEOPLE plug it into a wall socket, then switch it on. Then there is a tinkling noise, and the screen lights up. A moment later the picture floats into view. They change the channels by remote control. But all the channels are blank—probably, I think, because they haven't connected the set to an antenna. There has to be an antenna outlet somewhere in the apartment. I seem to remember the superintendent telling us where it was when we moved into this condominium. All you had to do was connect it. But I can't remember where it is. We don't own a television, so I've completely forgotten.

Yet somehow the TV PEOPLE don't seem bothered that they aren't picking up any broadcast. They give no sign of looking for the antenna outlet. Blank screen, no image—makes no difference to them. Having pushed the button and had the power come on, they've completed what they came to do.

The TV is brand-new. It's not in its box, but one look tells you it's new. The instruction manual and guarantee are in a plastic bag taped to the side; the power cable shines, sleek as a freshly caught fish.

All three TV PEOPLE look at the blank screen from here and there around the room. One of them comes over next to me and verifies that you can see the TV screen from where I'm sitting. The TV is facing straight toward me, at an optimum viewing distance. They seem satisfied. One operation down, says their air of accomplishment. One of the TV PEOPLE (the one who'd come over next to me) places the remote control on the table.

The TV PEOPLE speak not a word. Their movements come off in perfect order, hence they don't need to speak. Each of the three executes his prescribed function with maximum efficiency. A professional job. Neat and clean. Their work is done in no time. As an afterthought, one of the TV PEOPLE picks the clock up from the floor and casts a quick glance around the room to see if there isn't a more appropriate place to put it, but he doesn't find any and sets it back down. *TRPP Q SCHAOUS TRPP Q SCHAOUS*. It goes on ticking weightily on the floor. Our apartment is rather small, and a lot of floor space tends to be taken up with my books and the wife's reference materials. I am bound to trip on that clock. I heave a sigh. No mistake, stub my toes for sure. You can bet on it.

All three TV PEOPLE wear dark-blue jackets. Of who-knows-what fabric, but slick. Under them, they wear jeans and tennis shoes. Clothes and shoes all proportionately reduced in size. I watch their activities for the longest time, until I start to think maybe it's *my* proportions that are off. Almost as if I were riding backward on a roller coaster, wearing strong prescription glasses. The view is dizzying, the scale all screwed up. I'm thrown off balance, my customary world is no longer absolute. That's the way the TV PEOPLE make you feel.

Up to the very last, the TV PEOPLE don't say a word. The three of them check the screen one more time, confirm that there are no problems, then switch it off by remote control. The glow contracts to a point and flickers off with a tinkling noise. The screen returns to its expressionless, gray, natural state. The world outside is getting dark. I hear someone calling out to someone else. Anonymous footsteps pass by down the hall, intentionally loud as ever. *KRRSPUMK DUWB KRRSPUMK DUWB*. A Sunday evening.

The TV PEOPLE give the room another whirlwind inspection, open the door, and leave. Once again, they pay no attention to me whatsoever. They act as if I don't exist.

From the time the TV PEOPLE come into the apartment to the moment they leave, I don't budge. Don't say a word. I remain motionless, stretched out on the sofa, surveying the whole operation. I know what you're going to say: that's unnatural. Total strangers—not one but three—walk unannounced right into your apartment, plunk down a TV set, and you just sit there staring at them, dumbfounded. Kind of odd, don't you think?

I know, I know. But, for whatever reason, I don't speak up, I simply observe the proceedings. Because they ignore me so totally. And if you were in my position I imagine you'd do the same. Not to excuse myself, but *you* have people right in front of you denying your very presence like that, then see if you don't doubt whether you actually exist. I look at my hands half expecting to see clear through them. I'm devastated, powerless, in a trance. My body, my mind are vanishing fast. I can't bring myself to move. It's all I can do to watch the three TV PEOPLE deposit their television in my apartment and leave. I can't open my mouth for fear of what my voice might sound like.

The TV PEOPLE exit and leave me alone. My sense of reality comes back to me. These hands are once again my hands. It's only then I notice that the dusk has been swallowed by darkness. I turn on the light. Then I close my eyes. Yes, that's a TV set sitting there. Meanwhile, the clock keeps ticking away the minutes. *TRPP Q SCHAOUS TRPP Q SCHAOUS.*

Curiously, the wife makes no mention of the appearance of the television set in the apartment. No reaction at all. Zero. It's as if she doesn't even see it. Creepy. Because, as I said before, she's extremely fussy about the order and arrangement of furniture and other things. If someone dares to move anything in the apartment, even by a hair, she'll jump on it in an instant. That's her ascendancy. She knits her brows, then gets things back the way they were.

Not me. If an issue of *Home Ideas* gets put under an *An-An*, or a ballpoint pen finds its way into the pencil stand, you don't see me go to pieces. I don't even notice. This is her problem; I'd wear myself out living like her. Sometimes she flies into a rage. She tells me she can't abide my carelessness. Yes, I say, and sometimes I can't stand carelessness about universal gravitation and π and $E = mc^2$ either. I mean it. But when I say things like this she clams up, taking them as a personal insult. I never mean it that way; I just say what I feel.

That night, when she comes home, first thing she does is look around the apartment. I've readied a full explanation—how the TV PEOPLE came and mixed everything up. It'll be difficult to convince her, but I intend to tell her the whole truth.

She doesn't say a thing, just gives the place the once-over. There's a TV on the sideboard, the magazines are out of order on the table, the mantel clock is on the floor, and the wife doesn't even comment. There's nothing for me to explain.

"You get your own supper O.K.?" she asks me, undressing.

"No, I didn't eat," I tell her.

"Why not?"

"I wasn't really hungry," I say.

The wife pauses, half undressed, and thinks this over. She gives me a long look. Should she press the subject or not? The clock breaks up the protracted, ponderous silence. *TRPP Q SCHAOUS TRPP Q SCHAOUS*. I pretend not to hear; I won't let it in my ears. But the sound is simply too heavy, too loud to shut out. She, too, seems to be listening to it. Then she shakes her head and says, "Shall I whip up something quick?"

"Well, maybe," I say. I don't really feel much like eating, but I won't turn down the offer.

The wife changes into around-the-house wear and goes to the kitchen to fix *zosui* and *tamago-yaki* while filling me in on her friends. Who'd done what, who'd said what, who'd changed her hair style and looked so much younger, who'd broken up with her boyfriend. I know most of her friends, so I pour myself a beer and follow along, inserting attentive uh-huhs at proper intervals. Though in fact I hardly hear a thing she says. I'm thinking about the TV PEOPLE. That, and why she didn't remark on the sudden appearance of the television. No way she couldn't have noticed. Very odd. Weird, even. Something is wrong here. But what to do about it?

The food is ready, so I sit at the dining-room table and eat. Rice, egg, salt plum. When I've finished, the wife clears away the dishes. I have another beer, and she has a beer, too. I glance at the sideboard, and there's the TV set, with the power off, the remote-control unit sitting on the table. I get up from the table, reach for the remote control, and switch it on. The screen glows and I hear it tinkling. Still no picture. Only the same blank tube. I press the button to raise the volume, but all that does is increase the white-noise roar. I watch the snow-storm for twenty, thirty seconds, then switch it off. Light and sound vanish in an instant. Meanwhile, the wife has seated herself on the carpet and is flipping through *Elle*, oblivious of the fact that the TV has just been turned on and off.

I replace the remote control on the table and sit down on the sofa again, thinking I'll go on reading that long García Márquez novel. I always read after dinner. I might set the book down after thirty minutes, or I might read for two hours, but the thing is to read every day. Today, though, I can't get myself to read more than a page and a half. I can't concentrate; my thoughts keep returning to the TV set. I look up and see it, right in front of me.

I wake at half past two in the morning to find the TV still there. I get out of bed half hoping the thing has disappeared. No such luck. I go to the toilet, then plop down on the sofa and put my feet up on the table. I take the remote control in hand and try turning on the TV. No new developments in that department either; only a rerun of the same glow and noise. Nothing else. I look at it awhile, then switch it off.

I go back to bed and try to sleep. I'm dead tired, but sleep isn't coming. I shut my eyes and I see them. The TV PEOPLE carrying the TV set, the TV PEOPLE moving the clock out of the way, the TV PEOPLE transferring magazines to the table, the TV PEOPLE plugging the power cable into the wall socket, the TV PEOPLE checking the screen, the TV PEOPLE opening the door and silently exiting. They've stayed on in my head. They're in there walking around. I get back out of bed, go to the kitchen, and pour a double brandy into a coffee cup. I down the brandy and head over to the sofa for another session with Márquez. I open the pages, yet somehow the words won't sink in. The writing is opaque.

Very well, then, I throw García Márquez aside and pick up *Elle*. Reading *Elle* from time to time can't hurt anyone. But there isn't anything in *Elle* that catches my fancy. New hair styles and elegant white silk blouses and eateries that serve good beef stew and what to wear to the opera, articles like that. Do I care? I throw *Elle* aside. Which leaves me the television on the sideboard to look at.

I end up staying awake until dawn, not doing a thing. At six o'clock, I make myself some coffee. I don't have anything else to do, so I go ahead and fix ham sandwiches before the wife gets up.

"You're up awful early," she says drowsily.

"Mm," I mumble.

After a nearly wordless breakfast, we leave home together, and go our separate ways to our respective offices. The wife works at a small publishing house. Edits a natural-food and life-style magazine. "Shiitake Mushrooms Prevent Gout," "The Future of Organic Farming," you know the kind of magazine. Never sells very well, but hardly costs anything to produce; kept afloat by a handful of zealots. Me, I work in the advertising department of an electrical-appliance manufacturer. I dream up ads for toasters and washing machines and microwave ovens.

In my office building, I pass one of the TV PEOPLE on the stairs. If I'm not mistaken, it's one of the three who brought the TV the day before—probably the one who first opened the door, who didn't actually carry the set. Their singular lack of distinguishing features makes it next to impossible to tell them apart, so I can't swear to it, but I'd say I'm eight to nine out of ten on the mark. He's wearing the same blue jacket he had on the previous day, and he's not carrying anything in his hands. He's merely walking down the stairs. I'm walking up. I dislike elevators, so I generally take the stairs. My office is on the ninth floor, so this is no mean feat. When I'm in a rush I get all sweaty by the time I reach the top. Even so, getting sweaty has got to be better than taking the elevator, as far as I'm concerned. Everyone jokes about it: doesn't own a TV or a VCR, doesn't take elevators, must be a modern-day Luddite. Maybe a childhood trauma leading to arrested development. Let them think what they like. They're the ones who are screwed up, if you ask me.

In any case, there I am, climbing the stairs as always; I'm the only one on the stairs—almost nobody else uses them—when between the fourth and fifth floors I pass one of the TV PEOPLE coming down. It happens so suddenly I don't know what to do. Maybe I should say something?

But I don't say anything. I don't know what to say, and he's unapproachable. He leaves no opening; he descends the stairs so functionally, at one set tempo, with such regulated precision. Plus, he utterly ignores my presence, same as the day before. I don't even enter his field of vision. He slips by before I can think what to do. In that instant, the field of gravity warps.

At work the day is solid with meetings from the morning on. Important meetings on sales campaigns for a new product line. Several employees read reports. Blackboards fill with figures, bar graphs proliferate on computer screens. Heated discussions. I participate, although my contribution to the meetings is not that critical because I'm not directly involved with the project. So between meetings I keep puzzling things over. I voice an opinion only once. Isn't much of an opinion, either—something perfectly obvious to any observer—but I couldn't very well go without saying anything, after all. I may not be terribly ambitious when it comes to work, but so long as I'm receiving a salary I have to demonstrate responsibility. I summarize the various opinions up to that point and even make a joke to lighten the atmosphere. Half covering for my daydreaming about the TV PEOPLE. Several people laugh. After that one utterance, however, I only pretend to review the materials; I'm thinking about the TV PEOPLE. If they talk up a name for the new microwave oven, I certainly am not aware of it. My mind is all TV PEOPLE. What the hell was the meaning of that TV set? And why haul the TV all the way to my apartment in the first place? Why hasn't the wife remarked on its appearance? Why have the TV PEOPLE made inroads into my company?

The meetings are endless. At noon there's a short break for lunch. Too short to go out and eat. Instead, everyone gets sandwiches and coffee. The conference room is a haze of cigarette smoke, so I eat at my own desk. While I'm eating, the Section Chief comes around. To be perfectly frank, I don't like the guy. For no reason I can put my finger on: there's nothing you can fault him on, no single target for attack. He has an air of breeding. Moreover, he's not stupid. He has good taste in neckties, he doesn't wave his own flag or lord it over his inferiors. He even looks out for me, invites me out for the occasional meal. But there's just something about the guy that doesn't sit well with me. Maybe it's his habit of coming into body contact with people he's talking to. Men or women, at some point in the course of the conversation he'll reach out a hand and touch. Not in any suggestive way, mind you. No, his manner is brisk, his bearing perfectly casual. I wouldn't be surprised if some people don't even notice, it's so natural. Still—I don't know why—it does bother me. So whenever I see him, almost instinctively I brace myself. Call it petty, it gets to me.

He leans over, placing a hand on my shoulder. "About your statement at the meeting just now. Very nice," says the Section Chief warmly. "Very simply put, very pivotal. I was impressed. Points well taken. The whole room buzzed at that statement of yours. The timing was perfect, too. Yessir, you keep 'em coming like that."

And he glides off. Probably to lunch. I thank him straight out, but the honest truth is I'm taken aback. I mean, I don't remember a thing of what I said at the meeting. Why does the Section Chief have to come all the way over to my desk to praise me for *that*? There have to be more brilliant examples of *Homo loquens* around here. Strange. I go on eating my lunch, uncomprehending. Then I think about the wife. Wonder what she's up to right now. Out to lunch? Maybe I ought to give her a call, exchange a few words, anything. I dial the first three digits, have second thoughts, hang up. I have no reason to be calling her. My world may be crumbling, out of balance, but is that a reason to ring up her office? What can I say about all this anyway? Besides, I hate calling her at work. I set down the receiver, let out a sigh, and finish off my coffee. Then I toss the Styrofoam cup into the wastebasket.

At one of the afternoon meetings I see TV PEOPLE again. This time, their number has increased by two. Just as on the previous day, they come traipsing across the conference room, carrying a Sony color TV. A model one size bigger. Uh-oh. Sony's the rival camp. If, for whatever reason, any competitor's product gets brought into our offices, there's hell to pay, barring when other manufacturers' products are brought in for test comparison, of course. But then we take pains to remove the company logo—just to make sure no outside eyes happen upon it. Little do the TV PEOPLE care: the Sony mark is emblazoned for all to see. They open the door and march right into the conference room, flashing it in our direction. Then they parade the thing around the room, scanning the place for somewhere to set it down, until at last, not finding any location, they carry it backward out the door. The others in the room show no reaction to the TV PEOPLE. And they can't have missed them. No, they've definitely seen them. And the proof is they even got out of the way, clearing a path for the TV PEOPLE to carry their television through. Still, that's as far as it went: a reaction no more alarmed than when the nearby coffee shop delivered. They'd made it a ground rule not to acknowledge the presence of the TV PEOPLE. The others all knew they were there; they just acted as if they weren't.

None of it makes any sense. Does everybody know about the TV PEOPLE? Am I alone in the dark? Maybe the wife knew about the TV PEOPLE all along, too. Probably. I'll bet that's why she wasn't surprised by the television and why she didn't mention it. That's the only possible explanation. Yet this confuses me even more. Who or what, then, are the TV PEOPLE? And why are they always carrying around TV sets?

One colleague leaves his seat to go to the toilet, and I get up to follow. This is a guy who entered the company around the same time I did. We're on good terms. Sometimes we go out for a drink together after work. I don't do that with most people. I'm standing next to him at the urinals. He's the first to complain. "Oh, joy! Looks like we're in for more of the same, straight through to evening. I swear! Meetings, meetings, meetings, going to drag on forever."

"You can say that again," I say. We wash our hands. He compliments me on the morning meeting's statement. I thank him.

"Oh, by the way, those guys who came in with the TV just now . . ." I launch forth, then cut off.

He doesn't say anything. He turns off the faucet, pulls two paper towels from the dispenser, and wipes his hands. He doesn't even shoot a glance in my direction. How long can he keep drying his hands? Eventually, he crumples up his towels and throws them away. Maybe he didn't hear me. Or maybe he's pretending not to hear. I can't tell. But from the sudden strain in the atmosphere I know enough not to ask. I shut up, wipe my hands, and walk down the corridor to the conference room. The rest of the afternoon's meetings he avoids my eyes.

*   *   *

When I get home from work, the apartment is dark. Outside, dark clouds have swept in. It's beginning to rain. The apartment smells like rain. Night is coming on. No sign of the wife. I loosen my tie, smooth out the wrinkles, and hang it up. I brush off my suit. I toss my shirt into the washing machine. My hair smells like cigarette smoke, so I take a shower and shave. Story of my life: I go to endless meetings, get smoked to death, then the wife gets on my case about it. The very first thing she did after we were married was make me stop smoking. Four years ago, that was.

Out of the shower, I sit on the sofa with a beer, drying my hair with a towel. The TV PEOPLE's television is still sitting on the sideboard. I pick up the remote control from the table and push the on switch. Again and again I press, but nothing happens. The screen stays dark. I check the plug; it's in the socket all right. I unplug it, then plug it back in. Still no go. No matter how often I press the on switch, the screen does not glow. Just to be sure, I pry open the back cover of the remote-control unit, remove the batteries, and check them with my handy electrical-contact tester. The batteries are fine. At this point, I give up, throw the remote control aside, and slosh down more beer.

Why should it upset me? Supposing the TV did come on, what then? It would glow and crackle with white noise. Who cares, if that's all that'd come on?

I care. Last night it worked. And I haven't laid a finger on it since. Doesn't make sense.

I try the remote control one more time. I press slowly with my finger. But the result is the same. No response whatsoever. The screen is dead. Cold.

Dead cold.

I pull another beer out of the fridge and eat some potato salad from a plastic tub. It's past six o'clock. I read the whole evening paper. If anything, it's more boring than usual. Almost no article worth reading, nothing but inconsequential news items. But I keep reading, for lack of anything better to do. Until I finish the paper. What next? To avoid pursuing that thought any further, I dally over the newspaper. Hmm, how about answering letters? A cousin of mine has sent us a wedding invitation, which I have to turn down. The day of the wedding, the wife and I are going to be off on a trip. To Okinawa. We've been planning it for ages; we're both taking time off from work. We can't very well go changing our plans now. God only knows when we'll get the next chance to spend a long holiday together. And, to clinch it all, I'm not even that close to my cousin; haven't seen her in almost ten years. Still, I can't leave replying to the last minute. She has to know how many people are coming, how many settings to plan for the banquet. Oh, forget it. I can't bring myself to write, not now. My heart isn't in it.

I pick up the newspaper again and read the same articles over again. Maybe I ought to start preparing dinner. But the wife might be working late and could come home having eaten. Which would mean wasting one portion. And if I am going to eat alone I can make do with leftovers; no reason to make something up special. If she hasn't eaten, we can go out and eat together.

Odd, though. Whenever either of us knows he or she is going to be later than six, we always call in. That's the rule. Leave a message on the answering machine if necessary. That way, the other can coördinate: go ahead and eat alone, or set something out for the late arriver, or hit the sack. The nature of my work sometimes keeps me out late, and she often has meetings, or proofs to dispatch, before coming home. Neither of us has a regular nine-to-five job. When both of us are busy, we can go three days without a word to each other. Those are the breaks —just one of those things that nobody planned. Hence we always keep certain rules, so as not to place unrealistic burdens on each other. If it looks as though we're going to be late, we call in and let the other one know. I sometimes forget, but she, never once.

Still, there's no message on the answering machine.

I toss the newspaper, stretch out on the sofa, and shut my eyes.

I dream about a meeting. I'm standing up, delivering a statement I myself don't understand. I open my mouth and talk. If I don't, I'm a dead man. I have to keep talking. Have to keep coming out with endless blah-blah-blah. Everyone around me is dead. Dead and turned to stone. A roomful of stone statues. A wind is blowing. The windows are all broken; gusts of air are coming in. And the TV PEOPLE are here. Three of them. Like the first time. They're carrying a Sony color TV. And on the screen are the TV PEOPLE. I'm running out of words; little by little I can feel my fingertips growing stiffer. Gradually turning to stone.

I open my eyes to find the room aglow. The color of corridors at the Aquarium. The television is on. Outside, everything is dark. The TV screen is flickering in the gloom, static crackling. I sit up on the sofa, and press my temples with my fingertips. The flesh of my fingers is still soft; my mouth tastes like beer. I swallow. I'm dried out; the saliva catches in my throat. As always, the waking world pales after an all too real dream. But no, this is real. Nobody's turned to stone. What time is it getting to be? I look for the clock on the floor. *TRPP Q SCHAOUS TRPP Q SCHAOUS*. A little before eight.

Yet, just as in the dream, one of the TV PEOPLE is on the television screen. The same guy I passed on the stairs to the office. No mistake. The one who first opened the door to the apartment. I'm one hundred per cent sure. He stands there—against a bright, fluorescent white background, the tail end of a dream infiltrating my conscious reality—staring at me. I shut, then reopen my eyes, hoping he'll have slipped back to never-never land. But he doesn't disappear. Far from it. He gets bigger. His face fills the whole screen, getting closer and closer.

The next thing I know, he's stepping through the screen. Hands gripping the frame, lifting himself up and over, one foot after the other, like climbing out of a window, leaving a white TV screen glowing behind him.

He rubs his left hand in the palm of his right, slowly acclimating himself to the world outside the television. On and on, reduced right-hand fingers rubbing reduced left-hand fingers, no hurry. He has that all-the-time-in-the-world non-chalance. Like a veteran TV-show host. Then he looks me in the face.

"We're making an airplane," says my TV PEOPLE visitant. His voice has no perspective to it. A curious, paper-thin voice.

He speaks, and the screen is all machinery. Very professional fade-in. Just like on the news. First, there's an opening shot of a large factory interior, then it cuts to a closeup of the workspace, camera center. Two TV PEOPLE are hard at work on some machine, tightening bolts with wrenches, adjusting gauges. The picture of concentration. The machine, however, is unlike anything I've ever seen: an upright cylinder except that it narrows toward the top, with streamlined protrusions along its surface. Looks more like some kind of gigantic orange juicer than an airplane. No wings, no seats.

"Doesn't look like an airplane," I say. Doesn't sound like my voice either. Strangely brittle, as if the nutrients had been strained out through a thick filter. Have I grown so old all of a sudden?

"That's probably because we haven't painted it yet," he says. "Tomorrow we'll have it the right color. Then you'll see it's an airplane."

"The color's not the problem. It's the shape. That's not an airplane."

"Well, if it's not an airplane, what is it?" he asks me. If he doesn't know, and I don't know, then what *is* it?

"So, that's why it's got to be the color." The TV PEOPLE rep puts it to me gently. "Paint it the right color, and it'll be an airplane."

I don't feel like arguing. What difference does it make? Orange juicer or airplane—flying orange juicer?—what do I care? Still, where's the wife while all this is happening? Why doesn't she come home? I massage my temples again. The clock ticks on. TRPP Q SCHAOUS TRPP Q SCHAOUS. The remote control lies on the table, and next to it the stack of women's magazines. The telephone is silent, the room illuminated by the dim glow of the television.

The two TV PEOPLE on the screen keep working away. The image is much clearer than before. You can read the numbers on the dials, hear the faint rumble of machinery. TAABZHRAYBGG T A A B Z H R A Y B G G   A R P   A R R P TAABZHRAYBGG. This bass line is punctuated periodically by a sharp, metallic grating. AREEEENBT AREEENBT. And various other noises are interspersed through the remaining aural space; I can't hear anything clearly over them. Still, the two TV PEOPLE labor on for all they're worth. That, apparently, is the subject of this program. I go on watching the two of them as they work on and on. Their colleague outside the TV set also looks on in silence. At them. At that *thing*—for the life of me, it does not look like an airplane—that insane machine all black and grimy, floating in a field of white light.

The TV PEOPLE rep speaks up. "Shame about your wife."

I look him in the face. Maybe I didn't hear him right. Staring at him is like peering into the glowing tube itself.

"Shame about your wife," the TV PEOPLE rep repeats in exactly the same absent tone.

"How's that?" I ask.

"How's that? It's gone too far," says the TV PEOPLE rep in a voice like a plastic-card hotel key. Flat, uninflected, it slices into me as if it were sliding through a thin slit. "It's gone too far: she's out there."

"*It's gone too far: she's out there*," I repeat in my head. Very plain, and without reality. I can't grasp the context. Cause has effect by the tail and is about to swallow it whole. I get up and go to the kitchen. I open the refrigerator, take a deep breath, reach for a can of beer, and go back to the sofa. The TV PEOPLE rep stands in place in front of the television, right elbow resting on the set, and watches me extract the pull ring. I don't really want to drink beer at this moment; I just need to do something. I drink one sip, but the beer doesn't taste good. I hold the can in my hand dumbly until it becomes so heavy I have to set it down on the table.

Then I think about the TV PEOPLE rep's revelation, about the wife's failure to materialize. He's saying she's gone. That she isn't coming home. I can't bring myself to believe it's over. Sure, we're not the perfect couple. In four years, we've had our spats; we have our little problems. But we always talk them out. There are things we've resolved and things we haven't. Most of what we couldn't resolve we let ride. O.K., so we have our ups and downs as a couple. I admit it. But is this cause for despair? C'mon, show me a couple who don't have problems. Besides, it's only a little past eight. There must be some reason she can't get to a phone. Any number of possible reasons. For instance . . . I can't think of a single one. I'm hopelessly confused.

I fall back deep into the sofa.

How on earth is that airplane—if it is an airplane—supposed to fly? What propels it? Where are the windows? Which is the front, which is the back?

I'm dead tired. Exhausted. I still have to write that letter, though, to beg off from my cousin's invitation. My work schedule does not afford me the pleasure of attending. Regrettable. Congratulations, all the same.

The two TV PEOPLE in the television continue building their airplane, oblivious of me. They toil away; they don't stop for anything. They have an infinite amount of work to get through before the machine is complete. No sooner have they finished one operation than they're busy with another. They have no assembly instructions, no plans, but they know precisely what to do and what comes next. The camera ably follows their deft motions. Clear-cut, easy-to-follow camera work. Highly credible, convincing images. No doubt other TV PEOPLE (Nos. 4 and 5?) are manning the camera and control panel.

Strange as it may sound, the more I watch the flawless form of the TV PEOPLE as they go about their work, the more the thing starts to look like an airplane. At least, it'd no longer surprise me if it actually flew. What does it matter which is front or back? With all the exacting detail work they're putting in, it *has* to be an airplane. Even if it doesn't appear so—to them, it's an airplane. Just as the little guy said, "If it's not an airplane, then what is it?"

The TV PEOPLE rep hasn't so much as twitched in all this time. Right elbow still propped up on the TV set, he's watching me. I'm being watched. The TV PEOPLE factory crew keeps working. Busy, busy, busy. The clock ticks on. *TRPP Q SCHAOUS TRPP Q SCHAOUS.* The room has grown dark, stifling. Someone's footsteps echo down the hall.

Well, it suddenly occurs to me, maybe so. Maybe the wife *is* out there. She's gone somewhere far away. By whatever means of transport, she's gone somewhere far out of my reach. Maybe our relationship has suffered irreversible damage. Maybe it's a total loss. Only I haven't noticed. All sorts of thoughts unravel inside me, then the frayed ends come together again. "Maybe so," I say out loud. My voice echoes, hollow.

"Tomorrow, when we paint it, you'll see better," he resumes. "All it needs is a touch of color to make it an airplane."

I look at the palms of my hands. They have shrunk slightly. Ever so slightly. Power of suggestion? Maybe the light's playing tricks on me. Maybe my sense of perspective has been thrown off. Yet, my palms really do look shrivelled. Hey, now, wait just a minute! Let me speak. There's something I should say. I must say. I'll dry up and turn to stone if I don't. Like the others.

"The phone will ring soon," the TV PEOPLE rep says. Then, after a measured pause, he adds, "In another five minutes."

I look at the telephone; I think about the telephone cord. Endless lengths of phone cable linking one telephone to another. Maybe somewhere, at some terminal of that awesome megacircuit, is my wife. Far, far away, out of my reach. I can feel her pulse. Another five minutes, I tell myself. *Which way is front, which way is back?* I stand up and try to say something, but no sooner have I got to my feet than the words slip away.

STEVE RASNIC TEM
In the Trees

Steve Rasnic Tem grew up in the Appalachian Mountains of Virginia and now lives in Colorado. He is the author of an impressive number of fantasy and horror stories published in magazines and anthologies in the U.S. and U.K.

"In the Trees," reprinted from *Fantasy Tales* magazine, is a dark and moving story that climbs from the solid earth of reality up to the realms of fantasy just as the young child of the story climbs higher and higher in the trees. It is a story about a particular kind of fierce love and loving fear that parents of young children will recognize. For those of us who are not parents it strongly summons the ghosts of the children we have been.

—T.W.

In the Trees

STEVE RASNIC TEM

It was a good climbing tree, a good climbing tree for a good boy. And Will's son was a good boy. A wild boy, sure, but a good boy, a beautiful boy. A boy like Will himself could have been, if only he hadn't had to grow up so quickly. The fact was, Will had never been very good at being a boy. He'd never had the knack. At his son's age he'd been cautious and forced, an old man in the soft skin of a boy.

"Go to sleep, son," he said softly, a whisper from the old man he'd always been. He stood in the doorway and gazed at his son's head, small face and soft dark hair barely out of the comforter, sunk to his red ears in the pillow. "You need your rest. You can't understand that now, but take it from me, you'll never have enough rest for what lies ahead."

Will could see past the bed, out the window to where the climbing tree stood, its leaves lighting up with the moonlight. Will took another pull off his beer and wished it were whiskey. The climbing tree was a beautiful thing, standing out from the surrounding trees that formed the edge of "the grove"—more like a forest—that spread out from this edge of town seven miles before farm land started breaking it up.

But few of the trees seemed fit for climbing, and none of the others were this close to the house.

"I'm a good boy, aren't I, Dad?" his son spoke sleepily from his bed. But even in the sleepy voice Will could hear the anxiety that had *no* reason to be there. "I try to be good, don't I?"

"Of course, son. You're a good boy, a *fabulous* boy."

"Then don't make me go to sleep. I *can't* sleep."

Will knew this couldn't be true. This was just the boy's natural excitement talking, his anxiety, all the life in him rising to the top that made it hard for him just to lie down and rest, to permit the night to pass without his presence in it.

His son sounded sleepier the more he said. He wouldn't be surprised to hear his snores at any second. He had to go to sleep. Sleep was medicine. And he had to take his medicine. Had to grow up big and strong. And bury his old man someday if it came to that.

Will thought about what to say, tried to think about what his own father would have said, and drank slow and steady from the can, now lukewarm in his sweaty hand. "Tomorrow's another day," he finally managed, feebly. "You're young; you have a whole lifetime ahead. No sense rushing it; that was the mistake I made when I was a boy. I was always rushing things."

The wind picked up. The longest of the leafy branches thrashed the window. His son's dark head began to thrash, too, whipping back and forth across the pillow as if in fever.

"Stay still, son," Will implored, his hands shaking, full of pain. "That's no good. That's no good at all. You have to get your rest!"

"I can't sleep, Daddy! I just can't!"

Will moved to the side of the bed. It was a kid's bed, low and small; Will felt like a giant towering over it. "I'll help you sleep," he said, his own anxiety bubbling up at his throat. "I'll do anything I can."

Awkwardly Will dropped to his knees beside the bed. He put the can down on the rug, but it tipped over. Foam erupted from the opening and dribbled over the edge of the rug onto the wooden floor. But Will couldn't move his hands off his son's comforter. He reached over and stroked the good boy's hair, hair softer than anything in Will's experience. He felt the good boy's forehead for fever—not sure he would know a fever in a boy this small. He stroked the shallow rise of comforter that covered his chest and arms.

"I don't want to go to sleep, Daddy! I'm scared!"

"What are you afraid of?"

"I don't know," the good boy said, thrashing. "I never know." Will wasn't going to say there was nothing to be afraid of; he knew better.

Will looked around the room, for something, anything, that might calm his son down and let him sleep. And let Will sleep as well, for he knew he couldn't leave the room until a night's rightful relief for his son was well on its way.

A stuffed tiger, a bear, a red truck, a pillow decorated with tiny golden bells. His son barely looked at the toys as Will piled them up around his tiny, soft, thrashing head. "Had your prayers yet?" Will asked the beautiful, anxious boy, as if it was still more medicine he was talking about, still more magic. Will rubbed his hands together, prayerful-like, now desperate for another drink.

"No! I'm not sleeping!" his beautiful son cried, his tiny head red as blood, the wave of black hair across his forehead suddenly so like the greasy wing of a dead bird. Will made his pained hands into fists, not knowing whether he was going to caress or strike the good boy.

Will put his shaking hands together and prayed for his son to go to sleep.

"I want to climb the tree!" the good son suddenly cried.

And Will, who had never before permitted it, said, "Tomorrow. I'll let you climb the tree tomorrow."

* * *

Will sat on the floor in his son's dark bedroom, drinking a beer. He watched the beautiful face—no longer bright red, or dark, now pale silver in the moonlight that had slipped through the open window—as his son slept, dreaming the dreams all good boys dreamed, but which Will, who had grown up all too quickly, had forgotten.

Behind and above the headboard of the bed was the open window, and the climbing tree beyond. The moonlight had planted silver flames in its branches. The boy's head was perfectly still. The boy's head no longer thrashed, but the climbing tree continued to thrash in the wind, making the silver flames break and spread, shoot higher up the limbs of the tree.

Will watched his beautiful son's face, relieved at its peace, but could see his nervous, living dreams torturing the bright flaming limbs of the climbing tree.

Again, the beer had grown warm in his hand, but he continued to drink. Tomorrow his wife and daughter would be back from their trip. Maybe *she* could get their son to sleep. Maybe *she* could talk him down out of the climbing tree. Will had been crazy to agree to the climb—it wasn't *safe*, it had never been safe. He'd never let his beautiful boy climb the tree before, no matter how much he'd begged. Now he didn't understand how he could have given in so easily. He'd change his mind and tell the boy, but Will had never been able to break a promise to his son before.

The curtains floated up on either side of his son's window, flapping severely as if tearing loose. Will hugged himself and imagined his small, good son hugging him, protecting him from the chill wind of adult pain.

It was a good tree, an outstanding tree. Will drank and watched his beautiful son play in the uppermost branches of the climbing tree.

His son was better at climbing trees than he had ever been. His son braved things that had terrified the young Will, left him motionless and dumb. And old, so old the other young boys were strangers to him, wild beasts scrapping in the trees. His son was a much better boy than Will had been. His son had all the right talents for being a boy.

He was a wild boy, but a good boy. The boy loved it when the branches almost broke, bent so far they threatened to drop him on his head. The boy *laughed* at terror; it thrilled him. Like other boys Will had known once upon a time, his sweet boy had no sense about danger.

The boy shook the upper branches and made as if to fly off with the tree, laughing. Will imagined the tree up-rooting, then turning somersaults in the darkening, early evening air.

Behind him, the wife said, "Will, it's getting late. It's time to get him in." Will's wife knew about a boy's safety.

But much to his surprise, Will discovered he didn't want his son to come down just yet. As the sky grew darker and the wind increased Will took pride in the way the boy held fast to the uppermost branches, shaking them like some small, fierce animal, dancing among them like some unnatural spirit. *That's it, son! That's it*, he thought, throwing his head back and permitting the flat beer to gush down his throat. *Don't leave the trees for a life down here on the ground. It happens soon enough—you'll understand that someday.*

A sudden wind caught Will full in the face: his hair stood up and his eyes were forced closed. Another gust knocked the empty can out of his hand. He could almost feel himself up in the tree with his son, just another boy to join that good, wild boy. Will staggered to his feet. The wind took away his lawn chair. He moved forward toward the base of the tree, trying to remember what his clever son had done to begin the climb.

"Daddy, I want to climb, too." Will knew the tug on his pants. He looked down at his little girl, who was using his leg to block the wind.

"You're too small!" Will shouted down. But the wind was dragging his words away.

"You let *him*!" She began to cry.

Will picked his little girl up in his arms. "Too dangerous," he spoke into her ear.

"Will!" His wife's scream beside him warmed his ear. The wind had grown cold; he could feel ice in the wrinkles of his clothes.

He turned. Her face was white, floating in the cold black air. "It's going to be okay!" Will cried against the wind. "He's a *good* boy! A *great* boy! Don't you see? A much better boy than I ever was!"

Will turned back toward the tree, where his son played and laughed, his son's face hot and glorious in the wind, the moon laying shiny streaks into his dark hair. Lightning played in the distant boughs of the forest, moving toward the house. Will started toward the climbing tree, his wife and daughter clinging to him. But he remembered he no longer knew how to climb, and stopped halfway between the house and the tree.

His beautiful son stopped laughing and stared down at Will. Will brought a nervous hand up to his lips, then realized he had no beer. He felt a sudden panic as he knew his son had seen what life was like back on the ground.

Lightning began to ripple the trees. Up in the highest part of the tree, his beautiful son laughed and started climbing higher.

It was a good climbing tree. A wonderful climbing tree. Will had taught his good son not to be afraid to do things. Will had taught him the lessons Will had never known. Will had taught him not to be afraid to live.

"No!" Will cried out to the trees. "Come back! It's not safe!"

But in the trees there were boys laughing and playing, unafraid and with no sense of danger. Dark hair flew as the boys climbed higher, pushing and wrestling in the weak, thin upper branches of the forest. Lightning bleached their hair. Wind and electricity gave them wings.

"Will! Get him *back*!" his wife screamed.

"He's a good boy, he's a wild boy, he's a beautiful boy!" Will shouted above the wind.

The climbing tree rose up and did a somersault, the kind Will had always been afraid of doing. The forest floated up out of its roots and shouted. And all the boys in the trees laughed so hard they cried, in love with themselves and in love with each other.

And Will's beautiful son was gone, climbing *so* high, climbing to where Will had always been afraid to go.

GARRY KILWORTH
Truman Capote's Trilby: The Facts

One of the greatest pleasures about putting this collection together each year is looking beyond the newstand magazines and major publishers to find stories printed in out-of-the-way venues that the average reader is likely to have missed. The following story is one of these: a charming flight of fancy from the pages of the small British magazine *Back Brain Recluse*.

Garry Kilworth is an impressively versatile writer who contributes (as he did last year) two stories to this volume, one originally published as adult fantasy and one originally published for children. Kilworth was born in England but spent his childhood mainly in South Arabia, listening to arabesque tales that would influence his later writing. He has lived and worked in Africa, Asia and the Middle East; currently he and his wife live in Hong Kong. He is the author of *Hunter's Moon* and more than a dozen other novels and story collections.

—T.W.

Truman Capote's Trilby: The Facts

GARRY KILWORTH

I have never been a great lover of hats. For one thing they tend to crush one's hair and leave it looking like sweaty straw. For another, individual hats are never thoroughly in fashion these days and wearers are considered faintly eccentric. Even in the city they draw the occasional amused smile or nudge, unless seen on the head of someone stepping out of a Rolls Royce. Of course, there are places where a hat is completely acceptable, such as at sporting events—Ascot, or the boat race—but for people like me, on a modest income, buying a hat for a single occasion is an extravagance. Finally, I think my head is the wrong shape for most hats. Its supports headgear which moulds itself to the skull, like a ski hat, but tends to reshape less obsequious millinery into something almost grotesque in outward appearance.

It was, therefore, with some surprise that I found myself staring at the trilby in the window of Donne's of Oxford Street.

Purchasing a trilby requires special nerve and should really only be undertaken by a person with a charisma impossible to influence, like Bogart or the Orson Welles of *The Third Man*. The trilby has a personality, an ego, all of its own. If the wearer is not strong enough to resist alteration, it is better to steer clear of such forceful dominant items, the demi-gods and despots of hatlands and the high country.

In any case, the trilby has a dubious history, which is difficult to deny. It flaunts an ancestry which most of us would prefer to keep locked in a cupboard with all the other skeletons: forefathers that witnessed—let's not mince words—*took part in* such infamous deeds as the St. Valentine's Day Massacre, and later attended the funerals without so much as a droop of the brim. The Roaring Twenties and the trilby are inseparable. A gangster's hat. Phillip Marlowe gave it back some fictional respectability, but the taint remains. Of course, women too have worn the trilby, but since women tend to be promiscuous in the use of headwear we can assume that any honour regained from that quarter is open to question. In the forties, again, its reputation sank to a very dark level when the Gestapo adopted it (along with its constant companion, the trench coat) as part of their uniform, not to mention its sinister association with Papa Doc's Haitian secret police, the terrible *Tontons Macoute*. So, the trilby is not exactly a gentleman's hat, its motives are questionable to say the least, and it often ends its days perched on the back of an Australian head in some sweltering out-back creek, keeping off the flies.

It is a hat given to swaggering gestures and sloping cuteness, famed for its slouch.

Consequently, when I saw this particular trilby in the shop window, and felt a strong urge to buy it, I tried to allow my intellect to govern my emotions. I was shocked by the strength of those emotions. They produced fantasies the kind I used to have in my youth. I saw myself travelling on the Paris metro, men staring at me in envy and women attempting to attract my attention. These pretty pictures used to preceed a lot of purchases as a young man. Apparently they were still powerful enough to rule my head, because I found myself in the shop, self-consciously trying on the trilby. I left the place wearing it.

The effect on the city's populace was not startling, but I felt rather good just the same. The hat seemed a natural part of me, and I wondered, even after those first few paces along the pavement, how I had ever managed without it. Confidence entered my bones: my step was light. I passed a group of Italians, sitting outside the Café Munchen drinking beer. One of them pointed with his chin, the way Latins do, and the others looked and nodded gravely. They approved. Italians are known to have good dress sense, so this increased my feeling of well-being.

Once on the tube, if the women did not exactly jostle each other for a better view of my new hat, they certainly gave it second glances. My self-consciousness evaporated almost completely. In the shop the sales assistant had placed the hat on my head in a conventional position. I now tipped it at a rakish angle, emphasising, I was sure, my angular jaw. The world grew lighter.

Back at my two-roomed flat, I took the trilby and placed it where I could see it, on the dresser which also served as a desk. This piece of furniture stood exactly opposite the doorway between my kitchen-diner and the bedroom, and I made a meal then sat and studied the article from my position at the table. It was grey with a dark grey band. Not immediately exciting in its aspect, but there was a certain charm which gave me a possessive glow of satisfaction. This was *my* hat: no one else's. Also, there was an independence about this trilby which enhanced my feeling of ownership. This self-possessed hat had chosen *me*.

That evening I took the hat to see Harrison Ford's rugged-looking trilby in *Raiders of the Lost Ark*. We both admired the way it managed to remain on Ford's head, even during the most frantic stunts. Towards the end of the performance we were asked to leave because a woman sitting behind us could not see the screen, but by that time most of the best scenes were over.

The next morning I wore it to work. The journey was delightful, but on reaching the office in Theobald's Road, I arrived at the same time as Jason Rachman, one of the company's high-fliers.

"Nice lid," he said with a smirk, as we went through the double-doors together. "It's a trilby," I said, "not a *lid*."

He stopped, looking taken aback. I had never spoken to him as firmly as that before, and I think he was shocked at my assertiveness. He looked slightly confused for a moment, then said, "No, no—I'm serious. It suits you. I've often thought of buying a trilby myself—never had the nerve. Perhaps now that you've got one, I'll have a go. So long as you don't mind me copying . . ."

I was feeling magnanimous.

"Not at all," and I gave him the address of the shop. No one has ever asked me such things before.

At first I placed the hat on my desk, within reach, but one of the managers passed by and told me to put it on the hat rack at the entrance to the office. I had no choice.

The following Saturday I made a terrible mistake. I don't know what made me do it. I suppose, after one has taken a tremendous new step, a giant stride, the temptation to go much further is very strong. I remember as a younger man I went on a youth hostel tour of the Scottish Highlands, and it was so successful I considered a trip to Tibet. Of course, the latter would have been a disaster. I'm not equipped, mentally or physically, for scaling the Himalayas, but the bug had got me and I felt that I could take on anything that mountain ranges had to offer. Fortunately finances prevented me from making a complete idiot of myself.

Not so on Saturday. On Saturday I went the whole hog. I bought a fresh band for the crown of my trilby, a Big White Hunter thing that screamed at people from fifty yards away. A leopardskin band. How crass. How *stupid!* How kitsch. Who did I think I was? Hemingway?

The hat hated it of course. I wore the band for one morning only and then replaced it with the old grey ribbon. The leopardskin attracted the wrong sort of attention and made me feel vulnerable once more. After that experience, I never tried changing the hat again, and accepted it for what it was.

We settled into certain behaviour patterns, the trilby and I. One thing I learned was that it needed to be treated with respect and care. It was not a hat to be skimmed, James Stewart style, across the room, aimed at a peg or chair. Such undignified methods of removal were not to its liking, and I had not the lean grace of Mr. Stewart to enable me to bring the action off with the same aplomb. Also, contrary to Gene Kelly's doctrine, it did not improve for being danced through the streets in a downpour. Nor did it enjoy being crushed in a Cagney grip, or being battered into a shape reminiscent of Bogart's face. It was best placed, not tossed or jammed. It liked light, airy spaces, not dark corners. It enjoyed attention, but only for itself, not because of the angle at which it was worn, or how much of my brow showed beneath the brim.

We got on fine together, for several months. So well, in fact, that I began to take it for granted.

We made lots of new friends, who would call at the flat, or telephone to arrange an evening out: friends of both sexes. Although no really special relationship developed, these newcomers in my life became important to me.

There was Tag, a West Indian with a stylish beret; and Jake, a young Lancastrian who sported one of those colourful knitted caps. Then of course there was Beatrice, who always wore nice curled-brim bowlers: the kind of hat you often see on Cheltenham young ladies. Finally, there was Mona. Mona had seen *Annie Hall* six times and had consequently purchased a hat the twin of that cute, lopsided affair worn in the film by Diane Keaton.

Mona was my favourite. We once spent the night together and she put her Annie Hall hat under my trilby, so that they fitted snugly, one in the other.

"For company," she said.

Following in my footsteps, so to speak, Jason Rachman bought a trilby too, which he wore to the office, but I felt it was inferior to my own hat. It lacked refinement. Oh, it had a little panache and a certain sardonic humour, but its charm could not make up for its lack of sophistication, and it really was a rather shallow piece of headgear. Jason knew this, but he defended his trilby with a shrug and a smile, which was only right and proper.

As I said before, I began to take my trilby for granted, and that's when things started to go wrong between us.

Looking back on it, I suppose it was my fault. Things began to get pretty hectic at the office, especially after my promotion. I hardly had a minute to myself. My social life too, was a whirl of activity. Everything was done at a run, and, to my eternal shame, I forgot my trilby one evening, leaving it behind at the office.

The following morning I remembered it at about ten o'clock, but it was gone from its usual place on the rack. It eventually turned up behind someone's desk, dusty and covered in fluff. Anyway it was in a sorry state. I sent it to the cleaners and what with one thing and another was unable to retrieve it for two weeks.

Then I left it at home, several days running, simply forgetting to wear it. Unforgivable, but there it is: you don't realise the importance of these things at the time. Finally, the last straw was when I took Jason's trilby in mistake for my own. The next day, when we exchanged, correcting the error, I could see the experience had clearly upset my trilby quite badly. Jason had gone downhill a little since he had been passed over on the promotion ladder and tended to frequent bars and dives until the early hours of the morning. There were small stains on the brim and crown of my trilby and it had lost its shape in some steamy atmosphere.

That same evening, as I stepped out of the tube station at Tottenham Court Road, the hat blew off my head, sailed along Charing Cross Road, and got taken by a side-draught down Denmark Street. I ran after it, past the music shops and a rather sinister looking bookshop, but it had disappeared from the scene. I stood there for a while, by the small church on the corner, searching crannies and railings, but my hat had gone.

At first I tried to shrug it off. After all, it was only a hat, and there were plenty more of those to be had. Not that I actually *wanted* another hat (I told myself) since I seemed to have outgrown the need. I was more mature, more self-assured, and no longer concerned by the world and its ways. There were plenty of friends to visit and go out with, to the cinema or theatre. In fact a hat was rather an encumbrance. One had to find places to put it, or carry it in one's hand. Being without it was a kind of freedom. It had done me a favour, blowing away like that. I was free to go where I wished, with whom I wished, whether they were bare headed or not. Liberty is a heady tranquilizer, after a loss.

Unfortunately, my new friends did not turn out to be the kind of people I had previously thought. There were excuses and evasions, and they fell away from me with mumbled apologies. Even Mona. She told me one evening that we had better not see one another again, since she did not (after all) feel we were suited.

"It was fun," she said, "but our worlds are too far apart."

I think she felt embarrassed, walking along The Strand with a hatless man, because she remained a good two feet away and kept glancing down at the pavement, as if afraid of being recognised by someone she knew. She refused the offer to take her for a drink, saying she was on the wagon, and later that week I saw her in the company of a flat-capped fellow with a Plebeian brow. She cut me dead, in the street.

Anyway, all of my so-called new friends went the same way: towards the exit. I can't say it didn't upset me, because it did. I was terribly depressed. It was all so unfair.

There were problems at work, too. Some Japanese businessmen visited the firm and they were left in my hands. I was so distracted by the decline of my social life however, I unwittingly neglected them and the result was a reprimand from one of our directors.

"And do something about your appearance," said my boss afterwards. "You seem to have gone to seed lately. This company depends upon smart executives to give it a good image. A haircut would make a difference . . ."

After a week of sleepless nights, I reluctantly went looking for my lost trilby. I suppose I had hoped that it would turn up on its own, without effort on my part. Although I hadn't marked the leather headband, I had written my name and address on a piece of paper and tucked it inside. I scoured the found ads and rang various lost property offices, without success. Finally, I took to wandering the streets after work, searching the alleys. Once, I snatched the headgear off an old tramp, thinking it was my trilby, but I had made a mistake and had to apologise while the old fellow remonstrated with me, using the most obnoxious language. It took five pounds to get rid of him.

There was a period when I saw the trilby everywhere: on the tube, outside a cinema, going to work. But always, on closer inspection, it turned out to be a stranger which just happened to resemble my trilby superficially. Having once made an error in recognition, I was most careful not to handle these look-alikes, but the wearers often resented my staring, even from a distance, hurrying away into the crowd, or turning to glare at me.

Shortly after this period I lost my job through non-attendance at work. I didn't care any more. I began to hit the bottle.

Miserably, as the weeks went by, I toured the London streets, extending my area of search, and growing more despondent, and, yes, more resentful towards my erstwhile headwear. There were several million hats in London. What chance did I stand of finding one particular hat? The weeks crept into months, and gradually my frustration turned to anger, my anger to hatred. I convinced myself that my trilby was deliberately avoiding me. There were still times when I got morose and maudlin—when I missed it dreadfully—but many hours were spent over a glass bitterly regretting wasted dreams and shattered hopes. It seemed so silly—one breeze, one single breeze, and we had parted forever. My hatred bred a rage within me which was beyond my control. I told myself I would not be responsible for my actions, should I ever lay hands on that hat again. I bought myself another, a Sherlock Holmes deerstalker, and though we were not entirely compatible we were tolerant with one another, hoping to grow closer together as the relationship matured.

One day in October, when I was least expecting an encounter, I finally saw my old trilby plastered against a fence by the wind. I knew it instantly, though it had aged dramatically since I had last seen it. I went to it, picked it up, dusted it off—and rammed it into the nearest waste bin amongst some discarded Coke cans and cigarette packets! Remembering I had the trilby's replacement on my head I tipped my new deerstalker contemptuously at my ex, and hoped the humiliation was complete. I went home, determined to forget our association.

Six nights later the police came to my flat.

They questioned me concerning my whereabouts on an evening two nights previously. Eventually, they took me away, and in the presence of a lawyer, charged me with the murder of a woman whose corpse had been found near the Thames, close to Waterloo Bridge. A trilby—my hat, with name and address still inside the band—had been found pinned beneath her body. They later produced this item of clothing in court. Since it was associated with me it had gained the same sort of notoriety and attention from the gutter press as myself. However, it was its role as principal witness for the prosecution that seemed to suit it best. Like I said earlier, the trilby has a bad track record: you can't trust a trilby. When the prosecuting counsel pushed it in front of me, his accusations tying me in knots, it didn't help my case any when I threw lighter fuel on the brim and tried to set light to it.

However, at the last hour my own counsel called a witness to the stand who had seen the woman earlier the same evening that she died, and he stated that she 'had the face of a suicide'. (This remark was subsequently stricken from the record, but not from the minds of the jury). Coupled with this was a statement from a medical consultant who had independently examined the body. In his professional opinion the police doctor was mistaken. He himself was convinced that the dead woman could have sustained such injuries as a result of a fall, say from a bridge parapet onto concrete.

Despite the controversy which raged in the press, I was acquitted and walked from the courts 'a sadder but wiser man', though not without a stain on my character. There were those who were still convinced of my guilt, not least among them the police.

* * *

I never saw my hat again. The last I heard, it went on the stage. Someone had written a play around my court case, and the exhibit used in the actual court room where the trial took place was considered the main crowd puller at the theatre. My ex was a box office success, right from the opening night.

Since then a certain tabloid has fostered the tale that the hat was privately purchased by Truman Capote, shortly before his death: that it attended wild New York parties and was passed around superstars and celebrities. This is an extravagant claim, to which I give little credence. To my knowledge Mr. Capote preferred a more flamboyant form of headwear, such as a panama—certainly not second-hand grey trilbies, no matter how colourful their histories. Nevertheless, to most people my hat has become 'Truman Capote's trilby', for which unlikely title I should be grateful. My connection with the item has almost been forgotten: overshadowed by the charismatic influence of the famous author's name.

Good luck to it. I know one thing. I shall never trust a trilby again, as long as I live. They're not worth it. They use you up and then they blow away. And when they've had enough of the street life, they have the audacity to expect to be taken back again, no questions asked. They want the magic to last forever, and as everyone knows, things don't work out like that. Magical relationships grow into ordinary lives, sooner or later.

IAN R. MacLEOD
Green

Ian R. MacLeod is a British writer who has published a number of short stories in *Isaac Asimov's SF Magazine, Interzone, Amazing* and *Weird Tales*, including "1/72nd Scale" which was a recent Nebula Award nominee. MacLeod lives with his wife and their daughter in the West Midlands of England.

"Green" is a subtle and evocative tale set in that twilight landscape where the world of faery intersects with our own, the gardens and fields and ivy-covered woods where a dark shadow might be a fairy—or just a trick of light. It comes from the mid-December issue of *Isaac Asimov's*.

—T.W.

Green

IAN R. MacLEOD

There are many kinds of pest in a garden. Thrips and greenfly. Flea beetles, fairies, and fungi. Manslugs that nibble leaf-heraldry to mark the territory of their bearded king. Leatherjackets. Mealy bugs. An unmarshaled army bickering to bore a ripening fruit or wither a well-formed stem.

Mark knew them all. Their names had been his early words. His first memory was horror at the broken, weeping flesh of a blighted tomato. His second, the garden of his parents' cottage in the row at the south east corner of my Lord Widder's estate. Sitting in sunshine with the drone of the bees. Roses nodding with the weight of summer. The tawny wall. Everything high above, and the hot sky furthest of all, beyond reach even if he could persuade his legs to stand. Then there was movement. Something quick and brown. And there again; sheen of wings and ivory flicker of eyes and teeth in the wall shadow beneath the roses where plumes of lavender scented the air. He watched the tiny figure, something that moved in a world even wider and brighter than his own. Its movements were wild and sharp, like a bird's, hands darting to tuck the furry globes of lavender and push them into a tiny slung pouch. Its head flickered this way and that, looking for danger, and watching Mark, his presence, weighing up the threat.

Brownie. Mark knew the word. A brownie. And even then his gardener's instincts told him that this one was benign, that the lavender would thrive regardless of its attention. Mark wasn't sure what he did next. Maybe he laughed, perhaps he reached out a hand, but quick as a blink, the brownie was gone.

The wall shrank in a flurry of years until Mark could sit dangling his feet in the high grass on the far side. In the settling warmth of late afternoons, he would watch that special place amid the tunnel shadows of the orchard where the track from the estate gardens turned into sight. From the open kitchen window in the cottage behind, the clip of the chopping board, steam and the smell of vegetables seemed to draw his father into view, the hobble of his walk, the hump of his leather apron slung across his left shoulder.

Mark remembered the flash of excitement. Turning to call inside to his mother across the little stretch of their garden. And when he thought of those times, when he grew maudlin and tried to make sense of these things, he would always struggle to prolong that glance back through the open window, to penetrate the cooking shadows of the kitchen and glimpse the woman who breathed and lived and hummed to herself there. But even when he forced his mind into fantasy, she remained hidden by the play of summer light. A vague movement, nothing more than the shape of a cloud seen at night on a river. That was his sole memory of his mother.

In later years when he and his father were alone, he'd try to get him to talk about her. But his father's face would cloud with the same puzzlement that Mark recognized within himself. His lips would shape wordless sounds as though he too had lost his memories. And eventually, one way or another, he'd always tell the same story. How they'd honeymooned at the coast, walked the promenade in fresh new clothes like a couple of swells. A stall with striped awnings had offered daguerreotypes for a pound a throw and they'd stood out in the salt air, debating whether to have their likenesses taken. But it was almost all the money they had and the need for a meal and perhaps even a drink before they went back to the boarding house won the day. So, to his father's bitter regret, he had no face in a frame to remind him of the life he'd lost.

Mark and his father were close, sharing their forgetful grief, caring haphazardly for the cottage and each other, and, above all, responding to the growth of all things leafed, all things that came from the earth, all things green. Mark went to the school by the chestnut tree in the vale, but the other children found him vague and aloof. Not friend, nor enemy, nor prey. So Mark stood apart from the dusty rabble at playtime and participated woodenly in the organized games. His real lessons took place at home, with his father.

Their own cottage garden was small but, like the intricate petals of a rose, opened layer upon layer of wonder. In the evenings, free from school and work, they tended and watered, often so deep into the twilight that the soil became a dark mist in their hands. And his father, working in the big estate, clipping and hoeing for my Lord Widder, would sometimes bring home a gaudy broken bloom, a vegetable too huge for the pot yet still rejected as a dwarf in the competition greenhouses, or even—as with the blighted tomato—object lessons in decay and disease.

One day in autumn, his father trudged home through brown gusts of leaves and placed a barred wooden trap down on the kitchen table. Then he struck a lamp and held it close so that Mark could see what it was that whimpered and scurried inside.

"I stopped them from dropping this one in the water butt," he said, crouching down to level his face with Mark and the edge of the table. "Thought you might want to see it."

The creature put its hands to the bars and peered out, a prisoner in a tiny jail. It had damaged its wings in an initial attempt to escape; greenish-blue, they trailed at its back like torn scraps of paper. But now it seemed resigned to its confinement and tilted its head to watch as Mark and his father talked.

"Now, this is called a ferrish. They gather acorns, which no one minds." His father reached out and prodded a calloused finger, dark with ingrained dirt. The creature backed away from the bars. "But they torment the horses in the stables, though only the Devil knows exactly why and he isn't telling. My Lord Widder will not have his prize mounts tormented."

"Can I keep it?" Mark asked. "Keep it as a pet?"

His father shook his head. "It's a thing from the wild. Doesn't belong here with us any more than you or I belong up a tree." ·

"But please . . ."

Mark was uncharacteristically pleading and insistent. Although he didn't realize it, he was a lonely child at heart, withdrawing from the companionship of school-friends and the people on the estate as much from fear as from self-sufficiency. He could just picture the ferrish sitting—after weeks of slow and careful persuasion—on his shoulder like a magical parrot. The fun they would have together! The games!

Reluctantly, his father agreed.

Mark hurried into the deepening evening. He waded carelessly through the dead leaves and wind-flattened nettles that stretched down from the bottom of the garden to the misting river and retrieved the rabbit hutch that had lain there since the half-forgotten demise of Bobbity the year before. Brushing woodlice from its sides, he carried the big, awkward box back into the kitchen.

As his father stoked up the fire and chopped carrots and onions for dinner, Mark used his precocious skills as a maker to tack back the warped boards and tighten the loose mesh at the front. He worked on his knees on the worn firelit rug and the ferrish stared down at him from the table through the bars of the trap. He screwed doweling rods in as perches, scattered a few handfuls of straw and filled Bobbity's old bowl in the corner with water. It was dark now outside and food—acorns, he supposed—would have to wait until morning.

Mark surveyed his work on the hutch, taking proud, stew-scented breaths of the dim kitchen air. But he was unwilling to lift the trap and asked his father to take it down from the table.

"Slowly does it." His father wiped potato peelings from his hands and slid back the door of the trap, pressing it against the wider entrance to the hutch.

The ferrish cowered at the back, reluctant to come out. His father gave the little box a tap, then a gentle shake. Just as Mark was leaning down to peer inside, the ferrish flew from the trap, then, before he could close the door, out of the hutch again and into the kitchen.

Its chest heaving with a breathy, whistling sound, it perched on top of the frame of an old engraving by the closed door. Mark and his father moved towards it, their arms outstretched like zombies. Before they could close around the ferrish, it flitted between them and circled the room twice in quick and silent flight before swerving towards the window and bumping into the pane like a heavy moth. It fluttered to the floor and dragged itself towards a chair leg, briefly out of reach of their clasping hands. Slowly, quietly, they circled around both sides of the kitchen table, but the ferrish climbed into the air again, settling awkwardly on the stone rim of the sink. Back bent, body palpitating, wings bedraggled, it regarded them balefully as they approached once more.

The closer of the two, Mark scraped a chair out of the way and moved towards it, trying to look trustworthy, gentle. It obviously had little energy left.

"It's all right," he whispered. "Nothing to be afraid of."

The creature took off, batting by chance against Mark's outstretched hand. He felt the quick warmth clawing against his palm, but before he could close his fingers it was away.

Mark span around in time to see the ferrish dart towards the fire. The chimney, he thought. Of course, the chimney! But instead of flying upwards into the smoke drifting darkness and freedom, the ferrish dived into the heat.

There was a scream—neither of pain nor joy, but like the wind in the treetops on a wild night—and the flames briefly brightened. Then there was only stillness, and the rattle of the teakettle as it came slowly to the boil.

The ferrish's death was a sad lesson for Mark to learn. He carried the guilt with him for all of that winter; a long time for someone so young when the dark months stretch like a stony road lit only by the brightness of Christmas, holly berries and the occasional appearance of an impertinent mushroom. But it taught him that even in a garden, even in my Lord Widder's planned and regimented estate, there were many things that were wild, things that were free.

The earth awoke again. Summer followed spring, and Mark's reputation as a loner increased. In those precious hours when there was no school and little urgent work to be done in the garden at home, he would wander and explore the endless grounds of the Widder estate. There were, of course, strict rules as to where the young son of an under gardener could go—many of the workers lived out their whole lives on the estate without ever even glimpsing the distant, stately white porticos of the great house. These rules Mark never deliberately disobeyed. If he knew a place was forbidden, a laurel or an ivy wall that represented a boundary which only certain privileged gardeners were permitted to cross, he would turn away along less sacrosanct paths. He wandered, avoiding the gardeners and laborers who, seeing him in any part of the estate without any obvious purpose, invariably asked just what he thought he was doing. And, sometimes, he got lost.

In strange and unexplored parts of the garden, the distinctions between the permitted and the outlawed became deliciously vague. Not knowing whether he was allowed to be there was part of the joy of discovering new places, of getting lost, of crossing a stepping stone stream into a bluebell wood, of finding a marble chair engraved with seahorses overlooking a waterfall in a ferny dell.

Lord Widder's birthday in July was always a special day. In celebration, the entire estate was permitted a day of rest, something that never happened on Sundays and holy days despite the injunctions of the clergy. Then, there were always urgent tasks to be done in the garden, and of course the estate employees used what time they could to work for themselves on their own plots and houses. But, unlike God, when my Lord Widder decreed a day of rest, he meant it. And woe betide anyone found doing anything more strenuous than lifting a mug of tea.

So Mark set out across the orchard after breakfast with the whole day blissfully ahead of him. It was still early, but the sun was strong through the branches, the grass dry underfoot. Off down the slope to his left in the bowl of the valley where the prize Widder sheep grazed, the spire of Saint Pepper's, one of the estate churches, rose from a cluster of cottages and trees to prick the haze. The ave bell struck once, rippling the still air. Saint Pepper's and all the other churches throughout the estate would continue to strike the hour and half hour until dusk. When my Lord Widder had been much, much younger, the strike enumerated the years of his life, but now and for many years the stars came out before a full account could be given.

Through the white gate and along the raised track between the asparagus beds. Past the greenhouses. And more greenhouses. And yet more. A crystal garden on all sides, mirroring the flash of the sky. Inside, thick growths of cucumber and tomato billowed and clawed the glass like prisoners. Further on, stepping over hosepipes and wheelbarrows left in uncharacteristic abandon by workers careless in the knowledge that no one would be out to inspect their labors, greenhouse after greenhouse was filled with grapevines. Mark knew as well as any gardener that there were plenty of species of grape that could be grown outside on a south facing wall, but my Lord Widder was said to prefer the softer, sweeter texture of the more delicate varieties. Following the track between the greenhouses, Mark wondered how anyone, even an aristocrat, could eat so many grapes.

He eventually reached the mountainous privet hedge that marked the outermost boundary of the formal gardens. Here, the silence was still more obvious; on almost any other day of the year the privateers would be up on their ladders, clipping and trimming. Mark's father always said they were the happiest of all the workers on the estate. Privet suffers from few pests and seldom dies if properly mulched. It simply grows.

Mark followed the long shadow of the hedge to a white gate set in it like a door in a wall. He went through, down the dim tunnel under the hedge, thinking, although he'd only seen them in books, of a train racing under a hill towards a widening speck of light. Savoring the moment, he emerged into the heat.

Off in the distance, Saint Pepper's chimed another year of Lord Widder's life. The differing pitches of two other estate churches echoed from other directions moments later.

He was on familiar ground here. The mile-long avenue stretched from the perimeter, decked out with roses, dahlias and comical red hot pokers, leading him to a circular lake of grass centered by a great stone bird bath big enough to wash a griffon. This was one of his favorite places. From it, like doors leading from a giant hall, paths opened into the mysteries of the garden.

He took the way downhill through long grass and copses of oak. As the sun climbed, the trees gathered in larger masses, darker and thicker, until gradually, like falling into a dream, Mark found that they were all around him, over his head, shutting out all but splinters of the sun.

His toes stubbed upraised roots. Ropes of ivy tumbled into his face. The path was tentative and meandering, but the dense undergrowth gave him little choice but to follow. There was no birdsong, little noise but the faint sea murmur overhead. Mark gazed around in puzzled wonder as he walked, his gardener's instincts in turmoil. Never before had he seen a place where things were simply left to grow. Not checked, or weeded or staked or deadheaded or pruned.

The whisper of the topmost branches only added to the stillness. He jumped at the sound of a woodpecker hammering in the green shadows. As the path wound on between massive trunks and nettles, he stepped over a trail of marching ants. A squirrel darted up an oak and regarded him as it cleaned its whiskers, and further on he saw a half dozen manslugs chomping the succulent stems of a clump of wild rhubarb. Unafraid, they raised their heads towards him as he passed, their wet, fronded mouths gaping open as if they were about to break into song.

Then Mark saw a sea-horse. He stopped and stared. It was a little way off the track, swaying gently to and fro in the dreaming heat of the forest, its tail twined around a branch. He worked his way around towering foxgloves to get a better look. Sensing his presence, the sea-horse rippled its fins and drifted slowly, unconcernedly, into the air. Its scales, caught in a ribbon of sunlight, flashed rainbows. Entranced, Mark waded on through the undergrowth.

The sea-horse drifted ahead, unhurried. Mark stumbled after, his hands outstretched like a baby clutching for a bubble. A sea-horse of the air! Even after the experience with the ferrish, there was still a large part of him that wanted to touch, to understand.

Reaching a particularly thick stretch of bramble, the sea-horse floated high and over. Pushing his way blindly through, Mark suddenly felt the ground shoot from under him. He fell, down and out into brilliant sunlight.

Scratched, stung and muddied, he climbed out from the ankle-deep water of a ditch and looked around. He was in some unknown part of the landscaped gardens—the sea-horse had vanished. Then, ahead between a screen of holly, something bright flashed. Mark ran towards it, and found himself teetering at the stone lip of a wide pool. Carp glistened like gold in the shade beneath the lilies. Around the edge a boy was riding a bicycle. He tinkled his bell. Polished chrome sparked.

"Hey!"

Mark stepped out of the way in surprise, but the boy pulled up and dismounted.

He was about Mark's age, but fairer skinned and slightly taller. Freckles splattered his cheeks and joined in a dark stripe across his nose. The clothes he wore were almost as scruffy as Mark's, but still Mark could see they were conspicuously better made.

"And just who are you?"

Mark stammered his name.

"Adrian Widder."

The boy held out his hand. Mark had never shaken hands before, but he took it anyway.

"Not the left hand, stupid. The right. Like this."

"I see."

"Would you like a go on my bike? I don't mind."

Mark glanced down at the smooth lines, the bright red frame, the cream mudguards. "I can't ride."

"You can't do much, can you?"

Mark shrugged.

"Do you want to learn? I mean, anyone can do it as long as they're not an absolute and complete moron."

"Wouldn't mind."

They fell into step together, the wheels of the bicycle ticking and flashing between them.

The boy said, "It's easiest on the big lawn, softer if you fall. Up here, through the rose garden."

"Did you say your name was Widder?" Mark asked.

"Yes, I just told you. Adrian Widder. Are you this stupid naturally or do you take lessons?"

Mark ignored the taunt. He'd realized already that the boy didn't mean to hurt. "You can't be . . . Lord Widder . . . can you?"

"That's my father."

"It's his birthday."

"When?"

"Today."

"How do you know that?"

"Everyone on the estate knows," Mark said, glad that he was able to put Adrian right on something. "It's a special day. You must have heard the bells tolling."

Adrian shook his head. "Mother will have given him some present from me, I suppose. He's not here, anyway. Spends most of his time up in the capital with the King. The King needs him a lot."

"What for?"

"To fight, that sort of thing. Father's a great swordsman. I've read it in the papers."

They walked on through the rose garden. The bicycle tires sighed in the gravel. The bees droned. An easy silence fell between them, the sort that didn't demand to be filled by pointless words. For no reason he could easily explain, Mark liked Adrian Widder. He recognized another loner, and their mutual shyness had been overcome by the sheer accident of their meeting. There was no pressure, no reason why they should get on. Nobody *expected* them to be friends. And somehow, without trying, it became easy.

"Well, here we are." Adrian creaked open a gate in a wall.

Mark followed him through.

And stopped.

Adrian turned. "What is it? Come on!"

Mark stepped slowly across rich turf. Ahead in the midday sun, an immense lawn rolled on and on and on. And in the distant green shimmered the spires and domes of something that was too vast, too ornate to be called simply a building.

"That's the house," Adrian said offhandedly. "Haven't you ever seen a house before? Now, do you want to learn to ride or not?"

Mark did.

Adrian held the handlebars as Mark climbed on.

Mark fell off.

They tried again and again, Adrian shoving at the saddle to get him going and Mark's feet clawing uselessly at the pedals. And, every time, he fell off, down into the softness and the scent of the grass. It all happened so simply, so predictably, that they began to chuckle, then to laugh. Jaws aching, wiping tears from their eyes and noses, they continued. And the dogged stupidity of their repeated actions—Mark getting on, Mark falling off, Mark getting on again—made their laughter even better, even worse. Eventually, they had to lie down on the lawn, giggling in helpless spasms.

Mark was the first to recover. He sniffed, wiped his nose on the back of his hand, picked up the bicycle. Shoulders still shaking, Adrian propped himself up on his elbows to watch. Mark pushed off.

For once, his feet locked on the pedals. Miraculously, the bicycle started to roll forwards under him. He pedaled faster. The ground flashed by. It was wonderful, like flying. It could only be magic that kept the thing from falling over.

"Look!" he yelled. "Look at me!"

He glanced back towards Adrian, then gently tilted the handlebars to turn. Immediately, the bicycle became a wild thing again. It bucked, tossing him high into the air. The grass slammed into his face, a pedal banged his shin. They both started to laugh again.

As the afternoon flowed across the great blue sky, Mark learned—slowly and somewhat painfully—how to turn corners, how to start and, trickiest of all, how to stop. And gradually they moved down the lawn towards the house.

At about three, a dark-suited man emerged from a far door in a distant corner of the house and walked slowly over to them. Stretched on the grass as Adrian shot back and forth to demonstrate how to freewheel, Mark watched him advance. He was carrying a tray, and on it were tumblers and a huge jug of something that looked green and thirstquenching.

Adrian skidded to a halt. "Well done, Lawrence."

Lawrence placed the tray on the grass and looked at Mark oddly. Beads of sweat twinkled in the sunlight on his bald head. "I thought I should bring a glass for your friend as well."

"He's learning to ride my bicycle."

"I see . . ." Lawrence straightened up and began to walk slowly back towards the house. His bottom wobbled with each step. Mark and Adrian collapsed again into aching laughter. It was too painful, quite beyond the joke.

A short while later, as Mark was coming to terms with the discovery that the bicycle would continue to move even if you didn't pedal, the great French windows in the domed center of the house opened in a flash of sunlight.

Mark stopped the bicycle and dropped his feet from the pedals.

"Who's that?" he asked.

"Mother."

She was a lady dressed in white, carrying a white parasol. Even through the ghostly shimmer of the heat, Mark could tell she was beautiful. His thoughts struggled once again with the gaping memory of his own mother, the shadows inside that open kitchen window when he looked back from the wall. Please, he thought, make this the way she was.

"What a lovely day," she said, her clear voice and smile carrying ahead as she approached.

"This is Mark," Adrian said. "We met up at the fish pool. He's my friend."

"How do you do." She stopped in front of Mark and held out her hand. Still astride the bicycle, Mark felt stupid and awkward. But he knew which hand to offer.

"Hello," he said. Her hand felt strong and cool. "Your, um, lady."

She smiled again, her lovely face framed in the shade of the parasol. Her eyes were blue. They widened in gentle amusement. "Just hello is plenty," she said.

She glanced toward Adrian—who was brushing grass from his knees and standing up—then back toward Mark. "Can you cycle well?"

Mark grinned. "I couldn't at all until Adrian taught me."

"Just today?"

"Yes, just today."

"Congratulations, master Mark. You live on the estate?"

"Number three of the cottages up past the main orchards. My, er, father, he's an under gardener."

"What does he do?"

"Mostly berry fruits, I think. Some vegetables."

"It must be lovely, being a gardener, getting things to grow. Is that what you'd like to be?"

Mark nodded. No other option had ever occurred to him.

"You've got something stuck in your hair." She leaned forward. "Here." Close to, almost sharing the shade of the parasol, Mark could smell her scent. By the time she'd pulled back again and dropped the burr on the grass, he'd decided he was in love.

"Well." She twirled the parasol. "I'm afraid Adrian has to come inside now."

Adrian said, "But—"

"—No," she cut in firmly, without raising her voice. "You promised Master Ignatius that you'd finish that project. And a promise is a promise. Isn't that right, Mark?"

"Yes," Mark said. He realized that this wasn't a subject for negotiation. He climbed off the beautiful red and cream bicycle and wheeled it over to Adrian, who took it with the seriousness of a priest handling the sacrament. Without a word—children never understand the need for farewells—he followed his mother back towards the great house.

When Adrian had leaned the bicycle against the wall and the French windows had flashed shut again, Mark turned and ran like the wind.

The day after was a school day; it should have been an ordinary day. But Mark's father woke him early, a letter clasped awkwardly in his hand.

"This came," he said. "Just now as I was out doing a bit of weeding out the front. A man in uniform . . ."

Mark sat up and took the letter from him. He knew his father's reading was uncertain at the best of times. The paper was creased and slightly grubby from his father's fingers, but was a rich cream with an embossed red crest and letter heading and smelt of books and leather and luxury.

"It's about me," Mark said as comprehension and surprise trickled over him. "It says I've got to leave here and go as an apprentice gardener in the King's estate at Maldon."

"Now . . ." A half-hopeful smile crinkled his father's stubbled face. "That's foolishness, son. What does it really say?"

Mark glanced down at the letter again, almost doubting his own words. "That's what it says. I've got to leave here and go."

The black limousine came out of the rain, rumbling and splashing along the cart tracks to the cottage, pursued by drenched and shouting children and watched by arms-folded clusters of incredulous neighbors sheltering in porches and under dripping trees. The liveried driver took Mark's small case and held open the rear door. Mark descended into deep pile and leather. He hardly had time to glance back through the window and the rain before the cottages and his father had gone from sight.

It took most of the day to reach Maldon. Mark had to ask the driver to stop many times—he discovered that he suffered from travel sickness—but at least being ill gave him an excuse for his tears. He hardly noticed the world through which they passed, a world he had never seen before; cut off in his sickness by the rain-beaded windows, none of it seemed real, least of all the great forest that surrounded Maldon. As evening set in, the limousine lost its purr and strained grumpily up and down hills and roads tunneled by boughs and huge greenery. Wet fingers of bush and fern trailed and whispered along the panels or pushed themselves against the windows like sudden, eerie faces.

Finally, a great gate in a huge wall opened ahead. When they were through it was as though the forest had never been. After swishing along gravel roads across smooth acres of lake and lawn, the limousine finally stopped.

Mark stumbled out. The driver gave him back his case. The rain had faded and the air was evening dim, scented with green. Across the puddled and mossy paving a great, ivy clad building hunched its red roofs against forest hills and grey sky. So this was Maldon. Mark was impressed, but also a little disappointed; the house was no larger than the Widder house, and certainly less ornate.

"Where does the king live?" he wondered aloud, glancing along the rows of windows.

The driver snorted. "The castle is miles away, not that the king's ever there. This is just the hostel for the apprentices, for little oiks like you."

Mark hated Maldon from the start. After the initiations in the trembling darkness of the dormitory, after the forced fights and the preliminary beatings by the hostel masters, life settled into a bleak routine.

No reigning monarch had visited Maldon for more than fifty years. It continued to function, but, like the rain clouds that gathered so frequently on the surrounding hills, a greyness permeated the estate. The lawns and hedges were trimmed, exotic fruits were tended for the royal table, harvested, then left to rot. The solitary yearly rose that blossomed on the Culpen bush which traditionally was presented to the king on Saint Errig's day in July opened its petals, and let them fall. The king and his court preferred the diversions of the capital or, if they wanted to risk a little fresh air, there were more southerly retreats where the sun could be relied on.

In his misery—misery so predictable that Mark ceased to be conscious of it as anything other than normality—he still found comfort in all things green, all things that grew.

He soon realized that he knew tricks from his father that the gardeners at Maldon had somehow forgotten, or never known. How apple suckers, sawfly, and earwigs could be collected from fruit trees simply by hanging an open matchbox at the end of the branch. How a scatter of rose petals would draw the fairies away from the cabbages and a circle of clinker would keep the common slug at bay.

His knowledge brought mixed rewards. To stand out in any way from the other apprentices guaranteed a greater number of fights and beatings, but at the same time the hostel masters and under gardeners weren't foolish enough to turn away from good advice. Of course, they usually snatched the credit for Mark's efforts, for an eelworm-free crop of onions or an ancient rose restored to health, but at heart they were lazy and found undue success almost as trying as failure. Gradually, Mark was allowed to rise.

When he was sixteen, he was made an under gardener and allocated a little room of his own away from the dormitory. The previous occupant had hung himself with green gardening twine looped around the coat hook on the back of the door, but no ghosts disturbed Mark. In the evenings, he could sit by the open sash window where the ivy whispered and nodded and read books from the hostel's mildewed library, or simply gaze out at the green. The pines across the courtyard. The wild and misty hills in the distance.

He was appointed a full gardener at eighteen and a half. Although he was still the same solitary young man living in the same hostel room, Mark was grateful for the small privileges of rank and, in his own way, proud. Now that he had the freedom—and the money—he was able at last to take the charabanc out through the forest and the farmland far beyond to visit his father. He saw how the shapes of remembered trees on the Widder estate had changed; matured and broadened, or bowed into decrepitude. And past the gate and in the low walled garden in front of the kitchen window, he saw how lavender had choked the roses, how moss had darkened the patch of lawn. The man who greeted him, now stooped under a snowfall of white hair, trembled and avoided the eyes of his son. He was in awe of Mark; a gardener before the age of nineteen.

Mark lay sleepless that night in his childhood bedroom as he wondered at the change that had come between them. Was it fear, unfamiliarity, time? He got up from the narrow mattress and went to the window, pushing back the dusty cotton curtains. The moonlight was kind to the signs of neglect in the little garden below. The lawn looked smooth, the roses luxuriant. And then he saw a movement in the grey clouds of lavender beneath. A brownie gathering the fragrant buds.

He smiled and watched until the creature finally flitted away into the orchard, then returned to bed and slept soundly through to morning.

Maldon was in turmoil when Mark arrived back, travelsick and tired. Inexplicably, the king had announced that he was going to revive his traditional visit to Maldon on Saint Errig's day, less than a week away.

One of the senior gardeners called Mark to the offices by the orangery next morning. He deposited his umbrella in the hatstand and rapped on the third brass-plated door along the corridor where panicking clerks scuttled. Mr. Parkin bade Mark sit down facing the wide desk. He looked worried; his face was more deeply marbled with veins than ever, the files in the IN tray leaned precariously and the smell of drink was strong.

Mark had expected the interview—there were bound to be duties to be devolved, preparations to be discussed—but as Mr. Parkin spoke Mark realized that he was being given a far greater responsibility than he would have bargained for, or wished. Biddle, one of the few genuinely experienced gardeners, had been found lying on the marble bench beside the Culpen bush by an estate doctor collecting lichen that dawn, his leather apron soaked with dew and the slugs already feasting at his mouth and eyes. With just a few days to go, Mark would have to take over.

Afterward, Mark retrieved his umbrella and took the path between the willows around Blackroot Pool. It had already rained twice that morning, and between bursts of sunshine grey clouds were banking up once more over the hills. Every leaf, every blade of grass, was diamonded with moisture; to brush against a tree or bush guaranteed a soaking. But the estate was busy. Priveteers were clipping hedges, assistant gardeners were tying back peonies and laborers were mowing—mostly doing, Mark suspected, more harm than good in their panic. Of course, there *was* work to be done. Even in his anxiety about the Culpen bush and as the rain came down again, Mark still paused to snap the dead head off a rose and bent to pluck a shoot of bindweed from a flower bed, but his actions were gentle and instinctive. That was the way with a true gardener, not starting, not stopping, not hurrying, but understanding that the task never ends.

Mark had visited the far corner of the estate where the Culpen bush grew several times before. He'd been curious to see a plant that flowered so predictably, but he'd always misjudged the date and had never seen the bloom.

A long, wide avenue led to the garden of the Culpen bush. As Mark walked past the lines of elms through the thinning, drifting rain the dark Tudor arch at the far end slowly widened. The square little garden beyond that plain span of masonry was an obvious and possibly intentional anticlimax. Even with the sun breaking through after the rain it was dim and dull. Dense ivy climbed in the shadow of red brick walls, the highest of which, facing the Tudor arch, marked the final boundary of the estate. The oak forest beyond added to the shade, leaning over across the garden and whispering like an aunt admiring a baby. In the center, rising from a soggy square of grass, the Culpen bush spread its dark leaves.

Mark frowned as he looked around; it was a poor, lightless place, and the overhanging boughs of the forest would bring pests, insects, fungi, diseases, and fairies. The Culpen bush was fighting the odds to grow here at all. He walked around it. The outer leaves formed a ragged globe that almost matched his own height. A nerve of worry started to ache behind his eyes as he walked around it again, looking more carefully. There was no sign of a rose bud. And Mark knew where to look, *how* to look, what to expect. He wandered around the bush again and again, almost growing dizzy. But there was nothing. No sign. No rose.

He sat down on the wet marble bench facing the bush, then remembered Biddle and quickly stood up again. Had a rose ever blossomed on Saint Errig's day? Had anyone ever seen it? After all, more than fifty years had elapsed since it had been cut, placed on a velvet cushion and paraded before the king; a long time even— or especially—in a garden.

He knew it was pointless telling anyone. Whatever the facts of the case were, the blame would surely settle on him. He walked forward and touched the wet, dark leaves of the bush. And as he did so, he saw a graceful tiara spider at work, spinning a web that gleamed silver between the thorny stalks even in this shadowed place. He smiled despite himself. Perhaps the bush was truly special, perhaps a little magic flowed in its sap. All he could do was tend it, and pray.

Mark worked on the Culpen bush all day, bowed in its shadows. Using his bare hands, he softened and sifted the soil around the base of the plant, chasing the leatherback beetles away, bringing worms from nearby portions of the estate to burrow in some air. The rain came and went. He tried propping up the umbrella, but soon gave up and let the drops patter his head and back and the mud soak in at his knees. Eventually, it grew too dark to see clearly. He stood up, cloaked in the scent of earth, rubbing at the familiar gardener's ache in his back. The bush was a dim cloud now, the leaves no longer separable by sight. In jokey pretense that it had been a fine, uninterrupted day, the sky was deep and pinkish blue. Peering through the powdery air at the overhanging forest, Mark thought he could just make out the darting movements of the spinner fairies as they wove strands of dusk from bough to bough.

Mark wiped the worst of the mud from his hands on the grass, picked up his umbrella and set off back toward the hostel. The birds were silent. The stately avenue was eerily balanced between day and night, enfolded in glowing shadow.

He heard the rattle of a bell. The sound was odd in the close softness of the evening, yet instantly familiar. Up ahead amid the fading perspectives of the elms, he saw a figure on a bicycle. Curious, yet too tired to run, he increased his step, but when he reached the place there were only tracks shining on the wet grass like a snail's glitter.

Early next day, after a restless night and a dream of chasing something bright through a forest, Mark was back tending the Culpen bush. He worked fine ash into the soil with his fingers, then began the painstaking task of pinching the greenfly from the leaves and stems one by one. He was soon lost in the task, oblivious to the gusting wind that shivered the elms along the avenue and the leaning oaks, yet then, half buried in the bush, his face and arms scratched and bleeding from the thorns and his hands sticky with the sap-like juice of the greenfly, his concentration was suddenly broken by a sense of being watched.

He twisted out from under the bush. A barefoot child was standing close by, dressed in grubby brown. An equally brown and grubby bicycle was propped up against the ivy at the edge of the garden.

"Hello," she said.

Mark grunted discouragingly. He didn't enjoy being watched when he was working.

"You've been spending a lot of time inside that bush."

"It's the Culpen bush."

"Oh," She nodded. "Then it must be s'posed to flower soon."

Mark picked a thorn from his palm. "Four days from now, in fact. Not that there's any sign." He couldn't think of a reason not to tell her—just some grubby urchin, some laborer's child wandering the estate without permission.

"The flower's for the king?" she asked.

He stood up. "That's right."

The wind lifted wisps of light brown hair across her face. Mark was surprised at how tall she was, almost his own height. She was older than he'd thought, too. But then he was no expert, living a semi-monastic life at the hostel.

Mark shrugged and glanced back at the bush, feeling stupidly conscious that her eyes were on him. "I suppose I'll just have to hope . . ."

"That a bud suddenly appears?" She laughed. A little girl's laugh; fierce, absorbed, uncaring. The Culpen bush shivered in a sudden gust. "Well," she sniffed, "that would be magic, or a miracle."

Mark shrugged again as she turned away from him; so much, he thought, for sharing your problems.

She climbed back onto her bicycle, rang the bell and pedaled out of sight along the sighing avenue.

Dealing with the greenfly and tidying up the bush took him all of the rest of the day and the following morning, by which time the laborers were working their ladders along the avenue, trimming and cutting the elms—badly. Mark couldn't help noticing, and out of season—to make them look neat and soldierly for the king's procession to the Culpen bush. The shadowy little garden itself seemed to attract no attention; the laborers probably didn't know or care why the king was coming and the more senior staff in the estate would be too wrapped up in their own obsessions to think of anything as obvious as the absence of the Culpen rose. After he'd eaten his sandwiches sitting on the marble bench, Mark trimmed the ivy and the lawn with the shears he'd brought along. That was fairly easily done; the garden was too damp and shady to encourage quick growth.

Then he sat down again and stared at the Culpen bush. He tried thinking positively, he tried willing a flower to grow. Along the avenue, the rip of saws and falling, splintering timber grew closer, then receded. Once, he felt someone's presence behind him and turned, irritated, expecting to see the girl. There was no one there. He gauged it as an indication of the unhappy mood that the irritation then turned to disappointment.

Back at the hostel that evening, Mr. Parkin came to the refectory as Mark sat alone drinking tea.

"Dress rehearsal the day after tomorrow," he said, leaning over Mark and swaying a little. "Will everything be ready then?"

"Everything?"

"The rose."

"Yes." Mark nodded.

"Good." Mr. Parkin backed away, bumping painfully into the edge of a table.

It was foggy next morning. The elms along the avenue loomed. Mark felt sleepy and light-headed; he couldn't see beyond the next few days of his life. The dress rehearsal, the formal procession . . . Giants in the mist, barring his way.

The tiara spider had silvered the entire Culpen bush with its web. Mark sat down on the marble bench. Fog wreathed the boughs of the forest, hung from the ivy like rotting lace, closed off the sky.

A bell. The sound glittering in the thick air like a jewel, then closer, and with it the swish of bicycle tires on the soft grass. Mark waited expectantly.

"Hello." She dismounted, then came fully from the mist and sat beside him. "Any luck?"

She had changed from the grubby brown dress and looked considerably more presentable in a green blouse and skirt.

Mark shook his head.

"Never mind." She smiled, laid a hand on his shoulder.

Embarrassingly, Mark felt himself shiver. "It's too late to do anything," he said.

"Then forget about it. Why worry?"

Her eyes were green, brown, blue. Colors of autumn and summer, sadness and life. She was hardly a girl at all. A woman, yes. A woman. But even as Mark decided, the play of misty light changed her face and all he saw was a child.

She gave him an odd look, almost as though she'd been caught out.

"My name's Mark," he said.

"Mine's Fianna."

"Fiona?"

"No, Fianna." She spelt it out to him.

Mark nodded. He didn't want to hurt her feelings by commenting on her parents' obvious illiteracy—after all, his own father was hardly better.

She squirmed on the bench. "This is cold, cold and wet. You'll give yourself piles."

Mark said nothing. Even in the hostel he'd lived a sheltered life; he wasn't sure what piles were.

"Can you ride a bicycle?"

"I think so," he said. "I could once."

"Then why don't you try mine. It'll take your mind off the rose. I'll just sit here and get piles and watch."

The bicycle rested against the ivied wall. As Mark placed his hands on the old handlebars he was filled with doubt. After all these years, could he still make it balance and fly? He wheeled it out, finding the seat, the pedals, pushing off. The bicycle responded, became alive, drawing him into the mist.

He circled the walled garden, turning sharply around the rose bush, past Fianna on the bench. She clapped and cheered. Mark circled again, the quick mist opening and closing ahead and behind.

Dizzy, breathing hard, he finally braked and placed his feet on the soft, solid grass.

She ran over to him and placed a steadying hand upon his arm as he dismounted. "Well done!"

Mark no longer shivered at her touch, but Fianna's closeness brought an extraordinary feeling of softness, yearning. He blinked and found himself looking into her wide, beautiful eyes. The mist was thinning, forming a glowing nimbus around her hair.

She pulled back a little, releasing his arm.

"Thank you," Mark said " . . . for letting me try the bicycle."

"That's all right. I'd better go soon."

The wonderful feeling slackened as she drew away, like a wave hissing back across the shore, but when he passed the handlebars to her and their skin touched it came crashing in again.

"What are you going to do today?" she asked, backing off, her eyes lowered as she fiddled with the rusty chrome casing of the bell.

"I don't know," he said. "There's nothing left to do. I haven't touched the bush, or hardly looked at it."

"Then how can you be so sure a flower hasn't budded?" She turned the front wheel and climbed on the bicycle. "You can't be, can you?"

"No . . ."

"Good luck." She cycled off.

Mark walked slowly around the spider-webbed bush. The sky overhead was almost blue now. Something about the clearing mist made this normally shady place fill with brightness. The dewy, sparkling bush looked wonderful, Mark had to concede. It hardly needed a rose to decorate itself with. He watched the architect, the tiara spider with its jewel-like cluster of eyes, still embroidering leaf and branch. It paused, as though conscious of Mark's gaze, then moved gracefully on along a green stem to weave its silk around a fresh new rose bud.

Rising from a crag at the center of the estate, the ornate grey battlements of Maldon Castle hemmed the sky. On the day of the dress rehearsal, a red carpet slid like a tongue from the porticullis mouth, down the rhododendron screes of the crag and across the gardens, all the way to the Culpen bush.

The mock procession, the king's new equerry standing in for the king himself, left Maldon Castle at ten in the morning. The Head Master Gardener, the master gardeners, the chief horticulturists and others ranking high in the garden pyramid assumed, to their chagrin, third place in the procession behind the blue and silver ceremonial band that led the way through the pleasant sunshine and the courtiers in their tripping robes and feathered hats. The procession started off slowly and, striving for dignity, grew slower.

Mark stood waiting in the Culpen garden with a scatter of senior gardeners and minor officials. It was well after noon before he heard the first faint echo of the band as they turned into the top of the avenue. The sawn, clipped elms stood rigidly to attention.

The sound grew closer.

"Here they come," Mr. Parkin slurred, gripping a nearby shoulder for support. "Ready now."

Half an hour later, the mock procession arrived. The band stood fanfare along the sides of the avenue. The king's young equerry led the gaudy pack.

"So this is it," he said as they finally passed under the Tudor arch. "This place, this bush. Is *this* really what all the fuss is about?"

Silks and shufflings filled the garden. Beautiful patterns and colors. Tired faces, ugly with worry and responsibility. The Head Master Gardener made a rapid flanking movement to get beside the equerry.

"Tradition, my lord."

"Of course, tradition. Where would we be, eh?"

Peering around the surrounding heads, Mark saw that the equerry was indeed young. Little more than his own age. And oddly, frustratingly, he recognized him from somewhere.

"Then what happens next?"

"That's all . . . um . . ." The Head Master Gardener opened and closed his mouth like a fish.

"I grow bored," the equerry snapped. "Please let me have your views, sir. I'm hardly likely to know what goes on here, and neither's the bloody king."

"Well, the rose is placed on the very same cushion that . . . oh, here it is."

"I see. And where is the rose?"

"Ah. Let me . . . here. Yes. This."

"And who cuts it?"

The Head Master Gardener looked around, pleading for assistance. None was forthcoming. "Well . . . I . . ."

"How about someone from the estate?" the equerry suggested, his face puckered with irritation. "Some chappie who, oh, I don't know . . . How about the fellow who looks after the rose?"

"Of course, my lord."

The Head Master Gardener looked to the master gardeners, who looked to the senior gardeners.

"Step forward," Mr. Parkin lisped. "Go on."

Mark pushed his way awkwardly to the front of the crowd. "I tend the rose," he announced as feathers bobbed and heads turned towards him.

The equerry regarded him sullenly. "You're rather young, my friend. You really don't look the part. Still, we waste time and this is becoming boring. You'll have to do. What next?" He clapped his hands. His silk sleeves fluttered. "What next?"

The Head Master Gardener produced a pair of secateurs from the front of his embossed ceremonial apron. Mark took the cold metal in his hands and walked around the bush to the glorious, unfolding bloom. He felt let down, angry. Surely it wouldn't be like this tomorrow? Just some foolish ceremony?

"Then let us assume," the equerry said, "that the rose has been cut. It is placed on the cushion just so and our friend here brings it to the king. That's right, just *try* to pretend that I'm the king."

Mark took the old and rather threadbare cushion and walked towards the equerry. The bland face was maddeningly familiar. Across his nose and cheeks, Mark saw the faint stain of childhood freckles, and as he did so he remembered the wide lawn, the red and cream bicycle.

"You're Adrian Widder . . . my lord."

The equerry scowled. "I don't see what right you have to know or speak my name."

"But you taught me to ride your bicycle. That day, your father's birthday . . ."

Briefly, Mark believed he saw a glimmer of recognition, but then it vanished under irritation and disdain.

"You play a trick like that tomorrow before the king," the equerry hissed, his face growing pale and the old freckle marks showing more strongly, "and I swear you'll never dig a single turd of manure in any garden in the kingdom. Anyway . . ." he turned his back on Mark " . . . I think we've done enough. At this point, having accepted the rose—which he will pass back to me and I will toss behind a convenient bush—our beloved king will commence his progress back to the castle."

"Here," the Head Master Gardener said as they left, giving Mark back the silver secateurs. "You might as well keep these for tomorrow."

The crowd departed down the avenue, slowly fading from sight and hearing, leaving Mark standing alone in the walled garden. He pushed the secateurs into his apron pouch and sat down on the marble bench.

It was midafternoon. The birds were quiet. Hazy sunshine gilded the tops of the forest trees. He gazed at the Culpen bush, at the rose, its petals almost fully open from the bud in just one day. It was a miracle, no rose grew and unfurled that quickly. And all for what? He clenched and unclenched his fists, wondering if he was still capable of tears.

He'd never seen a rose of its like, or equal. Despite its size and the dense, heavy mass of its petals, it lifted proudly from its stem, seeking the sun that never graced the walled garden. Even sitting a good couple of yards away from it, Mark was bathed in the scent. It was unlike any other rose, bringing memories of wide lawns and clear skies, of a beautiful lady with a white parasol leaning close to him in sunlight. And it was partly that, Mark realized, that had triggered his memory of Adrian Widder. He shook his head. That was all in the past. Nothing remained, absolutely nothing.

The petals of the Culpen rose were white, but in the shade of their unfurling and in the deep and unrevealed heart was a blackness that went beyond shade or shadow or night. He breathed the fragrance again. It was too sweet and too bitter to ignore.

He heard the tinkle of a bicycle bell, the tick of approaching wheels. Fianna scooted in on one pedal and alighted smoothly, graceful as a swan, leaning the bicycle beside the Tudor arch.

"I've been watching the procession," she said. "I shouldn't really be on this bike. See, with my best clothes on."

She was barefoot as usual, but in a simple white dress. As she crossed the garden her image flickered dizzily in Mark's mind. Child, girl, woman, child . . .

"Has the rose come?" she asked.

"Yes." Mark's voice quavered. "It's here."

"Then let me see. And why do you look so glum?"

Mark crouched down beside the bloom. She leaned close behind him, but somehow from a vast, impossible height. Her scent, the scent of the rose, roared in his senses. The light and the darkness played over her young, old face, in the depths of her eyes.

She looked toward him. "You should be proud."

Mark swallowed, fighting for words through the dryness of his throat. She was Lady Widder, his dreams, his mother. "I am . . . I just can't let those people take it."

Mark stood up. His knees were trembling. She reached forward and pressed his hands into hers. Mark could feel the power passing between them in a delicious, aching rush. The shadowed garden waited, hushed in expectancy.

She took a step closer.

She kissed him.

When she drew back, letting go, she smiled at the seriousness of it all.

"It doesn't matter really, does it?" Mark said, dizzy with the sense of her reality. "The king, this bush?"

Gently, she shook her head.

"Look," Mark took the silver secateurs from his apron and gently clasped the Culpen rose between its thorns. The tiara spider scuttled out of his way along the broken web.

"I shouldn't—" she began.

But his mind was made up; he didn't hear the fear and urgency in her voice. He closed the jaws of the secateurs and lifted the incredible weight of the rose towards her.

The petals curled, writhing outwards, black spilling over white like ink through milk. The blackness turned to ash as the Culpen bush shivered in a sudden wind that caught the flaking remains, swirling them up into the arms of the forest.

Mark looked up at Fianna. The darkness was spreading, filling the white of her eyes, blistering and crinkling her dress and her skin. The wind increased, a tunnel billowing into the sky, swirling her hair like smoke. As she began to dissolve, flying upwards in ragged ash, the remains of her mouth opened into a scream, a sound neither of pain nor joy. Then she was swallowed in the shrieking wind, twirling into shadow, into nothing.

The wind quickly died. Mark stood alone by the flowerless bush. The still, damp shade settled in a cloak of sadness. There are many pests in a garden. Thrips. Manslugs. Greenfly. Fairies. Yes, that he had always known.

The old bicycle still rested beside the Tudor arch. He untangled the handlebars from the ivy and wheeled it over to the far wall, the forest wall. He leaned it there, settling it carefully before climbing onto the saddle and then, clasping the strongest stems, on up through the ivy towards the waiting boughs.

GARRY KILWORTH
Dark Hills, Hollow Clocks

Garry Kilworth's second contribution to this collection is a masterful dark cautionary tale about the Good Folk of the English woods. It comes from Kilworth's book of the same title containing ten fantasy tales that range from the otherworldly to the outrageous (including the story of a punk goblin in urban Scotland), published by Metheun Children's Books, U.K.

—T.W.

Dark Hills, Hollow Clocks

GARRY KILWORTH

My house is silent for a reason. The clock cases of my large collection of antique timepieces are now empty. Outside are the dark hills of Lancashire, equally as silent. I sit here in the dusk of my cottage parlor watching the smooth movements of the greatest clock of them all, as it disappears behind a crag, and wonder at my loss of fortune. I am too bemused to feel anguish at the moment. I am trying to sort through a puzzle, the solution of which will only satisfy my curiosity, not my frustration.

I have been collecting clocks for some twenty years, beginning with my first pay packet on leaving school. I went home with seven pounds, three of which was spent on the silver-cased pocket watch from the window of Jackson's junk shop. My *affairé* with timepieces began in earnest from that day. I find them fascinating instruments, with their precision-made wheels, springs, levers, rachets, cogs—delicate, yet needing strength for durability—but not until I was established in business did I have the funds to indulge seriously in their purchase.

Clockwork movements are the art of the engineer. Not for me paintings by the Impressionists, or sculptures by the Dadaists, or even functional architecture by the Bauhaus school. I love the look of brass behind glass, ornate ormolu cases, tulipwood grandfathers, faces with curlicued hands, centripetals on the frame, Roman numerals, deadbeat escapements, waggon-spring movements, pendulums, chains and weights, *tick-tock-tick-tock*, sounding brass and tinkling cymbal, dropping the quarter hours like metal lizards shedding their scales. I love moon and tide phase dials, and the dainty spiralling hairspring trembling with the ecstasy of its task. I love the rods and bells, the little hammers, that sound the chimes. I love, most of all, the precision, the teeth of the cogs fitting together like the fingers of tiny hands . . . yes, tiny hands . . . tiny hands. They were taken, all, all taken, by tiny little hands.

Last year I purchased a cottage in Thrushgill, attached to an old watermill no longer in use, and brought all my clocks up from the flat in Lancaster. I had metal grids fitted to the windows, and electronically operated bolts on the doors, until the place was as secure as a bank. All my hard-earned wealth was in these precious clocks and it was necessary to keep out any intruders.

I fought hard for my brass, as we Lancaster folk call it, and was determined to become a rich man before I was thirty. Made it too, a couple of years ahead of time. I began as a lowly engineer, but finished owning my own company, and if I had to tread on a few fingers on the way up, well, that was in the nature of the thing. Business is like that, isn't it? If it hadn't been me, it would have been someone else, someone even more determined, more ruthless. You have to recognize what you want and go for it, and if you pause for sentiment, you're lost.

Competitors had to go, too. You see, my factory turns out good traditional Lancashire cotton: one of the last firms to make a success of such an enterprise. A few handouts were necessary in the beginning, to stop the flow of imported materials, from India and places like that. Eventually I got my way and cleared most of the competition. But there was one, a locally produced muslin, so fine and light it could have been fashioned from dandelion fluff and cobwebs. Some cottage industry I guessed, up in the dark hills behind Thrushgill. It was a superior fabric, I could see that, but it wasn't exactly going to drive me out of business since, judging from the amount on the market, it could only be produced in small quantities. Being a jealous young man in those days, I didn't like losing *any* corner of the business, no matter how small, so I tried dropping my prices for a while, to attempt to force this rival off the market. I was only partially successful, but left it for more important things, such as expansion and increasing my exports.

One or two actions, I must admit, I now regret. There are men who are waiting patiently, simply to be around to stamp on my grave. I don't blame them for that. My ex-partner Joe is probably one of those. And people I've had to let go in my time, though I've never regarded myself as morally responsible for families, only for fulfilling my legal obligations as an employer. You can't afford to be emotional in business, or you go under. Never married. Never had time.

Then I bought the cottage in Thrushgill, near a rushy beck that tumbles from the crags. It has a long garden—something I've not owned before, always living above the offices of my factory—and I took some books out from the library in order to learn something about growing vegetables. I've never had much time for flowers, but producing one's own fare for the table, well, that's another thing.

The problem was, the garden faces north, so the shadow of the cottage is on it in the morning, and in the afternoon it is in the shade of those dark hills. However, I did my best with it, buying all the latest fertilizers and weedkillers and such. I don't hold with many modern innovations (*especially* quartz movements and digital watches: cold, soulless bits of wire covered in plastic), but it's my belief that one should take advantage of improvements in agriculture. This I duly did.

Right at the far left-hand corner of the garden is a wedge of ground where the midday sun manages to strike, as it slips between the corner of the house and the first crag of the ridge. It was here that I planted the blackcurrant bushes, in well-drained beds of peat and manure, dug and prepared as the book tells. They would have flourished, if it weren't for the blackfly.

"You need some poison dust," old Wacker, the local authority on such things told me. "A puff 'ere, a puff there. Give 'em a good going over. That'll knock the blighters for six."

This I duly did and was successful in ridding the bushes of blackfly.

Then I had problems with birds, stealing the early fruit. Having no protective nets to hand, I decided to dust some of the blackcurrants with poison dust, to teach the birds a lesson. It was a cruel thing to do, I see that now, but at the time I was very angry.

The following day was a fine summer's morning. Going down to the bottom of the garden to inspect the bushes, I found to my horror a small corpse lying on the ground under the blackcurrants. It was the body of a pixie, no doubt come down from the dark hills to steal the first of my fruit. My heart went cold. My grandmother had always told me that Lancashire fairies were normally benign creatures, who would never harm a child, but terrible if roused to fury.

"They have the patience of eel grass," she said. "You don't want to go upsetting the fairies around here, lad."

I had taken the life of a pixie! Unwittingly, perhaps, but would the fairies listen to my explanations? I very much doubted whether I would even be invited to my trial.

The pixie's body was smaller than that of a weasel: perhaps twenty centimeters long. I picked it up, quickly, and took it indoors, placing it on the scullery shelf amongst the flower pots and seed trays and other garden paraphernalia. There were some onions drying in there, and woody geranium stems that I had not cleared away. I placed these over the corpse, hiding it from view. Lancashire fairies are wild folk and have great difficulty entering human dwellings. My cottage is more secure than most, so I felt safer having him indoors. If I had just buried him, they might have discovered his grave.

That evening, I sat at my window, fearfully watching for small hands, small faces, to press themselves against the glass. I could imagine the grim expressions, the angry brows, and my knees trembled at the thought that they would come in their hundreds to drag me out to the crags to carry out whatever ghastly punishment such creatures devise for killers of their kin.

They did not come.

For several days I stayed in the cottage, neglecting my business in Lancashire, afraid to go beyond the doorjamb in case they were waiting for me amongst the ferns and grasses. Then, gradually, I came to the conclusion that no one had seen. Soon I was able to go out into the sunshine, and walk again through thickets and down amongst the gulleys. However, when I went to work I always double-locked the windows and doors, and blocked the chimney flue, to prevent any unauthorized entry of my property. They would need more than fairy guile to get past *my* guard.

Autumn came, then winter, and that February I took Wacker on as my gardener. I didn't want any more accidents to fall on my head. Wacker knew what he was doing amongst the weeds and vegetables. He had the knowledge of more than one lifetime, passed on by his earthy ancestors. Wacker liked to come in and look at my collection of clocks from time to time, and would shake his head in wonder, exclaiming, "Aye, like flowers of tin and tinsel, Mr. Roberts."

He would stand and listen to them chime, as if he were at a concert, listening to the world's greatest orchestra playing Mozart or Handel.

"Sheer delight," he would whisper. "They could be fuchsia bells made o' copper and brass."

Once, in mid-winter, I inspected the little body hidden on the scullery shelf, to find it had dried, just like a small cutting. The legs had become a fork, small knots where the knees had been, the two arms little twiggy projections from the main stem, and the long hair had shrivelled and looked for all the world like root tendrils. It seemed to have taken on the characteristics of both the geranium stems and the dried onions.

I put it back in its hiding place and forgot about it.

In the spring, I was full of myself. Business was booming. The cloth from the cottage industry, that flimsy but strong fabric which caused me small worry, had dropped away on the market to almost a rarity. Wherever it was located, the weavers were running out of something—probably raw materials.

My garden was flourishing under the green fingers of Wacker, who produced prize vegetables out of the most unlikely soils and positions. I had time to relax and oil my precious clocks. There was the Thomas Tompion in the study, the George Prior late eighteenth-century tortoiseshell with its small marine view above the face, my Breguet's *synchroniser* in the landing window niche, the French cartel, the English brass lantern-clock by Fromanteel made in 1670, and many many more. I loved them all. My heart lifted when I had time to work on them, tinker with them, keep them running smoothly.

One evening I came home to find a beautiful plant on the upright pianoforte. It was in an ordinary clay pot which had been placed on a cracked china saucer to protect the polished wood surface of the instrument. The plant had a faintly familiar appearance, though I had no idea what it was. There was just a single bloom, a magnificent scarlet trumpet-shaped flower, so heavy its stamens almost touched the surface of the piano.

Wacker was working at the bottom of the garden and I called him up to the house. He came up the path kicking the soil from his boots and then entered the scullery.

"Where on earth did *that* come from?" I asked him, pointing to the plant.

Wacker shifted his feet on the stone floor of the scullery as he peered around the parlour door at the plant.

"She's a beauty, that one. Found 'er on the scullery shelf, four little branches, just sproutin' green. Put 'er in that pot, and there she be."

Suddenly, the cozy feeling of well-being left me and a chill travelled through my whole body.

"But the flower, Wacker. It can't have bloomed in one afternoon, surely? When did it grow its flower?"

Wacker shifted his feet.

"Didn't *grow* it, like normal, if you see what I mean. After I potted 'er, she kind of *bled* the bloom. That's *best* way I can describe it. Sort of oozed out a drop o' red sap on stem. When I come back in, an hour later, there she hung in all her glory."

Horror replaced my feelings of perplexity.

"Throw it out," I said, coldly. "Now, you idiot. You should never have potted that . . . that *thing*."

"What?"

"Throw it away, Wacker," I shouted. "Didn't you hear me?"

Wacker turned, and left me, saying, "I heard all right, I ain't deaf, but I ain't being spoke to like that."

He slammed the door behind him.

I stared at the vile flower, that had grown from the husk of the dead pixie, and wondered if I would have the courage to throw it out myself. It was getting late. The purple lanes of the last shadows were stretching themselves on the lawn. Light drained from the sky, swirling down some invisible sluice behind the dark hills to the northeast.

"In the morning," I murmured, tossing my jacket over the back of a chair. "In the morning I'll take it out and burn it on a bonfire. Should have done it ages ago."

I spent the evening tinkering with a banjo clock and retired at eleven o'clock, thinking I would have to apologize to Wacker for my outburst. I planned to tell him I had been unwell and was not entirely responsible for my show of temper. Wacker was not one to hold a grudge and I was sure he would forgive me.

Some time later I woke with a start, having heard my name being called. I felt groggy, as one does when awakened from deep slumber. Putting on my dressing-gown, I went down the wooden staircase to see if there was anyone at the door. It occurred to me that Wacker might have been downing some ales at the local pub and had called by to put things to rights. As I reached the bottom step, all my clocks began chiming. Although I am used to the sound of their ticking, and their chimes, and am not awakened by them, for some reason the tinging and donging put fear into my heart. Twelve times the clamor repeated itself.

Midnight.

I stood on the final stair, looking into the eeriely-lit parlour, wondering. Why was I so frightened? What was it in here that made me so anxious?

Then I heard it.

"Mr. Roberts. Mr. Roberts. Murderer."

Terror almost clogged my throat, but I managed to cry out, "Who's there? Who's that?"

The words came again, from the direction of the piano, and I knew then what it was. The trumpet flower had called me from my bed. Its high tones were informing the world that I had carried out a deed as yet unconfessed. A full moon sat in a saddle between the dark hills beyond Thrushgill, illuminating my parlor, picking out my furniture. I saw the scarlet blossom tremble in the light.

"Mr. Roberts!" it shrieked.

Then they came.

At first, specks of light amongst the thistles, then small white faces at the windows, breathing chlorophyll, handprints like raindrops on the panes. They began rattling the glass, shaking the door on its hinges.

"Mr. Roberts!" cried the scarlet trumpet. "*Murderer!*"

The violence at the windows and doors increased.

I put my hands over my ears, yelling, "It wasn't my fault. I dusted for pests. It was an accident . . . an *accident!*"

But they would not go away, they would not leave me alone, and in the end I had to let them in. I flung open the door, shouting, "Don't hurt me. Don't touch me. Take what you want, but leave me here, please, leave me alone . . ."

They were silent then. They poured past me into the recesses of the house and began to dismantle my precious clocks. Four or five fairies at each device, quietly removing screws and pins, and taking out the works of each of my antique timepieces. The shells, the cases, they left behind, looking as if they had not been touched. Even the dust on them was undisturbed.

The fairies took the scarlet trumpet along with the vital innards of my priceless collection, and headed back for the dark hills. Leaving me, broken and bereft, amongst the silence of my hollow clocks.

That was over a month ago.

Sitting here now, staring at those hills, I have an idea that I may have been hoodwinked by those little people. You see, that fine muslin has begun to appear on the market in much greater quantities than ever before. Consider this, if you were to make a loom for tiny hands, it would have to be scaled down in size, would it not? All its parts would need to be in miniature: its cogs, levers, rachets. Fairies, we know, are not metalworkers, nor even good carpenters. Their skills are inclined towards more delicate creativity, like weaving. Any machinery they need, they have to modify from an existing contraption, perhaps originally fashioned for some entirely different purpose.

In short, I am now certain that my clockworks have become looms, or parts of such. In this day of the quartz movement in clocks and watches, those creatures out there must have despaired of finding replacement parts for the looms they have run over the previous several centuries. Now they have enough to last them for many years: my whole beautiful collection of antique timepieces.

What bothers me is whether it was all a fairy plan. Surely not? It was so elaborate, so full of chance. Too much was dependant on human reaction and odd circumstance.

Then again, are we humans not predictable creatures? Any animal that knows us, be it cat, dog or bird, can easily foretell what action we will take in any particular circumstance, even the most unusual of situations.

And are not fairy schemes, by the very nature of their planners, full of such embroideries as would startle any mortal with their twists and turns, their loops and twirls?

I don't know. I just don't know. I simply have the feeling, as I sit amongst my hollow clocks, staring at those dark hills, that I have been duped in more ways than one, since I have lost my precious collection of clocks and my business is fighting against the upsurge of an old rival I thought I had knocked out of existence.

It's a blessed puzzle, like some cobweb left on purpose over the staircase, that sticks to your nose, your eyelashes and your brows, and gums your fingers, as you try to sort through it.

JONATHAN CARROLL
The Panic Hand

Carroll, as his loyal readers know by now, is expert at depicting everyday people who turn a figurative corner into the fantastic and sometimes horrific realms of the physical/psychological world. In "The Panic Hand," which first appeared in the British magazine *Interzone*, and was reprinted in the winter issue of *Weird Tales*, a chance encounter on a train completely changes a traveler's views about reality. More importantly, and frighteningly, it is obliquely implied that he has been corrupted by the experience.

—E.D.

The Panic Hand

JONATHAN CARROLL

I'd just finished going through a time in life when one day bled into the next. Nothing worked, nothing smelled good, nothing smiled, nothing fit. Even my feet grew a little, for some mysterious reason, and I had to buy three pairs of new shoes. Figure that. Maybe my body was trying to burst out of its old, failed skin like a snake and form a new one.

In the middle of this black mess I met Celine Davenant. She lived in Munich, five easy hours away from Vienna on the train. With her beautifully smooth and reassuring voice, she worked reading the news on an English-language radio station up there.

After work Friday evenings I'd hurry over to the *Westbahnhof* and catch "The Rosenkavalier" to Munich. That was really the name of the train.

Sometimes Celine came to Vienna, but made no bones about the fact that she didn't like the city one bit. I told her the train trip was a pleasure for me and I looked forward to it. So we silently agreed for the time being to leave things as they were: she'd meet the train at the Munich *Hauptbahnhof* at 11.30 and our weekend would begin there amidst startled pigeons, travellers, the jerk and hoot of trains.

My first excited trip west, I made the mistake of buying a first-class ticket. But even there, the compartment was crowded with weekend people and their many bags. What I subsequently learned was to buy a second-class seat, arrive early, and go directly to the dining car. If I sat there until the town of Attnang-Puchheim, the train would have emptied by then and, strolling back to second class, I could have my pick of empty places.

The arrangement worked out well, particularly because the railroad served good food and it was delightful to sit eating by those large windows and watch the Austrian countryside slide by. Perchtoldsdorf, St Pölten, Linz. Station masters in red caps waved. Farmers in old pickup trucks, blank-faced. Unmoving people stood frozen at small stations, rural crossings, in the middle of who cares watching us click by. Dogs barked silently. I often saw deer grazing. Rabbits darted zigzags across open fields.

It took me away from my life, it took me closer to Celine.

What is the name of that pink and white lily that smells so strongly of pepper and spice? I can't remember, but it's one of my favourites. When they entered the dining car that evening it was the first thing I noticed. Both of them were wearing that marvelous flower in their hair. Maybe it was the second thing I noticed: it was hard not to be wide-eyed about their uniquely different beauty.

The woman was tall and splendid. She looked as though she'd been an actress earlier, or at least held perfect champagne glasses and looked out high windows at the Manhattan or Paris skyline. Now in her late thirties or early innings of forty, she'd come through the game strong and unimpeded. If there were lines on her face they made her look sexier, more knowing. The flower behind her ear said she had a sense of humour, give the world a smile. The flower behind her daughter's ear said here was an attentive, pleased mother. A rare combination.

The girl had the same russet-coloured hair and wide round eyes as her mother. At least I assumed it was the mother. They looked too much alike—senior and junior versions of the same great face. The face the girl would grow into in twenty-five years if she had luck.

I spent a good portion of every day thinking about Celine and how things would work out between us. I wanted them to work out and was hoping she did too. We hadn't talked about long-range plans because that sort of discussion comes after you have surveyed the new lands of your relationship and given long thought to where you want to drive in the first permanent posts. We liked many of the same things, couldn't get enough of each other in bed, but best of all, knew there was almost always something to talk about. Very few quiet spaces in our time together, and if they came, it was only because we were savouring the silent hum of contentment that is the real electricity of love.

When I started thinking about Celine, almost nothing could distract me. And I *was* thinking about her when the mother and daughter came into the dining car. So it shocked me to realize all thoughts of my friend had disappeared while I watched these two stunners cross . . . to my table.

"Do you mind if we sit here?"

The car was about a third full and there were a number of empty tables. Why did they want to sit here? I am a good-looking man and women generally like me, but they don't cross rooms for me. Particularly when they looked like this one.

"Please." I half-stood and gestured at the empty chairs. I could smell the flowers in their hair. The little girl was blushing and smiling and wouldn't look at me. Snatching the chair out so hard that it almost tipped over, she had to grab it with two hands at the last moment.

The mother grinned and put her hands to her cheeks. "Poor Heidi. She wanted to make such a good impression on you. She saw you walk down the platform at the station and actually jumped *out* of the train to see which car you went into. She made us wait till now so we wouldn't look too eager."

The girl looked daggers at mother; her secrets were being told, laughed at. I didn't think that was funny and tried to tell her with a smile and a small friendly shrug. She was sunburn red and wouldn't look at me after one fast, furtive glance.

Mama shook her head, still smiling and put out her slim hand. "I'm Francesca Pold. This is my daughter, Heidi. And you are?"

I said my name and shook the woman's warm hand. She held on a few seconds too long. I looked into her eyes to see if she was telling me something with that, but saw only "Wouldn't *you* like to know!" there. Her smile spread and she sat down.

Hmmmm.

"What are you reading? *Albanian Wonder Tales?* That sounds interesting." Without asking, she picked it up, opened it and started reading aloud. "Whether you believe it or doubt it, no matter. May all good things come to you who listen!"

Both mother and daughter burst out laughing. The laughter was exactly the same except one was high and young, the other deep and more experienced. It was charming.

"What a funny way to start a story! Are they fairy tales?" She put the book down on the table and the girl picked it right up.

"Yes. I like to read them. It's a hobby."

The woman nodded. Her expression said she fully approved. I'd scored points.

"What do you do for a living?"

"I sell computers to the East bloc."

"You sell computers and read fairy tales? A well-rounded man."

"That's nice to say, but it's probably only a bad case of arrested development."

That got me another approving smile.

She raised a hand for a waiter and one swept down on the table like a hawk. The world can be divided between people who can get a waiter's attention and those who can't.

Those who *can* have only to raise a tired or lazy finger and waiters lift their heads as if some secret radio signal has suddenly been beamed out on their private frequency. They arrive seconds later.

Those who can't, resort to finger snapping, and other embarrassing things but it does no good. They are unheard, invisible. They might as well rot. Francesca Pold got waiters. It wasn't surprising.

The two of them ordered and our chat continued. The girl pretended to be deeply involved in my fairytale book, but I often saw it slip down and her eyes —all attention and interest—watch carefully. Beautiful eyes. Large and smart, they had a kind of liquidness to them that made you think she was on the verge of crying. Yet that very quality made them more singular and attractive.

The mother was a gabber and although what she said was mostly interesting, it was easy to tune in and out on her monologue. More and more I found myself looking at the daughter. When their food came, I saw my chance.

"What's your favourite subject in school, Heidi?"

"Ma-ma-math-e-ma-ma-matics." Her jaw trembled up and down.

"Is that what you want to do when you get older?"

She shook her head and pointing at me, smiled. "C-C-C-Computers."

She had a tortuous, machine-gun stutter that grew worse as she got more excited. But it was also very plain she wanted to talk to me. Her mother made no attempt to interrupt or explain what Heidi said, even when some word or phrase was largely unintelligible. I liked that. They'd obviously worked it out between them and, handicapped as she was, the girl would grow up in a world where she was used to fighting her own battles.

I'd already had dinner but joined them for dessert when I saw how big and fresh the strawberries were they ordered. The three of us sat there and spooned them up while the sky lost the rest of its day. It was completely dark outside when we got up from the table.

"Where are you sitting?"

I smiled. "You mean what class am I in? Second, I'm afraid."

"Good, so are we! Do you mind if we sit with you?"

I liked to look at the woman, but was growing tired of her motor mouth. More and more looks passed between Heidi and me. I would have happily sat alone with the girl and her stutter for the rest of the trip to Munich (they were going there too), if that had been possible.

Despite being able to call waiters, Francesca appeared to have the mistaken idea that beauty also means license to go on about anything, ad infinitum. I pitied her daughter having to put up with it every day of her life.

But what could I say, no I don't want to sit with you? I could have, but it would've been rude and essentially wrong. We would sit together and Francesca would talk and I'd try to make Heidi's ride a little more pleasant.

As usual, most of the compartments were empty. Once settled, Francesca reached into her purse and took out a pack of cigarettes. That was surprising because she hadn't smoked at all till then. The brand was unfiltered Camels and she drew smoke way down into her lungs. While she puffed, Heidi and I talked about computers and the things she was doing with them at school. The girl knew a lot and I wondered what she would do with the skill when she grew older. That's one of the nice things about working with computers— you don't have to *say* a word to them and they'll still do your bidding. Even if Heidi retained her stutter in later life, computers would be a good profession for her to pursue because she could do wonderful, productive things without uttering a word.

To be young and suffering from the kind of affliction she carried on her tongue must have been as bad, in its way, as having a case of the worst acne. Only pimples usually go away when we get older. Stuttering stays around and doesn't pay much heed to a person's birth date or self-esteem.

She tried so damned hard to speak. No matter what subject we were discussing, there was something she wanted to say, but her words came out so slowly and painfully that at times I literally forgot what we'd been discussing after watching Heidi strain her way through the sentences.

Once when we were discussing computer games, she got completely hung up on the title of her favourite and her mother had to come in and help.

"The game she likes so much is called 'Panic Hand.' Have you ever played?"

"No, I've never even heard of it."

The girl tried explaining how it worked, but when none of it came out the right way, gave up and slumped in her seat. I knew she was about to cry. She'd tried but lost another game to her inner enemy: in living contrast to a gorgeous mother who had only to sit there and carry on her own boring, unending monologue.

But even Francesca was silent a while. The girl looked out the window, flushed and tight-lipped, while her mother smiled at me and smoked one cigarette after the other.

Suddenly Heidi looked at me and said: "Don't you th-th-think cigarette s-s-s-smo—king is c-c-c-c-ool? I d-d-d-do."

I shrugged. "Tried it when I was younger but never got the hang of it. I think it looks good in the movies."

Hearing this mild rebuff, the girl cringed down into her seat as if I'd hit her. Was she *that* sensitive?

I was looking at her, trying to catch her eye and wink, when her mother said "I'd like to sleep with you. I'd like to sleep with you right now. Right here."

"*What?*" I looked at Francesca. She had her hand on her blouse and was unbuttoning it.

"I said I want to sleep with you. Here."

"And what about Heidi?"

"She'll go into the corridor. We can pull the curtain." Her hand continued to climb down the buttons.

"No."

The blouse was open and a nice lilac frilly bra showed through against the stark white of her secret skin in there.

"Look, Francesca. Just wait, huh? Christ. Think about your daughter!"

The woman looked at the girl, then back at me. "You can sleep with her too. Would you rather? I can leave!" She laughed high and fully, winked at Heidi, then began to button herself back up. "See, honey, sometimes you don't need me. You just have to find a computer man."

"Just stop." I finally had the presence of mind to stand up and start for the door.

"D-d-d-d-don't go, please!" The girl grabbed my arm and held on hard. Her face was fear and shame. She got up out of her seat and put her arms around my neck. "Please don't go, please! I'll m-m-m-m-make her g-g-g-g-go aw-wa-wa-wa-wa-way!"

I hugged her back and, slowly easing her arms from around my neck, pushed her back into her seat at the same time. When I had her there, I turned to Francesca. Who wasn't there. Who wasn't anywhere. I was standing with my back to the door, so there was no way she could have gotten around me to get out.

Torn between a strong urge to get the hell out of there, and big curiosity to know what was going on, I more or less froze where I was and waited for something to decide the next move.

The train began to slow. The loudspeaker announced we'd arrived at Rosenheim, the last stop before Munich. I sat down. Heidi slid over next to me. Then she did something so erotic and wrong that I shiver to think of it, even now. Very gently, she took my hand and slid it under her skirt, between her child's legs. It was there a millisecond before I tried to pull it away. But couldn't because she held it there and she was much, *much* stronger than me. That power, more than where my hand rested, was what scared me. What was she, ten? Eleven? No eleven-year-old had that much strength.

When she spoke it was in a very normal, un-stuttering girl's voice. "Didn't you like her? Tell me what you like and I'll make it for you. I promise. Whatever you want!"

"What are you doing, Heidi? What are you doing?"

Her hand tightened on my own. It was so, so strong. "Didn't you think she was cool? The colour of her hair and the way she smoked those Camels? That's how I'll do it. That's what I want to be like when I'm old. That's how I'm going to make myself." Her eyes narrowed. "You don't believe me? You don't think she was cool? That's what I'll be like and every man will want me. They'll all want to touch me and listen to me talk. I'll have lots of stories and things. I'll be able to say whatever I want."

"Why can't you say it now?"

She squeezed my hand till I cried out. "Because I stutter! You heard! You think I was *kidding around*? I can't help it."

Trying to pry her hand off mine, I gave up. "Why can you talk normally now?"

"Because your hand's there. Men are going to want me all the time because I'll talk like her. I'll be beautiful and I'll talk beautifully."

"You made her?"

Her hand loosened a little. She looked at me, wanting a reaction. "Yes. You don't like her? All men like her. They always want her. Whenever she asks, they say yes. And if they want her then they'll want me too. 'Cause that's what I'll be like."

I had two choices—to play along and pretend, or tell the truth and hope . . . "She talks too much."

Heidi stopped squeezing my hand but kept it where it was. "What do you mean?"

"She talks too much. She's boring."

"B-B-B-oring?"

"Yes. She talks about herself too much and a lot of it isn't interesting. I stopped listening to her. I was paying more attention to you."

"Why? You didn't think she was pretty?"

"Pretty but dull."

"The other men didn't think that! They always wanted her! They always took her!"

"Not all men are the same. I like a woman to be interesting."

"More than pretty?" It was as if she were asking me things from a questionnaire. I had little choice but to answer.

In fact, the rest of the way to Munich she questioned me about "Francesca." Did I like her voice? What about her body? What was wrong with her stories? Would I have wanted to sleep with her if she'd been alone?

I never found out who the woman . . . "was." I did not want to make the girl angrier or more upset than she was for obvious reasons. I answered her questions as best I could and, believe me, there were a great many. I answered her right into the Munich train station where she stood up as the train was slowing and told me she had to go. Nothing more, nothing else. Sliding the glass door open, she gave me one last small smile and was gone.

What do I think happened? I think too many things. That Heidi had an idea for the perfect woman she wanted to be and created one out of her unhappiness to take her place until she could grow into her own adult skin. But she was young and made mistakes. What the young think is cool or sexy we grown-ups often smile at. That's one thought. Or she was a witch playing her own version of "Panic Hand," a game I naturally looked for but never found. Or . . . I don't know. It sounds completely dumb and helpless, but I *don't* know. I'm sorry if you're unsatisfied.

I saw her one last time. When I got off the train I saw her running down the platform and into the arms of a nice-looking couple who were delighted to see her. The man wouldn't put her down and the woman kept giving her kisses. She never turned around once.

But I walked far behind them anyway and was glad she didn't see me. Then there was Celine. And look who came with her so late at night! Fiona. The wonderful Fiona—Celine's daughter.

MICHAEL BLUMLEIN
Bestseller

In one life, Michael Blumlein is a practicing physician living in the San Francisco Bay area. In his other, he is the author of the novel *The Movement of Mountains* and the short works collected in *The Brains of Rats* (Scream/Press). Many of his stories, including "Bestseller," reflect his medical knowledge and use it to create some of the most fascinating, bizarre, and provocative science fiction/fantasy being produced in the short form today. "Bestseller" is also a sharp look at the plight of the artist—the insecurity of having to support one's self and one's family through one's art. The writer in this story finds a solution, albeit a—pardon the expression—radical, and somewhat appalling one. This piece first appeared in *Fantasy & Science Fiction*.

—E.D.

Bestseller

MICHAEL BLUMLEIN

October 20

I once believed that poverty was a desirable state, a way for an artist to focus his mind, to distinguish the inessential from the essential. I was younger then and needed less. A simple room with a bed, a chair, a table. An old typewriter, some pencils, a stack of clean paper. I prided myself on my economies, even though I could easily have found a job and lived otherwise. Asceticism seemed the proper breeding ground for a writer.

Things are different now. I have a family, and while poverty may serve some obscure personal purpose, I cannot accept it for my wife and son. They deserve better than recycled clothes and a tiny, dank apartment. Potato soup and week-old vegetables. Better than to hear me beg our landlord for a rent extension, or come home to a frigid apartment because the heat's been cut off. Indigence is no achievement.

I hate being poor.

October 21

Had a tough time with the book today. Dialogue felt flat, characters like they'd been collectively drugged. In the middle of asking myself what sense it meant to write something that didn't even hold my own interest, Tony called with the news that paperback rights to *In the Thicket* had been sold, but for only a fraction of what we'd hoped. And *Ordeal on the Neighbor's Lawn* had been remaindered. No big surprise, but enough to put an end to today's work. Tony gently asked about the new book, and I answered in vague but enthusiastic terms. "Commercial potential" were, I think, the words I used. They sounded less threatening coming from me than Tony, but after we hung up, their meaning seemed as baffling as ever. What the hell do I have to do to write a book that sells?

October 23

Nick goes through clothes like they were made of paper. Seems like every few days we're either patching something or making a trip to the Salvation Army. He's needed a new pair of shoes for a month now. I told him how Charlie Chaplin used a piece of bologna to patch a hole in his shoe in *Modern Times*. Nickie was intrigued.

"Where'd he get it?"

"From walking."

He looked at me, and I could see him thinking it through. "No," he said. "Where'd he get the bologna?"

October 27

After a week of toothache that wouldn't quit, Claire broke down and went to the dentist. The guy wanted to do a root canal and put in some kind of bridge. Four hundred bucks. Claire told him to pull it. I was furious.

"I can't believe you let him do that. It's your body, Claire. Teeth don't grow back."

"I'm not stupid," she said.

"I can't believe it. Four hundred bucks. Did you tell the asshole we don't have that kind of money?"

"That's enough, Matt."

"Did you?"

"Matt," she said, stopping me with one of her looks. "I've got plenty left."

It's hard to stay mad at a woman like Claire. That look of hers is a killer. To tell the truth, she's kind of cute with a gap in the middle of her smile.

October 29

Took Nick to the park after school, watched while he climbed the big cypress back of the tennis court. He's such a beauty, that boy. Nimble, fearless, reminded me of my own childhood, climbing like that. Young and invincible, one branch after another to the top of the tree. All sky up there. King of the world.

And even that time I fell, stepped on air instead of branch and plummeted twenty feet to the ground, even then something magical. Stunned, my rib cage vibrating like a string, I wandered through the forest in a trance. Finally made it home, bearing a lesson. The earth does not move when I strike it. Some things do not yield to my will.

Nick waved from the top of the cypress, and I caught myself praying he did not have to fall, hoping there was some other, easier way to learn.

On the way home, he kept lagging behind. Said that his leg hurt. Damn shoes, he probably got hung up coming down the tree. I promised we'd get a new pair as soon as a check comes.

November 1

Claire called from work in a state. They doubled the number of calls she has to take per hour, which of course makes the callers even angrier than they were to begin with. I took a break from the book and met her for lunch. She was nearly in tears.

"Some of the people are so rude. Over a goddamned dishwasher or some stupid toaster oven. Like their machine is more important than I am."

"Quit," I told her.

"This woman called today to complain that her husband's shirts weren't getting white enough. He's mad at her because he doesn't have a clean shirt to wear to work. So she calls and gets mad at me. Can you believe it?"

"What did you say to her?"

"I went through the whole routine, but she didn't want to hear. She just wanted to be mad. I don't need it."

"Everyone's mad," I said. "Quit."

"Don't keep saying that."

"You hate it."

"What I hate is when you make things sound so simple. It's like you're trying to fool me. You're telling a lie."

"It's no lie, Claire."

She looked away. "I'm not in the mood for this."

"Other people are just like us. They want their lives to live up to their dreams. They're trying to find a little hope."

"I can't believe yelling at me possibly helps." She shook her head and grumbled, eventually dismissing the subject with a sigh.

"Did you work today?"

"It was like pulling teeth, if you'll excuse the expression."

She didn't smile. "Has Tony seen any of it?"

"A couple of chapters. He thinks we can make some money. At least as much as *Thicket*."

"Not exactly a rousing endorsement."

"Forget Tony. We'll make money. If we don't, I'll find another way."

"Sure you would."

"I mean it."

She regarded me queerly, then took out her compact and freshened up her lips. After she'd gone, I stayed at the table, thinking over what I'd said. As a boy the possibilities of success abounded, but as an adult that same world seems far more difficult to locate. Nevertheless, my ambition remains fierce. This worries me sometimes. Am I lying to myself, as Claire seems to think? Could I ever truly give up writing?

* * *

November 4

Up day today. Words flew onto the page in a fury. Finished chapter 11, and, for the first time, everything seems in place. Jaime's beginning to come around . . . By the end he will have redeemed himself. The marriage of hope to sadness, it'll be a fitting conclusion. And just the kind of thing that'll sell.

November 5

Nick complains about his leg. Still tender from the tree, and he limps ever so slightly. Funny, when I was a kid, seems like I recovered from bumps and bruises overnight. Maybe it's just growing pains. Anyway, I gave him a couple of aspirin, which seemed to help. If he's not better by the time Claire gets her paycheck, I'll take him to the doctor.

November 8

During a lull in the writing, found myself looking through the want ads. All sorts of job opportunities and the accompanying visions of wealth. I let myself go, imagining the great adventures I could have as a filing clerk, memorizing long series of numbers, breathing paper dust and filing one folder after another. Or as a loan processor, recipient of all the hope and loathing people extend onto agents of finance. A cook, perhaps, knowing as I do the masterly craft of opening cans and heating their contents. Or a secretary, typing with clumsy fingers and answering the phone with cloaked civility. There was an opening for a librarian that sounded appealing, and on a whim I dialed the number. The woman, though pleasant, was unimpressed by the fact that I was a published author. In fact, in some subtle way, she seemed to hold it against me, as though I would be the last person on earth capable of helping a reader. When she discovered I lacked the proper college degree, she advised me not to apply for the job, and hung up. Her rejection upset me, and I quickly dialed another number, choosing an advertisement at random just to prove that I was at least capable of getting past a phone call. A man came on the line, and when I told him I was interested in a job, he asked if I had experience with the DBX 2000, the TAC 143, the QT 1522, and the BRT 6200. After a slight pause, I told him yes, I did have some knowledge of car engines, having worked extensively on my old Toyota before it blew a head gasket and died a year ago. There was a brief silence on his end of the line, and then he said he wasn't looking for jokers, and hung up.

I was deflated, feeling in some strange way that my manhood had been insulted. With unexpected determination, I searched the ads for anything to assuage my injured pride. Past dental assistants, escorts, and car salesmen. Machinists, cosmetic counterpersons, TV repairmen. None were remotely possible, and I was about to give up, when my eyes caught a box at the bottom of the page. "DONORS NEEDED," it read. "Good health the only requirement."

I called the number, and the most delightful woman answered. She represented a medical organization that was conducting a study, and if I was in good health, she would be happy to set up an appointment for an interview. Under further questioning, she explained that their research was in the field of organ transplantation, though she was quick to reassure me that the study required only a questionnaire and sample blood test. They were offering two hundred dollars to all those who enrolled. She concluded by saying, rather cryptically, that under the right circumstances, there was the opportunity for lucrative, full-time employment.

Her persuasiveness was such that I was about to make an appointment, when I realized that I had never really intended to go through with any of this. My whim had taken me further than I intended.

Thanking her, I hung up, disturbed at how close I had been to substituting some other project for the book. There's no question that money's tight, but we'll get by. The book will be finished before long, and once it sells, we'll get out of this rattrap life for good.

November 9

Walked down by the wharf this afternoon, reconstituting after a rough morning. The sharp, briny smell of salt water and fish was a tonic. The one-armed man at Scoma's, the big Italian with the crooked nose, was dumping palletfuls of crab into his chest-high vat of boiling water. Fat pink claws, severed from their bodies, floated to the surface.

I started to order one for dinner, then stopped when I realized the price. Instead, I bought a bag of fish guts and a couple of old heads. Thinking soup, but I couldn't bring myself to it. Ended up feeding the slop to some seals, who barked and clapped their flippers appreciatively.

On the way home, I passed a quadriplegic woman playing piano with her tongue. A newspaper clipping tacked on a board behind her told how she was a single mom supporting two kids. She did a nice job, particularly moving rendition of "Amazing Grace." Big hit with the tourists. I overheard someone say what courage she must have. Yes, I thought. Undeniably. And yet it occurred to me that she's only doing what she has to, what she knows, to survive.

November 11

Nick's leg no better, so took him to the hospital today. Doctor ordered an X ray and a blood test. Said there was something wrong in the bone, but he wasn't sure what. Wants to do another test next week, some kind of scan of the bone. I asked if it was absolutely necessary, and the look he gave me made me feel unfit to be alive. Of course we'll do the test. That's about it for Claire's paycheck.

November 12

Had a sweet lovemaking with Claire. It's been awhile. Unseasonably warm night kept us from having to huddle under blankets. She has such a beautiful body, the swale of her belly like some flawless planet, a geography made all the more perfect by the pale, thin scar half-hidden in her pubic hair where the doctors cut her open to deliver Nick. She told me once she had feared an ugly scar more than the surgery itself. She's still self-conscious, even though it's barely visible. She rarely lets me touch it, and I've stopped telling her it's as lovely as any of her natural landmarks. Lovelier, because it reminds me of her courage. She doesn't believe me.

Instead, I ask myself if I would have the same courage, given the opportunity. What would require it? Scars do not bother me. Nor am I especially frightened by the possibility of bodily injury. Some threat to my son? My wife? Undoubtedly. But for myself, only myself, what terrifies most is failure. It haunts my inner life, and I do whatever I can to avoid it. My act of courage, if it comes, will be to abandon ambition forever.

November 14

Finished chapter 12, one more to go. Even at this late stage, there are surprises. Jaime turned unexpectedly dour, revealing a side of himself that augurs darkly for the book. Suggests an ending I'd hoped to avoid. People are willing to consider suffering, but only as a tonic. Redemption must prevail.

But this book will be a success; I swear it. By the end, Jaime will reveal yet another layer, a deeper one. A wellspring of faith and abiding love. I know it's there. Even the hardest hearts will weep.

November 14

I came home today to find Claire yelling at Nick. He was standing beside the refrigerator, cowering and trying not to cry. Between them on the floor lay a mess of broken eggs. Claire lifted him roughly by the arms and moved him to the side. In a voice shaking with anger, she ordered him to his room.

When he was gone, I asked what had happened. She gave me a bleak look, then knelt on the floor and buried her face in her hands.

"I hate this," she muttered. "I hate it, hate it, hate it."

"I'll get some more."

She looked up accusingly. "With what?"

"You don't have to take it out on Nick."

She started to reply, then her eyes filled with tears.

"Claire. . . ."

She waved me away. "How does it get like this? Suddenly you see yourself doing something you never dreamed you could. That awful glimpse. The shame. . . ."

"Talk to him. Tell him."

"I wish we had money."

"We will."

"I don't mean a lot. Some." Wearily, she got to her feet. "It's not his fault."

She left the kitchen, and I stared at the mess. Half a dozen broken eggs is not a pretty sight. My responsibility? Maybe so.

Taking the rag in hand, I cleaned the floor, then went and found that ad in the newspaper. The same woman answered the phone, same cordial, pleasant voice. As though she were the guardian of some secret of contentment and happiness. I made the appointment to give her my blood.

November 16

The monkey sits on our head; we sit on the monkey. I finish the book, and an hour later the doctor calls to say that Nickie has cancer. Cancer. What is the heart to do? Between exhilaration at completing the book and this sudden grief, my heart chooses the latter. It is my son. They want to cut off his leg.

November 20

Another battery of tests. Doctors now unsure whether to amputate or try to cure with radiation and drugs. We are nearly broke. The two hundred dollars I'll have after tomorrow will stake us to another week, maybe two if we stretch it. Medical bills will just have to wait. By the time we get the second collection notice, the book should be sold.

November 21

The question of worthiness plagues me. Am I a good husband? A father? A writer? In moments of clarity, I see fame as the culmination of fear, success another name for sacrifice. Ambition has a way of being unforgiving.

The appointment was on Larkin Street, in a fancy old apartment building on Russian Hill. Its entrance was framed by marble pillars and lined by enormous stone urns the color of sand. At the top of the stairs was a glass door with a polished brass casing and a single doorbell. I was buzzed inside by a uniformed guard who asked my business. I gave him my name, which he checked on a clipboard before pointing me to a door at the rear of the lobby. It opened onto an old-fashioned elevator with a hand-operated metal gate. There were eight floors to the building, and I took the elevator to the top, where I stepped out into a carpet-lined hallway lit by a single large chandelier. Opposite me was a door with the number I'd been given.

A blue-suited man with a pleasant, generically handsome face let me in, addressing me by name without bothering to introduce himself. He was a head taller than I, and at least that much wider across the shoulders. His handshake was just firm enough to enforce the already unmistakable impression of latent strength.

He led me through a door into a second room many times larger than the first, full of furniture, sculptures, and paintings. I recognized a van Gogh, marveling at the quality of the reproduction, until I realized that it was probably the original. A brass head I had once seen in an art book lay casually propped on a table. Beside it was a richly upholstered couch, and, at the far end of the room, a grand piano, its black top gleaming.

The opulence was overwhelming, and it was some time before I ventured away from the door. Mindful of all the precious objects, I crossed to a picture window on the other side of the room. It was a relief to look out, like having a sip of plain water after a meal of sweets.

The view was breathtaking. To the west lay the city, to the north the bay, its water gray in the blunted afternoon light. I had the impression I was staring out from a gigantic eye, far from the poverty to which I was accustomed. It was a safe, antiseptic view, and for an instant the sun broke through the clouds, throwing a bright slit of light across the water. In that moment of beauty, I forgot my sorrow, but then a door closed, breaking the reverie.

I turned, expecting to see the totemlike man who had ushered me in. Instead, it was a woman. She had a youngish look about her, but moved with the deliberation of someone older. She wore a skirt and open-necked blouse, and her skin was either lightly tanned or else naturally dark. She introduced herself simply as Devora, and, as soon as she spoke, I recognized the voice of the woman on the telephone.

We sat opposite each other on the sofa, and I casually remarked that it was a beautiful room, not at all what I'd expected for a medical interview. She replied that there was no reason for research to be conducted in austerity, and went on to explain that the foundation she represented was small and personal enough to be attentive to such niceties.

"Those who work for us suffer few hardships," she said, then opened a folder on her lap and began with her questions.

Most pertained to my health, but others concerned my family, marriage, even my financial situation. Some were quite personal, and initially I was reluctant to discuss them. Devora was an attractive woman, her nails meticulously manicured, her hair just so. She wore several thin gold necklaces, which she had a habit of twirling through her fingers. It was a mannerism that, taken with her scrupulous beauty, called to mind a vanity that did not inspire my trust. In every other way, though, she seemed open and sincere, so that after a while I found myself willing to confide in her. I spoke briefly of my troubled career as a writer, my aspirations and current hopes for success. I mentioned Claire's dissatisfaction with work and, after a moment's hesitation, told her of the tumor in Nickie's leg. She made a note on her paper, then closed the folder and rewarded me with a look of sympathy and understanding.

"The human body can be so fragile," she said. "I'm very sorry."

"The doctors talk of a cure."

"Of course."

"He's receiving radiation and drugs. We're very hopeful."

"Certainly. And if the boy does not respond. What then?"

I was taken aback. "What kind of question is that?"

"You must have considered it."

"It's none of your business."

"Forgive me."

A silence ensued, which she seemed in no hurry to break.

"They'll have to cut it off," I muttered. "Give him some sort of fake leg."

"A prosthesis."

I nodded.

"If it were possible for your son to receive a real leg, one of flesh and blood, would you consent?"

"I don't understand."

"A living limb. A transplant."

"The doctors have never mentioned that."

"The operation is rarely done," she said with authority. "The donor requirements are so strict as to virtually prohibit it."

"Then why do you ask?"

"The foundation is interested in the attitudes people have toward transplantation."

"It must be expensive."

"Forgetting the cost."

I gave her a look.

"Come now. You're a writer. A thinker. Take it as a philosophical question." She played with a necklace. "If a limb were available, if it could be grafted on, would you consent?"

I sensed that some trap was being laid, but she did not seem the type. Still, I felt the need to consider carefully. I stood and walked to the window. The clouds now covered the whole of the city, bathing it in a marbled, celestial light.

"Yes," I said at length. "I'd consent. What father would not want his child whole?"

"It is a great gift."

"You have children?"

"One," she said without elaboration. She looked at her watch, then stood and smoothed her skirt. "You've been very patient."

She led me to a door opposite the one she had entered, and motioned me inside. When I realized she was not going to follow, I stopped and asked about the money.

"You'll receive a check within the week."

I hesitated briefly before asking if there were some way to be paid sooner. She started to say one thing, then stopped herself.

"Of course. I'll take care of it. And again, thanks for your cooperation."

She left, leaving me alone in this new room. It was small and windowless, unpleasantly lit by a fluorescent rectangle of overhead light. In the center was a narrow table, on either side of which was an armless plastic chair. In one corner was a sink, and in another, a refrigerator. Black-and-white photographs graced the walls, highly magnified views of people's faces. I was studying the lobe of an ear, when a man entered the room. He wore a white lab coat and looked uncannily like the man I had first met. He had me sit opposite him at the table, then opened a drawer and brought out a needle, syringe, and tourniquet. After tying the tourniquet around my arm, he slid the needle swiftly into a vein, causing the barest whisper of pain, and drew off five or six tubes of blood. He finished almost as soon as he had started, releasing the tourniquet and pasting a small bandage on top of the puncture wound. He marked the tubes with a pen, aligned them in a metal rack at the end of the table, then stood up with the rack in hand. He thanked me and pointed to a door, then turned and exited by another. Opening the one he had indicated, I found myself in the very first room I had entered.

I was disoriented, and stood for a moment wondering what to do. Just then, yet another door opened, and the man in the blue suit who had first greeted me appeared. From his vest pocket, he took out a plain white envelope, which he handed to me. I was embarrassed to look, but felt foolish not to, and ended up turning my back and quickly checking the contents. Satisfied, I slid the envelope in my coat pocket, thanked him, and left.

In the elevator I looked in the envelope again. Four fifty-dollar bills, as crisp as crackers. Easy money. It made me want to come back.

November 29

Tony is lukewarm on the book. He tries to be kind, says things like, "It's idio-syncratic. Challenging." He wants more of a resolution, meaning, if not complete sunshine, at least a healthy glow of happiness at the end. "Does Jaime have to suffer so much?" he asks. I feel like telling him to ask Jaime, instead reply that suffering is the human condition, is only a small step on the larger road to enlightenment. I tell him this is a story about love, and love involves sacrifice.

"We're just a breath away from paradise here," I hear myself saying. "Let the people judge. They've learned from their soap operas. They know how to pick a winner."

November 30

Got a letter from Devora and the Kingman Foundation today. Says if I'm interested in further work, to give them a call. I'm not. The conversation yesterday with Tony has left me surprisingly upbeat about my chances with the book. I'm a writer. I'll wait.

December 6

Nick is brave as hell. He limps all the time, obviously in pain, but he hardly ever complains. Worst thing for him is not being able to go out with the guys after school. By then he's so exhausted he has to come home for a nap. Sleeps until dinner. His appetite's off; doctors say the treatments will do that. Claire's a wreck, seeing him like this. Like part of herself has ceased to function properly. I'm not much better. We're barely eating, waking five, six times a night out of worry.

This thing's a family disease.

December 11

Met with Nick's doctors today. Grave men, but humane. Treatment not going as well as they'd hoped. Nick can't tolerate the doses they need to eradicate the tumor. All agreed to give it another couple of weeks. If no response, amputation.

I asked about a transplant. Difficult, they say, much harder than kidney or even heart. Cadavers don't work; donor has to be living and vital. Limbs remain viable for less than an hour after death.

"Obviously hard to find a living person willing to part with his leg," says one of the doctors.

"Prosthetics are getting better all the time," says another.

I ask about cost.

"A lot," says the doctor in charge.

"What? A hundred thousand?"

"More."

"Two?"

"After it's all over, probably half a million."

A daunting figure. I glance at Claire, who's staring at the floor, trying to contain herself. Anger rises in me, and then from nowhere an overwhelming sense of failure. Irrational as it is, I feel responsible.

December 13

The city is filled with the smoke from a brush fire a hundred miles to the east. Tiny white ashes float in the air, as though this were the Day of Judgment. People go methodically about their business without the slightest concern. I myself feel at the mercy of circumstances beyond my control, ironically the first breath of fresh air in months.

We are dead broke. It's a kind of freedom. Stark, but unencumbered by the swamp of egotism and pride. Now I have no choice but to get a job. I spread the want ads on the floor, poised with my foot to stamp at random, when the phone rings. It's Devora.

"You received our letter?" she asks.

"Letter?" I'm about to hang up, when I remember.

"We like to call to be sure," she says smoothly.

"Nicholas," I reply, embarrassed at my forgetfulness. "He's been a preoccupation."

"I understand."

Do you? I want to say, angry at her wealth and good health. Instead, I glance down at the newsprint under my foot. An ad for a school of technical and creative writing, promising exciting and rewarding careers. The ultimate self-indictment.

I tell her I'll take the job.

December 23

It's a funny kind of work. I've been poked and prodded by three different doctors, scanned by at least twice that many machines, had tubes passed down my throat and up my ass, blood drawn, eyes and ears checked, exercised, rested . . . . It goes on. Some of the tests are done in the Larkin Street apartment, but most in a private and fancy little clinic near Mission Bay. Everyone's nice as can be, making me feel a bit guilty. These tests would cost anyone else thousands, and here I am getting paid to do them. And paid handsomely. It's the easiest money I've ever earned.

As Devora has explained it, the foundation's work is in the area of clinical transplantation, and, according to her, they've been highly successful. My job, after this initial phase, will be to provide certain material, such as hair and skin, for grafting. My tissues have been matched to another man, who will receive them. Although the work will be intermittent, as long as I remain available, my salary will continue. Raises, she promises, will be frequent and generous.

January 22

It's been nearly a month now, and I've yet to be called on. From time to time, I find myself wondering what it will be . . . a small piece of skin, a tuft of hair? For the most part, though, I've been too busy to think about it.

We've moved into a beautiful new apartment at the tip of Grant Avenue. Three bedrooms, big kitchen, and a living room with a fireplace and a spectacular view of the bay. I spend hours just sitting in my armchair, beer in hand, luxuriating in the warmth of a well-heated room and the panorama of sky and water. We bought a television and VCR for Nickie to use while he's going through the exercises with his new leg. He's doing remarkably well, considering the amputation was little more than a month ago. Stump's all healed; he's got his energy back, raring to go. Amazing how he bounces back.

No word yet on the book, and, other than these entries, I'm not writing. I'm making good money as it is. Why torture myself to be rejected?

January 31

I was called today for my first "assignment." A few tufts of hair from the back of my scalp. They use an instrument that looks a little like an apple corer, but much smaller. Because my hair is so thick, the missing spots are hardly visible. The whole thing lasted about an hour, and now I am back home, sucking on a beer and watching the rain sweep across the city. It's a lovely sight, and I feel no need to improve on it.

February 10

Lately I've been wondering about the man on the other end. Devora says that someday I'll meet him, though she seems in no particular hurry. I gather that he's quite a bit older and not in the best of health. Selfishly, I find myself hoping that, even in sickness, he survives a long time.

The part of my scalp where they took the hair is virtually healed. The scabs came off yesterday, which makes the itching much less. The rectangle of skin from my inner thigh, however, is another matter. They used something called a microtome, which supposedly takes off only the thinnest of layers, but it feels as if they branded me with an iron. The area is all red and hurts like hell to touch.

I haven't been able to go out because my pants rub against it. No sex all this week.

February 15

Second week, and skin graft still not healed. Somehow it got infected, which isn't supposed to happen. Now I'm on antibiotics and bed rest to air it out. The doctors couldn't be nicer, but I'm not used to being sick. Makes me cantankerous. To top it off, Tony called with bad news. Because of disappointing sales of my first two books, they're not making an offer on the new one. Fine. Let them wither in the heat of my future fame and success.

February 20

Damn sore finally healed enough that Claire could touch me without my feeling she was sticking a knife in my leg. We made love gingerly, despite the weeks of pent-up desire. Afterward I found myself unconsciously fingering the scar on her belly. She didn't seem to mind, maybe because she was busy trying to arouse me again.

"This stays," she said.

"You bet."

"I mean it. It's one part I'll never let them take." Her face was hidden, and I couldn't tell if she was joking. The idea sent shivers down my spine.

February 24

I met Kingman Ho today, after whom the foundation is named. A tall man with a face that was once probably handsome, he was looking out the big picture window in the living room when I arrived. Devora introduced us, and I held out a hand that he did not immediately take. Instead, he looked at me from behind his thick glasses with eyes that were impossible to read. I remembered gazing out over the city on my first visit, thinking it lovely, though distant and dreamlike. The feeling I had as he looked at me was much the same but in reverse, as though I were a landscape of his own imagination. Either that or an article of clothing he was appraising.

It made me uncomfortable, and I became conscious of my imperfections: the faint scar on my cheek from a boyhood accident, the part of my nose that was broken in a fall. For some reason I felt I should apologize, but instead, I mumbled some inane comment about the view. He looked at me quizzically, as if surprised that I was capable of speech, and turned to Devora, who whispered something in his ear. He nodded and managed to smile at me, then left the room. Devora adjusted one of the necklaces at her throat.

"He likes you," she said, an assessment that seemed beyond the realm of anyone's knowledge. I asked what made her say so.

"He has no choice," she replied. "Kingman is ill. You may have noticed."

"He seemed distant."

"Renal osteodystrophy," she said cryptically. "His bones are like eggshells."

"He's in pain?"

"Great pain," she said. "Seldom will you meet a braver man."

I thought of Nick, who more than once has humbled me with his courage. "My son is brave."

She stared out the window, nodding ever so slightly. "They say that courage is contagious. How is the boy doing?"

"Well. He's already walking."

"The money is sufficient? There's been no interference with his care?"

"You've been more than generous."

She nodded again, this time turning to face me. "They say that that, too, is contagious."

She left the room before I had a chance to ask what she meant, and a moment later I followed, ushered out by the man in the blue suit.

At home tonight I looked up the disease in a book. Something having to do with kidney failure, the bones becoming wafer-thin because all the calcium leaches out. Later on, in bed, I found myself rubbing my flank, and Claire, sensing that something was troubling me, stilled me with her hand. Then she kissed where I had been rubbing, outlining the area with her tongue, as if to describe a future scar to match her own. An uncanny woman, choosing just the right moment to show her tenderness.

"I love you no matter who you are," she murmured, as she has so many times before. It makes all the difference.

February 27

Devora dropped by today, ostensibly to see the apartment and meet Claire. She wore a gay-looking dress with a scooped collar and the omnipresent gold chains at her throat. Claire was cordial but ill at ease, and I could tell from the beginning she was waiting for the visit to be over. At a certain point, she excused herself to make tea, and Devora used the opportunity to inform me of some upcoming work. At the same time, she handed me a "bonus" check of five thousand dollars. I stared at it for a moment, then folded it and put it away.

"Please don't mention this to Claire," I said, sensing it was unnecessary to ask. "It's always been hard for her to accept good fortune. I'll tell her later."

"Be politic when you do," said Devora. "I don't want her to fear me more than she does."

"What she fears is the sudden wealth."

"Perhaps." She was pensive. "And you?"

"I fear that it will end."

March 8

A week now since they took the kidney. Except for some pain when I turn or move fast, I don't even notice that it's gone. The initial shock of being asked to part with it has passed. So, too, the surprise that the recipient is Kingman Ho himself. Wealth makes its own rules. I look at it like this: if Nickie or Claire needed a kidney in order to live, would I offer one of mine? Without a second thought. So isn't what I'm giving them now nearly the same? A decent place to live, food when they're hungry, heat, clothing. By donating my kidney to Ho, I'm simply giving my family a life they deserve.

March 21

Attended a small party at the Larkin Street apartment this evening. After considerable persuasion, Claire agreed to come, and Nick joined us. We were met by the nameless man in the blue suit, who took our coats and ushered us into the living room. Devora stood beside the piano, drink in hand, talking to a woman who might well have been her twin. Kingman Ho was nearby, surrounded by a clump of judicious-looking, well-tailored men. Several couples stood by the window, taking in the magnificent view, and beyond them, warming themselves by the fireplace, two of the doctors who had examined me. A servant in a starched black dress brought us drinks, and, a few minutes later, a girl served us hors d'oeuvres from a silver tray. She couldn't have been more than a year or two older than Nick, though her manners were those of an adult well trained in service. She held out the tray to Nickie, who didn't know quite what to do. He looked to me for help, while the girl, in complete possession of herself, urged him to take one of her tidbits. I nodded my approval, then took one myself, a bit of a cracker heaped generously with caviar. It was delicious, and I had another.

At length, Devora came over with Kingman, clinging unashamedly to him as if he were some prize catch. I did not immediately grasp the significance of this. Admittedly, the man looked fitter than before, his color better, his attention crisper, but his stolid manner seemed a world away from Devora's youthfulness and vigor. She was a good twenty, even thirty years his junior, yet here she was nuzzling his neck like some restless colt. It occurred to me she might be a daughter, yet her attentions seemed anything but filial.

Kingman greeted me with more warmth than when we had first met. He held my hand longer than was necessary, using the opportunity to once again appraise me. This time I returned his scrutiny, and after a moment he smiled, releasing me with a muttered word of appreciation. He introduced himself to Claire, gracefully slipping her hand through his arm and steering her away.

"He seems to have recovered his health," I said dryly.

"Remarkably," replied Devora, looking after him. "He's a new man."

"Perhaps I should be flattered."

She considered this, then took a step closer. She was a little drunk. "For the first time in years, he performs like a man." She touched a necklace, smiling to herself. "I had all but forgotten. Imagine. Now I am called on to be a woman again. Who would have thought?"

"I'm happy for you," I said, but in truth I was not. It seemed wrong that Ho, already so much older than she, was performing with a body not wholly his. More than that, it seemed improper, as though I were being used in some strange and undignified way as a sex surrogate. This I had never agreed to, and I was about to say something, when Devora's look-alike interrupted us. She introduced herself, and I casually asked if the two of them were twins.

"You flatter me," said Devora.

"My mother knows the secret of youth," said the woman. She brushed a stray hair from Devora's cheek and whispered something in her ear. Devora nodded, and the woman, excusing herself, left.

"Mother?" I said. "To her? She can't be less than thirty."

"A beautiful girl," said Devora proudly.

"How old are you?"

She smiled coyly, touching one of her necklaces. Just then a piece of wood caught fire, momentarily brightening the room. It cast a sudden light on her throat, revealing a thin white scar at the base of her neck. I stared at it, then her eyes. They were laughing at me.

"The others are well hidden," she said.

"I'm embarrassed."

"Don't be." She lifted a glass of wine from a passing tray, holding it aloft as if in toast. "What greater act of creation than to create ourselves?"

Later that evening, watching the fog slip through the Gate, I happened to catch Nick out of the corner of an eye. He was sitting on the floor at the far end of the room, partially obscured by one of the piano legs. Kneeling next to him was the serving girl. At first I thought they were playing some game, so enrapt were they, but after edging a little closer, I saw they were doing something different entirely. Nick had his pant leg rolled up, and the girl was fingering his prosthesis. Inch by inch she was creeping up the leg, circling it one moment, stroking it the next, coddling it as though she were unearthing some priceless relic. Nick was utterly entranced, as mesmerized by the girl's attention as she was by his false limb. When she came to the edge of his pant leg, she'd stop and glance up, waiting for him to roll the pants up farther. Little by little the entire limb was becoming exposed.

By the look on his face, Nick seemed actually to be feeling the girl's touch, as though the intensity of her exploration were awakening some hitherto slumbering receptors in his phantom limb. There was a charge I could feel from across the room.

I was torn about what to do, feeling on the one hand that it was my responsibility as a father to intervene, and on the other, that to interrupt now might only reinforce the stigma of Nickie's handicap. The choice was made moot when one of the adult servants found the girl and with angry words pulled her from the room. The spell broken, Nickie became suddenly self-conscious, fumbling abashedly with his pant leg. I rushed over and helped him to his feet, saying nothing of what I had seen. I suggested it was time to leave, and, after looking quickly around the room, presumably for the girl, Nick agreed. I had an arm on his shoulder, but he shrugged me off, preferring to make his exit alone.

He fell asleep in the car on the way home, but a parent can never be sure. I decided to hold off telling Claire of the incident, and, to pass the time, I asked her opinion of Kingman Ho. They had spent nearly an hour together.

"I think there's something terribly wrong with him," she said. "We weren't together for ten minutes before I wanted to comfort him. A complete stranger. It's not what I expected."

"Suffering has a certain allure. Ho's been ill with one thing or another for years."

"When he speaks of himself, it's as though he were someone else. Once he said something—I don't remember what—and I found myself thinking, This is a man who lives in a mirror. A brittle, distant mirror."

"He's arrogant. And rich. I think he makes a point of staying aloof."

"He told me he holds himself in contempt. I asked him why, and he said for lacking the strength to die."

"He's posing, Claire. It's cocktail-party conversation."

"He scares me," she said, shivering against the cold and pulling Nick into her. "I wish we didn't depend on him."

"You have it backward," I told her, angry that she had been affected this way. "I'm the one who holds the aces. Kingman Ho depends on me."

May 3

Last month it was the small bones in my ear. A week later my right eye. It's amazing how quickly I adapt. Unless someone whispers to my left, I hear almost as well as before. And except for a certain flatness of vision, which becomes less noticeable each day, my eyesight is unchanged.

I run into Ho from time to time. He is polite, even cordial, and ironically, I'm now the one who's keeping a distance. There's little I have to say to him, and what I do usually comes out rudely. The fact is, I don't like him. He takes and takes like a spoiled child, and what does he give in return? Money. It's a cold reward.

Nevertheless, when we meet, I look for signs in him of recognition. I often find myself staring at his right eye, the brown one stippled with green, the one that is mine. It looks stony in his face, callous, yet every so often it takes on a gleam too familiar to ignore. I know your motives, it seems to say. You cannot lie.

Sometimes I want to claw the eye from his face.

May 5

Tony called . . . another rejection. I told him I don't care. For the first time that I remember, I feel liberated from the yoke of the marketplace.

May 17

There is something erotic to all this. It embarrasses me to say so because it sounds perverse. Yet each time they take part of my body, my sexuality becomes heightened. The toes were taken a week and a half ago, and since then I've been in a state of constant erection, having wet dreams nearly every night. Claire, always before my sexual match, has been eclipsed by this newfound desire. It's as if my unconscious, fearful of its survival, has panicked, triggering a surge of sexuality in the hopes of perpetuating my genetic stock before I suffer extinction.

At times I have the feeling I am approaching a new and primitive state, one of explosive creativity and gratification. The compulsion for language and abstract thought has become remote, making me wonder why I ever bothered writing at all. In comparison to the language of the body, words say so little.

Claire, who knows me better than I know myself, thinks I'm a little mad.

May 23

They want my arm. My right arm. Shoulder to fingertip. I'm afraid.

May 31

This past week has felt like a year. The fear of apprehension is with me constantly. The blue-suited bodyguard will appear, blandly crushing me in his arms and taking me back. Or Devora will arrive, bearing some new manner of persuasion. A subtle change of posture, a lilt in her voice, the veiled promise of some favor impossible to refuse. Or Kingman himself, man of few words, instigator of my flight. Armless now, with no finger to pull the trigger, no hand to make me dance at his insane command. He will come to beg for my limb.

Let him. Let him feel my contempt at his wealth and power. He is not a man. No man would do to me what he has done. More than anything, I fear my own uncertainty. I could tell them I'm through and put a stop to this thing once and for all. Or else give them the arm and be done with it. Why run?

Wealth and success are not easy to dismiss. What if Kingman dies? Kingman the Brute, the Cruel. My patron. What then?

June 3

The wind howls in the canyons, scouring the earth with sand. The heat of the desert sun is unbelievable. I hide in my motel room and wait. I'm convinced they know where I am. Why don't they come?

June 5

One's self-importance diminishes greatly out here. The desert is too big, too raw and exposed to suffer pride and deceit. I see that my hatred for Ho is little more than the mirage of my own inadequacy. I cannot despise him for wanting my arm, any more than I can despise my son for wanting a new leg. It's man's nature to fight disintegration and decay.

But more, I begin to see that Kingman Ho and I are linked. Each layer of skin, each organ that I give weds him more firmly to me. Ho is my creation. Running from him is tantamount to running from myself.

*   *   *

June 29

Absence is a stronger state than presence. It derives shape from the imagination, from loss and need. The arm has been gone for weeks, but when I close my eyes, it is still there. I feel sensations in thin air, pain, heat, motion. I hold a pencil, a cup of coffee in a phantom world, stroke Claire's back and feel the texture of her skin with a hand that can't be seen. But something exists—I know it—something that could not be severed from the tracts of memory.

I imagine the arm hanging from Kingman's side, attached to his nerves and muscles, moving to his command, but all the while maintaining a deeper program, untempered by conscious thought. I picture the hand accenting the air with my mannerisms, writing in my script, stroking Devora with my touch. The limb is a ghost, and I, the ghostwriter. As I serve Kingman, he serves me.

July 2

We have more money now than we know what to do with. Claire has quit her job, and Nick has private tutors to help him make up the time he's lost. I read rather than write, or else sit in the armchair with a beer and watch the bay change colors. I don't feel lazy. My job is to heal.

July 15

It's surprising how fast I recover from these operations. Just a few days ago, they took a piece of bone from my pelvis, and already I'm able to move around quite well. Except for the skin graft months ago, I've had no problems whatever. I can't say the same for Kingman. Even though our tissues are matched, he still seems to struggle through almost every procedure. His age must have something to do with it, and Devora says the drugs he takes to keep from rejecting my tissue get in the way of his healing. It's hard to see anyone suffer as he does. I pity him and sometimes wonder why he persists. Does he truly fear death, or is there some other reason that he prolongs his life? Perhaps immortality is a motive in itself.

July 18

Woke up from a dead sleep last night wondering, of all things, what Kingman had for dinner. Not simply the menu, but how he had eaten, and with whom. Was it a lively, high-spirited meal or tiresomely dull? A pleasure or, in his old age, a chore? Did he eat alone or with company? In suit and tie or more casually? What did he say?

It took me an hour to get back to sleep, and in the morning I needed two cups of coffee to wake up. As I poured the second, I tried to remember if I'd ever seen Kingman drink coffee? Black or with cream? One cup or two?

*   *   *

July 21

Why haven't they called? It's been nearly a week without a word. Something bad has happened; I know it. Two things come frightfully to mind. Kingman has finally gotten too sick to need me. Bad enough, but the other is worse.

They've found a new donor.

July 24

Finally. Early this morning, pitch black outside, the phone rang. It triggered a dream, and I reached out to Claire with my phantom limb. She murmured something and nestled into my empty socket. I picked up the receiver.

His voice was urgent, lacking its familiar polish and restraint. He demanded to see me immediately, insisting that I meet him at his apartment. I agreed, but when I asked what was the matter, the phone was already dead.

Outside, the fog had settled to ground level, as thick as if it had sprung from the earth itself. Kingman's building was all but invisible from the street, the tall Greek columns seemingly anchored to clouds. A night clerk let me in, saying that Mr. Ho was expecting me. I wiped the moisture from my face and hair and entered the elevator. At the eighth floor, I started to exit, when Kingman suddenly appeared, shoving me back inside. He pulled the gate shut, hit the down button, then stopped the elevator between floors.

"The records," he said, facing me with wild, bloodshot eyes. "Where are the records?"

I searched my mind for some previous mention of records. Something to orient me. But he did not wait for a reply.

"I need to know what they're doing. All of them. Earnest faces, yes, but none as honest as they pretend. I've tried to get messages out. It's some game, isn't it? Some imposter's ploy. . . ."

"Game? I don't understand."

"Why are they giving me four pills at night and only three in the morning? Tell me that, if you can."

"Four? Three?"

"It's a charade, isn't it? An imitation." He grinned, as though pleased with himself, but the look was quickly gone. "It moves on channels beyond what the others can detect. It's lost to them, but not to us. Tell me, who are the higher authorities? Who pulls the strings?

"I'm asking for your help," he said, more urgently now. "Tell me what to do. I hear them talk. Even behind my back, it's obvious what they're saying. But I will not be discouraged.

"They couldn't do this to an ordinary man. I see it, and I am above it. When I will it to stop, it will stop. Do you understand? It's my duty."

His voice was high-pitched, his manner desperate. He paced frantically, but careful not to touch me. All at once he stopped.

"Can you smell the decay? Even a strong person can't hold out forever. I need answers. Help me."

The man was clearly out of his mind, and I worried that the tiny space we were in was making him worse. I inched over to the elevator's control panel, eyeing the switch that would set us in motion, but as soon as I got close, he blocked my way. With a menacing look, he leaned against the panel, bracing himself with both feet planted firmly on the floor. He placed his palms together in an attitude of prayer or warning and shut his eyes.

For the first time, I got a good look at him. His hair was disheveled, his face mottled and red. His skin was marked by scores of tiny capillaries, many of which had burst. At one side of his neck, peeking above his shirt collar, was the edge of a recent skin graft. It was swollen and purple, with a crust that oozed yellowish liquid. I felt an urge to run, which was impossible, but also to comfort him. He seemed in furious pain, and had now put himself in a position of no escape. But when I stepped forward in an effort to help him, he opened his eyes and growled at me. I tried some words to calm him, but he only laughed, accusing me of trying to control him with my voice.

"I see what you're thinking," he said. "Trying to trick me with your deep tones. Don't you see that I'm your reflection? This is no joke."

He started humming to himself, a hysterical tune of his own making. Suddenly the elevator began to move. His head darted frantically from side to side, and he slapped at the control switch and the buttons. To no avail. Inexorably the car ascended, and, at the eighth floor, the blue-suited man was there to pull back the gate. Beside him, in slippers and bathrobe, stood Devora. The sight of her seemed to take something out of Kingman, who, having backed into a corner, let out a shuddering sigh and collapsed against the elevator wall.

We carried him into the apartment, and twenty minutes later Devora returned to tell me everything was all right.

"I must apologize for my husband's behavior." She offered me a drink, which I readily accepted. "Some of these drugs have such terrible effects."

"I don't know which of us was more scared."

"Him, I imagine." She took her drink to the window. "He's not himself these days."

"I'm not surprised."

She stiffened. "The irony does not escape me. But no, he's not." She sighed. "I suppose it's a wonder that things don't change any faster than they do."

I had no reply, and stared with her out the window, the reflection of our faces seeming to float in the fog.

"Have you ever written a book, then thrown it out? Destroyed it because it wasn't what you knew you could create, what you wanted to?"

"A book changes in the writing," I told her. "And then later, after. It could always become something else, something to cherish."

"Do you fall in love with what you write?"

"I suppose. Of a kind. It's always a stormy affair."

"But when things go bad, when they go astray, you know what to do."

I shrugged, and then all at once I understood what she was asking. "Someday Kingman will die," I told her. "Then you'll find out for yourself."

"I know how I'll act," she said quietly, as if she'd already planned it out. She seemed grateful to be able to tell me. "Is that shameful?"

"It's too early in the morning for shame."

"Yes." She touched a necklace and turned. "Do you find me attractive?"

I worked on my drink. She watched me and waited.

"You know the answer," I said at length. "You wouldn't have asked if you didn't."

"Vanity is such a scourge," she said with a self-deprecating little laugh.

I examined myself, my missing arm, toes, and the rest.

"Isn't it."

July 28

Tonight, after I read him a bedtime story, Nick grabbed onto my arm and wouldn't let go. After a few minutes, I asked him to stop, but he held on tighter.

"You have to stay," he said.

"Nickie, it's bedtime."

"I won't let you go."

"Three minutes," I said, relenting. "And then you sleep."

"You count."

The minutes passed, and when the time was up, Nickie still wouldn't let go.

"You have to leave your hand with me," he said.

"I've only got one left," I answered jokingly, touched by his possessiveness.

"Promise you won't take it away."

"I'm right next door, Nickie. I'm not going anywhere."

"Promise."

"I'm your father," I said. "You can't lose me." Gently, I pulled my arm away. "I love you, Nickie. I promise."

July 30

Claire and I naked in bed, her fingers working my back. One vertebra at a time, outlining each bone and muscle. I savor her touch, though I can't help wondering if she is taking inventory. When she reaches the nub at the bottom of my spine, the little upturning before it dives between the buttocks, she stops. I make sounds to indicate she should continue, but she is still. Then she starts to talk.

"When I was a kid, there was a boy. Joe something. He was older than I, with big buck teeth. Always popping his gum and showing his teeth. He used to get in corners and rub up against me. Front to back—front to front if I didn't turn around fast enough. It was awful."

"You just remembered?"

Absently, she touched me where she'd left off. "He had a tail."

"What?"

"A little tail. I didn't find out until later, after he had an operation to get rid of it. I was so happy when I heard."

"Why happy?"

"It seemed fair. Making me suffer like that, he should suffer, too."

"Is this some message, Claire? A parable?"

"It's true."

"What's true?"

She traces the scar on my flank, taking her time. "Would it have been different if Nickie had not lost his leg? I'd still be working, you still troubled and angry. Things balance out. There's a funny kind of logic to all this."

"We have money."

"I'm happy for that. But something else."

"I'm dense tonight, Claire. What's on your mind?"

"I don't know." She touches the nub at the bottom of my spine, rubbing it as if to conjure the proper explanation. "It has to do with self-respect. Knowing the measure of things. The limits.

"You can stop whenever you want, Matt. This is not for money; it's not for me or Nickie. You must know that."

"I have inklings."

"Will you stop?"

"When I'm done. Yes. I promise."

August 8

My face is bandaged so that only my mouth and nostrils are in contact with the air. Sometimes I think I am being reduced to the point that nothing will remain of me but holes. Mercifully, I am heavily drugged.

This last operation was a tough one, and it was complicated by an infection. I write this by Dictaphone, which someone, Claire probably, has left by the pillow. Kingman developed a sudden, overwhelming necrosis of his face, a result of one of the drugs he's on. The skin from forehead to chin, ear to ear sloughed off en masse. I was called in an emergency, and when I saw how he looked, the pain and fear in his eyes, I knew I would not refuse. So they brought me in and took my own face.

I am glad my eye is covered, because there are things I'd just as soon not see. Claire's look of woe, Nick's accusation and fear. I hear it well enough in their voices.

Tony called today, and, while someone held the phone, he jabbered on excitedly about an offer that promises a lot if I deliver a second book within a year. So much has happened these past months that I had to ask him the name of the book they want to buy. He laughed and told me, then asked if I thought I could write another so soon. It was my turn to laugh, a feeble sound that barely escaped my lips.

"It's nearly done."

"The diary?" he said. "You see it as a book?"

"Not that. The man. It's creation itself, Tony. Already I'm a success. Imagine, after all these years. You wait to see the door, and then you realize you've already walked through."

Someone is holding my hand. Claire, I think, though it might be Devora. Heavy sedation makes my senses less than keen.

Kingman has had a stroke. A massive one, and now his brain is dead. The news has the recurring and obsessive feel of a dream, yet all the substance and plausibility of reality.

His brain is dead.

A work of art must breathe life.

There seems only one thing left to do.

DELIA SHERMAN

Nanny Peters and the Feathery Bride

Delia Sherman was a 1989 Campbell Award nominee for Best New Writer in the sf/fantasy field on the basis of her unusually fine first novel, *Through a Brazen Mirror,* and several beautifully crafted short stories such as "Miss Carstairs and the Merman" and "A Maid on the Shore."

Though her previous work utilized motifs from British folk lore and balladry, set in distant imaginary lands or on the 19th-century coast of New England, in the following story Sherman has worked within a southern American folk tradition. The resulting tale is a pure delight.

Sherman comes from a southern family but grew up in New York City and now lives in Boston. She teaches writing at Boston University and has recently completed a second novel based on French history and folk lore. This piece first appeared in *Fantasy & Science Fiction.*

—*T.W.*

Nanny Peters and the Feathery Bride

DELIA SHERMAN

Nanny Peters? You ain't never heard of old Nanny Peters? My land, if that don't beat all! Well, you set yourself down right here on the porch swing, and I'll tell you about her.

Nanny Peters was half ox, half prairie dog, with jest a touch of the Rio Grande to leaven the mixture. She could hoe forty acres of beans, birth twenty calves, *and* set a good dinner on the table by noon, all without breakin' into a sweat over it. She had good, strong horse sense, and could tell a skunk from a woodchuck even on a dark night.

And cool! That woman was so cool, she didn't need an icehouse—she jest put the milk under the bed, and it'd keep a week or more. Why, she didn't even turn a hair when a big, sandy-white snake slithered in the front door one day, bold as brass. Nanny, she was scourin' the pots after a bean supper, and that snake sashayed right on up to her with his mouth wide open, showin' fangs like the horns on a Texas Longhorn.

Nanny hears him slidin' along on the floor (on account of the scales on his belly, see). So she waits for him to get real close, and then she jest grabs that snake ahind the jawbone and wraps him three times around her fist and commences to scour her good cast-iron pot her mama give her. She scrubs and scrubs with that snake until there warn't a lick of crust left in the pot, and the snake didn't have no more scales on his back than a baby has on her bottom—no, ma'am. But he was madder'n a wet hen, and drippin' pizen and leavin' burnt marks on the floor and all.

Well, Nanny lets go the end of his tail and cleans the chimney with it, the snake givin' her considerable help by whoppin' around against the bricks. By the time the chimney's clean, the snake's feelin' pretty humble, what with one thing and t'other. So Nanny tells him to expect more of the same should he think to call again, and then she takes and heaves him out the back door.

Now, old Nanny Peters bein' pretty strong in the arm from hoein' and scrubbin' and such, that snake sailed smack-dab across the state and landed five miles west of Albuquerque, New Mexico. He was half-bald down the back, and all covered with ashes, and his tail was cut to shreds from frailin' it on the chimney bricks, and (on account of he'd landed on his head) his skull was all flatted out. He got better by and by, but he warn't the same snake after—no, ma'am. His head stayed flatter'n a hotcake, and his new scales grew in patchy. What's worser yet, his tail healed in hard ridges that clattered together and kep him awake at night.

And that, jest in case you wondered, is why there's rattlesnakes.

But that's not what I set down to tell you about. Now, this here's the story, so you listen close.

Nanny Peters was a great quilter. In fact, some say she invented quiltin'. She could piece a double-size "Road to Texas" or "Tippecanoe" while the bread was risin', tack the top and the battin' and the back together while the oven heated, and quilt it solid before the crust turned brown. Something elegantifferously complicated, like "Grandmother's Flower Garden" or "Double Wedding Ring," might take her a mite longer. Her seams were so straight that people came from far away as Houston to check their yardsticks by 'em, and her stitches was so tiny you couldn't hardly see 'em, not even with a magnifying glass. And strong! My land, when the calico and battin' wore out, there'd still be little white chains of stitches left, like a skellerton, and you could use it for a fancy bed throw or maybe a pair of lace curtains.

Nanny's specialty was weddin' quilts, and this was the reason for that. Let a couple spend their weddin' night under one of Nanny's quilts, and they was set for life. Whatever kind of rip-staver a man had been before his weddin' night, he was a changed man ever after. If he'd been a boozer, he'd take the pledge. If he'd been a gambler, he'd clean forget the difference between a deuce and a three-spot. A brawler'd get religion, a spendthrift'd pinch pennies till they squealed, a layabout'd bounce to work like a cougar, and as for a ladies' man! Why, he'd rather crawl into a nest o' wildcats, heels foremost, than be catched lookin' at another woman.

This being the case, it won't come as no surprise that girls got in the way of asking Nanny Peters if she'd kindly make them a weddin' quilt. Why, it got to be that a girl wouldn't walk down the aisle until she had Nanny's quilt safely folded in brown paper and laid in her linen chest. Some Saturdays the girls'd be lined up from Nanny's front door clear to Amarillo, beggin' her for a quilt—nothing fancy, mind you, just "Log Cabin" or "Round the World" or "Drunkard's Path" and they'd wait for it, if 'twas all the same to her, seein' as the weddin' was next week. And Nanny almost always obliged 'em, providin' they was willin' to help with the cuttin' out.

But every once in a while, Nanny'd look at a girl, all bright and shy and eager to be hitched, and Nanny'd shake her head and say, "No."

Sometimes she'd say it sad, with a pat on the girl's shoulder or a cup of fresh coffee to make the "No" go down easier, and sometimes like she was too busy countin' clouds jest now, and would be so long as that girl was askin'. Some of those girls Nanny said "No" to married their men anyway, and every last one of 'em ended up plum ramsquaddled: dead, or so put about by their menfolk's bodaciousness that they might as well be dead and save theirselves the shame. It got so that Nanny's "No" was enough to break off an engagement, even if the couple'd been courtin' twenty years.

More than one girl tried to talk Nanny into changin' her mind, but when Nanny Peters said "No," it stayed said. Argufyin', cryin', shoutin', and bullraggin'—none of it budged her an inch. Only one time Nanny Peters ever came a country mile near to changin' her "No" to a "Yes," and that's the story I want to tell you.'

But first I got to tell you about Cora Mae Roberts.

Cora Mae Roberts, now, *she* was one winsome girl. Pretty as a picture, with eyes like Texas bluebonnets and curls so yaller that if her bonnet fell off while she was feedin' the chickens, you'd go plum blind lookin' at her. But only if the sun was shinin'—they warn't as yaller as all that when the sun was ahind a cloud. Her biscuits was like buckshot, her stitchin' like a picket fence, she could outscream a catamount, and she didn't have the sense God gave an armadillo—but every single man in the county was after her, from the widowman who owned the feedstore, to the deputy sheriff who hadn't nowhere to sleep but the jailhouse. By the time Cora Mae was sixteen years old, they was lined up five-deep around her daddy's ranch house, offering her everything from the moon to dresses from Pittsburgh if only she'd marry them.

Now, some of Cora Mae's suitors was good men, but some of them was more like coyotes on two legs. And the worst varmint of them all was one of her daddy's cowhands, a rip-tail roarer could whip his weight in wildcats and ride straight through a crab apple orchard on a flash of lightning. He was so hard he could kick fire out of a flint rock with his bare toes, and he had a thirst for whiskey would put a catfish to shame. His name was Jim Cleering, and he was the man of all men that Cora Mae Roberts wanted to marry.

Jim warn't long on patience or temperance or even on readin' or writin', but his worst enemy'd admit he was a pretty critter. He was so tall he didn't know when his feet was cold. There warn't no bunk long enough for him, but he didn't care nothin' 'bout that, 'cause his shoulders was so wide he couldn't get in the bunkhouse door anyhow, so he jest slep in the barn and scairt away the rats. His jaw was square as the jailhouse cornerstone and twice as hard. He was hairy as a bear and proud as an unbroke stallion, the yaller flower of the Texas plains. And if he warn't, there warn't a man still alive would say so.

Nanny Peters said so, though, and said it so loud you could hear it through three counties. "That man's no good," she told Cora Mae. "He's got more stalls than a good-sized stable, and if you can't see it, you'd miss a buzzard settin' on a dead cow. He'll spend your daddy's money and whup your tail until it's tough as saddle hide. Ain't a quilt around could reform that man, and that's a gospel fact."

Then she held open the door for Cora Mae to leave and the next girl to come in and say her piece.

Well. Cora Mae, she didn't think *her* piece was said yet. She wanted that man, and she wanted that quilt to tuck him up in, and she warn't going to leave Nanny's shack until she had it.

First she cries, whoopin' and hollerin' and pourin' salt water out her eyes until you couldn't tell the difference between Cora Mae Roberts and a four-star Texas thunderstorm. But Nanny jest fetches her bucket and a couple yards of petticoat flannel for a nose rag and leaves her to it.

Then Cora Mae screams, and, as I said before, she could outscream a catamount. On this occasion she extends herself some, and her screamin' was louder than three coyotes, two catamounts, and an entire tribe of Injuns, every one of them on the warpath. But Nanny jest rocks in her rockin' chair, sayin' less than nothing.

Then Cora Mae cusses, and I most teetotaciously hope you never hears the like of Cora Mae Roberts's cussin'. The words she said'd burn the ears right off your head and singe your eyeballs naked, for she'd learnt 'em off her sweetheart; and Jim Cleering, he had a gift for profanity. Well, Nanny sets and listens for a spell, until Cora Mae says a word made Nanny's hair jump straight out of her head, scatterin' hairpins every which way.

"Gal," says Nanny, real pleasant-like. "Gal, that ain't no way to address your elders." And quicker'n a mockingbird after a fly, she takes the bucket Cora Mae's cried into and douses Cora Mae with salt water, takin' the starch right out of her yaller curls and sendin' up clouds of steam where the cold water met the air she'd heated up with her cussin'. And while Cora Mae was drippin' and gaspin' like a landed catfish, Nanny takes her broom and sweeps her right on out the door.

But that's not the end of the story, not quite.

One thing you have to give Cora Mae, she warn't no quitter—no, ma'am. She'd set her heart on tamin' Jim Cleering with one o' Nanny's quilts, and she wouldn't rest until she was sure that colt was broke to the saddle and a quiet ride for a lady. She'd do it by fair means if she could, but she wouldn't stick at foul.

So Cora Mae thought and thought until her pore brain was smokin' like a prairie fire, and then she come up with what she thought was one bodaciously smart trick. She'd wait for a full moon, and then strip herself stark naked and roll around in the hog waller until she was all caked with sticky, smelly, sandy-brown Texas mud. Then she'd stick chicken feathers in the mud, and possum teeth and a couple of rattlesnake rattles and such, and she'd creep up to the foot of old Nanny Peter's bed and plumb *scare* a quilt out of her.

Come the full moon, and Cora Mae Roberts was ready. She rolled in that waller and rolled in the hen litter, stuck possum teeth on her buttocks and a rattlesnake rattle in her navel, caught some glowworms and stuck 'em in her hair, and she crep through the winder of Nanny's shack and commenced to wail and moan.

"Nanny Peters. Nanny Peters. This is the magic speakin' to you," she says.

Nanny sits up in her bed and reaches for her spectacles. "Hmm?" she says. "That so?"

Cora Mae, bein' put out that Nanny ain't quiverin' and beggin' for mercy, wails and moans a mite louder. "You made a mistake, Nanny Peters, a terrible mistake, and if you don't make it right, I'll haunt you and haunt you until the day you die."

"That so?"

"That's so. And I'll give you a taste of that hauntin' beginnin' right now." Cora Mae commenced to shake mud and feathers and chicken dirt, not to mention possum teeth and rattlesnake rattles, all over Nanny's bed and Nanny's clean floor.

And what does Nanny do? Does she squeeze that girl into jelly, or knock out five teeth and one of her eyes, or tie her fingers up in twenty-three separate knots? No, ma'am. Nanny takes a double-size blue-and-red "Rob Peter to Pay Paul" from the chest at the foot of her bed, wraps in brown paper, and hands it to Cora Mae Roberts.

"Here you are, Cora Mae," she says. "I hope this here quilt breaks Jim Cleering for you, 'cause he's in powerful need o' breakin', and that's a gospel fact."

Two weeks later, give or take a day, Cora Mae Roberts married Jim Cleering and went to bed with him under the blue-and-red quilt pieced in the pattern called "Rob Peter to Pay Paul." Three weeks later Jim Cleering was in The Silver Garter, twenty dollars in the hole to Wildcard Pete the gambler and too drunk to find his gun when the shootin' started. Cora Mae was home nursin' a broken jaw, which didn't stop her screamin' fit to be tied when they brought Jim home on a board with a bullet through his lung.

It was mighty tragic. Cora Mae never got over it. Of course she married lots of men after Jim: marryin' was one of her weaknesses, along with whiskey and cussin'. But she took the quilt back to Nanny right away after Jim's funeral, and she wouldn't take another one, not even though Nanny swore up hill and down dale that quilt hadn't had nothing to do with Jim breakin' her jaw and getting himself killed in the Silver Garter.

And I believe Nanny. I do indeed.

JACK WOMACK
Out of Sight, Out of Mind

❧

With the publication of his three sf novels *Ambient, Terraplane,* and *Heathern,* Kentuckian Jack Womack brought a fresh new sensibility into the field. He's quickly doing the same with the horror field. "Out of Sight, Out of Mind," his first published short story, is psychological horror. He has two other very edgy short stories either in print or about to be published. (I know, because I'm publishing them.) What all three of these very strange stories have in common is their intricate, dysfunctional, and doomed relationships. This piece is reprinted from *Walls of Fear.*

—E.D.

Out of Sight, Out of Mind

JACK WOMACK

"When he said he'd meet us at our office, we had our doubts he'd show," said Sherman, the lawyer for a branch of Lang's family Lang had never known. The blood trapped in his face by his tightly knotted tie appeared yellow beneath his muddy skin. "One of the bank officers claimed your cousin hadn't been in midtown for thirty years."

"Folklore," said Wenzel, Sherman's partner-in-law. Lang thought if you were to take a troll from beneath a bridge and dress him in a thousand-dollar suit, you could provide a twin for Wenzel.

"You expect a degree of elaboration, hearing these situations retold at distance. We offered to meet him at his house, but he demurred, telling us he'd have to dust." The three stepped from the cab onto Central Park West. "A small man, a deep voice. You'd have thought he was the size of a refrigerator to have heard him over the phone. He wore a zoot suit that looked almost new."

"Unexpected haberdashery for an eighty-year-old man," said Wenzel.

"He hadn't bathed since V-E Day, or so we believed. The windows in our office can be opened only in event of fire."

"Such awful weather lately," said Wenzel. "It gets this hot in Kentucky?"

"Tennessee," said Lang, glancing behind him to see what might be bounding toward them from the park's humid jungle. "Hotter. This a dangerous neighborhood?"

"Aren't they all?"

"The police usually get so involved in estate settlements up here?" Lang asked.

"If they're so inclined," said Wenzel, "dependent upon complications."

"He died in your office?"

"My office, actually," Sherman said. "I'd stepped out to get the agreement—"

"I got up to breathe," said Wenzel.

"When we returned, he was peaceful as life."

"Heart," said Wenzel. "You don't have your health, what've you got?"

They crossed the avenue when the light changed. Sirens wailed through the park, sounding as trapped animals. "In appearing and disappearing with such élan, he would have left an indelible impression in any event," Sherman continued. "While he sat in our waiting room, he stacked all the journals lying about into mathematically even piles. When we called him into our office, he pointed to our reference library and told us he read fifty thousand books a week."

"We leaned forward in our chairs," said Wenzel. They walked west down Ninety-fifth; spring breezes glued yellowed newspapers to their ankles. Two weather-worn cats padded by en route to the park.

"Why did the police want us to come up here?" Lang asked. "I'm afraid I didn't quite understand."

"That's the way they like it, Mr. Lang," said Wenzel. "We'll handle whatever they've uncovered."

"There're always problems when one dies intestate," said Sherman. "There're so many complications involved with the property—"

"In what way?" Lang asked.

"You'll see," said Wenzel. "We'd hoped not to involve you in this so directly. You said you never met him?"

"Dad told me he met him once, when they were tads," said Lang. "Thought he seemed a might touched."

"You could say that," Wenzel said. "A shame your father couldn't come up. Everyone should see New York before they die."

"Dad's in no rush."

"Your cousin was from the South originally as well?" asked Sherman, straightening his mustache with a tiny gold comb. Lang marveled at how closely he resembled the little man in the Monopoly game.

"Oh, yes." The lawyers nodded, and kept walking. Tree branches entwined above the street's thin green artery. Lang imagined himself strolling down an arbor through which a sewer ran, so overpowering was the smell of the street. The windows of the four-story brownstones lining the block held no more life than the eyes of subway passengers. As if through a bathroom window Lang saw, down the block, orange figures floating back and forth, seeming to hover above the pavement, contained within their own hazy world. Seven trash containers were stationed along the street's southern curb; countless cats prowled over their loads.

"He clutched a shopping bag from Peck and Peck, which went out of business when I was your age," Sherman went on. "The bag was stuffed with newspapers, sticks, several smaller bags, and a length of pipe. You saw the bowl of matchbooks on my desk, the ones imprinted with the name of our firm? He asked if he could have some, and emptied the bowl into his bag."

"Dad said he never met the sister," said Lang. "She was younger, I gather."

"By twenty years," said Wenzel. "An unexpected birth, probably. Their mother was nearly fifty and died not long after. Their father performed the delivery, it seems. He was an obstetrician, but family planning was so perfunctory in those days."

"Where is she?"

"We're not completely sure of her whereabouts," said Sherman. "Until we saw her name on the first mortgage, we were frankly unaware of her existence. No one at the bank remembered her, but then only one or two remembered *him*, so—"

"We told him we needed her signature as well. He quickly referred us to a court decision of eighteen years ago, appointing him her guardian. That was the last time he'd used a lawyer, he said, explaining that they never dealt with lawyers as their father had been a doctor," said Wenzel. "He said that when he listened, he heard her, but he only infrequently saw her."

The workers drifted through the fog, bouncing between house and dumpsters. Policepeople standing silently by slapped colorless powder from their dark blue uniforms as if tidying themselves after a drug raid. Lang grew cognizant of the fog's origin, approaching its grit; sparkling motes of dust billowed from the house, melding briefly into the air, settling again in layers upon the surroundings. Gray streaks highlighted the brown ivy smothering the facade. Sprayed across the front door were the faded words ROCK THIS HOUSE. Three workmen hauled a wooden pallet out the basement door; tied onto the pallet were five old cabinet radios and a car's front fender. A contraption resembling a children's slide ran from an attic window to the closet dumpster. Cats scattered whenever fresh wreckage poured onto them. Lang considered the dull glint in the house's unpierced eyes. "What did he cover the windows with?"

"Aluminum foil," said Wenzel. "Superfluous, considering."

"They're tearing the place down already?"

"Not yet."

A large blue truck blocked the sidewalk; hoses so thick as a heavy man's waist ran from the rear of its trailer through the basement windows. It was the largest vacuum cleaner Lang had ever seen; it screamed with a hurricane's roar, sucking up the cloud within, spewing it into the air without.

"So much about this case is atypical of our métier," said Wenzel. "There's the sergeant. Let me try to work my charms before we introduce you. We might be able to keep you out of it, Mr. Lang—"

"I'd like to go in—"

The sergeant was a slender woman half Lang's size wearing welder's goggles and gloves resembling those of a falconer. Wenzel sidled up to her as might any informant wishing for a deal. "He smiled, showing no teeth," Sherman continued. "We tried to hustle things along before we could be asphyxiated. To open, I remarked upon the bank's consideration in not having foreclosed upon the mortgage after seven years of nonpayment—"

"Seven years," Lang said. "Why hadn't they been evicted?"

"At the original time of foreclosure several notices went out. All were ignored. Bank representatives visited the house but couldn't get in."

"He kept them out?"

"In his fashion," said Sherman. "After so long the bank essentially gave up on attempting to seize their property. It must not have seemed worth the effort."

"Mighty nice banks you have up here," said Lang.

"On occasion. It could have been nothing more than the usual bureaucratic fumble. Time passed, people left, not even the computers cared after a while, and your cousin was left again to his devices. Late last year the developers of those adjacent lots notified the bank of their wish to purchase your cousin's property. By adding this lot to theirs, you see, twelve more floors of condominiums may be legally added to the tower they proposed. Your relatives' welfare became at once a matter of utmost concern."

As the sergeant spoke with Wenzel, she gestured at the house as if the architecture drove her to jubilation. The black hair she wore knotted up beneath her cap came loose and a skein unraveled beneath her visor. Their words disappeared within the shouts of workmen, the vacuum's howl, the rumble of debris descending the slide. "Their father built the house," said Sherman. "The family owned it outright, once. Your cousin took out a first mortgage, then a second."

"What did they need the money for?" asked Lang.

"He started collecting things," said Sherman.

Tabbies and marmalades slinked over the wreckage, pausing at moments to lick dirt from reddened muzzles. "Dad never mentioned this side of the family until you got in touch," said Lang. "He said his parents never talked about them."

"Most families live as if certain of their members exist in separate rooms, seen only if something's left ajar," said Sherman, staring at the house's gray ivy. "They must have had it hard. For ten years they lived without electricity, for five years without heat, for three years without water." He drew from his pocket a silk handkerchief and daubed the sweat from his forehead. "No record of when the phone was cut off. So, the bank sent letters. Messengers came around, but no one answered. At some point he realized his isolation needed interrupting, and so he called us from a pay phone, having seen our ad in the Voice—"

"Yo!" shouted the sergeant, waving them over. "Come here." When they traversed the fog, Lang coughed until he feared he'd spit blood; he imagined his lungs filling with sand, so granular grew the air's grain. Wenzel looked to have lost a case upon whose outcome his income depended. "You're the relative?" the sergeant asked Lang, who gasped for breath. "Do something about that cough. What's in your pocket? Take it out."

"I believe he's unarmed, Sergeant—" said Sherman.

"Out."

Lang withdrew the bulge she'd spotted and offered his holdings in his outstretched hand. "Matches," he said. Grimacing as she pulled off her goggles, she squinted against the dust with unshelled eyes. Cleaning the lenses on her shirtfront, she was careful not to scratch them on buttons or badge. As she rubbed them clean, they filmed over anew.

"Like father, like son," she said.

"They were cousins," said Lang. "I never met them."

"You were lucky," she said. "These two tell you anything about what we've got in here?"

"Until his presence was requested, our client's direct involvement in these details seemed nonessential," said Sherman.

"It's all right," Wenzel interrupted. "Mr. Lang doesn't have to come in if he doesn't want to. We do—"

"Thought you'd want to see for yourself," she said.

"Let's get on with it, Sergeant."

"You know my vacation should've started yesterday?" she asked. "Now they're telling me it'll be two weeks before they can get everything emptied out—"

"We're all middlemen here, Sergeant," said Wenzel.

"Somebody oughta suffer besides me," she said. "All right, get suited. I got to call in, be right back. Just hang." As she walked away, she stopped long enough to corner a workman and give him his assignment. He removed three orange coveralls from the cab of the vacuum truck and tossed them to Lang and his lawyers.

"You're sure you want to go in, Mr. Lang?" asked Wenzel.

"Why not? What are these for?" he asked, startled by the weight of the coverall he held.

"Precautions," said Sherman. As they tugged the work wear over their suits, he continued telling his tale. "From what we'd heard and from what we could discover, we were prepared to work around his personal eccentricities. Once he came in, we both began to believe that the roof wasn't quite on the house." Lang noticed that the material in the sleeves and legs of the suit was several times thicker than that in the body. "His beliefs made a certain sense. He might have reexamined his premises, but I have to admit there was a consistency to his logic—"

"Sounds like he was crazy to me," said Lang. "Nobody'd ever noticed before this?"

"When did anyone see him, Mr. Lang?" Wenzel asked. Lang yanked the suit's hood over his head, fitting the built-in goggles across his eyes and the filter insert into his mouth, grateful that it stole smell so well as dust from the air.

"We told him of the offer the bank made." Donning the coveralls effected metamorphosis; they appeared transformed into bright-hued roaches. "A onetime payment of two hundred thousand dollars to cover resettlement costs. They'll resell it for ten times that, certainly, but considering that they had the legal right to seize the property that day if they chose, it seemed quite fair to us. He didn't bite. The house fit them too well, he said."

The hood's filters made them hear one another's voices as if over a cheap telephone. "We suggested he look upon their offer as a gift and not as a demand," said Wenzel, "but he said a demand by any name still demanded. He couldn't lose what he'd saved, he said, not now—"

A workman shouted. A wooden hogshead rolled off the overhead track and exploded upon the pavement below in a shrapnel-burst of shattered crockery. The foreman, seeing that no one was hurt, spoke. "Break for lunch," he said. "Pass the word up."

A lump of kittens stirred in the nearest dumpster, crying for their mothers. "Were these their cats?" Lang asked.

"I suspect they're after the rats," said Wenzel. "Shoppers rushing to a holiday sale."

"Mr. Lang," Sherman asked, his eyes unreadable beneath the goggles, "are you by any chance claustrophobic?"

"Never before." The workmen shook free of the house's grip, filing off to lunch, each carrying away as they left some scrap of the accumulation: webs of string pitched into boxes, heaps of stained cloth, odd volumes of encyclopedias, treadless tires, headless dolls, skinned taxidermist's trophies, clocks without hands, type-writers without keys, televisions without tubes—archaeological *chotchkes* too quickly rediscovered to hold value.

"There's a certain disarray to the place," said Sherman.

"How can the house be big enough to hold so much?" Lang asked, looking again at the glutted dumpsters.

"They built these old brownstones with families in mind," said Sherman. "This one's standard, with additions. Four large rooms per floor, a kitchen and several bathrooms, small rooms serving as closets, servants' quarters in the attic and a full basement—"

"Less full," said Wenzel.

"The kitchen's split in half, they tell me. Part of it seems to have once been their father's office. There's much more space than it would appear, and he was adept at making things fit."

"Showtime," said the sergeant as she reappeared, tying a surgeon's mask around her face. "You two haven't been back here since the cleanup began, right?"

"There seemed no reason to return," said Sherman.

"And I'm guessing you've never been in New York?" she asked Lang; before he could answer, she continued to speak, as if he hadn't even been there to ask. "We'll go in through the basement," she said. "If it was good enough for him, it'll be good enough for us. The access's easier now. I can't make any guarantees at this point as to how much longer we can keep the papers out of this."

"We'll see to that," said Wenzel.

"It gets pretty bad in there. Don't make sudden movements. Watch your elbows. Keep an eye out for rats, in case. You can hear 'em all over the place, but the bastards hide. Don't get sick in your suits, you'll be sorry. If you feel the floor settling under you, be prepared to—" She paused. "Well, be prepared. If it starts getting to you, say something quick. Let's go."

They ducked, crossing the threshold beneath the stoop. Their filters didn't entirely subdue the house's miasma; a hallucinogenic blend of mildew, excrement, rat, rot, stale water and dust permeated the fine-lined mesh. Excavations laid bare the basement's front half. New growth stood among the virgin forest of floor supports.

"As they started taking the shit out, the floor began to sag," said the sergeant. "They put in all these extra beams. Solid oak," she said, striking one with her fist. She switched on her flash; the sound of animals scampering from the light came as the noise of a brush being drawn across sandpaper. Beyond the stairs lay an impenetrable canebrake of magazine stacks, columns of bound newspapers, pillars of books and journals. The lowest depths had been soaked for so long that they'd transmuted into black peat; the higher, drier ranges glistened all the same in the brief flickers of light. Lang, coming nearer, saw thousands of silverfish scurrying over the paper, busy converting their country into mulch.

"Goddamn—" he started to say, but couldn't think of what might follow.

"The drawbacks," said Wenzel, "of forever saving for that rainy day."

"Keep moving," said the sergeant, her voice powerful for one of her petite size. "No telling what we'll catch down here. I oughta be in Cuernavaca by now."

"Some remnant of socialization within his being prodded him to attempt explaining his efforts," Sherman said, continuing as they climbed the wet stairs. "At first we thought he rambled only to distract us, but soon we gathered it was something more, though it was hard to say what. He said the aborigines, the Indians, primitives of all lands, once possessed senses and abilities that we lost as civilization grew more oppressive. Being able to hear across vast distances, for example."

"To see the stars in daylight, he said," Wenzel picked up. "To smell the sun. He had an ear for phrasing. As we moderns became postmoderns—he didn't put it that way, but I don't remember everything like some people do—there were awarenesses that our parents took for granted that we had lost as well. In one generation history seemed to have been eliminated from the fabric of society, or at least the knowledge of history."

"To lose the past," Sherman said, "was to lose the soul."

Floodlamps put up by the workmen hung from a thick electric cord attached to the hall ceiling, sharpening shadows into knife-edges. Passageways ran between stacks of *National Geographic* and *Life*, around newspapers bundled into groups of thirty held fast with square knots. The rope nearest the floor was generally chewed through. Lang misstepped, bumped against a paper wall; a flare of pulp streamed outward in a sudden corona. The newspapers appeared hand-tinted; from top to bottom the colors deepened, from cream to lemon, to canary to mustard, to amber, then brown, then black.

"Tunnels and paths run all through the place," said the sergeant. "Turnarounds, false trails, dead ends. Don't see how he kept from getting lost in here himself."

"He remembered where everything was," said Wenzel. "He knew his labyrinth."

"This way first," she said. "Toward the kitchen. Watch your step, floor's a little loose through here. They told me the estimated weight load in here must be like sixty thousand pounds. Couldn't do this in a new place."

"One day he and his sister were cleaning the basement for what I suspect was the last time," said Sherman. "He made a joke about Fibber McGee's closet, and she didn't get the reference. It was a radio show. One of the characters had a closet, and every time he opened it, a ton of junk fell out—"

"Closets?" said the sergeant, "I'll show you closets. They're the neatest places in here. Look." Enough had been removed where they stood that she was able to open the nearest door, and they peered inside. Therein were a dozen shelves lined with pairs of men's shoes, the laces of each neatly knotted, the toes of each pair curling upward at an 80-degree angle. A chirping sound came from all around them, as if upon entering a pet shop they'd awakened all the birds.

"Bastards," she said. "There's poison all through here, hasn't done any good."

"At first, he said, he thought nothing more of his sister's incomprehension. It was no more than discovering that cultural baggage had been lost in transit," Sherman continued. "But the moment kept recurring to him, and so over the next few weeks, thinking that perhaps only his sister was unaware of a program he'd never missed, he tried dropping the reference into his conversation with others as young or younger than she, for in those days he hadn't yet climbed into his bottle and pulled the stopper in after him. He perceived, he said, that no one seemed to know what he was talking about. The more he thought about it, the more it disturbed him, until he grew so preoccupied with the ramifications as he understood them that he lay awake nights, unable to sweep his head clear."

Six refrigerators, each of a different decade's vintage, stood just inside the kitchen. As if to protect children, the doors of each were removed. Pots and pans buried the stove; dishware of a hundred patterns filled the sink. Space within had been made that they could move unhindered into the next room, the doctor's old office; it was almost empty. A long counter ran along one wall; a high cabinet was attached to the wall behind the countertop. An enormous nineteenth-century lock once sealed the cupboard, but someone had pried it away.

"Heredity makes the person before birth, he said," Sherman said, "but environment makes the person afterward. If the environment disappears, what happens to the person? It came to him as he lay there one night that life was so inessential that it might fade away as you watched. Sometimes, he said, he spent hours staring into the mirror, making sure he was still there."

"The notion of a Polaroid reversing itself," said Wenzel. "He wasn't an unintelligent man, but he discovered existentialism too late in life to deal with it so easily as might a freshman."

Foil covered the window above the counter, next to the cabinet; the sergeant ripped the shade away, pushing it aside with her glove. A trail of sunlight burned a path across the room; dust crystals shimmered in its beams.

"Theories need proof, and he sought proof," said Sherman, "throwing references into his conversation to see what might rise to the top with enough stirring. Bickford's cafeterias. The *Squalus*. Sapphire. Martin Dies. Grover Whalen. The Sea Beach Express. He said that, naturally, the youngest were the furthest gone. They didn't remember Reagan, and couldn't find their street on a map."

"He took it so personally," said Wenzel. "That's always bad to do. No one remembered anything he remembered, or so it struck him. Now, as we listened to him speak, we'd already been made aware of why he was so deeply affected as he set about exploring this problem, though we didn't make the connection until later."

"What do you mean?" asked Lang.

"Early on, in referring to the decision appointing him his sister's guardian, he quoted it, word for word, so near as we ourselves could recall, later reading it. He possessed, I believe, an eidetic memory. Whatever flew into its web forever stuck there."

"Take a look at this, now," said the sergeant, prying open the cabinet door, jerking away her hand before the roaches within could race up her arm. There were jars inside: pints arrayed along the top shelves, quarts upon the middle, half-gallons and larger on the bottom.

"No one cared anymore, he said," Sherman continued. "No one cared that so much was being lost, and the more that he realized was lost, the more he felt himself slipping away. Then one day he walked by a small shop over on Amsterdam—"

"Columbus," Wenzel corrected.

"An avenue. His agoraphobia hadn't become so pronounced yet," said Sherman. "In the window was something he hadn't seen for years. Log Cabin maple syrup, he said, came in tin cans resembling log cabins before the war, and now, years after Pearl Harbor, he found himself looking at one again. He bought it. When he brought it home, he put it on a table and stared at it for hours, allowing its image to resonate throughout his mind. His sister laughed, thinking it was a silly thing to buy, and even sillier to stare at; he said she asked him if he could see the future in it."

The sergeant lithely pulled herself onto the countertop, stirring loose clouds from its surface, and took down one of the pint jars as she descended. Her uniform was almost white with dust.

"For a time they were able to live off their inherited capital after he quit his job," said Sherman, "but in seeking new madeleines, he soon sent his money on its way, going to flea markets, weekend sales, apartment liquidations, wandering the streets window-shopping until something caught his eye."

From her back pocket the sergeant drew a rag and began removing the years from the jar. "Once he got started, it was hard to stop, he admitted," said Wenzel. "The mortgage money came and went, and came and went again. Luxuries fell by the wayside, then necessities, then all that remained was the need to continually rewrap with fresh bandages." The sergeant dropped her muddied rag onto the floor, having brought the jar from opacity into translucence. The jar bore a still-illegible label. Taking his handkerchief from his pocket, Sherman handed it to her, and with it she scrubbed harder, massaging the glass as if to warm it.

"What did it matter to preserve the past if in so doing you lost the present? I asked, dabbling in advocacy," said Sherman. "He said the present didn't trouble him so much as the fact he'd started too late to keep from losing his sister."

"Then she left?" Lang asked, expecting an answer, receiving none. "What is it? You believe she's dead, don't you? You said you weren't completely sure of her whereabouts?"

"Not completely," said the sergeant, pushing the cleaned jar into the sun's path. The rays hit the glass obliquely, forming a prism, throwing a blur of rainbow onto the gray wall opposite.

"Over time I gather he allowed the demands of collecting to supercede all other relationships," said Sherman. "It was too late to save her, he said; her sense of history had so atrophied, she didn't remember being his sister anymore."

Lang stared at the baby floating within its liquid fog. He couldn't read the spidery handwriting on the label from where he stood. Leaning into the light, Wenzel spoke the words aloud. " 'Janiceps. Gladys Murphy, 110 West 100th Street. Aborted June 16, 1904.' " Babies, truly; two squeezed into one body, as if they'd been pressed together to save space. Wenzel looked up at the shelves, the rows of jars. "The doctor had his own hobbies, it seems."

"Why would they have kept them?" Lang said, unable to keep his eyes off the swimmers.

"After so long they might have been looked on as members of the family," said Wenzel.

"What do you mean, she didn't remember being his sister?" Lang asked.

"We've since examined the court ruling, as we said, and the attendant medical reports. He was appointed her guardian because she had Alzheimer's, and the disease had so progressed, it's possible she never noticed anything out of the ordinary here at home."

The sergeant placed one of the quart jars in the light, one previously swept free of its surface crust. This jar's occupant was large enough to have been born. Seeing the splayed limbs, the face rising directly from the nape of the neck, Lang thought, and tried not to think, of bullfrogs he'd once, as a boy, gigged in ponds.

"They were surely close, once," said Sherman. "They never went far from the house, even when they could. That surely intensified the situation, over time."

" 'Roger,' " Wenzel read, studying this house's specifications. " 'Ancephalic. January 8' "—he coughed—" '1956.' "

"Then he fell silent, having seemed to run out of things to say," Sherman said. "He agreed to take home the proposal and think it over. That was good enough for us. When we left the room, he was just sitting there smiling, as if recalling a pleasant memory."

The sergeant removed a gallon jar from the bottom shelf, one seeming recently cleaned. "Cecily," she said, reading the label. "They reached the bedroom this morning, right before I called. Let's go." The quartet stepped out of the room, leaving the jars where they'd left them. The workmen were returning from lunch; Lang heard above the perpetual chirp their cries and shouts. They inched down the hall until they reached the stairwell; as they mounted the stairs, the wood cried beneath their feet. "People," the sergeant sighed, shrugging.

"He tried to save her," said Wenzel.

ÉILÍS NÍ DHUIBHNE

Midwife to the Fairies

Éilís Ní Dhuibhne was born in Dublin, Ireland in 1954. She has published short stories, poems and scholarly articles in Irish journals and newspapers; she has also worked as a librarian, archivist, folklore collector and lecturer and did her Ph.D. dissertation on folktales. *Midwife to the Fairies* is a beautifully rendered tale using folklore as a mirror held up to the real world. The story comes from the collection *Territories of the Voice: Contemporary Stories by Irish Women Writers*, edited by Louise DeSalvo, Kathleen Walsh D'Arcy and Katherine Hogan, published by Beacon Press in Boston. Prior to this publication, this story was published in the author's collection from the Irish Feminist publisher, Attic Press, titled *Blood and Water*.

—T.W.

Midwife to the Fairies

ÉILÍS NÍ DHUIBHNE

We were looking at the "Late Late." It wasn't much good this night, there was a fellow from Russia, a film star or an actor or something—I'd never heard tell of him—and some young one from America who was after setting up a prostitute's hotel or call-in service or something. God, what Gay wants with that kind I don't know. All done up really snazzy, mind you, like a model or a television announcer or something. And she made a mint out of it, writing a book about her experiences if you don't mind. I do have to laugh!

I don't enjoy it as much of a Friday. It was much better of a Saturday. After the day's work and getting the bit of dinner ready for myself and Joe, sure I'm barely ready to sit down when it's on. It's not as relaxing like. I don't know, I do be all het up somehow on Fridays on account of it being such a busy day at the hospital and all, with all the cuts you really have to earn your keep there nowadays! Saturday is busy too of course—we have to go into Bray and do the bit of shopping like, and do the bit of hoovering and washing. But it's not the same, I feel that bit more relaxed, I suppose it's on account of not being at work really. Not that I'd want to change that or anything. No way. Sixteen years of being at home was more than enough for me. That's not to say, of course, that I minded it at the time. I didn't go half-cracked the way some of them do, or let on to do. Mind you, I've no belief in that pre-menstrual tension and post-natal depression and what have you. I come across it often enough, I needn't tell you, or I used to, I should say, in the course of my duty. Now with the maternity unit gone of course all that's changed. It's an ill wind, as they say. I'll say one thing for male patients, there's none of this depression carry-on with them. Of course they all think they're dying, oh dying, of sore toes and colds in the head and anything at all, but it's easier to put up with than the post-natals. I'm telling no lie.

Well, anyway, we were watching Gaybo and I was out in the kitchen wetting a cup of tea, which we like to have around ten or so of a Friday. Most nights we wait till it's nearer bedtime, but on Fridays I usually do have some little treat I get on the way home from work in The Hot Bread Shop there on the corner of Corbawn Lane, in the new shopping centre. Some little extra, a few Danish pastries or doughnuts, some little treat like that. For a change more than anything. This night I'd a few Napoleons—you know, them cream slices with icing on top.

I was only after taking out the plug when the bell went. Joe answered it of course and I could hear him talking to whoever it was and I wondered who it could be at that hour. All the stories you hear about burglars and people being murdered in their own homes . . . there was a woman over in Dalkey not six months ago, hacked to pieces at ten o'clock in the morning. God help her! . . . I do be worried. Naturally. Though I keep the chain on all the time and I think that's the most important thing. As long as you keep the chain across you're all right. Well, anyway, I could hear them talking and I didn't go out. And after a few minutes I could hear him taking the chain off and letting whoever it was in. And then Joe came in to me and he says:

"There's a fellow here looking for you, Mary. He says it's urgent."

"What is it he wants? Sure I'm off duty now anyway, amn't I?"

I felt annoyed, I really did. The way people make use of you! You'd think there was no doctors or something. I'm supposed to be a nurse's aide, to work nine to five, Monday to Friday, except when I'm on nights. But do you think the crowd around here can get that into their heads? No way.

"I think you'd better have a word with him yourself, Mary. He says it's urgent like. He's in the hall."

I knew of course. I knew before I seen him or heard what he had to say. And I took off my apron and ran my comb through my hair to be ready. I made up my own mind that I'd have to go out with him in the cold and the dark and miss the rest of the "Late Late." But I didn't let on of course.

There was a handywoman in this part of the country and she used to be called out at all times of the day and night. But one night a knock came to her door. The woman got up at once and got ready to go out. There was a man standing at the door with a mare.

He was a young fellow with black hair, hardly more than eighteen or nineteen.

"Well," says I, "what's your trouble?"

"It's my wife," he said, embarrassed like. He'd already told Joe, I don't know what he had to be embarrassed about. Usually you'd get used to a thing like that. But anyway he was, or let on to be.

"She's expecting. She says it's on the way."

"And who might you be?"

"I'm her husband."

"I see," says I. And I did. I didn't come down in the last shower. And with all the carry-on that goes on around here you'd want to be thick or something not to get this particular message straight away. But I didn't want to be too sure of myself. Just in case. Because, after all, you can never be too sure of anything in this life. "And why?" says I to him then. "Why isn't she in hospital, where she should be?"

"There isn't time," he said, as bold as brass. See what I mean about getting used to it?

"Well," says I then, "closing maternity wards won't stop them having babies." I laughed, trying to be a bit friendly like. But he didn't see the joke. So, says I, "And where do you and your wife live?"

"We live on this side of Annamoe," he said, "and if you're coming we'd better be going. It's on the way, she said."

"I'll come," I said. What else could I say? A call like that has to be answered. My mother did it before me and her mother before her, and they never let anyone down. And my mother said that her mother had never lost a child. Not one. Her corporate works of mercy, she called it. You get indulgence. And anyway I pitied him, he was only a young fellow and he was nice-looking, too, he had a country look to him. But of course I was under no obligation, none whatever, so I said, "Not that I should come really. I'm off duty, you know, and anyway what you need is the doctor."

"We'd rather have you," he said.

"Well, just this time."

"Let's go then!"

"Hold on a minute, I'll get the keys of the car from Joe."

"Oh, sure I'll run you down and back, don't bother about your own car."

"Thank you very much," I said. "But I'd rather take my own, if it's all the same to you. I'll follow on behind you." You can't be too careful.

So I went out to start the car. But lo and behold, it wouldn't go! Don't ask me why, that car is nearly new. We got it last winter from Mike Byrne, my cousin that has the garage outside Greystones. There's less than thirty thousand miles on her and she was serviced only there a month before Christmas. But it must have been the cold or something. I tried, and he tried, and Joe, of course, tried, and none of us could get a budge out of her. So in the heel of the hunt I'd to go with him. Joe didn't want me to, and then he wanted to come himself, and your man . . . Sean O'Toole, he said his name was . . . said OK, OK, but come on quick. So I told Joe to get back inside to the fire and I went with him. He'd an old Cortina, a real old banger, a real farmer's car.

"Do not be afraid!" said the rider to her. "I will bring you home to your own doorstep tomorrow morning!"

She got up behind him on the mare.

Neither of us said a word the whole way down. The engine made an awful racket, you couldn't hear a thing, and anyway he was a quiet fellow with not a lot to say for himself. All I could see were headlights, and now and then a signpost: Enniskerry, Sallygap, Glendalough. And after we turned off the main road into the mountains, there were no headlights either, and no house-lights, nothing except the black night. Annamoe is at the back of beyonds, you'd never know you were only ten miles from Bray there, it's really very remote altogether. And their house was down a lane where there was absolutely nothing to be seen at all, not a house, not even a sheep. The house you could hardly see either, actually. It was kind of buried like at the side of the road, in a kind of a hollow. You wouldn't know it was there at all until it was on top of you. Trees all around it too. He pulled up in front of a big five-bar gate and just gave an almighty honk on the horn, and I got a shock when the gate opened, just like that, the minute he honked. I never saw who did it. But looking back now I suppose it was one of the brothers. I suppose they were waiting for him like.

It was a big place, comfortable enough, really, and he took me into the kitchen and introduced me to whoever was there. Polite enough. A big room it was, with an old black range and a huge big dresser, painted red and filled with all kinds of delph and crockery and stuff. Oh you name it! And about half a dozen people were sitting around the room, or maybe more than that. All watching the telly. The "Late Late" was still on and your one, the call-girl one, was still on. She was talking to a priest about unemployment. And they were glued to it, the whole lot of them, what looked like the mother and father and a whole family of big grown men and women. His family or hers I didn't bother my head asking. And they weren't giving out information for nothing either. It was a funny set up, I could see that as clear as daylight, such a big crowd of them, all living together. For all the world like in "Dallas."

Well, there wasn't a lot of time to be lost. The mother offered me a cup of tea, I'll say that for her, and I said yes, I'd love one, and I was actually dying for a cup. I hadn't had a drop of tea since six o'clock and by this time it was after twelve. But I said I'd have a look at the patient first. So one of them, a sister I suppose it was, the youngest of them, she took me upstairs to the room where she was. The girl. Sarah. She was lying on the bed, on her own. No heat in the room, nothing.

After a while they came to a steep hill. A door opened in the side of the hill and they went in. They rode until they came to a big house and inside there were lots of people, eating and drinking. In a corner of the house there lay a woman in labour.

I didn't say a word, just put on the gloves and gave her the examination. She was the five fingers, nearly into the second stage, and she must have been feeling a good bit of pain but she didn't let on, not at all. Just lay there with her teeth gritted. She was a brave young one, I'll say that for her. The waters were gone and of course nobody had cleaned up the mess so I asked the other young one to do it, and to get a heater and a kettle of boiling water. I stayed with Sarah and the baby came just before one. A little girl. There was no trouble at all with the delivery and she seemed all right but small. I'd no way of weighing her, needless to say, but I'd be surprised if she was much more than five pounds.

"By rights she should be in an incubator," I said to Sarah, who was sitting up smoking a cigarette, if you don't mind. She said nothing. What can you do? I washed the child . . . she was a nice little thing, God help her . . . I wrapped her in a blanket and put her in beside the mother. There was nowhere else for her. Not a cot, not even an old box. That's the way in these cases as often as not. Nobody wants to know.

I delivered the afterbirth and then I left. I couldn't wait to get back to my own bed. They'd brought me the cup of tea and all, but I didn't get time to drink it, being so busy and all. And afterwards the Missus, if that's what she was, wanted me to have a cup in the kitchen. But all I wanted then was to get out of the place. They were all so quiet and unfriendly like. Bar the mother. And even she wasn't going overboard, mind you. But the rest of them. All sitting like zombies looking at the late-night film. They gave me the creeps. I told them the child was too small, they'd have to do something about it, but they didn't let on they heard. The father, the old fellow, that is to say, put a note in my hand . . . it was worth it from that point of view, I'll admit . . . and said, "Thank you." Not a word from the rest of them. Glued to the telly, as if nothing was after happening. I wanted to scream at them, really. But what could I do? Anyway the young fellow, Sean, the father as he said himself, drove me home. And that was that.

Well and good. I didn't say a word about what was after happening to anyone, excepting of course to Joe. I don't talk, it's not right. People have a right to their privacy, I always say, and with my calling you've to be very careful. But to tell the truth they were on my mind. The little girl, the little baby. I knew in my heart and soul I shouldn't have left her out there, down there in the back of beyonds, near Annamoe. She was much too tiny, she needed care. And the mother. Sarah, was on my mind as well. Mind you, she seemed to be well able to look after herself, but still and all, they weren't the friendliest crowd of people I'd ever come across. They were not.

But that was that.

Until about a week later, didn't I get the shock of my life when I opened the evening paper and saw your one, Sarah, staring out at me. Her round baby face, big head of red hair. And there was a big story about the baby. Someone was after finding it dead in a shoebox, in a kind of rubbish dump they had at the back of the house. And she was arrested, in for questioning, her and maybe Sean O'Toole as well. I'm not sure. In for questioning. I could have dropped down dead there and then.

I told Joe.

"Keep your mouth shut, woman," he said. "You did your job and were paid for it. This is none of your business."

And that was sound advice. But we can't always take sound advice. If we could the world would be a different place.

The thing dragged on. It was in the papers. It was on the telly. There was questioning, and more questioning, and trials and appeals and I don't know what. The whole country was in on it.

And it was on my conscience. It kept niggling at me all the time. I couldn't sleep, I got so I couldn't eat. I was all het up about it, in a terrible state really. Depressed, that's what I was, me who was never depressed before in my life. And I'm telling no lie when I say I was on my way to the doctor for a prescription for

Valium when I realised there was only one thing to do. So instead of going down to the surgery, didn't I turn on my heel and walk over to the Garda barracks instead. I went in and I got talking to the sergeant straight away. Once I told them what it was about there was no delaying. And he was very interested in all I had to say, of course, and asked me if I'd be prepared to testify and I said of course I would. Which was the truth. I wouldn't want to but I would if I had to. Once I'd gone this far, of course I would.

Well, I walked out of that Garda station a new woman. It was a great load off my chest. It was like being to confession and getting absolution for a mortal sin. Not that I've ever committed a mortler, of course. But you know what I mean. I felt relieved.

Well and good.

Well. You'll never believe what happened to me next. I was just getting back to my car when a young fellow . . . I'd seen him somewhere before, I know that, but I couldn't place him. He might have been the fellow that came for me on the night, Sean, but he didn't look quite like him. I just couldn't place him at all . . . anyway, he was standing there, right in front of the car. And I said hello, just in case I really did know him, just in case it really was him. But he said nothing. He just looked behind him to see if anyone was coming, and when he saw that the coast was clear he just pulled out a big huge knife out of his breast pocket and pointed it at my stomach. He put the heart crossways in me. And then he says, in a real low voice, like a gangster in "Hill Street Blues" or something:

"Keep your mouth shut. Or else!"

And then he pushed a hundred pounds into my hand and he went off.

I was in bits. I could hardly drive myself home with the shock. I told Joe of course. But he didn't have a lot of sympathy for me.

"God Almighty, woman," he said, "what possessed you to go to the guards? You must be off your rocker. They'll be arresting you next!"

Well, I'd had my lesson. The guards called for me the next week but I said nothing. I said I knew nothing and I'd never heard tell of them all before, the family I mean. And there was nothing they could do, nothing. The sergeant hadn't taken a statement from me, and that was his mistake and my good luck I suppose, because I don't know what would have happened to me if I'd testified. I told a priest about the lie to the guards, in confession, to a Carmelite in White Friar Street, not to any priest I know. And he said God would understand. "You did your best, and that's all God will ask of you. He does not ask of us that we put our own lives in danger."

There was a fair one day at Baile an Droichid. And this woman used to make market socks and used to wash them and scour them and take them to the fair and get them sold. She used to make them up in dozen bunches and sell them at so much the dozen.

And as she walked over the bridge there was a great blast of wind. And who should it be but the people of the hill, the wee folk! And she looked among them and saw among them the same man who had taken her on the mare's back to see his wife.

"How are ye all? And how is the wife?" she said.

He stood and looked at her.

"Which eye do you see me with?" he asked.

"With the right eye," she said.

Before he said another word he raised his stick and stuck it in her eye and knocked her eye out on the road.

"You'll never see me again as long as you live," he said.

Sometimes I do think of the baby. She was a dawny little thing, there's no two ways about it. She might have had a chance, in intensive care. But who am I to judge?

JOE R. LANSDALE
The Phone Woman

Lansdale is best known for his redneck stories, which demonstrate a viciousness surprising when one meets the author, such a personable fellow in person. But last year's "The Steel Valentine," a brutal man's adventure/revenge story showed another of the many different styles Joe can write in—more in the tradition of his thrillers *Cold In July* and *Savage Season*. "The Phone Woman," this chilling little piece from *Night Visions* 8, exemplifies yet another style and is a good example of how we sometimes fool ourselves when we think we're "doing the right thing," with very mixed motives.

—E.D.

The Phone Woman

JOE R. LANSDALE

JOURNAL ENTRIES

A week to remember . . .

After this, my little white page friend, you shall have greater security, kept under not only lock and key, but you will have a hiding place. If I were truly as smart as I sometimes think I am, I wouldn't write this down. I know better. But, I am compelled.

Compulsion. It comes out of nowhere and owns us all. We put a suit and tie and hat on the primitive part of our brain and call it manners and civilization, but ultimately, it's just a suit and tie and a hat. The primitive brain is still primitive, and it compels, pulses to the same dark beat that made our less civilized ancestors and the primordial ooze before them, throb to simple, savage rhythms of sex, death and destruction.

Our nerves call out to us to touch and taste life, and without our suits of civilization, we can do that immediately. Take what we need if we've muscle enough. Will enough. But all dressed up in the trappings of civilization, we're forced to find our thrills vicariously. And eventually, that is not enough. Controlling our impulses that way, is like having someone eat your our for us. No taste. No texture. No nourishment. Pitiful business.

Without catering to the needs of our primitive brains, without feeding impulses, trying instead to get what we need through books and films and the lives of the more adventurous, we cease to live. We wither. We bore ourselves and others. We die. And are glad of it.

Whatcha gonna do, huh?

                    *   *   *

Saturday Morning, June 10th, Through Saturday 17th:

I haven't written in a while, so I'll cover a few days, beginning with a week ago today.

It was one of those mornings when I woke up on the wrong side of the bed, feeling a little out of sorts, mad at the wife over something I've forgotten and she probably hasn't forgotten, and we grumbled down the hall, into the kitchen, and there's our dog, a Siberian Husky—my wife always refers to him as a Suburban Husky because of his pampered life style, though any resemblance to where we live and suburbia requires a great deal of faith—and he's smiling at us, and then we see why he's smiling. Two reasons: (1) He's happy to see us. (2) He feels a little guilty.

He has reason to feel guilty. Not far behind him, next to the kitchen table, was a pile of shit. I'm not talking your casual little whoopsie-doo, and I'm not talking your inconvenient pile, and I'm not talking six to eight turds the size of large banannas. I'm talking a certified, pure-dee, goddamn prize winning SHIT. There were enough dog turds there to shovel out in a pickup truck and dump on the lawn and let dry so you could use them to build a adobe hut big enough to keep your tools in and have room to house your cat in the winter.

And right beside this sterling deposit, was a lake of piss wide enough and deep enough to go rowing on.

I had visions of a Siberian Husky hat and slippers, or possibly a nice throw rug for the bedroom, a necklace of dog claws and teeth; maybe cut that smile right out of his face and frame it.

But the dog-lover in me took over, and I put him outside in his pen where he cooled his dew-claws for a while. Then I spent about a half-hour cleaning up dog shit while my wife spent the same amount of time keeping our two year old son, Kevin, known to me as Fruit of My Loins, out of the shit.

Yep, Oh Great White Page of a Diary, he was up now. It always works that way. In times of greatest stress, in times of greatest need for contemplation or privacy, like when you're trying to get that morning piece off the Old Lady, the kid shows up, and suddenly it's as if you've been deposited inside an ant farm and the ants are crawling and stinging. By the time I finished cleaning up the mess, it was time for breakfast, and I got to tell you, I didn't want anything that looked like link sausage that morning.

So Janet and I ate, hoping that what we smelled while eating was the aroma of disinfectant and not the stench of shit wearing a coat of disinfectant, and we watched the kid spill his milk eighty-lebben times and throw food and drop stuff on the floor, and me and the wife we're fussing at each other more and more, about whatever it was we were mad about that morning—a little item intensified by our dog's deposits—and by the time we're through eating our meal, and Janet leaves me with Fruit of My Loins and his View Master and goes out to the laundry room to do what the room is named for—probably went out there to beat the laundry clean with rocks or bricks, pretending shirts and pants were my head—I'm beginning to think things couldn't get worse. About that time the earth passes through the tail of a comet or something, some kind of dimensional gate is opened, and the world goes weird.

There's a knock at the door.

At first I thought it was a bird pecking on the glass, it was that soft. Then it came again and I went to the front door and opened it, and there stood a woman about five feet tall wearing a long, wool coat, and untied, flared-at-the-ankles shoes, and a ski cap decorated with a silver pin. The wool ski cap was pulled down so tight over her ears her face was pale. Keep in mind that it was probably eighty degrees that morning, and the temperature was rising steadily, and she was dressed like she was on her way to plant the flag at the summit of Everest. Her age was hard to guess. Had that kind of face. She could have been twenty-two or forty-two.

She said, "Can I use your phone, mister? I got an important call to make."

Well, I didn't see any ready-to-leap companions hiding in the shrubbery, and I figured if she got out of line I could handle her, so I said, "Yeah, sure. Be my guest," and let her in.

The phone was in the kitchen, on the wall, and I pointed it out to her, and me and Fruit of My Loins, went back to doing what we were doing, which was looking at the View Master. We switched from Goofy to Winnie the Pooh, the one about Tigger in the tree, and it was my turn to look at it, and I couldn't help but hear that my guest's conversation with her mother was becoming stressful— I knew it was her mother because she addressed her by that title—and suddenly Fruit of My Loins yelled, "Wook, Daddy wook."

I turned and "wooked," and what do I see but what appears to be some rare tribal dance, possibly something having originated in higher altitudes where the lack of oxygen to the brain causes wilder abandon with the dance steps. This gal was all over the place. Fred Astaire with a hot coat hanger up his ass couldn't have been any brisker. I've never seen anything like it. Then, in mid-dossey-do, she did a leap like cheerleaders do, one of those things where they kick their legs out to the side, open up like a nut-cracker and kick the palms of their hands, then she hit the floor on her ass, spun, and wheeled as if on a swivel into the hallway and went out of sight. Then there came a sound from in there like someone on speed beating the bongos. She hadn't dropped the phone either. The wire was stretched tight around the corner and was vibrating like a big fish was on the line.

I dashed over there and saw she was lying crosswise in the hallway, bamming her head against the wall, clutching at the phone with one hand and pulling her dress up over her waist with the other, and she was making horrible sounds and rolling her eyes, and I immediately thought: this is it, she's gonna die. Then I saw she wasn't dying, just thrashing, and I decided it was an epileptic fit.

I got down and took the phone away from her, took hold of her jaw, got her tongue straight without getting bit, stretched her out on the floor away from the wall, picked up the phone and told her mama, who was still fussing about something or another, that things weren't so good, hung up on her in mid-sentence and called the ambulance.

I ran out to the laundry room, told Janet a strange woman was in our hallway pulling her dress over her head and that an ambulance was coming. Janet, bless her heart, has become quite accustomed to weird events following me around, and she went outside to direct the ambulance, like one of those people at the airport with light sticks.

I went back to the woman and watched her thrash awhile, trying to make sure she didn't choke to death, or injure herself, and Fruit of My Loins kept clutching my leg and asking me what was wrong. I didn't know what to tell him.

After what seemed a couple of months and a long holiday, the ambulance showed up with a whoop of siren, and I finally decided the lady was doing as good as she was going to do, so I went outside. On either side of my walk were all these people. It's like Bradbury's story "The Crowd." The one where when there's an accident all these strange people show up out of nowhere and stand around and watch.

I'd never seen but two of these people before in my life, and I've been living in this neighborhood for years.

One lady immediately wanted to go inside and pray for the woman, who she somehow knew, but Janet whispered to me there wasn't enough room for our guest in there, let alone this other woman and her buddy, God, so I didn't let her in.

All the other folks are just a jabbering, and about all sorts of things. One woman said to another: "Mildred, how you been?"

"I been good. They took my kids away from me this morning, though. I hate that. How you been?"

"Them hogs breeding yet?" one man says to another, and the other goes into not only that they're breeding, but he tells how much fun they're having at it.

Then here comes the ambulance boys with a stretcher. One of the guys knew me somehow, and he stopped and said, "You're that writer, aren't you?"

I admitted it.

"I always wanted to write. I got some ideas that's make a good book and a movie. I'll tell you about 'em. I got good ideas, I just can't write them down. I could tell them to you and you could write them up and we could split the money."

"Could we talk about this later?" I said. "There's a lady in there thrashing in my hallway."

So they went in with the stretcher, and after a few minutes the guy I talked to came out and said, "We can't get her out of there and turned through the door. We may have to take your back door out."

That made no sense to me at all. They brought the stretcher through and now they were telling me they couldn't carry it out. But I was too addled to argue and told them to do what they had to do.

Well, they managed her out the back door without having to remodel our home after all, and when they came around the edge of the house I heard the guy I'd talked to go, "Ahhh, damn, I'd known it was her I wouldn't have come."

I thought they were going to set her and the stretcher down right there, but they went on out to the ambulance and jerked open the door and tossed her and the stretcher inside like they were tossing a dead body over a cliff. You could hear the stretcher strike the back of the ambulance and bounce forward and slide back again.

I had to ask: "You know her?"

"Dark enough in the house there, I couldn't tell at first. But when we got outside, I seen who it was. She does this all the time, but not over on this side of town in a while. She don't take her medicine on purpose so she'll have fits when she gets stressed, or she fakes them, like this time. Way she gets attention. Sometimes she hangs herself, cuts off her air. Likes the way it feels. Sexual or something. She's damn near died half-dozen times. Between you and me, wish she'd go on and do it and save me some trips."

And the ambulance driver and his assistant were out of there. No lights. No siren.

Well, the two people standing in the yard that we knew were still there when I turned around, but the others, like mythical creatures, were gone, turned to smoke, dissolved, become one with the universe, whatever. The two people we knew, elderly neighbors, said they knew the woman, who by this time, I had come to think of as the Phone Woman.

"She goes around doing that," the old man said. "She stays with her mamma who lives on the other side of town, but they get in fights on account of the girl likes to hang herself sometimes for entertainment. Never quite makes it over the ridge, you know, but gets her mother worked up. They say her mother used to do that too, hang herself, when she was a girl. She outgrowed it. I guess the girl there . . . you know I don't even know her name . . . must have seen her mamma do that when she was little, and it kind of caught on. She has that 'lepsy stuff too, you know thrashing around and all, biting on her tongue?"

I said I knew and had seen a demonstration of it this morning.

"Anyway," he continued, "they get in fights and she comes over here and tries to stay with some relatives that live up the street there, but they don't cotton much to her hanging herself to things. She broke down their clothesline post last year. Good thing it was old, or she'd been dead. Wasn't nobody home that time. I hear tell they sometimes go off and leave her there and leave rope and wire and stuff laying around, sort of hoping, you know. But except for that time with the clothesline, she usually does her hanging when someone's around. Or she goes in to use the phone at houses and does what she did here."

"She's nutty as a fruitcake," said the old woman. "She goes back on behind here to where that little trailer park is, knocks on doors where the wet backs live, about twenty to a can, and they ain't got no phone, and she knows it. She's gotten raped couple times doing that, and it ain't just them Mex's that have got to her. White folks, niggers. She tries to pick who she thinks will do what she wants. She wants to be raped. It's like the hanging. She gets some kind of attention out of it, some kind of loving. Course, I ain't saying she chose you cause you're that kind of person."

I assured her I understood.

The old couple went home then, and another lady came up, and sure enough, I hadn't seen her before either, and she said, "Did that crazy ole girl come over here and ask to use the phone, then fall down on you and flop?"

"Yes, m'am."

"Does that all the time."

Then this woman went around the corner of the house and was gone, and I never saw her again. In fact, with the exception of the elderly neighbors and the Phone Woman, I never saw any of those people again and never knew where they came from. Next day there was a soft knock on the door. It was the Phone Woman again. She asked to use the phone.

I told her we'd had it taken out.

She went away and I saw her for several times that day. She'd come up our street about once every half hour, wearing that same coat and hat and those sad shoes, and I guess it must have been a hundred and ten out there. I watched her from the window. In fact I couldn't get any writing done because I was watching for her. Thinking about her lying there on the floor, pulling her dress up, flopping. I thought too of her hanging herself now and then, like she was some kind of suit on a hanger.

Anyway, the day passed and I tried to forget about her, then the other night, Monday probably, I went out on the porch to smoke one of my rare cigars (about four to six a year), and I saw someone coming down the dark street, and from the way that someone walked, I knew it was her, the Phone Woman.

She went on by the house and stopped down the road a piece and looked up and I looked where she was looking, and through the trees I could see what she saw. The moon.

We both looked at it a while, and she finally walked on, slow, with her head down, and I put my cigar out well before it was finished and went inside and brushed my teeth and took off my clothes, and tried to go to sleep. Instead, I lay there for a long time and thought about her, walking those dark streets, maybe thinking about her mom, or a lost love, or a phone, or sex in the form of rape because it was some kind of human connection, about hanging herself because it was attention and it gave her a sexual high . . . and then again, maybe I'm full of shit and she wasn't thinking about any of these things.

Then it struck me suddenly, as I lay there in bed beside my wife, in my quiet house, my son sleeping with his teddy bear in the room across the way, that maybe she was the one in touch with the world, with life, and that I was the one gone stale from civilization. Perhaps life had been civilized right out of me.

The times I had truly felt alive, in touch with my nerve centers, were in times of violence or extreme stress.

Where I had grown up, in Mud Creek, violence simmered underneath everyday life like lava cooking beneath a thin crust of earth, ready at any time to explode and spew. I had been in fights, been cut by knives. I once had a job bouncing drunks. I had been a bodyguard in my earlier years, had illegally carried a .38. On one occasion, due to a dispute the day before while protecting my employer, who sometimes dealt with a bad crowd, a man I had insulted and hit with my fists, pulled a gun on me, and I had been forced to pull mine. The both of us ended up with guns in our faces, looking into each other's eyes, knowing full well our lives hung by a thread and the snap of a trigger.

I had killed no one, and had avoided being shot. The Mexican stand-off ended with us both backing away and running off, but there had been that moment when I knew it could all be over in a flash. Out of the picture in a blaze of glory.

No old folks home for me. No drool running down my chin and some young nurse wiping my ass, thinking how repulsive and old I was, wishing for quitting time so she could roll up with some young stud some place sweet and cozy, open her legs to him with a smile and a sigh, and later a passionate scream, while in the meantime, back at the old folks ranch, I lay in the bed with a dead dick and an oxygen mask strapped to my face.

Something about the Phone Woman had clicked with me. I understood her suddenly. I understood then that the lava that had boiled beneath the civilized facade of my brain was no longer boiling. It might be bubbling way down low, but it wasn't boiling, and the realization of that went all over me and I felt sad, very, very sad. I had dug a grave and crawled into it and was slowly pulling the dirt in after me. I had a home. I had a wife. I had a son. Dirt clods all. Dirt clods filling in my grave while life simmered somewhere down deep and useless within me.

I lay there for a long time with tears on my cheeks before exhaustion took over and I slept in a dark world of dormant passion.

Couple days went by, and one night after Fruit of My Loins and Janet were in bed, I went out on the front porch to sit and look at the stars and think about what I'm working on—a novella that isn't going well—and what do I see but the Phone Woman, coming down the road again, walking past the house, stopping once more to look at the moon.

I didn't go in this time, but sat there waiting, and she went on up the street and turned right and went out of sight. I walked across the yard and went out to the center of the street and watched her back going away from me, mixing into the shadows of the trees and houses along the street, and I followed.

I don't know what I wanted to see, but I wanted to see something, and I found for some reason that I was thinking of her lying there on the floor in my hallway, her dress up, the mound of her sex, as they say in porno novels, pushing up at me. The thought gave me an erection, and I was conscious of how silly this was, how unattractive this woman was to me, how odd she looked, and then another thought came to me: I was a snob. I didn't want to feel sexual towards anyone ugly or smelly in a winter coat in the dead of summer.

But the night was cool and the shadows were thick, and they made me feel all right, romantic maybe, or so I told myself.

I moved through a neighbor's backyard where a dog barked at me a couple of times and shut up. I reached the street across the way and looked for the Phone Woman, but didn't see her.

I took a flyer, and walked on down the street toward the trailer park where those poor illegal aliens were stuffed in like sardines by their unscrupulous employers, and I saw a shadow move among shadows, and then there was a split in the trees that provided the shadows, and I saw her, the Phone Woman. She was standing in a yard under a great oak, and not far from her was a trailer. A pathetic air conditioner hummed in one of its windows.

She stopped and looked up through that split in the trees above, and I knew she was trying to find the moon again, that she had staked out spots that she traveled to at night; spots where she stood and looked at the moon or the stars or the pure and sweet black eternity between them.

Like the time before, I looked up too, took in the moon, and it was beautiful, as gold as if it were a great glob of honey. The wind moved my hair, and it seemed solid and purposeful, like a lover's soft touch, like the beginning of foreplay. I breathed deep and tasted the fragrance of the night, and my lungs felt full and strong and young.

I looked back at the woman and saw she was reaching out her hand to the moon. No, a low limb. She touched it with her finger tips. She raised her other hand, and in it was a short, thick rope. She tossed the rope over the limb and made a loop and pulled it taught to the limb. Then she tied a loop to the other end, quickly expertly, and put that around her neck.

Of course, I knew what she was going to do. But I didn't move. I could have stopped her, I knew, but what was the point? Death was the siren she had called on many a time, and finally, she had heard it sing.

She jumped and pulled her legs under her and the limb took her jump and held her. Her head twisted to the left and she spun about on the rope and the moonlight caught the silver pin on her ski cap and it threw out a cool beacon of silver light, and as she spun, it hit me once, twice, three times.

On the third spin her mouth went wide and her tongue went out and her legs dropped down and hit the ground and she dangled there, unconscious.

I unrooted my feet and walked over there, looking about as I went.

I didn't see anyone. No lights went on in the trailer.

I moved up close to her. Her eyes were open. Her tongue was out. She was swinging a little, her knees were bent and the toes and tops of her silly shoes dragged the ground. I walked around and around her, an erection pushing at my pants. I observed her closely, tried to see what death looked like.

She coughed. A little choking cough. Her eyes shifted toward me. Her chest heaved. She was beginning to breathe. She made a feeble effort to get her feet under her, to raise her hands to the rope around her neck.

She was back from the dead.

I went to her. I took her hands, gently pulled them from her throat, let them go. I looked into her eyes. I saw the moon there. She shifted so that her legs held her weight better. Her hands went to her dress. She pulled it up to her waist. She wore no panties. Her bush was like a nest built between the boughs of a snow-white elm.

I remembered the day she came into the house. Everything since then, leading up to this moment, seemed like a kind of perverse mating ritual. I put my hand to her throat. I took hold of the rope with my other hand and jerked it so that her knees straightened, then I eased behind her, put my forearm against the rope around her throat, and I began to tighten my hold until she made a soft noise, like a virgin taking a man for the first time. She didn't lift her hands. She continued to tug her dress up. She was trembling from lack of oxygen. I pressed myself against her buttocks, moved my hips rhythmically, my hard-on bound by my underwear and pants. I tightened the pressure on her throat.

And choked her.

And choked her.

She gave up what was left of her life with a shiver and a thrusting of her pelvis, and finally she jammed her buttocks back into me and I felt myself ejaculate, thick and hot and rich as shaving foam.

Her hands fell to her side. I loosened the pressure on her throat but clung to her for a while, getting my breath and my strength back. When I felt strong enough, I let her go. She swung out and around on the rope and her knees bent and her head cocked up to stare blindly at the gap in the trees above, at the honey-golden moon.

I left her there and went back to the house and slipped into the bedroom and took off my clothes. I removed my wet underwear carefully and wiped them out with toilet paper and flushed the paper down the toilet. I put the underwear in the clothes hamper. I put on fresh and climbed into bed and rubbed my hands over my wife's buttocks until she moaned and woke up. I rolled her on her stomach and mounted her and made love to her. Hard, violent love, my forearm around her throat, not squeezing, but thinking about the Phone Woman, the sound she had made when I choked her from behind, the way her buttocks had thrust back into me at the end. I closed my eyes until the sound that Janet made was the sound the Phone Woman made and I could visualize her there in the moonlight, swinging by the rope.

When it was over, I held Janet and she kissed me and joked about my arm around her throat, about how it seemed I had wanted to choke her. We laughed a little. She went to sleep. I let go of her and moved to my side of the bed and looked at the ceiling and thought about the Phone Woman. I tried to feel guilt. I could not. She had wanted it. She had tried for it many times. I had helped her do what she had never been able to manage. And I had felt alive again. Doing something on the edge. Taking a risk.

Well, journal, here's the question: Am I a sociopath?

No. I love my wife. I love my child. I even love my Suburban Husky. I have never hunted and fished, because I thought I didn't like to kill. But there are those who want to die. It is their one moment of life; to totter on the brink between light and darkness, to take the final, dark rush down a corridor of black, hot pain.

So, Oh Great White Pages, should I feel guilt, some inner torment, a fear that I am at heart a cold-blooded murderer?

I think not.

I gave the sweet gift of truly being alive to a woman who wanted someone to participate in her moment of joy. Death ended that, but without the threat of it, her moment would have been nothing. A stage rehearsal for a highschool play in street clothes.

Nor do I feel fear. The law will never suspect me. There's no reason to. The Phone Woman had a record of near suicides. It would never occur to anyone to think she had died by anyone's hand other than her own.

I felt content, in touch again with the lava beneath the primal crust. I have allowed it to boil up and burst through and flow, and now it has gone down once more. But it's no longer a distant memory. It throbs and rolls and laps just below, ready to jump and give me life. Are there others out there like me? Or better yet, others for me, like the Phone Woman?

Most certainly.

And now I will recognize them. The Phone Woman has taught me that. She came into my life on a silly morning and brought me adventure, took me away from the grind, and then she brought me more, much, much more. She helped me recognize the fine but perfect line between desire and murder; let me know that there are happy victims and loving executioners.

I will know the happy victims now when I see them, know who needs to be satisfied. I will give them their desire, while they give me mine.

This last part with the Phone Woman happened last night and I am recording it now, while it is fresh, as Janet sleeps. I think of Janet in there and I have a hard time imagining her face. I want her, but I want her to be the Phone Woman, or someone like her.

I can feel the urge rising up in me again. The urge to give someone that tremendous double-edged surge of life and death.

It's like they say about sex. Once you get it, you got to have it on a regular basis. But it isn't sex I want. It's something like it, only sweeter.

I'll wrap this up. I'm tired. Thinking that I'll have to wake Janet and take the edge off my need, imagine that she and I are going to do more than fornicate; that she wants to take that special plunge and that she wants me to shove her.

But she doesn't want that. I'd know. I have to find that in my dreams, when I nestle down into the happy depths of the primitive brain.

At least until I find someone like the Phone Woman, again, that is. Someone with whom I can commit the finest of adultry.

And until that search proves fruitful and I have something special to report, dear diary, I say, goodnight.

(For Ed Gorman)

T.E.D. KLEIN
Ladder

Klein is the author of the novella collection *Dark Gods*, from which one piece, "Nadelman's God," won the World Fantasy Award. He is also the author of the novel *The Ceremonies*.

Usually more comfortable in the novella length, Klein proves with "Ladder" that he can produce equally powerful work in a shorter length. Here, you have a clever variation of "God playing dice with the universe," first published in *Borderlands*.

—E.D.

Ladder

T. E. D. KLEIN

"When asked to identify the mood of our times, she answered, 'A desperate search for a pattern.' "

—Prof. Huston Smith on Rebecca West

i

Birth, I see now, was merely a rung on the ladder. Rather deflating, when you think about it; you live, you struggle, you learn and grow and suffer, and you realize, after nearly seventy years of searching, that your life has been nothing but a metaphor. It's not the sort of thing you see while you're living it, of course. It's like that Greek said, the one they used to teach in school: you can't judge whether your life is a success or a failure until its final moments. Though my memory's not so keen as it once was, I remember that remark; I suppose it must have stuck in my mind because, even as a very young boy, I was consumed with curiosity. How would my own life turn out? What would *I* judge it to be, as I lay dying? But now the question of its success or failure seems sadly beside the point—less important, anyhow, than the one raised by Dame Rebecca. The answer to that, too, has to wait until the end; you can't see the pattern while you're living it. And you certainly can't see it while you're busy being born, dragging that first chilly air into your lungs, already exiled, forlorn in the sunlight of a winter's morning, the damnable game already begun. Though I have no memory of the time, the first thing my eyes beheld was probably the heath, with the icy waters shimmering behind it . . . And it will likely be the last.

i i

The Firth of Lorne, that was the waters' name; can you think of a starting-place more fitting? It was fit, at least, for me, who have never married, never fathered children, never stayed in one place long enough to make a lasting friend (except the holy man), never owned any property but the tiny bungalow where, lying on my cot, an old Navy pillow propped up behind my back, I'm now scratching out this memoir. The Lords of Lorne once owned a third of Scotland; now the estuary that bears their name borders a region of deserted forts, ruined castles, and roofless crofts, their stone portals tumbled down and half concealed by meadow grass, the families that built them long since scattered to England or America or the other side of the world. Any of these houses, in their years of habitation, might have passed for the one where I was born, near the coast between Kilbride and Kilninver. Its low ceiling, heavy beams, and whitewashed plaster walls afforded barely space enough for the three of us, but as the beloved only child of two elderly parents, I was happy there. My father was a minister's son from Glasgow, my mother a MacDougall, of the clan whose ancient stronghold, now little more than rubble, stands on the island of Kerrera in Oban Bay. From the Esplanade at Oban, the region's largest port, you can still make out the ruins; as a child I liked to think of them as my ancestral castle. Beyond Kerrera lay the headwaters of the firth and, looming in the distance, the mountains of Mull. Steamers—they were called "puffers" in those days—plied among the islands, from Mull to Lismore, Colonsay, Coll, and the Outer Hebrides. Other boys dreamed of sailing on them, to see more of the world before they died; I was content where I was. I planned, in fact, to continue sheep-raising like my father; we had a flock of black-faced Argyllshires whose regular comings and goings from pasture to fold, daybreak to dusk, season to season, filled me with a sense of peace. Though we owned a car, our lives, by the standards of today, seem almost medieval in their simplicity. I remember doing schoolwork by lantern light, a single lantern for all three of us, and how we'd try to keep one coal glowing all night in the stove to light the fire again the next morning. It never occurred to me that the sight of glowing coals could ever be anything but precious . . . I loved the way the heath would change from green in spring to purple and gold in the fall, and how it gleamed like crystal in winter. I would gaze across it every day as the rattling old bus, its windows leaking draughts of icy air, drove us children to Church School in Kilninver. Over the doorway, I recall, carved into the granite, were foot-high letters spelling out the opening line of Saint John: *In the Beginning Was the Word*. I wasn't a clever student—I had trouble seeing the connections between things, even then —but I worked hard at pleasing my teachers. My parents were pious people, and I believed in a strict but fair Creator who, as they did, hid His kindly intentions behind a stern exterior. I remember how comforting it was to think of the Lord as a shepherd, and we His sheep . . . But then, one rainy night on the very eve of my graduation, just as my parents were returning from Oban in their car after buying me a new wool coat, a suit, and a bound set of *Youth's Companion*s, they were swept off the road by a freak storm; or perhaps it was the fault of a rain-smeared windscreen. The car, with their bodies, was discovered at the bottom of a glen. The coroner described it as "an act of God." Immediately my world changed forever. I was alone now. My father, I discovered, had not been as prudent as I'd thought; he'd borrowed over the years from a neighboring family of landowners and had left me in debt. I had to sell the farm to them—the house, the flock, the pastures. They offered to let me stay on, but I knew it was time for me to go. God, I told myself, had done this for a reason; He had plans for me.

Sensing that I'd been thrust out into the world like a sheep from the fold, I packed my things, ready to submit to His will.

i i i

Forth I went, my new suit in a satchel beneath my arm, to seek what I thought was my destiny. I had already sold my coat. My *Youth's Companions* lay unopened amid the pile of books I was leaving behind; my youth was over. I would have to make my own way now, settle in a town and learn a trade. I did know something about wool; I knew its grades, how to unkink it, how to make it take the dye. I was not, I told myself, entirely unprepared. Unlike my fellows, who dreamt of America, I had an idea that the course of my life—the pattern, if you will—lay toward the east; something, I see now, was calling me in that direction, toward my eventual encounter with the holy man and the secret he revealed. Into the Lorne flows the River Awe, cutting through the Pass of Brander from the Falls of Cruachan, and it was toward these magical names that I turned my steps. The heath was swimming in wildflowers, like foam on a choppy sea, as I walked to the highway and waited for a ride, wondering if I'd ever be coming back. Glen Mor, the Great Glen, lay ahead of me, sixty miles of waterway cutting across the highlands, from the Lynn of Lorne beside me in the west to Inverness in the east, where Loch Ness meets the Moray Firth and flows into the North Sea. The region that I passed through was as picturesque as I'd once been told, with menacing crags and pine-shadowed valleys, ghostly waterfalls and scenes of ancient slaughter. The land here had seen its share of blood; but beyond it, I knew, lay the wide world.

i v

Forts William (named for William III) and Augustus (for the Duke of Cumberland) stand guard on either side of the Glen, their broad streets sloping toward the great Caledonian Canal. Fort William, the first I reached, was noisy, traffic-clogged, and, I thought then, highly exciting; it was the largest town I'd ever seen, with handsome white houses, hotels crowded with vacationers, and the grey granite mass of Ben Nevis rising up behind it, its top obscured by clouds. One look at the women in the shops, all of whom seemed beautiful, and I resolved to go no farther; I would settle here. And I did . . . for a time. I put up at a cheap boarding house near the edge of town and found work in a tailor's shop, fitting hikers with tweed suits—in those days one dressed up to hike—and mending worn collars. I'd been employed there less than a month, however, when one morning I arrived to find the street filled with shouting firemen and the shop a smoking ruin. I don't know if they ever found the cause. At the time I suspected the landlord's younger son, who'd had a dispute with the tailor; now I suspect God, who has lightning at His command. It was clear to me, at any rate, that I had to move on. I continued eastward, to Fort Augustus, at the foot of Loch Ness, where anglers stalk salmon and Americans search for monsters. The King's Own High-landers were garrisoned at the fort there, and I soon found myself a job helping keep the books for a firm that made uniforms for these troops. And then I fell in love. I shan't write down her name; I haven't done so in half a century. Sometimes I manage to forget her; I think I prefer it that way. Anyhow, I hoped to marry her, and plans were made, and then she got ill—she had a brother in the garrison, where a fever was raging—and finally God took her. No use protesting; He simply had other plans for me, and the girl had gotten in the way. I see that now; it's why I'm writing this, so I'll see it all for what it was before I go. I wasn't supposed to linger at Augustus; my destiny—my great destiny—lay somewhere to the east. Pushing on to Inverness, I booked a passage for Edinburgh, where I found a ship to travel on, the *Saracen*. She was a rusted old tramp steamer, her twin smokestacks stained with grime, but they needed a purser on her and were willing to hire me. Besides, I liked her name. I signed on board, eager to see what God had in store for me.

v

Ports all over the world welcomed me in my quest. We docked at Lisbon, the Canaries, and Capetown, then sailed north to the Maldives and Bombay. In succeeding years I transferred to other ships and added new names to my catalogue of places seen. In a single year I saw Athens and Adelaide, Singapore and San Francisco. In another I did nothing but sail back and forth between Manila and Hong Kong. I saw a temple in Java where they worshipped small green spiders, and a woman in Ceylon who gave herself to snakes. I visited the New Hebrides and New Caledonia off Australia, lured by the Scottishness of their names, and the great port of New York, a universe away from the tiny ruined hamlet of the same name near my birthplace, at the edge of the Inverliever Forest and Loch Awe, where anglers feast on salmon and trout. The world left its marks on me, but I welcomed them. In Shanghai my face was slashed during a robbery, but I found the scar handsome. In Montevideo my nose was broken in a waterfront brawl, but I decided I liked it better that way. I was aimless, for once; I enjoyed it. I fell in love with travel. For a while, in the early years, I worried that God had forgotten me; then I hoped He had. Throughout these years I found myself employed with increasing frequency by the Britannic East India Company. The work—the purchase of shipboard supplies, the keeping of books—came easily now, and the Company and its concerns were seldom in my thoughts. But it seemed I was in theirs, because when the director of agricultural development unexpectedly took sick and died, they made me his successor.

v i

Posts in Gibraltar and, later, Bombay awaited me. Once again my life had changed drastically; after gallivanting across the globe, I was suddenly planted in an office.

I missed my vagabond days, but didn't have the strength to refuse the raise in pay. My first post, in Gibraltar, lasted exactly seven weeks; I was supposed to expedite the transfer of olive trees from Rabat to Madrid, but a Moroccan revolution cut off our supply. In Bombay, I had barely unpacked my bags before I was placed in charge of a plan designed to introduce Welsh Merino sheep into the south Indian state of Andhra Pradesh. The poor animals had been wrenched from their homes and shipped halfway around the world; I felt a kinship with them. I set up a small office in the interior, in a dusty little village whose name I could never pronounce. It seemed as remote as another planet, though the wrinkled grey hides of the elephants passing on the streets reminded me of the slopes of Ben Nevis. Only after we'd gotten set up did I discover that I'd arrived at the hottest time of year, in one of the hottest years on record. For once I didn't work hard; I sat there in my shirtsleeves and perspired. One morning a little old man, his face as brown and wrinkled as a walnut, strolled unannounced into my office. He was Mr. Nath, he told me in a shrill sing-song voice, "a holy man." His forthrightness amused me, and I told him to sit down. He'd come, he said, because the locals were complaining that I'd brought the heat wave with me. They feared that I was cursed. "Well," I said, not entirely joking, "perhaps I am"—and I proceeded to sketch the particulars of my life. "I feel," I said, "a little like a pawn, constantly being shunted from one scene to another at someone else's whim. I still believe there's a design to it all, but damned if I know what it is." Mr. Nath had been listening intently, nodding as I spoke. "All lives have a pattern," he said, "that we see in their beauty and completion only at the end. One man is the second son, and will be second in all things. One will forever be doomed to arrive too late. One will go from rich to poor and back again seven times in his life. Another will always take wrong advice. Another will win only one race, at the start, and thereafter will know nothing but defeat. One will make a miserable first marriage, and then his second wife will bring him only bliss. Another will rue every day but the last. Another's life will follow the pattern of a spiral, or a chess game, or the lines from a child's nursery song. But you, my friend—" Suddenly I saw his eyes widen. He was staring at a swarm of bugs that had just flown into the room, a seething little microcosm of darting energy and flashing wings, hovering just above our heads, humming in the morning heat. They were, I don't know, gnats, mosquitoes, tiny flies . . . India has so many. Their presence in my office was unremarkable; the door to the other rooms had been open, and the cloth screens were riddled with holes. What unnerved me was the manner of their coming, the sheer *abruptness* of it, as if they'd been rushed onto the stage by some great unseen hand. The little man seemed more upset than I. "Bugs," I said, shrugging. He shook his head, eyes round with horror. "No," he whispered. "*Pests!*" I mistook this for a reference to the plague, and thinking of my lost love, felt a stab of sadness. And at that moment, just as quickly as they came, the bugs vanished—simply melted into the air, as if that same great hand had wiped them off the board. The little man's eyes nearly popped from his head. He opened his mouth, made a strangled sound, and ran from the room. I was left staring at the place where the bugs had been, feeling more bemused than frightened. Those creatures didn't scare me, not then. But they scare me now. Because now I know what they were.

vii

The costs of running the Bombay branch proved to be too high, that's what I was informed, and I found myself abruptly—and, I might add, high-handedly—relieved of my post. Blame it on the dreadful heat I'd brought with me (for I'm more than half convinced I did), and on the drought that followed. No one had ever seen such weather; the Company's coffee crops withered, the sheep sickened and died, and the survivors had to be shipped north at considerable expense. Blame it on the war then raging in Europe, which more than doubled the price of doing business. Blame it on an act of God. All I knew is that I was suddenly being uprooted again, another chapter closed behind me. As I stood on the Bombay dock, gazing at the ship I'd soon be boarding while, around me, workers with ropes and pulleys strained to hoist cargo into the hold, I thought of the stable world I'd known as a child; I seemed to be inhabiting an entirely different place now, pushed from one scene to the next. These gloomy reflections were cut short by the high-pitched voice of Mr. Nath, who had come to see me off. I'd become friends with him following the incident in my office; and though it was the one subject on which he'd refused to talk further, I'd relished his insights on other matters—so much so, in fact, that I'd hired him as my assistant. He had accompanied me back to Bombay; he, too, was now jobless, but seemed much less downcast than I, and was looking forward to returning to his village. As he walked me up the gangplank, he listened impatiently as I complained once more about the turns my life had taken. "Surely," I said, "God must be behind these huge changes." He gave a little sigh before he spoke, as if this were something he'd been hoping to avoid. "Yes," he said, "and no. The changes you speak of are *maya*, illusion." We had reached the deck now; he gripped my arm and stared at me with, for the first time, a hint of urgency. "In the things that matter," he said, "the Lord works very slowly and deliberately, with a hand far more subtle than you imagine. Don't you know how He changes a dog into a cat?" He paused, smiled when he saw my bewilderment, and seemed about to answer his own question, when suddenly I saw him look past me; his eyes widened in horror, the way I'd seen before—with horror and, I think now, a kind of terrible understanding. A shadow fell across the deck, and I looked up, half expecting to see a swarm of insects. But something else darkened the sky: a rope had snapped, and an enormous wooden crate destined for the hold was hurtling down upon us. I stumbled back in time; Mr. Nath was not so lucky. The crate caught him almost head on, crushing him like a bug and bursting open on the deck, its puzzling contents spilling out and all but burying my friend.

viii

Coats, that's what the crate had contained; the word, in fact, was stenciled on the side. Greatcoats, dress coats, army issues, fancy leather affairs with epaulets and brass buttons. They lay scattered across the deck, some of them dropping into the warm blue water. I even think I saw my old woolen coat from Oban disappear beneath the waves. None of this made sense. The weather was hot in this part of the world, preternaturally hot at the moment, the climate muggy even at its best; these garments were as out of place here as a pair of snowshoes. Now, of course, as I set this down and read it over, the whole thing is comically clear; I must have been blind not to see it. But at the time my friend's last words, and the contents of the crate that had killed him, were sufficiently enigmatic that I spent most of the voyage pondering them. It was a shorter voyage than anyone expected. The ship, the *Jane Guy*, traveled south, then eastward, then south again. We kept clear of Japanese waters—there was still a war going on—but in those days nowhere was truly safe. Passengers took turns on deck, searching the horizon for a sign of danger. As I stood my watch one moonless night, preoccupied by thoughts of God and death, the ship gave a lurch, and somewhere metal echoed upon metal. Later a survivor would theorize about Japanese torpedoes, but it seemed to me that a piece of the ocean floor had simply risen up and speared us. However, there was no time for speculation. We were sinking.

ix

Boats were lowered over the side, passengers and crew having scrambled aboard, and those of us who could lay our hands on oars paddled madly away from the ship. My boat lost the others in the darkness. We heard the sound of distant screams and a great rushing of water, but when the sun rose we found ourselves alone. Several of us unfurled the single sail, but the canvas hung limp; there was no wind. The sun's gaze was as blank and pitiless as poets have warned. There were thirteen of us in the boat—we joked about it, of course—and it wasn't many days before the other twelve were dead. Half-starving and delirious, I shoved their bodies over the side to thwart temptation, and looked forward to dying myself. I felt like Ishmael or the Ancient Mariner; I couldn't understand why I'd been spared. That I *had* been immediately became clear, for no sooner did the last body hit the water than a sudden wind sprang up and filled the sail. The boat began to move. I can see God's hand in that wind now, and in the calm that preceded it as well. It is not a kindly hand; I wish now I'd had the courage to jump over the side and thwart it. But all I could do at the time was lie back, mumble a prayer of thanks, and let the boat carry me where it would. I no longer questioned the plans He had for me, though I must have lapsed into a sun-dazzled reverie of some sort: boyhood memories, faces, questions, words. But suddenly those thoughts were interrupted by a rhythmic thumping . . .

x

Beats of a drum were echoing across the water, above the pounding of surf. I
raised my head. Before me, in the distance, lay an island: coconut palms, thatched
huts, and a row of natives waiting for my boat to wash ashore. They reminded
me, as the boat drew nearer, of the black-faced sheep of my childhood . . . only
sheep had never worn bones in their noses, nor gazed at me so hungrily. I can
see even now, as in a fever dream, the group of them come toward me, dragging
my boat onto the beach. In the background women are tending a fire; the glowing
coals remind me of my boyhood. The largest of the men lifts me from the boat.
He ties my hands; he anoints my face; he drags me forward . . .

x i

. . . and heats a pot that's large enough to be my coffin. Wearily I whisper a final
prayer . . . Till at that moment, borne before a huge unnatural gust of wind, a
sailing ship appears on the horizon. The cartoon natives run away, and I am
saved. The ship meets a steamer which returns me to Scotland; I set foot once
more on my native soil. Still dazed and emaciated, a grey stick figure in cast-off
Navy clothes, I sink to my knees and praise God for his goodness; I consider
myself blessed. Later, as my weary legs carry me toward the house where I was
born, I believe I finally see the pattern He's imposed on my life: a madman's full
circle, clear around the globe.

x i i

The heath now stirs around me in the autumn wind. I have returned, like a piece
of ancient driftwood, to the spot where I began—though not, in fact, to my
parents' doorstep. Their cottage now stands empty like the others, roof rotten and
fallen in, a picturesque ruin. Instead, I'm now living in a tiny bungalow just
down the hill from it, on a small plot of what was once my parents' farm. The
land is subdivided now, along with the land of our neighbors, and a company
down in London is busy populating it with vacation homes. Tourists, hikers, and
holidaymakers now roam the hills where once I tended my father's flocks. The
old "puffers" have been replaced by diesel-powered vessels that take Americans
to Jura and Islay, and the deserted forts, those still in decent repair, have now
become museums. In one of them, devoted to local history and antiquities, I
recently had the novel experience—novel but eerily disorienting—of finding a
shelf of my own childhood books on display in a room labeled "Typical Crofter's
Cottage, Early 20th Century." I felt a queer burst of homesickness, seeing them
there in that reconstructed room; they looked as clean and well cared for as if my
mother were still alive to dust them. Among them were the bound *Youth's Companions* that circumstance had robbed me of the chance to read. I removed one

and sadly flipped through it. It fell open, as if by design, to a page entitled "Rainy Day Puzzles and Pastimes," below which my eye was caught by a familiar question: *"How do you change a Dog into a Cat?"* Heart pounding, I read on: *"By changing one letter at a time. This age-old game is called a 'Word Ladder,' for each change must make a new word. You can turn Dog into Cog, and Cog into Cot, and Cot into Cat—just three steps. Or you can do it in four, from Dog to Hog, to Hag, to Hat, to Cat. Or in five, from Dog to Bog, to Bag, to Bar, to Car, to Cat. In fact, the ladder may stretch as long as you like. The possibilities are endless!"* And, by God, they are—though at first I didn't understand; it's taken me this long to work it through. And now, at last, it's all laid out here in this memoir, the secret itinerary of my own career from "Birth" to "Firth," to "Forth," and on to "Forts" . . . and all for His amusement. All those deaths! The men of the *Jane Guy*, my father and mother, my friend Mr. Nath, the girl in Fort Augustus . . . Was it really for *this* that she had to die? To move me one rung down, from "Forts" to "Ports"? Couldn't He have spared her? Couldn't He have set me on a different course? I might have gone instead from "Forts" to "Forks," "Folks," "Folds," "Golds," "Gelds," "Melds," "Meads," "Meats," "Heats," and "Heath" . . . Or in an even more roundabout journey, from the "Posts" I once held, to "Poses," "Roses," "Ropes," "Rapes," "Races," "Faces," "Facts," "Fasts," "Fests," "Tests," "Tents," "Dents," "Depts.," and "Depth" (assuming the old cheat would allow Himself the use of an abbreviation near the end). But in my case He seems simply to have plumped for the easiest and most direct route—except, I now realize, for a single false step. The holy man must have noticed it at once. "Pests!" he'd cried. Not "Bugs!" but "Pests!"—a chapter that, in someone else's life, might well have followed "Posts." Those creatures, had they been permitted to remain, would likely have led me on an alternate route to "Tests," "Bests," "Beats," and "Heats," arriving precisely where I am today. Instead, God must have changed His mind—and erased that swarm of pests from the game so hurriedly that my friend saw what it meant. Perhaps, in the end, He simply found it easier to move from "Posts" to "Costs," and to drag in that dreadful crate of coats . . . Well, I always knew I was destined for something; I just never guessed it would be this. Saint John had it right, I see that now: In the Beginning Was the Word. Unfortunately for me, the word was "Birth," and it was all downhill from there. Below me now lies one more rung—the bottom rung, the one that follows "Heath." I'd rather cling to this one for a while, but I know that, like any true gamesman, God's going to have the last word.

STEVEN MILLHAUSER
Alice, Falling

"Alice, Falling" is a stylistic departure from many of the other stories in this volume and a fine example of the limitless ways a writer can approach fantasy material. First published in the literary journal *Anteaus*, it is a magical dreamscape of a story derived from Lewis Carroll's fantasy classic *Alice in Wonderland*.

Steven Millhauser teaches at Skidmore College and lives with his wife and children in Saratoga Springs, New York. He is the author of *Portrait of a Romantic, From the Realm of Morpheus, Edwin Mullhouse*, and *In the Penny Arcade*. His story "The Illusionist" (published in *Esquire* magazine and reprinted in last year's *Year's Best Fantasy & Horror*) won the 1989 World Fantasy Award. His most recent collection, *The Barnum Museum*, from which this story is reprinted, is highly recommended; it includes the bittersweet story "The Sepia Postcard" which is also one of the year's best fantasy tales.

—T.W.

Alice, Falling

STEVEN MILLHAUSER

Alice, falling, sees on the top shelf of the open cupboard a jar bearing the label RASPBERRY JAM, a yew-wood tea caddy with brass fastenings and a design of handpainted plants and flowers on the lid, and a tin of lemon snaps: the dark green top shows in the center an oval containing a colored head of Prince Albert. On the bottom shelf Alice sees a porcelain dessert plate with a gilt border and a center panel showing a young man in a tilted tricorne, red jacket, and white breeches, standing beside an oak tree; a bread knife with an ivory handle carved to show a boy holding wheat in his arms; and a silver-plated cream jug with a garland of silver-plated leaves and berries encircling the base. So slowly is Alice falling that she has time to take in all the details, to note the pink thistles on the lid of the tea caddy and the yellow buttons on the red jacket of the man on the dessert plate, to observe the faint reflections of her face above and below the label on the jar of raspberry jam.

Alice does not know how long she has been falling, but when she looks up she has the sense of a great shaft of darkness stretching interminably upward. In the alien tunnel-world she tries to think of the bright upper world, where her sister sits on a bank, under a tree, reading a book without pictures or conversations, but as she falls deeper and deeper it becomes harder for her thoughts to reach so high, as if each thought is a heavy rope that has to be hurled upward in the act of falling. And gradually, as she falls, a change comes about: the mysterious shaft or vertical tunnel through which she is falling begins to seem familiar to her, with its cupboards, its shelves, its lamplit bumps and hollows, while the upper world grows shadowy and strange; and as she falls she has to remind herself that somewhere far above, suddenly the air is blinding blue, white-and-yellow daisies grow in a green field, on a sloping bank her sister sits reading in sun-checked shade.

*   *   *

The dark walls of the shaft are faintly illuminated by globed oil lamps attached at irregular intervals to wrought-iron wall brackets: each bracket has the shape of an elongated S-curve turned sideways, and on the apex of the outermost curve sits a brass mermaid holding up a cylindrical chased-brass base with a brass adjustment knob; on the cylinder rests the globe of glass, topped by a slender glass stem. The light from the lamps permits Alice to observe the objects that abound on the walls. In addition to the cupboards with their shelves, she passes maps and pictures hung on pegs, including a black-and-white engraving of Scotland showing all the counties outlined in red, and a painting of a lion leaping onto the back of a horse: the horse's head is twisted backward, its teeth are bared, the flared nostrils are wide as teacups, and dark red streaks of blood course along the shiny brown sides; a pair of oak bookshelves holding *Twenty-five Village Sermons*, *Bewick's Birds*, Macauley's *History*, *The Fair Maid of Perth*, *The Life and Works of Edwin Landseer*, Pope's *Homer*, *Coke upon Lyttleton*, Rogers' *Pleasures of Memory*, *Sir Charles Grandison*, *Robberies and Murders of the Most Notorious Pirates*, Bayle's *Dictionary*, *Ivo and Verena*, *Pilgrim's Progress*, and *Gems of European Art*; a barometer in a case of walnut wood shaped like an anchor: the flukes of the anchor support the glass disc, in which is pictured Neptune riding a sea horse within a circle of words (RAIN, FAIR, CHANGE, STORMY); a niche containing a marble Venus and Cupid: the winged, curly-haired boy reaches for his bow, which his seated mother holds away: her robe has slipped to her lap, and one breast is visible above his reaching arm; and a Gothic-arch-topped set of small, glass-fronted shelves on which stand a barefoot porcelain girl holding a basket of flowers over one forearm, a pincushion set in a brass wheelbarrow and stuck with hat pins ornamented with china flowers, a playing-card box with a floral border and a center panel showing a castellated mansion in Tunbridge Wells, two small oval silhouettes framed in ivory and showing, respectively, a snub-nosed girl in a bonnet and a snub-nosed boy in a flat-brimmed hat, a red glass rose with green glass thorns, and a majolica snake devouring a toad.

Down, down, down. Would the fall *never* end? Alice has been falling for so long that she is beginning to grow uncertain. If the fall does end, then the vertical tunnel will be a connecting link, a transition, a bridge between the upper world and the unknown lower world; it will be unimportant in itself and, at the instant of ending, it will disappear. But if the fall never ends, then everything is changed: the fall itself becomes the adventure, and the tunnel through which she is falling becomes the unknown world, with its magic and mystery. Alice, looking about uncertainly, tries to decide whether she is on her way to an adventure or whether she is in the middle of one.

The shaft, well, or vertical tunnel down which Alice is falling has irregular walls of hard earth mixed with outcroppings of rock: granite, feldspar, and basalt. The hard earth is mostly dry, with occasional moist patches; here and there a trickle of dark water zigzags down, passing the edge of a map, slipping behind a cupboard's open door. Some of the cupboards have small dishes on top, placed back against the wall, as if to catch dripping water. The tunnel is a comfortable width for falling: Alice falls without fear of striking the walls, yet at any moment she can reach out and remove a jar from a shelf or adjust a tilted picture. Alice wonders how the shelves are reached from below. At first she imagines a very long ladder, but this presents difficulties even if the tunnel has a bottom, for how would such a long ladder get into such a narrow space? Next she imagines small openings in the walls, through which servants can enter the tunnel, but she sees no openings, no doors. Perhaps the answer is small birds who fly up from below, or from nests hidden in the darkness. It occurs to Alice that there may be another answer: the jars, the pictures, the maps, the lamps have always been here, unchanging. But how can that be? Alice, as she falls, feels a little frown creasing her forehead.

Falling, always falling, Alice closes her eyes and sees her sister on the bank under a tree, reading a book without pictures or conversations. The bank slopes down to a pool with reeds; the sun-shot shadow of the tree, a thick beech (*Fagus sylvatica*), trembles on the water. Circles of sun and shade move on her sister's hands. Deep in her book, Alice's sister scarcely hears the stir of leaves overhead, the distant cries of the shepherd boy, the lowing of the cattle, the rustle of Alice's dress. Gradually she becomes aware of a disturbance beside her; it is Alice, restless as always. It's difficult, thinks Alice's sister, to have a younger sister who won't ever sit still and let you read. Although Alice's sister is determined to keep her eyes fixed on the page, she feels that her attention has already been tugged away, it's as if she is being pulled out of a dream, the words are nothing but words now; irritably she places her finger at the end of a line. Raising her eyes, she is surprised to see Alice chasing a white rabbit across a field. With an impatient sigh, Alice's sister reaches into her pinafore pocket and removes a scrap of blue ribbon, which she places in her book before closing it. She rests the book carefully against a bare root. She then rises to her feet, brushing off her dress with sharp little flicks of the backs of her fingers, and begins to walk quickly after Alice through the field of daisies. When she comes to the rabbit hole under the hedge she stops and crouches down, pushing away the hedge branches, careful not to kneel on the ground. "Alice!" she calls, looking down into the dark hole. "Alice, are you there?" There is no answer. The hole is just large enough for her to enter, but it is very dirty, and very dark. For a while she looks down thoughtfully into the dark. Then she raises her head; in the distance she hears the tinkle of sheep bells; the sun burns down on the tall grass; reeds stir at the edge of the pool; under the leaning beech, sun and shade tremble on the grass, on the closed book, on a purple wildflower beside the bare root.

Down, down, down: she can't really see too much, down there in the dark. She can see the hem of her dress outspread by the wind of her slow falling, and the dark earthen wall of the vertical tunnel, broken here and there by eruptions of rock. The upper view is better, but it makes Alice dizzy: raising her eyes, and bending back her head, she can see the ocher bottom of a cupboard, and higher up, on the other side of the wall, the shadowy underside of a bookshelf supported by two wooden brackets shaped like elephant heads with uplifted trunks. Still higher up she sees a dim glow passing into upper darkness; the glow is from a lamp concealed by the cupboard. When Alice looks down again, she sees the top of a new object rising into view: a strip of dark wood carved with wooden leaves and wooden bunches of grapes. Beneath the strip of carved wood a glimmering mirror appears. Alice sees, at the top of the glass, her shiny black shoes with their narrow black ankle-straps and the bottoms of her blue stockings. The large mirror in its heavy frame of carved mahogany is shaped like a shield. In the dim glass Alice sees, as she falls, the outspread hem of her yellow dress, and then the bottom of her white pinafore with its blue stripe along the bottom border, and then the two pinafore pockets, each with a blue stripe along the top: one pocket holds a white handkerchief. And as if she is standing at the side of a stairway, watching someone appear at the high landing and start to descend, Alice sees in slow succession the white cotton belt, the puffed shoulder sleeves, the outspread yellow-brown hair, the dark, worried eyes under the dark eyebrows, the tense forehead; and already the shiny black shoes and blue stockings and pinafore pockets have disappeared, the bottom of the mirror is rising higher and higher, all at once the top of her head with its thick combed-back hair vanishes from view: and looking up she sees the bottom of the mirror rising higher and higher, floating away, slowly dissolving in the dark.

If only, Alice thinks to herself suddenly, I could let myself go! If only I could fall! For she feels, in her falling, a tension, as if she is holding herself taut against her fall. But a true fall, Alice thinks to herself, is nothing like this: it's a swoon, a release, it's like tugging at a drawer that suddenly comes unstuck. Alice, as she falls, is tense with alertness: she holds herself in readiness, though for what she isn't certain, she looks around eagerly, she takes in everything with sharpened awareness. Her fall is the opposite of a sleep: she has never been so awake. But if I were truly falling, Alice thinks to herself, then I would let myself go, myself go, myself go.

It occurs to Alice that she is of course dreaming. She has simply fallen asleep on the bank with her head in her sister's lap. Soon she will wake up, and the tunnel, the cupboards, the maps, the mirror, the jar of raspberry jam, all will vanish away, leaving only the bank of sun-patched shade, the sunny field, the distant farmyard. But suppose, Alice thinks to herself, the bank too is a dream? If the bank is a dream, then she will wake up somewhere else. But where will that be? Alice tries to think where she might wake up, if she doesn't wake up with her head in her sister's lap. Maybe she will wake up in Lapland, or China. But if she wakes up in Lapland, or China, will she still be Alice, or will she be someone else? Alice tries to imagine another Alice, dreaming: the other Alice has short brown hair, likes rice pudding, and has a cat called Arabella. But mightn't this Alice also be a dream? Who then is the dreamer? Alice imagines a series of Alices, each dreaming the other, stretching back and back, farther and farther, back and back and back and back and back.

*　*　*

On the afternoon of July 4, 1862, a boating party of five was to be seen on the Isis, heading up river from Oxford to Godstow. It was a cloudless blue day. Heat-haze shimmered over the meadows on both sides of the water. Charles Lutwidge Dodgson, mathematical tutor at Christ Church, Oxford, and deacon of the Church of England, having changed from the black clergyman's clothes he always wore in Oxford to white flannel trousers, black boots, and a white straw boater, sat facing the back of his friend Robinson Duckworth, who rowed stroke to Dodgson's bow. In the stern, facing Duckworth, sat the three Liddell sisters, daughters of the Dean of Christ Church: Edith, age 8; Alice, age 10; and Lorina, age 13. The girls, seated on cushions, wore white cotton frocks, white socks, black shoes, and hats with brims. In the boat stood a kettle and a large basket full of cakes; on river expeditions Dodgson liked to stop and take tea in the shadow of a haycock. "The story was actually composed and spoken *over my shoulder*," Duckworth recalled some years later, "for the benefit of Alice Liddell, who was acting as 'cox' of our gig. I remember turning round and saying, 'Dodgson, is this an extempore romance of yours?' And he replied: 'Yes, I'm inventing as we go along.'" Twenty-five years later Dodgson recalled: "I distinctly remember now, as I write, how, in a desperate attempt to strike out some new line of fairy-lore, I had sent my heroine straight down a rabbit-hole, to begin with, without the least idea what was to happen afterwards." He remembered the stillness of that afternoon: the cloudless blue sky, the watery mirror of the river, the tinkle of drops falling from the oars. Mrs. Hargreaves—as Dodgson always referred to Alice, after her marriage—also recalled the day sharply: the blazing summer afternoon, the heat-haze shimmering over the meadows, the shadow cast by the haycocks near Godstow.

Alice is growing thirsty, and as she falls slowly past a cupboard she opens the doors. She sees a bottle labeled GINGER BEER and grasps it as she falls, but the bottom of the bottle catches on the edge of the shelf and the bottle slips from her fingers. Alice covers her ears, widens her eyes, and opens her mouth to scream. But she sees the bottle of ginger beer falling lazily in front of her and not plunging down like a stone in a well. The bottle is tilted like the hand of a clock pointing to ten; at once Alice reaches out and seizes the bottle firmly. When she brings it close to her face she sees with disappointment that there is scarcely a swallow of ginger beer left. She wonders how long the bottle has been sitting on the shelf, for it simply won't do to drink from an old bottle, or one that has been used by someone else. She will have to speak to the housekeeper, if she ever finds one. How neat and clean the shelves are! The housekeeper must have a fine feather duster. But it must be a very long feather duster, to reach so high. Alice feels that her thoughts are growing confused, and without another moment's hesitation she raises the bottle to her lips and swallows the ginger beer. "Why," Alice says to herself in surprise, "this isn't ginger beer at all! It is nothing but soda water! I shall certainly have to speak to someone about this. Fancy if all labels meant something else, so that you never knew what you were going to eat. Please, Miss, would you care for more buttered toast? And out comes roast duck and dumplings.

But that isn't what I mean, exactly." Alice is no longer certain what she means, exactly; when she looks up she can see the cupboard vanishing in the dark. As she falls past another cupboard, she manages to place the bottle inside. At the last moment she realizes that the label is still not right, since the bottle is now empty. But, Alice thinks to herself as the cupboard rises into the dark, it isn't as wrong as it was before.

It occurs to Alice that the shaft is a prison: she cannot climb out, she cannot escape. It may be that she can stop falling, by reaching out and grasping the top of a cupboard, the edge of a niche, or a protruding piece of stone; but even if the cupboard does not tear out of the wall, even if the edge of the niche does not crumble, and the stone not break, what possible use will it be to hang there like a coat on a peg, while her fingers and arms grow tireder and tireder? There are no doors or windows in the walls of her prison, no stairs or ladders: it seems more sensible to keep falling, and to hope for an end of falling, than to stop and think about regaining the upper world. Perhaps if she had stopped very early in her fall, it might not have been too late. Alice tries to imagine herself sitting on top of a cupboard as she looks up and cries for help: her legs dangle against the cupboard doors, she grasps the rim of the cupboard top, she raises her face and shouts for her sister. It occurs to Alice that she has never once cried out, in all her falling; until this moment, when it is too late, the idea has never come to her.

Down, down, down: something must be wrong, Alice thinks to herself, for the fall should surely be over by now. And a doubt steals over her, like a cloud shadow over a pool on a summer's day. Did she do the right thing, when she jumped into the rabbit hole? Wasn't she guilty of a certain rashness? Shouldn't she have considered more carefully, before taking such a step? But the leap into the rabbit hole was the same as the leap to her feet beside her sister: it was the final motion of a single impulse, as if she had leaped from the bank directly into the rabbit hole. The mistake was to have jumped up in the first place. Alice tries to recall her feeling of restlessness on the bank, under the tree, beside her sister, but she recalls only the warm, drowsy shade, the sunny field of daisies, the blue, blue sky. Of course, it was the White Rabbit that made her jump up in excitement. But is a rabbit with a waistcoat and watch really so remarkable, when you stop to think about it? Was it really necessary for her to jump up without a moment's hesitation and run off so rashly, without considering anyone's feelings but her own? Her sister will be worried; when she looks up from her book, Alice will be gone; her day will be ruined. And is it possible, Alice thinks to herself, that the rabbit was only the usual sort of rabbit, after all? Is it possible that she had been daydreaming again, there on the bank beside her sister? Alice, doubting, feels a little burst of bitterness in her heart.

In the darkness, lit here and there by the dim glow of oil lamps, Alice feels a sudden revulsion: the tunnel walls oppress her, the cupboards bore her to death, she can't stand it for another second—and still she continues falling, past the always rising maps, the pictures, the cupboards, the bookshelves. She can hardly breathe in the dank, close air. It is like a long railway journey, without conversation and without any hope of taking tea. Above, the darkness pushes down on her like a column of stone; below, the darkness sweeps slowly upward, sticking to the dark above, increasing its height and weight. There is absolutely nothing to do. Do cats eat bats? Do bats eat cats? Do rats eat mats? Do blats eat clats? This can't go on much longer, Alice thinks to herself, and opens her mouth to scream, but does not scream.

There is no illustration of Alice falling, and so we must imagine the Tenniel drawing: Alice in black and white, falling against a dark background of minute cross-hatchings, upon which we can make out the bottom corner of a cupboard. Alice is wearing black shoes, white stockings with black shading, a white dress and white pinafore. Her long hair is lifted away from her face on both sides; her wide dress billows. Her elbows are held away from her sides and her forearms are held stiffly before her, at different heights; the fingers of the lower hand are spread tensely, the fingers of the upper hand are curved as if she is playing an invisible piano. Under her black eyebrows her black eyes are wide and brooding. The creases of her pinafore are indicated by several series of short parallel lines; the shadow of an arm across her pinafore shows as cross-hatching. In the lower right-hand corner is Tenniel's monogram: a large T crossed with a small J. The illustration is without a frame, and is fitted into the text in such a way that the words continue down the right-hand side of the drawing for most of the page before stretching across the entire width of the page for the last six lines. Alice is therefore falling alongside the text that describes her fall, and at the same time is enclosed by the text; if she falls any farther, she will bump into words. Pictured in the act of falling, Alice remains motionless: she is fixed forever in her fall.

There are four dreams of falling. The first is dreamed by Alice, asleep on the bank with her head in her sister's lap: she dreams of falling down a long vertical tunnel or well. The second is the dream that Alice tells her sister, when falling leaves wake her on the bank: her tale includes the story of the long fall through the dark well. The third is the dream of Alice's sister, alone on the bank, in the setting sun: she dreams of Alice telling her dream, which includes the story of the fall through the dark tunnel. The fourth is Alice's sister's dream of Alice as a grown woman: she dreams of grown-up Alice telling the dream of Wonderland to little children gathered about her. Alice is therefore caught in a circle of dream-falls: no sooner does she wake than she begins to fall again down the dark tunnel, as she recounts her dream to her sister, and no sooner does she run off to tea than she begins to fall again, in her sister's dream; and even as a grown woman she is still falling through the dark, as the bright-eyed children look up at her with eager faces. It appears, then, that Alice can never escape from her dream: once she plunges into the rabbit hole, once she leaves the safe, predictable world of her sister, she can never return; once she starts to fall, she can never stop falling.

* * *

Down, down, down: Alice tries not to be unhappy, for what would be the use of
that, but as she falls she bursts into sudden tears. "Come," Alice says to herself
rather sharply, "there's no use in crying like that!" And no sooner has she spoken
than she stops crying, for Alice always tries to listen to her own advice. She wipes
her cheeks with the backs of her hands; a few tears drip from her chin, and Alice
ignores them as she falls past a closed cupboard with six tiles over the doors. The
tiles show rustic figures in sepia, blue, and black: a shepherd resting under a tree,
a boy in a stream, a girl feeding tame rabbits, a woman and child resting from
collecting sticks, a seated girl with goat and kid, and a young woman carrying a
pail across a stream. The cupboard vanishes into the upper dark, and Alice,
glancing down, sees a curious sight: in the air directly under her chin there are
three tears, falling as she falls. For a while she watches the tears, pressing her
chin against her neck and frowning down to see them; then she lifts out the
handkerchief in her pinafore pocket and carefully wipes away the tears, as if she
is erasing them.

If only, Alice thinks to herself, I weren't so tired! If only I could rest! For it's
tiring to be always falling, falling down the rabbit hole. Alice wonders if it is
possible to rest awhile. She doesn't want to catch hold of a cupboard or bookshelf,
for fear of bringing it down; and in any case, to hang against a wall with your
legs resting on air is hardly Alice's idea of a proper way to rest. Indeed, the act
of falling requires no effort; Alice is puzzled why she should be tired of doing
something that requires no effort. Is it possible that the fall itself is a rest? Alice
tries to imagine what it would be like to sit on a chair as she falls. It would be
very pleasant, she thinks, to curl up in a corner of a great armchair and close her
eyes. But would there be room for an armchair in the narrow tunnel? Wouldn't
it knock against the cupboard doors? And if she should fall asleep, and tumble
out of the armchair, what then? But if she tumbled out of the armchair, wouldn't
she simply fall through the air, as she is doing now? Again Alice feels that she is
growing confused, and she decides to rest by raising her hands, interlocking her
fingers, and leaning her cheek on her clasped hands. For a while she falls this
way, with her eyes closed and her head resting lightly on her hands.

As in a dream, Alice remembers: she was sitting on the bank beside her sister. It
was hot, even in the shade. Her legs hurt from sitting on the ground, her stockings
itched, a gnat kept bumping against her hair. Her sister sat motionless over her
book and refused to look up—even her fingers gripping the edges of the book
were motionless, like table legs with claws gripping a ball, and her neck was bent
in a tense, unnatural way, which meant that she didn't want to be disturbed in
her reading. The grass was tickly and sharp. Alice's skin itched, but she also felt
an inner itching, as if all her bones needed to be scratched. Of course she loved
her sister dearly, but just at that moment she would have liked to pick up a stone
and crush her sister in the eyes. She was a wicked girl, to have thoughts like that.
Her brain felt hot. Her ankles itched. Her blood itched. She felt that at any
moment she was going to split open, like a seed pod. That was when, she remembers, she heard the noise in the grass.

*   *   *

Alice, raising her head abruptly, suddenly thinks of the White Rabbit: she had seen it pop down the rabbit hole and had gone down after it. He must therefore be under her, falling as she is falling. Of course, Alice reflects, it's possible that she alone has fallen down this endless well, while the White Rabbit has remained high above, in the tunnel-like part of the rabbit hole before the sudden drop. It's also possible that the White Rabbit has fallen much more swiftly than she, and has long ago come to the bottom, if there *is* a bottom. But Alice doesn't recall any other opening in the tunnel-like part of the rabbit hole; and the maps, the cupboards, the bookshelves all suggest a familiar, much-frequented portion of the White Rabbit's home. And then, there is actually no reason to think that the White Rabbit should fall more quickly than she. It is therefore very likely that the White Rabbit is just below her, falling in the dark; and so certain does her reasoning strike her that, looking down into the dark, she seems to see a faint motion there, in the blackness through which she is already passing.

Why, of course, Alice thinks to herself: the White Rabbit lives here. I am falling through the White Rabbit's home. Why hadn't she thought of it just that way before? But what a curious sort of home it was—more like a chimney, really. Alice has never heard of a chimney with maps and cupboards on the walls; it would never do to start a fire here. Is it perhaps an entrance hall? But what sort of entrance hall can it be, with no place to leave your visiting card and no stand to put your umbrella in? Is it a stairway, then? Alice wonders whether a stairway must have stairs in it, in order to be a stairway. And as she continues falling she looks with sudden interest, as if searching for a clue, at the crowded walls, where she sees a glass-covered engraving of two dogs fighting over the nest of a heron; a wall bracket shaped like a swan with lifted wings, supporting a marble statuette of Whittington Listening to the Bells of London: he is seated on a block carved with the word WHITTINGTON, his right hand is raised, his forefinger is pointing up, his head is cocked to one side; and a marble shelf holding a clock: the round dial is set in a dark blue porcelain vase surmounted by two white porcelain angels, and the vase rests on a pediment decorated with pink porcelain flowers. On the pediment, on each side of the vase, sits a naked child with flowers in his lap; one child holds up a butterfly, the other clutches an arrow. The hands are pointing to 2:05, and Alice wonders, as she falls past, whether the time is the same as the time on the bank, under the tree, where her sister sits reading, or whether it is some other time.

Falling through darkness, Alice imagines herself rising: past the clock, past the bottle of ginger beer, past the shield-shaped mirror, where she sees her hair pressed to the sides of her head, past the cupboard with the jar of raspberry jam, past so many shelves and maps and pictures that they begin to slide into each other like the dissolving views in the Polytechnic, higher and higher, until she reaches the place where the horizontal tunnel begins—and pulling herself onto the path, she makes her way through the dark toward a distant lightness, which reveals itself suddenly as the opening of the rabbit hole. Alice climbs out of the hole under the hedge into the brilliant day. Sunlight burns down on the field. The sky is the troubling blue of stained-glass windows or magic lantern slides. Across a field of knee-high grass she sees her sister reading a book on a sloping bank in the shade of a beech tree. The beech, the bank, the sister are very still, as if they are made of porcelain. Alice runs across the field with her hair streaming out behind her and comes to the shady bank. All is still. Her sister does not move, does not raise her eyes from the book. Over the far fields the bright blue sky burns down. All is still.

On her sister's lap, Alice lies dreaming. Leafshadows move on her face and arms. She is far from the long grass bending in the wind, from the pool rippling to the waving of the reeds, from the sheep bells tinkling, the cries of the shepherd boy, the lowing of the cows in the distance. Alice's sister doesn't want to disturb her sleep and sits very still in the warm shade of the bank. It is a hot, drowsy day. When Alice fell asleep, Alice's sister continued reading for a while, but now she has laid the book aside on the grass, for she is feeling a little sleepy herself, and it's difficult to read for very long without changing the position of your arm and hands, which she doesn't wish to do for fear of waking Alice. She watches Alice breathing gently in and out. Strands of hair lie rippling over Alice's cheek and shoulder; a single hair, escaping from the rest, curves across her cheek and lies at the corner of her mouth. Her forehead is smooth, but a slight tension shows between the eyebrows, which are darker than her hair: Alice is closed deeply in sleep. In the warm shade her sister feels drowsy, but she knows she must not sleep: she must watch over Alice, here on the shady bank. Sleep is strange, Alice's sister thinks to herself: you are there and not there. Alice seems far away, like a princess in a tower. Alice's sister would like to pick up her book again, but her hand remains motionless; she would like to shift her position, for her left leg is beginning to tingle, but she does not move. It is very quiet. Are we mistaken to see in the brightness and stillness of this afternoon an echo of the afternoon on the Isis? In the brightness a darkness forms: the tunnel is a shadow cast by the sunny day. May we perhaps think of a story as an internal shadow, a leap into the dark? In a distant field, cows are lowing. Under a shady tree, Alice's sister keeps watch. Deeply Alice lies sleeping.

A long, low hall lit by a row of oil lamps hanging from the ceiling. A row of many doors, evenly spaced, all around the hall. In the middle of the hall a small three-legged table made of glass: a tiny gold key lies on top. On the right-hand wall, a dark red curtain hanging to the floor. Behind the curtain, but not yet visible, a small door about fifteen inches high. Behind the small door, a garden of bright flowers and cool fountains. In the left-hand wall, rear, an opening: the entrance to a dark corridor or passage. The long passage leads to an unseen heap of sticks and dry leaves. Above the heap, a shaft, well, or vertical tunnel, stretching up into blackness.

Alice, falling, imagines that the tunnel comes to an end in a heap of sticks and dry leaves. In the instant that her foot touches the first stick, she realizes two things: that the tunnel does not exist, and that she is about to wake up with her head in her sister's lap. And indeed, already through the black wall she can see a shimmer of sun, the cupboards and maps are growing translucent, she can hear the tinkle of sheep bells in the fields. With a sharp, sudden motion of her mind she banishes the heap of sticks and dry leaves. And as when, in a darkened room, a heavy church or stone bridge becomes airy and impalpable, staining your hand with color as you pass your arm through the magic lantern's beam of dust-swirling light, so Alice's foot passes soundlessly through the heap of sticks and dry leaves, and she continues falling. Is it possible, Alice wonders, to resist the tug of the upper world, which even now, as she falls in darkness, entices her to wake? For should she wake, she would find herself on the bank, with itching bones, beside her sister, who will still be reading her book without pictures or conversations. Alice wonders whether it is possible to fall out of the bottom of a dream, into some deeper place. She would like to fall far, very far, so far that she will separate herself forever from the dreamer above, by whose waking she doesn't wish to be disturbed. Have they anything in common, really? Sooner or later the girl in her sister's lap will wake and rub her eyes. And in that moment she will sweep away the tunnel walls, the cupboards, the maps, the dark, replacing them with the tree, the book, the sun-dappled shade. But for dream-Alice the tree, the book, the sun-dappled shade are only a trembling and shimmering, a vanishing—for here there are only the hard walls of the tunnel, the solid shelves, the glistening glass jars, the lifted hair, the wind of her slow falling. And who's to say, Alice thinks to herself, that one's more a dream than the other? And is it possible, Alice wonders, that she will stop falling only when she releases herself utterly from the upper world, with its flickers of sunlight, its murmur of sheep bells, its green-blue shimmer of field and sky? Then in her toes she will feel the tingle of the end of falling. And with a sense of urgency, as if only now has she begun to fall, Alice bends her mind downward toward the upstreaming dark, looking expectantly at a map showing the Division of English Land by the Peace of 886 A.D. between King Alfred and the Danes, at a shelf on which sits a glass-domed arrangement of artificial leaves and flowers composed of knitting wool stitched over wire frames, at a painting in a carved gilt frame: in a parlor window-nook a woman with her hair parted in the middle is sitting in a maroon armchair with buttoned upholstery and an exposed frame of polished mahogany; in her lap she holds knitting needles and the beginning of a gray shawl, but her hands are idle, she is looking out the window; one gray strand leads to a ball of yarn on the floor, where a black kitten with green eyes and tilted head lifts one paw as if to strike the yarn-ball; the room is dark brown, but sunlight pours through the open window; in the yard stand blossoming apple trees; through the trees we see glimpses of a sun-flooded field; a brown stream, glinting with sunlight, winds like a path into the shimmering distance, vanishes into a dark wood.

ANGELA CARTER

Ashputtle: or, the Mother's Ghost

British author Angela Carter is one of the finest writers in the English language, and a veritable master of fnatasy fiction. Born in South Yorkshire in 1940, Carter published her first novel, *Shadow Dance*, in 1965; won the John Llewellyn Rhys Prize for her second novel, *The Magic Toyshop*; and won the Somerset Maugham Award for her third novel, *Several Perceptions*. She has since published several novels including *Heroes and Villains*, *The Infernal Desire Machines of Dr. Hoffman* and *Nights at the Circus*, several collections of short stories, plus two works of nonfiction: *The Sadeian Woman* and *Nothing Scared*. Of particular interest to fantasy readers are her translations of the fairy stores of Charles Perrault, and her collection of "adult fairy tales," *The Bloody Chamber*, from which her screenplay for the movie "The Company of Wolves" was drawn.

In *The Bloody Chamber*, and in the story that follows, Carter brilliantly reworks fairy tale motifs, infusing them with a dark sensuality and walking the fine line between fantasy and horror. It is a great pleasure to reprint "Ashputtle: or, The Mother's Ghost" here from its original publication in the March 13th issue of *The Village Voice*.

—T.W.

Although I haven't read them for a long time, I suspect that all fairy tales have their dark sides. Carter has been deft at stripping traditional fairy tales to their bare bones and rebuilding them, sometimes from the inside out, sometimes from a different point of view. Here, she deconstructs the tale of Cinderella, delving behind the masks of the "evil" stepmother and stepsisters with a feminist interpretation, attributing very believable motives to the participants.

—E.D.

Ashputtle: or, the Mother's Ghost

ANGELA CARTER

a) THE MUTILATED GIRLS

But although you can easily center the story not on Ashputtle but on the mutilated stepsisters, can think of it as a story about cutting bits off women so that they will *fit in*, nevertheless the story always begins with Ashputtle's mother, as though it is really always the story of her mother, even if, at the beginning of the story, she is already at death's door: "A rich man's wife fell sick, and, feeling that her end was near, she called her only daughter to her bedside."

Note the absence of the husband/father. Although the woman is defined by her relation to him ("a rich man's wife"), the daughter is unambiguously hers, as if hers alone, and the entire drama concerns only women, takes place almost exclusively among women, is a battle between two groups of women, on the one hand, Ashputtle and her mother, and, on the other, the stepmother and *her* daughters.

It is a drama between two female families in opposition to one another because of their rivalry over men (husband/father, husband/son), who seem no more than passive victims of their fancy and yet whose significance is absolute because it is ("a rich man," "a king's son") purely economic.

Ashputtle's father, the old man, is the first object of their desire and their dissension; the stepmother snatches him from the dead mother before her corpse is cold, as soon as her grip loosens. Then there is the young man, the potential bridegroom, the hypothetical son-in-law, for whose possession the mothers fight, using their daughters as instruments of war or as surrogates in the business of mating.

If the men, and the bank balances for which they stand, are the passive victims of the two grown women, then the girls, all three, are animated solely by the wills of their mothers. Even if Ashputtle's mother dies at the beginning of the story, her status as one of the dead only makes her position more authoritative; the mother's ghost dominates the narrative and is, in a real sense, the motive center, the event that makes all the other events happen.

The mother assures the daughter: "I shall always look after you and always be with you."

At this point, Ashputtle is nameless. She is her mother's daughter. That's all. It is the stepmother who names her Ashputtle, as a joke, and, in doing so, wipes out her real name, whatever that is, banishes her from the family, exiles her from the shared table to the lonely hearth, among the cinders, removes her contingent but honorable status as daughter and gives her, instead, the contingent but disreputable status of servant.

Her mother told Ashputtle she would always look after her but, untrustworthy, she died and the father married again, and gave Ashputtle an imitation mother with daughters of her own whom she loves with the same fierce passion as Ashputtle's mother did and still, posthumously, does, as we shall find out.

Now comes the vexed question: who shall be the daughters of the house? "Mine shall!" declares the stepmother and sets the freshly named nondaughter Ashputtle to sweep and scrub and sleep on the hearth while her own daughters lie between clean sheets in Ashputtle's bed. Ashputtle, no longer known as the daughter of her mother or of her father, either, goes by a dry, dirty, cindery nickname, for everything has turned to dust and ashes.

Meanwhile, the false mother sleeps in the bed where the real mother died and is, presumably, pleasured by the husband/father in that bed (unless there is no pleasure in it for her). We are not told what the father/husband does but we can make this assumption, that they share a bed.

And what can the real mother do? Burn as she might with love and anger, she is dead and buried.

The father, in this story, is a mystery to me. Is he so besotted with his new wife that he cannot see how his daughter is soiled with kitchen refuse and filthy from her ashy bed and always hard at work? If he sensed there was a drama at hand, he was content to leave the entire production to the women for, absent as he might be, always remember it is in *his* house that Ashputtle sleeps on the cinders, and he is the invisible link that binds both sets of mothers and daughters in their violent equation. He is the unmoved mover, the unseen organizing principle, like God, and, like God, up he pops in person, one fine day, to introduce an essential plot device.

Without the absent father, there would be no story because there would have been no conflict.

If they had been able to put aside these differences and discuss everything amicably, they'd have combined to expel the father. Then all the women could have slept in the one bed.

This is the essential plot device introduced by the father: he says, "I am about to take a business trip. What presents would my three girls like me to bring back for them?"

Note that: his *three* girls.

It occurs to me that perhaps the stepmother's daughters were really, all the time, his own daughters, just as much his own daughters as Ashputtle, his "natural" daughters, as they say, as though there is something inherently unnatural about legitimacy. *That* would realign the forces in the story. It would make his connivance with the ascendancy of the other girls more plausible. It would make the speedy marriage, the stepmother's hostility, more probable.

But it would also transform the story into something else, because it would provide motivation, and so on; it would mean I'd have to provide a past for all these people, that I would have to equip them with three dimensions, with tastes and memories, and I would have to think of things for them to eat and wear and say. It would transform "Ashputtle" from the bare necessity of fairy tale, with its characteristic copula formula, "and then," to the emotional and technical complexity of bourgeois realism. They would have to learn to think. Everything would change.

I will stick with what I know.

What presents do his three girls want?

"Bring me a silk dress," said his eldest girl. "Bring me a string of pearls," said the middle one. What about the third one, the forgotten one, called out of the kitchen on a charitable impulse and drying her hands, raw with housework, on her apron, bringing with her the smell of old fire?

"Bring me the first branch that knocks against your hat on the way home," said Ashputtle.

Why did she ask for that? Did she make an informed guess at how little he valued her? Or had a dream told her to use this random formula of unacknowledged desire, to allow blind chance to choose her present for her? Unless it was her mother's ghost, awake and restlessly looking for a way home, that came into the girl's mouth and spoke the request for her.

He brought her back a hazel twig. She planted it on her mother's grave and watered it with tears. It grew into a hazel tree. When Ashputtle came out to weep upon her mother's grave, the turtledove crooned: "I'll never leave you, I'll always protect you."

Then Ashputtle knew that the turtledove was her mother's ghost and she herself was still her mother's daughter and although she had wept and wailed and longed to have her mother back again, now her heart sank a little to find out that her mother, though dead, was no longer gone and henceforward she must do her mother's bidding.

Came the time for that curious fair they used to hold in that country, when all the resident virgins went to dance in front of the king's son so that he could pick out the girl he wanted to marry.

The turtledove was mad for that, for her daughter to marry the prince. You might think her own experience of marriage would have taught her to be wary but no, needs must, what else is a girl to do? The turtledove was mad for her daughter to marry so she flew in and picked up the new silk dress with her beak, dragged it to the open window, threw it down to Ashputtle. She did the same with the string of pearls. Ashputtle had a good wash under the pump in the yard, put on her stolen finery and crept out the back way, secretly, to the dancing grounds, but the stepsisters had to stay home and sulk because they had nothing to wear.

The turtledove stayed close to Ashputtle, pecking her ears to make her dance vivaciously, so that the prince would see her, so that the prince would love her, so that he would follow her and find the clue of the fallen slipper, for the story is not complete without the ritual humiliation of the other woman and the mutilation of her daughters.

The search for the foot that fits the slipper is essential to the enactment of this ritual humiliation.

The other woman wants that young man desperately. She would do anything to catch him. Not losing a daughter, but gaining a son. She wants a son so badly she is prepared to cripple her daughters. She takes up a carving knife and chops off her elder daughter's big toe, so that her foot will fit the little shoe.

Imagine.

Brandishing the carving knife, the woman bears down on her child, who is as distraught as if she had not been a girl but a boy and the old woman was after a more essential portion than a toe. No! she screams. Mother! No! Not the knife! No! But off it comes, all the same, and she throws it in the fire, among the ashes, where Ashputtle finds it, wonders at it, and feels both awe and fear at the phenomenon of mother love.

Mother love, which winds about these daughters like a shroud.

The prince saw nothing familiar in the face of the tearful young woman, one shoe off, one shoe on, displayed to him in triumph by her mother, but he said: "I promised I would marry whomever the shoe fitted so I will marry you," and they rode off together.

The turtledove came flying round and did not croon or coo to the bridal pair but sang a horrid song: "Look! look! there's blood in the shoe!"

The prince returned the ersatz ex-fiancée at once, angry at the trick, but the stepmother hastily lopped off her other daughter's heel and pushed *that* poor foot into the bloody shoe as soon as it was vacant so, nothing for it, a man of his word, the prince helped up the new girl and once again he rode away.

Back came the nagging turtledove: "look!" And, sure enough, the shoe was full of blood again.

(The shoe full of blood. Horrible. An open wound.)

"Let Ashputtle try," said the eager turtledove.

So now Ashputtle must put her foot into this hideous receptacle, still slick and warm and wet as it is, for nothing in any of the texts of this tale suggests the prince washed it out between the fittings. It was an ordeal in itself to put a naked foot into that bloody shoe but her mother, the turtledove, urged her to do so in a soft, cooing croon that could not be denied.

If she does not plunge without revulsion into this open wound, she won't be fit to marry. That is the song of the turtledove, while the other mad mother stood impotently by.

Ashputtle's foot, the size of the bound foot of a Chinese woman; a stump. Already an amputee, she put her foot in it.

"Look! look!" cried the turtledove in triumph, even as she betrayed the secret of her ghostly nature by becoming progressively more and more immaterial as Ashputtle stood up in the shoe and commenced to walk around, squelching but proud. "Her foot fits the shoe like a corpse fits a coffin!"

"See how well I look after you, my darling!"

b) THE BURNED CHILD

A burned child lived in the ashes. No, not really burned, more charred, a little bit charred, like a stick half-burned and picked off the fire. She looked like charcoal and ashes because she lived in the ashes since her mother died and the hot ashes burned her so she was scabbed and scarred. The burned child lived on the hearth, covered in ashes, as if she were still mourning.

After her mother died and was buried, her father forgot the mother and forgot the child and married the woman who used to rake the ashes, and that was why the child lived in the unraked ashes, and there was nobody to brush her hair so it stuck out like a mat nor to wipe the dirt off her scabbed face and she had no heart to do it for herself but she raked the ashes and slept beside the little cat and got the burned bits from the bottom of the pot to eat, scraping them out, squatting on the floor, by herself in front of the fire, not as if she were human, because she was still in mourning.

Her mother was dead and buried but felt perfect exquisite pain of love when she looked up through the earth and saw the burned child covered in ashes.

"Milk the cow, burned child, and bring back all the milk," said the stepmother, who used to rake the ashes and milk the cow, once upon a time, but the burned child did all that, now.

The ghost of the mother went into the cow.

"Drink milk, grow fat," said the mother's ghost.

The burned child pulled on the udder and drank enough milk before she took the bucket back and nobody saw, and time passed, she drank milk every day, she grew fat, she grew breasts, she grew up.

There was a man the stepmother wanted and asked into the kitchen to get his dinner but she made the burned child cook it, although the stepmother did all the cooking before. After the burned child cooked the dinner the stepmother sent her off to milk the cow.

"I want that man for myself," said the burned child to the cow.

The cow let down more milk, and more, and more, enough for the girl to have a drink and wash her face and wash her hands. When she washed her face, she washed the scabs off and now she was not burned at all, but the cow was empty.

"Give your own milk, next time," said the ghost of the mother inside the cow. "You've milked me dry."

The little cat came by. The ghost of the mother went into the cat.

"Your hair wants doing," said the cat. "Lie down."

The little cat unpicked her raggy lugs with its clever paws until the burned child's hair hung down nicely but it had been so snagged and tangled that the cat's claws were all pulled out before it was finished.

"Comb your own hair, next time," said the cat. "You've maimed me."

The burned child was clean and combed but stark naked.

There was a bird sitting in the apple tree. The ghost of the mother left the cat and went into the bird. The bird struck its own breast with its beak. Blood poured down onto the burned child under the tree. It ran over her shoulders and covered her front and covered her back. When the bird had no more blood, the burned child got a red silk dress.

"Make your own dress, next time," said the bird. "I'm through with that bloody business."

The burned child went into the kitchen to show herself to the man. She was not burned any more, but lovely. The man left off looking at the stepmother and looked at the girl.

"Come home with me and let your stepmother stay and rake the ashes," he said to her and off they went. He gave her a house and money. She did all right.

"Now I can go to sleep," said the ghost of the mother. "Now everything is all right."

c) THE TRAVELLING COSTUME

The cruel stepmother burned the orphan's face with a poker because she did not rake the ashes. The girl went to her mother's grave. Deep in the earth her mother said:

"It must be raining. Or else it is snowing. Unless there is a heavy dew tonight."

"It isn't raining, it isn't snowing, it's too early for the dew. But my tears are falling on your grave, mother."

The dead woman waited until night came. Then she climbed out and went to the house. The stepmother slept on a feather bed but the burned child slept on the hearth among the ashes. When the dead woman kissed her, the scar vanished. The girl woke up. The dead woman gave her a red dress.

"I had it when I was your age, I used it for travelling."

The girl put the travelling costume on. The dead woman took worms out of her eye sockets; they turned to jewels. The girl put on a handful of rings.

"Sell them as you need to."

They went together to the grave.

"Step into my coffin."

She trusted her mother. She stepped into the coffin. At once it turned into a coach and horses. The horses stamped, eager to be gone.

"Now go and seek your fortune, darling."

ADRIAN COLE
Face to Face

Adrian Cole lives in the West Country of Great Britain. He is the author of over fifty short stories and several novels mixing, science fiction, fantasy and horror, including *Blood Red Angel* and *The Dream Lords* trilogy.

"Face to Face," from *Dark Voices 2* (the revitalized *Pan Books of Horror*), starts off firmly in the science fiction genre and gradually develops into something quite different. It's what I call techno-horror.

—E.D.

Face to Face

ADRIAN COLE

When he woke up that morning, he had no idea anything was seriously wrong with him.

His head was stuffed with anxieties about the day's work ahead of him. *Damn Cartelli.* Where in hell was he? The senior programmer, of all people, gone for a week. No word, not even a call. They'd tried to contact him, but it was useless.

Holland couldn't believe Cartelli would just up and quit for another firm, not this way. It wasn't his style. Oh, he'd leave for a better offer, like most people. But he'd do it openly. No reason for cloak-and-dagger.

So now the work was piling up. How was Holland supposed to load up the new database on his own? He and Cartelli had put weeks into devising the program, a slick, sophisticated system that would really streamline things in Client Control. But Cartelli was the brains behind it, the *imagination*. Holland knew that he himself could follow a lead, take up someone else's idea and shape it. But the program was Cartelli's baby. Without him, it was going to be difficult to get the best from it.

Holland had put in too many hours since Cartelli's disappearance already for the good of his health. His head throbbed as he got out of bed. No good squinting at his watch as he fumbled it on. It was 7 A.M. and no amount of glaring was going to change that.

Dazedly he walked into the bathroom. The water felt good as he sloshed it over him. Cold, almost refreshing. He ungummed his eyes and studied the mirror. He looked blurred, which was how he felt. *Damn Cartelli.*

He ran the sink half full of hot water, getting ready for a shave. His morning shadow didn't look so bad today. He stroked his chin. It was smooth, as though he had already had a shave. He looked at himself more closely in the mirror. No sign of dark stubble. Well, that was fine. One less task.

Coffee was all he could take for breakfast. He left soon after.

On the Underground he stared vacantly ahead of him, not seeing the commuters packed in with him, functioning automatically, hardly thinking. But the database program began to loom large before his eyes, the endless information, the individual details, the details of individuals. Interlocking, interrelating, merging. Personal files, medical files. *Medical Files.* For a moment there was something . . .

Someone nudged him, an accident. They were forcing their way in, the tube too full. The usual morning crush. He murmured an unheard apology.

In the foyer of the glass building where he worked, he found himself glancing in a mirror. He felt guilty at not having had a shave. Absurd. But as he looked at his face, there was no sign of stubble, no dark stain on the cheeks and chin. He took the elevator before someone wondered at his odd self-attention.

He was seated at the console before anything else registered. He took out his tabulations, the streams of figures. But it was a language he spoke fluently.

The screen came on, a white rectangle. He saw himself reflected in it and leaned forward. His reflection was very clear, if not exactly a mirror image. He found himself studying his eyes. There were no lines, no signs of strain, no crow's feet. Same with the mouth. The visual display unit was flattering him. A reward for working together.

He punched in his requirements. The face dissolved, to be replaced with Cartelli's program, information. People as figures, as data. *Damn Cartelli.* Where was the bastard? He should be here. Helping with this monster.

His fingers began accessing Cartelli's file. Maybe there would be something here to indicate what the fool was up to.

FILE NOT FOUND.

The words blinked. Holland re-punched. But the message remained stubbornly fixed in the center of the screen. Mildly annoyed, Holland tried to access the file another way, by-passing the system. But half an hour later he was forced to admit that Cartelli's personal file was missing, just like the man himself. He tried the back-up system. Exasperated, he went to the old manual files. Nothing.

Another hour, and some terse exchanges with the secretaries, taught him that every record they had of Cartelli was gone. Only Cartelli could have done this. But how had he got his own manual files out? Not many people knew that there were any hard copy files left anyway.

Holland checked on other files. They were all there. He looked at his own. It was there.

Curiosity drew him deeper into the labyrinth of the file. Medical details. He knew them well enough. Mundane stuff. His health was good, apart from the additional stresses of the job. He didn't need a professional opinion in order to update the file.

There was a page of data missing.

It was blank, although on the screen there was something, ghostly lines, as though data were fading. A stupid concept. He stared at it. His own face loomed out of the screen, a slightly misshapen copy. He drew back.

He ran on through the file, checking to see if anything else was missing. There wasn't. He checked out the back-up. It was complete, so he restored the original file's missing page. For some curious reason it made him feel more secure.

The rest of the morning wore on remorselessly. He pumped in as much information as he could, building up the huge database. Apart from the select few clients, there were several thousand on the payroll of the company, and their paper files came in all kinds of sizes. Because of the complexity of Cartelli's program, converting the paper files could only be done by Holland and Cartelli himself. Part of the problem was the security.

The kind of medical research done by the company was highly confidential. Only the senior employees knew the full range of cosmetic surgery undertaken by the company, themselves under private contract. Holland and Cartelli were party to controversial stuff. Maybe that had something to do with Cartelli's disappearance.

Holland saw his superior, Adamley, for ten minutes that afternoon. No news of Cartelli.

"Something I don't know about?" said Holland. "Is he in trouble?"

Adamley shrugged. He seemed more interested in the streets of the city far below the plate glass. "Tell me, Holland. How safe is this client and personnel database you're building?"

"How easy is it to access? There's only the two of us can get in. When it's ready, the company can designate its users. No one else will be able to get in. It will be as tight as any system can be. And you can lock me and Cartelli out as well."

Adamley turned. There was no emotion, no hint of concern, though Holland knew it must be under his flesh like a barb. "Can you alter the system, as of now?"

Holland knew what he wanted. "Lock Cartelli out?"

"It's no use if he can access that information. Not if he's gone. He could be with anyone. With what he knows, the system would be a dangerous tool. In the wrong hands."

Adamley didn't have to elaborate. Holland knew what he meant. He could smell the stink of fear that competition brought. "I can alter it. Redirect all the prime access functions. I'll be the only one, though."

"We'll find someone else to work with you."

They would. It would be as dangerous to have only one man running the system as having Cartelli back if he was working for someone else. An industrial spy, whatever they called it.

Holland snatched a brief snack for lunch. A hot, flaking pasty and a pint of shandy. He didn't like to drink at dinner time, it broke up his concentration. In the noisy pub, he saw himself in a floor-to-ceiling mirror that he had always ignored in the past. This time he felt curiously uncomfortable sitting next to himself. The mirror was dirty, smeared. He couldn't see his face clearly.

He struggled with the pasty. It had gone cold, the pitifully small chunks of meat congealing. He couldn't swallow them properly, even with the help of the shandy.

As he pushed through the tables to leave, he abruptly sensed someone behind him, watching him. It came to him with an unreasonable force that it was Cartelli, hidden in the crowd. Turning, he saw only the contorted image of himself in the huge mirror, faceless and pathetic.

The afternoon wore on dully, more information swallowed by the hungry database. Holland was beginning to pick up on some of the refinements. Cartelli had linked things together superbly, the logic of the program exceptional.

It was while he was scanning the layouts and the intricate sub-data menus, that Holland came across the rogue file. Rogue because it had no business to be there. Cartelli had been amusing himself, or perhaps he had been trying to improve the program through a trial and error pattern. But this file should have been wiped off when he'd finished.

Intrigued, Holland studied the file. It was unusual. Instead of pulling information about a given subject from a number of different sources, this file seemed to be pulling information about a number of *subjects* and . . . what, creating a fact file on them? He couldn't be sure. He asked the machine for a graphic projection.

And gasped. But then he realized that Cartelli had evidently been having some fun. It was as though he had been playing the part of some mad surgeon, cobbling together a lunatic conglomerate of human organs and tissues. It might even have been the basis for some fantastic game, something for the open market. Who knew? It might have been the prototype for something very lucrative. There had been no limits to Cartelli's imagination.

Holland came out of the program, but could not bring himself to erase it from the computer's memory. Maybe he'd play with it himself sometime.

He went home tired, haggard. It was late.

He couldn't make any sense out of the film he tried to watch on TV. He flipped channels but everything was merging into one, and he found it impossible to keep track of the conversations, which might as well have been in a foreign tongue.

In the kitchen, cutting himself a late sandwich, he nicked his finger with the breadknife. He sucked on the blood for a moment. Under the glare of the bulb, he examined the minor damage. But he forgot the cut at once: his fingers were very smooth, printless. Where were the whirls, the many lines? Instinctively he stroked the side of his face. No five o'clock shadow. *After two days?* Still no stubble.

He looked at his hands again. If a gypsy had wanted to read his palms, he thought with a mirthless smile, she would have been disappointed. There was nothing there, as though every line, every crease, had been wiped off.

I need a good sleep, he thought. It came easily.

Adamley reached for the phone jerkily, surprising himself. Maybe his nerves were getting frayed by this whole business. But he recognized his own relief when he heard the voice on the other end of the line.

It was Holland.

"It's 9:30 A.M., Holland." It was an admonition.

"I'd have called you earlier, Mr. Adamley, but I've been asleep since 5:30. I was working from home until the early hours. I want to go on. Work from home today." The voice wasn't tired: it was feverish, Holland talking too fast.

"On the program?"

"I'm working on the database. I don't need to work from hard copy, today. I'm not installing new material from our files. I'm . . . changing things in the structure. I have a modem that links my home machine to our mainframe." Holland gabbled on some more, getting into jargon that Adamley only vaguely understood.

"Okay, Holland. Do what you need to. I want the system safe. But report here tomorrow. 8:30. I want an update."

Adamley put down the phone but it rang again.

Adamley knew the efficient, cold voice of his private investigator. "Anything?"

"Cartelli's still in the country. No one has seen him leave."

"What about our competitors?"

"No one has been approached by Cartelli. None of his friends have seen him for a week. I talked to his sister, Louisa. She called on him at his flat. She has her own key. Comes and goes as she pleases."

"I know the girl. She's clean?"

"Yes, I'm sure of that. No interest in computers. No contacts. Apparently she went to the flat nine days ago and Cartelli never showed up. No note, no phone call."

"You believe she knows nothing?" said Adamley.

"She appeared to be genuinely upset at Cartelli's disappearance. I'm sure she's no actress. I didn't think she was feigning her distress. She's very alarmed. She thinks he's in trouble. Kidnapped, or something like that."

Adamley snorted. "Does she?"

"He left in a hurry, but he took nothing, and he left no mess. I've almost nothing to go on."

Adamley nodded slowly. "Okay. I want you to put a man on Holland. From now. Every step he takes."

After the conversation Adamley wondered about the new work. Pull the plug? But the cost, the money the company had pumped into it. Where the hell was Cartelli?

"Who is it?" came the voice. It sounded annoyed, like someone had been interrupted in the bath, or worse, having sex. But the girl guessed that Holland wouldn't have answered if that had been the case.

"It's Louisa. Can I see you for a moment?"

The door opened, obscuring the man beyond. Louisa went into the flat, mildly surprised by the dim lighting. There was an eerie glow to the room adjoining the main suite, as though a TV had been left on, but Louisa had seen enough of her brother at work to recognize it for what it was. Holland had been using his screen.

The door thumped shut and Louisa turned to face Holland. She was quite stunning, even in her distress. Quite a contrast to Frank Cartelli, whose face was pinched and narrow, pocked and ridged unevenly. He had often joked, with more than a suggestion of bitterness, that God had lavished so much time creating his beautiful sister that he'd had nothing but scraps left for him.

In contrast to the lovely girl, Holland looked dreadful, his face white. His eyes

were a smudge, his mouth a thin, pale gash, his nose flat. If she had not known
it was Holland, she would never have recognized him in the street.

"Where's Frank?" he said, unable to keep a note of desperation out of his voice.
It was almost a wheeze, as though he had hardly enough energy to speak.

"I came here to ask you. Don't you know?"

He shook his head, going past her and into the room with the glow. She
followed him.

"This is insane!" she told him. "He can't just have gone off like this. There's
no reason."

Holland sat down at the screen as though he had already forgotten she was
there.

"I've said nothing to the police about this, but I think they should know.
Something is wrong. Well, don't you think so? Dammit, surely you know *something*. What was he working on? He said something about surgery. Was it illegal?"

"I can't find his file," murmured Holland, fingers working at the keyboard,
fluttering incredibly fast. The screen before him was blinking, the information
changing rapidly, whole sheets of it shifting, creating new patterns.

The girl watched it for a moment as if it would hypnotize her. But she shook
her head. "His file? What does his file matter? Will it tell us where he is?"

"It might. It contains every known thing about him. Right down to the last
gene." Holland turned to her as he spoke. The light from the screen shone on
his face, flattening it.

She drew back. In the false light he was featureless, his head like a naked,
empty balloon of flesh.

But he turned back to his work.

Quickly she went to the door, shaking her head, unable to go to him to confirm
that it was a trick of the light, her tired brain. This was hopeless. Holland was
obsessed with the machines, far more than Frank had been. She would get no
sense from him.

After she had gone, Holland felt himself beginning to sway, unable to focus
on the figures in front of him. The screen was like a pool of gray water. Whatever
swam beneath its surface was well hidden.

"Mr. Adamley?"

"Yes."

"Horton, sir, in Systems. We've disconnected the link with Mr. Cartelli's home
terminal. Shall we do the same with Mr. Holland's?"

"Is he working on it?"

"He was until about midday, sir. Since then he's been signed out of his program."

"Then disconnect. If he rings you, tell him I want to see him."

"Sir."

The voice on the end of the phone sounded like that of an invalid, short of breath.
Possibly an old, old man. But it was Holland.

"Holland, are you ill?" demanded Adamley. He had had reports that Holland had been in his flat all day. Cartelli's sister had visited him, understandably, but that was all. Asking the same questions they were all asking. She knew nothing, couldn't help. She'd gone to the police. But Adamley had known they would have to be told. He had the bland cover story ready for them.

Holland's exhausted voice answered. "My terminal is off."

"I authorized that. I don't want any more work done away from this office. Is that clear?"

"I need the terminal."

"Then come in. It will be available to you until eleven tonight. After that I'm scrapping Cartelli's work. All of it."

"No! You can't!"

Adamley sat up slowly, holding the phone as though it was the key piece in a game of chess. "And why not, Holland? Why can't I wipe that program clean?"

"You'll never find him. Listen, I think I know where he is. But you must let me handle this. You must do what I ask you, Mr. Adamley."

"I'm listening." He made it sound as though he had endless patience.

"I need access to Cartelli's machine, through this one of mine. His home machine."

"No."

"Then his office machine. Switch it on, and this one of mine. Lock his office. Don't let anyone in there."

Adamley kept his voice level. "I'm sorry, Holland, but if you want to use a machine, come in here."

There was a long pause. Eventually Holland spoke with a great effort. "I have to access the program."

"Then you'd better get in *here*."

"Lock Cartelli's office until I arrive. Please."

"No one is going to touch anything. But if you know where Cartelli is, you'd better enlighten me. The police are going to want explanations. Right now I don't have any. The company is going to find this embarrassing, Holland. We don't want that."

Adamley looked at the screen. It was on, but white and empty. The Systems Manager, Horton, sat at Cartelli's desk, his face pretending indifference, though his frustration seeped through in a tell-tale pinkish hue. Nothing was happening on the screen, the program defying whatever it was Horton was trying to do.

"I can't get in without the passwords. I've tried hacking—breaking in, sir. But it's no good. It's a very secure program."

"That's how it should be," grunted Adamley.

The phone rang and Horton jumped as if he had been electrocuted. But Adamley picked it up calmly enough. It was an internal call and he'd been expecting it.

"Send him straight in."

The door opened only a moment or two later. Surprisingly it was Cartelli's sister who stood there. Slightly dishevelled, her eyes tired and accusing, she still looked attractive. Amazing that that gargoyle Cartelli could be related to her.

Behind her there was a movement, and Holland, or what Adamley took to be Holland, stood there. Was he drunk? He almost had to lean on the door frame. He had a silk scarf wrapped around his lower face, as if he had just climbed off a motor bike, an idiotic thought, as he must have driven here by car. Only his eyes showed.

Horton gaped stupidly, but Adamley made a curt, dismissive gesture and the Systems Manager left the office quickly, a suggestion of guilt in his retreat. Both Holland and the girl ignored him. She watched Adamley, but Holland had eyes only for the screen. It lured him like a siren and he moved clumsily to the desk, sitting at the keyboard.

Adamley looked at his watch. Ten to eleven. Nearly everyone else had gone home. Holland had only just made the deadline.

"He rang me," the girl said sensing the need for an explanation. "He couldn't get here on his own."

"You'd better wait outside."

"You both had," said Holland, his mouth still muffled by the scarf.

Adamley was about to say something abrupt to him. Why cover his face so ridiculously? But something in the manner of the seated man deterred him. Instead he turned back to the girl and led her gently by the elbow out of the office, closing the door as he went.

Holland sat alone with the machine.

It was a while before he was able to gather his flagging energy and begin, but when he did so, he slipped into a natural flow, his hands moving with their usual smooth rhythm over the keys.

Access files. Okay. Cartelli's was still missing. His own was there, but again there were sections missing. He checked the back-up they had built into the system. To his horror he found it incomplete. He did a routine check on other personnel files. Some of them, too, were incomplete, as if Cartelli had for some reason taken pieces away. Why had he done this? So that only he would have control of the system? It didn't make sense.

During his routine checks, Holland came across the menu that gave him the opportunity to go into the client files. At the moment only he and Cartelli had the keys to get in. This was the most confidential information in the entire building. It related to the customers, the very rich clients whose names had been replaced by codes. Adamley knew their real identities. But he was paid a great deal of money to keep them secret.

Holland entered the system of client information. The biological detail was exhaustive. Everything a surgeon could wish for. And a surgeon using the specialized equipment housed here, programmed and controlled by a computer of infinite potential, could perform miracles.

Holland sat back, his breath coming in gulps. Perform miracles. Here. In one of the theaters.

He banged at the keys, looking for something else, a schedule. Dates, coded names. Treatment. He found it.

Tonight.

Lurching out of the chair, he got to the door, his hand flapping at it. He couldn't open it, but Adamley must have heard his efforts and it swung inwards.

"Theater," muttered Holland.

Adamley glanced across at the girl. She was sitting on one of the leather seats, still tired, her hopes worn thin. Adamley's face indicated clearly that he didn't want her involved. There would be a few guards on night patrol by now. Maybe he should get them to escort her home.

Holland tried to push past him.

"Please wait here," Adamley said as calmly to the girl as he could. She looked as if she might resist, but instead nodded and shrank back, as though she had given up the fight.

In the corridor, Adamley gripped Holland's arm. "You know you're not authorized to go near the theaters. What have you found?"

"Who's Steven S.?"

Adamley scowled, his anger deepening. "That isn't your concern. The clients are not, repeat, *not* your field. They're just codes in a file."

Holland shook his head stubbornly, still struggling down the corridor. "Steven S. is lying on an operating table. Now. With a robot surgeon, a *computer*, working on his face. Wiping it clean. Starting again. With new data."

Adamley drew back from the eyes, their coldness. Still the face was covered.

"Who is Steven S.?" repeated Holland.

"That's quite impossible."

They had moved down internal flights of stairs, half in darkness now. Beyond more corridors they stopped. The theaters were near at hand, silent, listening to their coming.

"His file is missing, like Cartelli's," said Holland thickly. "Wiped from the program."

"All right," said Adamley. He looked around him, his tongue running along his lips nervously. "Steven S. is dead. He died two days ago in his sleep. Natural causes. But only a few people know. He's . . . an important official. Most of our clients are important people. Who wiped his file? His death has been kept extremely quiet. He was due to be moved tomorrow, for the funeral. He *can't* be under the knife. Who wiped his file?"

"Cartelli. But the file isn't lost."

Adamley looked appalled, unable to fathom the nonsense Holland was giving him.

"It's been transferred. On to a disk. A soft disk. Along with Cartelli's."

Holland stood outside the door of one of the theaters. Its oval window was a black mirror, Holland a distorted smudge within it. "Who is supervising Steven S.'s operation?"

"No one, you fool. The man's dead."

Holland looked up and down the corridor for guards. There were none. Operations were often performed at night in these buildings. He pushed at the theater door. It resisted, but opened inward. In the room beyond, the lights were all but out. The computer had no need of human eyes to work by.

There were steeply tiered seats dropping down to a balcony overlooking the well of the surgery area. The two men went to the balcony, peering down into the glow. On the operating table beneath them, there was a body stretched out, covered in a spotless white sheet, only the head exposed. Delicate metal arms hovered over it, and light winked from the paper-thin surgical tools that dipped towards it.

Adamley looked appalled, his face terrible. "This isn't authorized!" he said in a whisper. "We have to stop it."

Holland shook his head. "The program is locked in to finish." He led the way round the balcony to an area of consoles, flicking on one of the screens. Its green light bathed the two men as they watched.

"Can't you do anything?" said Adamley. Should he ring for the night watch? They'd no reason to be around.

Holland ignored him. He worked at the keyboard. In a while he nodded. "They're here."

"What do you mean?"

"Cartelli copied his file and others on to disks. Then he brought them here. Inserted them in the operating computer, under a time lock. You, above all, know what we do here."

Adamley grimaced. Holland made it sound corrupt. "Holland, this is state-of-art cosmetic surgery. You understand our reasons for secrecy. Few people can afford it—"

"Yes, it's not for the likes of Cartelli and the ordinary working man. They have to live with their ugliness."

"Don't be a fool." But something in Holland's words alerted Adamley. He looked into the operating well. *Who is on the table?*

Holland tapped the screen, the file, the name in the upper right hand corner. "You've got to stop him—"

Slowly Holland undid the silk scarf that he had so carefully arranged about his lower face. As it came away, the green light suffused his smooth, alien features. The nose had almost disappeared, the mouth a tiny opening, far too small. The skin was like glass, polished and unblemished.

"I couldn't stop *this*," said Holland.

Adamley drew back in alarm. "What's wrong with you?"

"You tell me. I can't explain it. My files are incomplete, somehow corrupted by Cartelli's meddling. That goes for anyone else whose file he's changed. He's taken what he needs from us. And he's programmed that computer down there to fuse the information into a new face. For himself. All the files have been loaded."

Adamley stared down at the equipment. Could he see beads of blood on those precise blades? How far had it gone? "But what will he look like? Not—the man who died?"

Holland shook his head. "No, he's more subtle than that. Which is why he used other components. Whatever face Cartelli emerges with, you won't recognize it. It'll be new. But isn't that what this *art* is all about?"

Adamley drew in a long breath. He seemed to have brought his anger, his fear, under control. "Very well. When the machines have finished, I'll deal with the situation." He glanced at Holland, who was again fitting the scarf to his face. "And I'll see that you're given every opportunity to—"

Holland gestured vaguely with his arm, settling back to watch the patient work of the operating computer. In a moment he was alone.

Something nagged at his mind as he sat there. Cartelli's plan was too good. Too simple. Yet it would have worked. He would have got out without discovery, possibly a little embarrassment. No doubt he had another good job lined up. A man of his talent. And he would have chosen a face that would ensure him the attention he had never had. As many beautiful women as he desired. Holland shook his head. For a man of vision, it was a curiously adolescent dream.

Holland saw the slender arms of the robot rise above the table, folding back like the intricate limbs of a huge insect. Now he could see the exposed head. He leaned as far over the balcony as he dared to get a better view of the face.

There was none. The skin was pulled like the surface of a balloon over the face. Beneath it there were shapes, knuckling up as though the new face would break out of its skin like a butterfly emerging from a cocoon. Holland waited.

The layer of skin began to darken, peeling away, dead flesh.

Dead flesh? The words reverberated inside Holland's mind. *Dead flesh.* Cartelli had chosen as his subject for the main source of his operation a man who, two days ago, had died. But Cartelli had prepared his program days before that. He couldn't have known that the man would be dead. What difference would it make?

Holland watched, fear turning to shock as the new face thrust up from the blackened skin around it. One hugely bloated eye opened, opaque as a mirror, and the sagging mouth yawned as it tried to form words, the tongue flapping wetly, immense and obscene. Blood seeped from the distorted lips, which were like two engorged maggots, about to split down their length.

As the theater doors below were unlocked from outside the room, the thing on the bed at last managed a sound. Holland could not be sure whether it was a groan of agony or a distorted howl of bitter rage.

KAREL ČAPEK
The Dog's Tale

Karel Čapek (1890–1938) was a journalist, novelist and playright in Prague during a time of cultural renaissance before World War I and after the war when Czechoslovakia gained independence. He won international acclaim for his play *R.U.R.* (in which he coined the word "robot") and is best known for his book *War with the Newts*. He is also the author of the trilogy of novels: *Hordubal, Meteor,* and *An Ordinary Life*. Čapek has been described as a Czech Vonnegut or Swift, and described his own work as "literary Cubism, an attempt to discover the truth through the adoption of a variety of perspectives."

1990 marked the centennial celebration of Čapek's birth and was the occasion for Northwestern University Press's first English-language edition of Čapek's charming, humorous (and ultimately political) fairy and folk tales. *Nine Fairy Tales by Karel Čapek and One Thrown In for Good Measure* comes complete with the original Thurberesque line illustrations by Čapek's brother and is translated from the Czechoslovakian by Dagmar Herrmann.

—T.W.

The Dog's Tale

KAREL ČAPEK

Back in the days when my grandfather's wagon used to make the rounds of the villages in our parish, bringing bread to the villagers, and then returning to the mill with a wagonful of golden grain, everybody knew Peanut. Peanut, they would have told you, was the little dog that sat on the coach box beside old Šulitka the horseman and looked as if he were in charge of the whole business. And when the wagon slowed down, struggling up the hillside, Peanut started to bark, the wheels began to churn faster, old Šulitka cracked his whip, Ferda and Žanka, my grandpa's two horses, quickened their gallop, and the wagon clattered into the village in all its splendor, strewing the beautiful scent of God's bounty. Well, children, that's how the late Peanut used to ride around the whole parish.

Oh yes, in Peanut's time there were none of those cranky, crazy cars zooming everywhere. In those days one drove slowly, with class, and with a clamor. Nowadays, no driver can crack his whip or click his tongue at the horses the way the late Šulitka did—God rest his soul—and no driver has a companion as intelligent as Peanut, pushing forward, barking, and spreading terror. Today, when a car flies by it leaves behind its stench and if you look where it's gone, you can't even see it through the dust! Believe me, Peanut was a far more competent driver. A half hour before he pulled in, people pricked up their ears, sniffed, and said, "Aha!" Knowing that their bread was on the way, they would come out and stand on their doorsteps to welcome him with, "Good morning!" Then, Grandfather's wagon would roll into the village, with Šulitka clicking his tongue, and Peanut barking on the driver's seat. Hop! he would leap on Žanka's rump (did she have a rump!—God bless her!—wide as a table that could seat four people), and dance on Žanka's back, running from her collar to her tail and back to her collar again, barking with joy. "Ruff, ruff, what a drive! Žanka, Ferda and I, hurray!" Everyone marveled, "Good Lord, our daily bread's arriving, and with such pomp and glory as if the emperor himself were coming!" Well, as I said, drivers like those in Peanut's day I haven't seen since!

Did Peanut know how to bark! It sounded as if he were shooting off a gun. Bang!—to the right, at the geese who would run off in fright, not stopping till they found themselves at the market in Poličky, completely perplexed at how they had gotten there. Bang!—to the left, with such vigor that all the village pigeons flew up, circled and landed somewhere around Žaltman, close to the Prussian side of the border. That's how heartily Peanut could bark, that silly cur. It was a miracle his tail didn't fly off, as he wagged so lustily and with such joy over his mischief. Granted, he had something to be proud of. No general, mind you, not even a congressman, had that powerful a voice!

Yet, there was a time when Peanut did not know how to bark at all, although he was already quite grown, with teeth that tore up Grandpa's Sunday boots. Besides, I think I should tell you how Grandpa found Peanut (or it may have happened the other way around). Once, late at night, when Grandpa was coming home from the pub in a happy mood, singing along, perhaps to keep the evil spirits at bay, it so happened that he lost the tune and had to stop to look for it. While he was searching, he heard a whimper, a squeak, and a squeal coming from somewhere at his feet. He crossed himself and groped around to find out what it was. He felt a warm, shaggy, velvety soft little ball, that fit into the palm of his hand. As soon as he picked it up, it stopped whimpering and began sucking his finger as if it were made of honey. "I must have a look at it, whatever it is," Grandpa thought, and carried it home to the mill. Poor Grandma had been waiting for Grandpa to bid him good night, but now, even before she could bawl him out, Grandpa, the sly fellow, said, "Helen, see what I've brought you." Grandma held the furball up to the candlelight and, by golly, it was a puppy, a puny pup still blind and tawny, like a fresh hazelnut cracked out of its shell. "Now look at that. A puppy," said Grandpa. "Tell me, my dear, to whom do you belong?" Grandpa asked. Naturally, the little pup said nothing. He quivered on the table like a bundle of misery until his tail began to twitch, whimpering sorrowfully. Then, my goodness, a tiny puddle appeared beneath him, growing larger all the time, like a bad conscience. "Karl, Karl," said Grandma sternly, shaking her head. "Have you lost your mind? Without his mother, this puppy will wither away." Grandpa became frightened. "All right, Helen, now move quickly," he said, "warm some milk and get me a dinner roll." Grandma got everything ready, and Grandpa dipped a soft crumb into the milk, wrapped it up in the corner of his hanky, and made such a wonderful nipple that the puppy sucked it until his tummy looked like a drum.

"Karl, Karl," said Grandma, shaking her head again, "are you out of your mind? Tell me who'll warm the pup so he won't die of cold?" But Grandfather wasn't about to be deterred. He took the puppy and carried him straight to the stable. Good gracious, was it hot in there from all the hot air that Ferda and Žanka puffed out! Both horses had been asleep, but when their master walked in they lifted their heads and followed him with their wise, gentle eyes. "Listen, Žanka, listen, Ferda," said Grandpa, "this is Peanut. Here, take care of him, and don't harm him!" Then, he placed little Peanut on the straw in front of the horses.

Žanka sniffed the odd tiny creature and, smelling the scent of her master's hands, she whispered to Ferda, "He's all right." And so it was.

Peanut stayed in the stable. He was fed through the nipple made out of a handkerchief until his eyes opened and he could drink on his own from a little bowl. He was kept as warm as if he were with his mother and soon he grew into a rascal with a funny-looking head. Like any puppy he'd get confused: he wouldn't find his bottom to sit on, so he'd sit on his head instead, and when that would hurt, he'd wonder why. He wouldn't know what to make of his tail, so he'd chase it; he only knew how to count to two, so he'd get tangled in his four legs, and in the end he'd topple over, startled, showing his pink tongue that looked like a thin slice of ham. After all, every puppy is like, ah well, just like a little baby. Žanka and Ferda would have told you more about him—what trouble it was for them, old horses, always to be on guard for fear of treading on that silly dog. You know, my friends, a hoof is not a slipper; it needs to be lowered very softly, very gently so that a little creature on the ground doesn't squeal and whine in pain when stepped on. Children are trouble, that's what Žanka and Ferda would have told you.

Peanut grew into a really fine dog, happy and playful, just like any other. Yet, there was still something wrong with him. No one ever heard him bark or growl! All he managed was to squeal and to whine a little, but never to bark! Then one day Grandmother said to herself, "I'd like to know why this dog doesn't bark." She wondered about this for three days, walking around as if bereft of her soul. On the fourth, she said to Grandfather, "Would you know why our Peanut never barks?" Now it was Grandfather's turn to wonder. For three days he walked around shaking his head, and on the fourth, he said to Šulitka the horseman, "Do you know why Peanut never barks?" Šulitka took the question to heart. He went to the pub and pondered it for three days and three nights. When, on the fourth, he was finally ready to take a nap, his head was spinning. He called the owner over and pulled change out of his pocket to pay the bill. He kept counting the change, but the devil himself must have interfered, for he couldn't figure it out for the life of him. "Come on, Šulitka, didn't your mother teach you how to count?" asked the pub owner. At that, Šulitka stopped counting, tapped his forehead, and scurried off straight to Grandfather. "Master," he yelled at the door, "I've got it! Peanut doesn't bark because his mother never taught him how!"

"Well, I'll be . . ." said Grandpa. "You're right! Peanut never knew his mother and neither Ferda nor Žanka could ever teach him how to bark. There isn't another dog in the neighborhood . . . It certainly figures. Peanut can't even know what barking sounds like. I'll tell you what, Šulitka, you'll teach him how." So Šulitka sat beside Peanut in the stable and taught him how to bark. "Ruff, ruff, listen to how it's done," he began. "First, you must say rrrrr, here, in the throat, and then, at once, you let it burst from your mouth. Ruff, ruff! Rrrr, ruff!" Peanut didn't know why, but these sounds were music to his ears. Suddenly, out of sheer joy, he barked himself. That first bark came out a bit peculiar, like the screech of a knife on a plate. Listen, all beginnings are difficult. You didn't know your ABC's immediately either. Ferda and Žanka listened and wondered why old Šulitka was barking. In the end they just shrugged their shoulders and lost all respect for him. Peanut had an enormous talent for barking and he was a fast learner! When he went out with the wagon for the first time, yip!—he barked to the right, yip!—he barked to the left, as if he were shooting a gun. To his very last day he never tired of barking. He barked the whole blessed day long. It gave him such pleasure to have learned it so well.

Driving with Šulitka and riding on the wagon wasn't Peanut's only responsibility. Every evening he would make the rounds of the mill and the yard to see that everything was in place. He yapped at the hens to stop cackling like old women at the market. He would stand before Grandfather, wagging his tail and looking cocky, as if to say, "Time for bed, Karl, I'll take care of everything." Grandpa would praise him and then, blissfully content, go to sleep.

During the day, with Peanut running along, Grandfather often made the rounds of the villages and small towns to purchase wheat and other odd stuff, maybe cloverseed or lentils, or perhaps poppyseed. At night, on their way home, Peanut wasn't a bit scared. He always knew his way home even when Grandpa, himself, wasn't quite sure about it.

One day, after Grandpa had bought some seed, let me see, where was it . . . it must have been in Evilville, I guess, he stopped for a moment at the inn. Peanut was left outside. While he was waiting for his master, something delicious tickled his nose. The smell from the kitchen was so luscious that Peanut simply had to peek inside. There, upon my soul, were people dining on sausages! Peanut sat down and waited to see if perhaps a casing would fall under the table. While he waited, Grandpa's neighbor (now quickly, what was the man's name? I guess it was Youdal, well, let it be Youdal) Youdal pulled his wagon up to the inn. When Youdal found Grandfather at the bar, one word led to another, and not long after, the two neighbors clambered into Youdal's wagon, ready to go home together. Grandpa had forgotten all about Peanut and the two men drove off. Meanwhile, Peanut sat in the kitchen, begging for sausages. After their meal, the diners tossed the sausage skins to the cat curled on the hearth and Peanut was left empty-handed. Then he remembered Grandfather. He looked for him, sniffing all over the inn, but Grandpa was gone. When the innkeeper noticed, he said, "There Peanut, look," pointing with his hand, "your master went that way." Peanut understood and set off for home by himself. At first, he trudged alongside the road, but after a while he said to himself, "I'm no fool. Why don't I take a shortcut over the hill." So he went over the hill and through the forest. Twilight came and night fell, but Peanut wasn't the least bit afraid. "I've got nothing anyone could steal," he thought.

As the full moon came into view and the trees by the forest path parted to reveal a glade, the moon loomed over the treetops and all was so beautiful that Peanut's heart leaped in awe. The forest hummed softly as if playing the harp. Peanut ran through the forest, which had turned into a jet black tunnel. Suddenly a silvery light glistened before him. The sound of harps became louder and every hair on Peanut's back bristled. He crouched close to the ground, staring in a daze. Before him, there unfurled a silver-bright glade where fairy dogs were dancing. They were splendid white dogs, almost translucent, and so feathery light that they didn't even disturb the dew on the grass. They were fairy dogs for sure. Peanut knew that at once because they lacked that interesting, faint scent by which a dog can tell a real dog from a fairy. Peanut lay down in the wet grass and stared until his eyes were ready to pop out. The fairies danced, scampered, and played with each other, chased their tails, so gracefully and airily that not a single blade of grass moved beneath them.

Peanut watched very closely, for if one scratched or bit for fleas he would know it was only an ordinary white dog, rather than a fairy dog. None scratched or bit for fleas, leaving no doubt they were fairies. When the moon rose high, the fairies lifted their heads and began to howl and sing softly and enchantingly. Not even The National Theater Symphony Orchestra could have made more beautiful music. Peanut was moved to tears. He would have joined in had he not been afraid of spoiling it all.

After concluding their chorus, they lay down around an old, stately dog who must have been a valiant fairy or enchantress, all white and serene. "Tell us a story," the fairies implored.

The old fairy dog considered and then said, "I will tell you how dog created man. When the Lord created the whole world and all the animals, he chose a dog to be their leader, for the dog was the best and the wisest of them all. In Paradise all the animals lived, died, and were born again happy and content, except dogs who grew sadder by the day. So the Lord asked the dogs, 'Why are you so sad when all the other animals rejoice?' The oldest dog spoke, 'You see, dear Lord, the other animals have no need of anything, but we dogs have brains that tell us something exists that's superior to us, and that's you, O Creator! We can smell everything but we can't smell you and we miss that terribly. Therefore, O Lord, grant us our wish and create a god we can smell.' The good Lord smiled and said, 'Bring me some bones, and I will create a god for you whom you can smell.' The dogs scurried in all directions, and each returned with a bone: a lion's bone, a horse's bone, a camel's bone, and a cat's bone. In fact, there were bones of all the animals except a dog, for no dog would touch another dog's flesh or another dog's bone. When the pile of bones grew large, God made man out of it, a god the dogs could smell. Since man is made of the bones of every animal except the dog, he shares with the animals all their qualities: the strength of a lion, the perseverance of a camel, the craftiness of a cat, and the magnanimity of a horse, but he doesn't have the loyalty of a dog. No, man doesn't have a dog's faithfulness!"

"Tell us some more," the fairy dogs pleaded again.

The old fairy dog pondered and then continued. "I will tell you how dogs got to heaven. You know that after people die, their souls go up to the stars. It so happened that not a star was left for the souls of dogs, and so they had to be placed in the ground for their eternal rest. It remained this way until the time of Jesus Christ. When he was flogged and his blood was spilled, a hungry stray dog came by and lapped up the blood. 'Mary in heaven,' exclaimed the angels, 'that dog has received the blood of our Savior.' 'If that's the case,' said God, 'we will take his soul to heaven.' He created a new star, and attached a tail as a pointer on the way for dogs' souls. Barely did the first dog's soul reach the star, than it became so boundlessly happy it began running and scampering about the sky like a dog in a park, and it wouldn't follow its path like the rest of the stars. Now, these dog stars that romp about in the sky and wag their tails are called comets."

"Tell us some more," begged the fairy dogs a third time.

"I'll tell you," began the old fairy dog. "Long ago, here on earth, there was a dogs' kingdom and in it a large castle. People envied the dogs for their kingdom and practiced sorcery until the dogs' kingdom and their castle sank deep into the ground. Now, if you dug in the right spot, you would get to the cave where the dogs' treasure is buried."

"What is the dogs' treasure?" asked the fairies eagerly.

"It's a hall of exceptional beauty," the old fairy said. "The pillars are made of the choicest bones, and none of the bones are gnawed, not a single one. They are meaty like a goose leg still attached to the thigh. Then there is a throne built of smoked meat, and leading to it are steps of the purest bacon slabs. The slabs are covered with meat hash a finger thick—" Peanut could stand it no longer. He scooted out to the glade, yelping, "Where is this treasure? Where is this dogs' treasure?"

There was no one to answer him. All the fairy dogs, even the old one, were gone. Peanut rubbed his eyes. All he saw was a silvery glade. Not a blade of grass had been trampled by the fairies' dance, not a dewdrop had trickled to the ground. Alone, the still moon glimmered over the beautiful glade, surrounded by the black wall of the forest.

Once Peanut remembered that at home at least some water-soaked bread was waiting for him, he ran home as fast as his legs could carry him. From that day on, every now and then, when Peanut walked over the grass fields or through the woods with Grandfather, he would remember the dogs' sunken treasure deep in the ground and he would dig ferociously with all fours, burrowing a deep hole in the ground.

It's very likely that Peanut shared his secret with other dogs, and they in turn surely told it to others, and they again to more dogs, for now all dogs, at one time or another, when they remember the sunken kingdom, do the same thing: they dig holes in the ground, sniffing them longingly, hoping for a whiff from the depths of the earth of the succulent throne of their long-lost empire.

ELIZABETH MASSIE
Stephen

Elizabeth Massie was born and lives in Viginia. I first noticed her work in various small press magazines but it wasn't until "Hooked on Buzzer," which appeared in *Women of Darkness* in 1988, that I, as well as others, really started to sit up and take notice. Some of her most effective stories have nothing to do with the supernatural. The horror lies in the real-life circumstances, and/or the relationships she depicts so believably.

The moving and original "Stephen," from *Borderlands*, amply demonstrates her willingness to take chances with uncomfortable subjects.

—E.D.

STEPHEN

ELIZABETH MASSIE

Michael and Stephen shared a room at the rehabilitation center. Michael was a young man with bright, frantically moving eyes and an outrageous sense of non-stop, bitter humor. He had been a student at the center for more than a year, and with his disability, would most likely be there much longer. This was true, also, for the others housed on the first floor of the west wing. Severe cases, all of them, living at the center, studying food services, auto mechanics, computer operating, art, and bookkeeping, none of them likely to secure a job when released because when hiring the disabled, businesses would usually go for the students who lived on east wing and on the second floor. The center had amazing gadgets that allowed people like Michael to work machines and press computer keys and dabble in acrylics, but the generic factory or office did not go in for space-age, human-adaptive robotics. And Michael himself was a minor miracle of robotics.

Anne arrived at the center late, nearly ten thirty, although her meeting had been scheduled for ten o'clock. The cab dropped her off at the front walk and drove away, spraying fine gravel across her heels. Inside her shoes, her toes worked an awkward rhythm that neither kept them warm nor calmed her down. A cool November wind threw a piece of paper across the walk before her. On its tail followed the crumbled remains of a dead oak leaf. Anne's full skirt flipped and caught her legs in a tight embrace. It tugged, as if trying to pull her backward and away. In her mouth she tasted hair and sour fear. When she raked her fingers across her face the hair was gone, but not the fear.

The center was large and sterile, a modern bit of gray stone architecture. The largest building was marked with a sign to the left of the walkway: ADMINISTRATION AND ADMISSIONS. Almost the entire front of this building was composed of plate glass with borders of stone. Anne could not see behind the glass for the harsh glare of morning sun, but in the wind the glass seemed to bulge and ripple.

Like a river.

Like water.

"Christ."

Anne scrunched her shoulders beneath the weight of her coat and glanced about for a place to sit and compose herself. Yes, she was late, but screw them if they wanted to complain about volunteer help. There were several benches just off the walkway on the lawn, but she didn't want to sit in full view. And so she took the walk leading to the right, following along until it circled behind the main building beside what she assumed was a long, gray stone dormitory. The walk ended at a paved parking lot, marked off for visitors and deliveries. She crossed the lot, skirting cars and food trucks and large vans equipped for hauling wheelchairs, heading for a grove of trees on the other side. A lone man pushing an empty wheeled cot crossed in front of Anne and gave her a nod. She smiled slightly and then looked away.

The trees across the lot encircled a park. Picnic tables were clustered beneath the largest of the oaks, and concrete benches made a neat border about the pond in the center. The pond itself was small, no more than two acres, but it was dark and clearly deep. Dead cattails rattled on the water's edge. A short pier jutted into the water from the shore, with a weathered rowboat tethered to the end. Leaves blew spastic patterns on the black surface.

Anne sat on a bench and wrapped her fingers about her knees. There was no one else in the park. She looked at the brown grass at her feet, then at her hands on her knees, and then at the pond. The sight of the bobbing boat and the dull shimmering of the ripples made her stomach clamp. What a raw and ugly thing the pond was.

A cold thing, enticing and deadly, ready to suck someone under and drag them down into its lightless depths. Licking and smothering with its stinking embrace.

Phillip would have loved this pond.

Phillip would have thought it just right.

The fucking bastard.

If she was to go to the water's edge, she thought she might see his reflection there, grinning at her.

But she did not go. She sat on the concrete bench, her fingers turning purple with the chill, her breath steaming the air. She did not look at the pond again, but at the grass and her knees and the picnic tables. She studied the gentle slopes the paths made about the park, all accessible to wheeled means of movement. Accessible to the people who lived here. To the people Anne's mother had protected her from as a child; who her mother had hurried Anne away from on the street, whispering in her ear, "Don't stare, now, Anne. Polite people don't react. Do you hear me?

"There but for the grace of God go you, Anne. Don't look now. It's not nice."

Anne closed her eyes, but the vision of the park and the tables and the sloped pathways stayed inside her eyes. She could hear the wind on the pond.

"Damn you, Mother," she said. "Damn you, Phillip."

She sat for another twenty minutes.

When she crossed the parking lot again, her eyes in the sun and her hands in her pockets, her muscles were steeled and her face carried a tight, professional smile.

Janet Warren welcomed Anne into the center at ten fifty-six, barely mentioning the tardiness. She took Anne into her office, and, as assistant administrator, explained the functions of the center. She gave Anne a brief summary of the students with whom Anne would work, then led her off to the west wing.

Anne entered Michael's room after Janet gave an obligatory tap on the door. Michael grunted and Anne walked in, still holding her coat, which Janet had offered to take, clutched tightly to her stomach.

"Michael," said Janet to the man on the bed. "This is Miss Zaccaria, the lady I said would be coming to help us out."

Michael propped up on his elbow, straightening himself, patting his blanket down about the urinary bag as if it were an egg in an Easter basket. He gave Anne a wide grin.

"Well, if it ain't my dream lady come to see me in the flesh!" he crowed. "Are you real or just a vision of delight?"

Anne licked her lips and looked back at Janet Warren. "Thank you, Mrs. Warren. I'll be fine now. I'll let you know if we need anything."

"Hell, I know what I need," said Michael. "And she's standing right in front of me."

Janet nodded, her motion seeming to be both acknowledgment of what Anne had said and a sisterly confirmation of what she had come to do. Janet turned and left the room.

"Come on," said Michael, and Anne looked back at him.

"Come on? What do you mean?" There was only a small comfort in her professional ability at conversation. It wasn't enough to overcome her discomfort at seeing the physical form of Michael before her. He was legless, with hipbones flattened into a shovel-shaped protrusion. The thin blanket emphasized rather than hid his lower deformity. He was missing his right arm to the elbow, and there was no left arm at all. A steel hook clipped the air in cadence with the blinking of Michael's eyes.

"Come on and tell me. You ain't really no shrink, are you? I was expecting some shriveled-up old bitch. You really is my dream lady, ain't you?"

Anne focused on Michael's face and took a slow breath. "No, sorry," she said. "I'm from Associated Psychological. I'm a clinical social worker."

Michael grappled with a button and pressed it with the point of his hook. The bed rolled toward Anne. She held her position.

"No, you ain't. I dreamed about you last night. Dreamed I still had my parts and you was eating them nice as you please."

Anne's face went instantly hot. She could have kicked herself for not being ready for anything. "I was told you've had a rough time these past months," she said. "Not getting along with the other students like you used to do. I'd like to help."

"Sure. Just sit on my face for a few hours."

Anne glanced at the withered body, then back at his face. Of all the students she would be working with through the volunteer-outreach program, Michael was the most disabled. "Is that all you think about, Michael? Sex?"

"When it comes to sex," he said, "all I can *do* is think." He laughed out loud and wheeled closer. "You like me?"

"I don't know you yet. I hope we'll like each other."

"Why you here? We got shrinks. Two of them. You on a field trip?"

"Field trip?"

"You know, like them school kids. Sometimes the local schools bring in their junior high kids. Show them around. Let them take little look-sees. Tell them if they are bad enough and dive into shallow lakes or don't wear their seat belts, God'll make them just like us."

Anne cleared her throat and loosened her coat from her waist. "First of all, I'm here on a volunteer program. Until the new center is finished down state, there will continue to be more students than can be properly provided for. The center called on our association to help out temporarily. You are a student with whom I've been asked to work."

"Student." Michael spat out the word. "I'm thirty-one and I'm called a goddamn student."

"Second," Anne said, "I'm not on a field trip. I'm not here to stare. I'm here to help."

Michael shook his head, then eased off his elbow to a supine position. "So who else is on your list besides me?"

Anne opened the folded paper Janet had given her. "Randy Carter, Julia Powell, Cora Grant—"

"Cora'll drive you ape shit. She lost half her brain in some gun accident."

"And Ardie Whitesell. I might like Cora, Michael. Don't forget, I don't know her yet, either."

Michael sighed. "I don't need no shrink. What the fuck's your name?"

"Miss Zaccaria."

"Yeah, well, I'm okay. I don't need no shrink. Don't need one any more than old roomie over there." Michael tilted his head on his pillow, indicating a curtained corner of the room.

"Roomie?"

"Roommate. He don't need no shrink, neither. I don't 'cause I got things all figured out in this world. Nothing a little nookie can't cure." Michael looked at Anne and winked. "And roomie over there, he don't need one 'cause he's in some kind of damn coma. Not much fun to have around, you know."

Anne frowned, only then aware of the mechanical sounds softly emanating from the corner. The drawn curtain was stiff and white, hanging from the ceiling-high rod like a starched shroud. "What's wrong with your roommate?"

"Hell, what ain't wrong? Come over here." With a hissing of his arm, Michael rose again and clutched the bed switch, tapping buttons in a short series, and the bed spun around. The legless man rolled to the curtain. Anne followed.

Michael shifted onto his right side and took the curtain in his hook. "Stephen's been here longer'n me. He ain't on no shrink's list." Michael pulled the curtain back.

It was not registering what was before her that allowed her to focus on it as long as she did. There were machines there, a good number of them, crowded around a tiny bed like rumbling and humming steel wolves about a lone prey. Aluminum racks stood on clawed feet, heavy bags of various colored liquids hanging from them, oozing their contents into thin, clear tubes. A portable heart monitor beeped. Behind it, a utility sink held to the wall, various antiseptics and lotions and balms cluttering the shelf above. The rails of the bed were pulled up to full height. At one end of the mattress was a thin blanket, folded back and tucked down. And at the other end, a thin pillow. And Stephen.

Anne's coat and paper dropped to the floor. "Oh, my dear God."

"Weird, huh? I call him Head Honcho. I think he must be some doctor's experiment, you know, keeping him alive and all. Don't it beat all?"

On the pillow was a head, with black curled hair. Attached to the head, a neck, and below that a small piece of naked, ragged chest, barely large enough to house a heart and single lung. The chest heaved and shuddered, wires pulsing like obscene fishermen's lines. That was all there was of Stephen.

Anne's heart constricted painfully. She stepped backward.

"Nurses don't like him. Can't stand to touch him, 'though they shave him every three days. Doctor checks him nearly every day. Head Honcho don't do nothing but breathe. He ain't much but at least he don't complain about my music." Michael looked at Anne.

Anne turned away. Her stomach clenched, throwing fouled bile into her throat. "Hey, you leaving?"

"I need to see the others," she managed. And she went out of the west wing to the faculty rest room, where she lost her control and her lunch.

It was three days before Anne could bring herself to visit the center again. The AP partners were asking her for her volunteer hours chart, and as the newest member of the firm, she couldn't shrug it off. And so she returned. Her pulse was heavy in her neck and the muscles of her back were tight, but she decided she would not allow herself more than passing acknowledgment of them.

She talked with Cora in the art room. Cora had little to say, but seemed pleased with the attention Anne gave her painting. Randy was in the recreation hall with Ardie, playing a heated game of billiards, wheeling about the table with teeth gritted and chins hovering over cue sticks. Anne told them she'd visit later, after the match. Julia was shopping with her daughter, and Michael was in the pool on a red inner tube.

"Hey, Miss Zaccaria!" he called when he saw Anne peering through the water-steamed glass of the door. "Want to come in for a swim? I'm faster in the water. Bet I could catch you in a split second. What do you say?"

Anne pushed the door open and felt the onslaught of chlorine-heated mist. She did not go any closer to the pool. "I never learned to swim, Michael. Besides, I'm not exactly dressed for swimming."

"I don't want you *dressed* for swimming. What fun would that be?"

Anne wiped moisture from her forehead. "How long do you plan to swim? I thought we could visit outside. The day's turned out pretty fair. It's not as cold as it has been."

"I'm finished now, ain't I, Cindy?"

The pool-side attendant, who had been watching Michael spin around on his tube, shrugged. "If you say so." She pulled Michael's wheeled bed from the wall and moved it to the pool steps. "Get over to the side so I can get you out."

"Hey, Miss Zaccaria, do me a favor. My blue jacket is in my room. It's one of those Member's Only things. Anyway, I'm not real crazy about wind, even when it's warm. Would you get the jacket for me? Door's unlocked."

Anne's head was nodding as she thought, Oh, Christ, yes, I mind. "No problem," she said. She left the pool, telling herself the curtain was drawn.

They would always keep the curtain drawn.

Michael's door was indeed unlocked. The students of the center kept valuables in a communal vault, and the staff moved about the floor frequently, so chances of theft were slim. Anne went into the room, expecting the jacket to be in plain sight, prepared to lift it coolly and leave with her self-esteem intact.

But she did not see the jacket.

She checked Michael's small dresser, behind the straightbacked visitor's chair, in the plastic laundry basket beside the vacant spot where Michael's bed rested at night. It was not there.

Anne looked at the curtained corner. Certainly the jacket would not be behind the curtain. There was no reason to go there, no reason to look.

She walked to the curtain and edged over to the hemmed corner of the heavy material. It's not over there, she thought. Her hands began to sweat. She could not swallow.

She pulled the curtain back slowly. And let her gaze move to the bed.

Again, it was a flash image that recorded itself on her startled retinas before she looked away. The head was in the same place, eyes closed, dark hair in flat curls. The neck. The breathing, scarred half chest. Anne stared at the sink, counting, rubbing thumbs against index fingers, calming herself. She would look for Michael's jacket. There was a chair like that on Michael's side, and a laundry basket, although this one held no clothes, only white towels and washcloths. By the wall beside the sink was a pile of clothing, and Anne stepped closer to search through it. There were shirts, mostly, several pairs of shorts and underwear. And a blue jacket. Anne picked it up. She looked back at the small bed.

And the eyes in the head were open, and they were looking at her.

Anne's fingers clenched, driving nails into her palms. She blinked, and glanced back at the pile of clothes, pretending she hadn't seen the eyes. Chills raised tattoos up her shoulders, and adrenaline spoke loudly in her veins: leave now.

Her hands shook as they pawed through the clothes on the floor, acting as though she had more to find. Calm down. And leave.

But the voice made her stop.

"I didn't mean to stare," it said.

Anne flinched, and slowly stood straight. She looked at the bed.

The eyes were still open, still watching her.

Her own mouth opened before she had a chance to stop it, and she said, "I was looking for Michael's jacket." Leave now! cried the adrenaline. That thing did not say anything. It can't talk. It's comatose. It's brain dead. Leave *now!*

The eyes blinked, and Anne saw the muscles on the neck contract in a swallowing reflex. "Yes," it said. And the eyes closed. The whole ragged body seemed to shudder and shrink. It had gone to sleep again.

The jacket worked in Anne's fingers. Michael was in the pool, waiting for her. It's brain dead, Anne. Get hold of yourself. "Stephen?" she whispered.

But it did not open its eyes, nor move, and Anne took the jacket down to the pool where Michael was fuming about on his bed, spinning circles around the yawning attendant.

"So I store my stuff on Stephen's side of the room, 'cause he don't complain none. And when I get visitors they don't think I'm a slob. Nurses don't care. I get the stuff from over there into my laundry basket when its really dirty."

Anne was in Michael's visitor's chair. He was on his side, his gaze alternating between her, his hook, and the curtain.

"He's never complained to you?"

Michael chuckled shallowly. "You serious? He's in a coma, I told you already. Listen to this, if you don't believe me." Michael reached for the sleek black cassette player on the nightstand beside the bed. He pushed the switch, and an instant blast of heavy rock shattered the air. Above the shrieking guitars and pounding percussion, Anne could hear the sudden, angry calls from the neighboring students.

"Go, look, quick," Michael shouted over the music. "Go see before those damned nurses get here."

Anne shook her head, smiling tightly, brushing off the suggestion.

Michael would have none of it. "Shit, just go on and look at Dead-Head Honcho."

"I don't think it's my place to bother him."

"Get on now, the nurses are coming. I hear them damn squeaking shoes down the hall!"

Anne got up and looked behind the curtain. The head was silent and motionless. The eyes were closed.

"What'd I tell you? Deaf, dumb, blind, and in a coma. Sounds like hell to me, and God knows I seen hell up close myself."

"You have?" Anne went back to her chair. "What do you mean, you've seen it up close?"

"Look at me, Miss Zaccaria. You think the love of the Lord do this to me?"

There were then three nurses' heads at the door, clustered on the frame like Japanese beetles on a rose stem. "Turn that down, Michael, or the player's ours for the next week."

"Shit," said Michael. He grappled the button; pushed it off. "I ain't no goddamn student!" he told the nurses who were already gone. "It's my business how loud I play my music!"

"Tell me about your accident," said Anne. But she was thinking: Hell, oh, yes, it must be like hell, living in a coma.

But he's not in a coma. He is conscious. He is alive.

And when you are already in hell, what is hell to that?

Her next session with Michael was canceled because he was in the infirmary with the flu. And so Anne sought out Julia and spent an hour with her, and then with Cora, who did not want to talk but wanted Anne to paint a picture of a horse for her. Randy and Ardie were again at the billiard table and would have nothing to do with her. Then she visited the faculty lounge, and listened with feigned interest to the disgruntled banter and rehab shoptalk. A few questions were directed her way, and she answered them as cordially as possible, but she wanted to talk about Stephen. She wanted to know what they knew.

But she could not make herself bring up the subject. And so she went to the west wing, and let herself into Michael's unlocked room.

She went to the curtain and took the edge in her fingers. Her face itched but she shook it off. No, said the adrenaline. "Yes," she said. And she pulled the curtain back.

The tubes flowed, nutrients in, wastes out. The monitor beeped. Bags dripped and pumps growled softly. Anne moved to the end of the bed. She forced herself to see what was before her, what she needed to see, and not be distracted by the machinery about it.

The flesh of the chest twitched slightly and irregularly with the work of the wires. Every few seconds, the shuddering breath. It would be cold, Anne thought, yet the blanket was folded back at the foot of the bed, a regulatory piece of linen which served no purpose to the form on the pillow. With the wires and tubes, a blanket would be a hindrance. The neck did not move; swallowing was for the wakeful. The head as well did not move, except for the faint pulsing of the nostrils, working mindlessly to perform its assigned job.

Anne moved her hands to the railing of the bed. She slid around, moving along the side to the head of the bed. Her feet felt the floor cautiously as if the tiles might creak. She reached the pillow; her hands fell from the railing. Her face itched and again she refused to give in to it.

Through fear-chapped lips, she said, "Stephen?"

The monitor beeped. The chest quivered.

"Stephen?"

The sleeping face drew up as if in pain, and then the eyes opened. As the lids widened, the muscles of the cheeks seemed to ease. He blinked. His eyes were slate blue.

"I hope I'm not bothering you," she said.

"No," he said. And the eyes fluttered closed, and Anne thought he was asleep again. Her hands went to her face and scratched anxiously. She pulled them down.

Stephen's eyes opened. "No, you aren't bothering me. Why would you think that?"

"You were sleeping."

"I always sleep."

"Oh," Anne said.

"You've been spending time with Michael. What do you think of him?"

"He's . . . fine. It's good to spend time with him."

The head nodded, barely, sliding up and down the pillow, obviously an effort. "You are Miss Zaccaria."

"Anne," she said.

"Anne," he repeated. His eyes closed.

"Do you want me to go now?"

His eyes remained closed. "If you wish."

"Do you want me to?"

"No."

And so she stood those very long minutes, watching Stephen slip into sleep, trying to absorb the reality of what was before her, counting the beepings of the heart monitor.

Again the eyes opened. "You are still here."

"Yes."

"How long has it been?"

"Only a few minutes."

"I'm sorry."

"No, that's all right. I don't mind."

Stephen sighed. "Why don't you sit? There is a chair over there somewhere."

"I'll stand."

"Michael is wrong. I do mind his music. I hate it."

"I could ask him to keep it down."

"It's not the volume. It is the music. Music was created for movement, for involvement. I feel a straightjacket around my soul when Michael plays his music."

Anne said nothing for a moment. Stephen looked away from her, and then back again.

"Why do you let them think you are comatose?" Anne asked.

"That way I can sleep. When I sleep, there are dreams."

"What kind of dreams?"

"Ever the clinical social worker," said Stephen. And for the first time, a small smile crossed his lips.

Anne smiled also. "That's me," she said.

"My dreams are my own," he said. "I would never share them."

"All right."

"And I would not ask you to share yours," he said.

"No," said Anne.

"I'm tired," he said.

And when she was certain he was asleep once again, Anne left.

"I liked college, my studies there. The psyche of the human is so infinite and fascinating. I thought I could do something with all I'd learned. But I wasn't smart enough to become a doctor."

"How do you know?"

Anne shrugged. "I know."

"And so you are a therapist," said Stephen.

"Yes. It's important. Helping people."

"How do you help?"

"I listen to them. I help them find new ways of seeing situations."

"Do you like your patients?"

"I don't call them patients. They are clients."

"Do you like them?"

"Michael asked me something like that when we first met. He wanted to know if I liked him."

"Do you?"

Anne crossed her feet and angled her face away from Stephen. There was a lint ball on the floor by the bed. The nurses and orderlies were obviously not quick about their business here.

"Of course I do," she answered.

"That's good. If you like people you can help them."

"That's not a prerequisite, though. Liking them."

Stephen closed his eyes momentarily. Then he looked at Anne again. "You have a husband?"

"No."

"A boyfriend, certainly."

"No, not really. I've not wanted one." Anne hesitated. "It's not what you think."

"What do I think?"

"That I'm a lesbian or something."

"I haven't thought that."

"I'm not."

"You have family, though."

Anne's crossed arms drew in closer. Family, yes, she did. God knows what wonders she could have accomplished had it not been for her beloved family.

"A mother," she said. "An older brother."

"What are their names?"

"My mother is Audrey. My brother . . ." Suddenly Anne was acutely aware of the utility sink behind her. She could see it brimming with water, cold water, stopped up and ready. . . . "My brother's name is Phillip."

"Are you close?"

Anne's shoulders flinched at the nearness of the sink. Dark water; thick, stinking, and hungry water. Eager. She swallowed, then looked down at her hands. Pathetic things, she thought. She flexed them. Goddamn it all. She looked up at Stephen. His forehead was creased, with a barely discernible shadow over his eyes.

"Sure," she said. "We're close."

Then Stephen went to sleep. Anne stared at the dust ball and at the tubes running from beneath Stephen's ribs. And her fingers, wanting to move forward, were stopped, and were locked onto her lap like a colony of trapped souls.

* * *

Janet Warren was chuckling as she ushered Anne into the office. "It's no big deal," she said, obviously seeing through Anne's tight smile. "Honestly, I just want to talk with you for a minute."

Anne took one of the chairs that sat before the desk; Janet sat on the edge of the desk.

"It's Julia," Janet said.

Anne recrossed her arms and frowned slightly. "Julia? What's wrong with her?"

"Now, don't get me wrong. Sorry, I don't need to talk with you like that. You know what you're doing, you know how people react sometimes. I'm sure you've had clients freak out during sessions, things like that."

Anne said, "Certainly."

"Julia went a little crazy after your last visit. She started throwing things; she even threatened bodily harm to herself if you came back again."

"Mrs. Warren, certainly you don't think—"

"I don't think anything, Anne. We're in this together, remember? Julia has always been easily set off. It seems you remind her of someone she hated back when she was a child. In school, somewhere back then. You've done nothing wrong. As a matter of fact, you seem to be making real progress with Michael."

Anne tapped the rug lightly with the ball of her foot. "Michael likes to joke around. I seem to be a good receptacle for that."

"So be it," said Janet. "That could be just what he needs at this point."

"Yes, I believe so."

"So what I wanted to say was just forget about Julia for the time being. I'll get another volunteer assigned to her. With your own work at the association, I'm sure a smaller volunteer load won't disappoint you."

Anne nodded, stood, and started for the door. She turned back. "Mrs. Warren, what do you know about Stephen?"

"Stephen?"

"Michael's roommate."

"Ah, yes," Janet said. She slipped from the desk top and went around the desk to the swivel chair. She did not sit. "It may sound bad to say that we assigned Michael to that room because we didn't think any other student could tolerate Michael and his moods. Stephen's in a coma; you probably already how about that. We have brain waves, and they seem quite active, but who can figure what kinds of unconscious states the human can fall into? But whatever it is, Stephen is not to be disturbed. I would appreciate it if you would remind Michael to stay on his side of the curtain."

"Of course I will," said Anne.

"Thanks."

Anne looked out the office door, toward the activity in the main hall. Several wheelchaired students were talking with visitors; family, possibly. She looked again at Janet. "Before Stephen came here, who was he? I mean, what did he do?"

Janet sat and dug her fingers beneath a pile of manila folders, in search of a particular one. "What? Oh, music, he was a musician. A pianist. On the way up, I was told. Into classical concerts, things like that. A pity."

It felt as though cold water had been poured over Anne's lungs. She held her breath and slid her balled fists into her pockets. "And what," she began, "happened to him?"

The phone burred on the desk, and Janet raised an apologetic hand to Anne before picking up the receiver. She dropped to her seat with her "hello," and Anne left the office.

Michael seemed glad to be out of the infirmary. He waggled his eyebrows at Anne as she came into the room and raised himself up on his elbow. "Miss Zaccaria! Did you miss me?"

Anne sat in the visitor's chair. "Sure, Michael. Are you feeling better?"

Michael snorted. "Not a whole *hell* of a lot better, but enough to get me out of there. God, you should see the nurses they have for us sick students. The old ones all look like marines, and the young ones look like willing virgins. Like going from hot to cold and back to hot again all the time. It's enough to pop your nads, if you got some."

"Are you well enough to start back into the electronics program? You haven't done anything for nearly a month; and you know you can't stay unless you are working toward a future."

"I've been sick. I had my emotional problems, right? I mean, you can vouch for that. That's why you're here."

Anne scratched her calf. "You have to look at your goals, Michael. Without goals you just stay put in time and don't make progress."

"I got a goal."

"What's that?"

"To get my butt scratched. You ever scratch your butt with a hook?"

Anne shook her head.

"You scratch my butt for me, Miss Zaccaria?"

"Michael, don't start—"

"I ain't trying to be gross, honest. I just got an itch."

"Michael, it's not my place to do that. There are nurses."

"Tell me about it. Okay, then my back. You scratch my back? Please?"

Anne felt her hands catch her elbows. She sat straight, shifting as far from Michael as she could without getting up from the chair. "I'm not supposed to."

"Why?"

"I just can't. It's not professional. Therapists aren't supposed to touch clients."

"I'm not talking like you being my shrink now. Just my friend. Please. My back itches."

"No, Michael."

Michael was silent for a moment. He looked away from Anne, and studied a faint spot on his blanket. When he looked back, his face was pinched. "I ain't trying to be gross," he said softly. "How about my face? Can you scratch my nose for me?"

Anne, slowly, shook her head.

"Please," he said. "Nobody ever wants to touch me."

"I can't," said Anne.

Michael watched her, and then with a quick motion, he reached out and jabbed the play button on his tape player. Shrieking music cut the air. "Fine," he cried over it. "Sorry I asked. I didn't mean it, anyway. It was a joke. A butt scratch, shit, I just wanted a butt scratch for some jollies is all."

And then the nurses came and threatened Michael and he turned the music off.

"One of the last sets of visitors I had was quite a long time ago," said Stephen. "But it is one I'll never forget." He blinked, and his dark brows drew together, then apart. A strand of black, curled hair had been moved nearly into his eye, and Anne wondered what it would be like to reach out and push it back. "They were from a church. Pentecostal something. Holiness something. Young people, all of them. Neatly dressed, each in a pure white outfit that made me think of angry young angels. Even their Bibles were white. They didn't want to be here; I could hear them whispering behind the curtain. They were very frightened. But the leader, a young girl of about eighteen, quieted them, saying 'Even as you do it unto the least of the flock you do it unto Jesus.' And in they came, smiles flashing. The girl told me I needed to turn my life around, I needed to turn to the Lord. I told her I wasn't turning anywhere, couldn't she see that? She became flustered with my responses, then furious. I believe I was supposed to shake in the presence of their godly and bodily wholeness. Her face was as pale as her dress. When she finally ushered out her little group, she told me, 'You better accept the love of the Lord. There isn't anyone else in this world who would love something like you.' "

"Christ, Stephen."

"No, it's all right," he said. His eyes closed, held, then opened slightly. "It was a long time ago."

"You said one of the last sets of visitors were the church people. Who were the last?"

"Two insurance salesmen. I saw who they were, and went to sleep. I think they were more than relieved. I've been asleep most of the time since."

"Stephen."

"It's all right," he said. "Really."

Stephen shut his eyes. Anne watched his face. The nurses had done only a fair job of shaving. There was a small red cut on his chin. Then Stephen looked at her.

"Why wouldn't you touch Michael?"

Anne started. "You were listening."

"Yes."

"I can't. It's not part of the job, you know. People might take it the wrong way."

"Why are you a counselor, Anne?"

"So I can help people."

"There are lots of ways to help. Doctors, physical therapists, teachers."

"Yes." But they have to touch people. I can't touch, not now, not ever. Phillip touched me. Sweet God, he touched me and touching is nothing but pain and . . .

"Your family hoped you'd be a counselor?"

"No, I don't think it mattered to them." . . . anger and disgust. Touching is filth, degradation. It is losing control. Anne's feet were planted squarely on the floor. She was ready to run. Touching is cold and hateful, like putrid, black water.

"Tell me about your family."

"I already did."

"You have a mother. A brother."

"I already did!" Anne's hand flew to her mouth and pressed there. She had screamed. "Oh, God," she said then. "I'm sorry."

"It's all right."

Anne's throat felt swollen. She swallowed and it hurt. "I didn't mean to shout. It was rude."

"It's all right."

"Stephen," Anne began, and then hesitated. She inched herself forward on her chair. Stephen's eyes watched her calmly, and they were not eyes of a blue and frightening ocean, but of a blue and clear sky. She saw an understanding there, and she wanted to reach out for it.

She wanted it, but knew the only way to have it was to touch it.

She sat back. "Good night, Stephen," she said.

"Good night," he answered. And he slept.

Randy was being released from the center. The staff threw him a good-bye party, complete with balloons and ridiculous hats and noisemakers which Randy pretended to hate but obviously loved. He made a point of hooting his paper horn into the ear of everyone present. Randy had landed a job in the camera room of the local newspaper. His going away gift was a framed, fake newspaper front page, complete with the headline. "RANDY MYERS, AKA CLARK KENT, SECURES POSITION AT DAILY PRESS." Beneath the caption was a large black and white photo of Randy, cigar in teeth, leaning over the billiard table. A cue stick was in his hand.

"I taught him everything he knows," said Michael, as he looped about among the partyers. "He ought to take me with him, or he'll just make a mess of things."

Anne left in the midst of the hubbub and went down to the pond behind the administration building. The sky was overcast, and mist covered the algaed water.

Water, the dark trough of fears.

She stood beside the edge. The wind buffeted her.

Her mind, wearied, could not hold back the rush of memories.

Phillip, as a boy, touching Anne in secret. First as a game, then as an obsession. Anne growing up; Phillip growing up ahead of her, and his touching becoming even more cruel. His body heavy and harsh; his immense organ tearing into her relentlessly. Anne crying each night, knowing he would come to her and would have no love for anything except the sensation of his own explosive release. Phillip swearing that if she told anyone, he would kill her.

Anne, promising herself over and over that if she was not killed, she would never let this happen again. She would not touch or be touched.

And then came the night when Phillip decided blood would make it more rewarding. He was tired of the same old thing; he said he was going to change Anne just a little, like a sculptor changing a piece of clay to make it better. With the door locked and his underwear in Anne's mouth, he carved. He took off her little toes, stopping the blood with matches and suturing with his mother's sewing kit. He decorated her abdomen with a toothed devil face into which he rubbed ink from Anne's cartridge pen. Across her breasts he etched, "Don't fuck with me." The ink finished it off.

The next morning, Mother wanted to know why there were stains on the sheets. She accused Anne of having a boyfriend in at night. She shook Anne until the confession was made. Anne took off her nightgown and her slippers. Mother shrieked and wailed, clutching her hair and tearing hunks out. Then she said, "The grace of God has left you! You are one of those deformed creatures!"

Mother confronted Phillip.

Phillip killed Mother in the tub that evening with scalding water and an old shower curtain.

Then he had found Anne, hiding in the garage.

Anne doubled over and gagged on the bank of the pond. She could still taste the sludge and the slime from so many years ago. She drove her fists into the wall of her ribs, and with her head spinning, she retched violently. At her feet lay brown leaves, stirred into tiny, spiraling patterns by the wind and the spattering of her own vomit.

She wiped her mouth. She stood up. Her vision wavered, and it was difficult to stand straight.

She made her way to Michael's room.

Michael's tape player was on the bed table. Michael had left it on, though softly, and as Anne picked it up she could feel the faint hammering of the percussion. The player was slender and cool and Anne could wrap both hands about it easily. Much like Phillip's cock, when she was just a young girl. With a single jerk, she pulled the cord from the wall. The table teetered, then crashed to the floor. The music died in mid-beat.

Anne hauled the player, cord dragging, to Stephen's side of the room. There was sweat on her neck, and it dripped to her breasts and tickled like roach legs. She ignored it. Stephen was asleep. Anne threw the player into the sink and it shattered on the dulled enamel.

"This is for you, Stephen," she said. "No more music. You won't have to suffer it anymore."

She ran the water until the heat of it steamed her face and stung her eyes. She grabbed up the pieces of broken player and squeezed them. Sharp edges cut into her hands and she let the blood run.

"And this is for you, Phillip. Goddamn you to whatever hell there is in this world or the next."

She looked at Stephen's bed. He was awake, and watching her.

"Anne," he said.

Anne wiped her mouth with the back of her hand. Blood streaked her chin.
"Tell me, Anne."

"My brother killed my mother. Then he tried to kill me."

"Tell me."

Anne looked at the dead player in the sink. The hot water continued to run.
Anne could barely catch her breath in the heat. She stepped back and licked the
blood from her hands. "He tried to kill me. He was fucking me. Ever since I can
remember, he was fucking me, hurting me, and enjoying it like any other boy
would enjoy baseball." She turned to Stephen and held out her wounded hands.
"Touching is wrong. And he knew it. When Mother found out, he killed her.
He took me down the back road to the water treatment plant and threw me into
the settling pool. It was not deep, but I could not swim, and the bottom was slick
with sludge and it was rancid, Stephen, it was sewage and garbage, and I slipped
under and under and every time I came up Phillip would lean over the rail and
hit me with a broom handle. It was night, and I could no longer tell the difference
between up and down, it was all black and putrid and I couldn't breathe. Phillip
kept hitting me and hitting me. My blood ran into the sewage and when I screamed
I swallowed the sludge."

Anne moved closer to Stephen's bed, her hands raised.

"Someone heard us. Phillip was stopped and arrested. I spent a good deal of
time in the hospital, with concussions and infections."

Stephen watched between her bloodied hands and her face.

"I wanted to help people," Anne said. "I don't think I ever can. Phillip has
seen to that."

"Yes, you can."

"Tell me, Stephen. What can I do for you?"

Stephen sighed silently, his chest lifting then falling. His head rolled slightly
to the left, and he stared at the light above the bed.

"Love me," he said finally.

"I do, Stephen."

His eyes blinked, the light reflecting tiny sparks. He looked back at Anne. His
mouth opened, then closed. His jaw flexed and he licked his lips with his dry
tongue. "Love me," he said.

Anne hesitated. Then slowly, she lowered the side rail of the bed. She knelt
beside the bed and put her head onto the pillow beside Stephen. For a moment
she held still, and then she brought her hand up to touch Stephen's lips with her
fingers. They did not move, yet she could feel the soft blowing of his breath on
her skin.

She moved back then. Stephen watched her. Then he said, "You knew about
my music."

Anne nodded.

"My dreams are different now."

Anne nodded.

After a long moment, he said, "Anne, love me." His voice was certain, kind,
and sad.

Anne touched her face and it was hot and wet with the steam and her own sweat. She touched Stephen's face and it was fevered. She traced his cheekbone, his chin, his throat, and the damp, tendoned contour of his neck. She let her palm join her fingers, and felt slowly along his flesh among the myriad of tapes and tubes and wires. When she reached his heart, she pressed down. The beating quickened with the pressure, and Stephen moaned.

"That hurt," Anne said.

"No."

Anne stood straight. She unbuttoned her blouse and let it drop from her shoulders. She could not look at Stephen for fear of revulsion in his eyes. She removed her bra, and then slipped from her skirt and panties.

She looked at Stephen, and thought she saw him nod.

Anne climbed onto the foot of the bed. Beneath her knees the folded, unused blanket was cold. She moved forward, and bent over Stephen's body. Around her and beside her was the tangle of supports. Her body prickled; the veins in the backs of her hands flushed with icy fire. She tried to reach Stephen, but the web held her back.

"I can't," she said.

Stephen looked at her.

"These are in the way. I can't."

He said nothing.

And Anne, one by one, removed the web that kept her from him. She loosened the wires, she withdrew the needles, she pulled out the tubes. She touched the bruises and the marks on the pale skin. "I do love you," she said.

Anne lay with Stephen. Her hands were at first soft and tentative, then grew urgent, caressing his body, caressing her own. As she touched and probed and clutched, her fingers became his fingers. Gentle, intelligent fingers studying her and loving her.

Healing her.

She rode the current, rising and falling, her eyes closed. Stephen kissed her lips as she brought them to him, and her breasts as well, and as she lifted upward, he kissed the trembling, hot wetness between her thighs. She stretched her arms outward, reaching for the world, and then brought them down and about herself and Stephen, pulling inward to where there was nothing but them both. His breathing was heavy; her heart thundered. An electrical charge hummed in the pit of her stomach. It swelled and spread, moving downward. Anne opened her mouth to cry out silently to the ceiling. The charge stood her nerves on unbearable end, and it grew until it would hold no longer. The center of her being burst. She wailed with the pulses. And she fell, crumpled, when they were spent.

"Dear God," she whispered. She lay against Stephen, one hand entangled in the dark curls. Their warmth made her smile.

Her fear was gone.

Then she said, "Stephen, tell me. Only if you want. Why are you here? What put you in this place?"

Stephen said nothing. Anne hoped he had not slipped into sleep again.

"Stephen," she said, turning over, meaning to awaken him. "Tell me why you had to come to the center. What happened to you?"

Stephen said nothing. His closed eyes did not open.

Anne pressed her palm to his heart.

It was still.

The party was over. Back in the recreation hall, Anne could hear Michael tooting his paper horn and calling out, "Hey, Miss Zaccaria, where are you? I'm ready to give you that swimming lesson. What about you?"

The water in the pond did not move. The breeze had died down, and the mist was being replaced by an impenetrable fog that sucked the form and substance from the trees and the benches around the surface of the blackness.

There were leaves at her feet, and she kicked them off the edge of the bank and into the pond. Small circles radiated from the disturbances, little waves moving out and touching other waves.

Anne took off her shoes and walked barefoot to the end of the pier. The boat was still moored there, full of leaves.

The deep water below was as dark as Stephen's hair.

Some have their dreams, others nightmares.

Stephen had his dreams now. Dreams without end.

Amen.

And Anne would now accept her nightmare.

The leaves on the water were kind, and parted at her entrance.

PETER STRAUB

A Short Guide to the City

Straub is well-known as the author of such literate novels as *If You Could See Me Now*, *Shadowland*, *Koko*, and most recently, *Mystery*. But up until now he's only published a handful of short stories, a couple of them, like "The Juniper Tree," as powerful and disturbing as his best longer fiction. "A Short Guide to the City" appears in his collection *Houses Without Doors* (Dutton). Each story is a gem—from the short surrealistic "Something About a Death, Something About a Fire" to the chilling novella of insanity, "The Buffalo Hunter."

"A Short Guide . . ." takes the reader on a cold-blooded tour of an externally normal place of nightmares and dreams.

—E.D.

A Short Guide
to the City

PETER STRAUB

The viaduct killer, named for the location where his victims' bodies have been discovered, is still at large. There have been six victims to date, found by children, people exercising their dogs, lovers, or—in one instance—by policemen. The bodies lay sprawled, their throats slashed, partially sheltered by one or another of the massive concrete supports at the top of the slope beneath the great bridge. We assume that the viaduct killer is a resident of the city, a voter, a renter or property owner, a product of the city's excellent public school system, perhaps even a parent of children who even now attend one of its seven elementary schools, three public high schools, two parochial schools, or single nondenominational private school. He may own a boat or belong to the Book-of-the-Month Club, he may frequent one or another of its many bars and taverns, he may have subscription tickets to the concert series put on by the city symphony orchestra. He may be a factory worker with a library ticket. He owns a car, perhaps two. He may swim in one of the city's public pools or the vast lake, punctuated with sailboats, during the hot moist August of the city.

For this is a Midwestern city, northern, with violent changes of season. The extremes of climate, from ten or twenty below zero to up around one hundred in the summer, cultivate an attitude of acceptance in its citizens, of insularity— it looks inward, not out, and few of its children leave for the more temperate, uncertain, and experimental cities of the eastern or western coasts. The city is proud of its modesty—it cherishes the ordinary, or what it sees as the ordinary, which is not. (It has had the same mayor for twenty-four years, a man of limited-to-average intelligence who has aged gracefully and has never had any other occupation of any sort.)

Ambition, the yearning for fame, position, and achievement, is discouraged here. One of its citizens became the head of a small foreign state, another a famous bandleader, yet another a Hollywood staple who for decades played the part of the star's best friend and confidant; this, it is felt, is enough, and besides, all of these people are now dead. The city has no literary tradition. Its only mirror is provided by its two newspapers, which have thick sports sections and are comfortable enough to be read in bed.

The city's characteristic mode is *denial*. For this reason, an odd fabulousness permeates every quarter of the city, a receptiveness to fable, to the unrecorded. A river runs through the center of the business district, as the Liffey runs through Dublin, the Seine through Paris, the Thames through London, and the Danube through Budapest, though our river is smaller and less consequential than any of these.

Our lives are ordinary and exemplary, the citizens would say. We take part in the life of the nation, history courses through us for all our immunity to the national illnesses: it is even possible that in our ordinary lives . . . We too have had our pulse taken by the great national seers and opinion-makers, for in us you may find . . .

Forty years ago, in winter, the body of a woman was found on the banks of the river. She had been raped and murdered, cast out of the human community—a prostitute, never identified—and the noises of struggle that must have accompanied her death went unnoticed by the patrons of the Green Woman Taproom, located directly above that point on the river where her body was discovered. It was an abnormally cold winter that year, a winter of shared misery, and within the Green Woman the music was loud, feverish, festive.

In that community, which is Irish and lives above its riverfront shops and bars, neighborhood children were supposed to have found a winged man huddling in a packing case, an aged man, half-starved, speaking a strange language none of the children knew. His wings were ragged and dirty, many of the feathers as cracked and threadbare as those of an old pigeon's, and his feet were dirty and swollen. *Ull! Li! Gack!* the children screamed at him, mocking the sounds that came from his mouth. They pelted him with rocks and snowballs, imagining that he had crawled up from that same river which sent chill damp—a damp as cold as cancer—into their bones and bedrooms, which gave them earaches and chilblains, which in summer bred rats and mosquitos.

One of the city's newspapers is Democratic, the other Republican. Both papers ritually endorse the mayor, who though consummately political has no recognizable politics. Both of the city's newspapers also support the Chief of Police, crediting him with keeping the city free of the kind of violence that has undermined so many other American cities. None of our citizens goes armed, and our church attendance is still far above the national average.

We are ambivalent about violence.

We have very few public statues, mostly of Civil War generals. On the lakefront, separated from the rest of the town by a six-lane expressway, stands the cubelike structure of the Arts Center, otherwise called the War Memorial. Its rooms are hung with mediocre paintings before which schoolchildren are led on tours by their teachers, most of whom were educated in our local school system.

Our teachers are satisfied, decent people, and the statistics about alcohol and drug abuse among both students and teachers are very encouraging.

There is no need to linger at the War Memorial.

Proceeding directly north, you soon find yourself among the orderly, impressive precincts of the wealthy. It was in this sector of the town, known generally as the East Side, that the brewers and tanners who made our city's first great fortunes set up their mansions. Their houses have a northern, Germanic, even Baltic look which is entirely appropriate to our climate. Of gray stone or red brick, the size of factories or prisons, these stately buildings seem to conceal that vein of fantasy that is actually our most crucial inheritance. But it may be that the style of life —the invisible, hidden life—of these inbred merchants is itself fantastic: the multitude of servants, the maids and coachmen, the cooks and laundresses, the private zoos, the elaborate dynastic marriages and fleets of cars, the rooms lined with silk wallpaper, the twenty-course meals, the underground wine cellars and bomb shelters. . . . Of course we do not know if all of these things are true, or even if some of them are true. Our society folk keep to themselves, and what we know of them we learn chiefly from the newspapers, where they are pictured at their balls, standing with their beautiful daughters before fountains of champagne. The private zoos have been broken up long ago. As citizens, we are free to walk down the avenues, past the magnificent houses, and to peer in through the gates at their coach houses and lawns. A uniformed man polishes a car, four tall young people in white play tennis on a private court.

The viaduct killer's victims have all been adult women.

While you continue moving north you will find that as the houses diminish in size the distance between them grows greater. Through the houses, now without gates and coach houses, you can glimpse a sheet of flat grayish-blue—the lake. The air is free, you breathe it in. That is freedom, breathing this air from the lake. Free people may invent themselves in any image, and you may imagine yourself a prince of the earth, walking with an easy stride. Your table is set with linen, china, crystal, and silver, and as you dine, as the servants pass among you with the serving trays, the talk is educated, enlightened, without prejudice of any sort. The table talk is mainly about ideas, it is true, ideas of a conservative cast. You deplore violence, you do not recognize it.

Further north lie suburbs, which are uninteresting.

If from the War Memorial you proceed south, you cross the viaduct. Beneath you is a valley—the valley is perhaps best seen in the dead of winter. All of our city welcomes winter, for our public buildings are gray stone fortresses which, on days when the temperature dips below zero and the old gray snow of previous storms swirls in the avenues, seem to blend with the leaden air and become dreamlike and cloudy. This is how they were meant to be seen. The valley is called . . . it is called the Valley. Red flames tilt and waver at the tops of columns, and smoke pours from factory chimneys. The trees seem to be black. In the winter, the smoke from the factories becomes solid, like dark gray glaciers, and hangs in the dark air in defiance of gravity, like wings that are a light feathery gray at their tips and darken imperceptibly toward black, toward pitchy black at the point where these great frozen glaciers, these dirigibles, would join the body at the shoulder. The bodies of the great birds to which these wings are attached must be imagined.

In the old days of the city, the time of the private zoos, wolves were bred in the Valley. Wolves were in great demand in those days. Now the wolf-ranches have been entirely replaced by factories, by rough taverns owned by retired shop foremen, by spurs of the local railroad line, and by narrow streets lined with rickety frame houses and shoe-repair shops. Most of the old wolf-breeders were Polish, and though their kennels, grassy yards, and barbed-wire exercise runs have disappeared, at least one memory of their existence endures: the Valley's street signs are in the Polish language. Tourists are advised to skirt the Valley, and it is always recommended that photographs be confined to the interesting views obtained by looking down from the viaduct. The more courageous visitors, those in search of pungent experience, are cautiously directed to the taverns of the ex-foremen, in particular the oldest of these (the Rusty Nail and the Brace 'n' Bit), where the wooden floors have so softened and furred with lavings and scrubbings that the boards have come to resemble the pelts of long narrow short-haired animals. For the intrepid, these words of caution: do not dress conspicuously, and carry only small amounts of cash. Some working knowledge of Polish is also advised.

Continuing further south, we come to the Polish district proper, which also houses pockets of Estonians and Lithuanians. More than the city's sadly declining downtown area, this district has traditionally been regarded as the city's heart, and has remained unchanged for more than a hundred years. Here the visitor may wander freely among the markets and street fairs, delighting in the sight of well-bundled children rolling hoops, patriarchs in tall fur hats and long beards, and women gathering around the numerous communal water pumps. The sausages and stuffed cabbage sold at the food stalls may be eaten with impunity, and the local beer is said to be of an unrivaled purity. Violence in this district is invariably domestic, and the visitor may feel free to enter the frequent political discussions, which in any case partake of a nostalgic character. In late January or early February the "South Side" is at its best, with the younger people dressed in multilayered heavy woolen garments decorated with the "reindeer" or "snowflake" motif, and the older women of the community seemingly vying to see which of them can outdo the others in the thickness, blackness, and heaviness of her outergarments and in the severity of the traditional head scarf known as the babushka. In late winter the neatness and orderliness of these colorful folk may be seen at its best, for the wandering visitor will often see the bearded paterfamilias sweeping and shoveling not only his immaculate bit of sidewalk (for these houses are as close together as those of the wealthy along the lakefront, so near to one another that until very recently telephone service was regarded as an irrelevance), but his tiny front lawn as well, with its Marian shrines, crèches, ornamental objects such as elves, trolls, postboys, etc. It is not unknown for residents here to proffer the stranger an invitation to inspect their houses, in order to display the immaculate condition of the kitchen with its well-blackened wood stove and polished ornamental tiles, and perhaps even extend a thimble-glass of their own peach or plum brandy to the thirsty visitor.

Alcohol, with its associations of warmth and comfort, is ubiquitous here, and it is the rare family that does not devote some portion of the summer to the preparation of that winter's plenty.

For these people, violence is an internal matter, to be resolved within or exercised upon one's own body and soul or those of one's immediate family. The inhabitants of these neat, scrubbed little houses with their statues of Mary and cathedral tiles, the descendants of the hard-drinking wolf-breeders of another time, have long since abandoned the practice of crippling their children to ensure their continuing exposure to parental values, but self-mutilation has proved more difficult to eradicate. Few blind themselves now, but many a grandfather conceals a three-fingered hand within his embroidered mitten. Toes are another frequent target of self-punishment, and the prevalence of cheerful, even boisterous shops, always crowded with old men telling stories, which sell the hand-carved wooden legs known as "pegs" or "dollies," speaks of yet another.

No one has ever suggested that the viaduct killer is a South Side resident.

The South Siders live in a profound relationship to violence, and its effects are invariably implosive rather than explosive. Once a decade, perhaps twice a decade, one member of a family will realize, out of what depths of cultural necessity the outsider can only hope to imagine, that the whole family must die—*be sacrificed*, to speak with greater accuracy. Axes, knives, bludgeons, bottles, babushkas, ancient derringers, virtually every imaginable implement has been used to carry out this aim. The houses in which this act of sacrifice has taken place are immediately if not instantly cleaned by the entire neighborhood, acting in concert. The bodies receive a Catholic burial in consecrated ground, and a mass is said in honor of both the victims and their murderer. A picture of the departed family is installed in the church which abuts Market Square, and for a year the house is kept clean and dust-free by the grandmothers of the neighborhood. Men young and old will quietly enter the house, sip the brandy of the "removed," as they are called, meditate, now and then switch on the wireless or the television set, and reflect on the darkness of earthly life. The departed are frequently said to appear to friends and neighbors, and often accurately predict the coming of storms and assist in the location of lost household objects, a treasured button or Mother's sewing needle. After the year has elapsed, the house is sold, most often to a young couple, a young blacksmith or market vendor and his bride, who find the furniture and even the clothing of the "removed" welcome additions to their small household.

Further south are suburbs and impoverished hamlets, which do not compel a visit.

Immediately west of the War Memorial is the city's downtown. Before its decline, this was the city's business district and administrative center, and the monuments of its affluence remain. Marching directly west on the wide avenue which begins at the expressway are the Federal Building, the Post Office, and the great edifice of City Hall. Each is an entire block long and constructed of granite blocks quarried far north in the state. Flights of marble stairs lead up to the massive doors of these structures, and crystal chandeliers can be seen through many of the windows. The facades are classical and severe, uniting in an architectural landscape of granite revetments and colonnades of pillars. (Within, these grand and inhuman buildings have long ago been carved and partitioned into warrens illuminated by bare light bulbs or flickering fluorescent tubing, each tiny office with its worn counter for petitioners and a stamped sign proclaiming its function:

Tax—Excise, Dog Licenses, Passports, Graphs—Charts, Registry of Notary Publics, and the like. The larger rooms with chandeliers which face the avenue, reserved for civic receptions and banquets, are seldom used.)

In the next sequence of buildings are the Hall of Records, the Police Headquarters, and the Criminal Courts Building. Again, wide empty marble steps lead up to massive bronze doors, rows of columns, glittering windows which on wintry days reflect back the gray empty sky. Local craftsmen, many of them descendants of the city's original French settlers, forged and installed the decorative iron bars and grilles on the facade of the Criminal Courts Building.

After we pass the massive, nearly windowless brick facades of the Gas and Electric buildings, we reach the arching metal drawbridge over the river. Looking downriver, we can see its muddy banks and the lights of the terrace of the Green Woman Taproom, now a popular gathering place for the city's civil servants. (A few feet further east is the spot from which a disgruntled lunatic attempted and failed to assassinate President Dwight D. Eisenhower.) Further on stand the high cement walls of several breweries. The drawbridge has not been raised since 1956, when a corporate yacht passed through.

Beyond the drawbridge lies the old mercantile center of the city, with its adult bookstores, pornographic theaters, coffee shops, and its rank of old department stores. These now house discount outlets selling roofing tiles, mufflers and other auto parts, plumbing equipment, and cut-rate clothing, and most of their display windows have been boarded or bricked in since the civic disturbances of 1968. Various civic plans have failed to revive this area, though the cobblestones and gas street lamps installed in the optimistic mid-seventies can for the most part still be seen. Connoisseurs of the poignant will wish to take a moment to appreciate them, though they should seek to avoid the bands of ragged children that frequent this area at nightfall, for though these children are harmless they can become pressing in their pleas for small change.

Many of these children inhabit dwellings they have constructed themselves in the vacant lots between the adult bookstores and fast-food outlets of the old mercantile district, and the "tree houses" atop mounds of tires, most of them several stories high and utilizing fire escapes and flights of stairs scavenged from the old department stores, are of some architectural interest. The stranger should not attempt to penetrate these "children's cities," and on no account should offer them any more than the pocket change they request or display a camera, jewelry, or an expensive wristwatch. The truly intrepid tourist seeking excitement may hire one of these children to guide him to the diversions of his choice. Two dollars is the usual gratuity for this service.

It is not advisable to purchase any of the goods the children themselves may offer for sale, although they have been affected by the same self-consciousness evident in the impressive buildings on the other side of the river and do sell picture postcards of their largest and most eccentric constructions. It may be that the naive architecture of these tree houses represents the city's most authentic artistic expression, and the postcards, amateurish as most of them are, provide interesting, perhaps even valuable, documentation of this expression of what may be called folk art.

These industrious children of the mercantile area have ritualized their violence into highly formalized tattooing and "spontaneous" forays and raids into the tree houses of opposing tribes during which only superficial injuries are sustained, and it is not suspected that the viaduct killer comes from their number.

Further west are the remains of the city's museum and library, devastated during the civic disturbances, and beyond these picturesque, still-smoking hulls lies the ghetto. It is not advised to enter the ghetto on foot, though the tourist who has arranged to rent an automobile may safely drive through it after he has negotiated his toll at the gate house. The ghetto's residents are completely self-sustaining, and the attentive tourist who visits this district will observe the multitude of tents housing hospitals, wholesale food and drug warehouses, and the like. Within the ghetto are believed to be many fine poets, painters, and musicians, as well as the historians known as "memorists," who are the district's living encyclopedias and archivists. The "memorist's" tasks include the memorization of the works of the area's poets, painters, etc., for the district contains no printing presses or art-supply shops, and these inventive and self-reliant people have devised this method of preserving their works. It is not believed that a people capable of inventing the genre of "oral painting" could have spawned the viaduct killer, and in any case no ghetto resident is permitted access to any other area of the city.

The ghetto's relationship to violence is unknown.

Further west the annual snowfall increases greatly, for seven months of the year dropping an average of two point three feet of snow each month upon the shopping malls and paper mills which have concentrated here. Dust storms are common during the summers, and certain infectious viruses, to which the inhabitants have become immune, are carried in the water.

Still further west lies the Sports Complex.

The tourist who has ventured thus far is well advised to turn back at this point and return to our beginning, the War Memorial. Your car may be left in the ample and clearly posted parking lot on the Memorial's eastern side. From the Memorial's wide empty terraces, you are invited to look southeast, where a great unfinished bridge crosses half the span to the hamlets of Wyatt and Arnoldville. Construction was abandoned on this noble civic project, subsequently imitated by many cities in our western states and in Australia and Finland, immediately after the disturbances of 1968, when its lack of utility became apparent. When it was noticed that many families chose to eat their bag lunches on the Memorial's lakeside terraces in order to gaze silently at its great interrupted arc, the bridge was adopted as the symbol of the city, and its image decorates the city's many flags and medals.

The "Broken Span," as it is called, which hangs in the air like the great frozen wings above the Valley, serves no function but the symbolic. In itself and entirely by accident this great non-span memorializes violence, not only by serving as a reference to the workmen who lost their lives during its construction (its non-construction). It is not rounded or finished in any way, for labor on the bridge ended abruptly, even brutally, and from its truncated floating end dangle lengths of rusting iron webbing, thick wire cables weighted by chunks of cement, and bits of old planking material. In the days before access to the un-bridge was walled off by an electrified fence, two or three citizens each year elected to commit their suicides by leaping from the end of the span; and one must resort to a certain lexical violence when referring to it. Ghetto residents are said to have named it "Whitey," and the tree-house children call it "Ursula," after one of their own killed in the disturbances. South Siders refer to it as "The Ghost," civil servants, "The Beast," and East Siders simply as "that thing." The "Broken Span" has the violence of all unfinished things, of everything interrupted or left undone. In violence there is often the quality of *yearning*—the yearning for completion. For closure. For that which is absent and would if present bring to fulfillment. For the body without which the wing is a useless frozen ornament. It ought not to go unmentioned that most of the city's residents have never seen the "bridge" except in its representations, and for this majority the "bridge" is little more or less than a myth, being without any actual referent. It is pure idea.

Violence, it is felt though unspoken, is the physical form of sensitivity. The city believes this. Incompletion, the lack of referent which strands you in the realm of pure idea, demands release from itself. We are above all an American city, and what we believe most deeply we . . .

The victims of the viaduct killer, that citizen who excites our attention, who makes us breathless with outrage and causes our police force to ransack the humble dwellings along the riverbank, have all been adult women. These women in their middle years are taken from their lives and set like statues beside the pillar. Each morning there is more pedestrian traffic on the viaduct, in the frozen mornings men (mainly men) come with their lunches in paper bags, walking slowly along the cement walkway, not looking at one another, barely knowing what they are doing, looking down over the edge of the viaduct, looking away, dawdling, finally leaning like fishermen against the railing, waiting until they can no longer delay going to their jobs.

The visitor who has done so much and gone so far in this city may turn his back on the "Broken Span," the focus of civic pride, and look in a southwesterly direction past the six lanes of the expressway, perhaps on tiptoe (children may have to mount one of the convenient retaining walls). The dull flanks of the viaduct should just now be visible, with the heads and shoulders of the waiting men picked out in the gray air like brush strokes. The quality of their yearning, its expectancy, is visible even from here.

R.A. LAFFERTY

The Story of Little Briar-Rose, A Scholarly Study

R.A. Lafferty, one of the most original authors working today, is a Hugo Award–winning science fiction writer whose work sometimes crosses over the border into the field of fantasy. His novels include *The Devil is Dead*, *Past Master*, and *Fourth Mansions*, all Nebula Award nominees, and his short fiction has been collected in *Ringing Changes* and *Nine Hundred Grandmothers*. His delightfully idiosyncratic style of storytelling has made Lafferty something of a cult figure for the same reasons genre publishers have found him difficult to sell to a mass market audience. These days you have to seek out the small presses to read Lafferty's fiction, including Broken Mirrors Press (Box 473, Cambridge, MA 02338), Chris Drumm (Box 445, Polk City, IA 50226) and United Mythologies Press (Box 390, Station A, Weston, Ontario, Canada M9N 3N1.) It's well worth the search.

The following little tale, poking gentle fun at the solemn rhetoric of folklorists, comes from Steve Pasechnick's laudable new magazine *Strange Plasma* (Edgewood Press, P.O. Box 264, Cambridge, MA 02338) and is a fine example of why the fantasy field needs the small press publishers, who enliven our genre by bringing such offbeat and delightful works to the fantasy readership.

—T.W.

The Story of
Little Briar-Rose,
A Scholarly Study

R. A. LAFFERTY

> Thorny-Rose Dreamer, you sleep as though dead: Worlds within worlds
> within worlds in your head.
>> —Steep Dreams, Heinrich Kleinwolf

> The Dreamer is fifteen years old, and she has been fifteen years old for
> nearly a thousand years.
>> —Fairy Tales of Aragon, Alesandro Leija

We are investigating the story of Sleeping Beauty to see whether there are not
hidden in it the seeds of fuller happenings than those that are usually narrated.

Yes, there are indeed unused, hidden and explosive story riches in the Sleeping
Beauty Story. But these riches must remain hidden and unused, if not forever,
at least for a thousand years. For there would be world-wide turmoil in the hidden
parts of it were made known.

"World-wide turmoil?"

"Yes, even wider than the world. There would be turmoil in one entire mind
from one end of it to the other."

But first, there are a couple of loose ends that must be dealt with. Have you ever
noticed that most loose ends are found at the beginning?

We quote:

"In the tenth-century Europe and Near East, there was a general
feeling that the world would end in either the year 999 or 1000.

The popular prophets finally settled on the date of April 1 of the year
1000. (April First was at that time the first day of the year, so it was the
first All Fools' Day.) Many people, as the day approached, gave away all
that they owned to whomever wanted it. They sang a lot of and laughed
a lot and repented of their sins. Ninety-five percent of the people believed
that the End of the World was nigh, and they were glad to see that great
day coming. And five percent of the people believed that the world was
not about to end, and they acquired land titles and property titles from
all the True Believers. 'What monumental fools they are!' the skeptical
five percent cried. 'Oh, how the laugh is going to be on those fools!'

"But who was the laugh really on? For the world really did end at dawn of April 1 of the year 1000."

The Back Door of History, Arpad Arutinov

We quote again:

"In the year 410 of Restored Salvation, a Camel swallowed the entire world and retained it in its maw for a period of thirty-nine seconds. The beast then regurgitated the world again, and things went on as before. People had the feeling that something odd had happened, but they could not quite identify the feeling.

"In the year 785 B.C. a huge fish swallowed the entire Universe and retained it (not in its belly, but in a small space behind the pineal gland, the dreamer's gland, in its brain) for sixty-nine hours. A peculiarity of this manifestation was that each person in the world believed that he alone had been swallowed by the big fish, which became known as the Jonah-Fish in legend.

"Again, in the year 209 B.C. the pagan god Indra captured the entire Universe in his brain. As the Jonah-Fish had done, Indra set it in the small space behind his dreamer's gland (his pineal gland). The effect of this was that the Universe was existing only in the dreams of Indra and did not have an independent existence. But the experience gave Indra a headache, so after nine minutes he ejected the Universe again. Then the Universe teetered between an existence that was slightly more tenuous than its previous existence.

"These things really happened. They were not observational malfunctions. So what does the human community do when such massive and impossible things happen? It gives them a name and consigns them to being a footnote in the most obscure history it can find. The name given to these phenomena was 'Universal Inversion' or 'Topological Inversion', and mine was the most obscure history it could find."

Atrox Fabulinus

That takes care of the loose ends. They may not belong here, but it is a topological imperative that everything should be somewhere. Now we proceed to the story of Little Briar-Rose who came to be known as Sleeping Beauty.

The story presently is found in several different versions and forms. One of them is named THE SLEEPING BEAUTY IN THE WOODS, by Charles Perrault who lived from 1628 to 1703. The story appears in 1697 in a book titled "Accounts and Tales of Times Past by My Mother the Goose." In France of that day, 'Mother Goose Tales' had the same meaning as 'Old Wives Tales' had in England. But the "Mother Goose Nursery Rymes" published in London in 1760 owed nothing to Charles Perrault except the borrowed name 'Mother Goose.'

A second more modern version of the story was written by the Brothers Grimm

(Jacob who lived 1785–1863 and Wilhelm who lived 1786–1859). The story was in the "Household Tales" of the Grimms' that appeared between 1812 and 1822. It was named Little Briar-Rose (Dorn-Roschen). Though written more than a hundred years after the Perrault story, Little Briar-Rose is of an earlier recension. Using the technique of diffusion and parallelism, the tireless Brothers Grimm, sometimes employing as many as one hundred oral versions of a story from all Europe and the Near East, were able to reconstruct and to date approximately (so they believed) the original stories. They set the date-of-origin of Little Briar-Rose (its most popular name), or Sleeping Beauty (its second most popular name) as being close to, but not before, the year 1000.

The Brothers Grimm believed that the Story of Little Briar-Rose had a sort of predecessor in folk-lore named Noah and his Wonderful Ark.

What connection could there be between Noah and his Ark and the story of Sleeping Beauty? Oh, Noah was an enchanter, so he put all the birds and beasts on the Ark to sleep, and his wife and sons and his sons' wives too. "It's the easiest way to handle it," he said, "the hay bill for the beasts alone would break me." After he had put them all to sleep, Noah went up to the caboose (the little room with the window in the top of the Ark) and sat in the Captain's chair with his left eye open and his right eye closed in sleep. And he slept from the seventeenth day of the second month till the seventeenth day of the seventh month of what has been called 'The Year of The Big Flood.'

"Was the phenomena of Topological Inversion involved in either the Noah story or the Sleeper story?"

"How would we know if it was?"

A minor version of the Sleeping Beauty story is Tchaikovsky's Sleeping Beauty Ballet. The story is expressed more in the music and dance sequences than in its words and glosses.

Another minor version of the story is found in two songs by Stephen Foster: Beautiful Dreamer and Come Where My Love Lies Dreaming. The story is found entirely in the music and not at all in the words of these two songs.

And then there are several paintings which show the Sleeper's Castle surrounded by its bramble-bushes which merge into clouds, for the whole thing is free-floating in the sky—Well now, it is really free-floating in nothing at all, it is entirely outside space.

In the Perrault version there are eight fairies (seven good ones and one bad one). In the Grimm version there are no fairies at all. The two brothers, the crown princes of the fairy-tale industry, seldom used fairies. Instead of fairies, there were thirteen wise women, twelve good ones and one bad one.

The waking of the Sleeping Beauty Princess is contrived and artificial in all versions. Indeed, Jacob Grimm, in his old age and after the death of his brother Wilhelm, gave the opinion that the sleeping princess had not really wakened at all, that she was still sleeping after her 'century' had gone nine or ten times over. Jacob was even heard to mutter, "She must not wake, she must not wake. If she wakes up, then everything is finished." But Jacob Grimm had gone a bit dotty in his old age, and nobody inquired too closely as to what he meant.

*   *   *

Little Briar-Rose was an incomparably intricate and spacious and wise person. Since she had no speaking parts in any of the versions of her own story, it is something of a mystery how we know that she was so intricate and wise and spacious. but it's always been known about her. She became 'The Earthen Vessel Holding Treasure,' one selected out of many billions for the role.

Was there something mysterious about Briar Castle, the home of Little Briar-Rose? There is something mysterious about every castle; that's one of the requirements of being a castle. Was Briar Castle unusually large or in any way impressive?

"Not too large to fit behind the pineal gland (the dreamer's gland) in the human brain," says one peculiar voice.

"Be quiet, peculiar voice," we say. What evidence have we.

It impressed one poet who wrote:

> *"It's an older place than Eden*
> *And a taller town than Rome."*

Was Sleeping Beauty really as beautiful as has been made out? Yes, she was quite beautiful in form and face. However, though quite beautiful, there was more strength and intensity and scope in her fifteen-year-old face than there was softness and gentleness. Or, as Belloc has it in one of his poems:

> *"Her face was like a King's Command*
> *When all the swords are drawn."*

Even in her strange sleep, Little Briar-Rose was in command. This is especially evident in Tchaikovsky's Sleeping Beauty Ballet, in its music and dance sequences, more than in its glosses and words.

She must not wake, she must not wake!

"Hey, old Arpad Arutinov, if the world ended on April 1, of the year 1000, on the first April Fools' Day, as you say it did, how come we are still here?"

"You are not here, not quite here, not as you mean it. You are only here in a much more tenuous way, in a much more tenuous 'here.' "

"Why would the Lord of Eternity leave us in a tenuous state for near a thousand years?"

"For fun, perhaps, since a thousand years is less than one eyeblink to the Lord of Eternity."

"Hey, old Atrox Fabulinus, how much space is there behind the pineal gland in the human brain?"

"Not much space behind the pineal gland (the dreamer's gland) in the human brain, not much space at all. Barely enough space to contain the Universe."

Yes, of course the world ended at dawn of April 1 of the year 1000. That is proved by all sorts of evidence. No, there is nothing of the World remaining anywhere. There's a catch to that, however. To be completely inaccurate about the matter, we must state that one person has survived 'nowhere,' outside of space. She is in a deep sleep, and has been in deep sleep in her 'nowhere place' for nigh on to a thousand years. But she has deep dreams in her deep sleep, and all of us are items in her dreams.

Oh, don't carry on like that, folks. This isn't that bad at all. Consider the things that could have been.

What if the Camel that swallowed the entire World in the year 410 of Restored Salvation and retained it in his stomach for thirty-nine seconds, had retained it until the present time? What if all of us had been born and lived, and would die, in the crowded space of a camel's stomach! Anybody who has been in a camel's stomach for only thirty-nine seconds knows that it is a damnable place to be. The present circumstance is better.

What if, when in the year 785 B.C a huge fish had swallowed the entire universe and retained it for sixty-nine hours, the fish had retained it all until the present time? The circumstance for all of us would long since have become a situation of delirious insanity. The present circumstance is better.

What if, when in the year 209 B.C. the pagan god Indra captured the entire universe in his brain, he had retained it there until the present time instead of rejecting it after nine minutes? Oh, the awkward, misshapen, totally hideous dreams of Indra that we would then inhabit! The present circumstance is much better.

As it is, we are being dreamed by a pleasant, variegated mind, by a person of quiet sanity and balance and, yes, sweetness.

If we had been able to select, out of all the persons ever, the person we would most like to be dreamed by, could we have made a better selection than Little Briar-Rose?

End of Scholarly Study

K.W. JETER
The First Time

❦

K.W. Jeter is better known for his science fiction novels such as *Farewell Horizontal* and *Infernal Devices* (both St. Martin's Press/NAL) and film noir horror novels *In the Land of the Dead* (Onyx) and *The Night Man* (Onyx) than for his short fiction. "The First Time," is only his second published short story. It's brutal. It appeared in the anthology *Alien Sex* (Dutton).

—E.D.

The First Time

K. W. JETER

His father and his uncle decided it was about time. Time for him to come along. They went down there on a regular basis, with their buddies, all of them laughing and drinking beer right in the car, having a good time even before they got there. When they left the house, laying a patch of rubber out by the curb, he'd lie on his bed upstairs and think about them—at least for a little while, till he fell asleep—think about the car heading out on the long straight road, where there was nothing on either side except the bare rock and dirt and the dried-brown scrubby brush. With a cloud of dust rolling up behind them, his uncle Tommy could just floor it, one-handing the steering wheel, with nothing to do but keep it on the dotted line all the way down there. He lay with the side of his face pressed into the pillow, and thought of them driving, making good time, hour after hour, tossing the empties out the window, laughing and talking about mysterious things, things you only had to say the name of and everybody knew what you were talking about, without another word being said. Even with all the windows rolled down, the car would smell like beer and sweat, six guys together, one of them right off his shift at the place where they made the cinder blocks, the fine gray dust on his hands and matted in the dark black hair of his forearms. Driving and laughing all the way, until the bright lights came into view—he didn't know what happened after that. He closed his eyes and didn't see anything.

And when they got back—they always got back late at night, so even though they'd been gone nearly the whole weekend, and he'd gotten up and watched television and listened to his mom talking to her friends on the phone, and had something to eat and stuff like that, when his father and his uncle and their buddies got back, the noise of the car pulling up, with them still talking and laughing, but different now, slower and lower-pitched and satisfied—it was like it woke him up from the same sleep he'd fallen into when they'd left. All the other stuff was just what he'd been dreaming.

470

"You wanna come along?" His father had asked him, turning away from the TV. Just like that, no big deal, like asking him to fetch another beer from the fridge. "Me and Tommy and the guys—we're gonna go down there and see what's happening. Have a little fun."

He hadn't said anything back for a little while, but had just stared at the TV, the colors fluttering against the walls of the darkened room. His father hadn't had to say anything more than *down there*—he knew where that meant. A little knot, one he always had in his stomach, tightened and drew down something in his throat.

"Sure," he'd finally mumbled. The string with the knot in it looped down lower in his gut. His father just grunted and went on watching the TV.

He figured they'd decided it was time because he'd finally started high school. More than that, he'd just about finished his first year and had managed to stay out of whatever trouble his older brother had gotten into back then, finally causing him to drop out and go into the army and then god knew what—nobody had heard from his brother in a long time. So maybe it was as some kind of reward, for doing good, that they were going to take him along with them.

He didn't see what was so hard about it, about school. What made it worth a reward. All you had to do was keep your head down and not draw attention to yourself. And there was stuff to do that got you through the day: he was in the band, and that was okay. He played the baritone sax—it was pretty easy because they never got any real melodies to play, you just had to fart around in the background with everybody else. Where he sat was right in front of the trombone section, which was all older guys; he could hear them talking, making bets about which of the freshman girls would be the next to start shaving her legs. Plus they had a lot of jokes about the funny way flute players made their mouths go when they were playing. Would they still look that funny way when they had something else in their mouths? It embarrassed him because the flute players were right across from the sax section, and he could see the one he'd already been dating a couple of times.

One time, when they'd been alone, she'd given him a piece of paper that she'd had folded up in the back pocket of her jeans. The paper had gotten shaped round, the same shape as her butt, and he'd felt funny taking it and unfolding it. The paper was a mimeographed diagram that her minister at her Episcopalian youth group had given her and the rest of the girls in the group. It showed what parts of their bodies they could let a boy touch, at what stage. You had to be engaged, with a ring and everything, before you could unhook her bra. He'd kept the piece of paper, tucked in one of his books at home. In a way, it'd been kind of a relief, just to know what was expected of him.

It was what worried him about going down there, with his father and his uncle and the other guys—he didn't know what he was supposed to do when they got there. He lay awake the night before, wondering. He turned on the light and got out the piece of paper the girl who played the flute had given him, and looked at the dotted lines that made a sort of zone between the diagram's throat and navel, and another zone below that, that looked like a pair of underpants or the bottom half of a girl's two-piece swimsuit. Then he folded the paper back up and stuck it in the book where he kept it. He didn't think the diagram was going to do him any good where he was going.

"All right—let's get this show on the road." His uncle Tommy leaned out of the driver's-side window and slapped the door's metal. They always went down there in Tommy's car because it was the biggest, an old Dodge that wallowed like a boat even on the straightaways. The other guys chipped in for the gas. "Come on—let's move on out." Tommy's big yellow grin was even looser; he'd already gotten into the six-pack stowed down on the floor.

For a moment, he thought they'd all forgotten about taking him along. There were already five guys in the car when it'd pulled up in front of the house, and his father would make the sixth. He stood on the porch, feeling a secret hope work at the knot in his gut.

"Aw, man—what the hell were you guys thinking of?" The voice of one of the guys in the car floated out, across the warm evening air. It was Bud, the one who worked at the cinder block factory. "There's no way you can stick seven of us in here, and then drive all the way down there."

The guy next to Bud, in the middle of the backseat, laughed. "Well, hell—maybe you can just sit on my lap, then."

"Yeah, well, you can just sit on this." Bud gave him the finger, then drained the last from a can of beer and dropped it onto the curb. Bud pushed the door open and got out. "You guys just have a fine old time without me. I got some other shit to take care of."

Tommy's grin grew wider. "Ol' Bud's feeling his age. Since that little sweetheart last time fucked up his back for him."

"Your ass."

From the porch, he watched Bud walking away, the blue glow of the streetlights making the cinder block dust on Bud's workshirt go all silver. He couldn't tell if Bud had been really mad—maybe about him coming along and taking up space in the car—or if it was just part of the joke. A lot of the time he couldn't tell whether his father and his buddies were joking or not.

"Come on—" His father had already gotten in the car, up front, elbow hanging over the sill of the door. "What're you waiting for?"

He slid in the back. The seat had dust from Bud's shirt on it, higher up than his own shoulders. "Here we go," said his father, as his head rocked back into the cinder block dust. The guy next to him, his father's buddy, peeled a beer off a six-pack and handed it to him. He held it without opening it, letting the cold seep into his hands as the streets pivoted around and swung behind the car, until they were past the last streetlight and onto the straight road heading for the southern hills.

All the way down there, they talked about baseball. Or football, shouting over the radio station that Tommy had turned up loud. He didn't listen to them, but leaned his shoulder against the door, gulping breath out of the wind, his face stung red. For a long while he thought there was something running alongside the car, a dog or something, but faster than a dog could run, because his uncle Tommy had the car easily wound up to over seventy. The dog, or whatever it was, loped in the shadows at the side of the road, a big grin like Tommy's across its muzzle, its bright spark eyes looking right at him. But when another car came along, going the other way, the headlights making a quick scoop over the road, the dog wasn't there. Just the rocks and brush zooming by, falling back into the dark behind them. He pushed his face farther out into the wind, eyes squinted, the roar swallowing up the voices inside the car. The dog's yellow eyes danced like coins out there, keeping alongside and smiling at him.

"All *right*—we have uh-*rived*." His uncle Tommy beat an empty beer can against the curve of the steering wheel, then pitched it outside.

He looked up ahead, craning his neck to see around his father in the front seat. He could see a bridge, with lights strung up along it. And more lights beyond it, the town on the other side. He dropped back in his seat, combing his hair down into place with his fingers.

The lights, when they got across the bridge, were like Christmas lights, strings of little colored bulbs laced over the doorways of the buildings and even across the street, dangling up above, pushing back the night sky. There were other lights, too, the kind you'd see anywhere, blinking arrows that pointed to one thing or another, big yellow squares with the plastic strips for the black letters to stick on, covered in chicken wire to keep people's hands off.

Tommy let the car crawl along, inching through the traffic that had swallowed them up soon as they'd hit the town. So many other cars, all of them moving so slow, that people crossing the street, going from the lit-up doorways on one side to those on the other, just threaded their way through. Or if they were young guys, and the cars were bumper to bumper, they'd slap their hands down on a hood and a trunk lid and just vault over, with a little running step on the ridge of the bumpers halfway across, and just laughing and shouting to each other the whole time.

Even though it was so loud in the street—with all the car radios blaring away, with everybody's windows rolled down, and the even louder music thumping out of the doorways—he felt a little drowsy somehow. He'd drunk the beer his father's buddy had given him, and a couple more after that, and had gone on staring out at the dark rolling by the whole way down here. Now the street's noise rolled over him like the slow waves at the ocean's surface, far above him.

"Bail out, kid—let's go!" The guy beside him, in the middle of the backseat, was pushing him in the arm. His head lolled for a moment, neck limp, before he snapped awake. He looked around and saw his father and his uncle and the other guys all getting out of the car. Rubbing his eyes, he pushed the door open and stumbled out.

He followed them up the alley where they'd parked, out toward the lights and noise rolling in the street. It wasn't as bright and loud at this end; they'd left most of the action a couple of blocks back.

His father and his uncle were already down the street, laughing and swapping punches as they went, little boxing moves with feints and shuffles, like a couple of teenagers or something. His uncle Tommy was always carrying on, doing stuff like that, but he'd never seen his father so wild and happy. They had their arms around each other's shoulders, and their faces and chests lit up red as they stepped into one of the doorways, his father sweeping back a curtain with his hand. The light that had spilled out into the street blinked away as the curtain fell back into place. He broke into a run to catch up with the others.

Some kind of a bar—that was what it looked like and smelled like, the smell of spilled beer and cigarette smoke that had soaked into everything and made the air a thick blue haze around the lights. The others were already sitting around a table, one of the booths at the side; they'd left room for him at the end, and he slid in beside his uncle Tommy.

The man came around from behind the bar with a tray of beers, squat brown bottles sweating through the crinkly foil labels. He didn't know whether his father had already ordered, or whether the bartender already knew what they wanted, from all the times they'd been here before. He wasn't sure he'd get served, but it didn't seem to matter here how young he was; the bartender put a beer down in front of him, too. He took a pull at it as he looked around at the empty stage at one end of the room, with heavy red curtains draped around it and big PA speakers at the side. The other booths, and some of the tables in the middle, were crowded with bottles, men elbowing them aside as they leaned forward and talked, dropping the butts of their cigarettes into the empties.

Somebody poked him—it felt like a broom handle—and he looked around and saw a face grinning at him. A man short enough to look him straight in the eye where he sat; the grin split open to show brown teeth, except for two in front that were shining gold. The little man poked him again, with two metal tubes that had wires hooked to them, running back to a box that hung from a strap around the man's neck.

"Yeah, yeah—just take 'em." His father waggled a finger at the tubes, while digging with the other hand into his inside coat pocket. "Just hold on to 'em now. This is how they make you a man in these parts." His father came up with a dollar bill from a roll in the coat pocket and handed it over to the little man.

The tubes were about the size of the inside of a toilet paper roll, but shiny, and hard and cold to the touch. He looked at them sitting in his hands, then glanced up when he saw the little man turning a crank at the side of the box hanging around his neck.

An electric shock jumped out of the tubes, stinging his palms. He dropped them and jerked away. He looked around and saw his father and his buddies all roaring with laughter. Right beside him, his uncle Tommy was slapping the table with one hand, turning red and choking on a swallow of beer.

"Here—give 'em here." His father traded another dollar bill for the tubes, the wires dangling between the bottles as he took them from the little man. "Let 'er rip."

The little man turned the crank on the box, digging into it to make it go round faster and faster. His father winced with the first surge, then squeezed the tubes harder, hands going white-knuckled, teeth gritting together, lips drawn back. The crank on the box went around in a blur, until his father's hands flew open and the tubes clattered onto the table, knocking over one of the bottles. Beer foamed out and dribbled over the edge.

"Whoa! Jesus fucking Christ!" His father shook his hands, loose at the wrist. The guy sitting next over stuck out a palm and his father slapped it, grinning in triumph. The little man with the box did a kind of dance, laughing to show all the brown and gold teeth and pointing with a black-nailed finger. Then squatting down, the short legs bowing out, and cupping a hand to his crotch, acting like there was some cannonball-sized weight hanging there. The little man laughed and pointed to the man sitting in the booth again, then took another dollar bill and trotted away with the box and the tubes to another table.

He was looking at his father putting the roll of bills back into the coat pocket. His own hands still stung, and he wrapped them around the wet bottle in front of him to cool them.

"Yessir—that fucker'll sober you right up." His father signaled to the bartender. "I'm gonna need a couple more after that little bastard."

Somebody came walking over to the booth, but it wasn't the bartender. He looked up and saw one of the guys, one of his father's buddies—the guy hadn't been there the whole time they'd been messing around with the little man with the box.

"Lemme out." His uncle Tommy nudged him. "I think it's just about my turn."

He didn't know what his uncle meant, but he stood up and let Tommy slide out of the booth. The other guy took his place, sorting through the bottles on the table for the one that had been there before, that he hadn't finished.

Before he sat back down, he watched his uncle Tommy walking across the bar, squeezing past the backs of the chairs circled around the tables. There was a door in the corner with one of those wordless signs, a stick figure to indicate the men's room. But Tommy didn't head off toward that. His uncle pulled back the curtain hiding a doorway off to the side and disappeared behind it. He sat back down, but kept looking over at the curtain as he sipped at the beer that had grown warm in his hands.

Then—he didn't know how long it was—his uncle Tommy was back. Standing beside him, at the outside of the booth.

"Come on, fella—" Across the table, his father stabbed a thumb up in the air a couple of times. "Get up and let your old uncle siddown."

His uncle smelled different, sweat and something else. He got up, stepping back a little bit—the scent curled in his nostrils like something from an animal —and let his uncle slide into the booth.

He sat back down. His uncle Tommy had a big grin on his face. Around the table, he saw a couple of the other guys give a slow wink to each other, then tilt their beers up again.

Tommy glanced sidelong at him, then leaned over the table and spewed out a mouthful of blood. Enough of it to swamp across the tabletop, knocking the empty bottles over in the flood.

And he wasn't sitting in the booth then, next to his uncle. He'd jumped out of the booth, the way you would from the door of a rolling car; he stumbled and almost fell backward. Standing a couple of feet away, he listened to the men pounding the table and howling their laughter, louder than when the man with the box had shocked him.

"Tom, you shit-for-brains—" His father was red-faced, gasping for breath.

His uncle Tommy had a dribble of red going down his chin, like the finger of blood that had reached the edge of the table and dribbled over. Pretty drunk, his uncle smiled as he looked around the booth at the guys, pleased with the joke. His uncle turned and smiled at him, red seeping around the teeth in the sloppy grin.

The laughter dwindled away, the men shaking their heads and rubbing tears from the corners of their eyes. They all took long pulls at their beers. That was when he saw that there wasn't any room in the booth for him. They'd all shifted a little bit and taken up all the room; his uncle was sitting right at the end where he'd been.

They didn't say anything, but he knew what it meant. He turned around and looked across the bar, to the curtain that covered the doorway over there. It meant it was his turn now.

The woman ran her hand along the side of his neck. "You haven't been around here before, have you?" She smiled at him. Really smiled, not like she was laughing at him.

"No—" He shook his head. Her hand felt cool against the heat that had come rushing up under his skin. He pointed back over his shoulder. "I came with my dad, and his friends."

Her gaze moved past his eyes, up to where her fingers tangled around in his hair. "Uh-huh," she said. "I know your daddy."

She got up from the bed. He sat there watching her as she stood at a little shelf nailed to the wall. The shelf had a plastic-framed mirror propped up on it, and a towel and a bar of soap. She watched herself taking off her dangly earrings, gold ones, drawing the curved hooks out. She laid them down in front of the little mirror.

"Well, you don't have to worry none." She spoke to the mirror. "There's always a first time. Then it's easy after that." She rubbed a smudge away from the corner of her eye. "You'll see."

When he'd pulled aside the curtain and stepped into the dark—away from the bar's light, its noise of laughing and talking falling behind him—he hadn't even been able to see where he was, until he'd felt the woman take his hand and lead him a little farther along, back to where the doors to a lot of little rooms were lit up by a bulb hanging from the hallway's ceiling. One of the doors had opened and a man had come out and shoved past him in the narrow space, and he'd caught a whiff of the smell off the man, the same as had been on his uncle Tommy when he'd come back out to the booth.

When the woman had closed the door and come over to the bed to sit close by him, he'd held his breath for a moment, because he thought the scent would be on her too, that raw smell, like sweat, only sharper. But she smelled sweet, like something splashed on from a bottle, the kind women always had on their dressers. That made him realize that she was the first woman, the first female thing, he'd been near, for what seemed like days. All the way down here—in the car with his father and his uncle and their buddies, packed up tight with them as they'd gone barreling along in the night, and then crowded around the table in the booth, the same night rolling through the street outside, until their sweat was all he could smell, right down into his throat.

"Here—you don't want to get that all mussed up." The woman had on a white slip—it shone in the dim light as she came back toward the bed. "Let's take it off." She bent down, her dark hair brushing against his face, and started unbuttoning his shirt.

He felt cold, the sweat across his arms and shoulders chilling in the room's air. The woman sat down and leaned back against the bed's pillow, dropping his shirt to the floor. "Come a little closer." She stretched out her arms toward him.

"You see . . . there's nothing to be afraid of." Her voice went down to a whisper, yet somehow it filled the little room; it ate up all the space, until there was just the bed and her on it.

"We'll go real slow, so you won't get scared." She smiled at him, her hand tracing down his rib cage. She was a lot older than him; this close to her, he could see the tiny wrinkles around her eyes, the skin that had gone soft and tissuey around the bone, dark underneath it. The sweet smell covered up something else; when he breathed her breath, it slid down his throat and stuck there.

"Look . . ." She took his hand and turned his arm around, the pale skin underneath showing. She drew a fingernail along the blue vein that ran down to the pulse ticking away in his wrist.

She dropped his hand and held out her own arm. For just a second—then she seemed to remember something. She lifted her hips to pull the slip up, then shimmied the rest of the way out of it like a quick snakeskin. She threw it on the floor with his shirt.

"Now look . . ." She traced the vein in her arm. Her fingernail left a long thin mark along it. She did it again, the mark going deeper. Then a dot of red welled up around her nail, in the middle of her forearm. She dug the nail in deeper, then peeled back the white skin, the line pulling open from the inside of her elbow to her wrist.

"Look," she whispered again. She held the arm up to his face. The room was so small now, the ceiling pressing against his neck, that he couldn't back away. "Look." She held the long slit open, her fingers pulling the skin and flesh back. The red made a net over her hand, collecting in thicker lines that coursed to the point of her elbow and trickled off. A red pool had formed between her knee and his, where their weight pressed the mattress down low.

The blue line inside her arm was brighter now, revealed. "Go on," she said. "Touch it." She leaned forward, bringing her mouth close to his ear. "You have to."

He reached out—slowly—and lay his fingertips on the blue line. For a moment he felt a shock, like the one the man in the bar had given him. But he didn't draw his hand away from the slit the woman held open to him. Under his fingertips he felt the tremble of the blood inside.

Her eyelids had drawn down, so that she looked at him through her lashes. Smiling. "Don't go . . ." He saw her tongue move across the edges of her teeth. "There's more . . ."

She had to let go of the edges, to guide him. The skin and flesh slid against his fingers, under the ridge of his knuckles. He could still see inside the opening, past her hand and his.

She teased a white strand away from the bone. "Here . . ." She looped his fingers under the tendon. As his fingers curled around it, stretching and lifting it past the glistening muscle, the hand at the end of the arm, her hand, curled also. The fingers bent, holding nothing, a soft gesture, a caress.

He could barely breathe. When the air came into his throat, it was heavy with the woman's sweet smell, and the other smell, the raw, sharper one that he'd caught off his uncle.

"See?" The woman bent her head low, looking up through her lashes into his eyes. Her breasts glowed with sweat. Her hair trailed across her open arm, the ends of the dark strands tangling in the blood. "See—it's not so bad, is it?"

She wanted him to say no, she wanted him to say it was okay. She didn't want him to be frightened. But he couldn't say anything. The smell had become a taste lying on his tongue. He finally managed to shake his head.

Her smile was a little bit sad. "Okay, then." She nodded slowly. "Come on."

The hand at the end of the arm had squeezed into a fist, a small one because her hands were so small. The blood that had trickled down into her palm seeped out from between the fingers and thumb. With her other hand, she closed his fingers around the white tendon tugged up from inside. She closed her grip around his wrist and pulled, until the tendon snapped, both ends coming free from their anchor on the bone.

She made him lift his hand up, the ends of the tendon dangling from where it lay across his fingers. She had tilted her head back, the cords in her throat drawn tight.

"Come on . . ." She leaned back against the pillow. She pulled him toward her. One of her hands lay on the mattress, palm upward, open again, red welling up from the slit in her arm. With her other hand she guided his hand. His fingers made red smears across the curve of her rib cage. "Here . . ." She forced his fingertips underneath. "You have to push hard." The skin parted and his fingers sank in, the thin bone of the rib sliding across the tips.

"That's right . . ." She nodded as she whispered, eyes closed. "Now you've got it. . . ."

Her hand slid down from his, down his wrist and trailing along his forearm. Not holding and guiding him any longer, but just touching him. He knew what she wanted him to do. His fingers curled around the rib, the blood streaming down to his elbow as the skin opened wider. He lifted and pulled, and the woman's rib cage came up toward him, the ones higher snapping free from her breastbone, all of them grinding softly against the hinge of her spine.

His hand moved inside, the wing of her ribs spreading back. Her skin parted in a curve running up between her breasts. He could see everything now, the shapes that hung suspended in the red space, close to each other, like soft nestled stones. The shapes trembled as his hand moved between them, the webs of sinew stretching, the peeling open, the spongy tissue easing around his hand and forearm.

He reached up higher, his body above hers now, balancing his weight on his other hand hard against the mattress, deep in the red pool along her side. Her knees pressed into the points of his hips.

He felt it then, trembling against his palm. His hand closed around it, and he saw it in her face as he squeezed it tight into his fist.

The skin parted further, the red line dividing her throat, to the hinge of her jaw. She lifted herself up from the pillow, curling around him, the opening soft against his chest. She wrapped her arm around his shoulders to hold him closer to her.

She tilted her head back, pressing her throat to his mouth. He opened his mouth, and his mouth was full, choking him until he had to swallow. The heat streaming across his face and down his own throat pulsed with the trembling inside his fist.

He swallowed again now, faster, the red heat opening inside him.

It was lying on the bed, not moving. He stood there looking at it. He couldn't even hear it breathing anymore. The only sound in the little room was a slow dripping from the edge of the mattress onto the floor.

He reached down, fingertip trembling, and touched its arm. Its hand lay open against the pillow, palm upward. Underneath the red, the flesh was white and cold. He touched the edge of the opening in its forearm. Already, the blue vein and the tendon had drawn back inside, almost hidden. The skin had started to close, the ends of the slit becoming a faint white line, that he couldn't even feel, though he left a smeared fingerprint there. He pulled back his hand, then he turned away from the bed and stumbled out into the hallway with the single light bulb hanging from the ceiling.

They looked up and saw him as he walked across the bar. He didn't push the empty chairs aside, but hit them with his legs, shoving his way past them.

His uncle Tommy scooted over, making room for him at the booth. He sat down hard, the back of his head striking the slick padding behind him.

They had all been laughing and talking just before, but they had gone quiet now. His father's buddies fumbled with the bottles in front of them, not wanting to look at him.

His father dug out a handkerchief, a blue checked one. "Here—" A quiet voice, the softest he'd ever heard his father say anything. His father held out the handkerchief across the table. "Clean yourself up a little."

He took the handkerchief. For a long time, he sat there and looked down at his hands and what was on them.

They were all laughing again, making noise to keep the dark pushed back. His father and his uncle and their buddies roared and shouted and pitched the empties out the windows. The car barreled along, cutting a straight line through the empty night.

He laid his face into the wind. Out there, the dog ran at the edge of the darkness, its teeth bared, its eyes like bright heated coins. It ran over the stones and dry brush, keeping pace with the car, never falling behind, heading for the same destination.

The wind tore the tears from his eyes. The headlights swept across the road ahead, and he thought of the piece of paper folded in the book in his bedroom. The piece of paper meant nothing now, he could tear it into a million pieces. She'd know, too, the girl who played the flute and who'd given the piece of paper to him. She'd know when she saw him again, she'd know that things were different now, and they could never be the same again. They'd be different for her now, too. She'd know.

The tears striped his face, pushed by the wind. He wept in rage and shame at what had been stolen from him. Rage and shame that the woman down there, in the little room at the end of the street with all the lights, would be dead, would get to know over and over again what it was to die. That was what she'd stolen from him, from all of them.

He wept with rage and shame that now he was like them, he was one of them. He opened his mouth and let the wind hammer into his throat, to get out the stink and taste of his own sweat, which was just like theirs now.

The dog ran beside the car, laughing as he wept with rage and shame. Rage and shame at what he knew now, rage and shame that now he knew he'd never die.

IAN FRAZIER
Coyote v. Acme

Ian Frazier is the author of *Dating Your Mom, Great Plains,* and *Nobody Better, Better Than Nobody.* "Coyote v. Acme" is a dry and witty piece of fantasy that has tickled all of us who work on this book. What can I tell you about this story? You must read it for yourself. All I can say is that I haven't laughed so hard since John M. Ford put the same incorrigible coyote in his Hemingway pastiche, "The Helmstich Notebooks"—and both these pieces have taken on a new dimension now that my winter office is in desert mountains where coyotes howl beneath the windows at night.

"Coyote v. Acme" is reprinted from *The New Yorker* magazine. I hope you'll enjoy it as much as we have.

—T.W.

Coyote v. Acme

IAN FRAZIER

In The United States District Court,
Southwestern District, Tempe, Arizona
Case No. B19294, Judge Joan Kujava, Presiding

Wile E. Coyote, Plaintiff
-v.-
Acme Company, Defendant

Opening Statement of Mr. Harold Schoff, attorney for Mr. Coyote: My client,
Mr. Wile E. Coyote, a resident of Arizona and contiguous states, does hereby
bring suit for damages against the Acme Company, manufacturer and retail distributor of assorted merchandise, incorporated in Delaware and doing business in
every state, district, and territory. Mr. Coyote seeks compensation for personal
injuries, loss of business income, and mental suffering caused as a direct result
of the actions and/or gross negligence of said company, under Title 15 of the
United States Code, Chapter 47, section 2072, subsection (a), relating to product
liability.

Mr. Coyote states that on eighty-five separate occasions he has purchased of
the Acme Company (hereinafter, "Defendant"), through that company's mail-
order department, certain products which did cause him bodily injury due to
defects in manufacture or improper cautionary labelling. Sales slips made out to
Mr. Coyote as proof of purchase are at present in the possession of the Court,
marked Exhibit A. Such injuries sustained by Mr. Coyote have temporarily restricted his ability to make a living in his profession of predator. Mr. Coyote is
self-employed and thus not eligible for Workmen's Compensation.

Mr. Coyote states that on December 13th he received of Defendant via parcel
post one Acme Rocket Sled. The intention of Mr. Coyote was to use the Rocket
Sled to aid him in pursuit of his prey. Upon receipt of the Rocket Sled Mr.
Coyote removed it from its wooden shipping crate and, sighting his prey in the
distance, activated the ignition. As Mr. Coyote gripped the handlebars, the Rocket
Sled accelerated with such sudden and precipitate force as to stretch Mr. Coyote's
forelimbs to a length of fifty feet. Subsequently, the rest of Mr. Coyote's body
shot forward with a violent jolt, causing severe strain to his back and neck and
placing him unexpectedly astride the Rocket Sled. Disappearing over the horizon

at such speed as to leave a diminishing jet trail along its path, the Rocket Sled soon brought Mr. Coyote abreast of his prey. At that moment the animal he was pursuing veered sharply to the right. Mr. Coyote vigorously attempted to follow this maneuver but was unable to, due to poorly designed steering on the Rocket Sled and a faulty or nonexistent braking system. Shortly thereafter, the unchecked progress of the Rocket Sled brought it and Mr. Coyote into collision with the side of a mesa.

Paragraph One of the Report of Attending Physician (Exhibit B), prepared by Dr. Ernest Grosscup, M.D., D.O., details the multiple fractures, contusions, and tissue damage suffered by Mr. Coyote as a result of this collision. Repair of the injuries required a full bandage around the head (excluding the ears), a neck brace, and full or partial casts on all four legs.

Hampered by these injuries, Mr. Coyote was nevertheless obliged to support himself. With this in mind, he purchased of Defendant as an aid to mobility one pair of Acme Rocket Skates. When he attempted to use this product, however, he became involved in an accident remarkably similar to that which occurred with the Rocket Sled. Again, Defendant sold over the counter, without caveat, a product which attached powerful jet engines (in this case, two) to inadequate vehicles, with little or no provision for passenger safety. Encumbered by his heavy casts, Mr. Coyote lost control of the Rocket Skates soon after strapping them on, and collided with a roadside billboard so violently as to leave a hole in the shape of his full silhouette.

Mr. Coyote states that on occasions too numerous to list in this document he has suffered mishaps with explosives purchased of Defendant: the Acme "Little Giant" Firecracker, the Acme Self-Guided Aerial Bomb, etc. (For a full listing, see the Acme Mail Order Explosives Catalogue and attached deposition, entered in evidence as Exhibit C.) Indeed, it is safe to say that not once has an explosive purchased of Defendant by Mr. Coyote performed in an expected manner. To cite just one example: At the expense of much time and personal effort, Mr. Coyote constructed around the outer rim of a butte a wooden trough beginning at the top of the butte and spiralling downward around it to some few feet above a black X painted on the desert floor. The trough was designed in such a way that a spherical explosive of the type sold by Defendant would roll easily and swiftly down to the point of detonation indicated by the X. Mr. Coyote placed a generous pile of birdseed directly on the X, and then, carrying the spherical Acme Bomb (Catalogue # 78-832), climbed to the top of the butte. Mr. Coyote's prey, seeing the birdseed, approached, and Mr. Coyote proceeded to light the fuse. In an instant, the fuse burned down to the stem, causing the bomb to detonate.

In addition to reducing all Mr. Coyote's careful preparations to naught, the premature detonation of Defendant's product resulted in the following disfigurements to Mr. Coyote:

1. Severe singeing of the hair on the head, neck, and muzzle.

2. Sooty discoloration.

3. Fracture of the left ear at the stem, causing the ear to dangle in the aftershock with a creaking noise.

4. Full or partial combustion of whiskers, producing kinking, frazzling, and ashy disintegration.

5. Radical widening of the eyes, due to brow and lid charring

We come now to the Acme Spring-Powered Shoes. The remains of a pair of these purchased by Mr. Coyote on June 23rd are Plaintiff's Exhibit D. Selected fragments have been shipped to the metallurgical laboratories of the University of California at Santa Barbara for analysis, but to date no explanation has been found for this product's sudden and extreme malfunction. As advertised by Defendant, this product is simplicity itself: two wood-and-metal sandals, each attached to milled-steel springs of high tensile strength and compressed in a tightly coiled position by a cocking device with a lanyard release. Mr. Coyote believed that this product would enable him to pounce upon his prey in the initial moments of the chase, when swift reflexes are at a premium.

To increase the shoes' thrusting power still further, Mr. Coyote affixed them by their bottoms to the side of a large boulder. Adjacent to the boulder was a path which Mr. Coyote's prey was known to frequent. Mr. Coyote put his hind feet in the wood-and-metal sandals and crouched in readiness, his right forepaw holding firmly to the lanyard release. Within a short time Mr. Coyote's prey did indeed appear on the path coming toward him. Unsuspecting, the prey stopped near Mr. Coyote, well within range of the springs at full extension. Mr. Coyote gauged the distance with care and proceeded to pull the lanyard release.

At this point, Defendant's product should have thrust Mr. Coyote forward and away from the boulder. Instead, for reasons yet unknown, the Acme Spring-Powered Shoes thrust the boulder away from Mr. Coyote. As the intended prey looked on unharmed, Mr. Coyote hung suspended in air. Then the twin springs recoiled, bringing Mr. Coyote to a violent feet-first collision with the boulder, the full weight of his head and forequarters falling upon his lower extremities.

The force of this impact then caused the springs to rebound, whereupon Mr. Coyote was thrust skyward. A second recoil and collision followed. The boulder, meanwhile, which was roughly ovoid in shape, had begun to bounce down a hillside, the coiling and recoiling of the springs adding to its velocity. At each bounce, Mr. Coyote came into contact with the boulder, or the boulder came into contact with Mr. Coyote, or both came into contact with the ground. As the grade was a long one, this process continued for some time.

The sequence of collisions resulted in systemic physical damage to Mr. Coyote, viz., flattening of the cranium, sideways displacement of the tongue, reduction of length of legs and upper body, and compression of vertebrae from base of tail to head. Repetition of blows along a vertical axis produced a series of regular horizontal folds in Mr. Coyote's body tissues—a rare and painful condition which caused Mr. Coyote to expand upward and contract downward alternately as he walked, and to emit an off-key, accordionlike wheezing with every step. The distracting and embarrassing nature of this symptom has been a major impediment to Mr. Coyote's pursuit of a normal social life.

As the Court is no doubt aware, Defendant has a virtual monopoly of manufacture and sale of goods required by Mr. Coyote's work. It is our contention that

Defendant has used its market advantage to the detriment of the consumer of such specialized products as itching powder, giant kites, Burmese tiger traps, anvils, and two-hundred-foot-long rubber bands. Much as he has come to mistrust Defendant's products, Mr. Coyote has no other domestic source of supply to which to turn. One can only wonder what our trading partners in Western Europe and Japan would make of such a situation, where a giant company is allowed to victimize the consumer in the most reckless and wrongful manner over and over again.

Mr. Coyote respectfully requests that the Court regard these larger economic implications and assess punitive damages in the amount of seventeen million dollars. In addition, Mr. Coyote seeks actual damages (missed meals, medical expenses, days lost from professional occupation) of one million dollars; general damages (mental suffering, injury to reputation) of twenty million dollars; and attorney's fees of seven hundred and fifty thousand dollars. Total damages: thirty-eight million seven hundred and fifty thousand dollars. By awarding Mr. Coyote the full amount, this Court will censure Defendant, its directors, officers, shareholders, successors, and assigns, in the only language they understand, and reaffirm the right of the individual predator to equal protection under the law.

RICHARD CHRISTIAN MATHESON

Arousal

Matheson is a Renaissance man. He seems to have his hand in everything to do with writing—screenplays, teleplays, short stories, and soon a novel. I think he is one of the most effective writers of the very short story in horror today. "Red," originally published in *Night Cry* magazine and later appearing in his collection *Scars And Other Distinguishing Marks* (Scream/Tor) is a horror classic.

A little background about "Arousal": The story was originally commissioned for a group of horror shorts that I was putting together for *Omni* ("Two Minutes Forty-Five Seconds" was in that batch). I asked Richard for a sexual horror story. Because of its sexual nature I showed the story to my boss before I bought it, just to make sure it was all right. She gave it back to me saying she didn't think it was too offensive but she didn't see why it was horror. Ahem. But right before the story actually went into production, both she and the (male) managing editor got cold feet. So after offering it and having it turned down by both *Playboy* and *Penthouse* (I felt that since I commissioned the story I should help Richard resell it) I bought it again for *Alien Sex*.

The basic question here is can you get too much of a good thing?

—E.D.

Arousal

RICHARD CHRISTIAN MATHESON

She stared.

Trying to be sure. Trying to hide it.

He was somehow perfect, somehow virulent; handsome in a way that slit her restraint open. Drew her in. He was about thirty. By himself in the bar. The town, asleep ten stories below, was flat and black. Streetlights stared up, inspecting the hotel bar with orange eyes, and occasionally a sleepy police car would pass, roving pointlessly.

She stared more, wiping long nails with a napkin.

She was becoming sure. *It was in his eyes*.

The *thing*.

Maybe even more than the ones before.

She ordered another kamikaze and walked to the pay phone, passing him. He stared out the window, chewing on a match, and she noticed the way his index finger traced the edge of his beer as if touching a woman's body.

The look.

Every location, she found it.

When the company was done filming and she'd finished going over the next day's setups with whichever director she was currently working under, she'd grab the location van back to the hotel the studio had booked the production team into, pick up mail and messages at the front desk, and go to her room. Always exhausted, always hating being an assistant director. Hating not being the one to set the vision. Run the set.

Be in control.

Then she'd strip; shower. Let the water scratch fingernails down her body as she closed tired eyes. Try to let the sensations take over. Try to feel something. But she never did.

She couldn't.

The sensual voyage her girlfriends felt when they were alone and naked, touching their bodies, allowing their skin to respond, no longer interested her. Her body searched for greater responses. Searched for the one who could hold her the right way, touch her with the exact touch. Make her respond; transcend. Stare into her eyes when she came.

Stare with that look.

She stood at the phone and called collect. Her husband was asleep and when he answered told her he loved her. She said it back but kept watching the man. He was pressing his lips against the matchstick, gently sucking it in and out as she stared in unprotected fascination.

Her husband offered to wake the kids so they could tell her good-night.

"They miss Mommy," he told her, in a sweet voice she hated.

She didn't hear what he'd said then, and he told her again, asking if she were all right; she sounded tired, distracted. She laughed a little, making him go away by calming him. He told her again he loved her and wanted to be with her. To make love. She was silent, watching the man across the barroom, catching his glance as he tried to get the waitress's attention.

"Do you miss me?" her husband asked.

The man was looking at her. Her husband asked her if she was looking forward to making love when she got back into town. She kept staring at the man. Her husband asked again.

"Yes, darling. Of course I am. . . ."

But it was a lie. It never stopped being one. He did nothing for her. She wanted something that would make her forget who she was, what her life was. Something real.

Something unreal.

Her husband had gone to get the kids though she told him not to. He wouldn't listen, and when she lifted cold fingers from her closed eyes, head bowed in private irritation, the man was standing next to her, buying cigarettes from a machine.

"Say hello to Mommy, kids."

The kids spoke sleepily over the phone while the man stared at her, lighting his cigarette, eyes unblinking. She told them to go to sleep, and that she loved them. But she was watching the man's eyes moving down her face, slowly to her neck, her breasts. Further. He quickly looked back at her and she allowed the look to do whatever it wanted.

They went to his room.

Nothing was said. They made love all night and she clutched at the sheets on either side of her sweating stomach with both hands, bunching up the starched cotton, screaming. He touched her so faintly at one point, it felt like nothing more than a thought; a wish. Her body arched and tensed, the pillow beneath her head soaked.

He tied her to the bedposts with silk scarves and blew softly onto her salty mouth, gently kissed her eyelids. He circled his tongue around her ears and whispered rapist demands that made her come. He massaged her until her skin effervesced, until her fingers pulled wildly at the scarves that held her wrists to the bed. Until she moaned with such pleasure, she thought she was in someone else's body.

Or had left her own.

Everything he did aroused her like she'd never been and when he finally untied her, she slept against his chest, held in his soothing arms. She murmured over and over how incredible it had been, stunned by what he'd made her feel. What he was still making her feel.

He said the only thing he would.

"You won't forget tonight."

When she awakened at dawn, he was gone. No note, no sign. There was a knock on the door and she answered, wrapping a towel around herself. Room service rolled in a large breakfast, complete with omelet, café au lait, and a newspaper.

He'd taken care of everything.

She sat in bed and ate, untying the newspaper, aching sweetly from the evening, covered with tender welts and bite marks. The food tasted delicious and the flavors on her tongue made her want to make love. She smiled, listened to the birds outside her window. Their soft opera gave her goose bumps, and as she opened the newspaper, the sound of its crisp folds made her nipples tingle. She laughed a little, remembering the incredible way he'd licked and sucked them last night. They were still sensitive.

As she read, she sipped at her coffee and the creamy heat of it made her part her legs slightly as it spread over her tongue and ran down her throat, warm like sperm.

She began to breathe harder, sipping more, twisting her shoulders as a tingle ran delicate electricity across her shoulders; up her spine.

As she read the front page, she allowed her fingers to drift on the inky surface and could feel the words; their shape and length. The curve of the individual letters. The sound the sentences created in her mind.

She felt herself getting wet.

It was *fantastic*; her body responsive to every detail of the morning; its sounds, colors. Even the feel of the blanket, the scraping texture of the wool making her think about him, the hair on his chest and face. God, why hadn't she asked his name? He was the greatest lover she'd probably ever have and she knew it. She laughed out loud, feeling a strange, new woman inside coming forth; emerging.

The ice in the orange juice was melting and when it rubbed against the glass, the sound made her softly, involuntarily moan. She smiled and lit a cigarette, sensing an unfamiliar fulfillment in her cells and nerves. A happiness.

Lost control.

The cigarette flame gave off a heat she could actually feel and she began to perspire. She shook a bit, grinning, and blew the match out, watching the tiny curls of smoke that peeled from its blackened tip and smelled like the man's scent. She couldn't stop herself from sliding a trembling hand onto a breast. Her skin was hot and as the sounds of the birds got louder outside her window and the hotel began to wake up below her, making faraway morning sounds, she listened and began to groan pleasurably from the noise.

The smell of the unfinished food and the warm air from the heating vent felt like a caress, and her nipples got harder, her pubic hair more wet. Her eyes wandered lazily, sexually around the room and noticed the furniture; the way the fabric on the couch fit its plaid shapes together so perfectly, each cushion like the next. It made her shut her eyes in exquisite torture. She opened them and caught a glimpse of the ballpoint pen which the hotel provided on the bedside table. Its red color pleased her and she groaned happily. Her eyes drifted on. The ashtray on the floor, filled with crippled cigarettes and gum wrappers excited her, its smells and patterns making her think of making love, of the man entering her and . . .

She suddenly realized what was happening and noticed an article on the front page section of the paper about a grotesque murder that had occurred the night before. A family had been gunned down by two men in ski masks and as she imagined it, her fingers moved over her body, searching wildly, uncontrollably. Scratching, squeezing. Shivering. She didn't understand the sexual storm her body felt as her mind filled with images of bullets shredding skin, faces twisting in horror, bodies slumping.

The tensing percussion.

The shudder.

She began to come again.

She couldn't stop the orgasm and it drenched her like a toxic wave that rose high and fainted; collapsing, then rising again.

Her body was wet with sweat and her teeth bit into her bottom lip, making it bleed. She squeezed herself so hard she began to bruise, more bluish ponds growing under her skin. Her arms drew back to the bedposts and grabbed tightly to either as if crucified, fingers white; desperate. She screamed louder and louder, flailing, coming again and again, not able to stop the flood of sights, sounds; tactile impressions.

She saw her children and began to cry.

Then, in her mind, she could see the man's face. His easy smile. The way he touched her.

The *look*.

She passed out for a few moments but the sound of maids beginning to vacuum and cars honking outside awoke her and she couldn't stop her body from starting to respond again.

GWEN STRAUSS
The Waiting Wolf
The Beast

In 1990, Alfred A. Knopf published a wonderful slim volume of fairy tale poems for adult readers by Gwen Strauss, gorgeously illustrated with moody black-and-white drawings by Anthony Browne. Browne and Strauss met at a Simmons College symposium in Massachusetts, discovered a mutual fascination for the underlying psychological motifs in fairy tales, and created the Knopf collection, *Trail of Stones*.

About the poems, Strauss writes: "Whether it is a princess calling down a well, a witch seeking out her reflection, children following a trail into the woods, falling asleep or into blindness . . . [the protagonists of fairy tales] are enclosed within a private crisis. They have entered a dark wood where they must either face themselves, or refuse to, but they are given the choice to change. The momentum of self-revelation leads them toward metamorphosis, like a trail of stones drawing them into the dark forest."

—T.W.

The Waiting Wolf

GWEN STRAUSS

First, I saw her feet—
beneath a red pointed cloak
head bent forward
parting the woods,
one foot placed straight
in front of the other.

Then, came her scent.
I was meant to stalk her
smooth, not a twig snaps.
It is the only way I know;
I showed her flowers—
white dead-nettle, nightshade,
devil's bit, wood anemone.

I might not have gone further,
but then nothing ever remains
innocent in the woods.

When she told me about Grandmother,
I sickened. She placed herself on my path,
practically spilling her basket of breads and jams.

Waiting in this old lady's ruffled bed,
I am all calculation. I have gone this far—
dressed in Grandmother's lace panties,
flannel nightgown and cap,

puffs of breath beneath the sheet
lift and fall. I can see my heart tick.
Slightly. Slightly.

These are small lies for a wolf,
but strangely heavy in my belly like stones.
I will forget them as soon as I have her,
still, at this moment I do not like myself.

When she crawls into Grandma's bed,
will she pull me close, thinking:
This is my grandmother whom I love?

She will have the youngest skin
I have ever touched, her fingers unfurling
like fiddle heads in spring.

My matted fur will smell to her of forest
moss at night. She'll wonder about my ears,
large, pointed, soft as felt,
my eyes red as her cloak,
my leather nose on her belly.

But perhaps she has known who I am since the first,
since we took the other path
through the woods.

The Beast

GWEN STRAUSS

She left and winter has arrived;
the garden walls grown slick black ice.
I think of how I spied on her while she ate,
how I designed the menu
so she would struggle with her delicacy:
Asian noodles, escargot, partridge that clung
to the bone, lobster she had to peel
from the gaudy red shell.
When she unfurled the white inside, dipped
the soft meat into butter, and let it
dissolve in her pink mouth,
she could have been devouring my heart.

She sends notes:
charming dinner at Lady Belworth's
with father and sisters.
She wore the satin décolleté gown I gave her,
bare white shoulders, neck arched innocently as crocus.
She doesn't mention her plans to return.

The Count Esmire is my able escort, she writes,
so don't fret. Does he slip his handsome arm
beneath her elbow when she steps
onto the cobblestones of a distant city?
Loneliness pulls a tourniquet round my heart,
and I would rend the Count to pieces.

She sent a box of chocolates.
She sends them out of pity.
I feel as small as her smallest daily thought.

This morning's note:
My sisters need me a while longer,
dashed off in her quick pen.
I am a regret, a promise she can't keep.

I crawl on all fours.
I've dug up her rose bushes.
I'm sucking their ivory frozen roots.
I sleep in a pile of rotting mulch. She never comes.

Licking the ice in the fountain
I noticed I'm growing a tail, white, like her roses,
moth wings, snow, the colour of horror
on her face whenever I touched her.

The beast heart survives, waits, and grows uglier.
This morning I know, she is not coming back.

The heart is the last organ to die.
The heart waits. The heart eats away at anything.
The heart builds a prison. My heart mocks me,
beating a sound like her footsteps,
drawing near.

MICHAEL BISHOP

Snapshots from the Butterfly Plague

Michael Bishop lives in Pine Mountain, Georgia and is the author of several thought-provoking science fiction novels and many short stories, for which he has won the Nebula Award. Fantasy readers will know him best as the author of *Unicorn Mountain*, a contemporary southwestern fantasy that tackled the difficult subject of AIDS. He is also the author of the wacky and offbeat Kudzu Valley stories such as "The Yukio Mishima Cultural Association of Kudzu Valley, Georgia," first published in *Basilisk* (Ellen Kushner, editor) and highly recommended. Bishop's short story collections are *Blooded on Arachne* and *One Winter in Eden*.

"Snapshots from the Butterfly Plague" is less tongue-in-cheek than the Kudzu Valley stories, but equally inventive, thoughtful and original—Michael Bishop at his very best. It is reprinted from *Omni* magazine.

—T.W.

Snapshots from the Butterfly Plague

MICHAEL BISHOP

Two cruel Aprils ago, a swarm of monarchs—see-through amber and hosiery black—wheeled down on a baby carriage parked next to a boathouse on Mockingbird Lake. The butterflies landed on the baby's face, then clung there like a swaying tower of miniature flags. (Twenty Thousand Flags Over Georgia.)

From my bicycle on a trail above the boathouse, I saw it all. It never occurred to me to think those monarchs were murdering the kid, suffocating him the way Edward the Second's assassins crushed the poor king under a table. But the returning mother's scream, along with a whispery stampede of retreating infanticides, made me think again.

As everyone knows, incidents of lepidopteran hostility increased after that bewildering first incident. From Montreal to San Diego, kaleidoscopic kamikaze strikes on ballparks left dozens of players, and countless fans, battered almost to insensibility by siroccos of pitiless silk.

The culprits weren't monarchs only, but azures, swallowtails, metalmarks, hairstreaks: squadrons of flamboyant loveliness that dropped out of the sky or exploded from peach trees, wheat fields, cattle pastures.

And when butterfly silkstorms fanned into our cities, smearing windshields, appliquéing engine grilles, Osterizing themselves in revolving doors, cycloning through subway stations like opalescent confetti, randomly canonizing winos, bag ladies, and whores (even as, tenderly, they snuffed them), Uncle Sam mobilized the National Guard.

Frightened boys in combat gear gassed every butterfly-flooded urban canyon, or else they *shot to kill* with evil-looking automatic weapons. In fact, on the Fourth of July, in the parking lot of Atlanta/Fulton County Stadium, a platoon of burr-headed guardies machine-gunned a flight of anglewings, pearl crescents, and red admirals. The carnage—if that's the word—was spectacular. So was the noise.

Jodi-Marie and I watched from a wall above the parking lot. To us, the deafening *tat-tat-tat!* was like a firefight with the wash line of a shah: brocades disintegrating, Shantungs tattering in air, the entire blazing wardrobe of a royal household parachuting into orange and purple scrap.

"It's for the birds," Jodi-Marie said as we illegally pedaled the shoulder of Oklahoma's I-40 between Yukon and Hydro.

"What's for the birds?" I said. (Probably, it was fancying myself a Tour de France competitor on a day so hot it could have been radioactive.)

"Damn it, Dennis, I said, it's *like* that old flick, *The Birds*." Jodi-Marie reached out to halt me, bestriding the mountain bike I'd bought her like some leggy, Lycra-clad gal in a *Bicycle Guide* ad. "Except it's butterflies instead of birds."

Jodi-Marie hadn't been born when *The Birds* came out. Me, I'd been at Duke, digging the Beatles and pot-smoking my way to a hippy peacenik vision of Shangri-La.

Still, Jodi-Marie wanted points for the allusion—which, by then, was so old-hat I had to tell myself that she *did* deserve some credit; after all, it's hard to stay abreast of things when you're self-propellering your tassels in the Cheetah Lounge five to seven hours a night.

That's why she liked me: my inherited cash and my savvy about the world. I wasn't just some crusty old bum—I was a mature, and well-heeled, bicycle vagabond.

"*This time*," I began to say, "*the birds are on our side*"—but a highway patrol car swam out of the heat shimmer.

Smoky was debonair in his widebrim and shades. "Hey," he said, "you shouldn't be up here." (On the high, holy "Motorized Vehicles Only" macadam, he meant.) To illustrate his point, he told a story about some hitchhikers, over by Guthrie, set upon by a wheeling conflagration of scarlet swallowtails. They were driven screaming to their knees, not to mention their deaths, by yards and yards of belligerent red chiffon.

"They looked like men on fire—like they'd been whooshed by flamethrowers or something."

"Scarlet swallowtails are from the Philippines," I said. "You don't get them in temperate zones."

Smoky waved. The air did dizzying hulas over the concrete, out on the prairie. "This look 'temperate' to you, bubba?"

"It's just so hard to believe a bunch of silky butterflies can really kill people," Jodi-Marie said.

Smoky—his real name was Clayton McKenna—said, "A ton of nylon may be softer than a ton of bricks, but a ton's still a ton, missy." He told us that truckers, people in cars, bus passengers, and speeding Hell's Angels were probably safe, but that hikers and cyclists were "playing butterfly roulette."

Then, Good Samaritan-like, McKenna paced us four miles past El Reno to U.S. 270, which we followed northwest to Watonga, Woodward, Fort Supply, Forgan, and, eventually, the oxymoronically monickered Liberal, Kansas.

* * *

Actually, birds *weren't* our allies—not any longer. In only their past nine to twelve generations, an army of workaholic U.N. entomologists bemusedly reported, nearly every lepidopteran species worldwide had chemically mutated to secrete into its blood a sickening toxin—hydrogen cyanide—that no self-respecting bird or bat would ever want to taste again.

Besides, the bug men said, butterflies from every continent but Antarctica were now ecumenically flocking, as if joined in common cause to chasten humanity with their spectacular oneness. And, of course, if sheer beauty had no power to shame or reform, the little organza beasties weren't averse to pummeling the bejesus out of us with a myriad hallelujahing wings.

Seven miles up the nauseating zebra haze of Highway 83, due north of hayseed Liberal, our incandescent mountain bikes coasted into the lot of a dusty complex of cinderblock buildings called—I kid you not—LAAMAAR DE LONG'S HOLISTIC ECOLOGICAL GREAT PLAINS CHURCH & ROADSIDE MOTH-O-RAMA.

"Some damnfools say it's Nature biting back," Laamaar De Long told Jodi-Marie and me in the welcome cool of the moth-o-rama's parlor, "but that's a earthshoe liberal's two-bit notion of cosmic justice. I don't buy it."

Laamaar was a wide man, as wide as his given name, as wide as the G R E A T P L A I N S. Fifty or so, he put me in mind of a lumpy-faced critter from my daddy's favorite comic strip, *Pogo*—but whether hound, skunk, gator, or bear, I couldn't say, only that the gruff old coot was at once endearing and sinister.

"It isn't Nature biting back," he said. "It's God or something like Him souping up the ordinary with a whizz-bang glory."

Later, our admission money in hand, De Long walked Jodi-Marie and me through his bare-walled moth-o-rama. "These are the night fighters of God's holistic ecological invasion force. I've always been an after-hours guy, so it had to be moths I beelined for when going into, first, a business and, later, a religion."

We walked by glassed-in dioramas sheltering peacocks, lunas, regals, sphinx moths, owlets: an aviary of tender plumes hammering in the aqueous half-light of the viewing chambers.

"Nowadays, butterfly houses are 'in'—a dime a dozen," said De Long, "but my moth-o-rama's a one-of-a-kind affair. I'm damned proud of it."

The male lunas—pale green and glowing, like bioluminscent fungus—seemed especially restive. I wondered if their furred antennea were picking up the pheromone broadcasts of the females winging solo over the ticking evening wheat.

Jodi-Marie placed her hands on the glass, whispered consolingly to the moths, muttered that they deserved to be free, then said it was time to catch some muscle-restoring shuteye. Come morning, our itinerary long since decided, we'd strike out for Wolf Creek Pass, the Grand Canyon, Las Vegas, and, Jodi-Marie's own hubristic grail, Hollywood. (Hooray.)

"Make camp here on my grounds," De Long said. "You're my first real customers in days. I'd like the company."

Having taken a judgmental dislike to the old fellow, Jodi-Marie didn't want to accept. I convinced her it was okay.

* * *

A full moon floated over the wheat. It glimmered like a beach ball as we bucked on the canvas ground cloth in our thermoplastic tent.

Despite the Butterfly Plague now in process, we were biking to the coast so that Jodi-Marie could "become a star." She wasn't an unintelligent young woman, but she couldn't sing. Her voice was a metallic whine. She couldn't act, not even enough to disguise her distaste of Laamaar De Long from De Long himself. And once past her perfunctory B-girl bump & grind, she couldn't dance any better than a hamstrung sow tripping down a meat-packing line on its way to become Spam.

Nevertheless, in the plastic-defracted glow of the August moon, Jodi-Marie said, "I *am* going to make it. It's my destiny, Dennis. Remember that stripper who did it with fans?"

"Pardon me, Jodi girl, but I'm not *that* old."

"What was her name? Sally Something. Sally . . . Rand."

"Yeah, but she *didn't* use fans."

"Sure she did."

"It was feathers. Big ones. Ostrich plumes."

"Okay, okay. What difference does it make?"—but the kink in her voice said that the distance between fans and ostrich plumes was vast. Then, as if to dispel a gathering funk, she told me the dream she'd been having nightly for over a week:

She is sashaying down the runway of the biggest crystal palace since the world got into the business of World Fairing. Big-time exhibitionism. She herself is the fairest of the Fair, feathered in exotic lepidoptera from Africa, Asia, South and Central America, the palmy Caribbean: tailed batwings, languid owls with disturbing eyespots, yellow birdwings, Paris peacocks, tigers, emerald banded swallowtails, G I A N T purple emperors, modest zebras, blood-red flambeaux. They hide what she wants to hide. They show what she wants to show. They flutter when she struts. They crackle, sigh, and hover exactly when she wants them to.

Jodi-Marie's eyes had begun to glass in reverie. Butterflies swam in her pupils. I almost fell in love with her dream-stitched image of herself—her pied, and striated, and moiré-patterned self-infatuation.

"*Come back inside!*" boomed De Long from much too near us in the moon-burned night. "I'll break all my moth cases. You can let the fuzzy fellas shingle your pretty self for as long as it t-t-tickles your fancy, gal."

"Cripes!" said Jodi-Marie, pushing me off.

I fought to catch myself, to recover my shorts.

De Long blathered on: "My wife ran off with a weather-radio man six years ago. All I want's a look-see, gal. Isn't that what you want to give me? Isn't that what you've been dreaming of?" He peered down into our tent like a boozy sodbuster colossus.

"I was dreaming of *show business*," Jodi-Marie said. "What you snuck up on was private."

I got angry: "If it's a peep show you want, buy a VCR."

"Eskimos share their wives," De Long said reproachfully, then staggered back to his tinhorn moth-o-rama.

Jodi-Marie figured De Long for a would-be rapist; I argued that he was only a lonely, wifeless fool.

So we stayed, and tried to sleep, and the moon tumbled by like a ball in an exhausted roll-on deodorant.

Later: BOOM! BOOM! BOOM!

Our after-the-fact deductions told us that De Long had fired a 12-gauge shotgun at the panels in the moth-o-rama's roof, blasting holes in them, widening these holes, then blasting again—until every tin panel was a window and the moths in his dioramas (earlier freed by hammer slams) went helixing up through the holes like a tornado whirling black-and-white oragami toys, scissored scraps of celluloid, and weightless kernels of popcorn excelsior whoosingly upward: a tornado run in reverse on the drive-in-theater screen of the Seward County sky.

"They're heading toward the moon," Jodi-Marie said, "like moths toward a—"

"A flame," I concluded for her.

And, in fact, a superorganism of moths was climbing together to blot out the moon. Lepidoptera in the fields beyond the structure joined the escapees in windmilling aloft.

Jodi-Marie and I watched draft-borne argosies of the creatures bank, interthread, flap higher and wider, eclipse the stars, and greedily devour the slow-to-set moon. Then we packed up our gear and scrammed. For miles, though, we couldn't outpace the signs in the sky of an imaginative business gone horribly awry.

Killing the plants on which the larval caterpillars fed, said the hotshot U.N. entomologists, would knock out the berserk adults far more efficiently than machine-gunning them as they whirled over parking lots; better, even, than spraying them with chemicals while they basked in hardwood groves or wildflower meadows.

The entomologists were wrong: Every species worldwide had modified its feeding habits to such a degree that it could live on carrion as well as plants. We saw flocks of British Camberwell beauties, or mourning cloaks, perched like Ritz-dyed lichen on the carcasses of road kills: dead dogs, steamrollered cats, raw red opossums.

Almost overnight, in evolutionary terms, adult lepidoptera had become opportunistic scavengers. They also engaged in predation, slaying in wily bands whatever they wanted to eat.

But there was more: These new lepidoptera had abandoned the four-part life cycle of egg, caterpillar, chrysalis, imago—in favor of 1) sex between contending adults, 2) a three-or four-month pregnancy, and 3) the dropping of fully formed winged infants (as few as one, as many as a thousand) that scavenged, preyed, and grew, no matter the species, as large as a grown man's hand. Then they would fly off with the reconnoitering squadrons to which their parents still belonged.

Said one worried bug man, "I'm afraid that, today, the damned things are like souls: immortal."

For, although it was easy to kill free-lancing adults, it did appear that, left alone, these mutant lepidoptera *did not die.* Their biomass burgeoned like April kudzu. Meanwhile, silkworms, inchworms, bagworms, woolly bears—all the different makes of caterpillar—were conspicuous by their extinction.

Jodi-Marie and I had stopped to rest in a turnout at the top of Wolf Creek Pass. Near water birch, Englemann spruce, and aspens, I only half listened to her harangue about the necessity of choosing a stage name to replace her real surname, Woznicki.

Among a stand of wind-nudged aspens on the Pagosa Springs side of the mountain, one tree burned like a lamp sipping natural gas; the blaze of its foliage was a startling bluish white.

"*I'd like something sweet and happy-sounding,*" Jodi-Marie was saying, from far away. "*Something gay. Well, not gay. Joyful. Upbeat. Fun-like.*"

My bonfire tree was an aspen, but an albino, a breathtaking freak.

"*Like Jolley. Jodi-Marie Jolley. Or Goforth. Or Harmon—short for 'Harmony.' Whaddaya think?*"

A crash in the undergrowth near the burning tree. A rattling of leaves. A murmur. Faint snappings of branches. The leaves on my albino aspen burst into the San Juan Mountain sky and spread out overhead in bands of gaudy, living cirrocumulus.

The butterflies shooting from the aspen—huge mustard whites, slightly smaller azures—had scared me, but even more scary was the party of bare-chested savages trudging up the mountain toward our turnout. Eight or nine in all, they were young men and women (whites or chicanos, so far as I could tell) who had glued to their faces the scales of monarchs, sulphurs, blue tigers, British orange tips— even the prismatic scales of various unpigmented species—so that their faces sparkled like those of rain-forest Indians made up for ritual war.

"My God," Jodi-Marie said. (I heard her.) "Those women down there—they aren't even wearing halter tops."

I didn't say she was only barely wearing one herself. Besides, the savages did have capes, hand-painted linen wings that snagged the underbrush and glinted menacingly.

"Those are Mariposa People," I said. "Come on!"

But an arrow, colorfully fletched, lodged between the spokes of Jodi-Marie's front tire.

"*Now!*" I shouted, pulling it out and snapping it in two.

Together, plummeting, we rode the dropside of Wolf Creek Pass, coasting headlong to save our lives, falling handlebar by handlebar toward Pagosa Springs. Suddenly, a dreamy cloud of butterflies—lemon, ivory, sapphirine, emerald, scarlet, orange—loomed below us, smack in the middle of Highway 160.

"Duck your head," I cried. "Go through them! Stay inside the edging line!"

We were wearing helmets, our chin straps flying free, and when we hit that eddying, airborne palette, sky, mountain, and roadway disappeared. The world consisted solely of buoyant fabric scraps, nostril-tickling quilting squares. Waves of bitter insects filled my mouth. Sleeves of wind-plastered scales rippled from my arms. The highway was an unraveling gallery of Roualts, Chagalls, Klees, Pollocks, Mondrians.

Jodi-Marie and I broke from the silk squall. Wobbling crazily, we still might have wrecked, but an unpaved escape lane for runaway semis ski-sloped abruptly up to our right.

I shouted, *"Go up it! Go up!"*

She did. I did. We both did.

This uphill cut was bumpy and gravelly, but it rescued us from screaming ever faster downward, and when its gravity finally caught us, and we toppled, neither the Mariposa People nor the butterflies themselves were anywhere to be spied in the spruce-lined defile of Wolf Creek Pass.

"A bunch of crackpot millennarians," I said. "They think the end has come and the only way to save the world, and themselves, is to smear their faces with butterfly scales and sacrifice 'mundanes' like us to their Great Butterfly Manitou."

"Not really," Jodi-Marie said.

"That's the first lot I've ever seen, but it's plain what they wanted—namely, to kill us."

"You mean, they'd've left our bodies out as meat for a bunch of hungry butterflies?"

"You got it."

Later, walking our bikes, holding them back from the mountain's relentless tug, Jodi-Marie asked, "Why *mariposa?*"

"It means butterfly," I said. "In Spanish."

Later yet, in a motel in Pagosa Springs, Jodi-Marie, clad only in the wings of a big crimson towel, pirouetted for me.

"I've found my new name. 'Mariposa.' 'Jodi-Marie Mariposa.' "

"It's a syllable longer than your own name."

"Yeah, but it's prettier. And it goes with Marie."

I just looked at her. On the TV, I watched an entire program about mutating lepidoptera and their terrible impact—ecological, economic, emotional—on lands and peoples from the Philippines to the Seychelles.

We saw butterflies everywhere we rode: through the Ute country, on Arizona's Navajo reservations, tree-clinging festively in Kaibab National Forest, swooping in gala formations past the layer-cake strata of the Grand Canyon, eating dead animals on all the desert ranches between Cortez and Kingman.

It was scary to pass them. You had no idea if they were only scavenging or cagily biding their time. I'd have felt much less anxious sighting a tornado at twelve o'clock high.

Las Vegas was all neon glitz, but the painted ladies, mormons, clippers, striped blue crows, and crimson tips darting among the swimming pools and casinos made even Las Vegas's crisscrossing searchlights and jitterbugging electronic signs seem as prosaic as flashlight beams.

We stayed at Caesar's Palace, saw a stage show featuring thirty sequin-dusted girls, and fed more than five hundred quarters into the slots. At last, three citrus swallowtails in a row gave us a jackpot, and a welcome excuse to stop.

"You could probably get on here," I said. I meant as a chorus girl, but Jodi-Marie smiled wanly and shook her head.

"It's Hollywood or bust," she said.

I avoided the obvious joke, and, early that evening, we pedaled out of Vegas down Interstate 15, our handlebars laden with water bags: Neither of us was too keen on dying of thirst in the Devils Playground or some funky desert salina. But with the man-eating butterflies of the dying twentieth century, we were willing to take our chances.

It took us three days to bike the dry lakes of southeastern California. The only lepidoptera we chanced upon were singletons, because butterflies care for the yucca-spiked desert about as much as most people do.

In any case, we did a lot of riding at night. When we finally reached "civilization," the insane freeway grid that is Greater Los Angeles, we felt like two lost sand grains ourselves. We spent our first night in a motel not too far from Dodger Stadium. You could hear the traffic on the Hollywood Freeway, and the conch-shell roar of sun-tanned people in Hawaiian shirts, and the faint, recurring, businesslike cracks of either baseball bats or dreams.

"Maybe you'll be discovered," I told Jodi-Marie.

The pity was, standing with her on a balcony ledge somewhere on the bleak edge of Shangri-La-La Land, I understood, belatedly, that I wanted to discover her myself.

The plague grew worse. Galaxy arms of butterflies—hordes of skippers, moths, and swallowtails—reduced atmospheric visibility to a level prefigured only by the worst of L.A. smogs. You could not go outside without stepping on a carpet of wings, or breathing in a mist of scales, or overhearing the provocative whine of pastel membranes razoring the wind.

There was also the continuous noise of insect husks colliding. Air-conditioning systems clogged. Swimming pools began to resemble outdoor Oriental carpets. Unprotected infants died. Street people emigrated inland. The Hollywood sign took on a filigree of moving orchids.

The President declared Greater L.A. a federal disaster area—redundantly, in my opinion. The Environmental Protection Agency, with the California Department of Transportation, proposed spraying lepidoptera-specific poisons from water cannons mounted on trucks, boats, and helicopters. "Much too risky," said the mayor, and the plan was discreetly scrapped.

Meanwhile, Jodi-Marie "Mariposa" was getting nowhere but mauled in all her casting interviews—when, that is, she could hack her way down the butterfly-choked boulevards to her appointments, using a portfolio of publicity photographs as a machete.

Away from southern California, the Mariposa People slaughtered every member of a wealthy Texas oil family, the head of a prominent logging clan in Seattle, and a rich arms manufacturer and his wife in Ohio. At each site, they left messages accusing the government of "criminal inattention to the REAL NEEDS of the people."

All this was going on even as the funds I'd assumed bottomless were, according to a registered letter from my lawyer in Raleigh, steadily ebbing. Global crop failures and triple-digit inflation had a great deal to do with the depletion of my trust, but so did my life-style.

"Jodi-Marie," I said, "you'll never get a job until you find another stage name."

September, October, November—all gone. Our first Christmas in L.A. No tree in our bleak Koreatown walkup, but the starstruck wannabes on Sunset Boulevard had plenty of baubles, nose-rings, and tinsel-town pretensions to make up for the lack. When the daily Butterfly Alert was favorable, I would ride over to see them.

Jodi-Marie's new surname was O'Connor (in honor of a favorite teacher in Savannah). But in five weeks, it had landed her exactly as many parts—i.e., none—as had Mariposa. Then, three days before Christmas, she bicycled home from a longshot interview not far from the Rancho La Brea tar pits, to announce that she had been . . . "discovered!"

"Tonight," she said, showing me an address, "I've got to go for a screen test with a . . . a Mr. Marvyn Sabbatai."

"Okay," I said, smelling a rat. "I'm going with."

We took a cab. Mr. Oliver Lux, Sabbatai's aide, had given her the fare. We ended up at a house of cedar shakes and rustic stone off the Topanga Canyon Road. The oleagenous Lux appeared angry to see me, but he ushered us into a leather-padded room full of books and videocassettes. Then he left.

"Sabbatai's big-time," Jodi-Marie whispered. "Just look."

"Name a film he's directed."

"He's not exactly a director, Dennis."

"Great. Why are we here?"

"He's a producer, a special-effects man with cash. He's worked with Spielberg, Kubrick, Ridley Scott."

"Of course he has," I said.

Sabbatai's library was dimly lit. If you're legit, I thought, why isn't there a film-school diploma on your wall? The place felt like the sanctum of a latter-day opium-eater. Across from the door that Lux had exited by, another door quietly opened.

Sabbatai came through it. At first, all we could tell about him was that he was tall and slender and seemed to be wearing a rumpled dressing gown and a pair of silk pyjama bottoms as badly in need of pressing as his gown.

Marvyn Sabbatai was less a man then a papier-maché golem made up of, and animated by, the thousands of Asian black swallowtails comprising his gown and pyjamas. His hands and face also consisted of butterflies, but bronze, golden, or fuschia ones, with feathery earthtone moths all over his scalp for hair.

What sort of creature was this man? A human being? A robot of butterflies? A holographic special effect?

His entire body ceaselessly acrawl with beautiful insects, he turned about to face us as if my unspoken question were banal, its answer either irrelevant or unresolvably moot. He paced. He would not sit down. Finally, though, he halted.

"*You'll do,*" he whispered to Jodi-Marie. "*My faithful Oliver wasn't lying.*"

"Do for what?" I said.

It took a moment to realize that his whisper was actually a rubbing of wings at the anatomical focus of his "lips." He had "whispered" because what else can butterflies do to create sound? Thus, his "voice" was a chilling approximation of speech, something you might hear from a man with a cancer-gnawed larnyx.

"*Do for the film I'm going to produce.*"

"And what's that?" I asked.

"*My multimillion docudrama:* Hostile Butterflies. *Our lovely Miss O'Connor will play—humanity.*"

Sabbatai, gesturing, strode back and forth. Individual moths and butterflies detached themselves, briefly undulated away, then floated back to alight again among their fellows.

"*Are you afraid of insects, Jodi-Marie? Afraid of challenges? Afraid of stardom? Afraid of me?*"

"No, sir. I don't think so."

"*Then you won't mind butterflies landing on you. Or me, for that matter, touching you—here.*"

He approached to touch her, and I . . . well, to stop him, I tried to grab the lapels of his dressing gown. He flew apart. I fell through him. Jodi-Mari screamed. My hands sifted sparkling scales. Sabbatai—if he existed—had panicked into fragments, a minor riot of everywhere-skittering wings.

A door opened, Oliver Lux within it.

I scrambled to my feet. Parts of Sabbatai were shredded under my fingernails, parts were ground like mica or tinted Mylar into the burgundy carpet, other collops blossomed gaudily on his walls and bookshelves.

"Come on!" I said to Jodi-Marie.

I grabbed her hand. Our cab was still waiting, paid for in advance by Lux. We hightailed it out of Topanga.

"*You'll do,*" the night whispered. "*All of you will do.*"

January, February, March. And, all too cruelly, April again. Things had fallen apart. The center had not held. My money was gone. I'd hocked our bikes. Nowadays, we walked between Koreatown and Sunset Boulevard, or, depending on the status of the Butterfly Alert, scooted along the streets like bent-over soldiers.

Sabbatai, who had reputedly pulled himself together again, was orchestrating everything; or else the butterflies—maybe the more likely scenario—were orchestrating him: The filming of *Hostile Butterflies* was the only major project in the works in Hollywood. Clearly, the inhuman Mr. Sabbatai had put out a pheromonic casting call; greater L.A. had become, as I told the bewildered Jodi-Marie, a "mind-tripping Peter Max-ville."

A few freak thunderstorms gave us several days' relief, pelting butterflies out of the sky, plastering them like scrolls of flocked wallpaper to freeways, sidewalks, awnings, cars. But when the sun came out again, Sabbatai—who, according to *Variety*, had signed a fifteen-year-old hooker with AIDS for the symbolic role he'd almost given Jodi-Marie—reinvoked his potent legerdemain, and the city brimmed again with psychedelic silk.

In fact, a coalition of U.N. entomologists and meteorologists reported that 72% of the planet's lepidopterans had migrated, or were now satellite-trackably "in the act of migrating," to sunny southern California.

Jodi-Marie fell ill. Disappointment, existential ennui, and simple hunger drove her to the day-bed in our flat. Through our Venetian blinds, the ceaseless blur and hum of wings served only to amplify her little-girl delirium. I asked her if she wanted me to get her out of L.A. in a has-been-hippie friend's microbus.

"No, Dennis. This is where I belong."

Why, I had no earthly idea. I was surviving on peanut butter and stale bread. Jodi-Marie was getting by on lukewarm lemon tea and Skippy-flavored kisses.

One day in May, hacked off at God, I left her to the odors of sickness drenching our walkup.

Under the blizzard of insects rustling like palm fronds above Olympic Boulevard, I stumbled toward the studios. Along the way, I saw dozens of camerapeople busily filming Marvyn Sabbatai's latest, probably last, magnum opus.

They were everywhere. Squinting, aiming, shooting. Producing enough full-color footage to preserve the end of this world in complex celluloid montage for . . . not for our posterity, I guess, but for whoever or whatever succeeded us.

Sabbatai himself, magnificently reconstituted, stood swaying on a sixty-foot scaffold, visible from half a block away on Olympic. Gripping a huge megaphone of butterflies, he "whispered" through it as loudly as the Malibu surf: *"Full sun! Cameras! Action!"*

A third again as tall as his tower, he spoke to the sky over Los Angeles County and Santa Monica Bay. His exhortations had the unbrookable force of Yahwistic command. Monarchs, malachites, coppers—a thousand, thousand species—converged on the city, homed on Sabbatai's scaffold, geysered above it in an iridescent stalk as wide as teeming West Hollywood.

I fell to my knees. Stoplights blinked. Traffic halted. A blast-furnace wind hurricaned around me, stealing my breath and parching my lungs. But still I saw that the lepidoptera billowing aloft were not only rising, transfiguring sunlight, but spreading out atop their streaming pillar like the cap of an hallucinatory thermonuclear mushroom.

My air was gone. The ground was gone. The sun was gone. This was Armageddon. Sabbatai was its impresario. Then he mutated on the scaffold, coming to resemble—briefly, at least—Laamaar De Long, his body a carnation-and-chrysanthemum-covered effigy on a float in an upwardly mobile Rose Bowl Parade.

Sabbatai-De Long-Shiva the Destroyer. Therefore, the head of the Holistic Ecological Church of Liberty, Kansas, was also an usher into everlasting mystic liberty.

Butterflies were nibbling on my eyelids. Somebody indignantly shooed them away and helped me up.

Beneath the roiling mushroom cap sitting on our city, I hitched a ride on the back of a fume-stained van defeatedly sputtering east on Olympic.

Jodi-Marie was out of bed. Venetian blinds lay jumbled on the floor like spilled swords. The window overlooking Koreatown stood open. Butterflies wobbled around the room in a Mack Sennet frenzy. Jodi-Marie sat by the radiator under the window listlessly grabbing the insects, cramming them into her mouth.

"Good," she said, holding out a handful. "Try some, Dennis."

I seized her hand, brushed the crushed insects away. "They're foul," I told her. *"Foul!* You can't do this."

"Dennis, I'm hungry. You, too. Eat."

I guided her back to the day-bed. I laid a damp wash cloth over her eyes. I knelt beside her. I waited.

Later, dumbfounded, I watched her arch her back and die. "NO!" I cried.

(Outside, butterflies kept erupting heavenward.)

"Jodi-Marie Woznicki," I said, "I love you." Did I mean it? Or was saying so a sop to my own conscience? Then I remembered the dream she'd told me under the August moon at Laamaar De Long's, and I knew:

```
I AM                                                                I AM
   sashaying                                                     sashaying
      down the runway      \   /               down the runway
       of the biggest crystal   \   /            of the biggest crystal
   palace in the history of      V            palace in the history of
   such palaces since the world  {}      such palaces since the world
         got into the business  {{}}           got into the business
      of bigtime World Fairing, {{}}    of bigtime World Fairing,
         I myself the fairest   {{}}           I myself the fairest
      of the Fair in the bigtime {{{}}}      of the Fair in the bigtime
   exhibitionism by which I      {{}}        exhibitionism by which I
show the world my stuff,          {}             show the world my stuff,
strutting it with pride                           strutting it with pride
 and yes, oh yes,                                   and yes, oh yes,
the utmost utmost                                 the utmost utmost
life-affirming,                                     life-affirming,
self-affirming,                                     self-affirming,
validating                                              validating
LOVE                                                      LOVE
```

Was this a shallow vision? An empty faunching for celebrity?

Well, it wasn't the "vision" I loved: It was Jodi-Marie. No matter how childish or crass, her goal was higher than mine.

For mine was to drift, take my pleasure, and die.

Now I can heal myself, not quite at leisure, of the spiritual rot that once numbed me to everything about her I couldn't take in at a glance.

Beauty—the visible sort—has always slain me. Now it does so again: a lovely, silken megadeath.

Thanks to God and Marvyn Sabbatai, it slays us all: the quick and the dense, the naked and the overdressed, etc., etc., *for this is the way the world ends, this is the way the world ends—not with a bang but a flutter.*

But to hell with all that T. S. Eliot crap. Here's my epitaph for Jodie-Marie: HER TALENT WAS HER LOVINGKINDNESS. / SHE STAYED TRUE THROUGH THE BEAUTIFUL WORST.

Meanwhile, so many goddamned butterflies! Batwings, birdwings, peacocks, the whole iridescent, suffocating schmear.

To die beneath them is an exasperating loveliness, and I would do anything if, as a final boon, they would shape for me aloft the clear, forgiving face of Jodi-Marie Woznicki.

ISABEL ALLENDE
Two Words

South America has given us many of the masters (some say inventors and only true creators) of Magic Realist fiction from Borges to Asturias, García Márquez and others. Their fiction, using elements of the fantastic to augment and comment upon tales about the real world we live in, has had a strong influence during the latter half of this century not only on American writers but on the writers of many cultures as far distant as China, Japan, and the Soviet Union. Chilean novelist Isabel Allende is a strong representative of this tradition, with a short story newly translated into English by Canadian anthologist Alberto Manguel.

Allende was born in 1924 and fled from Chile to Venezuela during the military regime of General Pinochet, whose troops burned books and murdered her uncle. She is the author of *Eva Luna, Of Love and Shadows,* and the bestselling *House of Spirits* which tells the story of a country's rise and decline through the eyes of three generations of women and their ghosts.

"Two Words", translated by Margaret Sayers Peden, is a tale whose brevity belies its impact, commenting powerfully, as it does, on the power of language. It comes from Allende's new collection *The Stories of Eva Luna,* published by Atheneum. It can also be found in Alberto Manguel's excellent collection *Black Water 2,* published by Clarkson Potter.

—T.W.

Two Words

ISABEL ALLENDE

She went by the name of Belisa Crepusculario, not because she had been baptized with that name or given it by her mother, but because she herself had searched until she found the poetry of "beauty" and "twilight" and cloaked herself in it. She made her living selling words. She journeyed through the country from the high cold mountains to the burning coasts, stopping at fairs and in markets where she set up four poles covered by a canvas awning under which she took refuge from the sun and rain to minister to her customers. She did not have to peddle her merchandise because from having wandered far and near, everyone knew who she was. Some people waited for her from one year to the next, and when she appeared in the village with her bundle beneath her arm, they would form a line in front of her stall. Her prices were fair. For five centavos she delivered verses from memory, for seven she improved the quality of dreams; for nine she wrote love letters; for twelve she invented insults for irreconcilable enemies. She also sold stories, not fantasies but long, true stories she recited at one telling, never skipping a word. This is how she carried news from one town to another. People paid her to add a line or two: our son was born; so-and-so died; our children got married; the crops burned in the field. Wherever she went a small crowd gathered around to listen as she began to speak, and that was how they learned about each others' doings, about distant relatives, about what was going on in the civil war. To anyone who paid her fifty centavos in trade, she gave the gift of a secret word to drive away melancholy. It was not the same word for everyone, naturally, because that would have been collective deceit. Each person received his or her own word, with the assurance that no one else would use it that way in this universe or the Beyond.

Belisa Crepusculario had been born into a family so poor they did not even have names to give their children. She came into the world and grew up in an inhospitable land where some years the rains became avalanches of water that bore everything away before them and others when not a drop fell from the sky and the sun swelled to fill the horizon and the world became a desert. Until she was twelve, Belisa had no occupation or virtue other than having withstood hunger and the exhaustion of centuries. During one interminable drought, it fell to her to bury four younger brothers and sisters; when she realized that her turn was next, she decided to set out across the plains in the direction of the sea, in hopes that she might trick death along the way. The land was eroded, split with deep cracks, strewn with rocks, fossils of trees and thorny bushes, and skeletons of animals bleached by the sun. From time to time she ran into families who, like her, were heading south, following the mirage of water. Some had begun the march carrying their belongings on their back or in small carts, but they could barely move their own bones, and after a while they had to abandon their possessions. They dragged themselves along painfully, their skin turned to lizard hide and their eyes burned by the reverberating glare. Belisa greeted them with a wave as she passed, but she did not stop, because she had no strength to waste in acts of compassion. Many people fell by the wayside, but she was so stubborn that she survived to cross through that hell and at long last reach the first trickles of water, fine, almost invisible threads that fed spindly vegetation and farther down widened into small streams and marshes.

Belisa Crepusculario saved her life and in the process accidentally discovered writing. In a village near the coast, the wind blew a page of newspaper at her feet. She picked up the brittle yellow paper and stood a long while looking at it, unable to determine its purpose, until curiosity overcame her shyness. She walked over to a man who was washing his horse in the muddy pool where she had quenched her thirst.

"What is this?" she asked.

"The sports page of the newspaper," the man replied, concealing his surprise at her ignorance.

The answer astounded the girl, but she did not want to seem rude, so she merely inquired about the significance of the fly tracks scattered across the page.

"Those are words, child. Here it says that Fulgencio Barba knocked out El Negro Tiznao in the third round."

That was the day Belisa Crepusculario found out that words make their way in the world without a master, and that anyone with a little cleverness can appropriate them and do business with them. She made a quick assessment of her situation and concluded that aside from becoming a prostitute or working as a servant in the kitchens of the rich there were few occupations she was qualified for. It seemed to her that selling words would be an honorable alternative. From that moment on, she worked at that profession, and was never tempted by any other. At the beginning, she offered her merchandise unaware that words could be written outside of newspapers. When she learned otherwise, she calculated the infinite possibilities of her trade and with her savings paid a priest twenty pesos to teach her to read and write; with her three remaining coins she bought a dictionary. She poured over it from A to Z and then threw it into the sea, because it was not her intention to defraud her customers with packaged words.

* * *

One August morning several years later, Belisa Crepusculario was sitting in her tent in the middle of a plaza, surrounded by the uproar of market day, selling legal arguments to an old man who had been trying for sixteen years to get his pension. Suddenly she heard yelling and thudding hoofbeats. She looked up from her writing and saw, first, a cloud of dust, and then a band of horsemen come galloping into the plaza. They were the Colonel's men, sent under orders of El Mulato, a giant known throughout the land for the speed of his knife and his loyalty to his chief. Both the Colonel and El Mulato had spent their lives fighting in the civil war, and their names were ineradicably linked to devastation and calamity. The rebels swept into town like a stampeding herd, wrapped in noise, bathed in sweat, and leaving a hurricane of fear in their trail. Chickens took wing, dogs ran for their lives, women and children scurried out of sight, until the only living soul left in the market was Belisa Crepusculario. She had never seen El Mulato and was surprised to see him walking toward her.

"I'm looking for you," he shouted, pointing his coiled whip at her; even before the words were out, two men rushed her—knocking over her canopy and shattering her inkwell—bound her hand and foot, and threw her like a sea bag across the rump of El Mulato's mount. Then they thundered off toward the hills.

Hours later, just as Belisa Crepusculario was near death, her heart ground to sand by the pounding of the horse, they stopped, and four strong hands set her down. She tried to stand on her feet and hold her head high, but her strength failed her and she slumped to the ground, sinking into a confused dream. She awakened several hours later to the murmur of night in the camp, but before she had time to sort out the sounds, she opened her eyes and found herself staring into the impatient glare of El Mulato, kneeling beside her.

"Well, woman, at last you've come to," he said. To speed her to her senses, he tipped his canteen and offered her a sip of liquor laced with gunpowder.

She demanded to know the reason for such rough treatment, and El Mulato explained that the Colonel needed her services. He allowed her to splash water on her face, and then led her to the far end of the camp where the most feared man in all the land was lazing in a hammock strung between two trees. She could not see his face, because he lay in the deceptive shadow of the leaves and the indelible shadow of all his years as a bandit, but she imagined from the way his gigantic aide addressed him with such humility that he must have a very menacing expression. She was surprised by the Colonel's voice, as soft and well-modulated as a professor's.

"Are you the woman who sells words?" he asked.

"At your service," she stammered, peering into the dark and trying to see him better.

The Colonel stood up, and turned straight toward her. She saw dark skin and the eyes of a ferocious puma, and she knew immediately that she was standing before the loneliest man in the world.

"I want to be President," he announced.

The Colonel was weary of riding across that godforsaken land, waging useless wars and suffering defeats that no subterfuge could transform into victories. For years he had been sleeping in the open air, bitten by mosquitoes, eating iguanas and snake soup, but those minor inconveniences were not why he wanted to change his destiny. What truly troubled him was the terror he saw in people's eyes. He longed to ride into a town beneath a triumphal arch with bright flags and flowers everywhere; he wanted to be cheered, and be given newly laid eggs and freshly baked bread. Men fled at the sight of him, children trembled, and women miscarried from fright; he had had enough, and so he had decided to become President. El Mulato had suggested that they ride to the capital, gallop up to the Palace, and take over the government, the way they had taken so many other things without anyone's permission. The Colonel, however, did not want to be just another tyrant; there had been enough of those before him and, besides, if he did that, he would never win people's hearts. It was his aspiration to win the popular vote in the December elections.

"To do that, I have to talk like a candidate. Can you sell me the words for a speech?" the Colonel asked Belisa Crepusculario.

She had accepted many assignments, but none like this. She did not dare refuse, fearing that El Mulato would shoot her between the eyes, or worse still, that the Colonel would burst into tears. There was more to it than that, however; she felt the urge to help him because she felt a throbbing warmth beneath her skin, a powerful desire to touch that man, to fondle him, to clasp him in her arms.

All night and a good part of the following day, Belisa Crepusculario searched her repertory for words adequate for a presidential speech, closely watched by El Mulato, who could not take his eyes from her firm wanderer's legs and virginal breasts. She discarded harsh, cold words, words that were too flowery, words worn from abuse, words that offered improbable promises, untruthful and confusing words, until all she had left were words sure to touch the minds of men and women's intuition. Calling upon the knowledge she had purchased from the priest for twenty pesos, she wrote the speech on a sheet of paper and then signaled El Mulato to untie the rope that bound her anklès to a tree. He led her once more to the Colonel, and again she felt the throbbing anxiety that had seized her when she first saw him. She handed him the paper and waited while he looked at it, holding it gingerly between thumbs and fingertips.

"What the shit does this say," he asked finally.

"Don't you know how to read?"

"War's what I know," he replied.

She read the speech aloud. She read it three times, so her client could engrave it on his memory. When she finished, she saw the emotion in the faces of the soldiers who had gathered round to listen, and saw that the Colonel's eyes glittered with enthusiasm, convinced that with those words the presidential chair would be his.

"If after they've heard it three times, the boys are still standing there with their mouths hanging open, it must mean the thing's damn good, Colonel" was El Mulato's approval.

"All right, woman. How much do I owe you?" the leader asked.

"One peso, Colonel."

"That's not much," he said, opening the pouch he wore at his belt, heavy with proceeds from the last foray.

"The peso entitles you to a bonus. I'm going to give you two secret words," said Belisa Crepusculario.

"What for?"

She explained that for every fifty centavos a client paid, she gave him the gift of a word for his exclusive use. The Colonel shrugged. He had no interest at all in her offer, but he did not want to be impolite to someone who had served him so well. She walked slowly to the leather stool where he was sitting, and bent down to give him her gift. The man smelled the scent of a mountain cat issuing from the woman, a fiery heat radiating from her hips, he heard the terrible whisper of her hair, and a breath of sweetmint murmured into his ear the two secret words that were his alone.

"They are yours, Colonel," she said as she stepped back. "You may use them as much as you please."

El Mulato accompanied Belisa to the roadside, his eyes as entreating as a stray dog's, but when he reached out to touch her, he was stopped by an avalanche of words he had never heard before; believing them to be an irrevocable curse, the flame of his desire was extinguished.

During the months of September, October, and November the Colonel delivered his speech so many times that had it not been crafted from glowing and durable words it would have turned to ash as he spoke. He traveled up and down and across the country, riding into cities with a triumphal air, stopping in even the most forgotten villages where only the dump heap betrayed a human presence, to convince his fellow citizens to vote for him. While he spoke from a platform erected in the middle of the plaza, El Mulato and his men handed out sweets and painted his name on all the walls in gold frost. No one paid the least attention to those advertising ploys; they were dazzled by the clarity of the Colonel's proposals and the poetic lucidity of his arguments, infected by his powerful wish to right the wrongs of history, happy for the first time in their lives. When the Candidate had finished his speech, his soldiers would fire their pistols into the air and set off firecrackers, and when finally they rode off, they left behind a wake of hope that lingered for days on the air, like the splendid memory of a comet's tail. Soon the Colonel was the favorite. No one had ever witnessed such a phenomenon: a man who surfaced from the civil war, covered with scars and speaking like a professor, a man whose fame spread to every corner of the land and captured the nation's heart. The press focused their attention on him. Newspapermen came from far away to interview him and repeat his phrases, and the number of his followers and enemies continued to grow.

"We're doing great, Colonel," said El Mulato, after twelve successful weeks of campaigning.

But the Candidate did not hear. He was repeating his secret words, as he did more and more obsessively. He said them when he was mellow with nostalgia; he murmured them in his sleep; he carried them with him on horseback; he thought them before delivering his famous speech; and he caught himself savoring them in his leisure time. And every time he thought of those two words, he thought of Belisa Crepusculario, and his senses were inflamed with the memory of her feral scent, her fiery heat, the whisper of her hair, and her sweetmint breath in his ear, until he began to go around like a sleepwalker, and his men realized that he might die before he ever sat in the presidential chair.

"What's got hold of you, Colonel," El Mulato asked so often that finally one day his chief broke down and told him the source of his befuddlement: those two words that were buried like two daggers in his gut.

"Tell me what they are and maybe they'll lose their magic," his faithful aide suggested.

"I can't tell them, they're for me alone," the Colonel replied.

Saddened by watching his chief decline like a man with a death sentence on his head, El Mulato slung his rifle over his shoulder and set out to find Belisa Crepusculario. He followed her trail through all that vast country, until he found her in a village in the far south, sitting under her tent reciting her rosary of news. He planted himself, spraddle-legged, before her, weapon in hand.

"You! You're coming with me," he ordered.

She had been waiting. She picked up her inkwell, folded the canvas of her small stall, arranged her shawl around her shoulders, and without a word took her place behind El Mulato's saddle. They did not exchange so much as a word in all the trip; El Mulato's desire for her had turned into rage, and only his fear of her tongue prevented his cutting her to shreds with his whip. Nor was he inclined to tell her that the Colonel was in a fog, and that a spell whispered into his ear had done what years of battle had not been able to do. Three days later they arrived at the encampment, and immediately, in view of all the troops, El Mulato led his prisoner before the Candidate.

"I brought this witch here so you can give her back her words, Colonel," El Mulato said, pointing the barrel of his rifle at the woman's head. "And then she can give you back your manhood."

The Colonel and Belisa Crepusculario stared at each other, measuring one another from a distance. The men knew then that their leader would never undo the witchcraft of those accursed words, because the whole world could see the voracious-puma eyes soften as the woman walked to him and took his hand in hers.

LUCIUS SHEPARD
AND ROBERT FRAZIER

The All-Consuming

Shepard's name has often been associated with politically astute stories of self-discovery combined with descriptions of lush, psychotropic landscapes in Central and South America. His most recent book, *The Ends of the Earth* (Arkham), collects these stories in one beautiful package.

Robert Frazier is well-known in the science fiction field for his poetry. He and Bruce Boston are the creators of the "mutant rainforest," having written a series of poems about this hallucinatory, exotic land. A book collecting their material will be published by Ziesing.

"The All-Consuming," which takes place in the rainforest transformed by "chemical pollutants and radiation," is about obsession. A rich man wants to taste everything there is to be had in this odd jungle no matter the cost, no matter the consequences to his own health or psyche.

—E.D.

The All-Consuming

Lucius Shepard and Robert Frazier

Santander Jimenez was one of the towns that ringed the Malsueno, a kind of border station between the insane tangle of the rain forest and the more comprehensible and traditional insanity of the highlands. It was a miserable place of diesel smoke and rattling generators and concrete-block buildings painted in pastel shades of yellow, green and aqua, many with rusted Fanta signs over their doors, bearing names such as the Café of a Thousand Flowers or The Eternal Garden Bar or the Restaurant of Golden Desires, all containing fly-specked Formica tables and inefficient ceiling fans and fat women wearing grease-spattered aprons and discouraging frowns. Whores slouched beneath the buzzing neon marquee of the Cine Guevara. Drunks with bloody mouths lay in the puddles that mired the muddy streets. It was always raining. Even during the height of the dry season, the lake was so high that the playground beside it was half-submerged, presenting a surreal vista of drowned swing sets and seesaws.

To the west of town, separated from the other buildings by a wide ground strewn with coconut litter and flattened beer cans, stood a market—a vast tin roof shading a hive of green wooden stalls. It was there that the *marañeros* would take the curious relics and still more curious produce that they collected in the heart of the rain forest: stone idols whose eyes glowed with electric moss; albino beetles the size of house cats; jaguar bones inlaid with seams of mineral that flowed like mercury; lizards with voices as sweet as nightingales; mimick vines, parrot plants and pavonine, with its addictive spores that afforded one a transitory mental contact with the creatures of the jungle.

They were, for the most part, these *marañeros*, scrawny, rawboned men who wore brave tattoos that depicted lions and devils and laughing skulls. Their faces were scarred, disfigured by fungus and spirochetes, and when they walked out in the town, they were given a wide berth, not because of their appearance or their penchant for violence, which was no greater than that of the ordinary citizen, but because they embodied the dread mystique of the Malsueno, and in their tormented solitudes, they seemed the emblems of a death in life more frightening to the uninformed than the good Catholic death advertised by the portly priests at Santa Anna de la Flor del Piedra.

Scarcely anyone who lived in Santander Jimenez wanted to live there. A number of citizens had been driven to this extreme in order to hide from a criminal or politically unsound past. The most desperate of these were the marañeros—who but those who themselves were hunted would voluntarily enter the Malsueno to dwell for months at a time among tarzanals and blood vine and christomorphs? —and the most desperate of the marañeros, or so he had countenanced himself for 21 years, so many years that his desperation had mellowed to an agitated resignation, was a gaunt, graying man by the name of Arce Cienfuegos. In his youth, he had been an educator in the capital in the extreme west of the country, married to a beautiful woman, the father of an infant son, and had aspired to a career in politics. However, his overzealous pursuit of that career had set him at odds with the drug cartel; as a result, his wife and child had been murdered, a crime with which he had subsequently been charged, and he had been forced to flee to the Malsueno. For a time thereafter, he had been driven by a lust for revenge, for vindication, but when at last the drug cartel had been shattered, its leaders executed, revenge was denied him, and because those who could prove his innocence were in their coffins, the murder charge against him had remained open. Now, at the age of 48, his crime forgotten, although he might have returned to the capital, he was so defeated by time and solitude and grief he could no longer think of a reason to leave. Just as chemical pollutants and radiation had transformed the jungle into a habitat suitable to the most grotesque of creatures, living in the Malsueno had transformed him into a sour twist of a man who thrived on its green acids, its vegetable perversions, and he was no longer fit for life in the outside world. Or so he had convinced himself.

Nonetheless, he yearned for some indefinable improvement in his lot, and to ease this yearning, he had lately taken to penetrating ever more deeply into the Malsueno, to daring unknown territory, telling himself that perhaps in the depths of the jungle, he would find a form of contentment, but knowing to his soul that what he truly sought was release from an existence whose despair and spiritual malaise had come to outweigh any fleshly reward.

One day, toward the end of the rainy season, Arce received word that a man who had taken a room at the Hotel America 66, one Yuoki Akashini, had asked to see him. In general, visitors to Santander Jimenez were limited to scientists hunting specimens and the odd tourists gone astray, and since, according to his informant, Mr. Akashini fell into neither of those categories, Arce's curiosity was aroused. That evening, he presented himself at the hotel and informed the owner, Nacho Perez, a bulbous, officious man of 50, that he had an appointment with the Japanese gentleman. Nacho—who earned the larger part of his living by selling relics purchased from the marañeros at swindler's prices—attempted to pry information concerning the appointment out of him; but Arce, who loathed the hotel owner, having been cheated by him on countless occasions, kept his own counsel. Before entering room 23, he poked his head in the door and saw a short, crewcut man in his early 30s standing by a cot, wearing gray trousers and a T-shirt. The man glowed with health and had the heavily developed arms and chest of a weight lifter. His smile was extraordinarily white and fixed and wide.

"*Señor* Cienfuegos? Ah, excellent!" he said, and made a polite bow. "Please . . . come in, come in."

The room, which reeked of disinfectant, was of green concrete block and, like a jail cell, contained one chair, one cot, one toilet. Cobwebs clotted the transom and light was provided by a naked bulb dangling from a ceiling fixture. Mr. Akashini offered Arce the chair and took a position by the door, hands clasped behind his back and legs apart, like a soldier standing at ease.

"I am told," he said, his voice hoarse, his tone clipped, almost as if in accusation, "you know the jungle well." He arched an eyebrow, lending an accent of inquiry to these words.

"Well enough, I suppose."

Mr. Akashini nodded and made a rumbling noise deep in his throat—a sign of approval, Arce thought.

"If you're considering a trip into the jungle," he said, crossing his legs, "I'd advise against it."

"I do not require a guide," said Mr. Akashini. "I want you to bring me food."

Arce was nonplused. "There's a restaurant downstairs."

Mr. Akashini stood blinking, as if absorbing this information, then threw back his head and laughed uproariously. "Very good! A restaurant downstairs!" He wiped his eyes. "You have mistaken my meaning. I want you to bring me food from the jungle. Here. This will help you understand."

He crossed to the cot, where a suitcase lay open, and removed from it a thick leather-bound album, which he handed to Arce. It contained photographs and newspaper clippings that featured shots of Mr. Akashini at dinner. The text of the majority of the clippings was in Japanese, but several were in Spanish, and it was apparent from these—which bestowed upon Mr. Akashini the title of The All-Consuming—and from the photographs that he was not eating ordinary food but objects of different sorts: automobiles, among them a Rolls-Royce Corniche; works of art, including several important expressionist canvases and a small bronze by Rodin; cultural artifacts of every variety, mostly American, ranging from items such as one of Elvis Presley's leather-and-rhinestone jump suits, a guitar played by Jimi Hendrix and Lee Harvey Oswald's Carcano rifle—obtained at "an absurd cost," according to Mr. Akashini—to the structure of the first McDonald's restaurant, a meal that, ground to a powder and mixed with gruel, had taken a year to complete. Arce did not understand what had compelled Mr. Akashini to enter upon this strange gourmandizing, but one thing was plain: The man was wealthy beyond his wildest dreams, and although this did not overly excite Arce, for he had few wants, nevertheless, he was not one to let an opportunity for profit slip away.

"I am listed in the *Guinness Book of World Records*," said Mr. Akashini proudly.

"Three times." He held up three fingers in order to firmly imprint this fact on Arce's consciousness.

Arce tried to look impressed.

"I intend," Mr. Akashini went on, "to eat the Malsueno. Not everything in it, of course." He grinned and clapped Arce on the shoulder, as if to assure him of the limits of his appetite. "I wish to eat those things that will convey to me its essence. Things that embody the soul of the place."

"I see," said Arce, but failed to disguise the puzzlement in his voice.

"You are wondering, are you not," said Mr. Akashini, tipping his head to the side, holding up a forefinger like an earnest lecturer, "why I do this?"

"It's not my business."

"Still, you wonder." Mr. Akashini turned to the wall above his cot, again clasping his hands behind his back. He might have been standing on the bridge of a ship, considering a freshly conquered land. "I admit to a certain egocentric delight in accomplishment, but my desire to consume stems to a large degree from curiosity, from my love for other cultures, my desire to understand them. When I eat, you see, I understand. I cannot always express the understanding, but it is profound . . . more profound, I am convinced, than an understanding gained from study or travel or immersion in some facet of one culture or another. I know things about the United States that not even Americans know. I have tasted the inner mechanisms of American history, of the American experience. I have recently finished writing a book of meditations on the subject." He turned to Arce. "Now, it is my intention to understand the Malsueno, to derive from its mutations, from the furies of the radiation and chemicals and poisons that created them, a comprehension of its essence. So I have come to you for assistance. I will pay well."

He named a figure that elevated Arce's estimate of his wealth, and Arce signaled his acceptance.

"But how can you expect to eat poison and survive?" he asked.

"With caution." Mr. Akashini chuckled and patted his flat belly.

Arce pictured tiny cars, portraits, statuary, temples, entire civilizations in miniature inside Mr. Akashini's stomach, floating upon an angry sea like those depicted by the print maker Hokusai. The image infused the man's healthy glow with a decadent character.

"Please, have no fear about my capacity," said Mr. Akashini. "I am in excellent condition and accustomed to performing feats of ingestion. And I have implants that will neutralize those poisons that my system cannot handle. So, if you are agreed, I will expect my first meal tomorrow."

"I'll see to it." Arce came to his feet and, easing around Mr. Akashini, made for the door.

"Excuse, please!"

Arce turned and was met with a flash that blinded him for a moment; as his vision cleared, he saw his employer lowering a camera.

"See you at suppertime!" said Mr. Akashini.

He nodded and smiled as if he already understood everything there was to know about Arce.

*   *   *

Although determined to earn his fee, Arce did not intend to risk himself in the deep jungle for such a fool as Mr. Akashini appeared to be. Who did the man think he was to believe he could ingest the venomous essence of the Malsueno? Likely, he would be dead in a matter of days, however efficient his implants. And so the following afternoon, without bothering to put on protective gear, Arce walked a short distance into the jungle and cast about for something exotic and inedible . . . but nothing too virulent. He did not want to lose his patron so quickly. Soon he found an appropriate entree and secured it inside a specimen bag. At dusk, his find laid out in a box of transparent plastic with a small hinged opening, he presented himself at the hotel. Room 23 had undergone a few changes. The cot had been removed, and in its place was a narrow futon. Dominating the room, making it almost impossible to move, was a mahogany dinner table set with fine linens and silverware and adorned with a silver candelabrum. Mr. Akashini, attired in a dinner jacket and a black tie, was seated at the table, smiling his gleaming edifice of a smile.

"Ah!" he said. "And what do you have for me, *Señor* Cienfuegos?"

With a flourish, Arce deposited the box on the table and was rewarded by an appreciative sigh. In the dim light, his culinary offering—ordinary by the grotesque standards for the Malsueno—looked spectacularly mysterious: an 18-inch-long section of a rotten log, shining a vile, vivid green, with the swirls of phosphorescent fungus that nearly covered its dark, grooved surface; scuttling here and there were big spiders that showed a negative black against the green radiance, like intricate holes in a glowing film that was sliding back and forth . . . except now and again, they merged into a single many-legged blackness that pulsed and shimmered and grew larger still. Bathed in that glow, Mr. Akashini's face was etched into a masklike pattern of garish light and shadow.

"What are they?" he said, his eyes glued to the box.

For Mr. Akashini's benefit, Arce resorted to invention.

"They are among the great mysteries of the Malsueno," he said. "And thus, they have no name, for who can name the incomprehensible? They are insect absences, they live, they prey on life, and yet they are lightless and undefined, more nothing than something. They are common yet the essence of rarity. They are numberless, yet they are one."

At this, words failed him. He folded his arms and affected a solemn pose.

"Excellent!" whispered Mr. Akashini, leaning close to the lid of the box. He made one of his customary throaty growls. "You may leave now. I wish to eat alone so as to maximize my understanding."

That was agreeable to Arce, who had no wish to observe the fate of the spiders and the fungus-coated log. But as he turned to leave, pleased with the facility with which he had satisfied the terms of his employment, Mr. Akashini said, "You have provided me with a marvelous hors d'oeuvre, *señor*, but I expect much more of you. Is that clear?"

"Of course," said Arce, startled.

"No, not of course. There is nothing of course about what I've asked of you. I expect diligence. And even more than diligence, I expect zeal."

"As you wish."

"Yes," said Mr. Akashini, fitting his gaze to the glowing feast, his face again ordered by that impenetrable smile. "Exactly."

Although for weeks he obeyed Mr. Akashini's instructions and sought out ever more exotic and deadly suppers, to Arce's surprise, his employer did not sicken and die but thrived on his diet of poisons and claws and spore. His healthy glow increased, his biceps bulged like cannon balls, his eyes remained clear. It became a challenge to Arce to locate a dish that would weaken Mr. Akashini's resistance, that would at least cause him an upset stomach. He did not care for Mr. Akashini and had concluded that the man was something more sinister than a fool. And when Nacho asked again what was the nature of his business in room 23, Arce had no qualms about telling him, thinking that Nacho would make a joke of his employer's diet. But Nacho was incredulous and shook his fist at Arce. "I'm warning you," he said, "I won't have you taking advantage of my guests."

Arce understood that Nacho was concerned that he might be swindling Mr. Akashini and not cutting him in for a percentage. When he tried to clarify the matter, Nacho only threatened him again, demanded money, and Arce walked away in disgust.

It was evident by the way Mr. Akashini used his camera that he had no regard for anyone in the town. He would approach potential subjects, all smiles and bows, and proceed to pose them, making it plain that he was ridiculing the person whose photograph he was preparing to take. He posed confused, dignified old men with bouquets of flowers, he posed Nacho with a toy machine gun, he posed a young girl with an ugly birthmark on her cheek holding an armful of puppies. Afterward, he would once again smile and bow, but the smiles were sneers and the bows were slaps. Arce understood the uses of contempt—he had witnessed it among his own people in their harsh attitude toward Americans. Yet they were expressing the classic resentment of the poor toward the wealthy, and he could not fathom why Mr. Akashini, who was wealthier than an American, should express a similar attitude toward the poor. Perhaps, he thought, Mr. Akashini had himself been poor and was now having his revenge. But why revenge himself upon those who had never lorded it over him? Was his need to understand, to consume, part and parcel of a need to dominate and deride? All Arce knew of Japan had been gleaned from books dealing with the samurai, with knights, swords and a chill formal morality, and he had the notion that the values detailed in these books were of moment to Mr. Akashini, though in some distorted fashion. Yet, in the end, he could not decide if Mr. Akashini were as simple as he appeared or if there were more to him than met the eye, and he thought this might be a question to which not even his employer knew the answer.

Be he complicated or simple, one thing was apparent—Mr. Akashini did not know as much as he pretended. He could spout volumes of facts concerning the Malsueno. Yet his knowledge lacked the depth of experience, the unifying character of something known in the heart of the mind, and Arce could not accept the idea that consumption bestowed upon him a deeper comprehension. The things he claimed to understand of America—rock-and-roll music, say—he understood in a Japanese way, imbuing them with watered-down samurai principles and a neon romanticism redolent of contemporary Tokyo night-club values and B movies, thereby transforming them into devalued icons that bore little relation to the realities from which they had sprung.

However, Arce was not such a fool that he claimed to understand Mr. Akashini, and putting his doubts aside, he made an interior renewal of his contract and set himself to feed Mr. Akashini the absolute essence of the Malsueno, hoping to either prove or disprove the thesis. He was beginning to feel an odd responsibility to his job, to a man who—though he paid well—had shown him nothing but contempt, and while this conscientious behavior troubled him, being out of character with the person he believed he had become, he had no choice but to obey its imperatives.

Arce's searches carried him farther and farther afield and one morning found him in a clearing three days' trek from Santander Jimenez. Mr. Akashini would be occupied for the better part of a week in devouring his latest offering, which included lapis bees and lime ants, a section from the trunk of a gargantua garnished with its thorns, an entire duende cooked with blood vine, various fungi, all seasoned with powder ground from woohli bones and served with a variety of mushrooms. Thus, Arce, being in no particular hurry, stopped to rest and enjoy the otherworldly beauty of the clearing, its foliage a mingling of mineral brilliance and fairy shape such as occurred only within the confines of the Malsueno.

At the center of the clearing was a cloud pool, a ragged oval some 12 feet in diameter, whose quicksilver surface mirrored the surrounding foliage—yellow weeds; boulders furred with orange moss; mushrooms the size of parasols, their purple crowns mottled with spots of vermilion; mattes of dead lianas thick as boas; shrubs with spine-tipped viridian leaves that quested ceaselessly for some animal presence in which to inject their venom; and, dangling from above, the immense red leaves of a gargantua, each large enough to wrap about oneself several times.

Through gaps in the foliage, Arce could see the slender trunks of other gargantuas rising above the canopy, vanishing into a bank of low clouds. And in the middle distance, its translucent flesh barely visible against the overcast, a rainbird flapped up from a stinger palm and beat its way south against the prevailing wind. Arce watched it out of sight, captivated by the almost impalpable vibration of its wings, by the entirety of the scene, with its gaudy array of colors and exotic vitality. At times like this, he was able to shrug off the bitter weight of his past for a few moments and delight in the mystery he inhabited.

Once he had carefully inspected the area, he settled on a boulder and opened the face plate of his protective suit. The heat was oppressive after the coolness of the suit, and the air stank of carrion and sweet rot, yet it was refreshing to feel the breeze on his face. He took a packet of dried fruit from a pocket on his sleeve and ate, ever aware of the rustlings and cries and movement about him—there were creatures in this part of the jungle that could pluck him from his suit with no more difficulty than a man shelling a peanut, and they were not always easy to detect. Absently, he tossed a piece of apricot into the cloud pool and watched the silvery surface effloresce as it digested the fruit, ruffles of milky rose and lavender spreading from the point of impact toward the edges like the opening of a convulsed bloom. He considered collecting a vial of the fluid for Mr. Akashini—that would test the efficacy of his implants.

Yet to Arce's mind, the cloud pool did not embody the essence of the jungle but rather was a filigree, an adornment, and he doubted that he could provide his employer with any more quintessentially Malsuenan a meal than some of those he had already served him. Mr. Akashini had eaten fillet of tarzanal, woohli, ghost lemur, jaguar, malcoton; he had supped on stews of tar fish, manta bat, pezmiel, manatee; he had consumed stone, leaf, root, spore; he had gorged himself on sauces compounded of poison, feces, animal and plant excrescense of every kind; yet he appeared as healthy and ignorant as before. What, Arce thought, if it were the very efficacy of his implants that kept him from true understanding? Perhaps to attain such a state, one must be vulnerable to that which one wished to understand.

He unzipped another pocket on his sleeve and removed a packet of pavonine spores. Arce was no addict, but he enjoyed a taste of the drug now and again, and when attempting to seek out certain animals, he found it more than a little useful. He touched a spore-covered finger tip to his tongue, enough to sensitize him to his immediate environment. Within seconds, he felt a tightening at the back of his throat, a queasiness and a touch of vertigo. A violent cramp doubled him over, bringing tears and spots before his eyes. By the time the cramp had passed, he seemed to be crawling along a high branch of a gargantua, hauling himself along with knobby, hairy fingers tipped with claws, pushing aside heavy folds of dangling leaves with ropy patterns of veins, inflamed by a dark-red emotion that sharpened into lust as he was being lifted, shaken, pincers locked about his chitinous body and, above him, impossibly tall pale arcs of grass blades and the glowing white blur of an orchid sun; and then, fat with blood, he hung dazed and languorous in a shadowy place; and then he was leaping, his jaws wide, claws straining toward the flanks of a fleeing tapir; and then his mind went blank and still and calm, like a pool of emerald water steeped in a single thought; and then, his shadow casting a lake of darkness across a thicket of sapodilla bushes, he roared, on fire with the ecstasy of his strength and the exuberance of his appetites.

Less than three minutes after he had taken the pavonine, Arce came unsteadily to his feet and started hunting for the calm green mind that his mind had touched . . . like nothing he had touched before. Calm, and yet a calm compounded of a trillion minute violences, like the jungle itself in the hour before first light, brimming with hot potentials, but, for the moment, cool and peaceful and hushed. Whatever it had been was close by the pool, Arce was certain, and so he knew it could be nothing large. He overturned rocks with the toe of his boot, probed in the weeds with a rotten stick and at length unearthed a smallish snake with an intricate pattern of red and yellow and white tattooed across its black scales. It slithered away but did so with no particular haste, as if—rather than trying to elude capture—it was simply going on its way, and when Arce netted it, instead of twisting and humping about, it coiled up and went to sleep. Seeing this, Arce did not doubt that the snake's skull housed the mind he had contacted, and although he had no real feeling that the snake would implement Mr. Akashini's understanding, still he was pleased to have found something new and surprising to feed him.

On his return to Santander Jimenez, he served Mr. Akashini a meal that included a palm salad with diced snake meat. Then, leaving him to dine alone, he walked across town to the Salon Tia Flaca, a rambling three-story building of dark-green boards close to the market, and there secured the companionship of a whore for the night. The whore, his favorite, was named Expectacion and was a young thing, 19 or 20, pretty after the fashion of the women of the coast, slim and dark, with full breasts and a petulant mouth and black hair that tumbled like smoke about her shoulders. Once they had made love, she brought Arce rum with ice and lime and lay beside him and asked questions about his life whose answers were of no interest to her whatsoever. Arce realized that her curiosity was a charade, that she was merely fulfilling the forms of their unwritten contract, but nevertheless, he felt compelled to tell her about Mr. Akashini and the peculiar business between them, because by so doing, he hoped to disclose a pattern underlying it, something that would explain his new sense of responsibility, his complicity in this foolhardy mission.

When he was done, she propped herself up on an elbow, her pupils cored with orange reflections from the kerosene lamp, and said, "He pays you so much, and still you remain in Santander Jimenez?"

"It's as I've told you . . . I'm as happy here as anywhere. I've nowhere to go."

"Nowhere! You must be crazy! This"—she waved at the window, at the dark wall of the jungle beyond and the malfunctioning neons of the muddy little town—"*this* is nowhere! Even money can't change that. But the capital . . . with money. That's a different story."

"You're young," he said. "You don't understand."

She laughed. "The only way you can understand anything is to do it . . . Then it's not worth talking about. Tell that to your Japanese man. Anyway, you're the one who doesn't understand." She threw her arms about him, her breasts flattening against his chest. "Let's get out of here, let's steal the Jap's money and go to the capital. Even if the theft is reported, the police there don't care what happens in the Malsueno. You know that's true. They'll just file the report. Come on, *Papá!* I swear I'll make you happy."

Arce was put off by her use of the word *papá*, and said, "Do you think I'm a fool? In the capital, the minute I turned my back, you'd be off with the first good-looking boy who caught your eye."

"You are a fool to think I'm just a slut." She drew back and seemed to be searching his face. "I've been a whore since I was twelve, and I've learned all I need to know about good-looking boys. What gets my heart racing is somebody like you. Somebody rich and refined who'll keep me safe. I'd marry a guy like you in a flash. But even if I was the kind of woman you say, no injury I did you would be worse than what you're doing to yourself by staying here."

He thought he detected in her eyes a flicker of something more than reflected light, of an inner luminescence like that found in the eyes of a malcoton. It occurred to him that she herself was of the Malsueno, one of its creatures, the calm green habit of her thoughts every bit as inexplicable to him as the mind of the snake he had captured. And yet there was something in her that brought back memories of his dead wife—a mixture of energy and toughness that tempted him to believe not only in her but in himself, in the possibility that he could regain his energy and hope.

"Maybe someday," he told her. "I'll think about it."

"Don't kid yourself, *Papá*. I don't think it's in you." She arched her back, and her breasts rolled on her chest, drawing his eyes to the stiffened chocolate-colored nipples. "I guess you were born to be a *marañero*. But at least you've got good taste in whores."

She went astride him and made love to him with more enthusiasm than before, and as he arched beneath her, watching her in the dim light that penetrated the fall of her hair, which hung down about his head, walling him into a place of warm breath and musk, he imagined that he knew her, that he could see past the deceits and counterfeits in her rapt features to a place where she was in love not with him but with the security offered by his circumstance. Not truly in love but—like a beast that has spotted its prey—in the grip of a fierce opportunism, a feeling that might as well have been love for its delirium and consuming intensity.

The next day, when Arce visited the hotel, Nacho Perez, dressed in a sweat-stained *guayabera* and shorts, questioned him about his activities in room 23.

"What's going on up there?" he asked, mopping perspiration from his brow. "I won't have any funny business. Is he a drug addict? A pervert? What are you doing with him? He never lets anyone in the room, not even the maid. I won't tolerate this kind of behavior."

"You'll tolerate anything, Nacho," said Arce, "as long as you're paid to tolerate it. Ask your questions of Akashini."

"Listen to me . . ." Nacho began, but Arce caught him by the shirt front and said, "You bastard! Give me a reason—not a good reason, just a little one—and I'll cut you, do you hear?"

Nacho licked his lips and said, "I hear," but there was no conviction in his voice.

On reaching the room, Arce discovered that Mr. Akashini had spent a sleepless night. His color was poor, his brow clammy, his hands trembling. Yet when Arce suggested that he forgo his meal, the Japanese man said, "No, no! I'm all right." He passed a handkerchief across his brow. "Perhaps something simple. A few plants . . . some insects." Arce had no choice but to comply, and for several days thereafter, he served Mr. Akashini harmless meals from the edge of the jungle; yet despite this, whether because of the snake or simply because of a surfeit of poisons that had neutralized his implants, Mr. Akashini continued to deteriorate. His skin acquired the unhealthy shine of milk spore, his eyes were clouded, his manner distracted, and he grew so weak that it took him three tries to heave himself up from his chair. Nothing Arce said would sway him from his course.

"I feel"—Mr. Akashini had to swallow—"I feel as if I am . . . close to something."

Close to death, was Arce's thought, but it was not his place to argue, and he only shrugged.

"Yes," said Mr. Akashini, as if answering a question inaudible to Arce. He ran a palsied hand along the linen tablecloth, which—like its owner—displayed the effects of ill usage: stains, rips, embroideries of mildew. Even the candelabrum seemed afflicted, its surface tarnished. On a chipped plate were the remains of a meal: philosopher beetles thrashing in a stew of weeds and wild dog. "I . . . uh . . . ." Mr. Akashini's eyelids fluttered down and he gestured feebly at the plate. "Stay with me while I finish, will you?"

Astonished at this breach of custom, for Mr. Akashini had never before permitted him to remain with him while he ate, Arce took a seat on the futon and watched in silence as his employer laboriously swallowed down the stew. At last, he fell back in his chair, the muscles bunching in his jaw . . . or so Arce thought at first, his vision limited by the flickering candlelight. But then, to his horror, he realized that this was no simple muscular action. It appeared that a lump was moving beneath Mr. Akashini's skin, crawling crabwise across the cheek, along the cheekbone, then down along the hinge of the jaw and onto the neck, where it vanished as if submerging into the flesh. However, the truly horrifying aspect of this passage was that in its wake, the skin was suffused with blood, darkened, and the lump of muscle left—as a receding tide might reveal the configuration of the sand beneath—an expression such as Arce had never seen on any human face, one that seemed a rendering in human musculature of an emotion too poignant for such a canvas, embodying something of lust and fear but mostly a kind of feral longing. The expression faded, and Mr. Akashini, who had not moved for several minutes, his mouth wide open, let out a gurgling breath.

Certain that he was dead, Arce leaned over him and was further horrified to notice that the man's arms were freckled with vaguely phosphorescent patches of gray fungus. Closer inspection revealed other anomalies: three fingernails blackened and thick like chitin; strange whitish growths, like tiny outcroppings of crystal, inside the mouth; a cobweb of almost infinitesimally fine strands spanning the right eye. Arce's thoughts alternated between guilt and fear of implication in the death, but before he could decide how to proceed, Mr. Akashini stirred, giving him a start.

"I really believe that I am making progress," Mr. Akashini said with surprising vigor, and gave an approving growl.

Arce was inclined to let Mr. Akashini have his illusion, but a reflex of morality inspired him to say, "I think you're dying."

Mr. Akashini was silent for a long time. Finally, he said, "That is not important. I am making progress, nonetheless."

This confused Arce, causing him to wonder whether or not he had misjudged Mr. Akashini by labeling him a fool. But then he thought that his original judgment may have been correct, and that Mr. Akashini's judgment concerning his own enthusiasm must have been in error. Arce felt sympathy for him, and yet, contrasting Mr. Akashini's attitude with his own detachment, he envied him the rigor of his commitment.

"Will you continue to help me?" Mr. Akashini asked, and Arce, suddenly infected with a desire to know his employer, to comprehend the obscure drives that motivated him, could only say yes.

Mr. Akashini nodded toward his suitcase, which lay closed on the futon. "There . . . look beneath the clothing."

In the suitcase was a fat sheaf of traveler's checks. Arce handed them to Mr. Akashini, who—barely able to hold the pen—began endorsing them, saying, "You must keep them away from me . . . the people who would report my condition. Someone tries the door when you are away. I want nothing to interfere with . . . with what is happening."

Considering Nacho's suspicious questions and avaricious nature, Arce knew that Mr. Akashini's worries were well founded, yet he could not understand why his employer trusted him with such a vast sum of money. When he asked why, Mr. Akashini replied that he had no choice.

"Besides," he said, "you will not betray me. You have changed as much as I these past months, but one thing has not changed—you're an honest man, though you may not want to admit it."

Arce, convinced that because of his proximity to death, Mr. Akashini might have clearer sight than ordinary folk, asked how he had changed, but his employer had fallen asleep. Watching him, Arce thought it might be possible for him to know Mr. Akashini, and that they might have been friends, though only for a brief period. If they were both changing—and he believed they were, for he sensed change in himself the way he sometimes sensed the presence of a lurking animal in a shadowy thicket—then they were changing in different directions, and in passing, they were likely to experience a momentary compatibility at best.

Unable to care for Mr. Akashini every hour of the day, Arce recruited Expectacion to assist him, bestowing trust upon her with the same hopeful conviction with which Mr. Akashini had bestowed it upon him. Yet he was not so thoroughly trusting as his employer. When forced to be away from the room, he would leave valuables tucked into places where a cursory search would reveal them. Not once did he discover anything missing, and he took this for an emblem not of trustworthiness—he believed Expectacion had made a search—but of wisdom. He understood that she was interested less in making a minor profit than in changing her life, and since wisdom was an ultimately more reliable virtue than trustworthiness, he came to value her more and more, to dote upon the sweetness of her body and the bright particularity of her soul.

Yet as they watched Mr. Akashini being transformed into the artifact of his understanding, a strong bond developed between them, one that stopped short of untrustworthy passion and yet had many of the dependable consolations of love. It would have been unnatural had they not developed such a bond, because the event to which they were bearing witness was so monstrous it enforced union. Within the space of a few weeks, fungi of various sorts grew to cover much of Mr. Akashini's body, creating whorls of multicolored fur—saffron, lavender and gray. His visible skin became pale and puffy, prone to odd shiftings and spasms, and his right eye was totally obscured by glowing silver webs and green spiders scarcely bigger than pinheads, and more cobwebs spanned between his shoulders and neck and the walls, and a bubbled milky film coated his tongue, until finally, he had undergone a metamorphosis into a fearsome creature whose eyes glowed silver with greeny speckles in the darkened room, burning out from a head shaped like a tuber, his body sheathed in a mummy wrapping of cobwebs and moss, with stalks of mustard-colored fungi clumped like tiny cities here and there, a thing capable only of emitting croaked entreaties for food or asking that a photograph be taken. On one occasion, however, he appeared to regain something of his old spirit and strength and engaged Arce and Expectacion in conversation.

"You must not be concerned, my friends," he said. "This is glorious."

The effect of his lips, almost sealed with clots of fungus, splitting and the effortfully spoken words oozing forth, struck Arce as being more ghastly than glorious, but he refrained from saying as much.

"Why does it seem glorious?" he asked.

Mr. Akashini made a noise that approximated laughter, the heaving of his chest and diaphragm causing puffs of dusty spores to spurt into the air. The candle flames flickered; a faint tide of shadow lapped up his legs, then receded. "I . . ." he said. "I am . . . becoming."

Expectacion asked in a tremulous voice if he wanted water, and he turned his head toward her—the laborious motion of a statue coming to life after a centurieslong enchantment.

"Sitting here," he said, ignoring her question, "I am arrowing toward completion. Toward . . . everything I wanted to believe but never could. I understand. . . ."

"The Malsueno?" Arce asked. "You understand the Malsueno?"

"Not yet" was the answer. "I understand . . . not everything. But I had no understanding of anything before."

He appeared to drift off for a moment.

"What's happening to you?" Expectacion asked him.

"When I was young," he said, "I dreamed of becoming a samurai. . . ."

He gave another horrid laugh.

Expectacion looked perplexed, and Arce wondered if his employer were rambling as men would in the grip of fever; yet he could not quite believe that. He sensed a new rectitude in Mr. Akashini, one that accorded with the ideas about Japan he had gleaned from his reading. But neither could he accept that what he sensed was wholly accurate, because Mr. Akashini's horrifying appearance seemed to put the lie to the notion of beneficent change.

In that stomach where once he had envisioned cars and paintings and other oddments of culture, he now pictured a miniature jungle, and sometimes, on entering the room from the bright corridor, he would think that a demon with eyes of unreal fire had materialized in Mr. Akashini's chair. He and Expectacion spent hours on end sitting side by side, listening to the creaky whisperings of new growth emanating from the man's flesh, gazing at the awful pulsings of his chest and belly. Mr. Akashini was so self-involved that they were not embarrassed about making love in the room. Sex acted to diminish the miserable miracle before them and to make their vigil more tolerable, and if it had not been for Nacho's questions, knockings on the door and general harassment, they might have been happy.

Early one morning, before dawn, Arce went to buy breakfast for himself and Expectacion—they had slept poorly, disturbed by the noises of Mr. Akashini's body and his constant troubled movement. On returning, he heard angry voices issuing from room 23. The bulbous form of Nacho Perez was blocking the door. He was haranguing Expectacion, while two men—*marañeros*, judging by their tattoos—searched the suitcases, doing their utmost to avoid contact with Mr. Akashini, who sat motionless, emitting a faint buzzing, shifting now and again amid the fetters of his cobwebs, the shifts redolent not so much of muscular contractions as of vegetable reflex. In the dimness, due to the activity of microscopic spores, his glowing eyes appeared to be revolving slowly.

Arce drew his knife, but Nacho caught sight of him, seized Expectacion and barred an arm beneath her chin.

"I'll break her neck!" he said.

Expectacion threw herself about, trying to kick him, but when Nacho tightened his grip, she gave up struggling, other than to pluck feebly at his arm. Behind him, the two *marañeros* had drawn their knives. Arce recognized one of them—Gilberto Viera, a thin, sallow man with pocked skin and a pencil-line mustache.

"Gilberto," said Arce, "you remember the time on the Blanco Ojo? I helped you then. Help me now."

Gilberto looked ashamed but only lowered his eyes. The other man—taller, darker, with the nappy hair of a man born in the eastern mountains—asked Nacho, "What should we do?"

"Well," said Nacho, beaming at Arce, "that depends on our friend here."

"What do you want?" Arce had to exert tremendous restraint to resist aiming a slash at Nacho's double chin.

"There must be something," said Nacho archly, paying no attention to an intensification of Mr. Akashini's buzzing. "Isn't there, Arce?"

When Arce remained silent, he tightened his grip—Expectacion's feet were lifted off the ground and her face grew dark with blood. She dug her nails into Nacho's arm but with no effect.

"There's some money hidden behind one of the bricks," Arce said grudgingly. "Let her go."

Another flurry of buzzing from Mr. Akashini, accompanied by a series of throaty clicks, as if he were trying to speak. The two *marañeros* edged away from his chair, bumping against Nacho.

"Which brick is it?" Nacho asked, and Arce, thinking furiously of how he might extricate Expectacion from the fat man's grasp, was about to tell him, when—with the ponderous motion of a bloom bursting from its husk—Mr. Akashini came to his feet. With his glowing eyes and dark, deformed body, puffy strips of pallid skin showing through the fungus and moss like bandages, he was a gruesome sight. Gilberto tried to shove Nacho aside in an attempt to escape from the room. However, the other man spun about and slashed Mr. Akashini with his knife.

The knife passed through Mr. Akashini's side, its arc slowing as if encountering resistance of the sort that might be offered by sludge or mud; the dark fluid that leaked forth flowed with the sluggishness of syrup. Mr. Akashini staggered against the wall; his buzzing and clicking reached furious proportions, sounding like a nest of bees and crabs together. A tiny spider scuttled out from his right eye, diminishing its glow by a speck of green. His cheek bulged. One arm began to vibrate, his skin bubbled up in places, his chest puffed and deflated as if responding to the workings of an enormous flabby heart. Arce was repelled and retreated along the corridor, but when Mr. Akashini gave out a growly hum—of satisfaction, Arce thought—he realized that some fraction of his employer's personality was yet embedded within this vegetable demon. The man who had wielded the knife shrieked, and Nacho half-turned to see what had gone wrong, blocking the doorway entirely. Arce seized the opportunity to leap forward and stab him low in the back. The hotel owner squealed, clutching at the wound, and released Expectacion, who slumped to the floor and crawled away. Arce prepared to strike a second time, but the hotel owner lurched to the side, permitting him an unimpeded view into the room, and what he saw caused him to hesitate, allowing Nacho to stumble out of range.

Clouds of spores were pouring up from Mr. Akashini, filling the air with a whirling gray powder that reduced the flames of the candelabrum to pale yellow gleams, like golden tears hanging in the murk, and reduced the figures of the two *marañeros* to dimly perceived bulks that kicked and shuddered. One—Arce could not tell which—collapsed on the futon and the other crumpled beneath the dining table, both holding their throats and choking. Looming above them was Mr. Akashini, his luminous eyes the brightest objects in the room, the outline of his body nearly indistinguishable from the agitated gray motes around him, looking as ominous and eerie as a Fate. There was a flurrying at the edges of the body, along with a rustling sound—a horde of winged things were developing from the frays of skin, fluttering up to add a new density to the whirling spores, darkening the air further. Several danced out through the door: big carrion moths with charcoal wings. He must have inadvertently fed Mr. Akashini some of their eggs, Arce thought, and now they were hatching. And more than spores and moths were being born. Spiders, centipedes, insects of 100 varieties were burrowing up through his skin, pustules opening to reveal the heads of infant snakes and baby beetles, bulges erupting into larval flows, as the process of Mr. Akashini's understanding, a process of adaptation and fertilization and fecundity, at last reached fruition.

Within a minute or two, the room grew as dark as night, and yet still those strange silver eyes burned forth. It seemed to Arce that the body must have dissolved, that the eyes, thickly woven cobwebs, were suspended by a clever arrangement of strands. But then the eyes moved closer and he realized that Mr. Akashini was taking one unsteady step after another toward the door.

Expectacion caught Arce's arm. "Hurry!" she cried. "Nacho has gone for help!"

Turning, Arce saw that, indeed, the hotel owner was nowhere to be found, a snail's track of blood along the wall giving evidence of his passage toward the stairs.

"For Christ's sake, *Papá!*" Expectacion gave him a push. "Don't just stand there gawking."

"No, wait!"

Arce shook her off, ripped off his shirt and wrapped it about his face. Then he dashed into room 23, dived onto the floor and groped for the brick behind which he had hidden the money, trying not to breathe. Once he had secured the packet of checks, he scrambled to his feet and came face to face with Mr. Akashini— with a gray deformity, with newborn moths breaking free from a glutinous grain of skin and mold, with a shadow of a mouth, with tepid slow breath, with two eyes of green and cold silver. The webs of the eyes were a marvelous texture admitting to an infinite depth of interwoven strands, and Arce saw within them a tropic of green and silver, a loom of event and circumstance, and felt that if he were to continue staring, he would see not only the truth as Mr. Akashini had come to know it but also his truth and Expectacion's. Then he became afraid, and the eyes were again only webs, and the face before him, with its hideous growths, appeared a thing of incalculable menace. Yet the spores and the insects and the moths that had transformed the *marañeros* into anonymous heaps were keeping clear of him, and he realized even then that some relic of Mr. Akashini's soul was employing restraint.

Arce wanted to say something, to convey some good wish, but he could think of nothing that would not seem foolish. With mixed emotions, not sure what he should feel for Mr. Akashini, he retreated into the corridor, grabbed Expectacion by the arm and sprinted for the stairs.

A line of pink showed above the black wall of the jungle, and only a few stars pricked the indigo sky directly overhead; the neon signs over the bars were pale in the brightening air, and shadows were beginning to fill in the ruts in the muddy streets. The coolness of the night was already being dispelled. There were only a handful of people out—two drunks staggering along arm in arm; an old Indian man in rags hunkered down beside a door, smoking a pipe; farther along, a whore was yelling at a shirtless youth. Arce led Expectacion out of the hotel and started toward the jungle, but after about 20 yards, she balked.

"Where are you going?" she asked, pulling free of him.

"The Malsueno. We'll be safe there. I know places . . ."

"The hell with you! I'm not going in there!"

He made to grab her, but she danced away.

"You're nuts, *Papá!* Nacho'll have everybody looking for us! We have to get far away! The capital! That's the only place we'll be safe."

He stood gazing uncomprehendingly at her, seeing faces from another time, stung by old pains, experiencing a harrowing fear of displacement like that he had felt on being forced to flee the capital.

"Come on!" she shouted. "Nacho'll be here any second. We can take one of the cars parked back of the market."

"I can't."

"What do you mean, you can't?" She went back to him and pounded on his chest, her face twisted with anger and frustration. "You're going to get us killed . . . just standing here."

Although the blows hurt, he let her beat on him, ashamed of his fear and incapacity. Even when he saw Nacho turn the corner, at his back a group of *marañeros* armed with machetes, he was unable to take a step away from the place where he had hidden from memories and pain and life itself for all these years.

Expectacion, too, had begun to cry. "You really blew it, *Papá!* We had a chance, you and me." She went a few faltering steps toward the highway. "Damn you!" she said. "Damn you!" Then, with her arms pumping, she fled along the street.

In the other direction, Nacho was limping forward, holding his back with one hand, pointing at Arce with the other, while at his rear, like a squad of drunken soldiers, the *marañeros* whooped and brandished their machetes. Arce drew his knife, determined to make a final stand.

At that moment, however, torrents of spores and insects and serpents and unidentifiable scraps of life exploded from the windows and the door of the hotel, making it appear that the building had been filled to bursting with black fluid. A whirling cloud formed between Nacho and Arce. At its core, Arce thought he spotted a shadow, an indistinct manlike shape with glowing eyes, but before he could be certain of it, the edge of the cloud frayed and streams of insects raced toward him and stung his face and neck and arms.

Blinded, he staggered this way and that, harrowed by the insects, and then he ran and ran, the dark cloud sending forth rivers of tormenting winged things to keep him on his course. As he passed through the outskirts of town, a white pickup rocketed out of a side street and swerved to the side, barely missing him, coming to a rest against a light pole. Through the windshield, he made out Expectacion's startled face. Without thinking, desperate to escape the insects, he flung himself into the truck, began rolling up the window and shouted at her to drive. She gunned the engine and, pursued by the swarm, they fishtailed out onto the highway.

They drove into the hills with the sky reddening at their backs, and after experiencing a flurry of panic on recognizing the course that had been chosen for him, it seemed to Arce that with every mile—in a process of self-realization exactly contrary to Mr. Akashini's—he was shedding a coating of fear and habit and distorted view, as if a shell were breaking away from some more considered inner man. Not the man he had been but the man he had become without knowing it, tempered by years of solitary endeavor. He felt strong, directed, full of youthful enthusiasm.

He would go to the capital, he decided, not to inhabit the past but to build a future, to make of it a temple that would honor the eccentric brotherhood that existed between himself and Mr. Akashini, a brotherhood that he had not embraced, that he could not have acknowledged or understood before, that he did not wholly understand now, but whose consummation had filled him with the steel of purpose and the fire of intent. He realized that they were both men who had lost themselves, Mr. Akashini to the persuasions of arrogance and wealth, himself to the deprivations of pain and despair, and how because of the fortuitous propinquity of a peculiar ambition and a woman of energy and strength and a magical jungle, he at least had been afforded the opportunity to move on.

He could not take any such pleasure, however, in Mr. Akashini's death, and when he looked at Expectacion, the lines of her face aglow with pink light, when he felt the tenderness she had begun to rouse in him and saw the challenge she presented, the potential for poignant emotion, for grief and joy and love, those vital flavors he had rejected for so long, the prospect of an adventure with her was dimmed by regret that he had been unable to do more than speed Mr. Akashini to his end.

It wasn't fair, he thought.

He had done little, risked little, and yet he had won through to something real, whereas Mr. Akashini had only suffered and died among strangers far from home. This inequity caused Arce to think that perhaps he had won nothing, to wonder if everything he felt was the product of delusion. But as they climbed high into the hills, on glancing back toward Santander Jimenez, he saw there a sight that seemed to memorialize all that had happened: Trillions of insects and spores and things unnamable were spiraling above the miserable little town, a towering blackness that—despite a blustery wind—maintained its basic form, at one moment appearing to be the shadow of a great curved sword poised to deliver a sundering blow and at the next, a column of ashes climbing to heaven against the crimson pyre of the rising sun.

JONATHAN CARROLL
The Sadness of Detail

Jonathan Carroll is one of the most consistingly original writers working today, stepping effortlessly back and forth across the artificial line that's been drawn by critics and publishers between fantasy and mainstream fiction. "The Sadness of Detail," reprinted from *Omni* magazine, is typical of Carroll's work, taking real life characters, settings, events and giving them a darkly fantastical twist, exploring the tension between the real and the imagined. In the following story Carroll also explores the nature of creation itself, and does so compassionately, and with style. "The Sadness of Detail" is easily one of the very best stories of the year.

—T.W.

Jonathan Carroll has been astonishing readers for several years with his odd novels, which refuse to be categorized. His most recent, *A Child Across the Sky* (Doubleday) was nominated for the 1989 World Fantasy Award and his next one is *Outside the Dog Museum* (Macdonald—UK). "Mr. Fiddlehead," from last year's volume of this series, is being made into a feature film. It, too, was a nominee for the 1989 World Fantasy Award.

When I first read "The Sadness of Detail," Chesterton's novel *The Man Who Was Thursday*, a metaphysical mystery/comedy, immediately came to mind. Carroll's story is far more chilling.

—E.D.

The Sadness of Detail

JONATHAN CARROLL

I used to spend a lot of time at the Café Bremen. The coffee there is bitter and delicious, and the teal-blue velvet seats are as comfortable as old friends. The large windows greet the morning light like Herr Ritter, the waiter, greets anyone who comes in. You don't have to order much: a cup of tea or a glass of wine. The croissants come from the bakery next door and are delivered twice a day. Late in the evening, the café bakes its own specialty for the night-owl customers—"heavies," a kind of sugar doughnut the size of a pocket watch. A wonderful treat is to go in there late on a winter night and have a warm plate full of them.

The Bremen is open nineteen hours a day. December twenty-fourth is the only day of the year it's closed, but on Christmas it opens again, wearing green and red tablecloths, full of people in bright new sweaters or singles looking a little less lonely on a day when people should be home.

There are small, real pleasures in life—the latest issue of your favorite magazine, a fresh pack of cigarettes, the smell of things baking. You can have all of them in that café; you can be happy there without any of them.

I often went in to sit, look out the window, and hum. A secret vice. My husband sneaks candy bars, my mother reads movie magazines, I hum. Give me a free hour with nothing to do and a good window to stare out of and I'll gladly hum you all of Mahler's Fifth or any song off the Beatles' White Album.

I'm the first to admit I'm not very good at it, but humming is only meant for an audience of one, yourself, and anyone who eavesdrops does it at their own peril.

This happened on a late November afternoon when the whole town seemed one liquid glaze of reflected light and rain. A day when the rain is colder than snow and everything feels meaner, harder edged. A day to stay inside and read a book, drink soup out of a thick white cup.

I'd decided to treat myself to the Bremen because I was beat. Arguing with the children, a trip to the dentist, then endless shopping for invisible things—toilet paper, glue, salt. Things no one ever knows are there until they're gone and are then needed desperately. An invisible day where you exhaust yourself running around, doing thankless errands that are necessary but meaningless: the housewife's oxymoron.

Walking in, wet and loaded down with bags, I think I groaned with joy when I saw my favorite table was empty. I flew to it like a tired robin to its nest.

Herr Ritter came right over, looking elegant and very nineteenth century in his black suit and bow tie, a white towel as always draped carefully over his arm.

"You look very tired. A hard day?"

"A nothing day, Herr Ritter."

He suggested a piece of cream cake, damn the calories, but I ordered a glass of red wine instead. There was an hour before the kids would be home. An hour to let the knots inside slowly untie themselves while I looked out the window and watched the now-romantic rain. How long could it have been, two minutes? Three? Almost without knowing it, I'd begun to hum, but then from the booth behind, someone gave a loud, long "Sssh!"

Embarrassed, I turned and saw an old man with a very pink face glaring at me.

"Not everyone likes Neil Diamond, you know!"

The perfect end to a perfect day: Now I was on trial for humming "Holly Holy."

I made an "excuse me" face and was about to turn around again when, out of the corner of my eye, I noticed a number of photographs he had spread out on the table in front of him. Most of the pictures were of my family and me.

"Where did you get those?"

He reached behind him and, picking one up, handed it to me. Not looking at it, he said, "That is your son in nine years. He's wearing a patch because he lost that eye in an automobile accident. He wanted to be a pilot, as you know, but one needs good eyesight for that, so he paints houses instead and drinks a lot. The girl in the picture is the one he lives with. She takes heroin."

My son Adam is nine and the only thing that matters to him in the world is airplanes. We call his room the hangar because he's covered every wall with pictures of the Blue Angels, the British Red Arrows, and the Italian Frecce Tricolori precision flying teams. There are models and magazines and so many different airplane things in his room that it's a little overwhelming. Recently he spent a week writing to all of the major airlines (including Air Maroc and Tarom, the national airline of Romania), asking what one has to do to qualify as a pilot for their company. My husband and I have always been both charmed and proud of Adam's obsession and have never thought of him as anything but a future pilot. In the picture I held, our little boy with a crew cut and smart green eyes looked like a haggard eighteen-year-old panhandler. The expression on his face was a bad combination of boredom, bitterness, and no hope. It was obviously Adam in a few years, but a young man far past the end of his line, someone you'd sneer at or move to avoid if you saw him approaching on the street.

And the eye patch! Imagining the mutilation of one of our children is as

wrenching as the thought of them dead. None of that is . . . allowed. It cannot
be. And if, tragically, it does happen, then it is always our fault, no matter their
age or the circumstances. As parents, our wings must always be large enough to
cover and protect them from hurt or pain. It is in our contract with God when
we take on the responsibility of their lives. I remember so well the character in
Macbeth who, upon learning of the deaths of all his children, starts calling them
"chicks." "Where are all my little chicks?" The sight of my son wearing an eye
patch gave me the taste of blood in my mouth.

"Who are you?"

"Here's one of your husband after the divorce. He thinks that new mustache
is becoming. I think it's a little silly."

Willy has tried on and off for years to grow a mustache. Each one looked worse
than the last. Once in the middle of a very nasty fight, I said he always began
one at the same time as he began an affair. That stopped them.

In the picture, besides the mustache, he was wearing one of those typically
silly heavy-metal fan T-shirts (covered with flames and lightning) announcing a
group called Braindead. What was ominous about that was Adam had recently
brought home an album *by* Braindead and said they were "awesome."

"My name is Thursday, Frau Becker."

"Today is Thursday."

"That's right. If we'd met yesterday, I'd be Wednesday—"

"Who are you? What's this about? What are these pictures?"

"They're your future. Or rather, one of them. Futures are unstable, tricky
things. They depend on different factors.

"The way you're going now, the way you handle your life and those around
you, this is what will happen." He pointed to the picture I held and then opened
both hands in a gesture that said, "What can you do? That's the way it is."

"I don't believe it. Get away from me!" I moved to turn, but he touched my
shoulder.

"Your favorite smell is burning wood. You always lie when you say the first
person you ever slept with was Joe Newman. The first was really your parents'
handyman, Leon Bell."

No one knew that. Not my husband, my sister, no one. Leon Bell! I thought
of him so rarely. He was kind and gentle but it still hurt, and I was so scared
someone would come home and find us in my bed. "What do you want?" I asked.

He took the photograph out of my hand and put it back on the table with the
others.

"Futures can change. They're like the lines on our hands. Fate is a negotiable
thing. I'm here to negotiate with you."

"What do I have that you want?"

"Your talent. Remember the drawing you did the other night of the child under
the tree? I want it. Bring me the picture and your son'll be saved."

"That's all? It was only a sketch! It took ten minutes. I did it while watching
television!"

"Bring it to me here tomorrow at exactly this time."

"How can I believe you?"

He picked up a photograph that had been covered by the others. He held it in front of my eyes: my old bedroom. Leon Bell and me.

"I don't even know you. Why are you doing this to me?"

He slid the pictures together as if they were cards he was about to shuffle. "Go home and find that drawing."

I was pretty good once. Went to art school on a full scholarship and some of my teachers said I had the makings to be a real painter. But you know how I reacted to that? Got scared. I painted because I liked it. When people started looking carefully at my work and with their hands on their checkbooks, I ran away and got married. Marriage (and its responsibilities) is a perfect rock to hide behind when an enemy (parents, maturity, success) is out gunning for you. Squeeze down into a ball behind it and virtually nothing can touch you. For me, being happy didn't mean being a successful artist. I saw success as stress and demands I'd never be able to fulfill, thus disappointing people who thought I was better than I really was.

Just recently, now that the children were old enough to get their own snacks, I'd bought some expensive English oil paints and two stretched canvases. But I've been almost too embarrassed to bring them out because the only "art" I've done in the last years has been funny sketches for the kids or a little scribble at the bottom of a letter to a good friend.

Plus the sketchbook, my oldest friend. I'd always wanted to keep a diary but never had the kind of persistence that's needed to say something in writing about every day you live. My sketchbook is different because the day I began it, when I was seventeen, I promised myself to make drawings in there only when I wanted or when an event was so important (the birth of the kids, the day I discovered Willy was having an affair) that I had to "say" something about it. As an old woman I'd give it to my children and say, "These are things you didn't know. They aren't important now except to tell you more about me, if that interests you." Or maybe I'll only look at it, then sigh and throw it away.

I go through the book sometimes, but it generally depresses me, even the good parts, the nice memories. Because there is so much sadness in the details. How current and glamorous I thought I was, wearing striped bell-bottom pants to a big party just after we were married. Or one of Willy at his desk, smoking a cigar, so happy to be finishing the article on Fischer von Erlach that he had thought would make his career but which was never even published. I drew these things carefully and in great detail, but all I see now are the silly pants or the spread of his excited fingers on the typewriter. But if it depresses me, why do I continue drawing in the book? Because it is the only life I have and I am not pretentious enough to think I know answers now that might come to me when I'm older. I keep hoping thirty or forty years from now when I look at those drawings, I'll have some kind of revelation that will make parts of my life clearer to me.

I couldn't find the drawing he wanted. I went through everything: wastebaskets, drawers, the kids' old homework papers. How brutally panic can build when you can't find something needed! Whatever you are looking for becomes the most important object in the world, however trivial—a suitcase key, a year-old receipt from the gas company. Your apartment becomes an enemy—hiding the thing you need, indifferent to your pleas. It wasn't in my sketchbook, on the telephone table, stuck in a coat pocket. Neither the gray prairies under the beds nor the false pine and chemical smells in the kitchen closet offered anything. Would my son really lose his *eye* if I couldn't find one stupid little drawing? Yes, that's what the old man said. I believed him after seeing the picture of Leon and me together.

It was a terrible night, trying to be good old normal "Mom" to the family, while madly exploring every corner of our place for the picture. At dinner I casually asked if anyone had seen it in their travels. No one had. They were used to my drawings and doodles around the house. Now and then someone liked one and took it to their room but no luck with this one.

Throughout the evening I kept glancing at Adam, which gave me further reason to search. He had plain eyes but they were smart and welcoming. He looked straight at you in a conversation, gave you his full attention.

At midnight there were no further places to look. The drawing was gone. Sitting at the kitchen table with a glass of orange juice, I knew that there were only two things I could do when I met Thursday at the Bremen the next afternoon: Tell the truth or try and re-create from memory the drawing he demanded. It was such a simple sketch that I didn't think there would be much trouble drawing something that looked similar, but *exactly* the same? Not possible.

I went into the living room and got my clipboard. At least the paper would be the same. Willy bought the stuff by the ream because it was cheap and sturdy and we both liked using it. You didn't feel guilty crumpling up a piece if you'd made a mistake. I could easily see myself crumpling up that damned drawing and not thinking about it again. A child standing under a tree. A little girl in jeans. A chestnut tree. What was special about it?

It took five minutes to do, five minutes to be sure it was as I remembered, five more minutes with it in my lap, knowing it was hopeless. Fifteen minutes from start to finish.

The next afternoon, before I'd even sat down, Thursday was tapping an insistent finger on the marble table. "Did you find it? Do you have it?"

"Yes. It's in my bag."

Everything about him relaxed. His face went slack, the finger lay down with the rest of his palm on the table, he leaned back against the velvet seat. "That's great. Give it to me, please."

He was feeling better, but I wasn't. As coolly as I could, I pulled the wrinkled piece of paper out of my purse.

Before leaving the apartment I'd crumpled up the drawing into a tight ball to perhaps fool him a little. If he didn't look too closely, maybe I'd be safe. Maybe I wouldn't. There wasn't much chance of being lucky, but at that point what else could I hope for?

Yet watching how carefully he flattened out the paper and pored over it as if it were some unique and priceless document, I knew he'd notice the difference any moment and everything would go to hell from there. I took off my coat and slid into the booth.

He looked up from the picture. "You can hum if you'd like. I'll just be a minute."

I liked this café so much, but today it had been changed by this man into an unpleasant, menacing place where all I wanted to do was finish our business and leave. Even the sight of Herr Ritter standing there at the counter reading the newspaper was irritating. How could life go on so normally when the worst kind of magic was in the air, thick as cigar smoke?

"You have a good memory."

"What do you mean?"

He reached into his breast pocket and took out a piece of paper. Unfolding it, he held up the original drawing of the little girl under the tree I'd done.

"You had it!"

He nodded. "Both of us played tricks. I said you had it, you were trying to give me a copy and saying it was the original. Who was more dishonest?"

"But I couldn't find it because you had it! Why did you do that?"

"Because we had to see how well you remember things. It's very important."

"What about my son?" I asked. "Will he be all right?"

"I guarantee he will. I can show you a photograph of him then, but it might be better just knowing he'll be fine and will live a very contented life. Because of what you did for him here." He pointed to the second drawing. "Do you want to see the photograph of him?"

I was tempted but finally said no. "Just tell me if he'll be a pilot."

Thursday crossed his arms. "He'll be captain of a Concorde flying the Paris-to-Caracas route. One day his plane will be hijacked, but your Adam will do something so clever and heroic that he single-handedly will save the plane and the passengers. A genuinely heroic act. There'll even be a cover story about him in *Time* magazine titled 'Maybe There Are Still Heroes.' " He held up the drawing. "Your son. Because of this."

"What about my getting divorced?"

"Do you really want to know?"

"Yes, I do."

He took another piece of folded paper out of his pocket along with the nub of a pencil. "Draw a pear."

"A pear?"

"Yes. Draw a picture of a pear, then I can tell you."

I took the pencil and smoothed the paper on the table. "I don't understand any of this, Mr. Thursday."

A pear. A fat bottom and a half-so-fat top. A stem. A little cross-hatching to give it shadow and depth. One pear.

I handed it to him and he barely gave it a glance before folding it and putting it in another pocket.

"There will be a divorce because you will leave your husband, not vice versa, as you fear."

"But why would I do that?"

"Because Frank Elkin is coming for you."

I think if I had married Frank Elkin I would have been all right. I certainly loved him enough. But besides loving me too, he also loved parachuting. One day he jumped, pulled his rip cord, but nothing happened. How long ago was that, twenty years? Twenty-four?

"Frank Elkin is dead."

"He is, but you can change that."

The apartment was empty when we got back. Thursday said he would keep it empty until we finished what we had to do. In the bedroom I took my sketchbook out of the table beside the bed. That familiar gray and red cover. I remembered the day I'd bought it and paid for it with new coins. Somehow every coin I handed the salesgirl was gleaming like gold and silver. I was romantic enough to take that as a good omen.

In the living room again, I handed my book to Mr. Thursday, who took it from me without comment.

"Sit down."

"What will happen to the children?"

"If you want, the court will award them to you. You can prove your husband is an alcoholic and incapable of caring for them."

"But Willy doesn't drink!"

"You can change that."

"How? How can I change all these things? What do you mean?"

He opened the sketchbook and whipped quickly through it, not stopping or slowing anywhere. When he'd finished, he looked at me. "Somewhere in this book you've drawn pictures of God. I can't tell you which ones they are, but I just checked and they're here. Some people have this talent. Some have been able to write God, others can compose Him in music. I'm not talking about people like Tolstoy or Beethoven, either. They were only great artists.

"You know the sadness of detail, using your phrase. That is what makes you capable of transcendence.

"For the rest of your life, if you choose, I will come sometimes and ask you to do a drawing. Like the pear today. I'll ask for things like that, as well as copies of certain of the works in your sketchbook. I *can* say that your book is full of astounding work, Mrs. Becker. There are at least three different important drawings of God, one I've never even seen. Other things, too. We need this book and we need you, but unfortunately I cannot tell you more than that. Even if I were to show you which of your work is . . . transcendent, you wouldn't understand what I was talking about.

"You can do things we can't and vice versa. For us, bringing Frank Elkin back from the dead is no problem. Or saving your son." He held up my book with both hands. "But we can't do this, and that is why we need you."

"What if I were to say no?"

"We keep our word. Your son will still become a pilot, but you will sink deeper into your meager life until you will realize even more than now you've been suffocating in it for years."

"And if I give you the book and do your drawings?"

"You can have Frank Elkin and whatever else you want."

"Are you from heaven?"

Mr. Thursday smiled for the first time. "I can't honestly answer that because I don't know. That is why we need your drawings, Mrs. Becker. Because even God doesn't know or remember anymore. It is as if He has a kind of progressive amnesia. He forgets things, to put it simply. The only way we can get Him to remember is to show Him pictures like yours of Himself or play certain music, read passages from books. Only then does He remember and tell us the things we need to know. We are recording everything He says, but there are fewer and fewer periods of clarity. You see, the saddest thing of all is even He has begun to forget the details. And as He forgets, things change and go away. Right now they're small things—certain smells, forgetting to give this child arms, that man his freedom when he deserves it. Some of us who work for God don't know where we come from or if we are even doing the right thing. All we do know is His condition is becoming worse and something must be done quickly. When He sees your pictures, He is reminded of things, and sometimes He even becomes His old self again. We can work with Him then. But without your work, when we can't show Him pictures of Himself, images He once created, or words He spoke, He is only an old man with a failing memory. When His memory is gone, there will be nothing left."

I don't go to the Café Bremen anymore. A few days after I last met with Thursday I had a strange experience there that soured me on the place. I was in my favorite seat drawing the pig, the Rock of Gibraltar, and the ancient Spanish coin he had requested. Having just finished the coin, I looked up and saw Herr Ritter watching me closely from his place behind the counter. Too closely. I have to be careful about who I let see my drawings. Thursday said there are a great many around who would like nothing more than for a certain memory to disappear forever.

Honorable Mentions
1990

Joan Aiken, "Number Four, Bowstring Lane," *A Fit of Shivers.*
Ray Aldridge, "The Cold Cage," *The Magazine of Fantasy & Science Fiction,* Feb.
George J. Andrade, "Clowns," *Haunts,* Spring.
Patricia Anthony, "The Deer Lake Sightings," *Weird Tales,* Summer.
———, "The Murcheson Boy," *Weird Tales,* Fall.
Kim Antieau, "Great Expectations," *Cemetery Dance* Summer.
———, "At a Window Facing West," *Alfred Hitchcock Mystery Magazine,* mid-Dec.
Thomas Fox Averill, "The Man Who Ran With Deer," *Sonora Review* #18.
Scott Baker, "Alimentary Tract," *Universe 1.*
Robert Barnard, "Cupid's Dart," *Ellery Queen's Mystery Magazine,* May.
Donald Barthelme, "The King," (novella) HarperCollins.
Fran Barst, "Fishes of the Land, Cows of the Sea," (poem) *Ice River* #6.
Elsa Beckett, "Family Ties," *Fantasy Tales 2.*
Susan Beetlestone, "Heart of Santa Rosa" *Interzone* #38.
Judith R. Behunin, "Three Birds with One Stone," *Eldritch Tales* #23.
Thomas Berger, "Gibberish," *Playboy,* Dec.
Ruth Berman, "The Legend of the Mannikin Gulliver and Brobdingnag," (poem) *Isaac Asimov's Science Fiction Magazine,* July.
Elaine Bergstrom, "Net Songs," *The Women Who Walk Through Fire.*
Marcia Biederman, "Listen and Listen Good," *Sisters in Crime 3.*
Terry Bisson, "Bears Discover Fire," *IASFM,* Aug.
Michael Blumlein, "Shed His Grace," *Semiotext(e) SF; The Brains of Rats.*
Maclin Bocock, "The Baker's Daughter: A Tale of Holy Russia," *New Directions International Anthology of Prose & Poetry* #54.
Cecil Bonstein, "It Will Grow Again," *Best English Short Stories.*
Bruce Boston, "A Missionary of the Mutant Rain Forest," *IASFM,* Oct.
Gary Brandner, "Ugly," *Lovecraft's Legacy.*
Gary A. Braunbeck, "Afterthoughts," *After Hours* #8.
———, "To His Children in Darkness," *Cemetery Dance,* Fall.
Joseph Payne Brennan, "Shrouded Lake, " (poem) *Weirdbook* #25.
Alan Brennert, "Her Pilgrim Soul," *Her Pilgrim Soul.*
Eric Brown, "The Death of Cassandra Quebec," *Zenith 2.*
Sherrie Brown, "There are Worse Things," *Thin Ice 7.*
Edward Bryant, "The Loneliest Number," *Pulphouse* #7.
——— and Dan Simmons, "Dying is Easy, *Comedy* is Hard," *The Further Adventures of the Joker.*
Paul Buck, "Back Door Man," *New Crimes.*
Cliff Burns, "Invisible Boy," *Tesseracts 3.*
Rick Cadger, "A Pinch of . . . ," *Back Brain Recluse* #17.
Brad Cahoon, "The House in the Kudzu," *Grue 12.*
Carol Cail, "Roadkill," *Cemetery Dance,* Summer.
Elizabeth R. Caine, "The Body Beautiful," *Fear,* Sept.
Richard Calder, "The Lilim," *Interzone* #34.
Ramsey Campbell, "Needing Ghosts," (novella) Legend.

Elliott Capon, "Fun and Games at the Whacks Museum," *AHMM*, Dec.

Mary Caponegro, "Materia Prima," *The Star Café*.

Jonathan Carroll, "The Art of Falling Down," *Walls of Fear*.

——, "Black Cocktail," (novella) Legend.

——, "The Dead Love You," *Omni*, Dec.

——, "Tired Angel," *Weird Tales*, Winter '90/'91.

Michael Cassutt, "Curious Elation," *F & SF*, Sept.

Fred Chappell, "Free Hand," *Deathrealm*, #11.

Suzy McKee Charnas, "Evil Thoughts," *The SeaHarp Hotel*.

Mary Higgins Clark, "Voices in the Coalbin," *Sisters in Crime* 2.

Simon Clark, "Skinner Lane," *Blood & Grit*.

David Ira Cleary, "The Maintenance of Innocence," *New Pathways*, Nov.

Lisa R. Cohen, "The Dream of the Turtle King," *Pulphouse* #6.

Sherry Coldsmith, "Faking It," *Interzone* #42.

Michael R. Collings, "A Pound of Chocolates on St. Valentine's Day," *The Blood Review*, Jan.

——, "A Midnight Shooting on the Golden State Freeway . . . ," 2 *A.M.*, Aug.

J. L. Comeau, "Firebird," *The Women Who Walk Through Fire*.

Brian Cooper, "Bad Metal," *Fear* #20.

Gary William Crawford, "The Cabinets," *Fantasy Tales* 2.

Kara Dalkey, "A Prudent Obedience," *Festival Week*.

Colin Davis, "A Bad Season for Freaks," *Fear* #16.

Melinda Davis, "Something Like That Song Fanny Brice Used to Sing," *The Quarterly* 13.

Pamela Dean, "A Necessary Demise," *Festival Week*.

Don H. DeBrandt, "Payback," *Pulphouse* #9.

Charles de Lint, "Ghosts of Wind and Shadow," *Triskell Press*.

——, "Merlin Dreams in the Mondream Wood," *Pulphouse* #7.

——, "A Tattoo on Her Heart," *Pulphouse* #8.

Bradley Denton, "Captain Coyote's Last Hunt," *IASFM*, March.

——, "Jimmy Blackburn Flies a Kite," *F & SF*, Oct.

——, "The Murderer Chooses Sterility," *Pulphouse* #6.

Gardner R. Dozois, "Après Mois," *Omni*, Nov.

David L. Duggins, "Depth of Reflection," *Cemetery Dance*, Fall.

——, "Kid's Game," *Fear* #20.

——, "Seesaw," *Cemetery Dance*, Winter.

Scott Edelman, "True Love, and How it Ruined my Credit," *Deathrealm* #12.

Greg Egan, "The Caress," *IASFM*, Jan.

Tom Elliott, "Papa Jack," *New Blood*, Nov.-Dec.

——, "Thy Victory, Thy Sting," *Grue* 11.

Harlan Ellison, "Jane Doe #112," *EQMM*, Dec.

Carol Emshwiller, "Looking Down," *Verging on the Pertinent*.

——, "Moon Songs," *The Start of The End of It All and Other Stories*.

——, "Queen Kong," *Omni*, Jan.

M. J. Engh, "Penelope Comes Home," *Walls of Fear*.

Kelly Eskridge, "The Hum of Human Cities," *Pulphouse* #9.

John Farris, "Good Morning, Daddy," *Night Visions* 8.

Marina Fitch, "Just Give Me Your Hand," *Pulphouse* #9.

John M. Ford, "A Little Scene to Monarchize," (poem) *Speculative Engineering Production Chapbook*

Karen Joy Fowler, "The Night Wolf," *Skin of the Soul.*
Janet Fox, "Late Bloomer," *When the Black Lotus Blooms.*
Kristl Volk Franklin, "Act of Love," *Women of Darkness* 2.
Robert Frazier, "Descent into Eden," *Amazing*, Sept.
Esther M. Friesner, "Whammy," *F & SF*, July.
———, "The Weavers," *Tales of the Witchworld* 3.
C.S. Fuqua, "Graduation," *Grue* 12.
Stephen Gallagher, "The Back of His Hand," *Night Visions* 8.
———, "Comparative Anatomy," *Ibid.*
———, "Dead Man's Handle," *Ibid.*
———, "The Drain," *Fantasy Tales*, Spring.
Janice Galloway, "After The Rains," *Best English Short Stories* 2.
Craig Shaw Gardner, "Three Doors in a Double Room," *The SeaHarp Hotel.*
Peter T. Garrett, "Legions of the Night," *Fear* #17.
Mick Garris, "Joy," *Midnight Graffiti*, Spring.
Ray Garton, "Dr. Krusadian's Method," (novella) *Methods of Madness.*
———, "The Other Man," *Lovecraft's Legacy.*
———, "Something Kinky," *Methods of Madness.*
Nichola Germain, "Carlisle Hunter," *Fear* #13.
Molly Gloss, "Personal Silence," *IASFM*, Jan.
Marcus Gold, "The Vulture," *Dark Voices* 2.
J.B. Goodenough, "Nightmare," (poem) *Poetry.* Nov.
Ed Gorman, "The Man in the Long Black Sedan," *Borderlands.*
———, "The Monster," *Cemetery Dance*, Spring.
Charles L. Grant, "Alice Smiling," *Fantasy Tales*, Spring.
———, "Pinto Rider," *Black Lotus.*
Daryl Gregory, "In the Wheels," *F & SF*, Aug.
John Griesemer, "Box of Light," *IASFM*, Nov.
Robert Grossmith, "Company," *Best English Short Stories* 2.
Karen Haber, "His Spirit Wife," *F & SF*, Aug.
Jana Hakes, "Daddy's Little Pumpkin," (poem) *Doppelganger* 12.
Joe Haldeman, "Eighteen years old, October eleventh," (poem) *IASFM*, Aug.
Melissa Mia Hall, "Listening," *Skin of the Soul.*
———, "Revelations," *The SeaHarp Hotel.*
Elizabeth Hand and Paul Witcover, "Jangletown," *Joker.*
Ian Harding, "State of the Art," *Fear* #13.
Glyn Hardwick, "The Elixer," *EQMM*, April.
Jeanne Hart, "Missing Person," *Sisters in Crime* 2.
Gregor Hartmann, "Details at Six," *After Hours* #6.
Sharon Hashimoto, "The Mirror of Matsuyama," (poem) *Poetry*, Aug.
Barb Hendee, "China Dolls in Red Lagoons," *Cemetery Dance*, Winter.
Lynn S. Hightower, "Daddy's Coming Home," *Women of Darkness* 2.
Elizabeth Hillman, "Orestes' Last Song," (poem) *Fantasy Macabre* #13.
Russell Hoban, "The Man With the Dagger," *Best English Short Stories* 11.
Brian Hodge, "Childhood at the Lost and Found," *The Horror Show*, Spring.
Barry Hoffman, "Talk Dirty to Me," *Cemetery Dance*, Fall.
Nina Kiriki Hoffman, "Broken Things," *Deathrealm* #13.
———, "Moving Sale," *Grue* 12.
———, "Pouring the Foundations of a Nightmare," (poem) *AHMM*, April.
———, "Reflected Light," *Amazing*, July.

Nancy Holder, "Message Found in a Bottle II or, An Invitation from Your Captain," *Pulphouse* #7.

Martha Hollander, "You, Me and the Thing," (poem) *The Game of Statues*.

Robert Hood, "Dreams of Death," *AHMM*, July.

Leslie Alan Horvitz, "A Muse for Mr. Kalish," *The SeaHarp Hotel*.

Janette Turner Hospital, "The Loss of Faith," *Best English Short Stories 2*.

Ian Hunter, "Fearwheeling," *Fear* #20.

Rachel Ingalls, "Faces of Madness," *Esquire*, July.

Simon D. Ings, "The Braining of Mother Lamprey," *Interzone* #36.

———, "The Dead," *REM*, Aug.

Stefan Jackson, "Art is Anything You Can Get Away With," *Cemetery Dance*, Fall.

K.W. Jeter, "Blue on One End, Yellow on the Other," *Midnight Graffiti*, Spring.

Gary David Johnson, "Galatea," *2 A.M.* #15.

Gary Jonas, "By Death Abused," (chapbook) *Roadkill Press*.

Gwyneth Jones, "Grandmother's Footsteps," *Walls of Fear*.

Stuart M. Kaminski, "The Man Who Laughs," *Joker*.

Peg Kerr, "Debt in Kind," *Weird Tales*, Fall.

Garry Kilworth, "In the Country of Tattooed Men," *Omni*, Sept.

———, "Inside the Walled City," *Walls of Fear*.

———, "Networks," *Fantasy Tales 2*.

Stephen King, "The Moving Finger," *F&SF*, Dec.

James Kisner, "12 Items or Less," *New Blood* #7.

Shelia Kohler, "The Apartment," *Miracles in America*.

Kathe Koja, "Command Performance," *Amazing*, Nov.

Francis Korn, "More Amalias Than You Can Bear," *The Antioch Review*, Vol. 47, #4.

Mercedes R. Lackey, "An Object Lesson," *Domains of Darkover*.

Roberta Lannes, "Apostate in Denim," *Iniquities* #1.

Joe R. Lansdale, "Drive-In Date," *Night Visions 8*.

———, "Incident on and Off a Mountain Road," *Ibid*.

———, "Steppin' Out, Summer, '68," *Ibid*.

Janet LaPierre, "The Man Who Loved His Wife," *Sisters in Crime 3*.

Kristine Larson, "Scarlet," *Tales of the Unanticipated* #7.

Tanith Lee, "The Nightmare's Tale," *Women of Darkness 2*.

Melissa Lentricchia, "No-Chickens-to-Count Blues," *Guarantees*.

Primo Levi, "Angelic Butterfly," *The Sixth Day and Other Tales*.

———, "The Sleeping Beauty in the Fridge: A Winter's Tale" (translated from the Italian by Raymond Rosenthal), *Ibid*.

Brad Linaweaver, "The Lon Chaney Factory," *Black Lotus*.

Bentley Little, "The Beach," *Eldritch Tales* #23.

Brian Lumley, "The Thief Immortal," *Weirdbook* #25.

T.J. MacGregor, "The Works," *Sisters in Crime 2*.

John Maclay, "A Younger Woman," *Borderlands*.

Ian MacLeod, "1/72nd scale," *Weird Tales*, Fall.

——— "Well-Loved," *Interzone* #34.

Elissa Malcohn and Sylvia Alkoff, "Two Sestinas/Across the Border" (poems), *Tales of the Unanticipated* #7.

Albert J. Manachino, "Death and the Pointing Dog," *Thin Ice* 7.

William Marconette, Jr., "The Black Box," *Haunts*, Summer.

Raymond Marshall, "Visitor," *Thin Ice* 7.

Graham Masterton, "5a Bedford Row," *The Horror Show*, Spring.

————, "Will," *Lovecraft's Legacy.*

Lia Matera, "Destroying Angel," *Sisters in Crime 2.*

Richard Christian Matheson & William Relling, Jr., "Wonderland," *Cemetery Dance,* Summer.

Ardath Mayhar, "The Little Finger of the Left Hand," *Weird Tales,* Summer.

Taylor McCafferty, "Playing Dolls," *AHMM,* Feb.

Robert R. McCammon, "Beauty," *The SeaHarp Hotel.*

————, "On a Beautiful Summer's Day, He Was," *Joker.*

Sharyn McCrumb, "Remains to Be Seen," *Mummy Stories.*

Patricia A. McKillip, "Fortune's Children," *Tales of the Witchworld 3.*

Rick McMahan, "The Mojo Hand," *After Hours #8.*

Steven Millhauser, "The Invention of Robert Herendeen," *The Barnum Museum.*

————, "The Sepia Postcard," *Ibid.*

Lee Moler, "Suicide Note," *Borderlands.*

Thomas F. Monteleone, "The Cutty Black Sow," *Cemetery Dance,* Spring.

A. R. Morlan, "Size of a Silver Dollar," *Women of the West.*

————, "The Redemption of Pop Gee," *Pulphouse #7.*

Pat Murphy, "Bones," *IASFM,* May.

Will Murray, "Bone," *Joker.*

Yvonne Navarro, "Memories," *Pulphouse #7.*

S. Newman, "Vindolanda in Winter," *F & SF,* Dec.

William F. Nolan, "Gobble, Gobble!," *Weird Tales,* Winter 90/91.

Philip Nutman, "Full Throttle," *Splatterpunks.*

Joyce Carol Oates, "Why Don't You Come Live With Me It's Time," *Tikkun,* Vol. 5, No. 4.

Jerry Oltion, "The Signing," *Pulphouse #9.*

William C. Orem, "Fire," *After Hours #* 8.

Barbara Owens, "A Marty Kind of Guy," *EQMM,* Sept.

Mike O'Driscoll, "Sailor on the Sea of Tranquility," *BBR #6.*

Marco Palmieri, "Best of All," *Joker.*

Karen Parker, "Chet and Emily: A Strange Silence," *AHMM,* July.

T. L. Parkinson, "The Sex Club," *Semiotext(e) SF.*

Norman Partridge, "Cosmos," *Noctulpa #4.*

J. A. Paul, "The Time Between," *AHMM,* March.

Jack Pavey, "The Killer," *Not One of Us #6.*

————, "The Rabbit," *Cemetery Dance,* Summer.

Keith Peterson, "Kneecap Carbone and the Theory of Relativity," *EQMM,* Feb.

Gary L. Phillips, "Birds of Fire," *Deathrealm #12.*

Adrian Nikolas Phoenix, "Point of View," *Pulphouse #7.*

Dennis Post, "A House Occupied," *Fantasy Macabre #13.*

Alex Quiroba, "Breaking Up," *West/Word #1.*

Mark Rainey, "Deep Wood," *The Sterling Web,* Summer.

————, "The Grim," *Noctulpa #4.*

Marta Randall, "A Question of Magic," *Tales of the Witchworld 3.*

Derek Raymond, "Every Day is a Day in August," *New Crimes.*

Robert Reed, "Busybody," *F & SF,* Jan.

————, "Chaff," *F & SF,* May.

Garfield Reeves-Stevens, "Masks," *Joker.*

Michey Zucker Reichert, "The Ulfjarl's Stone," *Dragon Magazine,* (Month?)

Ruth Rendell, "The Fish Sitter," *EQMM,* June.

Keith Roberts, "Mrs. Byres and the Dragon," *IASFM*, Aug.
John Maddox Roberts, "Skinsuit," *F & SF*, Nov.
Russell Roberts, "Whistlin' Slim," *Pulphouse #6*.
Kim Stanley Robinson, "Before I Wake," *IASFM*, April.
Mary Rosenblum, "The Awakening," *Pulphouse #9*.
John Rosenman, "Jesse's Hair," *The Tome*, Sept.
Michael Rothschild, "A Land Without Fossils," *Wondermonger*.
Nicholas Royle, "Negatives," *Interzone #35*.
———, "D. GO," *Interzone #41*.
James Sallis, "The Need," *EQMM*, April.
Jessica Amanda Salmonson, "Black the Water," (poem) *Fantasy Tales 2*.
———, "Sheeted Traveler," (poem) *Eldritch Tales #23*.
Robert Sampson, "Sacred to Women," *Weird Tales*, Winter '90/'91.
David J. Schow, "Incident on a Rainy Night in Beverly Hills," *Seeing Red*.
———, "Monster Movies," *Weird Tales*, Spring; *Lost Angels*.
———, "Night Bloomer," *Weird Tales*, Spring.
Ann K. Schwader, "Glassgirl," (poem) *The Tome #4*.
Darrell Schweitzer, "Soft," *Weird Tales*, Spring.
———, and Jason van Hollander, "The Throwing Suit," *The Horror Show*, Spring.
———, and Jason van Hollander, "The Unmaker of Men," *Weird Tales*, Fall.
Howard Seabrook, "Faces in Concrete," *Grue 11*.
Carol Severance, "Whispering Cane," *Tales of the Witchworld 3*.
Sarah Shankman, "Say You're Sorry," *Sisters in Crime 3*.
Charles Sheffield, "Health Care System," *IASFM*, Sept.
Rick Shelley, "Eats," *Unique*, Sept./Oct.
Lucius Shepard, "Skull City," *IASFM*, July.
Lewis Shiner, " Scales," *Alien Sex*.
———, "White City," *IASFM*, June.
David B. Silva, "Metastasis," *Cemetery Dance*, Spring.
Dan Simmons, "Banished Dreams," (chapbook) Roadkill Press.
———, "Entropy's Bed at Midnight," (chapbook), Lord John Press.
Dean Wesley Smith, "Bryant Street," *2 A.M. #15*.
James Robert Smith, "Moving," *Black Lotus*,
Michael Marshall Smith, "The Man Who Drew Cats," *Dark Voices 2*.
Melinda M. Snodgrass, "Silent Voices of the Clay," *Pulphouse #9*.
Midori Snyder, "Skin Deep," *Pulphouse #7*.
Nancy Springer, "Snickerdoodles," *Weird Tales*, Summer.
———, "#20," *Ibid*.
Brian Stableford, "Behind the Wheel, " *Dark Voices 2*.
David Starkey, "Ready," *Grue 12*.
Kiel Stuart, "The Mirror of Dorian Gray, *After Hours #7*.
Peter Straub, "Something About a Death, Something About a Fire," *Houses Without Doors*.
Brad Strickland, "Snow Dove," *Black Lotus*.
Tim Sullivan, "Midnight Glider," *Iniquities #1*.
Lisa Swallow, "Dirty Pain," *Women of Darkness 2*.
David A. Sydney, "Hair Care," *Deathrealm #11*.
D.W. Taylor, "Wangdang Sweet Poontang," *Pulphouse #7*.
L.A. Taylor, "The Guide Dog," *AHMM*, July.
Melanie Tem, "Lightning Rod," *Skin of the Soul*.

————, "Rain Shadow," *Women of the West*.

Steve Rasnic Tem, "Aquarium," *The SeaHarp Hotel*.

————, "Fairytales," (chapbook) *Roadkill Press*.

————, "My Wife With the Yellow Hair," 2 A.M., #15.

Sheri S. Tepper, "The Gazebo," *F & SF*, October.

Jeffrey Thomas, "The Yellow House," *After Hours* #8.

Joyce Thompson, "Boat People," *Pulphouse* #7.

————, "Dancing Holes," *Pulphouse* #6.

Lois Tilton, "The Drought," *Women of Darkness 2*.

Peter Treymayne, "The Mongfind," *Weirdbook* #25.

Lisa Tuttle, "Bits and Pieces," *Pulphouse* #9.

————, "Lizard Lust," *Interzone* #39.

————, "Mr. Elphinstone's Hands," *Skin of the Soul*.

Robert Twohy, "At a Rest Stop South of Portland," *EQMM*, Jan.

Robert E. Vardeman, "Blood Lilies," *The SeaHarp Hotel*.

Karl Edward Wagner, "But You'll Never Follow Me," *Borderlands*.

————, "Cedar Lane," *Walls of Fear*.

Ian Watson, "Gaudi's Dragon," *IASFM*, Oct.

————, "Happy Hour," *Walls of Fear*.

————, "In Her Shoes," *Weird Tales*, Fall.

————, "Stalin's Teardrops," *Weird Tales*, Winter '90/'91.

Don Webb, "Djinn," *Interzone* #41.

Edward Wellen, "Overkill," *Cults of Horror*.

Robert Westall, "The Call," *The Call & Other Stories*.

————, "The Red House Clock," *Ibid*.

————, "Uncle Otto at Denswick Park," *Ibid*.

————, "Women and Home," *Ibid*.

Dale White, "Double Occupancy," *Thin Ice 7*.

J. W. Whitehead, "The Right Thing," *EQMM*, June.

Cherry Wilder, "Alive in Venice," *Dangerous Voices 2*.

————, "Anzac Day," *Skin of the Soul*.

Kate Wilhelm, "And the Angels Sing," *Omni*, May.

Chet Williamson, "The Assembly of the Dead," *Noctulpa* #4.

————, "The Cairnwell Horror," *Walls of Fear*.

————, "The Heart's Desire," *Weird Tales*, Fall.

————, "His Two Wives," *Iniquities* #1.

————, "Muscae Volitantes," *Borderlands*.

————, "The Treasure of the Nassasalars," *Weird Tales*, Fall.

Connie Willis, "Cibola," *IASFM*. Dec.

F. Paul Wilson, " 'Definitive Therapy,' " *Joker*.

————, "Midnight Mass," (novella, chapbook) *Axolotl*.

————, "Pelts," (chapbook) *Footsteps Press*.

————, "The Barrens," (novella) *Lovecraft's Legacy*.

Gahan Wilson, "Four Boys in All," *Wigwag*, Aug.

————, "H.P.L.,"(novella) *Lovecraft's Legacy*.

————, "Mr. Ice Cold," *Omni*, April.

Ken Wisman, "Brother Endle," *Eldritch Tales* #22.

Gene Wolfe, "The Haunted Boardinghouse," *Walls of Fear*.

————, "The Monday Man," *Monochrome: The Readercon Anthology*.

————, "Lord of the Land," *Lovecraft's Legacy*.

N. Lee Wood, "Memories that Dance Like Dust in the Summer Heat," *Amazing*, June.
Patricia C. Wrede, "The Lover's Night Out," *Festival Week*.
————, "The Sword-Seller," *Tales of the Witchworld* 3.
William F. Wu, "The Caravan of Death," *Pulphouse* #6.
Scott D. Yost, "The Breakdown," *Starshore*, Fall.
Mary Frances Zambreno, "The Fire Rider," *Marion Zimmer Bradley's Fantasy Magazine*, #7.

About the Editors

ELLEN DATLOW is the fiction editor of *Omni* magazine, and has edited several anthologies, including *The Books of Omni Science Fiction* (Zebra), *Blood Is Not Enough* (William Morrow/Berkley Books), and *Alien Sex* (E. P. Dutton). She has published a number of award-winning stories by outstanding authors during her tenure at *Omni*. Upcoming projects include *A Whisper of Blood* (Morrow), (November 1991). She lives in Manhattan.

TERRI WINDLING, a four-time winner of the World Fantasy Award, was for many years the Fantasy Editor for Ace Books. Now she is a Consulting Editor for Tor Books in New York; she also runs the Endicott Studio, which recently relocated to the mountains of the Southwest. specializing in book publishing projects and art for exhibition. She created the "Adult Fairy Tales" series of novels (Ace/Tor) and the "Borderland" urban fantasy books for teenagers (NAL/Tor/HBJ), and has edited a number of fiction anthologies. She lives in Tuscon, Arizona and Devon, England.

About the Artist

THOMAS CANTY is one of the most distinguished artists working in the fantasy field. He has won World Fantasy Awards for his distinctive book jacket and cover illustrations; and he is a noted book designer working in the fantasy, horror, mystery, and mainstream fields, as well as with various small presses. He has also created children's picture book series for St. Martin's Press and Ariel Books. He lives in Massachusetts.

About the Packager

JAMES FRENKEL is the publisher of Bluejay Books, which was a major publisher of science fiction and fantasy from 1983 to 1986. Since then he has been a consulting editor for Tor Books and for Macmillan's Collier Nucleus books, and a packager. Editor of Dell's science fiction in the late 1970s, he has published some of the finest new science fiction and fantasy authors, including Greg Bear, Orson Scott Card, Judith Tarr, John Varley, and Joan D. Vinge. He lives with his wife and two children in Chappaqua, New York.